TALES OF MYSTERY & THE SUPE

General Editor

IRISH GHO

IRISH
GHOST STORIES

Personally I have no bone to pick with graveyards,
I take the air there willingly, perhaps more
willingly than elswhere, when take the air I must.

SAMUEL BECKETT (1906–1989)

WORDSWORTH EDITIONS

For my husband
ANTHONY JOHN RANSON
with love from your wife, the publisher
Eternally grateful for your
unconditional love

Readers who are interested in other titles from
Wordsworth Editions are invited to visit our
website at www.wordsworth-editions.com

For our latest list and a full mail order service contact
Bibliophile Books, Unit 5 Datapoint,
South Crescent, London E16 4TL
Tel: +44 (0) 20 74 74 24 74
Fax: +44 (0) 20 74 74 85 89
orders@bibliophilebooks.com
www.bibliophilebooks.com

First published 2011 by Wordsworth Editions Limited
8B East Street, Ware, Hertfordshire SG12 9HJ

ISBN 978 1 84022 660 7

Text © Wordsworth Editions Limited 2011

Wordsworth® is a registered trademark of
Wordsworth Editions Limited

Wordsworth Editions is
the company founded in 1987 by
MICHAEL TRAYLER

Typeset in Great Britain by Antony Gray
Printed and bound by Clays Ltd, St Ives plc

CONTENTS

The Rival Dreamers

MICHAEL BANIM

Mr Washington Irving has already given to the public a version of an American legend, which, in a principal feature, bears some likeness to the following transcript of a popular Irish one. It may, however, be interesting to show this very coincidence between the descendants of a Dutch transatlantic colony and the native peasantry of Ireland, in the superstitious annals of both. Our tale, moreover, will be found original in all its circumstances, that alluded to only excepted.

Shamus Dempsey returned a silent, plodding, sorrowful man, though a young one, to his poor home, after seeing laid in the grave his aged decrepit father. The last rays of the setting sun were glorious, shooting through the folds of their pavilion of scarlet clouds; the last song of the thrush, chanted from the bough nearest to his nest, was gladdening; the abundant though but half-matured crops around breathed of hope for the future. But Shamus's bosom was covered with the darkness that inward sunshine alone can illumine. The chord that should respond to song and melody had snapped in it; for him the softly undulating fields of light-green wheat, or the silken surfaced patches of barley, made a promise in vain. He was poor, penniless, friendless, and yet groaning under responsibilities; worn out by past and present suffering, and without a consoling prospect. His father's corpse had been just buried by a subscription among his neighbours, collected in an old glove, a penny or a halfpenny from each, by the most active of the humble community to whom his sad state was a subject of pity. In the wretched shed which he called 'home', a young wife lay on a truss of straw, listening to the hungry cries of two little children, and awaiting her hour to become the weeping mother of a third. And the recollection that but for an act of domestic treachery experienced by his father and himself, both would have been comfortable and respectable in the world, aggravated the bitterness of the feeling in which Shamus contemplated this lot. He could himself faintly call to mind a time of early childhood, when he lived with his parents in a roomy house, eating and sleeping and dressing well, and surrounded by servants and workmen; he further remembered that a day of great affliction came, upon which strange and rude persons forced their way into the house; and, for some cause his infant observation did not reach, father, servants, and workmen (his mother had just died), were all turned out upon the road, and doomed to seek the shelter of a mean roof. But his father's discourse, since he gained the years of manhood, supplied Shamus with an explanation of all these circumstances, as follows.

Old Dempsey had been the youngest son of a large farmer, who divided his lands between two elder children, and destined Shamus's father to the Church, sending him abroad for education, and, during its course, supplying him with liberal allowances. Upon the eve of ordination, the young student returned home to visit his friends; was much noticed by neighbouring small gentry of each religion; at the house of one of the opposite persuasion from his, met a sister of the proprietor, who had a fortune in her own right; abandoned his clerical views for her smiles; eloped with her; married her privately; incurred thereby the irremovable hostility of his own family; but, after a short time, was received, along with his wife, by his generous brother-in-law, under whose guidance both became reputably settled in the house to which Shamus's early recollections pointed, and where, till he was about six years old, he passed indeed a happy childhood.

But, a little previous to this time, his mother's good brother died unmarried, and was succeeded by another of her brothers, who had unsuccessfully spent half his life as a lawyer in Dublin, and who, inheriting little of his predecessor's amiable character, soon showed himself a foe to her and her husband, professedly on account of her marriage with a Roman Catholic. He did not appear to their visit, shortly after his arrival in their neighbourhood, and he never condescended to return it. The affliction experienced by his sensitive sister, from his conduct, entailed upon her a premature accouchement, in which, giving birth to a lifeless babe, she unexpectedly died. The event was matter of triumph rather than of sorrow to her unnatural brother. For, in the first place, totally unguarded against the sudden result, she had died intestate; in the next place, he discovered that her private marriage had been celebrated by a Roman Catholic priest, consequently could not, according to law, hold good; and again, could not give to her nominal husband any right to her property, upon which both had hitherto lived, and which was now the sole means of existence to Shamus's father.

The lawyer speedily set to work upon these points, and with little difficulty succeeded in supplying for Shamus's recollections a day of trouble, already noticed. In fact, his father and he, now without a shilling, took refuge in a distant cabin, where, by the sweat of his parent's brow, as a labourer in the fields, the ill-fated hero of this story was scantily fed and clothed, until maturer years enabled him to relieve the old man's hand of the spade and sickle, and in turn labour for their common wants.

Shamus, becoming a little prosperous in the world, rented a few acres adjacent to his cabin and – married. The increase of his fields did not quite keep pace with the increases of his cares, in the persons of newcomers, for whose well being he was bound to provide. His ray of success in life soon became overclouded, by the calls of the landlord and the tithe-proctor. In truth, three years after his marriage, he received a notice which it were vain to oppose, to quit both his farm and his cabin, and leave his few articles of furniture behind.

At this juncture his father was bedridden, and his wife advanced in her third pregnancy. He put on his hat, walked to the door, fixed his eyes upon the ruins of an old abbey which stood on the slope of an opposite hill, and formed his plan for present measures. By the next evening he had constructed a wattled shed, covered with rushes and leaves, against a gable in the interior of the ruin. Clearing away the nettles and other rank weeds enclosed by his new house, he discovered a long slab on which was carved a cross and letters illegible to his eye; this he made his hearthstone. To furnish the abode, he fetched two large stones, as seats for his wife and himself, shook straw in either corner, and laid in a bundle of twigs. Then he went to the cabin that was no longer his, sent on his wife and two children to the abbey, followed with his father on his back, and laid him upon one of the straw couches. Two days afterwards the old man was a corpse. From his pauper funeral we now see Shamus returning, and to such a home does he bend his heavy steps.

If to know that the enemy of his father and mother did not thrive on the spoils of his oppression could have yielded Shamus any consolation in his lot, he had long ago become aware of circumstances calculated to give this negative comfort. His maternal uncle enjoyed, indeed, his newly acquired property only a few years after it came into his possession. Partly on account of his cruelty to his relations, partly from a meanness and vulgarity of character, which soon displayed itself in his novel situation, and which, it was believed, had previously kept him in the lowest walks of his profession as a Dublin attorney, he found himself neglected and shunned by the gentry of his neighbourhood. To grow richer than anyone who thus insulted him, to blazon abroad reports of his wealth, and to watch opportunities of using it to their injury, became the means of revenge adopted by the parvenu. His legitimate income not promising a rapid accomplishment of this plan, he ventured, using precautions that seemingly set suspicion at defiance, to engage in smuggling adventures on a large scale, for which his proximity to the coast afforded a local opportunity. Notwithstanding all his pettifogging cleverness, the ex-attorney was detected, however, in his illegal traffic, and fined to an amount which swept away half his real property. Driven to desperation by the publicity of his failure, as well as by the failure itself, he tried another grand effort to retrieve his fortune; was again surprised by the revenue officers; in a personal struggle with them, at the head of his band, killed one of their boys; immediately absconded from Ireland; for the last twenty years had not been authentically heard of; but, it was believed, lived under an assumed name in London, deriving an obscure existence from some mean pursuit, of which the very nature enabled him to gratify propensities to drunkenness and other vices, learned during his first career in life.

All this Shamus knew, though only from report, inasmuch as his uncle had exiled himself while he was yet a child, and without previously having become known to the eyes of the nephew he had so much injured. But if Shamus occasionally drew a bitter and almost savage gratification from the downfall of his inhuman persecutor, no recurrence to the past could alleviate the misery of his present situation. He passed under one of the capacious open arches of the old abbey, and then entered his squalid shed reared against its wall, his heart as shattered and as trodden down as the ruins around him. No words of greeting ensued between him and his equally hopeless wife, as she sat on the straw of her bed, rocking to sleep, with feeble and mournful cries, her youngest infant. He silently lighted a fire of

withered twigs on his ready-furnished hearthstone; put to roast
among their embers a few potatoes which he had begged during the
day; divided them between her and her crying children; and as the
moon, rising high in the heavens, warned him that night asserted
her full empire over the departed day, Shamus sunk down upon the
couch from which his father's mortal remains had lately been borne,
supperless himself, and dinnerless, too, but not hungry; at least not
conscious or recollecting that he was.

His wife and little ones soon slept soundly, but Shamus lay for
hours inaccessible to nature's claims for sleep as well as for food.
From where he lay he could see, through the open front of his
shed, out into the ruins abroad. After much abstraction of his own
thoughts, the silence, the extent, and the peculiar desolation of the
scene, almost spiritualised by the magic effect of alternate moonshine
and darkness, of objects and of their parts, at last diverted his mind,
though not to relieve it. He remembered distinctly, for the first
time, where he was – an intruder among the dwellings of the dead;
he called to mind, too, that the present was their hour for revealing
themselves among the remote loneliness and obscurity of their
crumbling and intricate abode. As his eye fixed upon a distant stream
of cold light or of blank shadow, either the wavering of some
feathery herbage from the walls, or the flitting of some night bird
over the roofless aisle, made motion which went and came during
the instant of his alarmed start, or else some disembodied sleeper
around had challenged and evaded his vision, so rapidly as to baffle
even the accompaniment of thought. Shamus would, however, recur,
during these entrancing aberrations, to his more real causes for
terror; and he knew not, and to this day cannot distinctly tell whether
he waked or slept, when a new circumstance absorbed his attention.
The moon struck fully, under his propped roof, upon the carved slab
he had appropriated as a hearthstone, and turning his eye to the
spot, he saw the semblance of a man advanced in years, though not
very old, standing motionless, and very steadfastly regarding him;
the still face of the figure shone like marble in the nightbeam,
without giving any idea of the solidity of that material; the long and
deep shadows thrown by the forehead over the eyes, left those
unusually expressive features vague and uncertain. Upon the head
was a close-fitting black cap, the dress was a loose-sleeved, plaited
garment of white, descending to the ground, and faced and otherwise
checked with black, and girded round the loins; exactly the costume

which Shamus had often studied in a little framed and glazed print, hung up in the sacristy of the humble chapel recently built in the neighbourhood of the ruin, by a few descendants of the great religious fraternity to whom, in its day of pride, the abbey had belonged. As he returned very inquisitively, though, as he avers, not now in alarm, the fixed gaze of his midnight visitor, a voice reached him, and he heard these strange words: 'Shamus Dempsey, go to London Bridge, and you will be a rich man.'

'How will that come about, your reverence?' cried Shamus, jumping up from the straw.

But the figure was gone; and he stumbling among the black embers on the remarkable place where it had stood, he fell prostrate, experiencing a change of sensation and of observance of objects around, which might be explained by supposing a transition from a sleeping to a waking state of mind.

The rest of the night he slept little, thinking of the advice he had received, and of the mysterious personage who gave it. But he resolved to say nothing about his vision, particularly to his wife, lest, in her present state of health, the frightful story might distress her; and, as to his own conduct respecting it, he determined to be guided by the future – in fact, he would wait to see if his counsellor came again. He did come again, appearing in the same spot at the same hour of the night, and wearing the same dress, though not the same expression of feature; for the shadowy brows now slightly frowned, and a little severity mingled with the former steadfastness of look.

'Shamus Dempsey, why have you not gone to London Bridge, and your wife so near the time when she will want what you are to get by going there? Remember this is my second warning.'

'Musha, your reverence, an' what am I to do on Lunnon Bridge?'

Again he rose to approach the figure; again it eluded him. Again a change occurred in the quality of the interest with which he regarded the admonition of his visitor. Again he passed a day of doubt as to the propriety of undertaking what seemed to him little less than a journey to the world's end, without a penny in his pocket, and upon the eve of his wife's accouchement, merely in obedience to a recommendation which, according to his creed, was not yet sufficiently strongly given, even were it under any circumstances to be adopted. For Shamus had often heard, and firmly believed, that a dream or a vision, instructing one how to procure riches, ought to be experienced three times before it became entitled to attention.

He lay down, however, half hoping that his vision might thus recommend itself to his notice. It did so.

'Shamus Dempsey,' said the figure, looking more angry than ever, 'you have not yet gone to London Bridge, although I hear your wife crying out to bid you go. And, remember, this is my third warning.'

'Why, then, tundher-an-ouns, your reverence, just stop and tell me – '

Ere he could utter another word the holy visitant disappeared, in a real passion at Shamus's qualified curse; and at the same moment, his confused senses recognised the voice of his wife, sending up from her straw pallet the cries that betoken a mother's distant travail. Exchanging a few words with her, he hurried away, professedly to call up, at her cabin window, an old crone who sometimes attended the very poorest women in Nance Dempsey's situation.

'Hurry to her, Noreen, acuishla, and do the best it's the will of God to let you do. And tell her from me, Noreen,' – he stopped, drawing in his lip, and clutching his cudgel hard.

'Shamus, what ails you, avick?' asked old Noreen; 'what ails you, to make the tears run down in the grey o' the morning?'

'Tell her from me,' continued Shamus, 'that it's from the bottom o' the heart I'll pray, morning and evening, and fresh and fasting, maybe, to give her a good time of it; and to show her a face on the poor child that's coming, likelier than the two that God sent afore it. And that I'll be thinking o' picturing it to my own mind, though I'll never see it far away.'

'Musha, Shamus, what are you speaking of?'

'No matter, Noreen, only God be wid you, and wid her, and wid the weenocks; and tell her what I bid you. More-be-token, tell her that poor Shamus quits her in her throuble, with more love from the heart out than he had for her the first day we came together; and I'll come back to her, at any rate, sooner or later, richer or poorer, or as bare as I went; and maybe not so bare either. But God only knows. The top o' the morning to you, Noreen, and don't let her want the mouthful o' praties while I'm on my thravels. For this' – added Shamus, as he bounded off to the consternation of old Noreen – 'this is the very morning and the very minute that, if I mind the dhrame at all at all, I ought to mind it; ay, without ever turning back to get a look from her, that 'ud kill the heart in my body entirely.'

Without much previous knowledge of the road he was to take, Shamus walked and begged his way along the coast to the town where he might hope to embark for England. Here, the captain of a merchantman agreed to let him work his passage to Bristol, whence he again walked and begged into London.

Without taking rest or food, Shamus proceeded to London Bridge, often put out of his course by wrong directions, and as often by forgetting and misconceiving true ones. It was with old London Bridge that Shamus had to do (not the old one last pulled down, but its more reverend predecessor), which, at that time, was lined at either side by quaintly fashioned houses, mostly occupied by shop-keepers, so that the space between presented, perhaps, the greatest thoroughfare then known in the Queen of Citics. And at about two o'clock in the afternoon, barefooted, ragged, fevered, and agitated, Shamus mingled with the turbid human stream, that roared and chafed over the, as restless and as evanescent, stream which buffeted the arches of old London Bridge. In a situation so novel to him, so much more extraordinary in the reality than his anticipation could have fancied, the poor and friendless stranger felt overwhelmed. A sense of forlornness, of insignificance, and of terror, seized upon his faculties. From the store, or the sneers, or the jostle of the iron-nerved crowd, he shrank with glances of wild timidity, and with a heart as wildly timid as were his looks. For some time he stood or staggered about, unable to collect his thoughts, or to bring to mind what was his business there. But when Shamus became able to refer to the motive of his pauper journey, from his native solitudes into the thick of such a scene, it was no wonder that the zeal of super-stition totally subsided amid the astounding truths he witnessed. In fact, the bewildered simpleton now regarded his dream as the merest chimera. Hastily escaping from the thoroughfare, he sought out some wretched place of repose suited to his wretched condition, and there mooned himself asleep, in half accusations at the thought of poor Nance at home, and in utter despair of all his future prospects.

At daybreak the next morning he awoke, a little less agitated, but still with no hope. He was able, however, to resolve upon the best course of conduct now left open to him; and he arranged immediately to retrace his steps to Ireland, as soon as he should have begged sufficient alms to speed him a mile on the road. With this intent he hastily issued forth, preferring to challenge the notice of chance passengers, even at the early hour of dawn, than to venture again in the middle of the day, among the dreaded crowds of the vast city. Very few, indeed, were the passers-by whom Shamus met during his straggling and stealthy walk through the streets, and those of a description little able or willing to afford a halfpenny to his humbled, whining suit, and to his spasmed lip and watery eye. In what direction he went Shamus did not know; but at last he found himself entering upon the scene of his yesterday's terror. Now, however, it presented nothing to renew its former impression. The shops at the sides of the bridge were closed, and the occasional stragglers of either sex who came along inspired Shamus, little as he knew of a great city, with aversion rather than with dread. In the quietness and security of his present position, Shamus was both courageous and weak enough again to summon up his dream.

'Come,' he said, 'since I *am* on Lunnon Bridge, I'll walk over every stone of it, and see what good that will do.'

He valiantly gained the far end. Here one house, of all that stood upon the bridge, began to be opened; it was a public house, and, by a sidelong glance as he passed, Shamus thought that, in the person of a red-cheeked, red-nosed, sunk-eyed, elderly man, who took down the window-shutters, he recognised the proprietor. This person looked at Shamus, in return, with peculiar scrutiny. The wanderer liked neither his regards nor the expression of his countenance, and quickened his steps onward until he cleared the bridge.

'But I'll walk it over at the other side, now,' he bethought, after allowing the publican time to finish opening his house, and retire out of view.

But, repassing the house, the man still appeared, leaning against his door-jamb, and as if waiting for Shamus's return, whom, upon this second occasion, he eyed more attentively than before.

'Sorrow's in him,' thought Shamus, 'have I two heads on me, that I'm such a sight to him? But who cares about his pair of ferret-eyes? I'll thrudge down the middle stone of it, at any rate!'

Accordingly he again walked towards the public house, keeping the middle of the bridge.

'Good-morrow, friend,' said the publican, as Shamus a third time passed his door.

'Sarvant kindly, sir,' answered Shamus, respectfully pulling down the brim of his hat, and increasing his pace.

'An early hour you choose for a morning walk,' continued his new acquaintance.

'Brave and early, faix, sir,' said Shamus, still hurrying off.

'Stop a bit,' resumed the publican. Shamus stood still. 'I see you're a countryman of mine – an Irishman; I'd know one of you at a look, though I'm a long time out of the country. And you're not very well off on London Bridge this morning, either.'

'No, indeed, sir,' replied Shamus, beginning to doubt his skill in physiognomy, at the stranger's kind address; 'but as badly off as a body 'ud wish to be.'

'Come over to look for the work?'

'Nien, sir; but come out this morning to beg a ha'penny, to send me a bit of the road home.'

'Well, here's a silver sixpence without asking. And you'd better sit on the bench by the door here, and eat a crust and a cut of cheese, and drink a drop of good ale, to break your fast.'

With profuse thanks, Shamus accepted this kind invitation; blaming himself at heart for having allowed his opinion of the charitable publican to be guided by the expression of the man's features. 'Handsome is that handsome does,' was Shamus's self-correcting reflection.

While eating his bread and cheese, and drinking his strong ale, they conversed freely together, and Shamus's heart opened more and more to his benefactor. The publican repeatedly asked him what had brought him to London; and though half out of prudence, and half out of shame, the dreamer at first evaded the question, he felt it at last impossible to refuse a candid answer to his generous friend.

'Why, then, sir, only I am such a big fool for telling it to you, it's what brought me to Lunnon Bridge was a quare dhrame I had at home in Ireland, that tould me just to come here, and I'd find a pot of goold'; for such was the interpretation given by Shamus to the vague admonition of his visionary counsellor.

His companion burst into a loud laugh, saying after it – 'Pho, pho, man, don't be so silly as to put faith in nonsensical dreams of that kind. Many a one like it I have had, if I would bother my head with them. Why, within the last ten days, while you were dreaming of finding a pot of gold on London Bridge, I was dreaming of finding a pot of gold in Ireland.'

'Ullaloo, and were you, sir?' asked Shamus, laying down his empty pint.

'Ay, indeed; night after night, an old friar with a pale face, and dressed all in white and black, and a black scullcap on his head, came to me in a dream, and bid me go to Ireland, to a certain spot in a certain county that I know very well, and under the slab of his tomb, that has a cross and some old Romish letters on it, in an old abbey I often saw before now, I'd find a treasure that would make me a rich man all the days of my life.'

'Musha, sir,' asked Shamus, scarce able prudently to control his agitation, 'and did he tell you that the treasure lay buried there ever so long under the open sky and the ould walls?'

'No; but he told me I was to find the slab covered in by a shed, that a poor man had lately built inside the abbey for himself and his family.'

'Whoo, by the powers!' shouted Shamus, at last thrown off his guard by the surpassing joy derived from this intelligence, as well as by the effects of the ale; and, at the same time, he jumped up, cutting caper with his legs, and flourishing his shillelah.

'Why, what's the matter with you?' asked his friend, glancing at him a frowning and misgiving look.

'We ax pardon, sir,' Shamus rallied his prudence. 'An' sure sorrow a thing is the matter wid me, only the dhrop, I believe, made me do it, as it ever and always does, good luck to it for the same. An' isn't what we were spaking about the biggest raumaush [nonsense] undher the sun, sir? Only it's the laste bit in the world quare to me, how you'd have the dhrame about your own country, that you didn't see for so many years, sir – for twenty long years, I think you said, sir?' Shamus had now a new object in putting his sly question.

'If I said so, I forgot,' answered the publican, his suspicions of Shamus at an end. 'But it is about twenty years, indeed, since I left Ireland.'

'And by your speech, sir, and your dacency, I'll engage you were in a good way in the poor place, afore you left it?'

'You guess correctly, friend.' (The publican gave way to vanity). 'Before misfortunes came over me, I possessed, along with a good hundred acres besides, the very ground that the old ruin I saw in the foolish dream I told you stands upon.'

'An' so did my curse-o'-God's uncle,' thought Shamus, his heart's blood beginning to boil, though, with a great effort, he kept himself seemingly cool. 'And this is the man fornent me, if he answers another word I'll ax him. Faix, sir, and sure that makes your dhrame quarer than ever; and the ground the ould abbey is on, sir, and the good acres round it, did you say they lay somewhere in the poor county myself came from?'

'What county is that, friend?' demanded the publican again with a studious frown.

'The ould County Monaghan, sure, sir,' replied Shamus, very deliberately.

'No, but the county of Clare,' answered his companion.

'Was it?' screamed Shamus, again springing up. The cherished hatred of twenty years imprudently bursting out, his uncle lay stretched at his feet, after a renewed flourish of his cudgel. 'And do you know what you are telling it to this morning? Did you ever hear that the sisther you kilt, left a bit of a *gorsoon* behind her, that one day or other might overhear you? Ay,' he continued, keeping down the struggling man, '*it is* poor Shamus Dempsey that's kneeling by you; ay, and that has more to tell you. The shed built over the old friar's tombstone was built by the hands you feel on your throttle, and that tombstone is his hearthstone; and' – continued Shamus, beginning to bind the prostrate man with a rope, snatched from a bench near them – 'while you lie here awhile, an' no one to help you, in the cool of the morning, I'll just take a start of you on the road home, to lift the flag and get the threasure; and follow me if you dare! You know there's good money bid for your head in Ireland – so here goes. Yes, faith and wid this – *this* to help me on the way!' He snatched up a heavy purse which had fallen from his uncle's pocket in the struggle. 'And sure, there's neither hurt nor harm in getting back a little of a body's own from you. A bright good-morning, uncle dear!'

Shamus dragged his manacled relative into the shop, quickly shut to and locked the door, flung the key over the house into the Thames, and the next instant was running at headlong speed.

He was not so deficient in the calculations of common sense as to think himself yet out of his uncle's power. It appeared, indeed, pretty certain, that neither for the violence done to his person, nor for the purse appropriated by his nephew, the outlawed murderer would raise a hue and cry after one who, aware of his identity, could deliver him up to the laws of his country. But Shamus felt certain that it would be a race between him and his uncle for the treasure that lay under the friar's tombstone. His simple nature supplied no stronger motive for a pursuit on the part of a man whose life now lay in the breath of his mouth. Full of his conviction, however, Shamus saw he had not a moment to lose until the roof of his shed in the old abbey again sheltered him. So, freely making use of his uncle's guineas, he purchased a strong horse in the outskirts of London, and to the surprise, if not under heavy suspicions of the vendor, set off at a gallop upon the road by which he had the day before gained the great metropolis.

A ship was ready to sail at Bristol for Ireland; but, to Shamus's discomfort, she waited for a wind. He got aboard, however, and in the darksome and squalid hold often knelt down and, with clasped hands and panting breast, petitioned Heaven for a favourable breeze. But from morning until evening the wind remained as he had found it, and Shamus despaired. His uncle, meantime, might have reached some other port, and embarked for their country. In the depth of his anguish he heard a brisk bustle upon deck, clambered up to investigate its cause, and found the ship's sails already half unfurled to a wind that promised to bear him to his native shores by the next morning. The last light of day yet lingered in the heavens: he glanced, now under way, to the quay of Bristol. A group who had been watching the departure of the vessel, turned round to note the approach to them of a man who ran furiously towards the place where they stood, pointing after her, and evidently speaking with vehemence, although no words reached Shamus's ear. Neither was his eye sure of this person's features, but his heart read them distinctly. A boat shot from the quay; the man stood up in it, and its rowers made a signal.

Shamus stepped to the gangway, as if preparing to hurl his pursuer into the sea. The captain took a speaking-trumpet, and informing the boat that he could not stop an instant, advised her to wait for another merchantman, which would sail in an hour. And during and after his speech his vessel plowed cheerily on, making as much way as she was adapted to accomplish.

Shamus's bosom felt lightened of its immediate terror, but not freed of apprehension for the future. The ship that was to sail in an hour haunted his thoughts: he did not leave the deck, and, although the night proved very dark, his anxious eyes were never turned from the English coast. Unusual fatigue and want of sleep now and then overpowered him, and his senses swam in a wild and snatching slumber; but from this he would start, carrying out and clinging to the cordage, as the feverish dream of an instant presented him with the swelling canvas of a fast sailing ship, which came suddenly bursting through the gloom of midnight, alongside of his own. Morning dawned, really to unveil to him the object of his fears following almost in the wake of her rival. He glanced in the opposite direction, and beheld the shores of Ireland; in another hour he jumped upon them; but his enemy's face watched him from the deck of the companion vessel, now not more than a few ropes' lengths distant.

Shamus mounted a second good horse, and spurred towards home. Often did he look back, but without seeing any cause for increased alarm. As yet, however, the road had been level and winding, and therefore could not allow him to span much of it at a glance. After noon, it ascended a high and lengthened hill, surrounded by wastes of bog. As he gained the summit of this hill, and again looked back, a horseman appeared, sweeping to its foot. Shamus galloped at full speed down the now quickly falling road; then along its level continuation for about a mile; and then up another eminence, more lengthened, though not so steep as the former; and from it still he looked back, and caught the figure of the horseman breaking over the line of the hill he had passed. For hours such was the character of the chase; until the road narrowed and began to wind amid an uncultivated and uninhabited mountain wilderness. Here Shamus's horse tripped and fell; the rider, little injured, assisted him to his legs, and, with lash and spur, reurged him to pursue his course. The animal went forward in a last effort, and, for still another span of time well befriended his rider. A rocky valley, through which both had been galloping, now opened at its further end, presenting to Shamus's eye, in the distance, the sloping ground, and the ruin which, with is mouldering walls, encircled his poor home; and the setting sun streamed golden rays through the windows and rents of the old abbey.

The fugitive gave a weak cry of joy, and lashed his beast again. The cry seemed to be answered by a shout; and a second time, after a wild plunge, the horse fell, now throwing Shamus off with a force that left him stunned. And yet he heard the hoofs of another horse come thundering down the rocky way; and, while he made a faint effort to rise on his hands and look at his pursuer, the horse and horseman were very near, and the voice of his uncle cried, 'Stand!' at the same time that the speaker fired a pistol, of which the ball struck a stone at Shamus's foot. The next moment his uncle, having left his saddle, stood over him, presenting a second pistol, and he spoke in a low but distinct voice.

'Spawn of a beggar! This is not merely for the chance of riches given by our dreams, though it seems, in the teeth of all I ever thought, that the devil tells truth at last. No, nor it is not quite for the blow; but it is to close the lips that, with a single word, can kill me. You die, to let me live!'

'Help!' aspirated Shamus's heart, turning itself to Heaven; 'help me but now, for the sake of the goold either, but for the sake of them that will be left on the wild world widout me; for them help me, great God!'

Hitherto his weakness and confusion had left him passive. Before his uncle spoke the last words, his silent prayer was offered, and Shamus had jumped upon his assailant. They struggled, and dragged each other down. Shamus felt the muzzle of the pistol at his breast; heard it snap – but only snap; he seized and mastered it, and once more the uncle was at the mercy of his nephew. Shamus's hand was raised to deal a good blow; but he checked himself, and addressed the almost senseless ears of his captive.

'No; you're my mother's blood, and a son of hers will never draw it from your heart; but I can make sure of you again – stop a bit.'

He ran to his own prostrate horse, took off its bridle and its saddle-girth, and with both secured his uncle's limbs, beyond all possibility of the struggler being able to escape from their control.

'There,' resumed Shamus, 'lie there till we have time to send an ould friend to see you, that, I'll go bail, will take good care of your four bones. And do you know where I'm going now? You tould me, on Lunnon Bridge, that you knew that, at least' – pointing to the abbey – 'ay, and the quare ould hearthstone that's to be found in it. And so, look at this, uncle, honey' – he vaulted upon his relation's horse – 'I'm just goin' to lift it off o' the barrel-pot full of good ould goold, and you have only to cry halves, and you'll get it, as sure as that the big divvle is in the town you came from.'

Nance Dempsey was nursing her new-born babe, sitting up in her straw, and doing very well after her late illness, when old Noreen tottered in from the front of the ruin, to tell her that 'the body they were just speaking about was driving up the hill mad, like as if 'twas his own sprit in great troble.' And the listener had not recovered from her surprise, when Shamus ran into the shed, flung himself kneeling by her side, caught her in his arms, then seized her infant, covered it with kisses, and then, roughly throwing it in her lap, turned to the fireplace, raised one of the rocky seats lying near it, poised the ponderous mass over the hearthstone, and shivered into pieces, with one crash, that solid barrier between him and his visionary world of wealth.

'It's cracked he is, out an' out, of a certainty,' said Nance, looking terrified at her husband.

'Nothing else am I,' shouted Shamus, after groping under the broken slab; 'an', for a token, get along with yourself out of this, owld gran!'

He started up and seized her by the shoulder. Noreen remonstrated. He stooped for a stone; she ran; he pursued her to the arches of the ruin. She stopped halfway down the descent. He pelted her with clods to the bottom, and along a good piece of her road homewards; and then danced back into his wife's presence.

'Now, Nance,' he cried, 'now that we're by ourselves, what noise is this like?'

'And he took out han'fuls after han'fuls of the ould goold, afore her face, my dear,' added the original narrator of this story.

'An' after the gaugers and their crony, Ould Nick, ran off with the uncle of him, Nance and he, and the childer, lived together in their father's and mother's house; and if they didn't live and die happy, I wish that you and I may.'

The Three Wishes

WILLIAM CARLETON

In ancient times there lived a man called Billy Dawson, and he was known to be a great rogue. They say he was descended from the family of the Dawsons, which was the reason, I suppose, of his carrying their name upon him.

Billy, in his youthful days, was the best hand at doing nothing in all Europe; devil a mortal could come next or near him at idleness; and, in consequence of his great practice that way, you may be sure that if any man could make a fortune by it he would have done it.

Billy was the only son of his father, barring two daughters, but they have nothing to do with the story I'm telling you. Indeed it was kind father and grandfather for Billy to be handy at the knavery as well as the idleness, for it was well known that not one of their blood ever did an honest act, except with a roguish intention. In short, they were altogether a *dacent* connection and a credit to the name. As for Billy, all the villainy of the family, both plain and ornamental, came down to him by way of legacy, for it so happened that the father, in spite of all his cleverness, had nothing but his roguery to *lave* him.

Billy, to do him justice, improved the fortune he got. Every day advanced him farther into dishonesty and poverty, until, at the long run, he was acknowledged on all hands to be the completest swindler and the poorest vagabond in the whole parish.

Billy's father, in his young days, had often been forced to acknowledge the inconvenience of not having a trade, in consequence of some nice point in law, called the 'Vagrant Act,' that sometimes troubled him. On this account he made up his mind to give Bill an occupation, and he accordingly bound him to a blacksmith; but whether Bill was to *live* or *die* by *forgery* was a puzzle to his father – though the neighbours said that *both* was most likely. At all events, he was put apprentice to a smith for seven years, and a hard card his master had to play in managing him. He took the proper method, however, for Bill was so lazy and roguish that it would vex a saint to keep him in order.

'Bill,' says his master to him one day that he had been sunning himself about the ditches, instead of minding his business, 'Bill, my boy, I'm vexed to the heart to see you in such a bad state of health. You're very ill with that complaint called an *all-overness*; however,' says he, 'I think I can cure you. Nothing will bring you about but three or four sound doses every day of a medicine called "the oil o' the hazel". Take the first dose now,' says he, and he immediately banged him with a hazel cudgel until Bill's bones ached for a week afterward.

'If you were my son,' said his master, 'I tell you that, as long as I could get a piece of advice growing convenient in the hedges, I'd have you a different youth from what you are. If working was a sin, Bill, not an innocenter boy ever broke bread than you would be. Good people's scarce, you think; but however that may be, I throw it out as a hint, that you must take your medicine till you're cured, whenever you happen to get unwell in the same way.'

From this out he kept Bill's nose to the grinding stone, and whenever his complaint returned he never failed to give him a hearty dose for his improvement.

In the course of time, however, Bill was his own man and his own master, but it would puzzle a saint to know whether the master or the man was the more precious youth in the eyes of the world.

He immediately married a wife, and devil a doubt of it, but if *he* kept *her* in whiskey and sugar, *she* kept *him* in hot water. Bill drank and she drank; Bill fought and she fought; Bill was idle and she was idle; Bill whacked her and she whacked Bill. If Bill gave her one black eye, she gave him another, *just to keep herself in countenance*. Never was there a blessed pair so well met, and a beautiful sight it was to see them both at breakfast time, blinking at each other across the potato basket, Bill with his right eye black, and she with her left.

In short, they were the talk of the whole town; and to see Bill of a morning staggering home drunk, his shirt sleeves rolled up on his smutted arms, his breast open, and an old tattered leather apron, with one corner tucked up under his belt, singing one minute and fighting with his wife the next – she, reeling beside him with a discoloured eye, as aforesaid, a dirty ragged cap on one side of her head, a pair of Bill's old slippers on her feet, a squalling child on her arm – now cuffing and dragging Bill, and again kissing and hugging him! Yes, it was a pleasant picture to see this loving pair in such a state!

This might do for a while, but it could not last. They were idle, drunken, and ill conducted; and it was not to be supposed that they would get a farthing candle on their words. They were, of course, *druv* to great straits; and faith, they soon found that their fighting and drinking and idleness made them the laughing sport of the neighbours; but neither brought food to their *childhre*, put a coat upon their backs, nor satisfied their landlord when he came to look for his own. Still, the never a one of Bill but was a funny fellow with strangers, though, as we said, the greatest rogue unhanged.

One day he was standing against his own anvil, completely in a brown study – being brought to his wit's end how to make out a breakfast for the family. The wife was scolding and cursing in the house, and the naked creatures of children squalling about her knees for food. Bill was fairly at an amplush, and knew not where or how to turn himself, when a poor, withered old beggar came into the forge, tottering on his staff. A long white beard fell from his chin, and he looked as thin and hungry that you might blow him, one would think, over the house. Bill at this moment had been brought to his senses by distress, and his heart had a touch of pity toward the old man, for, on looking at him a second time, he clearly saw starvation and sorrow in his face.

'God save you, honest man!' said Bill.

The old man gave a sigh, and raising himself with great pain on his staff, he looked at Bill in a very beseeching way.

'Musha. God save you kindly!' says he. 'Maybe you could give a poor, hungry, helpless ould man a mouthful of something to ait? You see yourself I'm not able to work; if I was, I'd scorn to be beholding to anyone.'

'Faith, honest man,' said Bill, 'if you knew who you're speaking to, you'd as soon ask a monkey for a churnstaff as me for either mate or money. There's not a blackguard in the three kingdoms so fairly on the *shaughran* as I am for both the one and the other. The wife within is sending the curses thick and heavy on me, and the *childhre's* playing the cat's melody to keep her in comfort. Take my word for it, poor man, if I had either mate or money I'd help you, for I know particularly well what it is to want them at the present spaking; an empty sack won't stand, neighbour.'

So far Bill told him truth. The good thought was in his heart, because he found himself on a footing with the beggar; and nothing brings down pride, or softens the heart, like feeling what it is to want.

'Why, you are in a worse state than I am,' said the old man; 'you have a family to provide for, and I have only myself to support.

'You may kiss the book on that, my old worthy,' replied Bill; 'but come, what I can do for you I will; plant yourself up here beside the fire, and I'll give it a blast or two of my bellows that will warm the old blood in your body. It's a cold, miserable, snowy day, and a good heat will be of service.'

'Thank you kindly,' said the old man; 'I *am* cold, and a warming at your fire will do me good, sure enough. Oh, but it *is* a bitter, bitter day; God bless it!'

He then sat down, and Bill blew a rousing blast that soon made the stranger edge back from the heat. In a short time he felt quite comfortable, and when the numbness was taken out of his joints, he buttoned himself up and prepared to depart.

'Now,' says he to Bill, 'you hadn't the food to give me, but *what you could you did*. Ask any three wishes you choose, and be they what they may, take my word for it, they shall be granted.'

Now, the truth is, that Bill, though he believed himself a great man in point of 'cuteness, wanted, after all, a full quarter of being square, for there is always a great difference between a wise man and a knave. Bill was so much of a rogue that he could not, for the blood of him, ask an honest wish, but stood scratching his head in a puzzle.

'Three wishes!' said he. 'Why, let me see – did you say *three*?'

'Ay,' replied the stranger, 'three wishes – that was what I said.'

'Well,' said Bill, 'here goes – aha! – let me alone, my old worthy! – faith I'll overreach the parish, if what you say is true. I'll cheat them in dozens, rich and poor, old and young; let me alone, man – I have it here,' and he tapped his forehead with great glee. 'Faith, you're the sort to meet of a frosty morning, when a man wants his breakfast; and I'm sorry that I have neither money nor credit to get a bottle of whiskey, that we might take our morning together.'

'Well, but let us hear the wishes,' said the old man; 'my time is short, and I cannot stay much longer.'

'Do you see this sledge hammer?' said Bill, 'I wish, in the first place, that whoever takes it up in their hands may never be able to lay it down till I give them lave; and that whoever begins to sledge with it may never stop sledging till it's my pleasure to release him.

'Secondly – I have an armchair, and I wish that whoever sits down in it may never rise out of it till they have my consent.

'And, thirdly – that whatever money I put into my purse, nobody may have power to take it out of it but myself!'

'You Devil's rip!' says the old man in a passion, shaking his staff across Bill's nose. 'Why did you not ask something that would sarve you both here and hereafter? Sure it's as common as the market cross, that there's not a vagabone in His Majesty's dominions stands more in need of both.'

'Oh! by the elevens,' said Bill, 'I forgot that altogether! Maybe you'd be civil enough to let me change one of them? The sorra purtier wish ever was made than I'll make, if only you'll give me another chance at it.'

'Get out, you reprobate,' said the old fellow, still in a passion. 'Your day of grace is past. Little you knew who was speaking to you all this time. I'm St Moroky, you blackguard, and I gave you an opportunity of doing something for yourself and your family; but you neglected it, and now your fate is cast, you dirty, bog-trotting profligate. Sure, it's well known what you are! Aren't you a byword in everybody's mouth, you and your scold of a wife? By this and by that, if ever you happen to come across me again, I'll send you to where you won't freeze, you villain!'

He then gave Bill a rap of his cudgel over the head and laid him at his length beside the bellows, kicked a broken coal scuttle out of his way, and left the forge in a fury.

When Billy recovered himself from the effects of the blow and began to think on what had happened, he could have quartered himself with vexation for not asking great wealth as one of the wishes at least; but now the die was cast on him, and he could only make the most of the three he pitched upon.

He now bethought him how he might turn them to the best account, and here his cunning came to his aid. He began by sending for his wealthiest neighbours on pretence of business, and when he got them under his roof he offered them the armchair to sit down in. He now had them safe, nor could all the art of man relieve them except worthy Bill was willing. Bill's plan was to make the best bargain he could before he released his prisoners; and let him alone for knowing how to make their purses bleed. There wasn't a wealthy man in the country he did not fleece. The parson of the parish bled heavily; so did the lawyer; and a rich attorney, who had retired from practice, swore that the Court of Chancery itself was paradise compared to Bill's chair.

This was all very good for a time. The fame of his chair, however, soon spread; so did that of his sledge. In a short time neither man, woman, nor child would darken his door; all avoided him and his fixtures as they would a spring gun or mantrap. Bill, so long as he fleeced his neighbours, never wrought a hand's turn; so that when his money was out he found himself as badly off as ever. In addition to all this, his character was fifty times worse than before, for it was the general belief that he had dealings with the old boy. Nothing now could exceed his misery, distress, and ill temper. The wife and he and their children all fought among one another. Everybody hated them, cursed them, and avoided them. The people thought they were acquainted with more than Christian people ought to know. This, of course, came to Bill's ears, and it vexed him very much.

One day he was walking about the fields, thinking of how he could raise the wind once more; the day was dark, and he found himself, before he stopped, in the bottom of a lonely glen covered by great bushes that grew on each side. 'Well,' thought he, when every other means of raising money failed him, 'it's reported that I'm in league with the old boy, and as it's a folly to have the name of the connection without the profit, I'm ready to make a bargain with him any day – so,' said he, raising his voice, 'Nick, you sinner, if you be convenient and willing why stand out here; show your best leg – here's your man.'

The words were hardly out of his mouth when a dark, sober-looking old gentleman, not unlike a lawyer, walked up to him. Bill looked at the foot and saw the hoof. 'Morrow, Nick,' says Bill.

'Morrow, Bill,' says Nick. 'Well, Bill, what's the news?'

'Devil a much myself hears of late,' says Bill; 'is there anything *fresh* below?'

'I can't exactly say, Bill; I spend little of my time down now; the Tories are in office, and my hands are consequently too full of business here to pay much attention to anything else.'

'A fine place this, sir,' says Bill, 'to take a constitutional walk in; when I want an appetite I often come this way myself – hem! *High* feeding is very bad without exercise.'

'High feeding! Come, come, Bill, you know you didn't taste a morsel these four-and-twenty hours.'

'You know that's a bounce, Nick. I ate a breakfast this morning that would put a stone of flesh on you, if you only smelt at it.'

'No matter; this is not to the purpose. What's that you were muttering to yourself a while ago? If you want to come to the brunt, here I'm for you.'

'Nick,' said Bill, 'you're complate; you want nothing barring a pair of Brian O'Lynn's breeches.'

Bill, in fact, was bent on making his companion open the bargain, because he had often heard that, in that case, with proper care on his own part, he might defeat him in the long run. The other, however, was his match.

'What was the nature of Brian's garment?' enquired Nick.

'Why, you know the song,' said Bill:

> Brian O'Lynn had no breeches to wear,
> So he got a sheep's skin for to make him a pair;
> With the fleshy side out and the woolly side in,
> 'They'll be pleasant and cool,' says Brian O'Lynn.

'A cool pare would sarve you, Nick.'

'You're mighty waggish today, Misther Dawson.'

'And good right I have,' said Bill; 'I'm a man snug and well to do in the world; have lots of money, plenty of good eating and drinking, and what more need a man wish for?'

'True,' said the other; 'in the meantime it's rather odd that so respectable a man should not have six inches of unbroken cloth in his apparel. You're as naked a tatterdemalion as I ever laid my eyes on; in full dress for a party of scarecrows, William?'

'That's my own fancy, Nick; I don't work at my trade like a gentleman. This is my forge dress, you know.'

'Well, but what did you summon me here for?' said the other; 'you may as well speak out, I tell you, for, my good friend, unless you do, I shan't. Smell that.'

'I smell more than that,' said Bill; 'and by the way, I'll thank you to give me the windy side of you – curse all sulphur, I say. There, that's what I call an improvement in my condition. But as you *are* so stiff,' says Bill, 'why, the short and long of it is – that – ahem – you see I'm – tut – sure you know I have a thriving trade of my own, and that if I like I needn't be at a loss; but in the meantime I'm rather in a kind of a so – so – don't you *take*?'

And Bill winked knowingly, hoping to trick him into the first proposal.

'You must speak aboveboard, my friend,' says the other. 'I'm a man of few words, blunt and honest. If you have anything to say, be plain. Don't think I can be losing my time with such a pitiful rascal as you are.'

'Well,' says Bill. 'I want money, then, and am ready to come into terms. What have you to say to that, Nick?'

'Let me see – let me look at you,' says his companion, turning him about. 'Now, Bill, in the first place, are you not as finished a scarecrow as ever stood upon two legs?'

'I play second fiddle to you there again,' says Bill.

'There you stand, with the blackguards' coat of arms quartered under your eye, and – '

'Don't make little of *black*guards,' said Bill, 'nor spake disparagingly of your *own* crest.'

'Why, what would you bring, you brazen rascal, if you were fairly put up at auction?'

'Faith, I'd bring more bidders than you would,' said Bill, 'if you were to go off at auction tomorrow. I tell you they should bid *downward* to come to your value, Nicholas. We have no coin *small* enough to purchase you.'

'Well, no matter,' said Nick. 'If you are willing to be mine at the expiration of seven years, I will give you more money than ever the rascally breed of you was worth.'

'Done!' said Bill. 'But no disparagement to my family, in the meantime; so down with the hard cash, and don't be a *neger*.'

The money was accordingly paid; but as nobody was present, except the giver and receiver, the amount of what Bill got was never known.

'Won't you give me a luck penny?' said the old gentleman.

'Tut,' said Billy, 'so prosperous an old fellow as you cannot want it; however, bad luck to you, with all my heart! and it's rubbing grease to a fat pig to say so. Be off now, or I'll commit suicide on you. Your absence is a cordial to most people, you infernal old profligate. You have injured my morals even for the short time you have been with me, for I don't find myself so virtuous as I was.'

'Is that your gratitude, Billy?'

'Is it gratitude *you* speak of, man? I wonder you don't blush when you name it. However, when you come again, if you bring a third eye in your head you will see what I mane, Nicholas, *ahagur*.'

The old gentleman, as Bill spoke, hopped across the ditch on his way to *Downing* street, where of late 'tis thought he possesses much influence.

Bill now began by degrees to show off, but still wrought a little at his trade to blindfold the neighbours. In a very short time, however, he became a great man. So long indeed as he was a poor rascal, no decent person would speak to him; even the proud servingmen at the 'big house' would turn up their noses at him. And he well deserved to be made little of by others, because he was mean enough to make little of himself. But when it was seen and known that he had oceans of money, it was wonderful to think, although he was *now* a greater blackguard than ever, how those who despised him before began to come round him and court his company. Bill, how-ever, had neither sense nor spirit to make those sunshiny friends know their distance; not he – instead of that he was proud to be seen in decent company, and so long as the money lasted, it was, 'hail fellow well met' between himself and every fair-faced *spunger* who had a horse under him, a decent coat to his back, and a good appetite to eat his dinners. With riches and all, Bill was the same man still; but, somehow or other, there is a great difference between a rich profligate and a poor one, and Bill found it so to his cost in *both* cases.

Before half the seven years was passed, Bill had his carriage and his equipages; was hand and glove with my Lord This, and my Lord That; kept hounds and hunters; was the first sportsman at the Curragh; patronised every boxing ruffian he could pick up; and betted night and day on cards, dice, and horses. Bill, in short, *should* be a blood, and except he did all this, he could not presume to mingle with the fashionable bloods of his time.

It's an old proverb, however, that 'what is got over the Devil's back is sure to go off under it,' and in Bill's case this proved true. In short, the old boy himself could not supply him with money so fast as he made it fly; it was 'come easy, go easy,' with Bill, and so sign was on it, before he came within two years of his time he found his purse empty.

And now came the value of his summer friends to be known. When it was discovered that the cash was no longer flush with him – that stud, and carriage, and hounds were going to the hammer – whish! off they went, friends, relations, pot companions, dinner caters, black-legs, and all, like a flock of crows that had smelled gunpowder. Down Bill soon went, week after week and day after day, until at last he was obliged to put on the leather apron and take to the hammer again; and not only that, for as no experience could make him wise, he once more began his taproom brawls, his quarrels with Judy, and took to his 'high feeding' at the dry potatoes and salt. Now, too, came the cutting tongues of all who knew him, like razors upon him. Those that he scorned because they were poor and himself rich now paid him back his own with interest; and those that he measured himself with, because they were rich, and who only countenanced him in consequence of his wealth, gave him the hardest word in their cheeks. The Devil mend him! He deserved it all, and more if he had got it.

Bill, however, who was a hardened sinner, never fretted himself down an ounce of flesh by what was said to him or of him. Not he; he cursed, and fought, and swore, and schemed away as usual, taking in everyone he could; and surely none could match him at villainy of all sorts and sizes.

At last the seven years became expired, and Bill was one morning sitting in his forge, sober and hungry, the wife cursing him, and children squalling as before; he was thinking how he might defraud some honest neighbour out of a breakfast to stop their mouths and his own, too, when who walks in to him but old Nick to demand his bargain.

'Morrow, Bill!' says he with a sneer.

'The Devil welcome you!' says Bill. 'But you have a fresh memory.'

'A bargain's a bargain between two *honest* men, any day,' says Satan; 'when I speak of honest men, I mean yourself and *me*, Bill'; and he put his tongue in his cheek to make game of the unfortunate rogue he had come for.

'Nick, my worthy fellow,' said Bill, 'have bowels; you wouldn't do a shabby thing; you wouldn't disgrace your own character by putting more weight upon a falling man. You know what it is to get a *comedown* yourself, my worthy; so just keep your toe in your pump, and walk off with yourself somewhere else. A *cool* walk will sarve you better than my company, Nicholas.'

'Bill, it's no use in shirking,' said his friend; 'your swindling tricks may enable you to cheat others, but you won't cheat *me*, I guess. You want nothing to make you perfect in your way but to travel; and travel you shall under my guidance, Billy. No, no – I'm not to be swindled, my good fellow. I have rather a – a – better opinion of

myself, Mr D., than to think that you could outwit one Nicholas
Clutie, Esq. – ahem!'

'You may sneer, you sinner,' replied Bill, 'but I tell you that I have
outwitted men who could buy and sell you to your face. Despair,
you villain, when I tell you that *no attorney* could stand before me.'

Satan's countenance got blank when he heard this; he wriggled
and fidgeted about and appeared to be not quite comfortable.

'In that case, then,' says he, 'the sooner I *deceive* you the better; so
turn out for the *Low Countries*.'

'Is it come to that in earnest?' said Bill. 'Are you going to act the
rascal at the long run?'

' 'Pon honour, Bill.'

'Have patience, then, you sinner, till I finish this horseshoe – it's
the last of a set I'm finishing for one of your friend the attorney's
horses. And here, Nick, I hate idleness; you know it's the mother of
mischief; take this sledge hammer and give a dozen strokes or so, till
I get it out of hands, and then here's with you, since it must be so.'

He then gave the bellows a puff that blew half a peck of dust in
Clubfoot's face, whipped out the red-hot iron, and set Satan sledging
away for bare life.

'Faith,' says Bill to him, when the shoe was finished, 'it's a
thousand pities ever the sledge should be out of your hand; the
great *Parra Gow* was a child to you at sledging, you're such an able
tyke. Now just exercise yourself till I bid the wife and *childhre*
goodbye, and then I'm off.'

Out went Bill, of course, without the slightest notion of coming
back; no more than Nick had that he could not give up the sledging,
and indeed neither could he, but was forced to work away as if he
was sledging for a wager. This was just what Bill wanted. He was
now compelled to sledge on until it was Bill's pleasure to release
him; and so we leave him very industriously employed, while we
look after the worthy who outwitted him.

In the meantime Bill broke cover and took to the country at large;
wrought a little journey work wherever he could get it, and in this
way went from one place to another, till, in the course of a month, he
walked back very coolly into his own forge to see how things went on
in his absence. There he found Satan in a rage, the perspiration
pouring from him in torrents, hammering with might and main upon
the naked anvil. Bill calmly leaned back against the wall, placed his
hat upon the side of his head, put his hands into his breeches pockets,

and began to whistle *Shaun Gow's* hornpipe. At length he says, in a very quiet and good-humoured way: 'Morrow, Nick!'

'Oh!' says Nick, still hammering away. 'Oh! you double-distilled villain (hech!), may the most refined ornamental (hech!) collection of curses that ever was gathered (hech!) into a single nosegay of ill fortune (hech!) shine in the buttonhole of your conscience (hech!) while your name is Bill Dawson! I denounce you (hech!) as a double-milled villain, a finished, hot-pressed knave (hech!), in comparison of whom all the other knaves I ever knew (hech!), attorneys included, are honest men. I brand you (hech!) as the pearl of cheats, a tiptop take-in (hech!). I denounce you, I say again, for the villainous treatment (hech!) I have received at your hands in this most untoward (hech!) and unfortunate transaction between us; for (hech!) unfortunate, in every sense, is he that has anything to do with (hech!) such a prime and finished impostor.'

'You're very warm, Nicky,' says Bill; 'what puts you into a passion, you old sinner? Sure if it's your own will and pleasure to take exercise at my anvil, *I'm* not to be abused for it. Upon my credit, Nicky, you ought to blush for using such blackguard language, so unbecoming your grave character. You cannot say that it was I set you a-hammering at the empty anvil, you profligate.

'However, as you are so very industrious, I simply say it would be a thousand pities to take you from it. Nick, I love industry in my heart, and I always encourage it, so work away; its not often you spend your time so creditably. I'm afraid if you weren't at that you'd be worse employed.'

'Bill, have bowels,' said the operative; 'you wouldn't go to lay more weight on a falling man, you know; you wouldn't disgrace your character by such a piece of iniquity as keeping an inoffensive gentleman, advanced in years, at such an unbecoming and rascally job as this. Generosity's your top virtue, Bill; not but that you have many other excellent ones, as well as that, among which, as you say yourself, I reckon industry; but still it is in generosity you shine. Come, Bill, honour bright, and release me.'

'Name the terms, you profligate.'

'You're above terms, William; a generous fellow like you never thinks of terms.'

'Goodbye, old gentleman!' said Bill very coolly; 'I'll drop in to see you once a month.'

'No, no, Bill, you infern – a – a – . You excellent, worthy, delightful

fellow, not so fast; not so fast. Come, name your terms, you sland –
My dear Bill, name your terms.'

'Seven years more.'

'I agree; but – '

'And the same supply of cash as before, down on the nail here.'

'Very good; very good. You're rather simple, Bill; rather soft, I
must confess. Well, no matter. I shall yet turn the tab – a – hem!
You are an exceedingly simple fellow, Bill; still there will come a
day, my *dear* Bill – there will come – '

'Do you grumble, you vagrant? Another word, and I double the
terms.'

'Mum, William – mum; *tace* is Latin for a candle.'

'Seven years more of grace, and the same measure of the needful
that I got before. Ay or no?'

'Of grace, Bill! Ay! ay! ay! There's the cash. I accept the terms.
Oh, blood! The rascal – of grace! Bill!'

'Well, now drop the hammer and vanish,' says Billy; 'but what
would you think to take this sledge, while you stay, and give me a –
Eh! Why in such a hurry?' he added, seeing that Satan withdrew in
double-quick time.

'Hollo! Nicholas!' he shouted. 'Come back; you forgot something!'
And when the old gentleman looked behind him, Billy shook the
hammer at him, on which he vanished altogether.

Billy now got into his old courses; and what shows the kind of
people the world is made of, he also took up with his old company.
When they saw that he had the money once more and was sowing it
about him in all directions, they immediately began to find excuses
for his former extravagance.

'Say what you will,' said one, 'Bill Dawson's a spirited fellow and
bleeds like a prince.'

'He's a hospitable man in his own house, or out of it, as ever
lived,' said another.

'His only fault is,' observed a third, 'that he is, if anything, too
generous, and doesn't know the value of money; his fault's on the
right side, however.'

'He has the spunk in him,' said a fourth; 'keeps a capital table,
prime wines, and a standing welcome for his friends.'

'Why,' said a fifth, 'if he doesn't enjoy his money while he lives, he
won't when he's dead; so more power to him, and a wider throat to
his purse.'

Indeed, the very persons who were cramming themselves at his expense despised him at heart. They knew very well, however, how to take him on the weak side. Praise his generosity, and he would do anything; call him a man of spirit, and you might fleece him to his face. Sometimes he would toss a purse of guineas to this knave, another to that flatterer, a third to a bully, and a fourth to some broken-down rake – and all to convince them that he was a sterling friend – a man of mettle and liberality. But never was he known to help a virtuous and struggling family – to assist the widow or the fatherless, or to do any other act that was truly useful. It is to be supposed the reason of this was that as he spent it, as most of the world do, in the service of the Devil, by whose aid he got it, he was prevented from turning it to a good account. Between you and me, dear reader, there are more persons acting after Bill's fashion in the same world than you dream about.

When his money was out again, his friends played him the same rascally game once more. No sooner did his poverty become plain than the knaves began to be troubled with small fits of modesty, such as an unwillingness to come to his place when there was no longer anything to be got there. A kind of virgin bashfulness prevented them from speaking to him when they saw him getting out on the wrong side of his clothes. Many of them would turn away from him in the prettiest and most delicate manner when they thought he wanted to borrow money from them – all for fear of putting him to the blush for asking it. Others again, when they saw him coming toward their houses about dinner hour, would become so confused, from mere gratitude, as to think themselves in another place; and their servants, seized, as it were, with the same feeling, would tell Bill that their masters were 'not at home.'

At length, after travelling the same villainous round as before, Bill was compelled to betake himself, as the last remedy, to the forge; in other words, he found that there is, after all, nothing in this world that a man can rely on so firmly and surely as his own industry. Bill, however, wanted the organ of common sense, for his experience – and it was sharp enough to leave an impression – ran off him like water off a duck.

He took to his employment sorely against his grain, but he had now no choice. He must either work or starve, and starvation is like a great doctor – nobody tries it till every other remedy fails them. Bill had been twice rich; twice a gentleman among blackguards, but always a blackguard among gentlemen, for no wealth or acquaintance with decent society could rub the rust of his native vulgarity off him. He was now a common blinking sot in his forge; a drunken bully in the taproom, cursing and browbeating everyone as well as his wife; boasting of how much money he had spent in his day; swaggering about the high doings he carried on; telling stories about himself and Lord This at the Curragh; the dinners he gave – how much they cost him – and attempting to extort credit upon the strength of his former wealth. He was too ignorant, however, to know that he was publishing his own disgrace and that it was a mean-spirited thing to be proud of what ought to make him blush through a deal board nine inches thick.

He was one morning industriously engaged in a quarrel with his wife, who, with a three-legged stool in her hand, appeared to mistake his head for his own anvil; he, in the meantime, paid his addresses to her with his leather apron, when who steps in to jog his memory about the little agreement that was between them but old Nick. The wife, it seems, in spite of all her exertions to the contrary, was getting the worst of it; and Sir Nicholas, willing to appear a gentleman of great gallantry, thought he could not do less than take up the lady's quarrel, particularly as Bill had laid her in a sleeping posture. Now Satan thought this too bad, and as he felt himself under many obligations to the sex, he determined to defend one of them on the present occasion; so as Judy rose, he turned upon the husband and floored him by a clever facer.

'You unmanly villain,' said he, 'is this the way you treat your wife? 'Pon honour Bill, I'll chastise you on the spot. I could not stand by, a spectator of such ungentlemanly conduct, without giving up all claim to gallant – ' Whack! The word was divided in his mouth by the blow of a churnstaff from Judy, who no sooner saw Bill struck than she nailed Satan, who 'fell' once more.

'What, you villain! That's for striking my husband like a murderer behind his back,' said Judy, and she suited the action to the word. 'That's for interfering between man and wife. Would you murder the poor man before my face, eh? If he bates me, you shabby dog you, who has a better right? I'm sure it's nothing out of your pocket. Must you have your finger in every pie?'

This was anything but *idle* talk, for at every word she gave him a remembrance, hot and heavy. Nicholas backed, danced, and hopped; she advanced, still drubbing him with great perseverance, till at length he fell into the redoubtable armchair, which stood exactly behind him. Bill, who had been putting in two blows for Judy's one, seeing that his enemy was safe, now got between the Devil and his wife, *a situation that few will be disposed to envy him.*

'Tenderness, Judy,' said the husband; 'I hate cruelty. Go put the tongs in the fire, and make them red-hot. Nicholas, you have a nose,' said he.

Satan began to rise but was rather surprised to find that he could not budge.

'Nicholas,' says Bill, 'how is your pulse? You don't look well; that is to say, you look worse than usual.'

The other attempted to rise but found it a mistake.

'I'll thank you to come along,' said Bill. 'I have a fancy to travel under your guidance, and we'll take the *Low Countries* in our way, won't we? Get to your legs, you sinner; you know a bargain's a bargain between two *honest* men, Nicholas, meaning *yourself* and *me*. Judy, are the tongs hot?'

Satan's face was worth looking at as he turned his eyes from the husband to the wife and then fastened them on the tongs, now nearly at a furnace heat in the fire, conscious at the same time that he could not move out of the chair.

'Billy,' said he, 'you won't forget that I rewarded you generously the last time I saw you, in the way of business.'

'Faith, Nicholas, it fails me to remember any generosity I ever showed you. Don't be womanish. I simply want to see what kind of stuff your nose is made of and whether it will stretch like a rogue's conscience. If it does we will flatter it up the chimly with red-hot tongs, and when this old hat is fixed on the top of it, let us alone for a weathercock.'

'Have a *fellow-feeling*, Mr Dawson; you know we ought not to dispute. Drop the matter, and I give you the next seven years.'

'We know all that,' says Billy, opening the red-hot tongs very coolly.

'Mr Dawson,' said Satan, 'if you cannot remember my friendship to yourself, don't forget how often I stood your father's friend, your grandfather's friend, and the friend of all your relations up to the tenth generation. I intended, also, to stand by your children after you, so long as the name of Dawson – and a respectable one it is – might last.'

'Don't be blushing, Nick,' says Bill; 'you are too modest; that was ever your failing; hold up your head, there's money bid for you. I'll give you such a nose, my good friend, that you will have to keep an outrider before you, to carry the end of it on his shoulder.'

'Mr Dawson, I pledge my honour to raise your children in the world as high as they can go, no matter whether they desire it or not.'

'That's very kind of you,' says the other, 'and I'll do as much for your nose.'

He gripped it as he spoke, and the old boy immediately sung out; Bill pulled, and the nose went with him like a piece of warm wax. He then transferred the tongs to Judy, got a ladder, resumed the tongs, ascended the chimney, and tugged stoutly at the nose until he got it five feet above the roof. He then fixed the hat upon the top of it and came down.

'There's a weathercock,' said Billy; 'I defy Ireland to show such a beauty. Faith, Nick, it would make the purtiest steeple for a church in all Europe, and the old hat fits it to a shaving.'

In this state, with his nose twisted up the chimney, Satan sat for some time, experiencing the novelty of what might be termed a peculiar sensation. At last the worthy husband and wife began to relent.

'I think,' said Bill, 'that we have made the most of the nose, as well as the joke; I believe, Judy, it's long enough.'

'What is?' says Judy.

'Why, the joke,' said the husband.

'Faith, and I think so is the nose,' said Judy.

'What do you say yourself, Satan?' said Bill.

'Nothing at all, William,' said the other; 'but that – ha! ha! – it's a good joke – an excellent joke, and a goodly nose, too, as it *stands*. You were always a gentlemanly man, Bill, and did things with a grace; still, if I might give an opinion on such a trifle – '

'It's no trifle at all,' says Bill, 'if you spake of the nose.'

'Very well, it is not,' says the other; 'still, I am decidedly of opinion that if you could shorten both the joke and the nose without further violence, you would lay me under very heavy obligations, which I shall be ready to acknowledge and *repay* as I ought.'

'Come,' said Bill, 'shell out once more, and be off for seven years. As much as you came down with the last time, and vanish.'

The words were scarcely spoken, when the money was at his feet and Satan invisible. Nothing could surpass the mirth of Bill and his wife at the result of this adventure. They laughed till they fell down on the floor.

It is useless to go over the same ground again. Bill was still incorrigible. The money went as the Devil's money always goes. Bill caroused and squandered but could never turn a penny of it to a good purpose. In this way year after year went, till the seventh was closed and Bill's hour come. He was now, and had been for some time past, as miserable a knave as ever. Not a shilling had he, nor a shilling's worth, with the exception of his forge, his cabin, and a few articles of crazy furniture. In this state he was standing in his forge as before, straining his ingenuity how to make out a breakfast, when Satan came to look after him. The old gentleman was sorely puzzled how to get at him. He kept skulking and sneaking about the forge for some time, till he saw that Bill hadn't a cross to bless himself with. He immediately changed himself into a guinea and lay in an open place where he knew Bill would see him. 'If,' said he. 'I once get into his possession, I can manage him.' The honest smith took the bait, for it was well gilded; he clutched the guinea, put it into his purse, and closed it up. 'Ho! Ho!' shouted the Devil out of the purse. 'You're caught, Bill; I've secured you at last, you knave you. Why don't you despair you villain, when you think of what's before you?'

'Why, you unlucky ould dog,' said Bill, 'is it there you are? Will you always drive your head into every loophole that's set for you? Faith, Nick *achora*, I never had you bagged till now.'

Satan then began to tug and struggle with a view of getting out of the purse, but in vain.

'Mr Dawson,' said he, 'we understand each other. I'll give the seven years additional and the cash on the nail.'

'Be aisey, Nicholas. You know the weight of the hammer, that's enough. It's not a whipping with feathers you're going to get, anyhow. Just be aisey.'

'Mr Dawson, I grant I'm not your match. Release me, and I double the case. I was merely trying your temper when I took the shape of a guinea.'

'Faith and I'll try yours before I lave it, I've a notion.' He immediately commenced with the sledge, and Satan sang out with a considerable want of firmness. 'Am I heavy enough!' said Bill.

'Lighter, lighter, William, if you love me. I haven't been well latterly, Mr Dawson – I have been delicate – my health, in short, is in a very precarious state, Mr Dawson.'

'I can believe *that*,' said Bill, 'and it will be more so before I have done with you. Am I doing it right?'

'Bill,' said Nick, 'is this gentlemanly treatment in your own respectable shop? Do you think, if you dropped into my little place, that I'd act this rascally part toward you? Have you no compunction?'

'I know,' replied Bill, sledging away with vehemence, 'that you're notorious for giving your friends a *warm* welcome. Devil an ould youth more so; but you must be daling in bad coin, must you? However, good or bad, you're in for a sweat now, you sinner. Am I doin' it purty?'

'Lovely, William – but, if possible, a little more delicate.'

'Oh, how delicate you are! Maybe a cup o' tay would sarve you, or a little small gruel to compose your stomach?'

'Mr Dawson,' said the gentleman in the purse, 'hold your hand and let us understand one another. I have a proposal to make.'

'Hear the sinner anyhow,' said the wife.

'Name your own sum,' said Satan, 'only set me free.'

'No, the sorra may take the toe you'll budge till you let Bill off,' said the wife; 'hould him hard, Bill, barrin' he sets you clear of your engagement.

'There it is, my posy,' said Bill; 'that's the condition. If you don't give *me up*, here's at you once more – and you must double the cash you gave the last time, too. So, if you're of that opinion, say *ay* – leave the cash and be off.'

The money appeared in a glittering heap before Bill, upon which he exclaimed, 'The *ay* has it, you dog. Take to your pumps now, and fair weather after you, you vagrant; but, Nicholas – Nick – here, here – ' The other looked back and saw Bill, with a broad grin upon him, shaking the purse at him. 'Nicholas, come back,' said he. 'I'm short a guinea.' Nick shook his fist and disappeared.

It would be useless to stop now, merely to inform our readers that Bill was beyond improvement. In short, he once more took to his old habits and lived on exactly in the same manner as before. He had two sons – one as great a blackguard as himself, and who was also named after him; the other was a well-conducted, virtuous young man called James, who left his father and, having relied upon his own industry and honest perseverance in life, arrived afterward to great wealth and built the town called Castle Dawson, which is so called from its founder until this day.

Bill, at length, in spite of all his wealth, was obliged, as he himself said, 'to travel' – in other words, he fell asleep one day and forgot to awaken; or, in still plainer terms, he died.

Now, it is usual, when a man dies, to close the history of his life and adventures at once; but with our hero this cannot be the case. The moment Bill departed he very naturally bent his steps toward the residence of St Moroky, as being, in his opinion, likely to lead him toward the snuggest berth he could readily make out. On arriving, he gave a very humble kind of a knock, and St Moroky appeared.

'God save your Reverence!' said Bill, very submissively.

'Be off; there's no admittance here for so poor a youth as you are,' said St Moroky.

He was now so cold and fatigued that he cared like where he went, provided only, as he said himself, 'he could rest his bones and get an air of the fire.' Accordingly, after arriving at a large black gate, he knocked, as before, and was told he would get *instant* admittance the moment he gave his name.

'Billy Dawson,' he replied.

'Off, instantly,' said the porter to his companions, 'and let His Majesty know that the rascal he dreads so much is here at the gate.'

Such a racket and tumult were never heard as the very mention of Billy Dawson created.

In the meantime, his old acquaintance came running toward the gate with such haste and consternation that his tail was several times nearly tripping up his heels.

'Don't admit that rascal,' he shouted; 'bar the gate – make every chain and lock the bolt fast – I won't be safe – and I won't stay here, nor none of us need stay here, if he gets in – my bones are sore yet after him. No, no – begone, you villain – you'll get no entrance here – I know you too well.'

Bill could not help giving a broad, malicious grin at Satan, and, putting his nose through the bars, he exclaimed, 'Ha! you ould dog, I have you afraid of me at last, have I?'

He had scarcely uttered the words, when his foe, who stood inside, instantly tweaked him by the nose, and Bill felt as if he had been gripped by the same red-hot tongs with which he himself had formerly tweaked the nose of Nicholas.

Bill then departed but soon found that in consequence of the inflammable materials which strong drink had thrown into his nose, that organ immediately took fire, and, indeed, to tell the truth, kept burning night and day, winter and summer, without ever once going out from that hour to this.

Such was the sad fate of Billy Dawson, who has been walking without stop or stay, from place to place, ever since; and in consequence of the flame on his nose, and his beard being tangled like a wisp of hay, he has been christened by the country folk Will-o'-the-Wisp, while, as it were, to show the mischief of his disposition, the circulating knave, knowing that he must seek the coldest bogs and quagmires in order to cool his nose, seizes upon that opportunity of misleading the unthinking and tipsy night travellers from their way, just that he may have the satisfaction of still taking in as many as possible.

The Gollan

A. E. COPPARD

There was once a peasant named Goose who had worked his back crooked with never a thank-ye from providence or man, and he had a son, Gosling, whom the neighbours called the Gollan for short. The Gollan was an obedient child and strong, though not by nature very willing. He was so obedient that he would do without question whatever anybody told him to do. One day he was bringing his mother three eggs in a basket and he met a rude boy.

'Hoi,' called the rude boy, 'are those eggs the bouncing eggs?'

'Are they?' enquired the Gollan.

'Try one and see,' the rude boy said.

The Gollan took one of the eggs from the basket and dropped it to the ground, and it broke.

'Haw!' complained the rude one, 'you did not do it properly. How could an egg bounce if you dropped it so? You must throw it hard and it will fly back into your hand like a bird.'

So the Gollan took another and dashed it to the ground and waited. But the egg only lay spilled at his feet.

'No, no, no! Stupid fellow!' the rude boy cried. 'Look. Throw the other one up in the air high as you can and all three will bounce back into your basket.'

So the Gollan threw the last egg up on high, but it only dropped beside the others and all lay in a slop of ruins.

'Oh dear! What will my mother say? Oh dear!' wept the Gollan.

The rude boy merely put his thumb to his nose and ran off upon his proper business, laughing.

The Gollan grew up a great powerful fellow, and whatever anyone told him to do, it might be simple, it might be hard, he did it without repining, which shows that he had a kind heart anyway, though he had little enough inclination to work; indeed he had no wish to at all.

One day his father said to him: 'My son, you are full of strength and vigour, you are the prop of my old age and the apple of my two eyes. Take now these five and twenty pigs and go you to market and dispose of them. Beware of false dealing, and you may hear wonders.'

'What wonders should I hear?'

'Mum,' said his father, 'is the word. Say nothing and scare nobody.'

He gave him two noggins of ale and off went the Gollan. And it was a queer half and half day, however, but full of colour. There were poppies in the green corn, charlock in the Swedes, and weak sunlight in the opaline sky. He tried to drive the pigs but they had their minds set upon some other matters and would not go where they should because of distractions and interruptions. There was the green corn, there were the swedes, and there were heifers in the lane, lambs afield, and hens in every hedge, so before he had gone a mile the pigs were all astray.

'I don't care where those pigs go,' then said the Gollan to himself. 'I don't trouble about those pigs as long as I have my strength and vigour.' So he lay down under a nut hazel-bush and was soon sleeping.

In the course of time – long or short makes no odds – he heard someone whistling shrilly, and waking up he looked about him to the right hand and to the left and soon saw a person caught hard and fast in a catchpole, a little plump man with a red beard and bright buckled shoes.

'Well met, friend!' the little man called out. 'Pray release me from this trap and I will make your fortune.' So the Gollan went and put out all his strength and vigour, with a heave and a hawk and a crash, until he had drawn the little plump man out of the trap and set him free.

'Thanks, friend,' said the leprechaun – for he was that and no less, not like any man you ever read about. 'You have done me a kind service. Ask any reward you will and I will give it.'

'Sir,' said the Gollan, 'there is no matter about that. I am the prop of my father's age and the apple of his two eyes. I have strength and vigour with which I work for what I need.'

'Unhappy is that man,' the leprechaun answered, 'who serves his need and not his choice. You have strength and vigour, but how do you use it?'

The Gollan drew himself up proudly: 'I can crack rocks and hew trees.'

'Well, then,' replied the other, 'crack on, and hew.'

'Alas,' the Gollan explained, 'I have four fingers and a thumb on one hand, four fingers and a thumb on the other, all of them able – but not one of them willing.' And he confided to the leprechaun that it was his doom and distress to be at the beck and call of everyone because of his strength and vigour, and he with no heart to refuse to do a deed required of him.

'That cannot be endured. I can easily remedy it,' said the leprechaun. 'I will make you invisible to mankind, except only when you are asleep. Nobody will be able to see you when you are awake and walking, therefore they will not be able to give you a task of any kind.'

So he made the Gollan invisible there and then, and no one saw the Gollan any more, save his parents when he was sleeping, and his life became a bed or roses and a bower of bliss. Where is the Gollan? – people would say. But though they knew he was thereabout they could not set eyes on him and they could not find him. If the Gollan were only with us – they would say – he would do this tiresome labour, he would do it well. But as he was no longer visible to them they could not catch him and they could not ask him. The Gollan would be about in the sunlight day after day doing nothing at all, and got so blown up with pride that he thought: 'I am invisible, no one can task me in my strength and vigour. I am king of all the unseen world, and that is as good as twenty of these other kings. I live as I choose, and I take my need as I want it.'

But though it was all very grand to be invisible the Gollan soon found out that there was small blessing in it. He could be seen by none save when he slept, but the truth is neither could he see anybody – man, woman, or child. No one could hear him, but then he himself could hear no one – man, woman, or child. It was the same way with smelling, touching and tasting. Animals and birds he could see, and he could talk to them, but they were so hard of understanding that he might as well have conversed with a monument or a door. Sure, he had kept his wits but he had lost his five senses, and that is cruel fortune.

After a while his heart grew weary for the sight of his friends and the talk and sounds of people, he was tired of seeing animals and birds only, so he went to a hawk he knew that had the most piercing gaze, and said: 'Friend, lend me your two eyes for a while and I will pawn you my own for their safe return.'

'Will I? Will I?' mused the hawk.

'You will!' the Gollan sternly said.

So they exchanged, but the Gollan was greatly deceived by these hawk eyes. He went about wearing them far and near, and he saw thousands of mice and birds and moles, but those eyes never set their gaze on a single human creature, good, bad, or medium. What was worse, rascally things, they never seemed to want to! The farther he wandered the more sure it became that those eyes were merely looking out for moles and voles and suchlike. He saw nothing else except a jackass with fine upstanding ears straying in a bethistled waste whom he accosted: 'Friend, lend me your two ears for a while. I will pawn you my own for their safe return.'

'Will you? Won't you?' mused the ass.

'I will,' declared the Gollan, for he longed to hear human speech again, or a song to cheer him.

So they exchanged. But the Gollan was more deceived and bewildered than ever, for he never caught the sound of any pleasant human talk. What he heard was only an ass's bald portion, vile oaths, denunciations, and abuse. And although it all rushed into one ear and quickly fell out of the other, it was not good hearing at all; it was not satisfactory. When he heard a pig grunting not far off he hastened to the pig, saying: 'Friend, lend me your nose. I will pawn you mine for its safe return.'

'Ask me no more,' said the pig, surveying him with a rueful smile as he suffered the Gollan to make the exchange.

But something kept the Gollan from smelling anything save what a pig may smell. Instead of flowers, the odour of fruit, or the cook's oven, the swinish nostrils delighted only in the vapours of swill and offal and ordure. Surely – thought the Gollan – it is better to be invisible and senseless than to live thus. So he tried no further, but gave back the eyes, the ears, and the nose and received his pledges again.

Now at that time the king of the land was much put about by the reason of a little pond that lay in front of his palace. It was a meager patch of water and no ways good.

'If only this were a lake,' sighed the king, 'a great lake of blue water with neat waves and my ships upon it and my swans roving and my snipe calling and my fish going to and fro, my realm would be a great realm and the envy of the whole world.'

And one day, as he was wandering and wondering what he could do about this, he came upon the Gollan lying on a green bank drowsing and dreaming. Of course when the king set eyes on him, he saw him and knew him.

'Hoi, Gollan!' the king roared at him. 'Stretch out that water for me!' Just like that. The Gollan woke up and at once became invisible again, but he was so startled at being roared at that without thinking, just absent-mindedly, he stretched out the water of the king's pond and there and then it became a fine large lake with neat waves and ships and swans and suchlike, beautiful – though when he learned the right of it the Gollan was crabby and vexed, 'I am the king of the unseen world, and that's as good as any twenty of these other kings.' Still, he could not alter it back again. Whatever he did had to stay as it was once done: it could neither be changed nor improved.

However, by the reason of his fine new lake and ships the king's realm became the envy of all other nations, who began to strive after it after it and attack it. The king was not much of a one for martial dispositions and so the whole of his country was soon beleaguered and the people put to miserable extravagances.

Now although the Gollan could not directly see or hear anything of this, yet one way and another he came to know something of the misfortune, and then he was worn to a tatter with rage and fury by the reason he was such a great one for the patriotism. And he was powerless to help now his five senses were gone from him.

'O, what sort of a game is this,' he thought, 'now the world is in ruins and I have no more senses than a ghost or a stone! I had the heart of an ass when I took that red-haired villain out of his trap and had his reward. Reward! Take it back! Take it back, you palavering old crow of a catchpole! You have cramped me tight and hauled me to a grave. Take it back, you!'

'Well met, friend,' a voice replied, and there was the old leprechaun bowing before him. 'Your wish is granted.'

True it was. They were standing beside a field of corn ripe and ready, waving and sighing it was. The Gollan could hear once more, he could touch, taste, and smell again, and he could see his own royal king as clear as print on a page of history hurrying down the road towards them.

'What else can I do for you?' asked the little red-haired man.

'I fancy,' said the Gollan, jerking his thumb towards the king, 'he is running to ask me for a large great army.'

'You shall have that,' said the leprechaun, vanishing away at the king's approach.

'Gollan,' the king says, 'I want a large great army.'

'Yes, Sir,' says the Gollan. 'Will you have the grenadiers, the bombardiers, or men of the broadsword?'

He said he would have the bombardiers.

Well, the Gollan made a pass of his hand over that field of corn, and the standing stalks at once began to whistle and sway sideways. Before you could blink a lash there they were, 50,000 men and noblemen, all marking time, all dressed to glory with great helmets and eager for battle.

'Gollan,' says the king, 'will you undertake the command of this my noble army?'

'I will that, Sir.'

'Lead on, then,' says the king, and 'may the blood of calamity never splash upon one single rib of the whole lot of you.'

Which, it is good to say, it never did. The Gollan then marched them straightway to battle by the shore of the lake.

'Get ready now,' cried General Gollan, 'here comes the artillery with their big guns!'

The bombardiers began to prepare themselves and first gave a blast on their trumpets, but the enemy got ready sooner and fired off a blast on all their culverins, mortars, and whatnot. Ah, what a roar they let out of that huge and fatal cannonade! It would have frightened the trunk of a tree out of its own bark, and at the mere sound of it every man of General Gollan's army toppled to the earth like corn that is cut, never to rise again.

'What is it and all!' cried the distracted Gollan. 'Is this another joke of that palavering old crow of a catchpole? By the soul of my aunty!' he exclaimed, as he surveyed his exposed position amid all those fallen bombardiers, so neat, so gallant, so untimely dead, 'By the soul of my aunty I think I'd rather be invisible now!'

In a twink he was invisible once more, and his five senses gone again; but none of his friends ever had time to enquire what became of him because the conquering general painfully exterminated them all.

Unseen, unknown, the good Gollan lived on for many years in great privation, and when he at last came to die (though nobody knew even about that) he had grown mercifully wise and wrote his own epitaph – though nobody ever saw it: 'To choose was my need, but need brooks no choosing'.

The Eyes of the Dead

DANIEL CORKERY

I

If he had not put it off for three year Johns Spillane's homecoming would have been that of a famous man. Bonfires would have been lighted on the hilltops of Rossamara, and the ships passing by, twenty miles out, would have wondered what they meant.

Three years ago, the *Western Star*, an Atlantic liner, one night tore her iron plates to pieces against the cliff-like face of an iceberg, and in less than an hour sank in the waters. Of the seven hundred and eighty-nine human souls aboard her one only had been saved, John Spillance, able seaman, of Rossamara in the country of Cork. The name of the little fishing village, his own name, his picture, were in all the papers of the world, it seemed, not only because he alone had escaped, but by reason of the manner of that escape. He had clung to a drift of wreckage, must have lost consciousness for more than a whole day, floated then about on the ocean for a second day, for a second night, and had arrived at the threshold of another dreadful night when he was rescued. A fog was coming down on the waters. It frightened him more than the darkness. He raised a shout. He kept on shouting. When safe in the arms of his rescuers his breathy, almost inaudible voice was still forcing out some cry which they interpreted as Help! Help!

That was what had struck the imagination of men – the half-insane figure sending his cry over the waste of waters, the fog thickening, and the night falling. Although the whole world had read also of the groping rescue ship, of Spillane's bursts of hysterical laughter, of his inability to tell his story until he had slept eighteen hours on end, what remained in the memory was the lonely figure sending his cry over the sea.

And then, almost before his picture had disappeared from the papers, he had lost himself in the great cities of the States. To

Rossamara no world had come from himself, nor for a long time from any acquaintance; but then, when about a year had gone by, his sister or mother as they went up the road to Mass of a Sunday might be stopped and informed in a whispering voice that John had been seen in Chicago, or, it might be, in New York, or Boston, or San Francisco, or indeed anywhere. And from the meagreness of the messages it was known, with only too much certainty, that he had not, in exchanging sea for land, bettered his lot. If once again his people had happened on such empty tidings of him, one knew it by their bowed and stilly attitude in the little church as the light whisper of the Mass rose and fell about them.

When three years had gone by he lifted the latch of his mother's house one October evening and stood awkwardly in the middle of the floor. It was nightfall and not a soul had seen him break down from the ridge and cross the roadway. He had come secretly from the ends of the earth.

And before he was an hour in their midst he rose up impatiently, timidly, and stole into his bed.

'I don't want any light,' he said, and as his mother left him there in the dark, she heard him yield his whole being to a sigh of thankfulness. Before that he had told them he felt tired, a natural thing, since he had tramped fifteen miles from the railway station in Skibbereen. But day followed day without his showing any desire to rise from the bedclothes and go abroad among the people. He had had enough of the sea, it seemed; enough too of the great cities of the States. He was a pity, the neighbours said; and the few of them who from time to time caught glimpses of him, reported him as not yet having lost the scared look that the ocean had left on him. His hair was grey or nearly grey, they said, and, swept back fiercely from his forehead, a fashion strange to the place, seemed to pull his eyes open, to keep them wide open, as he looked at you. His moustache also was grey, they said, and his cheeks were grey too, sunken and dark with shadows. Yet his mother and sister, the only others in the house, were glad to have him back with them; at any rate, they said, they knew where he was.

They found nothing wrong with him. Of speech neither he nor they ever had had the gift; and as day followed day, and week week, the same few phrases would carry them through the day and into the silence of night. In the beginning they had thought it natural to speak with him about the wreck; soon, however, they came to know

that it was a subject for which he had no welcome. In the beginning
also, they had thought to rouse him by bringing the neighbour to his
bedside, but such visits instead of cheering him only left him sunken
in silence, almost in despair. The priest came to see him once in a
while, and advise the mother and sister, Mary her name was, to treat
him as normally as they could, letting on that his useless presence
was no affliction to them nor even a burden. In time John Spillane
was accepted by all as one of those unseen ones, or seldom-seen
ones, who are to be found in every village in the word – the bedridden, the struck-down, the aged – forgotten of all except the few
faithful creatures who bring the cup to the bedside of a morning,
and open the curtains to let in the sun.

2

In the nearest house, distant a quarter-mile from them, lived Tom
Leane. In the old days before John Spillane went to sea, Tom had
been his companion, and now of a night-time he would drop in if he
had any story worth telling or if, on the day following, he chanced to
be going back to Skibbereen, where he might buy the Spillanes such
goods as they needed, or sell a pig for them, slipping it in among his
own. He was a quiet creature, married, and struggling to bring up
the little family that was thickening about him. In the Spillanes' he
would, dragging at the pipe, sit on the settle, and quietly gossip with
the old woman while Mary moved about on the flags putting the
household gear tidy for the night. But all three of them, as they kept
up the simple talk, were never unaware of the silent listener in the
lower room. Of that room the door was kept open; but no lamp was
lighted within it; no lamp indeed was needed, for a shaft of light
from the kitchen struck into it showing one or two of the religious
pictures on the wall and giving sufficient light to move about in.
Sometimes the conversation would drift away from the neighbourly
doings, for even to Rossamara tidings from the great world abroad
would sometimes come; in the middle of such gossip, however, a
sudden thought would strike Tom Leane, and, raising his voice, he
would blurt out: 'But sure 'tis foolish for the like of me to be talking
about these far-off places, and that man inside after travelling the
world, over and thither.' The man inside, however, would give no
sign whatever whether their gossip had been wise or foolish. They

might hear the bed creak, as if he had turned with impatience at their mention of his very presence.

There had been a spell of stormy weather, it was now the middle of February, and for the last five days at twilight the gale seemed always to set in for a night of it. Although there was scarcely a house around that part of the southwest Irish coast that had not some one of its members, husband or brother or son, living on the sea, sailoring abroad or fishing the home waters or those of the Isle of Man – in no other house was the strain of a spell of disastrous weather so noticeable in the faces of its inmates. The old woman, withdrawn into herself, would handle her beads all day long, her voice every now and then raising itself, in forgetfulness, to a sort of moan not unlike the wind's upon which the younger woman would chide her with a 'Sh! sh!' and bend vigorously upon her work to keep bitterness from her thoughts. At such a time she might enter her brother's room and find him raised on his elbow in the bed, listening to the howling winds, scared it seemed, his eyes fixed and wide open. He would drink the warm milk she had brought him, and hand the vessel back without a word. And in the selfsame attitude she would leave him.

The fifth night instead of growing in loudness and fierceness the wind died away somewhat. It became fitful, promising the end of the storm; and before long they could distinguish between the continuous groaning and pounding of the sea and the sudden shout the dying tempest would fling among the treetops and the rocks. They were thankful to note such signs of relief; the daughter became more active, and the mother put by her beads. In the midst of a sudden sally of the wind's the latch was raised, and Tom Leane gave them greeting. His face was rosy and glowing under his sou'wester; his eyes were sparkling from the sting of the salty gusts. To see him, so sane, so healthy, was to them like a blessing. 'How is it with ye?' he said, cheerily, closing the door to.

'Good, then, good, then,' they answered him, and the mother rose almost as if she would take him by the hand. The reply meant that nothing unforeseen had befallen them. He understood as much. He shook a silent head in the direction of the listener's room, a look of enquiry in his eyes, and this look Mary answered with a sort of hopeless upswing of her face. Things had not improved in the lower room.

The wind died away, more and more; and after some time streamed by with a shrill steady undersong; all through, however, the crashing of the sea on the jagged rocks beneath kept up an unceasing clamour. Tom had a whole budget of news for them. Finny's barn had been stripped of its roof; a window in the chapel had been blown in; and Largy's store of fodder had been shredded in the wind; it littered all the bushes to the east. There were rumours of a wreck somewhere; but it was too soon yet to know what damage the sea had done in its five days' madness. The news he had brought them did not matter; what mattered was his company, the knitting of their half-distraught household once again to humankind. Even when at last he stood up to go, their spirits did not droop, so great had been the restoration.

'We' re finished with it for a while anyhow,' Tom said, rising for home.

'We are, we are; and who knows, it mightn't be after doing all the damage we think.'

He shut the door behind him. The two women had turned towards the fire when they thought they again heard his voice outside. They wondered at the sound; they listened for his footsteps. Still staring at the closed door, once more they heard his voice. This time they were sure. The door reopened, and he backed in, as one does from an unexpected slap of rain in the face. The light struck outwards, and they saw a white face advancing. Some anxiety, some uncertainty, in Tom's attitude as he backed away from that advancing face, invaded them so that they too became afraid. They saw the stranger also hesitating, looking down his own limbs. His clothes were dripping; they were clung in about him. He was bare headed. When he raised his face again, his look was full of apology. His features were large and flat, and grey as a stone. Every now and then a spasm went through them, and they wondered what it meant. His clab of a mouth hung open; his unshaven chin trembled. Tom spoke to him: 'You'd better come in; but 'tis many another house would suit you better than this.'

They heard a husky, scarce-audible voice reply: 'A doghouse would do, or a stable.' Bravely enough he made an effort to smile.

'Oh, 'tisn't that at all. But come in, come in.' He stepped in slowly and heavily, again glancing down his limbs. The water running from his clothes spread in a black pool on the flags. The young woman began to touch him with her finger tips as with some instinctive sympathy, yet could not think, it seemed, what was best to be done. The mother, however, vigorously set the fire-wheel at work, and

Tom built up the fire with bog-timber and turf. The stranger mean-while stood as if half-dazed. At last, as Mary with a candle in her hand stood pulling out dry clothes from a press, he blurted out in the same husky voice, Welsh in accent: 'I think I'm the only one!'

They understood the significance of the words, but it seemed wrong to do so.

'What is it you're saying?' Mary said, but one would not have recognised the voice for hers, it was so toneless. He raised a heavy sailor's hand in an awkward taproom gesture: 'The others, they're gone, all of them.'

The spasm again crossed his homely features, and his hand fell. He bowed his head. A coldness went through them. They stared at him. He might have thought them inhuman. But Mary suddenly pulled herself together, leaping at him almost: 'Sh! Sh!' she said, 'speak low, speak low, low,' and as she spoke, all earnestness, she towed him first in the direction of the fire, and then away from it, haphazardly it seemed. She turned from him and whispered to Tom: 'Look, take him up into the loft, and he can change his clothes. Take these with you, and the candle, the candle.' And she reached him the candle eagerly. Tom led the stranger up the stairs, it was more like a ladder, and the two of them disappeared into the loft. The old woman whispered: 'What was it he said?'

' 'Tis how his ship is sunk.'

'Did he says he was the only one?'

'He said that.'

'Did himself hear him?' She nodded towards her son's room.

'No, didn't you see me pulling him away from it? But he'll hear him now. Isn't it a wonder Tom Wouldn't walk easy on the boards!'

No answer from the old woman. She had deliberately seated her-self in her accustomed place at the fire, and now moaned out: 'Aren't we in a cruel way, not knowing how he'd take a thing!'

'Am I better tell him there's a poor seaman after coming in on us?'

'Do you hear them above! Do you hear them!'

In the loft the men's feet were loud on the boards. The voice they were half-expecting to hear they then heard break in on the clatter of the boots above: 'Mother! Mother!'

'Yes, child, yes.'

'Who's aloft? Who's going around like that, or is it dreaming I am?'

The sounds from above were certainly like what one hears in a ship. They thought of this, but they also felt something terrible in that voice they had been waiting for: they hardly knew it for the voice of the man they had been listening to for five months.

'Go in and tell him the truth,' the mother whispered. 'Who are we to know what's right to be done. Let God have the doing of it.' She threw her hands in the air.

Mary went in to her brother, and her limbs were weak and cold. The old woman remained seated at the fire, swung round from it, her eyes towards her son's room, fixed, as the head itself was fixed, in the tension of anxiety.

After a few minutes Mary emerged with a strange alertness upon her: 'He's rising! He's getting up! 'Tis his place, he says. He's quite good.' She meant he seemed bright and well. The mother said: 'We'll take no notice of him, only just as if he was always with us.'

'Yes.'

They were glad then to hear the two men in the loft groping for the stair head. The kettle began to splutter in the boil, and Mary busied herself with the table and tea cups.

The sailor came down, all smiles in his ill-fitting, haphazard clothes. He looked so overjoyed one might think he would presently burst into song.

3

'The fire is good,' he said. 'It puts life in one. And the dry clothes too. My word, I'm thankful to you, good people; I'm thankful to you.' He shook hands with them all effusively.

'Sit down now; drink up the tea.'

'I can't figure it out; less than two hours ago, out there . . . As he spoke he raised his hand towards the little porthole of a window, looking at them with his eyes staring. 'Don't be thinking of anything, but drink up the hot tea,' Mary said.

He nodded and set to eat with vigour. Yet suddenly he would stop, as if he were ashamed of it, turn half-round and look at them with beaming eyes, look from one to the other and back again; and they affably would nod back at him. 'Excuse me, people,' he would say, 'excuse me.' He had not the gift of speech, and his too-full heart could not declare itself. To make him feel at his ease, Tom Leane sat down away from him, and the women began to find something to do about the room. Then there were only little sounds in the room: the breaking of the eggs, the turning of the fire-wheel, the wind going by. The door of the lower room opened silently, so silently that none of them heard it, and before they were aware, the son of the house, with his clothes flung on loosely, was standing awkwardly in the middle of the floor, looking down on the back of the sailorman bent above the table. 'This is my son,' the mother thought of saying. 'He was after going to bed when you came in.'

The Welshman leaped to his feet, and impulsively, yet without many words, shook John Spillane by the hand, thanking him and all the household. As he seated himself again at the table John made his way silently towards the settle from which, across the room, he could see the sailor as he bent over his meal.

The stranger put the cup away from him, he could take no more; and Tom Leane and the womenfolk tried to keep him in talk, avoiding, as by some mutual understanding, the mention of what he had come through. The eyes of the son of the house were all the time fiercely buried in him. There came a moment's silence in the general chatter, a moment it seemed impossible to fill, and the sailorman swung his chair half-round from the table, a spoon held in his hand lightly: 'I can't figure it out. I can't nohow figure it out. Here I am, fed full like a prize beast; and warm – Oh, but I'm thankful – and all my mates,' with the spoon he was pointing towards the sea – 'white, and cold like dead fish! I can't figure it out.'

To their astonishment a voice travelled across the room from the settle.

'Is it how ye struck?'

'Struck! Three times we struck! We struck last night, about this time last night. And off we went in a puff! Fine, we said. We struck again. 'Twas just coming light. And off again. But when we struck the third time, 'twas like that!' He clapped his hands together; 'She went in matchwood! 'Twas dark. Why, it can't be two hours since!'

'She went to pieces?' the same voice questioned him.

'The *Nan Tidy* went to pieces, sir! No one knew what had happened or where he was. 'Twas too sudden. I found myself clung about a snag of rock. I hugged it.'

He stood up, hoisted as from within.

'Is it you that was on the look-out?'

'Me! We'd all been on the look-out for three days. My word, yes, three days. We were stupefied with it!'

They were looking at him as he spoke, and they saw the shiver again cross his features; the strength and warmth that the food and comfort had given him fell from him, and he became in an instant the half-drowned man who had stepped in to them that night with the clothes sagging about his limbs, ' 'Twas bad, clinging to that rock, with them all gone! 'Twas lonely! Do you know, I was so frightened I couldn't call out.' John Spillane stood up, slowly, as if he too were being hoisted from within.

'Were they looking at you?'

'Who?'

'The rest of them. The eyes of them.'

'No,' the voice had dropped, 'no, I didn't think of that!' The two of them stared as if fascinated by each other.

'You didn't!' It seemed that John Spillane had lost the purpose of his questioning. His voice was thin and weak; but he was still staring with unmoving, puzzled eyes at the stranger's face. The abashed creature before him suddenly seemed to gain as much eagerness as he had lost: his words were hot with anxiety to express himself adequately: 'But now, isn't it curious, as I sat there, there at that table, I thought somehow they would walk in, that it would be right for them, somehow, to walk in, all of them!'

His words, his eager lowered voice, brought in the darkness outside, its vastness, its terror. They seemed in the midst of an unsubstantial world. They feared that the latch would lift, yet dared not glance at it, lest that should invite the lifting. But it was all one to the son of the house, he appeared to have gone away into some mood of his own; his eyes were glaring, not looking at anything or anyone close at hand. With an instinctive groping for comfort, they all, except him, began to stir, to find some little homely task to do: Mary Handled the tea ware, and Tom his pipe, when a rumbling voice, very indistinct, stilled them all again. Words, phrases, began to reach them – that a man's eyes will close and he on the lookout, close in spite of himself, that it wasn't fair, it wasn't fair, it wasn't fair! And lost in his agony, he began to glide through them, explaining, excusing the terror that was in him: 'All round. Staring at me. Blaming me. A sea of them. Far, far! Without a word out of them, only their eyes in the darkness, pale like candles!'

Transfixed, they glared at him, at his round-shouldered sailor's back disappearing again into his den of refuge. They could not hear his voice any more, they were afraid to follow him.

The Dead Smile

FRANCIS MARION CRAWFORD

I

Sir Hugh Ockram Smiled as he sat by the open window of his study, in the late August afternoon, and just then a curiously yellow cloud obscured the low sun, and the clear summer light turned lurid, as if it had been suddenly poisoned and polluted by the foul vapours of a plague. Sir Hugh's face seemed, at best, to be made of fine parchment drawn skintight over a wooden mask, in which two eyes were sunk out of sight, and peered from far within through crevices under the slanting, wrinkled lids, alive and watchful like two toads in their holes, side by side and exactly alike. But as the light changed, then a little yellow glare flashed in each. Nurse Macdonald said once that when Sir Hugh smiled he saw the faces of two women in hell – two dead women he had betrayed. (Nurse Macdonald was a hundred years old.) And the smile widened, stretching the pale lips across the discoloured teeth in an expression of profound self-satisfaction, blended with the most unforgiving hatred and contempt for the human soul. The hideous disease of which he was dying had touched his brain. His son stood beside him, tall, white, and delicate as an angel in a primitive picture, and though there was deep distress in his violet eyes as he looked at his father's face, he felt the shadow of that sickening smile stealing across his own lips and parting them and drawing them against his will. And it was like a bad dream, for he tried not to smile and smiled the more. Beside him, strangely like him in her wan, angelic beauty, with the same shadowy golden hair, the same sad violet eyes, the same luminously pale face, Evelyn Warburton rested one hand upon his arm. And as she looked into her uncle's eyes, and could not turn her own away, she knew that the deathly smile was hovering on her own red lips, drawing them tightly across her little teeth, while two bright tears ran down her cheeks to her mouth, and dropped from the upper to the lower lip while she smiled – and the smile was like the shadow of death and the seal of damnation upon her pure, young face.

'Of course,' said Sir Hugh very slowly, and still looking out at the trees, 'if you have made up your mind to be married, I cannot hinder you, and I don't suppose you attach the smallest importance to my consent – '

'Father!' exclaimed Gabriel reproachfully.

'No, I do not deceive myself,' continued the old man, smiling terribly. 'You will marry when I am dead, though there is a very good reason why you had better not – why you had better not,' he repeated very emphatically, and he slowly turned his toad eyes upon the lovers.

'What reason?' asked Evelyn in a frightened voice.

'Never mind the reason, my dear. You will marry just as if it did not exist.' There was a long pause. 'Two gone,' he said, his voice lowering strangely, 'and two more will be four – all together – for ever and ever, burning, burning, burning bright.'

At the last words his head sank slowly back, and the little glare of the toad eyes disappeared under the swollen lids, and the lurid cloud passed from the westering sun, so that the earth was green again and the light pure. Sir Hugh had fallen asleep, as he often did in his last illness, even while speaking.

Gabriel Ockram drew Evelyn away, and from the study they went out into the dim hall, softly closing the door behind them, and each audibly drew breath, as though some sudden danger had been passed. They laid their hands each in the other's and their strangely-alike eyes met in a long look, in which love and perfect understanding were darkened by the secret terror of an unknown thing. Their pale faces reflected each other's fear.

'It is his secret,' said Evelyn at last. 'He will never tell us what it is.'

'If he dies with it,' answered Gabriel, 'let it be on his own head!'

'On his head!' echoed the dim hall. It was a strange echo, and some were frightened by it, for they said that if it were a real echo it should repeat everything and not give back a phrase here and there, now speaking, now silent. But Nurse Macdonald said that the great hall would never echo a prayer when an Ockram was to die, though it would give back curses ten for one.

'On his head!' it repeated quite softly, and Evelyn started and looked round.

'It is only the echo.' said Gabriel, leading her away.

They went out into the late afternoon light, and sat upon a stone seat behind the chapel, which was built across the end of the east wing. It was very still, not a breath stirred, and there was no sound near them. Only far off in the park a songbird was whistling the high prelude to the evening chorus.

'It is very lonely here,' said Evelyn, taking Gabriel's hand nervously, and speaking as if she dreaded to disturb the silence. 'If it were dark, I should be afraid.'

'Of what? Of me?' Gabriel's sad eyes turned to her.

'Oh no! How could I be afraid of you? But of the old Ockrams – they say they are just under our feet here in the north vault outside the chapel, all in their shrouds, with no coffins, as they used to bury them.'

'As they always will – as they will bury my father, and me. They say an Ockram will not lie in a coffin.'

'But it cannot be true – these are fairy tales – ghost stories!' Evelyn nestled nearer to her companion, grasping his hand more tightly, and the sun began to go down.

'Of course. But there is a story of old Sir Vernon, who was beheaded for treason under James II. The family brought his body back from the scaffold in an iron coffin with heavy locks, and they put it in the north vault. But ever afterwards, whenever the vault was opened to bury another of the family, they found the coffin wide open, and the body standing upright against the wall, and the head rolled away in a corner, smiling at it.'

'As Uncle Hugh smiles?' Evelyn shivered.

'Yes, I suppose so,' answered Gabriel, thoughtfully. 'Of course I never saw it, and the vault has not been opened for thirty years – none of us have died since then.'

'And if – if Uncle Hugh dies – shall you – ' Evelyn stopped, and her beautiful thin face was quite white.

'Yes. I shall see him laid there too – with his secret, whatever it is.' Gabriel sighed and pressed the girl's little hand.

'I do not like to think of it,' she said unsteadily. 'O Gabriel, what can the secret be? He said we had better not marry – not that he forbade it – but he said it so strangely, and he smiled – ugh!' Her small white teeth chattered with fear, and she looked over her shoulder while drawing still closer to Gabriel. 'And, somehow, I felt it in my own face – '

'So did I,' answered Gabriel in a low, nervous voice. 'Nurse Macdonald – ' He stopped abruptly.

'What? What did she say?'

'Oh – nothing. She has told me things – they would frighten you, dear. Come, it is growing chilly.' He rose, but Evelyn held his hand in both of hers, still sitting and looking up into his face.

'But we shall be married, just the same – Gabriel! Say that we shall!'

'Of course, darling – of course. But while my father is so very ill it is impossible – '

'O Gabriel, Gabriel dear! I wish we were married now!' cried Evelyn in sudden distress. 'I know that something will prevent it and keep us apart.'

'Nothing shall!'

'Nothing?'

'Nothing human,' said Gabriel Ockram, as she drew him down to her.

And their faces, that were so strangely alike, met and touched – and Gabriel knew that the kiss had a marvellous savour of evil, but on Evelyn's lips it was like the cool breath of a sweet and mortal fear. And neither of them understood, for they were innocent and young. Yet she drew him to her by her lightest touch, as a sensitive plant shivers and waves its thin leaves, and bends and closes softly upon what it wants, and he let himself be drawn to her willingly, as he would if her touch had been deadly and poisonous; for she strangely loved that half voluptuous breath of fear and he passionately desired the nameless evil something that lurked in her maiden lips.

'It is as if we loved in a strange dream,' she said.

'I fear the waking,' he murmured.

'We shall not wake, dear – when the dream is over it will have already turned into death, so softly that we shall not know it. But until then – '

She paused, and her eyes sought his, and their faces slowly came nearer. It was as if they had thoughts in their red lips that foresaw and foreknew the deep kiss of each other.

'Until then – ' she said again, very low, and her mouth was nearer to his.

'Dream – till then,' murmured his breath.

Nurse Macdonald was a hundred years old. She used to sleep sitting all bent together in a great old leathern armchair with wings, her feet in a bag footstool lined with sheepskin, and many warm blankets wrapped about her, even in summer. Beside her a little lamp always burned at night by an old silver cup, in which there was something to drink.

Her face was very wrinkled, but the wrinkles were so small and fine and near together that they made shadows instead of lines. Two thin locks of hair, that was turning from white to a smoky yellow again, were drawn over her temples from under her starched white cap. Every now and then she woke, and her eyelids were drawn up in tiny folds like little pink silk curtains, and her queer blue eyes looked straight before her through doors and walls and worlds to a far place beyond. Then she slept again, and her hands lay one upon the other on the edge of the blanket; the thumbs had grown longer than the fingers with age, and the joints shone in the low lamplight like polished crab-apples.

It was nearly one o'clock in the night, and the summer breeze was blowing the ivy branch against the panes of the window with a hushing caress. In the small room beyond, with the door ajar, the girl-maid who took care of Nurse Macdonald was fast asleep. All was very quiet. The old woman breathed regularly, and her in-drawn lips trembled each time as the breath went out, and her eyes were shut.

But outside the closed window there was a face, and violet eyes were looking steadily at the ancient sleeper, for it was like the face of Evelyn Warburton, though there were eighty feet from the sill of the window to the foot of the tower. Yet the cheeks were thinner than Evelyn's, and as white as a gleam, and her eyes stared, and the lips were not red with life, they were dead and painted with new blood.

Slowly Nurse Macdonald's wrinkled eyelids folded themselves back, and she looked straight at the face at the window while one might count ten.

'Is it time?' she asked in her little old, faraway voice.

While she looked the face at the window changed, for the eyes opened wider and wider till the white glared all round the bright violet, and the bloody lips opened over gleaming teeth, and stretched

and widened and stretched again, and the shadowy golden hair rose
and streamed against the window in the night breeze. And in answer
to Nurse Macdonald's question came the sound that freezes the
living flesh.

That low moaning voice that rises suddenly, like the scream of a
storm, from a moan to a wail, from a wail to a howl, from a howl to
the fear-shriek of the tortured dead – he who has heard knows, and
he can bear witness that the cry of the banshee is an evil cry to hear
alone in the deep night. When it was over and the face was gone,
Nurse Macdonald shook a little in her great chair, and still she
looked at the black square of the window, but there was nothing
more there, nothing but the night, and the whispering ivy branch.
She turned her head to the door that was ajar, and there stood the
girl in her white gown, her teeth chattering with fright.

'It is time, child.' said Nurse Macdonald. 'I must go to him, for it
is the end.'

She rose slowly, leaning her withered hands upon the arms of the
chair, and the girl brought her a woollen gown and a great mantle,
and her crutch-stick, and made her ready. But very often the girl
looked at the window and was unjointed with fear, and often Nurse
Macdonald shook her head and said words which the maid could not
understand.

'It was like the face of Miss Evelyn,' said the girl at last, trembling.

But the ancient woman looked up sharply and angrily, and her
queer blue eyes glared. She held herself by the arm of the great chair
with her left hand, and lifted up her crutch-stick to strike the maid
with all her might. But she did not.

'You are a good girl,' she said, 'but you are a fool. Pray for wit,
child, pray for wit – or else find service in another house than
Ockram Hall. Bring the lamp and help me under my left arm.'

The crutch-stick clacked on the wooden floor, and the low heels
of the woman's slippers clappered after her in slow triplets as Nurse
Macdonald got toward the door. And down the stairs each step she
took was a labour in itself, and by the clacking noise the waking
servants knew that she was coming, very long before they saw her.

No one was sleeping now, and there were lights and whisperings
and pale faces in the corridors near Sir Hugh's bedroom, and now
someone went in, and now someone came out, but everyone made
way for Nurse Macdonald, who had nursed Sir Hugh's father more
than eighty years ago.

The light was soft and clear in the room. There stood Gabriel Ockram by his father's bedside, and there knelt Evelyn Warburton, her hair lying like a golden shadow down her shoulders, and her hands clasped nervously together. And opposite Gabriel, a nurse was trying to make Sir Hugh drink. But he would not, and though his lips were parted, his teeth were set. He was very, very thin and yellow now, and his eyes caught the light sideways and were as yellow coals.

'Do not torment him,' said Nurse Macdonald to the woman who held the cup. 'Let me speak to him, for his hour is come.'

'Let her speak to him,' said Gabriel in a dull voice.

So the ancient woman leaned to the pillow and laid the feather-weight of her withered hand, that was like a brown moth, upon Sir Hugh's yellow fingers, and she spoke to him earnestly, while only Gabriel and Evelyn were left in the room to hear.

'Hugh Ockram,' she said, 'this is the end of your life; and as I saw you born, and saw your father born before you, I am come to see you die. Hugh Ockram, will you tell me the truth?'

The dying man recognised the little faraway voice he had known all his life, and he very slowly turned his yellow face to Nurse Macdonald; but he said nothing. Then she spoke again.

'Hugh Ockram, you will never see the daylight again. Will you tell the truth?'

His toad-like eyes were not dull yet. They fastened themselves on her face.

'What do you want of me?' he asked, and each word struck hollow on the last. 'I have no secrets. I have lived a good life.'

Nurse Macdonald laughed – a tiny, cracked laugh, that made her old head bob and tremble a little, as if her neck were on a steel spring. But Sir Hugh's eyes grew red, and his pale lips began to twist.

'Let me die in peace,' he said slowly.

But Nurse Macdonald shook her head, and her brown, mothlike hand left his and fluttered to his forehead.

'By the mother that bore you and died of grief for the sins you did, tell me the truth!'

Sir Hugh's lips tightened on his discoloured teeth.

'Not on earth,' he answered slowly.

'By the wife who bore your son and died heartbroken, tell me the truth!'

'Neither to you in life, nor to her in eternal death.'

His lips writhed, as if the words were coals between them, and a great drop of sweat rolled across the parchment of his forehead. Gabriel Ockram bit his hand as he watched his father die. But Nurse Macdonald spoke a third time.

'By the woman whom you betrayed, and who waits for you this night, Hugh Ockram, tell me the truth!'

'It is too late. Let me die in peace.'

The writhing lips began to smile across the set yellow teeth, and the toad eyes glowed like evil jewels in his head.

'There is time,' said the ancient woman. 'Tell me the name of Evelyn Warburton's father. Then I will let you die in peace.'

Evelyn started back, kneeling as she was, and stared at Nurse Macdonald, and then at her uncle.

'The name of Evelyn's father?' he repeated slowly, while the awful smile spread upon his dying face.

The light was growing strangely dim in the great room. As Evelyn looked, Nurse Macdonald's crooked shadow on the wall grew gigantic. Sir Hugh's breath came thick, rattling in his throat, as death crept in like a snake and choked it back. Evelyn prayed aloud, high and clear.

Then something rapped at the window, and she felt her hair rise upon her head in a cool breeze, as she looked around in spite of herself. And when she saw her own white face looking in at the window, and her own eyes staring at her through the glass, wide and fearful, and her own hair streaming against the pane, and her own lips dashed with blood. She rose slowly from the floor and stood rigid for one moment, till she screamed once and fell back into Gabriel's arms. But the shriek that answered hers was the fear-shriek of the tormented corpse, out of which the soul cannot pass for shame of deadly sins, though the devils fight in it with corruption, each for their due share.

Sir Hugh Ockram sat upright in his deathbed, and saw and cried aloud: 'Evelyn!' His harsh voice broke and rattled in his chest as he sank down. But still Nurse Macdonald tortured him, for there was a little life left in him still.

'You have seen the mother as she waits for you, Hugh Ockram. Who was this girl Evelyn's father? What was his name?'

For the last time the dreadful smile came upon the twisted lips, very slowly, very surely now, and the toad eyes glared red, and the parchment face glowed a little in the flickering light. For the last time words came.

'They know it in hell.'

Then the glowing eyes went out quickly, the yellow face turned waxen pale, and a great shiver ran through the thin body as Hugh Ockram died.

But in death he still smiled, for he knew his secret and kept it still, on the other side, and he would take it with him, to lie with him for ever in the north vault of the chapel where the Ockrams lie uncoffined in their shrouds – all but one. Though he was dead, he smiled, for he had kept his treasure of evil truth to the end, and there was none left to tell the name he had spoken, but there was all the evil he had not undone left to bear fruit.

As they watched – Nurse Macdonald and Gabriel, who held Evelyn still unconscious in his arms while he looked at the father – they felt the dead smile crawling along their own lips – the ancient crone and the youth with the angel's face. Then they shivered a little, and both looked at Evelyn as she lay with her head on his shoulder, and, though she was very beautiful, the same sickening smile was twisting her mouth too, and it was like the foreshadowing of a great evil which they could not understand.

But by and by they carried Evelyn out, and she opened her eyes and the smile was gone. From far away in the great house the sound of weeping and crooning came up the stairs and echoed along the dismal corridors, for the women had begun to mourn the dead master, after the Irish fashion, and the hall had echoes of its own all that night, like the far-off wail of the banshee among forest trees.

When the time was come they took Sir Hugh in his winding-sheet on a trestle bier, and bore him to the chapel and through the iron door and down the long descent to the north vault, with tapers, to lay him by his father. And two men went in first to prepare the place and came back staggering like drunken men, and white, leaving their lights behind them.

But Gabriel Ockram was not afraid, for he knew. And he went in alone and saw that the body of Sir Vernon Ockram was leaning upright against the stone wall, and that his head lay on the ground near by with the face turned up, and the dried leathern lips smiled horribly at the dried-up corpse, while the iron coffin, lined with black velvet, stood open on the floor.

Then Gabriel took the thing in his hands, for it was very light, being quite dried by the air of the vault, and those who peeped in from the door saw him lay it in the coffin again, and it rustled a little, like a bundle of reeds, and sounded hollow as it touched the sides and the bottom. He also placed the head upon the shoulders and shut down the lid, which fell to with a rusty spring that snapped.

After that they laid Sir Hugh beside his father, with the trestle bier on which they had brought him, and they went back to the chapel.

But when they saw one another's faces, master and men, they were all smiling with the dead smile of the corpse they had left in the vault, so that they could not bear to look at one another until it had faded away.

3

Gabriel Ockram became Sir Gabriel, inheriting the baronetcy with the half-ruined fortune left by his father, and still Evelyn Warburton lived at Ockram Hall, in the south room that had been hers ever since she could remember anything. She could not go away, for there were no relatives to whom she could have gone, and besides there seemed to be no reason why she should not stay. The world would never trouble itself to care what the Ockrams did on their Irish estates, as it was long since the Ockrams had asked anything of the world.

So Sir Gabriel took his father's place at the dark old table in the dining room, and Evelyn sat opposite to him, until such time as their mourning should be over, and they might be married at last. And meanwhile their lives went on as before, since Sir Hugh had been a hopeless invalid during the last year of his life, and they had seen him but once a day for a little while, spending most of their time together in a strangely perfect companionship.

But though the late summer saddened into autumn, and autumn darkened into winter, and storm followed storm, and rain poured on rain through the short days and the long nights, yet Ockram Hall seemed less gloomy since Sir Hugh had been laid in the north vault beside his father. And at Christmastide Evelyn decked the great hall with holly and green boughs, and huge fires blazed on every hearth. Then the tenants were all bidden to a New Year's dinner, and they ate and drank well, while Sir Gabriel sat at the head of the table.

Evelyn came in when the port wine was brought, and the most respected of the tenants made a speech to propose her health.

It was long, he said, since there had been a Lady Ockram. Sir Gabriel shaded his eyes with his hand and looked down at the table, but a faint colour came into Evelyn's transparent cheeks. But, said the grey-haired farmer, it was longer still since there had been a Lady Ockram so fair as the next was to be, and he gave the health of Evelyn Warburton.

Then the tenants all stood up and shouted for her, and Sir Gabriel stood up likewise, beside Evelyn. And when the men gave the last and loudest cheer of all, there was a voice not theirs, above them all, higher, fiercer, louder – a scream not earthly, shrieking for the bride of Ockram Hall. And the holly and the green boughs over the great chimney piece shook and slowly waved as if a cool breeze were blowing over them. But the men turned very pale, and many of them sat down their glasses, but others let them fall upon the floor for fear. And looking into one another's faces, they were all smiling strangely, a dead smile, like dead Sir Hugh's. One cried out words in Irish, and the fear of death was suddenly upon them all so that they fled in panic, falling over one another like wild beasts in the burning forest, when the thick smoke runs along the flame, and the tables were overset, and drinking glasses and bottles were broken in heaps, and the dark red wine crawled like blood upon the polished floor.

Sir Gabriel and Evelyn stood alone at the head of the table before the wreck of the feast, not daring to turn to see each other, for each knew that the other smiled. But his right arm held her and his left hand clasped her right as they stared before them, and but for the shadows of her hair one might not have told their two faces apart. They listened long, but the cry came not again, and the dead smile faded from their lips, while each remembered that Sir Hugh Ockram lay in the north vault, smiling in his winding-sheet, in the dark, because he had died with his secret.

So ended the tenants' New Year's dinner. But from that time on Sir Gabriel grew more and more silent, and his face grew even paler and thinner than before. Often without warning and without words, he would rise from his seat, as if something moved him against his will, and he would go out into the rain or the sunshine to the north side of the chapel, and sit on the stone bench, staring at the ground as if he could see through it, and through the vault below, and through the white winding-sheet in the dark, to the dead smile that would not die.

Always when he went out in that way Evelyn came out presently and sat beside him. Once, too, as in summer, their beautiful faces came suddenly near, and their lids drooped, and their red lips were almost joined together. But as their eyes met, they grew wide and wild, so that the white showed in a ring all round the deep violet, and their teeth chattered, and their hands were like hands of corpses, each in the other's for the terror of what was under their feet, and of what they knew but could not see.

Once, also, Evelyn found Sir Gabriel in the Chapel alone, standing before the iron door that led down to the place of death, and in his hand there was the key to the door, but he had not put it in the lock. Evelyn drew him away, shivering, for she had also been driven in waking dreams to see that terrible thing again, and to find out whether it had changed since it had lain there.

'I'm going mad,' said Sir Gabriel, covering his eyes with his hand as he went with her. 'I see it in my sleep, I see it when I am awake – it draws me to it, day and night – and unless I see it I shall die!'

'I know,' answered Evelyn, 'I know. It is as if threads were spun from it, like a spider's, drawing us down to it.' She was silent for a moment, and then she stared violently and grasped his arm with a man's strength, and almost screamed the words she spoke. 'But we must not go there!' she cried. 'We must not go!'

Sir Gabriel's eyes were half shut, and he was not moved by the agony on her face.

'I shall die unless I see it again,' he said, in a quiet voice not like his own. And all that day and that evening he scarcely spoke, thinking of it, always thinking, while Evelyn Warburton quivered from head to foot with a terror she had never known.

She went alone, on a grey winter's morning, to Nurse Macdonald's room in the tower, and sat down beside the great leathern easy chair, laying her thin white hand upon the withered fingers.

'Nurse,' she said, 'what was it that Uncle Hugh should have told you, that night before he died? It must have been an awful secret – and yet, though you asked him, I feel somehow that you know it, and that you know why he used to smile so dreadfully.'

The old woman's head moved slowly from side to side.

'I can only guess – I shall never know,' she answered slowly in her cracked little voice.

'But what do you guess? Who am I? Why did you ask who my father was? You know I am Colonel Warburton's daughter, and my mother was Lady Ockram's sister, so that Gabriel and I are cousins. My father was killed in Afghanistan. What secret can there be?'

'I do not know. I can only guess.'

'Guess what?' asked Evelyn imploringly, and pressing the soft withered hands, as she leaned forward. But Nurse Macdonald's wrinkled lids dropped suddenly over her queer blue eyes, and her lips shook a little with her breath as if she were asleep.

Evelyn waited. By the fire the Irish maid was knitting fast, and the needles clicked like three or four clocks ticking against each other. And the real clock on the wall solemnly ticked alone, checking off the seconds of the woman who was a hundred years old, and had not many days left. Outside the ivy branch beat the window in the wintry blast, as it had beaten against the glass a hundred years ago.

Then as Evelyn sat there she felt again the waking of a horrible desire – the sickening wish to go down, down to the thing in the north vault, and to open the winding-sheet, and see whether it had changed, and she held Nurse Macdonald's hands as if to keep herself in her place and fight against the appalling attraction of the evil dead.

But the old cat that kept Nurse Macdonald's feet warm, lying always on the bag footstool, got up and stretched itself, and looked up into Evelyn's eyes, while its back arched, and its tail thickened and bristled, and its ugly pink lips drew back in a devilish grin, showing its sharp teeth. Evelyn stared at it, half fascinated by its ugliness. Then the creature suddenly put out one paw with all its claws spread, and spat at the girl, and all at once the grinning cat was like the smiling corpse far down below, so that Evelyn shivered down to her small feet and covered her face with her free hand lest Nurse Macdonald should wake and see the dead smile there, for she could feel it.

The old woman had already opened her eyes again, and she touched her cat with the end of her crutch-stick, whereupon its back went down and its tail shrunk, and it sidled back to its place in the bag footstool. But its yellow eyes looked up sideways at Evelyn, between the slits of its lids.

'What is it that you guess, Nurse?' asked the young girl again.

'A bad thing – a wicked thing. But I dare not tell you, lest it might not be true, and the very thought should blast your life. For if I guess right, he meant that you should not know, and that you two should marry, and pay for his old sin with your souls.'

'He used to tell us that we ought not to marry – '

'Yes – he told you that, perhaps – but it was as if a man put poisoned meat before a starving beast, and said "do not eat", but never raised his hand to take the meat away. And if he told you that you should not marry, it was because he hoped you would, for of all men living or dead, Hugh Ockram was the falsest man that ever told a cowardly lie and the cruelest that ever hurt a weak woman, and the worst that ever loved a sin.'

'But Gabriel and I love each other,' said Evelyn very sadly.

Nurse Macdonald's old eyes looked far away, at sights seen long ago, and that rose in the grey winter air amid the mists of an ancient youth.

'If you love, you can die together,' she said very slowly. 'Why should you live, if it is true? I am a hundred years old. What has life given me? The beginning is fire, the end is a heap of ashes, and between the end and the beginning lies all the pain in the world. Let me sleep, since I cannot die.'

Then the old woman's eyes closed again, and her head sank a little lower upon her breast.

So Evelyn went away and left her asleep, with the cat asleep on the bag footstool; and the young girl tried to forget Nurse Macdonald's words, but she could not, for she heard them over and over again in the wind, and behind her on the stairs. And as she grew sick with fear of the frightful unknown evil to which her soul was bound, she felt a bodily something pressing her, and pushing her, and forcing her on, and from the other side she felt threads that drew her mysteriously, and when she shut her eyes, she saw in the chapel behind the altar the low iron door through which she must pass to go to the thing.

And as she lay awake at night, she drew the sheet over her face, lest she should see shadows on the wall beckoning her, and the sound of her own warm breath made whisperings in her ears, while she held the mattress with her hands to keep from getting up and going to the chapel. It would have been easier if there had not been a way thither through the library, by a door which was never locked. It would be fearfully easy to take her candle and go softly through the sleeping house. And the key of the vault lay under the altar behind a stone that turned. She knew that little secret. She could go alone and see.

But when she thought of it, she felt her hair rise on her head, and first she shivered so that the bed shook, and then the horror went through her in a cold thrill that was agony again, like a myriads of icy needles boring into her nerves.

4

The old clock in Nurse Macdonald's tower struck midnight. From her room she could hear the creaking chains and weights in their box in the corner of the staircase, and overheard the jarring of the rusty lever that lifted the hammer. She had heard it all her life. It struck eleven strokes clearly and then came the twelfth, with a dull half-stroke, as though the hammer were too weary to go on, and had fallen asleep against the bell.

The old cat got up from the bag footstool and stretched itself, and Nurse Macdonald opened her ancient eyes and looked slowly round the room by the dim light of the night lamp. She touched the cat with her crutch-stick and it lay down upon her feet. She drank a few drops from her cup and went to sleep again.

But downstairs Sir Gabriel sat straight up as the clock struck, for he had dreamed a fearful dream of horror, and his heart stood still, till he awoke at its stopping, and it beat again furiously with his breath, like a wild thing set free. No Ockram had ever known fear waking, but sometimes it came to Sir Gabriel in his sleep.

He pressed his hands on his temples as he sat up in bed, and his hands were icy cold, but his head was hot. The dream faded far, and in its place there came the sick twisting of his lips in the dark that would have been a smile. Far off, Evelyn Warburton dreamed that the dead smile was on her mouth, and awoke, starting with a little moan, her face in her hands shivering.

But Sir Gabriel struck a light and got up and began to walk up and down his great room. It was midnight, and he had barely slept an hour, and in the north of Ireland the winter nights are long.

'I shall go mad,' he said to himself, holding his forehead. He knew that it was true. For weeks and months the possession of the thing had grown upon him like a disease, till he could think of nothing without thinking first of that. And now all at once it outgrew his strength, and he knew that he must be its instrument or lose his mind – that he must do the deed he hated and feared if he could fear

anything, or that something would snap in his brain and divide him
from life while he was yet alive. He took the candlestick in his hand,
the old-fashioned heavy candlestick that had always been used by
the head of the house. He did not think of dressing, but went as he
was, in his silk nightclothes and his slippers, and he opened the
door. Everything was very still in the great old house. He shut the
door behind him and walked noiselessly on the carpet through the
long corridor. A cool breeze blew over his shoulder and blew the
flame of his candle straight out from him. Instinctively he stopped
and looked round, but all was still, and the upright flame burned
steadily. He walked on, and instantly a strong draft was behind him,
almost extinguishing the light. It seemed to blow him on his way,
ceasing whenever he turned, coming again when he went on –
invisible, icy.

Down the great staircase to the echoing hall he went, seeing
nothing but the flame of the candle standing away from him over
the guttering wax, while the cold wind blew over his shoulder and
through his hair. On he passed through the open door into the
library, dark with old books and carved bookcases, on through the
door in the shelves, with painted shelves on it, and the imitated
backs of books, so that one needed to know where to find it – and it
shut itself after him with a soft click. He entered the low-arched
passage, and though the door was shut behind him and fitted tightly
in its frame, still the cold breeze blew the flame forward as he
walked. And he was not afraid, but his face was very pale, and his
eyes were wide and bright, looking before him, seeing already in
the dark air the picture of the thing beyond. But in the chapel he
stood still, his hand on the little turning stone tablet in the back of
the stone altar. On the tablet were engraved the words, '*Clavis
sepulchri Clarissimorum Dominorum De Ockram*' – ('the key to the
vault of the most illustrious lord of Ockram'). Sir Gabriel paused
and listened. He fancied that he heard a sound far off in the great
house where all had been so still, but it did not come again. Yet he
waited at the last, and looked at the low iron door. Beyond it, down
the long descent, lay his father uncoffined, six months dead, corrupt,
terrible in his clinging shroud. The strangely preserving air of
the vault could not yet have done its work completely. But on the
thing's ghastly features, with their half-dried, open eyes, there would
still be the frightful smile with which the man had died – the smile
that haunted.

As the thought crossed Sir Gabriel's mind, he felt his lips writhing, and he struck his own mouth in wrath with the back of his hand so fiercely that a drop of blood ran down his chin and another, and more, falling back in the gloom upon the chapel pavement. But still his bruised lips twisted themselves. He turned the tablet by the simple secret. It needed no safer fastening, for had each Ockram been confined in pure gold, and had the door been wide, there was not a man in Tyrone brave enough to go down to the place, saving Gabriel Ockram himself, with his angel's face and his thin, white hands, and his sad unflinching eyes. He took the great gold key and set it into the lock of the iron door, and the heavy, rattling noise echoed down the descent beyond like footsteps, as if a watcher had stood behind the iron and were running away within, with heavy dead feet. And though he was standing still, the cool wind was from behind him, and blew the flame of the candle against the iron panel. He turned the key.

Sir Gabriel saw that his candle was short. There were new ones on the altar, with long candlesticks, and he lit one and left his own burning on the floor. As he set it down on the pavement his lip began to bleed again, and another drop fell upon the stones.

He drew the iron door open and pushed it back against the chapel wall, so that it should not shut of itself while he was within, and the horrible draft of the sepulchre came up out of the depths in his face, foul and dark. He went in, but though the fetid air met him, yet the flame of the tall candle was blown straight from him against the wind while he walked down the easy incline with steady steps, his loose slippers slapping the pavement as he trod.

He shaded the candle with his hand, and his fingers seemed to be made of wax and blood as the light shone through them. And in spite of him the unearthly draft forced the flame forward, till it was blue over the black wick, and it seemed as if it must go out. But he went straight on, with shining eyes.

The downward passage was wide, and he could not always see the walls by the struggling light, but he knew when he was in the place of death by the larger, drearier echo of his steps in the greater space and by the sensation of a distant blank wall. He stood still, almost enclosing the flame of the candle in the hollow of his hand. He could see a little, for his eyes were growing used to the gloom. Shadowy forms were outlined in the dimness, where the biers of the Ockrams stood crowded together, side by side, each with its straight, shrouded corpse, strangely preserved by the dry air, like the empty shell that the locust sheds in summer. And a few steps before him he saw clearly the dark shape of headless Sir Vernon's iron coffin, and he knew that nearest to it lay the thing he sought.

He was as brave as any of those dead men had been, and they were his fathers, and he knew that sooner or later he should lie there himself, beside Sir Hugh, slowly drying to a parchment shell. But he was still alive, and he closed his eyes a moment, and three great drops stood on his forehead.

Then he looked again, and by the whiteness of the winding sheet he knew his father's corpse, for all the others were brown with age; and, moreover, the flame of the candle was blown towards it. He made four steps till he reached it, and suddenly the light burned straight and high, shedding a dazzling yellow glare upon the fine linen that was all white, save over the face, and where the joined hands were laid on the breast. And at those places ugly stains had spread, darkened with outlines of the features and of the tight-clasped fingers. There was a frightful stench of drying death.

As Sir Gabriel looked down, something stirred behind him, softly at first, then more noisily, and something fell to the stone floor with a dull thud and rolled up to his feet; he started back, and saw a withered head lying almost face upward on the pavement, grinning at him. He felt the cold sweat standing on his face, and his heart beat painfully.

For the first time in all his life that evil thing which men call fear was getting hold of him, checking his heart strings as a cruel driver checks a quivering horse, clawing at his backbone with icy hands, lifting his hair with freezing breath climbing up and gathering in his midriff with leaden weight.

Yet presently he bit his lip and bent down, holding the candle in one hand, to lift the shroud back from the head of the corpse with the other. Slowly he lifted it.

Then it clove to the half-dried skin of the face, and his hand shook as if someone had struck him on the elbow, but half in fear and half in anger at himself, he pulled it, so that it came away with a little ripping sound. He caught his breath as he held it, not yet throwing it back, and not yet looking. The horror was working in him, and he felt that old Vernon Ockram was standing up in his iron coffin, headless, yet watching him with the stump of his severed neck.

While he held his breath he felt the dead smile twisting his lips. In sudden wrath at his own misery, he tossed the death-stained linen backward, and looked at last. He ground his teeth lest he should shriek aloud.

There it was, the thing that haunted him, that haunted Evelyn Warburton, that was like a blight on all that came near him.

The dead face was blotched with dark stains, and the thin, grey hair was matted about the discoloured forehead. The sunken lids were half open, and the candle light gleamed on something foul where the toad eyes had lived.

But yet the dead thing smiled, as it had smiled in life; the ghastly lips were parted and drawn wide and tight upon the wolfish teeth, cursing still, and still defying hell to do its worst – defying, cursing, and always and for ever smiling alone in the dark.

Sir Gabriel opened the winding-sheet where the hands were, and the blackened, withered fingers were closed upon something stained and mottled. Shivering from head to foot, but fighting like a man in agony for his life, he tried to take the package from the dead man's hold. But as he pulled at it the claw-like fingers seemed to close more tightly, and when he pulled harder the shrunken hands and arms rose from the corpse with a horrible look of life following his motion – then as he wrenched the sealed packet loose at last, the hands fell back into their place still folded.

He set down the candle on the edge of the bier to break the seals from the stout paper. And, kneeling on one knee, to get a better light, he read what was within, written long ago in Sir Hugh's queer hand.

He was no longer afraid.

He read how Sir Hugh had written it all down that it might perchance be a witness of evil and of his hatred; how he had loved Evelyn Warburton, his wife's sister; and how his wife had died of a broken heart with his curse upon her, and how Warburton and he had fought side by side in Afghanistan, and Warburton had fallen; but Ockram had brought his comrade's wife back a full year later, and little Evelyn, her child, had been born in Ockram Hall. And next, how he had wearied of the mother, and she had died like her sister with his curse on her. And then, how Evelyn had been brought up as his niece, and how he had trusted that his son Gabriel and his daughter, innocent and unknowing, might love and marry, and the souls of the women he had betrayed might suffer another anguish before eternity was out. And, last of all, he hoped that someday, when nothing could be undone, the two might find his writing and live on, not daring to tell the truth for their children's sake and the world's word, as man and wife.

This he read, kneeling beside the corpse in the north vault, by the light of the altar candle; and when he had read it all, he thanked God aloud that he had found the secret in time. But when he rose to his feet and looked down at the dead face it was changed, and the smile was gone from it for ever, and the jaw had fallen a little, and the tired dead lips were relaxed. And then there was a breath behind him and close to him, not cold like that which had blown the flame of the candle as he came, but warm and human. He turned suddenly.

There she stood, all in white, with her shadowy golden hair – for she had risen from her bed and had followed him noiselessly, and had found him reading, and had herself read over his shoulder. He started violently when he saw her, for his nerves were unstrung – and then he cried out her name in the still place of death: 'Evelyn!'

'My brother!' she answered, softly and tenderly, putting out both hands to meet his.

Master and Man

THOMAS CROFTON CROKER

Billy Mac Daniel was once as likely a young man as ever shook his brogue at a patron [a festival held in honour of some patron saint], emptied a quart or handled a shillelagh; fearing for nothing but the want of drink; caring for nothing but who should pay for it; and thinking of nothing but how to make fun over it; drunk or sober, a word and a blow was ever the way with Billy Mac Daniel; and a mighty easy way it is of either getting into or of ending a dispute. More is the pity that, through the means of his thinking, and fearing, and caring for nothing, this same Billy Mac Daniel fell into bad company; for surely the good people are the worst of all company anyone could come across.

It so happened that Billy was going home one clear frosty night not long after Christmas; the moon was round and bright; but although it was as fine a night as heart could wish for, he felt pinched with cold.

'By my word,' chattered Billy, 'a drop of good liquor would be no bad thing to keep a man's soul from freezing in him; and I wish I had a full measure of the best.'

'Never wish it twice, Billy,' said a little man in a three-cornered hat, bound all about with gold lace, and with great silver buckles in his shoes, so big that it a wonder how he could carry them, and he held out a glass as big as himself, filled with as good liquor as eye ever looked on or lip tasted.

'Success, my little fellow,' said Billy Mac Daniel nothing daunted, though well he knew the little man to belong to the *good people*; 'here's your health, anyway, and thank you kindly; no matter who pays for the drink'; and he took the glass and drained it to the very bottom without ever taking a second breath to it.

'Success,' said the little man; 'and you're heartily welcome, Billy; but don't think to cheat me as you have done others – out with your purse and pay me like a gentleman.'

'Is it I pay you?' said Billy; 'could I not just take you up and put you in my pocket as easily as a blackberry?'

'Billy Mac Daniel,' said the little man, getting very angry, 'you shall be my servant for seven years and a day, and that is the way I will be paid; so make ready to follow me.'

When Billy heard this he began to be very sorry for having used such bold words toward the little man; and he felt himself, yet could not tell how, obliged to follow the little man the livelong night about the country, up and down, and over hedge and ditch, and through bog and brake, without any rest.

When morning began to dawn the little man turned round to him and said, 'You may now go home, Billy, but on your peril don't fail to meet me in the Fort-field tonight; or if you do it may be the worse for you in the long run. If I find you a good servant, you will find me an indulgent master.'

Home went Billy Mac Daniel; and though he was tired and weary enough, never a wink of sleep could he get for thinking of the little man; but he was afraid not to do his bidding, so up he got in the evening, and away he went to the Fort-field. He was not long there before the little man came towards him and said, 'Billy, I want to go a long journey tonight; so saddle one of my horses, and you may saddle another for yourself, as you are to go along with me, and may be tired after your walk last night.'

Billy thought this very considerate of his master, and thanked him accordingly: 'But,' said he, 'if I may be so bold, sir, I would ask which is the way to your stable, for never a thing do I see but the fort here, and the old thorn tree in the corner of the field, and the stream running at the bottom of the hill, with the bit of bog over against us.'

'Ask no questions, Billy,' said the little man, 'but go over to that bit of bog, and bring me two of the strongest rushes you can find.'

Billy did accordingly, wondering what the little man would be at; and he picked two of the stoutest rushes he could find, with a little bunch of brown blossom stuck at the side of each, and brought them back to his master.

'Get up, Billy,' said the little man, taking one of the rushes from him and striding across it.

'Where shall I get up, please your honour?' said Billy.

'Why, upon horseback, like me, to be sure,' said the little man.

'Is it after making a fool of me you'd be,' said Billy, 'bidding me get a horseback upon that bit of a rush? Maybe you want to persuade me that the rush I pulled but a while ago out of the bog over there is a horse?'

'Up! up! and no words,' said the little man, looking very angry; 'the best horse you ever rode was but a fool to it.' So Billy, thinking all this was in joke, and fearing to vex his master, straddled across the rush. 'Borram! Borram! Borram!' cried the little man three times (which, in English, means to become great), and Billy did the same after him; presently the rushes swelled up into fine horses, and away they went full speed; but Billy, who had put the rush between his legs, without much minding how he did it, found himself sitting on horseback the wrong way, which was rather awkward, with his face to the horse's tail; and so quickly had his steed started off with him that he had no power to turn round, and there was therefore nothing for it but to hold on by the tail.

At last they came to their journey's end, and stopped at the gate of a fine house. 'Now, Billy,' said the little man, 'do as you see me do, and follow me close; but as you did not know your horse's head from his tail, mind that your own head does not spin round until you can't tell whether you are standing on it or your heels; for remember that old liquor, though able to make a cat speak, can make a man dumb.'

The little man then said some queer kind of words, out of which Billy could make no meaning; but he contrived to say them after him for all that; and in they both went through the keyhole of the door, and through one keyhole after another, until they got into the wine-cellar, which was well stored with all kinds of wine.

The little man fell to drinking as hard as he could, and Billy noway disliking the example, did the same. 'The best of masters are you, surely,' said Billy to him; 'no matter who is the next; and well pleased will I be with your service if you continue to give me plenty to drink.'

'I have made no bargain with you,' said the little man, 'and will make none; but up and follow me.' Away they went, through keyhole after keyhole; and each mounting upon the rush which he left at the hall door, scampered off, kicking the clouds before them like snow-balls, as soon as the words, 'Borram, Borram, Borram,' had passed their lips.

When they came back to the Fort-field the little man dismissed Billy, bidding him to be there the next night at the same hour. Thus did they go on, night after night, shaping their course one night here, and another night there; sometimes north, and sometimes east, and sometimes south, until there was not a gentleman's wine-cellar in all Ireland they had not visited, and could tell the flavour of every wine in it as well, ay, better than the butler himself.

One night when Billy Mac Daniel met the little man as usual in the Fort-field, and was going to the bog to fetch the horses for their journey, his master said to him, 'Billy, I shall want another horse tonight, for maybe we may bring back more company than we take.' So Billy, who now knew better than to question any order given to him by his master, brought a third rush, much wondering who it might be that would travel back in their company, and whether he was about to have a fellow-servant. 'If I have,' thought Billy, 'he shall go and fetch the horses from the bog every night; for I don't see why I am not, every inch of me, as good a gentleman as my master.'

Well, away they went, Billy leading the third horse, and never stopped until they came to a snug farmer's house, in the county Limerick, close under the old castle of Carrigogunniel, that was built, they say, by the great Brian Boru. Within the house there was great carousing going forward, and the little man stopped outside for some time to listen; then turning round all of a sudden, said, 'Billy, I will be a thousand years old tomorrow!'

'God bless us, sir,' said Billy; 'will you?'

'Don't say these words again, Billy,' said the little old man, 'or you will be my ruin forever. Now Billy, as I will be a thousand years in the world tomorrow, I think it is full time for me to get married.'

'I think so too, without any kind of doubt at all,' said Billy, 'if ever you mean to marry.'

'And to that purpose,' said the little man, 'have I come all the way to Carrigogunniel; for in this house, this very night, is young Darby Riley going to be married to Bridget Rooney; and as she is a tall and comely girl, and has come of decent people, I think of marrying her myself, and taking her off with me.'

'And what will Darby Riley say to that?' said Billy.

'Silence' said the little man, putting on a mighty severe look; 'I did not bring you here with me to ask questions,' and without holding further argument, he began saying the queer words which had the power of passing him through the keyhole as free as air, and which Billy thought himself mighty clever to be able to say after him.

In they both went; and for the better viewing the company, the little man perched himself up as nimbly as a cock-sparrow upon one of the big beams which went across the house over all their heads, and Billy did the same upon another facing him; but not being much accustomed to roosting in such a place, his legs hung down as untidy as may be, and it was quite clear he had not taken pattern after the way in which the little man had bundled himself up together. If the little man had been a tailor all his life, he could not have sat more contentedly upon his haunches.

There they were, both master and man, looking down upon the fun that was going forward; and under them were the priest and piper, and the father of Darby Riley, with Darby's two brothers and his uncle's son; and there were both the father and the mother of Bridget Rooney, and proud enough the old couple were that night of their daughter, as good right they had; and her four sisters, with brand-new ribbons in their caps, and her three brothers all looking as clean and as clever as any three boys in Munster, and there were uncles and aunts, and gossips and cousins enough besides to make a full house of it; and plenty was there to eat and drink on the table for everyone of them, if they had been double the number.

Now it happened, just as Mrs Rooney had helped his reverence to the first cut of the pig's head which was placed before her, beautifully bolstered up with white savoys, that the bride gave a sneeze, which made everyone at the table start, but not a soul said 'and bless us'. All thinking that the priest would have done so, as he ought if he had done his duty, no one wished to take the word out of his mouth, which, unfortunately, was preoccupied with pig's head and greens. And after a moment's pause the fun and merriment of the bridal feast went on without the pious benediction.

Of this circumstance both Billy and his master were no inattentive spectators from their exalted stations. 'Ha!' exclaimed the little man, throwing one leg from under him with a joyous flourish, and his eye twinkled with a strange light, while his eyebrows became elevated into the curvature of Gothic arches; 'Ha!' said he, leering down at the bride, and then up at Billy, 'I have half of her now, surely. Let her sneeze but twice more, and she is mine, in spite of priest, mass-book, and Darby Riley.'

Again the fair Bridget sneezed; but it was so gently, and she blushed so much, that few except the little man took, or seemed to take, any notice; and no one thought of saying 'God bless us.'

Billy all this time regarded the poor girl with a most rueful expression of countenance; for he could not help thinking what a terrible thing it was for a nice young girl of nineteen, with large blue eyes, transparent skin, and dimpled cheeks, suffused with health and joy, to be obliged to marry an ugly little bit of a man, who was a thousand years old, barring a day.

At this critical moment the bride gave a third sneeze, and Billy roared out with all his might, 'God save us!' Whether this exclamation resulted from his soliloquy, or from the mere force of habit, he never could tell exactly himself; but no sooner was it uttered than the little man, his face glowing with rage and disappointment, sprung from the beam on which he had perched himself, and shrieking out in the shrill voice of a cracked bagpipe, 'I discharge you from my service, Billy Mac Daniel – take *that* for your wages,' gave poor Billy a most furious kick in the back, which sent his unfortunate servant sprawling upon his face and hands right in the middle of the supper table.

If Billy was astonished, how much more so was everyone of the company into which he was thrown with so little ceremony. But when they heard his story, Father Cooney laid down his knife and fork, and married the young couple out of hand with all speed; and Billy Mac Daniel danced the Rinka at their wedding, and plenty he did drink at it too, which was what he thought more of than dancing.

The Legend of Knockgrafton

THOMAS CROFTON CROCKER

There was once a poor man who lived in the fertile glen of Aherlow, at the foot of the gloomy Galtee mountains, and he had a great hump on his back: he looked just as if his body had been rolled up and placed upon his shoulders; and his head was pressed down with the weight so much that his chin, when the was sitting, used to rest upon his knees for support. The country people were rather shy of meeting him in any lonesome place, for though, poor creature, he was as harmless and as inoffensive as a new-born infant, yet his deformity was so great that he scarcely appeared to be a human creature, and some ill-minded persons had set strange stories about him afloat. He was said to have a great knowledge of herbs and charms; but certain it was that he had a mighty skilful hand in plaiting straws and rushes into hats and baskets, which was the way he made his livelihood.

Lusmore, for that was the nickname put upon him by reason of his always wearing a sprig of the fairy cap, or lusmore (the foxglove), in his little straw hat, would ever get a higher penny for his plaited work than anyone else, and perhaps that was the reason why some-one, out of envy, had circulated the strange stories about him. Be that as it may, it happened that he was returning one evening from the pretty town of Cahir toward Cappagh, and as little Lusmore walked very slowly, on account of the great hump upon his back, it was quite dark when he came to the old moat of Knockgrafton, which stood on the right-hand side of his road.

Tired and weary was he, and no ways comfortable in his own mind at thinking how much farther he had to travel, and that he should be walking all the night; so he sat down under the moat to rest himself, and began looking mournfully enough upon the moon, which, 'Rising in clouded majesty, at length Apparent Queen, unveil'd her peerless light, And o'er the dark her silver mantle threw.'

Presently there rose a wild strain of unearthly melody upon the ear of little Lusmore; he listened, and he thought that he had never heard such ravishing music before. It was like the sound of many voices, each mingling and blending with the other so strangely that they seemed to be one, though all singing different strains, and the words of the song were these: '*Da Luan, Da Mort, Da Luan, Da Mort, Da Luan, Da Mort.*' There would be a moment's pause, and then the round of melody went on again.

Lusmore listened attentively, scarcely drawing his breath lest he might lose the slightest note. He now plainly perceived that the singing was within the moat; and though at first it had charmed him so much, he began to get tired of hearing the same round sung over and over so often without any change; so availing himself of the pause when '*Da Luan, Da Mort*', had been sung three times, he took up the tune, and raised it with the words '*agus Da Dardeen*', and then went on singing with the voices inside of the moat, '*Da Luan, Da Mort*', finishing the melody, when the pause again came, with '*agus Da Dardeen*'. [The words *La Luan, Da Mort agus Da Dardeen* are Irish for 'Monday, Tuesday, and Wednesday too.']

The fairies within Knockgrafton, for the song was a fairy melody, when they heard this addition to the tune, were so much delighted that, with instant resolve, it was determined to bring the mortal among them, whose musical skill so far exceeded theirs, and little Lusmore was conveyed into their company with the eddying speed of a whirlwind.

Glorious to behold was the sight that burst upon him as he came down through the moat, twirling round and round, with the lightness of a straw, to the sweetest music that kept time to his motion. The greatest honour was then paid him, for he was put above all the musicians, and he had servants tending upon him, and everything to his heart's content, and a hearty welcome to all; and, in short, he was made as much of as if he had been the first man in the land.

Presently Lusmore saw a great consultation going forward among the fairies, and, notwithstanding all their civility, he felt very much frightened, until one stepping out from the rest came up to him and said:

'Lusmore! Lusmore!
Doubt not, nor deplore,
For the hump which you bore
On your back is no more;

Look down on the floor,
And view it, Lusmore! Lusmore!'

When these words were said poor little Lusmore felt himself so light, and so happy, that he thought he could have bounded at one jump over the moon, like the cow in the history of the cat and the fiddle; and he saw, with inexpressible pleasure, his hump tumble down upon the ground from his shoulders. He then tried to lift up his head, and he did so with becoming caution, fearing that he might knock it against the ceiling of the grand hall, where he was; he looked round and round again with the greatest wonder and delight upon everything, which appeared more and more beautiful; and, overpowered at beholding such a resplendent scene, his head grew dizzy, and his eyesight became dim. At last he fell into a sound sleep, and when he awoke he found that it was broad daylight, the sun shining brightly, and the birds singing sweetly; and that he was lying just at the foot of the moat of Knockgrafton, with the cows and sheep grazing peacefully round about him. The first thing Lusmore did, after saying his prayers, was to put his hand behind to feel for his hump, but no sign of one was there on his back, and he looked at himself with great pride, for he had now become a well-shaped, dapper little fellow, and more than that, found himself in a full suit of new clothes, which he concluded the fairies had made for him.

Toward Cappagh he went, stepping out as lightly, and springing up at every step as if he had been all his life dancing-master. Not a creature who met Lusmore knew him without his hump, and he had a great work to persuade everyone that he was the same man – in truth he was not, so far as the outward appearances went.

Of course it was not long before the story of Lusmore's hump got about, and a great wonder was made of it. Through the country, for miles round, it was the talk of everyone, high and low.

One morning, as Lusmore was sitting contented enough at his cabin door, up came an old woman to him and asked him if he could direct her to Cappagh.

'I need give you no directions, my good woman,' said Lusmore, 'for this is Cappagh; and whom may you want here?'

'I have come,' said the woman, 'out of Decie's country, in the country of Waterford, looking after one Lusmore, who, I have heard tell, had his hump taken off by the fairies; for there is a son of a gossip of mine who has got a hump on him that will be his death;

and maybe, if he could use the same charm as Lusmore the hump may be taken off him. And now I have told you the reason of my coming so far: 'tis to find out about this charm, if I can.'

Lusmore, who was ever a good-natured little fellow, told the woman all the particulars, how he had raised the tune for the fairies at Knockgrafton, how his hump had been removed from his shoulders, and how he had got a new suit of clothes into the bargain.

The woman thanked him very much, and then went away quite happy and easy in her own mind. When she came back to her gossip's house, in the county of Waterford, she told her everything that Lusmore had said and they put the little humpbacked man, who was a peevish and cunning creature from his birth, upon a car, and took him all the way across the county. It was a long journey, but they did not care for that, so the hump was taken from off him; and they brought him, just at nightfall, and left him under the old moat of Knockgrafton.

Jack Madden, for that was the humpy man's name, had not been sitting there long when he heard the tune going on within the moat much sweeter than before; for the fairies were singing it the way Lusmore had settled their music for them, and the song was going on: 'Da Luan, Da Mort, Da Luan, Da Mort, Da Luan, Da Mort, agus Da Dardeen', without ever stopping. Jack Madden, who was in a great hurry to get quit of his hump, never thought of waiting until the fairies had done, or watching for a fit opportunity to raise the tune higher again than Lusmore had; so having heard them sing it over seven times without stopping, out he bawls, never minding the time or the humour of the tune, or how he could bring his words in properly, 'agus Da Dardeen, agus Da Hena', thinking that if one day was good, two were better; and that if Lusmore had one new suit of clothes given him, he should have two. [Da Hena is Thursday.]

No sooner had the words passed his lips than he was taken up and whisked into the moat with prodigious force; and the fairies came crowding round about him with great anger, screeching and screaming, and roaring out: 'Who spoiled our tune? Who spoiled our tune?' and one stepped up to him above all the rest, and said:

'Jack Madden, Jack Madden
Your words come so bad in
The tune we felt glad in;
This castle you're had in,

That your life we may sadden;
Here's two humps for Jack Madden!'

And twenty of the strongest fairies brought Lusmore's hump, and put it down upon poor Jack's back, over his own, where it became fixed as firmly as if it was nailed on with twelve-penny nails, by the best carpenter that ever drove one. Out of their castle they then kicked him; and in the morning, when Jack Madden's mother and her gossip came to look after their little man, they found him half dead, lying at the foot of the moat, with the other hump upon his back. Well to be sure, how they did look at each other! but they were afraid to say anything, lest a hump might be put upon their own shoulders. Home they brought the unlucky Jack Madden with them, as downcast in their hearts and their looks as ever two gossips were; and what through the weight of his other hump, and the long journey, he died soon after, leaving, they say, his heavy curse to anyone who would go to listen to fairy tunes again.

The Haunted Cellar

THOMAS CROFTON CROKER

There are few people who have not heard of the Mac Carthys – one of the real old Irish families, with the true Milesian blood running in their veins as thick as buttermilk. Many were the clans of this family in the south; as the Mac Carthymore – and the Mac Carthy-reagh – and the Mac Carthy of Muskerry; and all of them were noted for their hospitality to strangers, gentle and simple.

But not one of that name, or of any other, exceeded Justin Mac Carthy, of Ballinacarthy, at putting plenty to eat and drink upon his table; and there was a right hearty welcome for everyone who should share it with him. Many a wine cellar would be ashamed of the name if that at Ballinacarthy was the proper pattern for one. Large as that cellar was, it was crowded with bins of wine, and long rows of pipes, and hogsheads, and casks, that it would take more time to count than any sober man could spare in such a place, with plenty to drink about him, and a hearty welcome to do so.

There are many, no doubt, who will think that the butler would have little to complain of in such a house; and the whole country round would have agreed with them, if a man could be found to remain as Mr MacCarthy's butler for any length of time worth speaking of; yet not one who had been in his service gave him a bad word.

'We have no fault,' they would say, 'to find with the master, and if he could but get anyone to fetch his wine from the cellar, we might everyone of us have grown grey in the house and have lived quiet and contented enough in his service until the end of our days.'

' 'Tis a queer thing that, surely,' thought young Jack Leary, a lad who had been brought up from a mere child in the stables of Ballinacarthy to assist in taking care of the horses, and had occasionally lent a hand in the butler's pantry: – ' 'Tis a mighty queer thing, surely, that one man after another cannot content himself with the best place in the house of a good master, but that everyone of them must quit, all through the means, as they say, of the wine cellar. If the master, long life to him! would but make me his butler, I warrant never the word more would be heard of grumbling at his bidding to go to the wine cellar.'

Young Leary, accordingly, watched for what he conceived to be a favourable opportunity of presenting himself to the notice of his master.

A few mornings after, Mr Mac Carthy went into his stableyard rather earlier than usual, and called loudly for the groom to saddle his horse, as he intended going out with the hounds. But there was no groom to answer, and young Jack Leary led Rainbow out of the stable.

'Where is William?' enquired Mr Mac Carthy.

'Sir?' said Jack; and Mr Mac Carthy repeated the question.

'Is it William, please your honour?' returned Jack; 'why, then, to tell the truth, he had just *one* drop too much last night.'

'Where did he get it?' said Mr Mac Carthy; 'for since Thomas went away the key of the wine cellar has been in my pocket, and I have been obliged to fetch what was drunk myself.'

'Sorrow a know I know,' said Leary, 'unless the cook might have given him the *least taste* in life of whiskey. But,' continued he, performing a low bow by seizing with his right hand a lock of hair, and pulling down his head by it, while his left leg, which had been put forward, was scraped back against the ground, 'may I make so bold as just to ask your honour one question?'

'Speak out, Jack,' said Mr Mac Carthy.

'Why, then, does your honour want a butler?'

'Can you recommend me one,' returned his master, with the smile of good-humour upon his countenance, 'and one who will not be afraid of going to my wine cellar?'

'Is the wine cellar all the matter?' said young Leary; 'devil a doubt I have of myself then for that.'

'So you mean to offer me your services in the capacity of butler?' said Mr Mac Carthy, with some surprise.

'Exactly so,' answered Leary, now for the first time looking up from the ground.

'Well, I believe you to be a good lad, and have no objection to give you a trial.'

'Long may your honour reign over us, and the Lord spare you to us!' ejaculated Leary, with another national bow, as his master rode off; and he continued for some time to gaze after him with a vacant stare, which slowly and gradually assumed a look of importance.

'Jack Leary,' said he, at length, 'Jack – is it Jack?' in a tone of wonder; 'faith, 'tis not Jack now, but Mr John, the butler;' and with an air of becoming consequence he strided out of the stableyard towards the kitchen.

It is of little purport to my story, although it may afford an instructive lesson to the reader, to depict the sudden transition of nobody into somebody. Jack's former stable companion, a poor superannuated hound named Bran, who had been accustomed to receive many an affectionate pat on the head, was spurned from him with a kick and an 'Out of the way, sirrah.' Indeed, poor Jack's memory seemed sadly affected by this sudden change of situation. What established the point beyond all doubt was his almost for-getting the pretty face of Peggy, the kitchen wench, whose heart he had assailed but the preceding week by the offer of purchasing a gold ring for the fourth finger of her right hand, and a lusty imprint of good will upon her lips.

When Mr Mac Carthy returned from hunting, he sent for Jack Leary – so he still continued to call his new butler. 'Jack,' said he, 'I believe you are a trustworthy lad, and here are the keys of my cellar. I have asked the gentlemen with whom I hunted today to dine with me, and I hope they may be satisfied at the way in which you will wait on them at table; but, above all, let there be no want of wine after dinner.'

Mr John having a tolerably quick eye for such things, and being naturally a handy lad, spread his cloth accordingly, laid his plates and knives and forks in the same manner be had seen his pre-decessors in office perform these mysteries, and really, for the first time, got through attendance on dinner very well.

It must not be forgotten, however, that it was at the house of an Irish country squire, who was entertaining a company of booted and spurred fox-hunters, not very particular about what are considered matters of infinite importance under other circumstances and in other societies.

For instance, few of Mr Mac Carthy's guests (though all excellent and worthy men in their way) cared much whether the punch produced after soup was made of Jamaica or Antigua rum; some even would not have been inclined to question the correctness of good old Irish whiskey; and, with the exception of their liberal host himself, everyone in company preferred the port which Mr Mac Carthy put on his table to the less ardent flavour of claret – a choice rather at variance with modern sentiment.

It was waxing near midnight, when Mr Mac Carthy rung the bell three times. This was a signal for more wine; and Jack proceeded to the cellar to procure a fresh supply, but it must be confessed not without some little hesitation.

The luxury of ice was then unknown in the south of Ireland; but the superiority of cool wine had been acknowledged by all men of sound judgment and true taste.

The grandfather of Mr Mac Carthy, who had built the mansion of Ballinacarthy upon the site of an old castle which had belonged to his ancestors, was fully aware of this important fact; and in the construction of his magnificent wine cellar had availed himself of a deep vault, excavated out of the solid rock in former times as a place of retreat and security. The descent to this vault was by a flight of steep stone stairs, and here and there in the wall were narrow passages – I ought rather to call them crevices; and also certain projections, which cast deep shadows, and looked very frightful when anyone went down the cellar stairs with a single light: indeed, two lights did not much improve the matter, for though the breadth of the shadows became less, the narrow crevices remained as dark and darker than ever.

Summoning up all his resolution, down went the new butler, bearing in his right hand a lantern and the key of the cellar, and in his left a basket, which he considered sufficiently capacious to contain an adequate stock for the remainder of the evening: he arrived at the door without any interruption whatever; but when he put the key, which was of an ancient and clumsy kind – for it was before the days of Bramah's patent – and turned it in the lock, he thought he heard a strange kind of laughing within the cellar, to which some empty bottle that stood upon the floor outside vibrated so violently that they struck against each other: in this he could not be mistaken, although he may have been deceived in the laugh, for the bottles were just at his feet, and he saw them in motion.

Leary paused for a moment, and looked about him with becoming caution. He then boldly seized the handle of the key, and turned it with all his strength in the lock, as if he doubted his own power of doing so; and the door flew open with a most tremendous crash, that if the house had not been built upon the solid rock would have shook it from the foundation.

To recount what the poor fellow saw would be impossible, for he seems not to have known very clearly himself: but what he told the cook the next morning was, that he heard a roaring and bellowing like a mad bull, and that all the pipes and hogsheads and casks in the cellar went rocking backwards and forwards with so much force that he thought everyone would have been staved in, and that he should have been drowned or smothered in wine.

When Leary recovered, he made his way back as well as he could to the dining room, where he found his master and the company very impatient for his return.

'What kept you?' said Mr Mac Carthy in an angry voice; 'and where is the wine ? I rung for it half an hour since.'

'The wine is in the cellar, I hope, sir,' said Jack, trembling violently; 'I hope 'tis not all lost.'

'What do you mean, fool?' exclaimed Mr Mac Carthy in a still more angry tone: 'why did you not fetch some with you?'

Jack looked wildly about him, and only uttered a deep groan.

'Gentlemen,' said Mr Mac Carthy to his guests, 'this is too much. When I next see you to dinner, I hope it will be in another house, for it is impossible I can remain longer in this, where a man has no command over his own wine cellar, and cannot get a butler to do his duty. I have long thought of moving from Ballinacarthy; and I am now determined, with the blessing of God, to leave it tomorrow. But wine shall you have were I to go myself to the cellar for it.' So saying, he rose from table, took the key and lantern from his half-stupified servant, who regarded him with a look of vacancy, and descended the narrow stairs, already described, which led to his cellar.

When he arrived at the door, which he found open, he thought he heard a noise, as if of rats or mice scrambling over the casks, and on advancing perceived a little figure, about six inches in height, seated astride upon the pipe of the oldest port in the place, and bearing a spigot upon his shoulder. Raising the lantern, Mr Mac Carthy contemplated the little fellow with wonder: he wore a red nightcap on his head; before him was a short leather apron, which now, from his attitude, fell rather on one side; and he had stockings of a light blue colour, so long as nearly to cover the entire of his legs; with shoes, having huge silver buckles in them, and with high heels (perhaps out of vanity to make him appear taller). His face was like a withered winter apple; and his nose, which was of a bright crimson colour, about the tip wore a delicate purple bloom, like that of a plum; yet his eyes twinkled 'like those mites of candied dew in money nights – ' and his mouth twitched up at one side with an arch grin.

'Ha, scoundrel!' exclaimed Mr Mac Carthy, 'have I found you at last? disturber of my cellar – what are you doing there?'

'Sure, and master,' returned the little fellow, looking up at him with one eye, and with the other throwing a sly glance towards the spigot on his shoulder, 'a'n't we going to move tomorrow? and sure you would not leave your own little Cluricaune Naggeneen behind you?'

'Oh!' thought Mr Mac Carthy, 'if you are to follow me, master Naggeneen, I don't see much use in quitting Ballinacarthy.' So filling with wine the basket which young Leary in his fright had left behind him, and locking the cellar door, he rejoined his guests.

For some years after Mr Mac Carthy had always to fetch the wine for his table himself, as the little Cluricaune Naggeneen seemed to feel a personal respect towards him. Notwithstanding the labour of these journeys, the worthy lord of Ballinacarthy lived in his paternal mansion to a good round age, and was famous to the last for the excellence of his wine, and conviviality of his company; but at the time of his death, the same conviviality had nearly emptied his wine cellar; and as it was never so well filled again, nor so often visited, the revels of master Naggeneen became less celebrated, and are now only spoken of among the legendary lore of the country. It is even said that the poor little fellow took the declension of the cellar so to heart, that he became negligent and careless of himself, and that he has been sometimes seen going about with hardly a *skreed* to cover him.

Legend of Bottle Hill

THOMAS CROFTON CROKER

It was in the good days when the little people, most impudently called fairies, were more frequently seen than they are in these unbelieving times, that a farmer, named Mick Purcell, rented a few acres of barren ground in the neighbourhood of the once celebrated preceptory of Mourne, situated about three miles from Mallow, and thirteen from 'the beautiful city called Cork.' Mick had a wife and family. They all did what they could, and that was but little, for the poor man had no child grown up big enough to help him in his work; and all the poor woman could do was to mind the children, and to milk the one cow, and to boil the potatoes, and carry the eggs to market to Mallow; but with all they could do, 'twas hard enough on them to pay the rent. Well, they did manage it for a good while; but at last came a bad year, and the little grain of oats was all spoiled, and the chickens died of the pip, and the pig got the measles, – she was sold in Mallow and brought almost nothing; and poor Mick found that he hadn't enough to half pay his rent, and two gales were due.

'Why, then, Molly,' says he, 'what'll we do?'

'Wisha, then, mavournene, what would you do but take the cow to the fair of Cork and sell her?' says she; 'and Monday is fair day, and so you must go tomorrow, that the poor beast may be rested *again* the fair.'

'And what'll we do when she's gone?' says Mick, sorrowfully.

'Never a know I know, Mick; but sure God won't leave us without Him, Mick; and you know how good He was to us when poor little Billy was sick, and we had nothing at all for him to take, – that good doctor gentleman at Ballydahin come riding and asking for a drink of milk; and how he gave us two shillings; and how he sent the things and bottles for the child, and gave me my breakfast when I went over to ask a question, so he did; and how he come to see Billy, and never left off his goodness till he was quite well?'

'Oh! you are always that way, Molly, and I believe you are right
after all, so I won't be sorry for selling the cow; but I'll go tomorrow,
and you must put a needle and thread through my coat, for you
know 'tis ripped under the arm.'

Molly told him he should have everything right; and about twelve
o'clock next day he left her, getting a charge not to sell his cow
except for the highest penny. Mick promised to mind it, and went
his way along the road. He drove his cow slowly through the little
stream which crosses it, and runs under the old walls of Mourne. As
he passed he glanced his eye upon the towers and one of the old
elder trees, which were only then little bits of switches.

'Oh, then, if I only had half of the money that's buried in you,
'tisn't driving this poor cow I'd be now! Why, then, isn't it too bad
that it should be there covered over with earth, and many a one
besides me wanting? Well if it's God's will, I'll have some money
myself coming back.'

So saying he moved on after his beast. 'Twas a fine day, and the
sun shone brightly on the walls of the old abbey as he passed under
them. He then crossed an extensive mountain tract, and after six
long miles he came to the top of that hill – Bottle-hill 'tis called
now, but that was not the name of it then, and just there a man
overtook him. 'Good morning,' says he. 'Good morning, kindly,'
says Mick, looking at the stranger, who was a little man, you'd
almost call him a dwarf, only he wasn't quite so little neither: he had
a bit of an old wrinkled, yellow face, for all the world like a dried
cauliflower, only he had a sharp little nose, and red eyes, and white
hair, and his lips were not red, but all his face was one colour, and
his eyes never were quiet, but looking at everything, and although
they were red they made Mick feel quite cold when he looked at
them. In truth, he did not much like the little man's company; and
he couldn't see one bit of his legs nor his body, for though the day
was warm, he was all wrapped up in a big great coat. Mick drove his
cow something faster, but the little man kept up with him. Mick
didn't know how he walked, for he was almost afraid to look at him,
and to cross himself, for fear the old man would be angry. Yet he
thought his fellow-traveller did not seem to walk like other men,
nor to put one foot before the other, but to glide over the rough
road – and rough enough it was – like a shadow, without noise and
without effort. Mick's heart trembled within him, and he said a
prayer to himself, wishing he hadn't come out that day, or that he

was on Fair-hill, or that he hadn't the cow to mind, that he might run away from the bad thing – when, in the midst of his fears, he was again addressed by his companion.

'Where are you going with the cow, honest man?'

'To the fair of Cork, then,' says Mick, trembling at the shrill and piercing tones of the voice.

'Are you going to sell her?' said the stranger.

'Why, then, what else am I going for but to sell her?'

'Will you sell her to me?'

Mick started – he was afraid to have anything to do with the little man, and he was more afraid to say no.

'What'll you give for her?' at last says he.

'I'll tell you what, I'll give you this bottle,' says the little one, pulling a bottle from under his coat.

Mick looked at him and the bottle, and, in spite of his terror, he could not help bursting into a loud fit of laughter.

'Laugh if you will,' said the little man, 'but I tell you this bottle is better for you than all the money you will get for the cow in Cork – ay, than ten thousand times as much.'

Mick laughed again. 'Why then,' says he, 'do you think I am such a fool as to give my good cow for a bottle – and an empty one, too? Indeed, then, I won't.'

'You had better give me the cow, and take the bottle – you'll not be sorry for it.'

'Why, then, and what would Molly say? I'd never hear the end of it; and how would I pay the rent? and what should we all do without a penny of money.'

'I tell you this bottle is better to you than money; take it, and give me the cow. I ask you for the last time, Mick Purcell.'

Mick started.

'How does he know my name?' thought he.

The stranger proceeded: 'Mick Purcell, I know you, and I have regard for you; therefore do as I warn you, or you may be sorry for it. How do you know but your cow will die before you go to Cork?'

Mick was going to say 'God forbid!' but the little man went on (and he was too attentive to say anything to stop him; for Mick was a very civil man, and he knew better than to interrupt a gentleman, and that's what many people, that hold their heads higher, don't mind now).

'And how do you know but there will be much cattle at the fair, and you will get a bad price, or maybe you might be robbed when you are coming home? but what need I talk more to you, when you are determined to throw away your luck, Mick Purcell.'

'Oh! no, I would not throw away my luck, sir,' said Mick; 'and if I was sure the bottle was as good as you say, though I never liked an empty bottle, although I had drank the contents of it, I'd give you the cow in the name – '

'Never mind names,' said the stranger, but give me the cow; I would not tell you a lie. Here, take the bottle, and when you go home do what I direct exactly.'

Mick hesitated.

'Well, then goodbye, I can stay no longer: once more, take it, and be rich; refuse it, and beg for your life, and see your children in poverty, and your wife dying for want – that will happen to you, Mick Purcell!' said the little man with a malicious grin, which made him look ten times more ugly than ever.

'Maybe, 'tis true,' said Mick, still hesitating: he did not know what to do – he could hardly help believing the old man, and at length, in a fit of desperation, he seized the bottle. 'Take the cow,' said he, 'and if you are telling a lie, the curse of the poor will be on you.'

'I care neither for your curses nor your blessings, but I have spoken truth, Mick Purcell, and that you will find tonight, if you do what I tell you.'

'And what's that?' says Mick.

'When you go home, never mind if your wife is angry, but be quiet yourself, and make her sweep the room clean, set the table out right, and spread a clean cloth over it; then put the bottle on the ground, saying these words: "Bottle, do your duty", and you will see the end of it.'

'And is this all?' says Mick.

'No more,' said the stranger, 'Goodbye, Mick Purcell – you are a rich man.'

'God grant it!' said Mick, as the old man moved after the cow, and Mick retraced the road towards his cabin: but he could not help turning back his head, to look after the purchaser of his cow, who was nowhere to be seen.

'Lord between us and harm!' said Mick. 'He can't belong to this earth; but where is the cow?' She too was gone, and Mick went homeward muttering prayers, and holding fast the bottle.

'And what would I do if it broke?' thought he. 'Oh! but I'll take care of that;' so he put it into his bosom, and went on anxious to prove his bottle, and doubting of the reception he should meet from his wife; balancing his anxieties with his expectation, his fears with his hopes, he reached home in the evening, and surprised his wife, sitting over the turf fire in the big chimney.

'Oh! Mick, are you come back? Sure you weren't at Cork all the way What has happened to you? Where is the cow? Did you sell her? How much money did you get for her? What news have you? Tell us everything about it?'

'Why then, Molly, if you'll give me time, I'll tell you all about it. If you want to know where the cow is, 'tisn't Mick can tell you, for the never a know does he know where she is now.

'Oh! then, you sold her; and where's the money?'

'Arrah! stop awhile, Molly, and I'll tell you all about it.'

'But what is that bottle under your waistcoat ?' said Molly, spying its neck sticking out. 'Why, then, be easy now, can't you,' says Mick, 'till I tell it to you;' and putting the bottle on the table, 'That's all I got for the cow.'

His poor wife was thunderstruck. 'All you got! and what good is that, Mick? Oh! I never thought you were such a fool; and what'll we do for the rent, and what – '

'Now, Molly,' says Mick, 'can't you hearken to reason? Didn't I tell you how the old man, or whatsomever he was, met me, – no, he did not meet me neither, but he was there with me – on the big hill, and how he made me sell him the cow, and told me the bottle was the only thing for me?'

'Yes, indeed, the only thing for you, you fool!' said Molly, seizing the bottle to hurl it at her poor husband's head; but Mick caught it and quietly for he minded the old man's advice; loosened his wife's grasp, and placed the bottle again in his bosom. Poor Molly sat down crying, while Mick told her his story, with many a crossing and blessing between him and harm. His wife could not help believing him, particularly as she had as much faith in fairies as she had in the priest, who indeed never discouraged her belief in the fairies; may be, he didn't know she believed in them, and may be, he believed in them himself. She got up, however, without saying one word, and began to sweep the earthen floor with a bunch of heath; then she tidied up everything, and put out the long table, and spread the clean cloth, for she had only one, upon it, and Mick, placing the bottle on the ground, looked at it, and said, 'Bottle, do your duty.'

'Look there! look there, mammy!' said his chubby eldest son, a boy about five years old – 'look there! look there!' and he sprang to his mother's side, as two tiny little fellows rose like light from the bottle, and in an instant covered the table with dishes and plates of gold and silver, full of the finest victuals that ever were seen, and when all was done went into the bottle again. Mick and his wife looked at everything with astonishment they had never seen such plates and dishes before, and didn't think they could ever admire them enough; the very sight almost took away their appetites; but at length Molly said, 'Come and sit down, Mick, and try and eat a bit: sure you ought to be hungry after such a good day's work.'

'Why, then, the man told no lie about the bottle.' Mick sat down, after putting the children to the table; and they made a hearty meal, though they couldn't taste half the dishes. 'Now,' says Molly, 'I wonder will those two good little gentlemen carry away these fine things again?' They waited, but no one came; so Molly put up the dishes and plates very carefully, saying, 'Why, then, Mick, that was no lie sure enough: but you'll be a rich man yet, Mick Purcell.'

Mick and his wife and children went to their bed, not to sleep, but to settle about selling the fine things they did not want, and to take more land. Mick went to Cork and sold his plate, and bought a horse and cart, and began to show that he was making money; and they did all they could to keep the bottle a secret; but for all that, their landlord found it out, for he came to Mick one day, and asked him where he got all his money – sure it was not by the farm; and he bothered him so much, that at last Mick told him of the bottle.

His landlord offered him a deal of money for it, but Mick would not give it, till at last he offered to give him all his farm for ever: so Mick, who was very rich, thought he'd never want any more money, and gave him the bottle: but Mick was mistaken – he and his family spent money as if there was no end of it; and to make the story short, they became poorer and poorer, till at last they had nothing left but one cow; and Mick once more drove his cow before him to sell her at Cork fair, hoping to meet the old man and get another bottle. It was hardly daybreak when he left home, and he walked on at a good pace till he reached the big hill: the mists were sleeping in the valleys and curling like smoke wreaths upon the brown heath around him. The sun rose on his left, and just at his feet a lark sprang from its grassy couch and poured fourth its joyous matin song, ascending into the clear blue sky,

'Till its form like a speck in the airiness blending,
And thrilling with music, was melting in light.'

Mick crossed himself, listening as he advanced to the sweet song of the lark, but thinking, notwithstanding, all the time of the little old man; when, just as he reached the summit of the hill, and cast his eyes over the extensive prospect before and around him, he was startled and rejoiced by the same well-known voice: 'Well, Mick Purcell, I told you you would be a rich man.'

'Indeed, then, sure enough I was, that's no lie for you, sir. Good morning to you, but it is not rich I am now – but have you another bottle, for I want it now as much as I did long ago; so if you have it, sir, here is the cow for it.'

'And here is the bottle,' said the old man, smiling; 'you know what to do with it.'

'Oh! then, sure I do, as good right I have.'

'Well, farewell for ever, Mick Purcell: I told you you would be a rich man.'

'And goodbye to you, sir,' said Mick, as he turned back; 'and good luck to you, and good luck to the big hill – it wants a name, Bottle-hill – goodbye, sir, goodbye': so Mick walked back as fast as he could, never looking after the white-faced little gentleman and the cow, so anxious was he to bring home the bottle. Well, he arrived with it safely enough, and called out as soon as he saw Molly, 'Oh! sure I've another bottle!'

'Arrah! then, have you? why, then, you're a lucky man, Mick Purcell, that's what you are.'

In an instant she put everything right; and Mick, looking at his bottle, exultingly cried out, 'Bottle, do your duty.' In a twinkling, two great stout men with big cudgels issued from the bottle (I do not know how they got room in it), and belaboured poor Mick and his wife and all his family, till they lay on the floor, when in they went again. Mick, as soon as he recovered, got up and looked about him; he thought and thought, and at last he took up his wife and his children; and, leaving them to recover as well as they could, he took the bottle under his coat and went to his landlord, who had a great company: he got a servant to tell him he wanted to speak to him, and at last he came out to Mick.

'Well, what do you want now?'

'Nothing, sir, only I have another bottle.'

'Oh! ho! is it as good as the first?'

'Yes, sir, and better; if you like I will show it to you before all the ladies and gentlemen.'

'Come along, then.' So saying, Mick was brought into the great hall, where he saw his old bottle standing high up on a shelf: 'Ah! ha!' says he to himself, 'maybe I won't have you by and by.'

'Now,' says his landlord, 'show us your bottle.' Mick set it on the floor, and uttered the words: in a moment the landlord was tumbling on the floor; ladies and gentlemen, servants and all, were running, and roaring, and sprawling, and kicking, and shrieking. Wine cups and salvers were knocked about in every direction, until the landlord called out, 'Stop those two devils, Mick Purcell, or I'll have you hanged.'

'They never shall stop,' said Mick, 'till I get my own bottle that I see up there at top of that shelf.'

'Give it down to him, give it down to him, before we are all killed!' says the landlord.

Mick put his bottle in his bosom: in jumped the two men into the new bottle, and he carried them home. I need not lengthen my story by telling how he got richer than ever, how his son married his landlord's only daughter, and how he and his wife died when they were very old, and how some of the servants, fighting at their wake, broke the bottles; but still the hill has the name upon it; ay, and so 'twill be always Bottle-hill to the end of the world, and so it ought, for it is a strange story.

Daniel O'Rourke

THOMAS CROFTON CROKER

People may have heard of the renowned adventures of Daniel O'Rourke, but how few are there who know that the cause of all his perils, above and below, was neither more nor less than his having slept under the walls of the Pooka's tower. I knew the man well. He lived at the bottom of Hungry Hill, just at the right-hand side of the road as you go toward Bantry. An old man was he, at the time he told me the story, with grey hair and red nose; and it was on the 25th of June, 1813, that I heard it from his own lips, as he sat smoking his pipe under the old poplar tree, on as fine an evening as ever shone from the sky. I was going to visit the caves in Dursey Island, having spent the morning at Glengariff.

'I am often *axed* to tell it, sir,' said he, 'so that this is not the first time. The master's son, you see, had come from beyond foreign parts in France and Spain, as young gentlemen used to go before Buonaparte or any such was heard of; and sure enough there was a dinner given to all the people on the ground, gentle and simple, high and low, rich and poor. The *ould* gentlemen were the gentlemen after all, saving your honour's presence. They'd swear at a body a little, to be sure, and, maybe, give one a cut of a whip now and then, but we were no losers by it in the end; and they were so easy and civil, and kept such rattling houses, and thousands of welcomes; and there was no grinding for rent, and there was hardly a tenant on the estate that did not taste of his landlord's bounty often and often in a year; but now it's another thing. No matter for that, sir, for I'd better be telling you my story.

'Well, we had everything of the best, and plenty of it; and we ate, and we drank and we danced, and the young master by the same token danced with Peggy Barry, from the *Bohereen* – a lovely young couple they were, though they are both low enough now. To make a long story short, I got, as a body may say, the same thing as tipsy almost, for I can't remember ever at all, no ways, how it was I left the place; only I did leave it, that's certain. Well, I thought for all that, in myself, I'd just step to Molly Cronohan's, the fairy woman, to speak a word about the bracket heifer that was bewitched; and so as I was crossing the stepping-stones of the ford of Ballyashenogh, and as looking up at the stars and blessing myself – for why? it was Lady-day – I missed my foot, and souse I fell into the water. "Death alive!" thought I, "I'll be drowned now!" However, I began swimming, swimming, swimming away for the dear life, till at last I got ashore, somehow or other, but never the one of me can tell how, upon a *dissolute* island.

'I wandered and wandered about there, without knowing where I wandered, until at last I got into a big bog. The moon was shining as bright as day, or your fair lady's eyes, sir (with the pardon for mentioning her), and I looked east and west, and north and south, and every way, and nothing did I see but bog, bog, bog – I could never find out how I got into it; and my heart grew cold with fear, for sure and certain I was that it would be my *berrin* place. So I sat down upon a stone which, as good luck would have it, was close by me, and I began to scratch my head, and sing the *Ullagone* – when all of a sudden the moon grew black, and I looked up, and saw something for all the world as if it was moving down between me and it, and I could not tell what it was. Down it came with a pounce, and looked at me full in the face; and what was it but an eagle? as fine a one as ever flew from the kingdom of Kerry. So he looked at me in the face, and says he to me, "Daniel O'Rourke," says he, "how do you do?" "Very well, I thank you, sir," says I; "I hope you're well"; wondering out of my senses all the time how an eagle came to speak like a Christian. "What brings you here, Dan?" says he. "Nothing at all, sir," says I; "only I wish I was safe home again." "Is it out of the island you want to go, Dan?" says he. " 'Tis, sir," says I: so I up and told him how I had taken a drop too much, and fell into the water; how I swam to the island; and how I got into the bog and did not know my way out of it. "Dan," says he, after a minute's thought, "though it is very improper for you to get drunk on Lady-day, yet as you are a decent, sober man, who 'tends mass well and never flings stones at me or mine, nor cries out after us in the fields – my life for yours," says he; "so get up on my back, and grip me well for fear you'd fall off, and I'll fly you out of the bog." "I am afraid," says I, "your honour's making game of me; for who ever heard of riding horseback on an eagle before?" " 'Pon the honour of a gentleman," says he, putting his right foot on his breast, "I am quite in earnest: and so now either take my offer or starve in the bog – besides, I see that your weight is sinking the stone."

'It was true enough as he said, for I found the stone every minute going from under me. I had no choice; so thinks I to myself, faint heart never won fair lady, and this is fair persuadance. "I thank your honour," says I, "for the loan of your civility; and I'll take your kind offer."

'I therefore mounted upon the back of the eagle, and held him tight enough by the throat, and up he flew in the air like a lark. Little I knew the trick he was going to serve me. Up – up – up, God knows how far up he flew. "Why then," said I to him – thinking he did not know the right road home – very civilly, because why? I was in his power entirely; "sir," says I, "please your honour's glory, and with humble submission to your better judgment, if you'd fly down a bit, you're now just over my cabin, and I could be put down there, and many thanks to your worship."

' "*Arrah*, Dan," said he, "do you think me a fool? Look down the next field, and don't you see two men and a gun? By my word it would be no joke to be shot this way, to oblige a drunken blackguard that I picked up off of a *could* stone in a bog." "Bother you," said I to myself, but I did not speak out, for where was the use? Well, sir, up he kept flying, flying, and I asking him every minute to fly down, and all to no use. "Where in the world are you going, sir?" says I to him. "Hold your tongue, Dan," says he: "mind your own business, and don't be interfering with the business of other people." "Faith, this is my business, I think," says I. "Be quiet, Dan," says he: so I said no more.

'At last where should we come to, but to the moon itself. Now you can't see it from this, but there is, or there was in my time, a reaping-hook sticking out of the side of the moon, this way (drawing the figure thus, Ω, on the ground with the end of his stick).

' "Dan," said the eagle, "I'm tired with this long fly; I had no notion 'twas so far." "And my lord, sir,' said I, "who in the world *axed* you to fly so far – was it I? Did not I beg and pray and beseech you to stop half an hour ago?" "There's no use talking, Dan," said he; "I'm tired bad enough, so you must get off, and sit down on the moon until I rest myself." "Is it sit down on the moon?" said I, "is it upon that little round thing, then? why, then, sure I'd fall off in a minute, and be *kilt* and spilt and smashed all to bits; you are a vile deceiver – so you are." "Not at all, Dan, said he; "you can catch fast hold of the reaping-hook that's sticking out of the side of the moon, and 'twill keep you up." "I won't then," said I. "Maybe not," said he, quite quiet. "If you don't, my man, I shall just give you a shake, and one slap of my wing, and send you down to the ground, where every bone in your body will be smashed as small as a drop of dew on a cabbage-leaf in the morning." "Why, then, I'm in a fine way," said I to myself, "ever to have come along with the likes of you;" and so giving him a hearty curse in Irish, for fear he'd know what I said, I got off his back with a heavy heart, took hold of the reaping hook, and sat down upon the moon, and a mighty cold seat it was, I can tell you that.

'When he had me there fairly landed, he turned about on me, and said: "Good morning to you, Daniel O'Rourke," said he; 'I think I've nicked you fairly now. You robbed my nest last year' ('twas true enough for him, but how he found it out is hard to say), "and in return you are freely welcome to cool your heels dangling upon the moon like a cockthrow."

' "Is that all, and is this the way you leave me, you brute, you," says I. "You ugly, unnatural *baste*, and is this the way you serve me at last? Bad luck to yourself, with your hook'd nose, and to all your breed, you blackguard." 'Twas all to no manner of use; he spread out his great big wings, burst out a-laughing, and flew away like lightning. I bawled after him to stop; but I might have called and bawled for ever, without his minding me. Away he went, and I never saw him from that day to this sorrow fly away with him! You may be sure I was in a disconsolate condition, and kept roaring out for the bare grief, when all at once a door opened right in the middle of the moon, creaking on its hinges as if it had not been opened for a month before, I suppose they never thought of greasing 'em, and out there walks – who do you think, but the man in the moon himself? I knew him by his bush.

' "Good-morrow to you, Daniel O'Rourke," said he; "how do you do?" "Very well, thank your honour," said I. "I hope your honour's well." "What brought you here, Dan?" said he. So I told him how I was a little overtaken in liquor at the master's, and how I was cast on a dissolute island, and how I lost my way in the bog, and how the thief of an eagle promised to fly me out of it and how, instead of that, he had fled me up to the moon.

' "Dan," said the man in the moon, taking a pinch of snuff when I was done, "you must not stay here." "Indeed, sir," says I, " 'tis much against my will I'm here at all; but how am I to go back?" "That's your business," said he; "Dan, mine is to tell you that here you must not stay; so be off in less than no time." "I'm doing no harm," says I, "only holding on hard by the reaping-hook, lest I fall off." "That's what you must not do, Dan," says he. "Pray, sir," say I, "may I ask how many you are in family, that you would not give a poor traveller lodging: I'm sure 'tis not so often you're troubled with strangers coming to see you, for 'tis a long way." "I'm by myself, Dan," says he; "but you'd better let go the reaping-hook." "Faith, and with your leave," says I, "I'll not let go the grip, and the more you bid me, the more I won't let go; – so I will." "You had better, Dan," says he again. "why, then, my little fellow," says I, taking the whole weight of him with my eye from head to foot, "there are two words to that bargain; and I'll not budge, but you may if you like." "We'll see how that is to be," says he; and back he went, giving the door such a great bang after him (for it was plain he was huffed) that I thought the moon and all would fall down with it.

'Well, I was preparing myself to try strength with him, when back again he comes, with the kitchen cleaver in his hand, and, without saying a word, he gives two bangs to the handle of the reaping-hook that was keeping me up, and *whap*! it came in two. "Good-morning to you, Dan," says the spiteful little old blackguard, when he saw me cleanly falling down with a bit of the handle in my hand; I thank you for your visit and fair weather after you, Daniel.' I had not time to make answer to him, for I was tumbling over and over and rolling and rolling, at the rate of a fox-hunt. "God help me!" says I, "but this is a pretty pickle for a decent man to be seen in at this time of night: I am now sold fairly." The word was not out of my mouth when, *whiz*! what should fly by close to my ear but a flock of wild geese, all the way from my own bog of Ballyasheenogh, else how should they know *me*? The *ould* gander, who was their general, turning about his head, cried out to me, "Is that you, Dan?" "The same," said I, not a bit daunted now at what he said, for I was by this time used to all kinds of *bedevilment*, and, besides, I knew him of ould. "Good-morrow to you," says he, "Daniel O'Rourke; how are you in health this morning?" "Very well, sir," says I, "I thank you kindly," drawing my breath, for I was mightily in want of some. "I hope your honour's the same." "I think 'tis falling you are, Daniel," says he. "You may say that, sir," says I. "And where are you going all the way so fast?" said the gander. So I told him how I had taken the drop, and how I came on the island, and how I lost my way in the bog, and how the thief of an eagle flew me up to the moon, and how the man in the moon turned me out. "Dan," said he, "I'll save you: put out your hand and catch me by the leg, and I'll fly you home." "Sweet is your hand in a pitcher of honey, my jewel," says I, though all the time I thought within myself that I don't much trust you; but there was no help, so I caught the gander by the leg, and away I and the other geese flew after him fast as hops.

'We flew, and we flew, and we flew, until we came right over the wide ocean. I knew it well, for I saw Cape Clear to my right hand, sticking up out of the water. "Ah, my lord,' said I to the goose, for I thought it best to keep a civil tongue in my head anyway, "fly to land if you please." "It is impossible, you see, Dan"; said he, "for a while, because you see we are going to Arabia." "To Arabia!" said I; "that's surely some place in foreign parts, far away. Oh! Mr Goose: why then, to be sure, I'm a man to be pitied among you." "Whist, whist, you fool," said he, "hold your tongue; I tell you Arabia is a very decent sort of place, as like West Carbery as one egg is like another, only there is a little more sand there."

'Just as we were talking, a ship hove in sight, scudding so beautiful before the wind. "Ah! then, sir," said I, "will you drop me on the ship, if you please?" "We are not fair over it," said he; "if I dropped you now you would go splash into the sea." "I would not," says I; "I know better than that, for it is just clean under us, so let me drop now at once."

' "If you must, you must," said he; "there, take your way"; and he opened his claw, and faith he was right – sure enough I came down plump into the very bottom of the salt sea! Down to the very bottom I went, and I gave myself up then forever, when a whale walked up to me, scratching himself after his night's sleep, and looked me full in the face, and never the word did he say, but lifting up his tail, he splashed me all over again with the cold salt water till there wasn't a dry stitch upon my whole carcass! and I heard somebody saying – 'twas a voice I knew, too – "Get up, you drunken brute, off o' that," and with that I woke up and there was Judy with a tub full of water, which she was splashing all over me for, rest her soul! though she was a good wife, she never could bear to see me in drink, and had a bitter hand of her own.

' "Get up," said she again: "and of all places in the parish would no

place *sarve* your turn to lie down upon but under the *ould* walls of
Carrigapooka? an *uneasy* resting I am sure you had of it." And sure
enough I had: for I was fairly bothered out of my senses with eagles,
and men of the moons, and flying ganders, and whales, driving me
through bogs, and up to the moon, and down to the bottom of the
green ocean. If I was in drink ten times over, long would it be before
I'd lie down in the same spot again, I know that.'

The Blood-Drawing Ghost

JEREMIAH CURTIN

There was a young man in the parish of Drimoleague, county Cork, who was courting three girls at one time, and he didn't know which of them would he take; they had equal fortunes, and any of the three was as pleasing to him as any other.

One day when he was coming home from the fair with his two sisters, the sisters began: 'Well, John,' said one of them, 'why don't you get married? Why don't you take either Mary, or Peggy, or Kate?'

'I can't tell you that,' said John, 'till I find which of them has the best wish for me.'

'How will you know?' asked the other.

'I will tell you that as soon as any person will die in the parish.'

In three weeks' time from that day an old man died. John went to the wake and then to the funeral. While they were burying the corpse in the graveyard, John stood near a tomb which was next to the grave, and when all were going away, after burying the old man, he remained standing a while by himself, as if thinking of something; then he put his blackthorn stick on top of the tomb, stood a while longer, and on going from the graveyard left the stick behind him. He went home and ate his supper. After supper John went to a neighbour's house where young people used to meet of an evening, and the three girls happened to be there that time. John was very quiet, so that everyone noticed him.

'What is troubling you this evening, John?' asked one of the girls.

'Oh, I am sorry for my beautiful blackthorn,' said he.

'Did you lose it?'

'I did not,' said John; 'but I left it on the top of the tomb next to the grave of the man who was buried today and whichever of you three will go for it is the woman I'll marry. Well, Mary, will you go for my stick?' asked he.

'Faith, then, I will not,' said Mary.

'Well, Peggy, will you go?'

'If I were without a man forever,' said Peggy, 'I wouldn't go.'

'Well, Kate,' said he to the third, 'will you go for my stick? If you go I'll marry you.'

'Stand to your word,' said Kate, 'and I'll bring the stick.'

'Believe me, that I will,' said John.

Kate left the company behind her, and went for the stick. The graveyard was three miles away and the walk was a long one. Kate came to the place at last and made out the tomb by the fresh grave. When she had her hand on the blackthorn, a voice called from the tomb: 'Leave the stick where it is and open this tomb for me.'

Kate began to tremble and was greatly in dread, but something was forcing her to open the tomb – she couldn't help herself.

'Take the lid off now,' said the dead man when Kate had the door open and was inside in the tomb, 'and take me out of this – take me on your back.'

Afraid to refuse, she took the lid from the coffin, raised the dead man on her back, and walked on in the way he directed. She walked about the distance of a mile. The load, being very heavy, was near breaking her back and killing her. She walked half a mile farther and came to a village; the houses were at the side of the road.

'Take me to the first house,' said the dead man.

She took him.

'Oh, we cannot go in here,' said he, when they came near. 'The people have clean water inside, and they have holy water, too. Take me to the next house.'

She went to the next house.

'We cannot go in there,' said he, when she stopped in front of the door. 'They have clean water, and there is holy water as well.'

She went to the third house.

'Go in here,' said the dead man. 'There is neither clean water nor holy water in this place; we can stop in it.'

They went in.

'Bring a chair now and put me sitting at the side of the fire. Then find me something to eat and to drink.'

She placed him in a chair by the hearth, searched the house, found a dish of oatmeal and brought it. 'I have nothing to give you to drink but dirty water,' said she.

'Bring me a dish and a razor.'

She brought the dish and the razor.

'Come, now,' said he, 'to the room above.'

They went up to the room, where three young men, sons of the man of the house, were sleeping in bed, and Kate had to hold the dish while the dead man was drawing their blood.

'Let the father and mother have that,' said he, 'in return for the dirty water,' meaning that if there was clean water in the house he wouldn't have taken the blood of the young men.

He closed their wounds in the way that there was no sign of a cut on them. 'Mix this now with the meal, get a dish of it for yourself and another for me.'

She got two plates and put the oatmeal in it after mixing it, and brought two spoons. Kate wore a handkerchief on her head; she put this under her neck and tied it; she was pretending to eat, but she was putting the food to hide in the handkerchief till her plate was empty.

'Have you your share eaten?' asked the dead man.

'I have,' answered Kate.

'I'll have mine finished this minute,' said he, and soon after he gave her the empty dish. She put the dishes back in the dresser and didn't mind washing them. 'Come, now,' said he, 'and take me back to the place where you found me.'

'Oh, how can I take you back; you are too great a load; 'twas killing me you were when I brought you.' She was in dread of going from the house again.

'You are stronger after that food than what you were in coming; take me back to my grave.'

She went against her will. She rolled up the food inside the handkerchief. There was a deep hole in the wall of the kitchen by the door, where the bar was slipped in when they barred the door; into this hole she put the handkerchief. In going back she shortened the road by going through a big field at command of the dead man. When they were at the top of the field she asked, was there any cure for those young men whose blood was drawn?

'There is no cure,' said he, 'except one. If any of that food had been spared, three bits of it in each young man's mouth would bring them to life again, and they'd never know of their death.'

'Then,' said Kate in her own mind, 'that cure is to be had.'

'Do you see this field?' asked the dead man.

'I do.'

'Well, there is as much gold buried in it as would make rich people of all who belong to you. Do you see the three *leachtans* [piles of small stones]? Underneath each pile of them is a pot of gold.'

The dead man looked around for a while; then Kate went on, without stopping, till she came to the wall of the graveyard, and just then they heard the cock crow.

'The cock is crowing,' said Kate; 'it's time for me to be going home.'

'It is not time yet,' said the dead man; 'that is a bastard cock.'

A moment after that another cock crowed. 'There the cocks are crowing a second time,' said she.

'No,' said the dead man, 'that is a bastard cock again; that's no right bird.' They came to the mouth of the tomb and a cock crowed the third time.

'Well,' said the girl, 'that must be the right cock.'

'Ah, my girl, that cock has saved your life for you. But for him I would have you with me in the grave for evermore, and if I knew this cock would crow before I was in the grave you wouldn't have the knowledge you have now of the field and the gold. Put me into the coffin where you found me. Take your time and settle me well. I cannot meddle with you now, and 'tis sorry I am to part with you.'

'Will you tell me who you are?' asked Kate.

'Have you ever heard your father or mother mention a man called Edward Derrihy or his son Michael?'

'It's often I heard tell of them,' replied the girl.

'Well, Edward Derrihy was my father; I am Michael. That blackthorn that you came for tonight to this graveyard was the lucky stick for you, but if you had any thought of the danger that was before you, you wouldn't be here. Settle me carefully and close the tomb well behind you.'

She placed him in the coffin carefully, closed the door behind her, took the blackthorn stick, and away home with Kate. The night was far spent when she came. She was tired, and it's good reason the girl had. She thrust the stick into the thatch above the door of the house and rapped. Her sister rose up and opened the door.

'Where did you spend the night?' asked the sister. 'Mother will kill you in the morning for spending the whole night from home.'

'Go to bed,' answered Kate, 'and never mind me.'

They went to bed, and Kate fell asleep the minute she touched the bed, she was that tired after the night.

When the father and mother of the three young men rose next

morning, and there was no sign of their sons, the mother went to the room to call them, and there she found the three dead. She began to screech and wring her hands. She ran to the road screaming and wailing. All the neighbours crowded around to know what trouble was on her. She told them her three sons were lying dead in their bed after the night. Very soon the report spread in every direction. When Kate's father and mother heard it they hurried off to the house of the dead men. When they came home Kate was still in bed; the mother took a stick and began to beat the girl for being out all the night and in bed all the day.

'Get up now, you lazy stump of a girl,' said she, 'and go to the wake-house; your neighbour's three sons are dead.'

Kate took no notice of this. 'I am very tired and sick,' said she. 'You'd better spare me and give me a drink.'

The mother gave her a drink of milk and a bite to eat, and in the middle of the day she rose up.

' 'Tis a shame for you not to be at the wake-house yet,' said the mother; 'hurry over now.'

When Kate reached the house, there was a great crowd of people before her and great wailing. She did not cry, but was looking on. The father was as if wild, going up and down the house wringing his hands.

'Be quiet,' said Kate. 'Control yourself.'

'How can I do that, my dear girl, and my three fine sons lying dead in the house?'

'What would you give,' asked Kate, 'to the person who would bring life to them again?'

'Don't be vexing me,' said the father.

'It's neither vexing you I am nor trifling,' said Kate. 'I can put the life in them again.'

'If it was true that you could do that, I would give you all that I have inside the house and outside as well.'

'All I want from you,' said Kate, 'is the eldest son to marry and *Gort na Leachtan* [the field of the stone heaps] as fortune.'

'My dear, you will have that from me with the greatest blessing.'

'Give me the field in writing, from yourself, whether the son will marry me or not.'

He gave her the field in his handwriting. She told all who were inside in the wake house to go outside the door, every man and woman of them. Some were laughing at her and more were crying, thinking it was mad she was. She bolted the door inside, and went to the place where she left the handkerchief, found it, and put three bites of the oatmeal and the blood in the mouth of each young man, and as soon as she did that the three got their natural colour, and they looked like men sleeping. She opened the door, then called on all to come inside, and told the father to go and wake his sons.

He called each one by name, and as they woke they seemed very tired after their night's rest; they put on their clothes, and were greatly surprised to see all the people around. 'How is this?' asked the eldest brother.

'Don't you know of anything that came over you in the night?' asked the father.

'We do not,' said the sons. 'We remember nothing at all since we fell asleep last evening.'

The father then told them everything, but they could not believe it. Kate went away home and told her father and mother of her night's journey to and from the graveyard, and said that she would soon tell them more.

That day she met John.

'Did you bring the stick?' asked he.

'Find your own stick,' said she, 'and never speak to me again in your life.'

In a week's time she went to the house of the three young men, and said to the father, 'I have come for what you promised me.'

'You'll get that with my blessing,' said the father. He called the eldest son aside then and asked would he marry Kate, their neighbour's daughter. 'I will,' said the son. Three days after that the two were married and had a fine wedding. For three weeks they enjoyed a pleasant life without toil or trouble; then Kate said, 'This will not do for us; we must be working. Come with me tomorrow and I'll give yourself and brothers plenty to do, and my own father and brothers as well.'

She took them next day to one of the stone heaps in *Gort na Leachtan*. 'Throw these stones to one side,' said she.

They thought that she was losing her senses, but she told them that they'd soon see for themselves what she was doing. They went to work and kept at it till they had six feet deep of a hole dug; then they met with a flat stone three feet square and an iron hook in the middle of it.

'Sure there must be something underneath this,' said the men.

They lifted the flag, and under it was a pot of gold. All were very happy then. 'There is more gold yet in the place,' said Kate. 'Come, now, to the other heap.' They removed that heap, dug down, and found another pot of gold. They removed the third pile and found a third pot full of gold. On the side of the third pot was an inscription, and they could not make out what it was. After emptying it, they placed the pot by the side of the door.

About a month later a poor scholar walked the way, and as he was going in at the door he saw the old pot and the letters on the side of it. He began to study the letters.

'You must be a good scholar if you can read what's on that pot,' said the young man.

'I can,' said the poor scholar, 'and here it is for you. There is a deal more at the south side of each pot.'

The young man said nothing, but putting his hand in his pocket, gave the poor scholar a good day's hire. When he was gone, they went to work and found a deal more of gold at the south side of each stone heap. They were very happy then and very rich, and bought several farms and built fine houses, and it was supposed by all of them in the latter end that it was Derrihy's money that was buried under the *leachtans*, but they could give no correct account of that, and sure why need they care? When they died, they left property to make their children rich to the seventh generation.

St Martin's Eve

JEREMIAH CURTIN

In Iveragh, not very far from the town of Cahirciveen, there lived a farmer named James Shea with his wife and three children, two sons and a daughter. The man was peaceable, honest, and very charitable to the poor, but his wife was hard hearted, never giving even a drink of milk to a needy person. Her younger son was as bad in every way as herself, and whatever the mother did he always agreed with her and was on her side.

This was before the roads and cars were in the Kerry Mountains. The only way of travelling in those days, when a man didn't walk, was to ride sitting on a straw saddle, and the only way to take anything to market was on horseback in creels.

It happened, at any rate, that James Shea was going in the beginning of November to Cork with two firkins of butter, and what troubled him most was the fear that he'd not be home on St Martin's night to do honour to the saint. For never had he let that night pass without drawing blood in honour of the saint.

To make sure, he called the elder son and said, 'if I am not at the house on St Martin's night, kill the big sheep that is running with the cows.'

Shea went away to Cork with the butter, but could not be home in time. The elder son went out on St Martin's eve, when he saw that his father was not coming, and drove the sheep into the house.

'What are you doing, you fool, with that sheep?' asked the mother.

'Sure, I'm going to kill it. Didn't you hear my father tell me that there was never a St Martin's night but he drew blood, and do you want to have the house disgraced?'

At this the mother made sport of him and said: 'Drive out the sheep and I'll give you something else to kill by and by.'

So the boy let the sheep out, thinking the mother would kill a goose.

He sat down and waited for the mother to give him whatever she had to kill. It wasn't long till she came in, bringing a big tomcat they had, and the same cat was in the house nine or ten years.

'Here,' said she, 'you can kill this beast and draw its blood. We'll have it cooked when your father comes home.'

The boy was very angry and spoke up to the mother: 'Sure the house is disgraced for ever,' said he, 'and it will not be easy for you to satisfy my father when he comes.'

He didn't kill the cat, you may be sure; and neither he nor his sister ate a bite of supper, and they were crying and fretting over the disgrace all the evening.

That very night the house caught fire and burned down; nothing was left but the four walls. The mother and younger son were burned to death, but the elder son and his sister escaped by some miracle. They went to a neighbour's house, and were there till the father came on the following evening. When he found the house destroyed and the wife and younger son dead he mourned and lamented. But when the other son told him what the mother did on St Martin's eve, he cried out: 'Ah, it was the wrath of God that fell on my house; if I had stopped at home till after St Martin's night, all would be safe and well with me now.'

James Shea went to the priest on the following morning, and asked would it be good or lucky for him to rebuild the house.

'Indeed,' said the priest, 'there is no harm in putting a roof on the walls and repairing them if you will have Mass celebrated in the house before you go to live in it. If you do that all will be well with you.'

[Shea spoke to the priest because people are opposed to repairing or rebuilding a burnt house, and especially if any person has been burned in it.]

Well, James Shea put a roof on the house, repaired it, and had Mass celebrated inside. That evening as Shea was sitting down to supper what should he see but his wife coming in the door to him. He thought she wasn't dead at all. 'Ah, Mary,' said he, ' 'tis not so bad as they told me. Sure, I thought it is dead you were. Oh, then you are welcome home; come and sit down here; the supper is just ready.'

She didn't answer a word, but looked him straight in the face and walked on to the room at the other end of the house. He jumped up, thinking it's sick the woman was, and followed her to the room to help her. He shut the door after him. As he was not coming back for a long time the son thought at last that he'd go and ask the father why he wasn't eating his supper. When he went into the room he saw no sign of his mother, saw nothing in the place but two legs from the knees down. He screamed out for his sister and she came.

'Oh, merciful God!' screamed the sister.

'Those are my father's legs!' cried the brother, 'and Mary, don't you know the stockings, sure you knitted them yourself, and don't I know the brogues very well?'

They called in the neighbours, and, to the terror of them all, they saw nothing but the two legs and feet of James Shea.

There was a wake over the remains that night, and the next day they buried the two legs. Some people advised the boy and girl never to sleep a night in the house, that their mother's soul was lost, and that was why she came and ate up the father, and she would eat themselves as well.

The two now started to walk the world, not caring much where they were going if only they escaped the mother. They stopped the first night at a farmer's house not far from Killarney. After supper a bed was made down for them by the fire, in the corner, and they lay there. About the middle of the night a great noise was heard outside, and the woman of the house called to her boys and servants to get up and go to the cow-house to know why the cows were striving to kill one another. Her own son rose first. When he and the two servant boys went out they saw the ghost of a woman, and she in chains. She made at them, and wasn't long killing the three.

Not seeing the boys come in, the farmer and his wife rose up, sprinkled holy water around the house, blessed themselves and went out, and there they saw the ghost in blue blazes and chains around her. In a coop outside by himself was a March cock. [A cock hatched in March from a cock and hen hatched in March.]

He flew down from his perch and crowed twelve times. That moment the ghost disappeared.

Now the neighbours were roused, and the news flew around that the three boys were killed. The brother and sister didn't say a word to anyone, but, rising up early, started on their journey, begging God's protection as they went. They never stopped nor stayed till they came to Rathmore, near Cork, and, going to a farmhouse, the boy asked for lodgings in God's name.

'I will give you lodgings in His name,' said the farmer's wife.

She brought warm water for the two to wash their hands and feet, for they were tired and dusty. After supper a bed was put down for them, and about the same hour as the night before there was a great noise outside.

'Rise up and go out,' said the farmer's wife, 'some of the cows must be untied.'

'I'll not go out at this hour of the night, if they are untied itself,' said the man, 'I'll stay where I am, if they kill one another, for it isn't safe to go out till the cock crows; after cockcrow I'll go out.'

'That's true for you,' said the farmer's wife, 'and, upon my word, before coming to bed, I forget to sprinkle holy water in the room, and to bless myself.'

So taking the bottle hanging near the bed, she sprinkled the water around the room and toward the threshold, and made the sign of the cross. The man didn't go out until cockcrow. The brother and sister went away early, and travelled all day. Coming evening they met a pleasant-looking man who stood before them in the road.

'You seem to be strangers,' said he, 'and where are you going?'

'We are strangers,' said the boy, 'and we don't know where to go.'

'You need go no farther. I know you well, your home is in Iveragh. I am St Martin, sent from the Lord to protect you and your sister. You were going to draw the blood of a sheep in my honour, but your mother and brother made sport of you, and your mother wouldn't let you do what your father told you. You see what has come to them; they are lost for ever, both of them. Your father is saved in heaven, for he was a good man. Your mother will be here soon, and I'll put her in the way that she'll never trouble you again.'

Taking a rod from his bosom and dipping it in a vial of holy water he drew a circle around the brother and sister. Soon they heard their mother coming, and then they saw her with chains on her, and the rattling was terrible, and flames were rising from her. She came to where they stood, and said: 'Bad luck to you both for being the cause of my misery.'

'God forbid that,' said St Martin. 'It isn't they are the cause, but yourself, for you were always bad. You would not honour me, and now you must suffer for it.'

He pulled out a book and began to read, and after he read a few minutes he told her to depart and not be seen in Ireland again till the day of judgment. She rose in the air in flames of fire, and with such a noise that you'd think all the thunders of heaven were roaring and all the houses and walls in the kingdom were tumbling to the ground.

The brother and sister went on their knees and thanked St Martin. He blessed them and told them to rise, and, taking a little tablecloth out of his bosom, he said to the brother: 'Take this cloth with you and keep it in secret. Let no one know that you have it. If you or your sister are in need go to your room, close the door behind you and bolt it. Spread out the cloth then, and plenty of everything to eat and drink will come to you. Keep the cloth with you always; it belongs to both of you. Now go home and live in the house that your father built, and let the priest come and celebrate Monday Mass in it, and live the life that your father lived before you.'

The two came home, and brother and sister lived a good life. They married, and when either was in need that one had the cloth to fall back on, and their grandchildren are living yet in Iveragh. And this is truth, every word of it, and it's often I heard my poor grandmother tell this story, the Almighty God rest her soul, and she was the woman that wouldn't tell a lie. She knew James Shea and his wife very well.

The Witch Hare

DUBLIN UNIVERSITY MAGAZINE (1839)

About the commencement of the last century there lived in the vicinity of the once famous village of Aghavoe a wealthy farmer, named Bryan Costigan. This man kept an extensive dairy and a great many milch cows and every year made considerable sums by the sale of milk and butter. The luxuriance of the pasture lands in this neighbourhood has always been proverbial; and, consequently, Bryan's cows were the finest and most productive in the country, and his milk and butter the richest and sweetest, and brought the highest price at every market at which he ordered these articles for sale.

Things continued to go on thus prosperously with Bryan Costigan, when, one season all at once, he found his cattle declining in appearance, and his dairy almost entirely profitless. Bryan, at first, attributed this change to the weather, or some such cause, but soon found or fancied reasons to assign it to a far different source. The cows, without any visible disorder, daily declined, and were scarcely able to crawl about on their pasture; many of them, instead of milk, gave nothing but blood; and the scanty quantity of milk which some of them continued to supply was so bitter that even the pigs would not drink it; while the butter which it produced was of such a bad quality, and stunk so horribly, that the very dogs would not eat it. Bryan applied for remedies to all the quacks and 'fairy-women' in the country – but in vain. Many of the imposters declared that the mysterious malady in his cattle went beyond *their* skill; while others, although they found no difficulty in tracing it to superhuman agency, declared that they had no control in the matter, as the charm under the influence of which his property was made away with, was too powerful to be dissolved by anything less than the special inter-position of Divine Providence. The poor farmer became almost distracted; he saw ruin staring him in the face; yet what was he to do? Sell his cattle and purchase others! No; that was out of the question, as they looked so miserable and emaciated that no one would even take them as a present, while it was also impossible to sell to a butcher, as the flesh of one which he killed for his own family was as black as a coal, and stunk like any putrid carrion.

The unfortunate man was thus completely bewildered. He knew not what to do; he became moody and stupid; his sleep forsook him by night, and all day he wandered about the fields, among his 'fairy-stricken' cattle like a maniac.

Affairs continued in this plight, when one very sultry evening in the latter days of July, Bryan Costigan's wife was sitting at her own door, spinning at her wheel, in a very gloomy and agitated state of mind. Happening to look down the narrow green lane which led from the high road to her cabin, she espied a little old woman barefoot, and enveloped in an old scarlet cloak, approaching slowly, with the aid of a crutch which she carried in one hand, and a cane or walking-stick in the other. The farmer's wife felt glad at seeing the odd-looking stranger; she smiled, and yet she knew not why, as she neared the house. A vague and indefinable feeling of pleasure crowded on her imagination; and, as the old woman gained the threshold, she bade her 'welcome' with a warmth which plainly told that her lips gave utterance but to the genuine feelings of her heart.

'God bless this good house and all belonging to it,' said the stranger as she entered.

'God save you kindly, and you are welcome, whoever you are,' replied Mrs Costigan.

'Hem, I thought so,' said the old woman with a significant grin. 'I thought so, or I wouldn't trouble you.'

The farmer's wife ran, and placed a chair near the fire for the stranger, but she refused, and sat on the ground near where Mrs Costigan had been spinning. Mrs Costigan had now time to survey the old hag's person minutely. She appeared of great age; her countenance was extremely ugly and repulsive; her skin was rough and deeply embrowned as if from long exposure to the effects of some tropical climate; her forehead was low, narrow, and indented with a thousand wrinkles; her long grey hair fell in matted elf-locks from beneath a white linen skull cap; her eyes were bleared, blood-sotten, and obliquely set in their sockets, and her voice was croaking, tremulous, and, at times, partially inarticulate. As she squatted on the floor, she looked round the house with an inquisitive gaze; she peered pryingly from corner to corner, with an earnestness of look, as if she had the faculty, like the Argonaut of old, to see through the very depths of the earth, while Mrs C. kept watching her motions with mingled feelings of curiosity, awe, and pleasure.

'Mrs,' said the old woman, at length breaking silence, 'I am dry with the heat of the day; can you give me a drink?'

'Alas!' replied the farmer's wife, 'I have no drink to offer you except water, else you would have no occasion to ask me for it.'

'Are you not the owner of the cattle I see yonder?' said the old hag, with a tone of voice and manner of gesticulation which plainly indicated her foreknowledge of the fact.

Mrs Costigan replied in the affirmative, and briefly related to her every circumstance connected with the affair, while the old woman still remained silent, but shook her grey head repeatedly and still continued gazing round the house with an air of importance and self-sufficiency.

When Mrs C. had ended, the old hag remained a while as if in a deep reverie; at length she said: 'Have you any of the milk in the house?'

'I have,' replied the other.

'Show me some of it.'

She filled a jug from a vessel and handed it to the old sybil, who smelled it, then tasted it, and spat out what she had taken on the floor.

'Where is your husband?' she asked.

'Out in the fields,' was the reply.

'I must see him.'

A messenger was despatched for Bryan, who shortly after made his appearance.

'Neighbour,' said the stranger, 'your wife informs me that your cattle are going against you this season.'

'She informs you right,' said Bryan.

'And why have you not sought a cure?'

'A cure!' re-echoed the man; 'why, woman, I have sought cures until I was heartbroken, and all in vain; they get worse every day.'

'What will you give me if I cure them for you?'

'Anything in our power,' replied Bryan and his wife, both speaking joyfully, and with a breath.

'All I will ask from you is a silver sixpence, and that you will do everything which I will bid you,' said she.

The farmer and his wife seemed astonished at the moderation of her demand. They offered her a large sum of money.

'No,' said she, 'I don't want your money; I am no cheat, and I would not even take sixpence, but that I can do nothing till I handle some of your silver.'

The sixpence was immediately given her, and the most implicit obedience promised to her injunctions by both Bryan and his wife, who already began to regard the old beldame as their tutelary angel.

The hag pulled off a black silk ribbon or filet which encircled her head inside her cap, and gave it to Bryan, saying: 'Go, now, and the first cow you touch with this ribbon, turn her into the yard, but be sure you don't touch the second, nor speak a word until you return; be also careful not to let the ribbon touch the ground, for, if you do, all is over.'

Bryan took the talismanic ribbon and soon returned, driving a red cow before him.

The old hag went out, and, approaching the cow, commenced pulling hairs out of her tail, at the same time singing some verse in the Irish language, in a low, wild, and unconnected strain. The cow appeared restive and uneasy, but the old witch still continued her mysterious chant until she had the ninth hair extracted. She then ordered the cow to be drove back to her pasture, and again entered the house.

'Go, now,' said she to the woman, 'and bring me some milk from every cow in your possession.'

She went, and soon returned with a large pail filled with a frightful-looking mixture of milk, blood, and corrupt matter. The old woman got it into the churn, and made preparations for churning.

'Now,' she said, 'you both must churn, make fast the door and windows, and let there be no light but from the fire; do not open your lips until I desire you, and by observing my direction, I make no doubt but, ere the sun goes down, we will find out the infernal villain who is robbing you.'

Bryan secured the doors and windows, and commenced churning. The old sorceress sat down by a blazing fire which had been specially lighted for the occasion, and commenced singing the same wild song which she had sung at the pulling of the cow hairs, and after a little time she cast one of the nine hairs into the fire, still singing her mysterious strain, and watching, with intense interest, the witching process.

A loud cry, as if from a female in distress, was now heard

approaching the house; the old witch discontinued her incantations, and listened attentively. The crying voice approached the door.

'Open the door quickly,' shouted the charmer.

Bryan unbarred the door, and all three rushed out the yard, when they heard the same cry down the *boreheen*, but could see nothing.

'It is all over,' shouted the old witch; 'something has gone amiss, and our charm for the present is ineffectual.'

They now turned back quite crestfallen, when, as they were entering the door, the sybil cast her eyes downward, and perceiving a piece of horseshoe nailed on the threshold, she vociferated: 'Here I have it; no wonder our charm was abortive. The person that was crying abroad is the villain who has your cattle bewitched; I brought her to the house, but she was not able to come to the door on account of that horseshoe. Remove it instantly, and we will try our luck again.'

Bryan removed the horseshoe from the doorway, and by the hag's directions placed it on the floor under the churn, having previously reddened it in the fire.

They again resumed their manual operations. Bryan and his wife began to churn, and the witch again to sing her strange verses, and casting her cow hairs into the fire until she had them all nearly exhausted. Her countenance now began to exhibit evident traces of vexation and disappointment. She got quite pale, her teeth gnashed, her hand trembled, and as she cast the ninth and last hair into the fire, her person exhibited more the appearance of a female demon than of a human being.

Once more the cry was heard, and an aged red-haired woman was seen approaching the house quickly.

'Ho, ho!' roared the sorceress, 'I knew it would be so; my charm has succeeded; my expectations are realised, and here she comes, the villain who has destroyed you.'

'What are we to do now?' asked Bryan.

'Say nothing to her,' said the hag; 'give her whatever she demands, and leave the rest to me.'

The woman advanced screeching vehemently, and Bryan went out to meet her. She was a neighbour, and she said that one of her best cows was drowning in a pool of water – that there was no one at home but herself, and she implored Bryan to go rescue the cow from destruction.

Bryan accompanied her without hesitation; and having rescued the cow from her perilous situation, was back again in a quarter of an hour.

It was now sunset, and Mrs Costigan set about preparing supper.

During supper they reverted to the singular transactions of the day. The old witch uttered many a fiendish laugh at the success of her incantations, and enquired who was the woman whom they had so curiously discovered.

Bryan satisfied her in every particular. She was the wife of a neighbouring farmer; her name was Rachel Higgins; and she had been long suspected to be on familiar terms with the spirit of darkness. She had five or six cows; but it was observed by her sapient neighbours that she sold more butter every year than other farmers' wives who had twenty. Bryan had, from the commencement of the decline in his cattle, suspected her for being the aggressor, but as he had no proof, he held his peace.

'Well,' said the old beldame, with a grim smile, 'it is not enough that we have merely discovered the robber; all is in vain if we do not take steps to punish her for the past, as well as to prevent her inroads for the future.'

'And how will that be done?' said Bryan.

'I will tell you; as soon as the hour of twelve o'clock arrives tonight, do you go to the pasture, and take a couple of swift-running dogs with you; conceal yourself in some place convenient to the cattle; watch them carefully; and if you see anything, whether man or beast, approach the cows, set on the dogs, and if possible make them draw the blood of the intruder; then *all* will be accomplished. If nothing approaches before sunrise, you may return, and we will try something else.'

Convenient there lived the cowherd of a neighbouring squire. He was a hardy, courageous young man, and always kept a pair of very ferocious bulldogs. To him Bryan applied for assistance, and he cheerfully agreed to accompany him, and, moreover, proposed to fetch a couple of his master's best greyhounds, as his own dogs, although extremely fierce and bloodthirsty, could not be relied on for swiftness. He promised Bryan to be with him before twelve o'clock, and they parted.

Bryan did not seek sleep that night; he sat up anxiously awaiting the midnight hour. It arrived at last, and his friend, the herdsman, true to his promise, came at the time appointed. After some further admonitions from the *Collough*, they departed. Having arrived at the field, they consulted as to the best position they could choose for concealment. At last they pitched on a small brake of fern, situated at the extremity of the field, adjacent to the boundary ditch, which was thickly studded with large, old white-thorn bushes. Here they crouched themselves, and made the dogs, four in number, lie down beside them, eagerly expecting the appearance of their as yet unknown and mysterious visitor.

Here Bryan and his comrade continued a considerable time in nervous anxiety, still nothing approached, and it became manifest that morning was at hand; they were beginning to grow impatient, and were talking of returning home, when on a sudden they heard a rushing sound behind them, as if proceeding from something endeavouring to force a passage through the thick hedge in their rear. They looked in that direction, and judge of their astonishment, when they perceived a large hare in the act of springing from the ditch, and leaping on the ground quite near them. They were now convinced that this was the object which they had so impatiently expected, and they were resolved to watch her motions narrowly.

After arriving to the ground, she remained motionless for a few moments, looking around her sharply. She then began to skip and jump in a playful manner, now advancing at a smart pace toward the cows and again retreating precipitately, but still drawing nearer and nearer at each sally. At length she advanced up to the next cow, and sucked her for a moment; then on to the next, and so respectively to every cow on the field – the cows all the time lowing loudly, and appearing extremely frightened and agitated. Bryan, from the moment the hare commenced sucking the first, was with difficulty restrained from attacking her; but his more sagacious companion suggested to him that it was better to wait until she would have done, as she would then be much heavier, and more unable to effect her escape than at present. And so the issue proved; for being now done sucking them all, her belly appeared enormously distended, and she made her exit slowly and apparently with difficulty. She advanced toward the hedge where she had entered, and as she arrived just at the clump of ferns where her foes were couched, they started up with a fierce yell, and hallooed the dogs upon her path.

The hare started off at a brisk pace, squirting up the milk she had sucked from her mouth and nostrils, and the dogs making after her rapidly. Rachel Higgins's cabin appeared, through the grey of the morning twilight, at a little distance; and it was evident that puss seemed bent on gaining it, although she made a considerable circuit through the fields in the rear. Bryan and his comrade, however, had their thoughts, and made toward the cabin by the shortest route, and had just arrived as the hare came up panting and almost exhausted, and the dogs at her very scut. She ran round the house, evidently confused and disappointed at the presence of the men, but at length made for the door. In the bottom of the door was a small, semicircular aperture, resembling those cut in fowl-house doors for the ingress and egress of poultry. To gain this hole, puss now made a last and desperate effort, and had succeeded in forcing her head and shoulders through it, when the foremost of the dogs made a spring and seized her violently by the haunch. She uttered a loud and piercing scream, and struggled desperately to free herself from his grip, and at last succeeded, but not until she left a piece of her rump in his teeth. The men now burst open the door; a bright turf fire blazed on the hearth, and the whole floor was streaming with blood. No hare, however, could be found, and the men were more than ever convinced that it was old Rachel, who had, by the assistance of some demon, assumed the form of the hare, and they now determined to have her if she were over the earth. They entered the bedroom, and heard some smothered groaning, as if proceeding from someone in extreme agony. They went to the corner of the room from whence the moans proceeded, and there, beneath a bundle of freshly-cut rushes, found the form of Rachel Higgins, writhing in the most excruciating agony, and almost smothered in a pool of blood. The men were astounded; they addressed the wretched old woman, but she either could not, or would not, answer them. Her wound still bled copiously; her tortures appeared to increase, and it was evident that she was dying. The aroused family thronged around her with cries and lamentations; she did not seem to heed them, she got worse and worse, and her piercing yells fell awfully on the ears of the bystanders. At length she expired, and her corpse exhibited a most appalling spectacle, even before the spirit had well departed.

Bryan and his friend returned home. The old hag had been previously aware of the fate of Rachel Higgins, but it was not known by what means she acquired her supernatural knowledge. She was delighted at the issue of her mysterious operations. Bryan pressed her much to accept of some remuneration for her services, but she utterly rejected such proposals. She remained a few days at his house, and at length took her leave and departed, no one knew whither.

Old Rachel's remains were interred that night in the neighbouring churchyard. Her fate soon became generally known, and her family, ashamed to remain in their native village, disposed of their property, and quitted the country forever. The story, however, is still fresh in the memory of the surrounding villagers; and often, it is said, amid the grey haze of a summer twilight, may the ghost of Rachel Higgins, in the form of a hare, be seen scudding over her favourite and well-remembered haunts.

The Brown Man

GERALD GRIFFIN

In a lonely cabin, in a lonely glen, on the shores of a lonely lough in one of the most lonesome districts of west Munster, lived a lone woman named Guare. She had a beautiful girl, a daughter named Nora. Their cabin was the only one within three miles round them every way. As to their mode of living, it was simple enough, for all they had was one little garden of white cabbage, and they had eaten that down to a few heads between them, a sorry prospect in a place where even a handful of *prishoc* weed was not to be had without sowing it.

It was a very fine morning in those parts, for it was only snowing and hailing, when Nora and her mother were sitting at the door of their little cottage, and laying out plans for the next day's dinner. On a sudden, a strange horseman rode up to the door. He was strange in more ways than one. He was dressed in brown, his hair was brown, his eyes were brown, his boots were brown, he rode a brown horse, and he was followed by a brown dog.

'I'm come to marry you, Nora Guare,' said the Brown Man.

'Ax my mother fusht, if you plaise, sir,' said Nora, dropping him a curtsy.

'You'll not refuse, ma'am,' said the Brown Man to the old mother, 'I have money enough, and I'll make you daughter a lady, with servants at her call, and all manner of fine doings about her.' And so saying, he flung a purse of gold into the widow's lap.

'Why then the heavens speed you and her together, take her away with you, and make much of her,' said the old mother, quite bewildered with all the money.

'Agh, agh,' said the Brown Man, as he placed her on his horse behind him without more ado. 'Are you all ready now?'

'I am!' said the bride. The horse snorted, and the dog barked, and almost before the word was out of her mouth, they were all whisked away out of sight. After travelling a day and a night, faster than the wind itself, the Brown Man pulled up his horse in the middle of the Mangerton mountain, in one of the most lonesome places that eye ever looked on.

'Here is my estate,' said the Brown Man.

'A'then, is it this wild bog you call an estate?' said the bride.

'Come in, wife; this is my palace,' said the bridegroom.

'What! a clay-hovel, worse than my mother's!'

They dismounted, and the horse and the dog disappeared in an instant, with a horrible noise, which the girl did not know whether to call snorting, barking, or laughing.

'Are you hungry?' said the Brown Man. 'If so, there is your dinner.'

'A handful of raw white-eyes [potatoes] and a grain of salt!'

'And when you are sleepy, here is you bed,' he continued, pointing to a little straw in a corner, at sight of which Nora's limbs shivered and trembled again. It may be easily supposed that she did not make a very hearty dinner that evening, nor did here husband either.

In the dead of the night, when the clock of Muckross Abbey had just tolled one, a low neighing at the door and a soft barking at the window were heard. Nora feigned sleep. The Brown Man passed his hand over her eyes and face. She snored. 'I'm coming,' said he, and he arose gently from her side. In half an hour after she felt him by her side again. He was cold as ice.

The next night the same summons came. The Brown Man rose. The wife feigned sleep. He returned, cold. The morning came.

The next night came. The bell tolled at Muckross, and was heard across the lakes. The Brown Man rose again, and passed a light before the eyes of the feigning sleeper. None slumber so sound as they who *will* not wake. Her heart trembled, but her frame was quiet and firm. A voice at the door summoned the husband.

'You are very long coming. The earth is tossed up, and I am hungry. Hurry! Hurry! Hurry! if you would not lose all.'

'I'm coming!' said the Brown Man. Nora rose and followed instantly. She beheld him at a distance winding through a lane of frost-nipped sallow trees. He often paused and looked back, and once or twice retraced his steps to within a few yards of the tree, behind which she had shrunk. The moonlight, cutting the shadow close and dark about her, afforded the best concealment. He again proceeded, and she followed. In a few minutes the reached they old Abbey of Muckross. With a sickening heart she saw him enter the churchyard. The wind rushed through the huge yew tree and startled her. She mustered courage enough, however, to reach the gate of the churchyard and look in. The Brown Man, the horse, and the dog, were there seated by an open grave, eating something and glancing their brown, fiery eyes about in every direction. The moonlight shone full on them and her. Looking down towards here shadow on the earth, she started with horror to observe it move, although she was herself perfectly still. It waved its black arms, and motioned her back. What the feasters said, she understood not, but she seemed still fixed in the spot. She looked once more on her shadow; it raised one hand, and pointed the way to the lane; then slowly rising from the ground, and confronting her, it walked rapidly off in that direction. She followed as quickly as might be.

She was scarcely in her straw, when the door creaked behind, and her husband entered. He lay down by her side and started.

'Uf! Uf!' said she, pretending to be just awakened, 'how cold you are, my love!'

'Cold, inagh? Indeed you're not very warm yourself, my dear, I'm thinking.'

'Little admiration I shouldn't be warm, and you laving me alone this way at night, till my blood is snow broth, no less.'

'Umph!' said the Brown Man, as he passed his arm round her waist. 'Ha! your heart is beating fast?'

'Little admiration it should. I am not well, indeed. Them praties and salt don't agree with me at all.'

'Umph!' said the Brown Man.

The next morning as they were sitting at the breakfast table together. Nora plucked up a heart and asked leave to go to see her mother. The Brown Man, who ate nothing, looked at her in a way that made her think he knew all. She felt her spirit die away within her.

'If you only want to see your mother,' said he, 'there is no occasion for your going home. I will bring her to you here. I didn't marry you to be keeping you gadding.'

The Brown Man then went out and whistled for his dog and his horse. They both came; and in a very few minutes they pulled up at the old widow's cabin-door.

The poor woman was very glad to see her son-in-law, though she did not know what could bring him so soon.

'Your daughter sends her love to you, mother,' says the Brown Man, the villain, 'and she'd be obliged to you for a *loand* of a *shoot* of your best clothes, as she's going to give a grand party, and the dressmaker has disappointed her.'

'To be sure and welcome,' said the mother; and making up a bundle of clothes, she put them into his hands.

'Whogh! whogh!' said the horse as they drove off, 'that was well done. Are we to have a mail of her?'

'Easy, ma-coppuleen, and you'll get your 'nough before night,' said the Brown Man, 'and you likewise, my little dog.'

'Boh!' cried the dog, 'I'm in no hurry – I hunted down a doe this morning that was fed with milk from the horns of the moon.'

Often in the course of that day did Nora Guare go to the door, and cast her eye over the weary flat before it, to discern, if possible, the distant figures of her bridegroom and mother. The dusk of the second evening found her alone in the desolate cot. She listened to every sound. At length the door opened, and an old woman, dressed in a new jock, and leaning on a staff, entered the hut. 'O mother, are you come?' said Nora, and was about to rush into her arms, when the old woman stopped her.

'Whisht! whisht! my child! – I only stepped in before the man to know how you like him? Speak softly, in dread he'd hear you – he's turning the horse loose, in the swamp, abroad, over.'

'O mother, mother! such a story!'

'Whisht! easy again – how does he use you?'

'Sarrow worse. That straw my bed, and them white-eyes – and bad ones they are – all my diet. And 'tisn't that same, only – '

'Whisht! easy, again! He'll hear you, maybe – Well?'

'I'd be easy enough only for his own doings. Listen, mother. The fusht night, I came about twelve o'clock – '

'Easy, speak easy, eroo!'

'He got up at the call of the horse and the dog, and out a good hour. He ate nothing next day. The second night, and the second day, it was the same story. The third – '

'Husht! husht! Well, the third night?'

'The third night I said I'd watch him. Mother, don't hold my hand so hard . . . He got up, and I got up after him . . . Oh, don't laugh, mother, for 'tis frightful . . . I followed him to Muckross churchyard . . . Mother, mother, you hurt my hand . . . I looked in at the gate – there was great moonlight three, and I could see everything as plain as day.'

'Well, darling – husht! softly! What did you see?'

'My husband by the grave, and the horse . . . Turn your head aside, mother, for your breath is very hot . . . and the dog and they eating. – Ah, you are not my mother!' shrieked the miserable girl, as the Brown Man flung off his disguise, and stood before her, grinning worse than a blacksmith's face through a horse-collar. He just looked at her one moment, and then darted his long fingers into her bosom, from which the red blood spouted in so many streams. She was very soon out of all pain, and a merry supper the horse, the dog, and the Brown Man had that night, by all accounts.

Teig O'Kane and the Corpse

DOUGLAS HYDE

There was once a grown-up lad in the County Leitrim, and he was strong and lively, and the son of a rich farmer. His father had plenty of money, and he did not spare it on the son. Accordingly, when the boy grew up he liked sport better than work, and, as his father had no other children, he loved this one so much that he allowed him to do in everything just as it pleased himself. He was very extravagant, and he used to scatter the gold money as another person would scatter the white. He was seldom to be found at home, but if there was a fair, or a race, or a gathering within ten miles of him, you were dead certain to find him there. And he seldom spent a night in his father's house, but he used to be always out rambling, and, like Shawn Bwee long ago, there was: 'grádh gach cailin i mbrollach a léine, the love of every girl in the breast of his shirt,' and it's many's the kiss he got and he gave, for he was very handsome, and there wasn't a girl in the country but would fall in love with him, only for him to fasten his two eyes on her, and it was for that someone made this *rann* [verse] on him:

> Look at the rogue, it's for kisses he's rambling,
> It isn't much wonder, for that was his way;
> He's like an old hedgehog, at night he'll be scrambling
> From this place to that, but he'll sleep in the day.

At last he became very wild and unruly. He wasn't to be seen day or night in his father's house, but always rambling or going on his *kailee* (evening visit) from place to place and from house to house, so that the old people used to shake their heads and say to one another, 'It's easy seen what will happen to the land when the old man dies; his son will run through it in a year, and it won't stand him that long itself.'

He used to be always gambling and card-playing and drinking, but his father never minded his bad habits, and never punished him. But it happened one day that the old man was told that the son had ruined the character of a girl in the neighbourhood, and he was greatly angry, and he called the son to him, and said to him, quietly and sensibly – 'Avic,' says he, 'you know I loved you greatly up to this, and I never stopped you from doing your choice thing whatever it was, and I kept plenty of money with you, and I always hoped to leave you the house and land, and all I had after myself would be gone; but I heard a story of you today that has disgusted me with you. I cannot tell you the grief that I felt when I heard such a thing of you, and I tell you now plainly that unless you marry that girl I'll leave house and land and everything to my brother's son. I never could leave it to anyone who would make so bad a use of it as you do yourself, deceiving women and coaxing girls. Settle with yourself now whether you'll marry that girl and get my land as a fortune with her, or refuse to marry her and give up all that was coming to you; and tell me in the morning which of the two things you have chosen.'

'Och! *Domnoo Sheery*! father, you wouldn't say that to me, and I such a good son as I am. Who told you I wouldn't marry the girl?' says he.

But his father was gone, and the lad knew well enough that he would keep his word too; and he was greatly troubled in his mind, for as quiet and as kind as the father was, he never went back on a word that he had once said, and there wasn't another man in the country who was harder to bend than he was.

The boy did not know rightly what to do. He was in love with the girl indeed, and he hoped to marry her sometime or other, but he would much sooner have remained another while as he was, and follow on at his old tricks – drinking, sporting, and playing cards; and, along with that, he was angry that his father should order him to marry, and should threaten him if he did not do it.

'Isn't my father a great fool,' says he to himself. 'I was ready enough, and only too anxious, to marry Mary; and now since he threatened me, faith I've a great mind to let it go another while.'

His mind was so much excited that he remained between two notions as to what he should do. He walked out into the night at last to cool his heated blood, and went on to the road. He lit a pipe, and as the night was fine he walked and walked on, until the quick pace made him begin to forget his trouble. The night was bright, and the moon half full. There was not a breath of wind blowing, and the air was calm and mild. He walked on for nearly three hours, when he suddenly remembered that it was late in the night, and time for him to turn. 'Musha! I think I forgot myself,' says he; 'it must be near twelve o'clock now.'

The word was hardly out of his mouth, when he heard the sound of many voices, and the trampling of feet on the road before him. 'I don't know who can be out so late at night as this, and on such a lonely road,' said he to himself.

He stood listening, and he heard the voices of many people talking, but he could not understand what they were saying. 'Oh, *wirra!*' says he, 'I'm afraid. It's not Irish or English they have; it can't be they're Frenchmen!' He went on a couple of yards further, and he saw well enough by the light of the moon a band of little people coming towards him, and they were carrying something big and heavy with them. 'Oh, murder!' says he to himself, 'sure it can't be that they're the good people that's in it!' Every *rib* [strand] of hair that was on his head stood up, and there fell a shaking on his bones, for he saw that they were coming to him fast.

He looked at them again, and perceived that there were about twenty little men in it, and there was not a man at all of them higher than about three feet or three feet and a half, and some of them were grey, and seemed very old. He looked again, but he could not make out what was the heavy thing they were carrying until they came up to him, and then they all stood round about him. They threw the heavy thing down on the road, and he saw on the spot that it was a dead body.

He became as cold as the Death, and there was not a drop of blood running in his veins when an old little grey *maneen* came up to him and said, 'Isn't it lucky we met you, Teig O'Kane?'

Poor Teig could not bring out a word at all, nor open his lips, if he were to get the world for it, and so he gave no answer.

'Teig O'Kane,' said the little grey man again, 'isn't it timely you met us?'

Teig could not answer him.

'Teig O'Kane,' says he, 'the third time, isn't it lucky and timely that we met you?'

But Teig remained silent, for he was afraid to return an answer, and his tongue was as if it was tied to the roof of his mouth.

The little grey man turned to his companions, and there was joy in his bright little eye. 'And now,' says he, 'Teig O'Kane hasn't a word, we can do with him what we please. Teig, Teig,' says he, 'you're living a bad life, and we can make a slave of you now, and you cannot withstand us, for there's no use in trying to go against us. Lift that corpse.'

Teig was so frightened that he was only able to utter the two words, 'I wont't'; for as frightened as he was he was obstinate and stiff, the same as ever.

'Teig O'Kane won't lift the corpse,' said the little *maneen* with a wicked little laugh, for all the world like the breaking of a *lock* [bundle] of dry *kippeens* [twigs], and with a little harsh voice like the striking of a cracked bell. 'Teig O'Kane won't lift the corpse – make him lift it'; and before the word was out of his mouth they had all gathered round poor Teig, and they all talking and laughing through each other.

Teig tried to run from them, but they followed him, and a man of them stretched out his foot before him as he ran, so that Teig was thrown in a heap on the road. Then before he could rise up the fairies caught him, some by the hands and some by the feet, and they held him tight, in a way that he could not stir, with his face against the ground. Six or seven of them raised the body then, and pulled it over to him, and left it down on his back. The breast of the corpse was squeezed against Teig's back and shoulders, and the arms of the corpse were thrown around Teig's neck. Then they stood back from him a couple of yards, and let him get up. He rose, foaming at the mouth and cursing, and he shook himself, thinking to throw the corpse off his back. But his fear and his wonder were great when he found that the two arms had a tight hold round his own neck, and that the two legs were squeezing his hips firmly, and that, however strongly he tried, he could not throw it off, any more than a horse can throw off its saddle. He was terribly frightened then, and he thought he was lost. 'Ochone! for ever,' said he to himself, 'it's the bad life I'm leading that has given the good people this power over me. I promise to God and Mary, Peter and Paul, Patrick and Bridget, that I'll mend my ways for as long as I have to live, if I come clear out of this danger – and I'll marry the girl.'

The little grey man came up to him again, and said he to him, 'Now, Teig*een*,' says he, 'you didn't lift the body when I told you to lift it, and see how you were made to lift it; perhaps when I tell you to bury it, you won't bury it until you're made to bury it!'

'Anything at all that I can do for your honour,' said Teig, 'I'll do it,' for he was getting sense already, and if it had not been for the great fear that was on him, he never would have let that civil word slip out of his mouth.

The little man laughed a sort of laugh again. 'You're getting quiet now, Teig,' says he. 'I'll go bail but you'll be quiet enough before I'm done with you. Listen to me now, Teig O'Kane, and if you don't obey me in all I'm telling you to do, you'll repent it. You must carry with you this corpse that is on your back to Teampoll-Démus, and you must bring it into the church with you, and make a grave for it in the very middle of the church, and you must raise up the flags and put them down again the very same way, and you must carry the clay out of the church and leave the place as it was when you came, so that no one could know that there had been anything changed. But that's not all. Maybe that the body won't be allowed to be buried in that church; perhaps some other man has the bed, and, if so, it's likely he won't share it with this one. If you don't get leave to bury it in Teampoll-Démus, you must carry it to Carrick-fhad-vic-Orus, and bury it in the churchyard there; and if you don't get it into that place, take it with you to Teampoll Ronan; and if that churchyard is closed on you, take it to Imlogue-Fada; and if you're not able to bury it there, you've no more to do than to take it to Kill-Breedya, and you can bury it there without hindrance. I cannot tell you what one on those churches is the one where you will have leave to bury that corpse under the clay, but I know that it will be allowed you to bury him at some church or other of them. If you do this work rightly, we will be thankful to you, and you will have no cause to grieve; but if you are slow or lazy, believe me we shall take satisfaction of you.'

When the grey little man had done speaking, his comrades laughed and clapped their hands together. 'Glic! Glic! Hwee! Hwee!' they all cried; 'go on, go on, you have eight hours before you till daybreak, and if you haven't this man buried before the sun rises, you're lost.' They struck a fist and a foot behind on him, and drove him on in the road. He was obliged to walk, and to walk fast, for they gave him no rest.

He thought himself that there was not a wet path, or a dirty *boreen* [lane], or a crooked contrary road in the whole county, that he had not walked that night. The night was at times very dark, and whenever there would come a cloud across the moon he could see nothing, and then he used often to fall. Sometimes he was hurt, and sometimes he escaped, but he was obliged always to rise on the moment and to hurry on. Sometimes the moon would break out clearly, and then he would look behind him and see the little people following at his back. And he heard them speaking among themselves, talking and crying out, and screaming like a flock of seagulls; and if he was to save his soul he never understood as much as one word of what they were saying.

He did not know how far he had walked, when at last one of them cried out to him, 'Stop here!' He stood, and they all gathered round him.

'Do you see those withered trees over there?' says the old boy to him again. 'Teampoll-Démus is among those trees, and you must go in there by yourself, for we cannot follow you or go with you. We must remain here. Go on boldly.'

Teig looked from him, and he saw a high wall that was in places half broken down, and an old grey church on the inside of the wall, and about a dozen withered old trees scattered here and there round it. There was neither leaf nor twig on any of them, but their bare crooked branches were stretched out like the arms of an angry man when he threatens. He had no help for it, but was obliged to go forward. He was a couple of hundred yards from the church, but he walked on, and never looked behind him until he came to the gate of the churchyard. The old gate was thrown down, and he had no difficulty in entering. He turned then to see if any of the little people were following him, but there came a cloud over the moon, and the night became so dark that he could see nothing. He went into the churchyard, and he walked up the old grassy pathway leading to the church. When he reached the door, he found it locked. The door was large and strong, and he did not know what to do. At last he drew out his knife with difficulty, and stuck it in the wood to try if it were not rotten, but it was not.

'Now,' said he to himself, 'I have no more to do; the door is shut, and I can't open it.'

Before the words were rightly shaped in his own mind, a voice in his ear said to him, 'Search for the key on the top of the door, or on the wall.'

He started. 'Who is that speaking to me?' he cried, turning round; but he saw no one. The voice said in his ear again, 'Search for the key on the top of the door, or on the wall.'

'What's that?' said he, and the sweat running from his forehead; 'who spoke to me?'

'It's I, the corpse, that spoke to you!' said the voice.

'Can you talk?' said Teig.

'Now and again,' said the corpse.

Teig searched for the key, and he found it on the top of the wall. He was too much frightened to say any more, but he opened the door wide, and as quickly as he could, and he went in, with the corpse on his back. It was as dark as pitch inside, and poor Teig began to shake and tremble.

'Light the candle,' said the corpse.

Teig put his hand in his pocket, as well as he was able, and drew out a flint and steel. He struck a spark out of it, and lit a burnt rag he had in his pocket. He blew it until it made a flame, and he looked round him. The church was very ancient, and part of the wall was broken down. The windows were blown in or cracked, and the timbers of the seats were rotten. There were six or seven old iron candlesticks left there still, and in one of these candlesticks Teig found the stump of an old candle, and he lit it. He was still looking round him in the strange and horrid place in which he found himself, when the cold corpse whispered in his ear, 'Bury me now, bury me now; there is a spade and turn the ground.' Teig looked from him, and he saw a spade lying beside the altar. He took it up, and he placed the blade under a flag that was in the middle of the aisle, and leaning all his weight on the handle of the spade, he raised it. When the first flag was raised it was not hard to raise the others near it, and he moved three or four of them out of their places. The clay that was under them was soft and easy to dig, but he had not thrown up more than three or four shovelfuls when he felt the iron touch something soft like flesh. He threw up three or four more shovelfuls from around it, and then he saw that it was another body that was buried in the same place.

'I am afraid I'll never be allowed to bury the two bodies in the same hole,' said Teig, in his own mind. 'You corpse, there on my back,' says he, 'will you be satisfied if I bury you down here?' But the corpse never answered him a word.

'That's a good sign,' said Teig to himself. 'Maybe he's getting quiet,' and he thrust the spade down in the earth again. Perhaps he hurt the flesh of the other body, for the dead man that was buried there stood up in the grave, and shouted an awful shout. 'Hoo! Hoo!! Hoo!!! Go! go!! go!!! or you're a dead, dead, dead man!' And then he fell back in the grave again. Teig said afterwards, that of all the wonderful things he saw that night, that was the most awful to him. His hair stood upright on his head like the bristles of a pig, the cold sweat ran off his face, and then came a tremor over all his bones, until he thought that he must fall.

But after a while he became bolder, when he saw that the second corpse remained lying quietly there, and he threw in the clay on it again, and he smoothed it overhead, and he laid down the flags carefully as they had been before. 'It can't be that he'll rise up any more,' said he.

He went down the aisle a little further, and drew near to the door, and began raising the flags again, looking for another bed for the corpse on his back. He took up three or four flags and put them aside, and then he dug the clay. He was not long digging until he laid bare an old woman without a thread upon her but her shirt. She was more lively than the first corpse, for he had scarcely taken any of the clay away from about her, when she sat up and began to cry, 'Ho, you *bodach* (clown)! Ha, you *bodach*! Where has he been that he got no bed?'

Poor Teig drew back, and when she found that she was getting no answer, she closed her eyes gently, lost her vigour, and fell back quietly and slowly under the clay. Teig did to her as he had done to the man – he threw the clay back on her, and left the flags down overhead.

He began digging again near the door, but before he had thrown up more than a couple of shovelfuls, he noticed a man's hand laid bare by the spade. 'By my soul, I'll go no further, then,' said he to himself; 'what use is it for me?' And he threw the clay in again on it, and settled the flags as they had been before.

He left the church then, and his heart was heavy enough, but he shut the door and locked it, and left the key where he found it. He sat down on a tombstone that was near the door, and began thinking. He was in great doubt what he should do. He laid his face between his two hands, and cried for grief and fatigue, since he was dead certain at this time that he never would come home alive. He made another attempt to loosen the hands of the corpse that were squeezed round his neck, but they were as tight as if they were clamped; and the more he tried to loosen them, the tighter they squeezed him. He was going to sit down once more, when the cold, horrid lips of the dead man said to him, 'Carrick-fhad-vic-Orus,' and he remembered the command of the good people to bring the corpse with him to that place if he should be unable to bury it where he had been.

He rose up, and looked about him. 'I don't know the way,' he said.

As soon as he had uttered the word, the corpse stretched out suddenly its left hand that had been tightened round his neck, and kept it pointing out, showing him the road he ought to follow. Teig went in the direction that the fingers were stretched, and passed out of the churchyard. He found himself on an old rutty, stony road, and he stood still again, not knowing where to turn. The corpse stretched out its bony hand a second time, and pointed out to him another road – not the road by which he had come when approaching the old church. Teig followed that road, and whenever he came to a path or road meeting it, the corpse always stretched out its hand and pointed with its fingers, showing him the way he was to take.

Many was the crossroad he turned down, and many was the crooked *boreen* he walked, until he saw from him an old burying-ground at last, beside the road, but there was neither church nor chapel nor any other building in it. The corpse sequeezed him tightly, and he stood. 'Bury me, bury me in the burying-ground,' said the voice.

Teig drew over towards the old burying-place, and he was not more than about twenty yards from it, when, raising his eyes, he saw hundreds and hundreds of ghosts – men, women, and children – sitting on the top of the wall round about, or standing on the inside of it, or running backwards and forwards, and pointing at him, while he could see their mouths opening and shutting as if they were speaking, though he heard no word, nor any sound among them at all.

He was afraid to go forward, so he stood where he was, and the moment he stood, all the ghosts became quiet, and ceased moving. Then Teig understood that it was trying to keep him from going in, that they were. He walked a couple of yards forwards, and immediately the whole crowd rushed together towards the spot to which he was moving, and they stood so thickly together that it seemed to him that he never could break through them, even though he had a mind to try. But he had no mind to try it. He went back broken and dispirited, and when he had gone a couple of hundred yards from the burying-ground, he stood again, for he did not know what way he was to go. He heard the voice of the corpse in his ear, saying 'Teampoll-Ronan,' and the skinny hand was stretched out again, pointing him out the road.

As tired as he was, he had to walk, and the road was neither short nor even. The night was darker than ever, and it was difficult to make his way. Many was the toss he got, and many a bruise they left on his body. At last he saw Teampoll-Ronan from him in the distance, standing in the middle of the burying-ground. He moved over towards it, and thought he was all right and safe, when he saw no ghosts nor anything else on the wall, and he thought he would never be hindered now from leaving his load off him at last. He moved over to the gate, but as he was passing in, he tripped on the threshold. Before he could recover himself, something that he could not see seized him by the neck, by the hands, and by the feet, and bruised him, and shook him, and chocked him, until he was nearly dead; and at last he was lifted up, and carried more than a hundred yards from that place, and then thrown down in an old dyke, with the corpse still clinging to him.

He rose up, bruised and sore, but feared to go near the place again, for he had seen nothing the time he was thrown down and carried away.

'You corpse, up on my back?' said he, 'shall I go over again to the churchyard?' – but the corpse never answered him.

'That's a sign you don't wish me to try it again,' said Teig.

He was now in great doubt as to what he ought to do, when the corpse spoke in his ear, and said, 'Imlogue-Fada.'

'Oh, murder!' said Teig, 'must I bring you there? If you keep me long walking like this, I tell you I'll fall under you.'

He went on, however, in the direction the corpse pointed out to him. He could not have told, himself, how long he had been going, when the dead man behind suddenly squeezed him, and said, 'There!'

Teig looked from him, and he saw a little low wall, that was so broken down in places that it was no wall at all. It was in a great wide field, in from the road; and only for three or four great stones at the corners, that were more like rocks than stones, there was nothing to show that there was either graveyard or burying-ground there.

'Is this Imlogue-Fada? Shall I bury you here?' said Teig.

'Yes,' said the voice.

'But I see no grave or gravestone, only this pile of stones,' said Teig.

The corpse did not answer, but stretched out its long fleshless hand to show Teig the direction in which he was to go. Teig went on accordingly, but he was greatly terrified, for he remembered what had happened to him at the last place. He went on, 'with his heart in his mouth,' as he said himself afterwards; but when he came to within fifteen or twenty yards of the little low square wall, there broke out a flash of lightning, bright yellow and red, with blue streaks in it, and went round about the wall in one course, and it swept by as fast as the swallow in the clouds, and the longer Teig remained looking at it the faster it went, till at last it became like a bright ring of flame round the old graveyard, which no one could pass without being burnt by it. Teig never saw, from the time he was born, and never saw afterwards, so wonderful or so splendid a sight as that was. Round went the flame, white and yellow and blue sparks leaping out from it as it went, and although at first it had been no more than a thin, narrow line, it increased slowly until it was at last a great broad band, and it was continually getting broader and higher, and throwing out more brilliant sparks, till there was never a colour on the ridge of the earth that was not to be seen in that fire; and lightning never shone and flame never flamed that was so shining and so bright as that.

Teig was amazed; he was half dead with fatigue, and he had no courage left to approach the wall. There fell a mist over his eyes, and there came a *soorawn* [wave of vertigo] in his head, and he was obliged to sit down upon a great stone to recover himself. He could see nothing but the light, and he could hear nothing but the whirr of it as it shot round the paddock faster than a flash of lightning.

As he sat there on the stone, the voice whispered once more in his ear, 'Kill-Breedya'; and the dead man squeezed him so tightly that he cried out. He rose again, sick, tired, and trembling, and went forward as he was directed. The wind was cold, and the road was bad, and the load upon his back was heavy, and the night was dark, and he himself was nearly worn out, and if he had very much farther to go he must have fallen dead under his burden.

At last the corpse stretched out its hand, and said to him, 'Bury me there.'

'This is the last burying-place,' said Teig in his own mind; 'and the little grey man said I'd be allowed to bury him in some of them, so it must be this; it can't be but they'll let him in here.'

The first faint streak of the ring of day was appearing in the east, and the clouds were beginning to catch fire, but it was darker than ever, for the moon was set, and there were no stars.

'Make haste, make baste!' said the corpse; and Teig hurried

forward as well as he could to the graveyard, which was a little place on a bare hill, with only a few graves in it. He walked boldly in through the open gate, and nothing touched him, nor did he either hear or see anything. He came to the middle of the ground, and then stood up and looked round him for a spade or shovel to make a grave. As he was turning round and searching, he suddenly perceived what startled him greatly – a newly-dug grave right before him. He moved over to it, and looked down, and there at the bottom he saw a black coffin. He clambered down into the hole and lifted the lid, and found that (as he thought it would be) the coffin was empty. He had hardly mounted up out of the hole, and was standing on the brink, when the corpse, which had clung to him for more than eight hours, suddenly relaxed its hold of his neck, and loosened its shins from round his hips, and sank down with a plop into the open coffin.

Teig fell down on his two knees at the brink of the grave, and gave thanks to God. He made no delay then, but pressed down the coffin lid in its place, and threw in the clay over it with his two hands, and when the grave was filled up, he stamped and leaped on it with his feet, until it was firm and hard, and then he left the place.

The sun was fast rising as he finished his work, and the first thing he did was to return to the road, and look out for a house to rest himself in. He found an inn at last; and lay down upon a bed there, and slept till night. Then he rose up and ate a little, and fell asleep again till morning. When he awoke in the morning he hired a horse and rode home. He was more than twenty-six miles from home where he was, and he had come all that way with the dead body on his back in one night.

All the people at his own home thought that he must have left the country, and they rejoiced greatly when they saw him come back. Everyone began asking him where he had been, but he would not tell anyone except his father.

He was a changed man from that day. He never drank too much; he never lost his money over cards; and especially he would not take the world and be out late by himself of a dark night.

He was not a fortnight at home until he married Mary, the girl he had been in love with, and it's at their wedding the sport was, and it's he was the happy man from that day forward, and it's all I wish that we may be as happy as he was.

The Field of Boliauns

JOSEPH JACOBS

One fine day in harvest – it was indeed Ladyday in harvest, that everybody knows to be one of the greatest holidays in the year – Tom Fitzpatrick was taking a ramble through the ground, and went along the sunny side of a hedge; when all of a sudden he heard a clacking sort of noise a little before him in the hedge. 'Dear me,' said Tom, 'but isn't it surprising to hear the stonechatters singing so late in the season?' So Tom stole on, going on the tops of his toes to try if he could get a sight of what was making the noise, to see if he was right in his guess. The noise stopped; but as Tom looked sharply through the bushes, what should he see in a nook of the hedge but a brown pitcher, that might hold about a gallon and a half of liquor; and by and by a little wee teeny tiny bit of an old man, with a little *motty* of a cocked hat stuck upon the top of his head, a deeshy daushy leather apron hanging before him, pulled out a little wooden stool, and stood up upon it, and dipped a little piggin into the pitcher, and took out the full of it, and put it beside the stool, and then sat down under the pitcher, and began to work at putting a heel-piece on a bit of a brogue just fit for himself. 'Well, by the powers,' said Tom to himself, 'I often heard tell of the Lepracauns, and, to tell God's truth, I never rightly believed in them – but here's one of them in real earnest. If I go knowingly to work, I'm a made man. They say a body must never take their eyes off them, or they'll escape.'

Tom now stole on a little further, with his eye fixed on the little man just as a cat does with a mouse. So when he got up quite close to him, 'God bless your work, neighbour,' said Tom.

The little man raised up his head, and 'Thank you kindly,' said he.

'I wonder you'd be working on the holiday!' said Tom.

'That's my own business, not yours,' was the reply.

'Well, maybe you'd be civil enough to tell us what you've got in the pitcher there?' said Tom.

'That I will with pleasure,' said he; 'it's good beer.'

'Beer!' said Tom. 'Thunder and fire! where did you get it?'

'Where did I get it, is it? Why, I made it. And what do you think I made it of?'

'Devil a one of me knows,' said Tom; 'but of malt, I suppose, what else?'

'There you're out. I made it of heath.'

'Of heath!' said Tom, bursting out laughing; 'sure you don't think me to be such a fool as to believe that?'

'Do as you please,' said he, 'but what I tell you is the truth. Did you never hear tell of the Danes?'

'Well, what about them?' said Tom.

'Why, when they were here they taught us to make beer out of the heath, and the secret's in my family ever since.'

'Will you give a body a taste of your beer?' said Tom.

'I'll tell you what it is, young man, it would be fitter for you to be looking after your father's property than to be bothering decent quiet people with your foolish questions. There now, while you're idling away your time here, there's the cows have broke into the oats, and are knocking the corn all about.'

Tom was taken so by surprise with this that he was just on the very point of turning round when he recollected himself; so, afraid that the like might happen again, he made a grab at the Lepracaun, and caught him up in his hand; but in his hurry he overset the pitcher, and spilled all the beer, so that he could not get a taste of it to tell what sort it was. He then swore that he would kill him if he did not show him where his money was. Tom looked so wicked and so bloody-minded that the little man was quite frightened; so says he, 'Come along with me a couple of fields off, and I'll show you a crock of gold.'

So they went, and Tom held the Lepracaun fast in his hand, and never took his eyes from off him, though they had to cross hedges and ditches, and a crooked bit of bog, till at last they came to a great field all full of boliauns, and the Lepracaun pointed to a big boliaun, and says he, 'Dig under that boliaun, and you'll get the great crock all full of guineas.'

Tom in his hurry had never thought of bringing a spade with him, so he made up his mind to run home and fetch one; and that he might know the place again he took off one of his red garters, and tied it round the boliaun.

Then he said to the Lepracaun, 'Swear ye'll not take that garter away from that boliaun.' And the Lepracaun swore right away not to touch it.

'I suppose,' said the Lepracaun, very civilly, 'you have no further occasion for me?'

'No,' says Tom; 'you may go away now, if you please, and God speed you, and may good luck attend you wherever you go.'

'Well, goodbye to you, Tom Fitzpatrick,' said the Lepracaun; 'and much good might it do you when you get it.'

So Tom ran for dear life, till he came home and got a spade, and then away with him, as hard as he could go, back to the field of boliauns; but when he got there, lo and behold! not a boliaun in the field but had a red garter, the very model of his own, tied about it; and as to digging up the whole field, that was all nonsense, for there were more than forty good Irish acres in it. So Tom came home again with his spade on his shoulder, a little cooler than he went, and many's the hearty curse he gave the Lepracaun every time he thought of the neat turn he had served him.

Darby O'Gill and the Leprechaun

HERMINIE KAVANAGH

The news that Darby O'Gill had spint six months with the Good People spread fast and far and wide.

At fair or hurlin' or market he would be backed be a crowd agin some convaynient wall and there for hours men, women, and childher, with jaws dhroppin' and eyes bulgin'd, stand ferninst him listening to half-frightened questions or to bould, mystarious answers.

Alway, though, one bit of wise adwise inded his discoorse: 'Nayther make nor moil nor meddle with the fairies,' Darby'd say. 'If you're going along the lonely boreen at night and you hear, from some fairy fort, a sound of fiddles, or of piping, or of sweet woices singing, or of little feet pattherin' in the dance, don't turn your head, but say your prayers an' hould on your way. The pleasures the Good People'll share with you have a sore sorrow hid in them, an' the gifts they'll offer are only made to break hearts with.'

Things went this a-way till one day in the market, over among the cows, Maurteen Cavanaugh, the schoolmasther – a cross-faced, argifying ould man he was – conthradicted Darby pint blank. 'Stay a bit,' says Maurteen, catching Darby by the coat-collar. 'You forget about the little fairy cobbler, the leprechaun,' he says. 'You can't deny that to catch the leprechaun is great luck entirely. If one only fix the glance of his eye on the cobbler, that look makes the fairy a presner – one can do anything with him as long as a human look covers the little lad and he'll give the favours of three wishes to buy his freedom,' says Maurteen.

At that Darby, smiling high and knowledgeable, made answer over the heads of the crowd.

'God help your sinse, honest man!' he says. 'Around the favours of thim same three wishes is a bog of thricks an' cajolories and conditions that'll defayt the wisest.

'First of all, if the look be taken from the little cobbler for as much as the wink of an eye, he's gone forever,' he says. 'Man alive, even when he does grant the favours of the three wishes, you're not safe, for, if you tell anyone you've seen the leprechaun, the favours melt like snow, or if you make a fourth wish that day – whiff! they turn to smoke. Take my advice – nayther make nor moil nor meddle with the fairies.'

'Thrue for ye,' spoke up long Pether McCarthy, siding in with Darby. 'Didn't Barney McBride, on his way to early mass one May morning, catch the fairy cobbler sewing an' workin' away under a hedge. "Have a pinch of snuff, Barney agra," says the leprechaun, handing up the little snuffbox. But, mind ye, when my poor Barney bint to take a thumb an' finger full, what did the little villain do but fling the box, snuff and all, into Barney's face. An' thin, while the poor lad was winkin' and blinkin', the leprechaun gave one leap and was lost in the reeds.

'Thin, again, there was Peggy O'Rourke, who captured him fair an' square in a hawthorn-bush. In spite of his wiles she wrung from him the favours of the three wishes. Knowing, of course, that if she towld of what had happened to her the spell was broken and the wishes wouldn't come thrue, she hurried home, aching and longing to in some way find from her husband Andy what wishes she'd make.

'Throwing open her own door, she said, "What would ye wish for most in the world, Andy dear? Tell me an' your wish'll come thrue," says she. A peddler was crying his wares out in the lane. "Lanterns, tin lanterns!" cried the peddler. "I wish I had one of thim lanterns," says Andy, careless, and bendin' over to get a coal for his pipe, when, lo and behold, there was the lantern in his hand.

'Well, so vexed was Peggy that one of her fine wishes should be wasted on a palthry tin lantern, that she lost all patience with him. "Why thin, bad scran to you!" says she – not mindin' her own words – "I wish the lantern was fastened to the ind of your nose!"

'The word wasn't well out of her mouth till the lantern *was* hung swinging from the ind of Andy's nose in a way that the wit of man couldn't loosen. It took the third and last of Peggy's wishes to relayse Andy.'

'Look at that, now!' cried a dozen voices from the admiring crowd. 'Darby said so from the first.'

Well, after a time people used to come from miles around to see Darby and sit under the sthraw-stack beside the stable to adwise with our hayro about their most important business – what was the best time for the settin' of hins, or what was good to cure colic in childher, an' things like that.

Any man so parsecuted with admiration an' hayrofication might aisily feel his chest swell out a bit, so it's no wondher that Darby set himself up for a knowledgeable man.

He took to talkin' slow an' shuttin' one eye whin he listened, and he walked with a knowledgeable twist to his chowlders. He grew monsthrously fond of fairs and public gatherings where people made much of him, and he lost every ounce of liking he ever had for hard worruk.

Things wint on with him in this way from bad to worse, and where it would have inded no man knows, if one unlucky morning he hadn't rayfused to bring in a creel of turf his wife Bridget had axed him to fetch her. The unfortunate man said it was no work for the likes of him.

The last word was still on Darby's lips whin he rayalised his mistake, an' he'd have given the world to have the sayin' back again.

For a minute you could have heard a pin dhrop. Bridget, instead of being in a hurry to begin at him, was crool dayliberate. She planted herself in the door, her two fists on her hips, an' her lips shut.

The look Julius Sayser'd trow at a servant-girl he'd caught stealing sugar from the rile cupboard was the glance she waved up and down from Darby's toes to his head, and from his head to his brogues agin.

Thin she began an' talked steady as a fall of hail that has now an' then a bit of lightning an' tunder mixed in it.

The knowledgeable man stood purtendin' to brush his hat and tryin' to look brave, but the heart inside of him was meltin' like butther.

Bridget began aisily be carelessly mentioning a few of Darby's best known wakenesses. Afther that she took up some of them not so well known, being ones Darby himself had sayrious doubts about having at all. But on these last she was more savare than on the first. Through it all he daren't say a word – he only smiled lofty and bitther.

'Twas but natural next for Bridget to explain what a poor crachure her husband was the day she got him, an what she might have been if she had married ayther one of the six others who had axed her. The step for her was a little one, thin, to the shortcomings and misfortunes of his blood relations, which she follyed back to the blaggardisms of his fourth cousin, Phelim McFadden.

Even in his misery poor Darby couldn't but marvel at her wondherful memory.

By the time she began talking of her own family, and especially about her Aunt Honoria O'Shaughnessy, who had once shook hands with a Bishop, and who in the rebellion of '98 had turn a brick at a Lord Liftenant, whin he was riding by, Darby was as wilted and as forlorn-looking as a roosther caught out in the winther rain.

He lost more pride in those few minutes than it had taken months to gather an' hoard. It kept falling in great drops from his forehead.

Just as Bridget was lading up to what Father Cassidy calls a pur-roar-ration – that being the part of your wife's discoorse whin, after telling you all she's done for you, and all she's stood from your relaytions, she breaks down and cries, and so smothers you entirely – just as she was coming to that, I say, Darby scrooged his caubeen down on his head, stuck his fingers in his two ears, and, making one grand rush through the door, bolted as fast as his legs could carry him down the road toward Sleive-na-mon Mountains.

Bridget stood on the step looking afther him, too surprised for a word. With his fingers still in his ears, so that he couldn't hear her commands to turn back, he ran without stopping till he came to the willow tree near Joey Hooligan's forge. There he slowed down to fill his lungs with the fresh, sweet air.

'Twas one of those warm-hearted, laughing autumn days which steals for a while the bonnet and shawl of the May. The sun, from a sky of feathery whiteness, laned over, telling jokes to the worruld, an' the goold harvest-fields and purple hills, lasy and continted, laughed back at the sun. Even the blackbird flying over the haw tree looked down an' sang to those below, 'God save all here'; an' the linnet from her bough answered back quick an' sweet, 'God save you kindly, sir!'

With such pleasant sight and sounds an' twitterings at every side, our hayro didn't feel the time passing till he was on top of the first hill of the Sleive-na-mon Mountains, which, as everyone knows, is called the Pig's Head.

It wasn't quite lonesome enough on the Pig's Head, so our hayro plunged into the walley an' climbed the second mountain – the Divil's Pillow where 'twas lonesome and desarted enough to shuit anyone.

Beneath the shade of a tree, for the days was warm, he set himself down in the long, sweet grass, lit his pipe, and let his mind go free. But, as he did, his thoughts rose together like a flock of frightened, angry pheasants, an' whirred back to the owdacious things Bridget had said about his relations.

Wasn't she the mendageous, humbrageous woman, he thought, to say such things about as illegant stock, as the O'Gills and the O'Gradys?

Why, Wullum O'Gill, Darby's uncle, at that minute, was head butler at Castle Brophy, and was known far an' wide as being one of the foinest scholars an' as having the most beautiful pair of legs in all Ireland!

This same Wullum O'Gill had tould Bridget in Darby's own hearing, on a day when the three were going through the great picture-gallery at Castle Brophy, that the O'Gills at one time had been Kings in Ireland.

Darby never since could raymember whether this time was before the flood or afther the flood. Bridget said it was durin' the flood, but surely that sayin' was nonsinse.

Howsumever, Darby knew his Uncle Wullum was right, for he often felt in himself the signs of greatness. And now as he sat alone on the grass, he said out loud: 'If I had me rights I'd be doing nothing all day long but sittin' on a throne, an' playin' games of forty-five with the Lord Liftenant an' some of me generals. There never was a lord that likes good ating or dhrinking betther nor I, or who hates worse to get up airly in the morning. That last disloike I'm tould is a great sign entirely of gentle blood the worruld over,' says he.

As for the wife's people, the O'Hagans an' the O'Shaughnessys, well – they were no great shakes, he said to himself, at laste so far as looks were concerned. All the handsomeness in Darby's childher came from his own side of the family. Even Father Cassidy said the childher took afther the O'Gills.

'If I were rich,' said Darby, to a lazy ould bumble-bee who was droning an' tumbling in front of him, 'I'd have a castle like Castle Brophy, with a great picture-gallery in it. On one wall I'd put the picture of the O'Gills and the O'Gradys, and on the wall ferninst them I'd have the O'Hagans an' the O'Shaughnessys.'

At that ideah his heart bubbled in a new and fierce deloight. 'Bridget's people,' he says agin, scowling at the bee, 'would look four times as common as they raylly are, whin they were compared in that way with my own relations. An' whenever Bridget got rampageous I'd take her in and show her the difference betwixt the two clans, just to punish her, so I would.'

How long the lad sat that way warming the cowld thoughts of his heart with drowsy, pleasant dhrames an' misty longings he don't rightly know, whin – tack, tack, tack, tack, came the busy sound of a little hammer from the other side of a fallen oak.

'Be jingo!' he says to himself with a start, ' 'tis the leprechaun that's in it.'

In a second he was on his hands an' knees, the tails of his coat flung across his back, an' he crawling softly toward the sound of the hammer. Quiet as a mouse he lifted himself up on the mossy log to look over, and there before his two popping eyes was a sight of wondheration.

Sitting on a white stone an' working away like fury, hammering pegs into a little red shoe, half the size of your thumb, was a bald-headed ould cobbler of about twice the hoight of your hand. On the top of a round, snub nose was perched a pair of horn-rimmed spectacles, an' a narrow fringe of iron-grey whuskers grew undher his stubby chin. The brown leather apron he wore was so long that it covered his green knee-breeches an' almost hid the knitted grey stockings.

The leprechaun – for it was he indade – as he worked, mumbled an' mutthered in great discontent: 'Oh, haven't I the hard, hard luck,' he said. 'I'll never have thim done in time for her to dance in tonight. So, thin, I'll be kilt entirely,' says he. 'Was there ever another quane of the fairies as wearing on shoes an' brogues an' dancin' slippers? Haven't I the – ' Looking up, he saw Darby.

'The top of the day to you, dacint man!' says the cobbler, jumpin' up. Giving a sharp cry, he pinted quick at Darby's stomach. 'But, wirra, wirra, what's that wooly, ugly thing you have crawling an' creepin' on your weskit?' he said, purtendin' to be all excited.

'Sorra thing on my weskit,' answered Darby, cool as ice, 'or any-where else that'll make me take my two bright eyes off'n you – not for a second,' says he.

'Well! Well! will you look at that, now?' laughed the cobbler. 'Mark how quick an' handy he took me up! Will you have a pinch of snuff, clever man?' he axed, houlding up the little box.

'Is it the same snuff you gave Barney McBride a while ago?' axed Darby, sarcastic. 'Lave off your foolishness,' says our hayro, growin' fierce, 'and grant me at once the favours of the three wishes, or I'll have you smoking like a herring in my own chimney before night-fall,' says he.

At that the leprechaun, seeing that he but wasted time on so knowledgeable a man as Darby O'Gill, surrendhered, and granted the favours of the three wishes.

'What is it you ask?' says the cobbler, himself turning on a sudden very sour an' sullen.

'First an' foremost,' says Darby, 'I want a home of my ansisthers, an' it must be a castle like Castle Brophy, with pictures of my kith an' kin on the wall, and then facing them pictures of my wife Bridget's kith an' kin on the other wall.'

'That favour I give ye, that wish I grant ye,' says the fairy, making the shape of a castle on the ground with his awl.

'What next?' he grunted.

'I want goold enough for me an' my generations to enjoy in grandeur the place forever.'

'Always the goold,' sneered the little man, bending to dhraw with his awl on the turf the shape of a purse.

'Now for your third and last wish. Have a care!'

'I want the castle set on this hill – the Divils Pillow – where we two stand,' says Darby. Then sweeping with his arm, he says, 'I want the land about to be my demesne.'

The leprechaun stuck his awl on the ground. 'That wish I give you, that wish I grant you,' he says. With that he straightened himself up, and grinning most aggravaytin' the while, he looked Darby over from top to toe. 'You're a foine, knowledgeable man, but have a care of the fourth wish!' says he.

Bekase there was more of a challenge than friendly warning in what the small lad said, Darby snapped his fingers at him an' cried: 'Have no fear, little man! If I got all Ireland ground for making a fourth wish, however small, before midnight I'd not make it. I'm going home now to fetch Bridget an' the childher, and the only fear or unaisiness I have is that you'll not keep your word, so as to have the castle here ready before us when I come back.'

'Oho! I'm not to be thrusted, amn't I?' screeched the little lad, flaring into a blazing passion. He jumped upon the log that was betwixt them, and with one fist behind his back shook the other at Darby.

'You ignorant, suspicious-minded blaggard!' says he. 'How dare the likes of you say the likes of that to the likes of me!' cried the cobbler. 'I'd have you to know,' he says, 'that I had a repitation for truth an' voracity ayquil if not shuperior to the best, before you were born!' he shouted. 'I'll take no high talk from a man that's afraid to give words to his own wife if whin she's in a tantrum!' says the leprechaun.

'It's aisy to know you're not a married man,' says Darby, mighty scornful, 'bekase if you – '

The lad stopped short, forgetting what he was going to say in his surprise an' aggaytation, for the far side of the mountain was waving up an' down before his eyes like a great green blanket that is being shook by two women, while at the same time high spots of turf on the hillside toppled sidewise to level themselves up with the low places. The enchantment had already begun to make things ready for the castle. A dozen foine trees that stood in a little grove bent their heads quickly together, and thin by some inwisible hand they were plucked up by the roots an' dhropped aside much the same as a man might grasp a handful of weeds an' fling them from his garden.

The ground under the knowledgeable man's feet began to rumble an' heave. He waited for no more. With a cry that was half of gladness an' half of fear, he turned on his heel an' started on a run down into the walley, leaving the little cobbler standing on the log, shouting abuse after him an' ballyraggin' him as he ran.

So excited was Darby that, going up the Pig's Head, he was nearly run over by a crowd of great brown building stones which were moving down slow an' ordherly like a flock of driven sheep – but they moved without so much as bruising a blade of grass or bendin' a twig, as they came.

Only once, and that at the top of the Pig's Head, he trew a look back.

The Divil's Pillow was in a great commotion; a whirlwind was sweeping over it – whether of dust or of mist he couldn't tell.

Afther this, Darby never looked back again or to the right or the left of him, but kept straight on till he found himself, panting and pufflng, at his own kitchen door. 'Twas tin minutes before he could spake, but at last, whin he tould Bridget to make ready herself and the childher to go up to the Divil's Pillow with him, for once in her life that raymarkable woman, without axing, How comes it so, What rayson have you, or Why should I do it, set to work washing the childer's faces.

Maybe she dabbed a little more soap in their eyes than was needful, for 'twas a habit she had; though this time if she did, not a whimper broke from the little hayros. For the matther of that, not one word, good, bad or indifferent, did herself spake till the whole family were trudging down the lane two by two, marching like sojers.

As they came near the first hill along its sides the evening twilight turned from purple to brown, and at the top of the Pig's Head the darkness of a black night swooped suddenly down on them. Darby hurried on a step or two ahead, an' resting his hand upon the large rock that crowns the hill, looked anxiously over to the Divil's Pillow. Although he was ready for something foine, yet the greatness of the foineness that met his gaze knocked the breath out of him.

Across the deep walley, and on top of the second mountain, he saw lined against the evening sky the roof of an imminse castle, with towers an' parrypets an' battlements. Undher the towers a thousand sullen windows glowed red in the black walls. Castle Brophy couldn't hould a candle to it.

'Behold!' says Darby, flinging out his arm, and turning to his wife, who had just come up – 'behold the castle of my ansisthers who were my forefathers!'

'How,' says Bridget, quick and scornful – 'how could your aunt's sisters be your four fathers?'

What Darby was going to say to her he don't just raymember, for at that instant from the right-hand side of the mountain came a cracking of whips, a rattling of wheels, an' the rush of horses, and, lo and behold! a great dark coach with flashing lamps, and drawn by four coal-black horses, dashed up the hill and stopped beside them. Two shadowy men were on the driver's box.

'Is this Lord Darby O'Gill?' axed one of them, in a deep, muffled woice. Before Darby could reply, Bridget took the words out of his mouth.

'It is!' she cried, in a kind of a half cheer, 'an' Lady O'Gill an' the childher.'

'Then hurry up!' says the coachman. 'Your supper's gettin' cowld.'

Without waiting for anyone Bridget flung open the carriage door, an' pushin' Darby aside jumped in among the cushions. Darby, his heart sizzlin' with vexation at her audaciousness, lifted in one after another the childher, and then got in himself.

He couldn't undherstand at all the change in his wife, for she had always been the odherliest, modestist woman in the parish.

Well, he'd no sooner shut the door than crack went the whip, the horses gave a spring, the carriage jumped, and down the hill they went. For fastness there was never another carriage-ride like that before nor since. Darby hildt tight with both hands to the window, his face pressed against the glass. He couldn't tell whether the horses were only flying or whether the coach was falling down the hill into the walley. By the hollow feeling in his stomach he thought they were falling. He was striving to think of some prayers when there came a terrible jolt which sint his two heels against the roof an' his head betwixt the cushions. As he righted himself the wheels began to grate on a graveled road, an' plainly they were dashing up the side of the second mountain.

Even so, they couldn't have gone far whin the carriage dhrew up in a flurry, an' he saw through the gloom a high iron gate being slowly opened.

'Pass on,' said a voice from somewhere in the shadows; 'their supper's getting cowld.'

As they flew undher the great archway, Darby had a glimpse of the thing which had opened the gate, and had said their supper was getting cowld. It was standing on its hind legs – in the darkness he couldn't be quite sure as to its shape, but it was ayther a Bear or a Loin.

His mind was in a pondher about this when, with a swirl an' a bump, the carriage stopped another time, an' now it stood before a broad flight of stone steps which led up to the main door of the castle. Darby, half afraid, peering out through the darkness, saw a square of light high above him which came from the open hall door. Three sarvants in livery stood waiting on the thrashol.

'Make haste, make haste!' says one, in a doleful voice; 'their supper's gettin' cowld.'

Hearing these words, Bridget imagetely bounced out, an' was half-way up the steps before Darby could ketch her an' hould her till the childher came up.

'I never in all my life saw her so owdacious,' he says, half cryin', an' linkin' her arm to keep her back, an' thin, with the childher following two by two, according to size, the whole family payraded up the steps, till Darby, with a gasp of deloight, stopped on the thrashol of a splendid hall. From a high ceiling hung great flags from every nation an' domination, which swung and swayed in the dazzlin' light. Two lines of men and maid servants dhressed in silks an' satins an' brocades, stood facing aich other, bowing an' smiling an' wavin' their hands in welcome. The two lines stretched down to the goold stairway at the far ind of the hall. For half of one minute Darby, every eye in his head as big as a tay-cup, stood hesitaytin'. Thin he said, 'Why should it flutther me? Arrah, ain't it all mine? Aren't all these people in me pay? I'll engage it's a pritty penny all this grandeur is costing me to keep up this minute.' He trew out his chist. 'Come on, Bridget!' he says; 'let's go into the home of my ansisthers.'

Howandever, scarcely had he stepped into the beautiful place whin two pipers with their pipes, two fiddlers with their fiddles, two flute-players with their flutes, an' they dhressed in scarlet an' goold, stepped out in front of him, and thus to maylodius music the family proudly marched down the hall, climbed up the goolden stairway at its ind, an' thin turned to enter the biggest room Darby had ever seen.

Something in his sowl whuspered that this was the picture-gallery.

'Be the powers of Pewther!' says the knowledgeable man to himself, 'I wouldn't be in Bridget's place this minute for a hatful of money! Wait, oh just wait, till she has to compare her own relations with my own foine people! I know how she'll feel, but I wondher what she'll say,' he says.

The thought that all the unjust things, all the unraysonable things Bridget had said about his kith an' kin were just going to be disproved and turned against herself, made him proud an' almost happy.

But wirrasthrue! He should have raymembered his own adwise not to make nor moil nor meddle with the fairies, for here he was to get the first hard welt from the little leprechaun.

It was the picture-gallery sure enough, but how terribly different everything was from what the poor lad expected. There on the left wall, grand an' noble, shone the pictures of Bridget's people. Of all the well-dressed, handsome, proud-appearing persons in the whole worruld, the O'Hagans an' the O'Shaughnessys would compare with the best. This was a hard enough crack, though a crushinger knock was to come. Ferninst them on the right wall glowered the O'Gills and the O'Gradys, and of all the ragged, sheep-stealing, hangdog-looking villains one ever saw in jail or out of jail, it was Darby's kindred.

The place of honour on the right wall was given to Darby's fourth cousin, Phelem McFadden, an' he was painted with a pair of handcuffs on him. Wullum O'Gill had a squint in his right eye, and his thin legs bowed like hoops on a barrel.

If you have ever at night been groping your way through a dark room, and got a sudden, hard bump on the forehead from the edge of the door, you can undherstand the feelings of the knowledgeable man.

'Take that picture out!' he said, hoarsely, as soon as he could speak. 'An' will someone kindly inthrojuice me to the man who med it? Bekase,' he says, 'I intend to take his life! There was never a crass-eyed O'Gill since the world began,' says he.

Think of his horror an' surprise whin he saw the left eye of Wullum O'Gill twist itself slowly over toward his nose and squint worse than the right eye.

Purtending not to see this, an' hoping no one else did, Darby fiercely led the way over to the other wall.

Fronting him stood the handsome picture of Honoria O'Shaugh-nessy, an' she dhressed in a shuit of tin clothes like the knights of ould used to wear – armour I think they calls it.

She hildt a spear in her hand with a little flag on the blade, an' her smile was proud and high.

'Take that likeness out, too,' says Darby, very spiteful; 'that's not a dacint shuit of clothes for any woman to wear!'

The next minute you might have knocked him down with a feather, for the picture of Honoria O'Shaughnessy opened its mouth an' stuck out its tongue at him.

'The supper's getting cowld, the supper's getting cowld!' someone cried at the other ind of the picture gallery. Two big doors were swung open, an' glad enough was our poor hayro to folly the musicianers down to the room where the ating an' drinking were to be thransacted.

This was a little room with lots of looking-glasses, and it was bright with a thousand candles, and white with the shining-ist marble. On the table was biled beef an' reddishes an' carrots an' roast mutton an' all kinds of important ating an' drinking. Beside there stood fruits an' sweets an' – but, sure, what is the use in talkin'?

A high-backed chair stood ready for aich of the family, an' 'twas a lovely sight to see them all whin they were sitting there – Darby at the head, Bridget at the foot, the childher – the poor little paythriarchs – sitting bolt upright on aich side, with a bewigged and befrilled serving-man standing haughty behind every chair.

The atin' and dhrinkin' would have begun at once – in throth there was already a bit of biled beef on Darby's plate – only that he spied a little silver bell beside him. Sure, 'twas one like those the quality keep to ring whin they want more hot wather for their punch, but it puzzled the knowledgeable man, and 'twas the beginning of his misfortune.

'I wondher,' he thought, 'if 'tis here for the same raison as the bell is at the Curragh races – do they ring this one so that all at the table will start ating and dhrinking fair, an' no one will have the advantage, or is it,' he says to himself agin, 'to ring whin the head of the house thinks everyone has had enough. Haven't the quality quare ways! I'll be a long time learning them,' he says.

He sat silent and puzzling an' staring at the biled beef on his plate, afeard to start in without ringing the bell, an' dhreadin' to risk ringing it. The grand sarvants towered cowldly on every side, their chins tilted, but they kep' throwing over their chowlders glances so scornful and haughty that Darby shivered at the thought of showing any uncultivaytion.

While our hayro sat thus in unaisy contimplation an' smouldherin' mortification an' flurried hesitaytion, a powdhered head was poked over his chowlder, and a soft, beguiling voice said, 'Is there anything else you'd wish for?'

The foolish lad twisted in his chair, opened his mouth to spake, and gave a look at the bell; shame rushed to his cheeks, he picked up a bit of the biled beef on his fork, an' to consale his turpitaytion gave the misfortunit answer: 'I'd wish for a pinch of salt, if you plaze,' says he.

'Twas no sooner said than came the crash. Oh, tunderation an' murdheration, what a roaring crash it was! The lights winked out together at a breath an' left a pitchy, throbbing darkness. Overhead and to the sides was a roaring, smashing, crunching noise, like the ocean's madness when the winthry storm breaks agin the Kerry shore, an' in that roar was mingled the tearing and the splitting of the walls and the fading of the chimneys. But through all this confusion could be heard the shrill, laughing woice of the leprechaun. 'The clever man med his fourth grand wish' it howled.

Darby – a thousand wild woices screaming an' mocking above him – was on his back kicking and squirming and striving to get up, but some load hilt him down, an' something bound his eyes shut.

'Are you kilt, Bridget asthore?' he cried; 'Where are the childher?' he says.

Instead of answer there suddenly flashed a fierce an' angry silence, an' its quickness frightened the lad more than all the wild confusion before.

'Twas a full minute before he dared to open his eyes to face the horrors which he felt were standing about him; but when courage enough to look came, all he saw was the night-covered mountain, a purple sky, and a thin, new moon, with one trembling goold star a hand's space above its bosom.

Darby struggled to his feet. Not a stone of the castle was left, not a sod of turf but what was in its ould place; every sign of the little cobbler's work had melted like April snow. The very trees Darby had seen pulled up by the roots that same afternoon now stood a waving blur below the new moon, an' a nightingale was singing in their branches. A cricket chirped lonesomely on the same fallen log which had hidden the leprechaun.

'Bridget! Bridget!' Darby called agin an' agin. Only a sleepy owl on a distant hill answered.

A shivering thought jumped into the boy's bewildered sowl – maybe the leprechaun had stolen Bridget an' the childher.

The poor man turned, and for the last time darted down into the night-filled walley.

Not a pool in the road he waited to go around, not a ditch in his path he didn't leap over, but ran as he never ran before till he raiched his own front door.

His heart stood still as he peeped through the window. There were the childher croodled around Bridget, who sat with the youngest asleep in her lap before the fire, rocking back an' forth, an' she crooning a happy, continted baby-song.

Tears of gladness crept into Darby's eyes as he looked in upon her. 'God bless her!' he says to himself. 'She's the flower of the O'Hagans and the O'Shaughnessys, and she's a proud feather in the caps of the O'Gills and the O'Gradys.'

'Twas well he had this happy thought to cheer him as he lifted the door-latch, for the manest of all the little cobbler's spiteful thricks waited in the house to meet Darby – nayther Bridget nor the childher raymembered a single thing of all that had happened to them during the day. They were willing to make their happy-davitts that they had been no farther than their own petatie-patch since morning.

Hairy Rouchy

PATRICK KENNEDY

There was once a widow woman, as often there was, and she had three daughters. The eldest and the second eldest were as handsome as the moon and the evening star, but the youngest was all covered with hair, and her face was as brown as a berry, and they called her Hairy Rouchy. She lighted the fire in the morning, cooked the food, and made the beds, while her sisters would be stringing flowers on a hank, or looking at themselves in the glass, or sitting with their hands across. 'No one will ever come to marry us in this lonesome place,' said the eldest, one day; 'so you and I,' said she to the second sister, 'may as well go seek our fortune.' 'That's the best word you ever spoke,' said the other. 'Bake our cake and kill our cock, mother, and away we go.' Well, so she did. 'And now, girls,' said she, 'which will you have, half this with my blessing, or the whole of it with my curse?' 'Curse or no curse, mother, the whole of it is little enough.'

Well, they set off, and says Hairy Rouchy to her mother when they got to the end of the lane, 'Mother, give me your blessing, and a quarter of the griddle cake, I must go after these girls, for I fear ill luck is in their road.' She gave her blessing and the whole of the cake, and she went off running, and soon overtook them. 'Here's Hairy Rouchy,' says the eldest, 'she'll make a show of us. We'll tie her to this big stone.' So they tied her to the big stone and went their way, but when they were a quarter of a mile further, there she was three perches behind them. Well, they were vexed enough, and the next clamp of turf they passed, they made her lie down, and piled every sod of it over her.

When they were a quarter of a mile further they looked back again, and there was the girl three perches behind them, and weren't they mad! To make a long story short, they fastened her in a pound, and they put the tying of the three smalls on her, and fastened her to a tree. The next quarter of a mile she was up by their side, and at last they were tired, and let her walk behind them.

Well, they walked and they walked till they were tired, and till the greyness of night came round them, and they saw a light at a distance. When they came up, what was it but a giant's house, and great sharp teeth were in the heads of himself, and his wife, and his three daughters. Well, they got lodging, and when sleep time was coming they were put into one bed, and the giant's daughters' bed touched the head of theirs. Well becomes my brave Hairy Rouchy, when the giant's daughters were asleep, she took off the hair necklaces from her own neck and the necks of her sisters, and put them on the giant's daughters' necks, and she put their gold and silver and diamond necklaces on the necks of her sisters and herself, and then watched to see what would happen.

The giant and his wife were sitting by the fire, and says he, 'Won't these girls make a fine meat pie for us tomorrow.' 'Won't they,' says she, and she smacked her lips, 'but I'll have some trouble singeing that hairy one.' 'They are all asleep now,' says he, and he called in his red-headed *giolla* [servant]. 'Go and put them strangers out of pain,' says he. 'But how'll I know them from your daughters,' says the giolla. 'Very easy, they have only hair necklaces round their necks.'

Well, you may all guess what happened. So the night faded away, and the morning came, and what did the giant see at the flight of darkness, when the gate was opened by the cowboy, but Hairy Rouchy walking out through it after her two sisters. Down the stairs he came, five at a time, and out of the bawn he flew, and *magh go bragh* with him after the girls. The eldest screamed out, and the second eldest screamed out, but the youngest took one under each arm, and if she didn't lay leg to ground, you may call me a storyteller. She ran like the wind, and the giant ran like the north wind; the sparks of fire he struck out of the stones hit her on the back, and the sparks of fire she struck out of the stones scorched his face. At last they came near the wide and deep river that divided his land from the land of the King of Spain, and into that land he daren't pass. Over the wide deep river went Hairy Rouchy with a high, very active bound, and after her went the giant. His heels touched the bank, and back into the water went his head and body. He dragged himself out on his own side, and sat down on the bank, and looked across, and this is what he said: 'You're there, Hairy Rouchy,' says he. 'No thanks to you for it,' says she. 'You got my three daughters killed,' says he. 'It was to save our own lives,' says she. 'When will you come to see me again,' says he. 'When I have business,' says she. 'Divel be in your road,' says he. 'It's better pray than curse,' says she.

The three girls went on till they came to the King of Spain's castle, where they were well entertained, and the King's eldest son and the eldest sister fell in love with one another, and the second son and the second sister fell in love with one another, and poor Hairy Rouchy fell in love with the youngest son, but he didn't fall in love with her.

Well, the next day, when they were at breakfast, says the King to her, 'Good was your deed at the giant's house, and if you only bring me the talking golden quilt that's covering himself and his wife, my eldest son may marry your eldest sister.' 'I'll try, says she, 'worse than lose I can't.'

So that night, when the giant and his wife were fast asleep, the quilt felt a hand pulling it off the bed. 'Who are you?' says the quilt. 'Mishe' [myself], says the girl, and she pulled away. 'Waken, master,' says the quilt, 'someone is taking me away.' 'And who's taking you away?' says he. 'It's mische that's doing it,' says the quilt. 'Then let mishe stop his tricks, and not be disturbing us.' 'But I tell you, mishe is carrying me off.' 'If mishe says another word, I'll get up and throw him in the fire.' So the poor quilt had nothing to do but hold its tongue.

'But,' says the giant's wife, after a few minutes, 'maybe the divel bewitched the quilt to walk off with itself.' 'Faith and maybe so,' says the giant; 'I'll get up and look.' So he searched the room, and the stairs, and the hall, and the bawn, and the bawn gate was open, 'Mile mollachd,' says he; 'Hairy Rouchy was here,' and to the road he took. But when he was on the hill she was in the hollow, and when he was in the hollow she was on the hill, and when he came to the hither side of the river she was on the thither. 'You're there, Hairy Rouchy,' says he. 'No thanks to you,' says she. 'You took away my speaking golden quilt,' says he. 'It was to get my eldest sister married,' says she. 'When will you come back?' 'Divel be in your road,' says he. 'It's better pray than curse,' says she; and the same night the speaking golden quilt was covering the Kind and Queen of Spain.

Well, the wedding was made, but there was little notice taken of poor Hairy Rouchy, and she spent a good part of the day talking to a poor travelling woman that she often relieved at home and that was come by accident as far as Spain.

So the next day, when they were at breakfast again, says the King,

'Hairy Rouchy, if you bring me tomorrow morning, the *chloive solais* [sword of light] that hangs at the giant's bed's head, my second son will marry your second sister.' 'I'll make the trial,' says she; 'worse than lose I can't.'

Well, the next night the giant's wife was boiling his big pot of gruel, and Hairy Rouchy was sitting by the chimbly on the straws that covered the ridge pole, and dropping fistfuls of salt into the pot. 'You put too much salt in this porridge,' says the giant to his wife, when he was supping it. 'I'm sure I didn't put in more than four spoonfuls,' says she. 'Well, well, that was the right size; still it tastes mortial salty.'

When he was in bed he cries out, 'Wife, I'll be a piece of cured bacon before morning if I don't get a drink.' 'Oh, then, purshuin to the sup of water in the house,' says she. 'Well, call up the giolla out of the settle, and let him bring a pailful from the well.' So, the giolla got up in a bad humour, scratching his head, and went to the door with the pail in his hand. There was Hairy Rouchy by the jamb, and maybe she didn't dash fistfuls of sand and salt into his eyes. 'Oh, master, master,' says he, 'the sky is as black as your hat, and it's pelting hailstones on me; I'll never find the well.' 'Here you *onshuch*, take the sword of light, and it will show you the way.'

So he took the *chloive solais*, and made his way to the well, and while he was filling the pail he laid the sword on the ground. That was all the girl wanted. She snatched it up, waved it round her head, and the light flashed over hills and hollows. 'If you're not into the house like a shot,' says she, 'I'll send your head half a mile away.' The poor giolla was only too glad to get off, and she was soon flying like the wind to the river, and the giant hot foot after her. When she was in the hollow he was on the hill . . .

'You're a very good girl, indeed,' says the King of Spain to Hairy Rouchy, the morning after the second marriage. 'You deserve a reward. So bring me the giant's *puckawn* [a goat-sprite] with the golden bells round his neck as soon as you like, and you must get my youngest son for a husband.' 'But maybe he won't have me,' says she. 'Indeed an' I will,' says the prince; 'so good a sister can't make a bad wife.' 'But I'm all hairy and brown,' says she. 'That's no sin,' says the prince.

Sure enough, the night after, she was hard and fast in the giant's outhouse, stuffing the puckawn's bells with the marrow of the elder; and when she thought the job was well finished she was leading

him out. She had a band on his mouth, but when my brave puck
found he couldn't bawl, he took to rear and kick like a puck as he
was. Out came the elder marrow from three of the bells, and the
sound that came from them was enough to waken the dead. She
drove him at his full speed before her, but after came the giant like
a storm. She could escape him if she liked, but she would not
return without puck, and bedad she was soon pinned and brought
back to the giant's big kitchen. There was his wife and the giolla,
and if he wasn't proud to show them his prisoner there's not a
glove in Wexford.

'Now, ma'am,' says he to her, 'I have you safe after all the mischief
you done me. If I was in your power what would you do to me?' 'Oh,
wouldn't I tie you up to the ceiling in a sack, you ould tyrant, and go
myself and giolla to the wood, cut big clubs, and break every bone in
your body one after another. Then if there was any life left in you,
we'd make a fire of the green boughs underneath, and stifle the little
that was left out of you.' 'The very thing I'll do with you,' says he.

So he put her in a sack, tied her up to the beam that went across
the kitchen, and went off with the giolla to the wood to cut down the
clubs and green branches, leaving his wife to watch the prisoner.
She expected to hear crying and sobbing from out of the sack, but
the girl did nothing but shout and laugh. 'Is it mad, you are,' says
she, 'and death so near you?' 'Death indeed. Why, the bottom of the
sack is full of diamonds, and pearls, and guineas, and there is the
finest views all round me you ever see – castles, and lawns, and lakes,
and the finest flowers.' 'Is it lies you're telling?' 'Oh, dickens a lie. If
I'd let you up, but I won't, you'd see and feel it all.'

But the giant's wife over-persuaded her, and when she was
loosened, and got the other into the sack, she tied her hard and fast,
ran to the outhouse, threw a rope round the puckawn's neck, and he
and she were soon racing like the wind toward the river. The giant
and the giolla were soon back, and he wondered where his wife
could be. But he saw the sack still full, and the two began to whack it
like so many blacksmiths. 'Oh, Lord,' says the poor woman, 'it's
myself that's here.' But she roared out, 'Ah, sure, I'm your wife,
don't kill me for goodness sake.' 'Be the laws,' says the giolla, 'it's
the mistress. Oh, bad luck to you, Hairy Rouchy; this is your doing.
Run and catch her, master, while I take the poor mistress down, and
see what I can do for her.' Off went the big fellow like a *bowarra*, but
when he came to this side of the river, panting and puffing, there

was the girl and his darling puckawn on the other side, and she ready to burst her sides with the laughing.

'You're there, my damsel,' 'No thanks, etc.' So the scolding match went on to the end and then says he, 'If you were in my place and I in yours now, what would you do?' 'I'd stoop down and drink the river dry to get at you.' But she didn't stop to see whether he was fool enough to take her advice, but led her goat to the palace. Oh, wasn't there great joy and clapping of hands when the golden bells were heard a-ringing up the avenue, and into the big bawn. She didn't mind how anyone looked but the youngest prince; and though he didn't appear very rejoiced, there was a kind of smile in his face, and she was satisfied.

Well, the next morning, when they were all setting out to the church, and the bridegroom was mounted on his horse, and the bride getting into the coach, she asked him for leave to take the poor travelling woman in along with her. 'It's a queer request,' says he, 'but do as you like; you must have some reason for it.' Well, when all were dismounting or getting out of their coaches, he went to open the door for his bride, and the sight almost left his eyes; for there sitting fornent him was the most beautiful young woman he ever beheld. She had the same kind innocent look that belonged to Hairy Rouchy, but she had also the finest colour in her face, and neck, and hands, and her hair, instead of the tangled brake it used to be, was nicely plaited and curled, and was the finest dark brown in the world.

Glad enough she was to see the joy and surprise in his face, and if they were not the happy bride and bridegroom I never saw one. When they were talking by themselves, she told him that an enchantment was laid on her when she was a child, and she was always to remain the fright she was, till someone would marry her for the sake of her disposition. The travelling woman was her guardian fairy in disguise. There were two unhappy marriages and one happy one in the King of Spain's family, and I'll let everyone here guess which was which.

The Ghosts and the Game of Football

PATRICK KENNEDY

There was once a poor widow woman's son that was going to look for service, and one winter's evening he came to a strong farmer's house, and this house was very near an old castle. 'God save all here,' says he, when he got inside the door. 'God save you kindly,' says the farmer. 'Come to the fire.' 'Could you give me a night's lodging?' says the boy.

'That we will, and welcome, if you will only sleep in a comfortable room in the old castle above there; and you must have a fire and candlelight, and whatever you like to drink; and if you're alive in the morning I'll give you ten guineas.' 'Sure. I'll be 'live enough if you send no one to kill me.' 'I'll send no one to kill you, you may depend. The place is haunted ever since my father died, and three or four people that slept in the same room were found dead next morning. If you can banish the spirits I'll give you a good farm and my daughter, so that you like one another well enough to be married.' 'Never say't twice. I've a middling safe conscience, and don't fear any evil spirit that ever smelled of brimstone.'

Well and good, the boy got his supper, and then they went up with him to the old castle, and showed him into a large kitchen, with a roaring fire in the grate, and a table, with a bottle and glass, and tumbler on it, and the kettle ready on the hob. They bade him good-night and Godspeed, and went off as if they didn't think their heels were half swift enough. 'Well,' says he to himself, 'if there's any danger, this prayer-book will be usefuller than either the glass or tumbler.' So he kneeled down and read a good many prayers, and then sat by the fire, and waited to see what would happen. In about a quarter of an hour, he heard something bumping along the floor overhead till it came to a hole in the ceiling. There it stopped, and cried out, 'I'll fall, I'll fall.' 'Fall away,' says Jack, and down came a pair of legs on the kitchen floor. They walked to one end of the room, and there they stood, and Jack's hair had like to stand upright on his head along with them. Then another crackling and whacking came to the hole, and the same words passed between the thing above and Jack, and down came a man's body, and went and stood upon the legs. Then comes the head and shoulders, till the whole man, with buckles in his shoes and knee-breeches, and a big flapped waistcoat and a three-cocked hat, was standing in one corner of the room. Not to take up your time for nothing, two more men, more old-fashioned dressed than the first, were soon standing in two other corners. Jack was a little cowed at first; but found his courage growing stronger every moment, and what would you have of it, the three old gentlemen began to kick a *puckeen* [football] as fast as they could, the man in the three-cocked hat playing again' the other two.

'Fair play is bonny play,' says Jack, as bold as he could; but the terror was on him, and the words came out as if he was frightened in his sleep; 'so I'll help *you*, sir.' Well and good, he joined the sport, and kicked away till his shirt was ringing wet, savin' your presence, and the ball flying from one end of the room to the other like thunder, and still not a word was exchanged. At last the day began to break, and poor Jack was dead beat, and he thought, by the way the three ghosts began to look at himself and themselves, that they wished him to speak.

So, says he, 'Gentlemen, as the sport is nearly over, and I done my best to please you, would you tell a body what is the reason of your coming here night after night, and how could I give you rest, if it is rest you want?' 'Them is the wisest words,' says the ghost with the three-cocked hat, 'you ever said in your life. Some of those that came before you found courage enough to take a part in our game, but no one had *misnach* [energy] enough to speak to us. I am the father of the good man of the next house, that man in the left corner is my father, and the man on my right is my grandfather. From father to son we were too fond of money. We lent it at ten times the honest interest it was worth; we never paid a debt we could get over, and almost starved our tenants and labourers.

'Here,' says he, lugging a large drawer out of the wall; 'here is the gold and notes that we put together, and we were not honestly entitled to the one half of it; and here,' says he, opening another drawer, 'are bills and memorandums that'll show who were wronged, and who are entitled to get a great deal paid back to them. Tell my son to saddle two of his best horses for himself and yourself, and keep riding day and night, till every man and woman we ever wronged be rightified. When that is done, come here again some night; and if you don't hear or see anything, we'll be at rest, and you may marry my granddaughter as soon as you please.'

Just as he said these words, Jack could see the wall through his body, and when he winked to clear his sight, the kitchen was as empty as a noggin turned upside down. At that very moment the farmer and his daughter lifted the latch, and both fell on their knees when they saw Jack alive. He soon told them everything that happened, and for three days and nights did the farmer and himself ride about, till there wasn't a single wronged person left without being paid to the last farthing.

The next night Jack spent in the kitchen he fell asleep before he was after sitting a quarter of an hour at the fire, and in his sleep he thought he saw three white birds flying up to heaven from the steeple of the next church.

Jack got the daughter for his wife, and they lived comfortably in the old castle; and if ever he was tempted to hoard up gold, or keep for a minute a guinea or a shilling from the man that earned it through the nose, he bethought him of the ghosts and the game of football.

The Watcher

SHERIDAN LE FANU

It is now more than fifty years since the occurrences which I am about to relate caused a strange sensation in the gay society of Dublin. The fashionable world, however, is no recorder of traditions; the memory of selfishness seldom reaches far; and the events which occasionally disturb the polite monotony of its pleasant and heartless progress, however stamped with the characters of misery and horror, scarcely outlive the gossip of a season, and (except, perhaps, in the remem–brance of a few more directly interested in the consequences of the catastrophe) are in a little time lost to the recollection of all. The appetite for scandal, or for horror, has been sated; the incident can yield no more of interest or novelty; curiosity, frustrated by impenetrable mystery, gives over the pursuit in despair; the tale has ceased to be new, grows stale and flat; and so, in a few years, enquiry subsides into indifference.

Somewhere about the year 1794, the younger brother of a certain baronet, whom I shall call Sir James Barton, returned to Dublin. He had served in the navy with some distinction, having commanded one of his Majesty's frigates during the greater part of the American war. Captain Barton was now apparently some two or three-and-forty years of age. He was an intelligent and agreeable companion, when he chose it, though generally reserved, and occasionally even moody. In society, however, he deported himself as a man of the world and a gentleman. He had not contracted any of the noisy brusqueness sometimes acquired at sea, on the contrary, his manners were remarkably easy, quiet, and even polished. He was in person about the middle size, and somewhat strongly formed; his coun-tenance was marked with the lines of thought, and on the whole wore an expression of gravity and even of melancholy. Being, how-ever, as we have said, a man of perfect breeding, as well as of affluent circumstances and good family, he had, of course, ready access to the best society of the metropolis, without the necessity of any other credentials. In his personal habits Captain Barton was economical. He occupied lodgings in one of the then fashionable streets in the south side of the town, kept but one horse and one servant, and though a reputed free-thinker, he lived an orderly and moral life, indulging neither in gaming, drinking, nor any other vicious pursuit, living very much to himself, without forming any intimacies, or choosing any companions, and appearing to mix in gay society rather for the sake of its bustle and distraction, than for any opportunities which it offered of interchanging either thoughts or feelings with its votaries. Barton was therefore pronounced a saving, prudent, unsocial sort of a fellow, who bid fair to maintain his celibacy alike against stratagem and assault, and was likely to live to a good old age, die rich and leave his money to a hospital.

It was soon apparent, however, that the nature of Captain Bartons plans had been totally misconceived. A young lady, whom we shall call Miss Montague, was at this time introduced into the fashionable world of Dublin by her aunt, the Dowager Lady Rochdale. Miss Montague was decidedly pretty and accomplished, and having some natural cleverness, and a great deal of gaiety, became for a while the reigning toast. Her popularity, however, gained her, for a time, nothing more than that unsubstantial admiration which, however pleasant as an incense to vanity is by no means necessarily antecedent to matrimony, for, unhappily for the young lady in question, it was an understood thing, that, beyond her personal attractions, she had no kind of earthly provision. Such being the state of affairs, it will readily be believed that no little surprise was consequent upon the appearance of Captain Barton as the avowed lover of the penniless Miss Montague.

His suit prospered, as might have been expected, and in a short time it was confidentially communicated by old Lady Rochdale to each of her hundred and fifty particular friends in succession, that Captain Barton had actually tendered proposals of marriage, with her approbation, to her niece, Miss Montague, who had, moreover, accepted the offer of his hand, conditionally upon the consent of her father, who was then upon his homeward voyage from India, and expected in two or three months at furthest. About his consent there could be no doubt. The delay, therefore, was one merely of form; they were looked upon as absolutely engaged, and Lady Rochdale, with a vigour of old-fashioned decorum with which her niece would, no doubt, gladly have dispensed, withdrew her thenceforward from all further participation in the gaieties of the town. Captain Barton was a constant visitor as well as a frequent guest at the house, and was permitted all the privileges and intimacy which a betrothed suitor is usually accorded. Such was the relation of parties, when the mysterious circumstances which darken this narrative with inexplicable melancholy first began to unfold themselves.

Lady Rochdale resided in a handsome mansion at the north side of Dublin, and Captain Bartons lodgings, as we have already said, were situated at the south. The distance intervening was considerable, and it was Captain Barton's habit generally to walk home without an attendant, as often as he passed the evening with the old lady and her fair charge. His shortest way in such nocturnal walks lay, for a considerable space, through a line of streets which had as yet been merely laid out, and little more than the foundations of the houses constructed. One night, shortly after his engagement with Miss Montague had commenced, he happened to remain usually late, in company only with her and Lady Rochdale. The conversation had turned upon the evidences of revelation, which he had disputed with the callous scepticism of a confirmed infidel. What were called 'French principles' had, in those days, found their way a good deal into fashionable society, especially that portion of it which professed allegiance to Whiggism, and neither the old lady nor her charge was so perfectly free from the taint as to look upon Captain Barton's views as any serious objection to the proposed union. The discussion had degenerated into one upon the supernatural and the marvellous, in which he had pursued precisely the same line of argument and ridicule. In all this, it is but true to state, Captain Barton was guilty of no affectation; the doctrines upon which he insisted were, in reality, but too truly the basis of his own fixed belief, if so it might be called; and perhaps not the least strange of the many strange circumstances connected with this narrative, was the fact that the subject of the fearful influences we are about to describe was himself, from the deliberate conviction of years, an utter disbeliever in what are usually termed preternatural agencies.

It was considerably past midnight when Mr Barton took his leave, and set out upon his solitary walk homeward. He rapidly reached the lonely road, with its unfinished dwarf walls tracing the foundations of the projected rows of houses on either side. The moon was shining mistily, and its imperfect light made the road he trod but additionally dreary; that utter silence, which has in it something indefinably exciting, reigned there, and made the sound of his steps, which alone broke it, unnaturally loud and distinct. He had proceeded thus some way, when on a sudden he heard other footsteps, pattering at a measured pace, and, as it seemed, about two score steps behind him. The suspicion of being dogged is at all times unpleasant; it is, however, especially so in a spot so desolate and lonely: and this suspicion became so strong in the mind of Captain Barton, that he abruptly turned about to confront his pursuers, but, though there was quite sufficient moonlight to disclose any object upon the road he had traversed, no form of any kind was visible.

The steps he had heard could not have been the reverberation of his own, for he stamped his foot upon the ground, and walked briskly up and down, in the vain attempt to wake an echo. Though by no means a fanciful person, he was at last compelled to charge the sounds upon his imagination, and treat them as an illusion. Thus satisfying himself, he resumed his walk, and before he had proceeded a dozen paces, the mysterious footfalls were again audible from behind, and this time, as if with the special design of showing that the sounds were not the responses of an echo, the steps sometimes slackened nearly to a halt, and sometimes hurried for six or eight strides to a run, and again abated to a walk.

Captain Barton, as before, turned suddenly round, and with the same result; no object was visible above the deserted level of the road. He walked back over the same ground, determined that, whatever might have been the cause of the sounds which had so disconcerted him, it should not escape his search; the endeavour, however, was unrewarded. In spite of all his scepticism, he felt something like a superstitious fear stealing fast upon him, and, with these unwonted and uncomfortable sensations, he once more turned and pursued his way. There was no repetition of these haunting sounds, until he had reached the point where he had last stopped to retrace his steps. Here they were resumed, and with sudden starts of running, which threatened to bring the unseen pursuer close up to the alarmed pedestrian. Captain Barton arrested his course as formerly; the unaccountable nature of the occurrence filled him with vague and almost horrible sensations, and, yielding to the excitement he felt gaining upon him, he shouted, sternly, 'Who goes there?'

The sound of one's own voice, thus exerted, in utter solitude, and followed by total silence, has in it something unpleasantly exciting, and he felt a degree of nervousness which, perhaps, from no cause had he ever known before. To the very end of this solitary street the steps pursued him, and it required a strong effort of stubborn pride on his part to resist the impulse that prompted him every moment to run for safety at the top of his speed. It was not until he had reached his lodging, and sat by his own fireside, that he felt sufficiently reassured to arrange and reconsider in his own mind the occurrences which had so discomposed him: so little a matter, after all, is sufficient to upset the pride of scepticism, and vindicate the old simple laws of nature within us.

Mr Barton was next morning sitting at a late breakfast, reflecting upon the incidents of the previous night, with more of inquisitiveness than awe – so speedily do gloomy impressions upon the fancy disappear under the cheerful influences of day – when a letter just delivered by the postman was placed upon the table before him. There was nothing remarkable in the address of this missive, except that it was written in a hand which he did not know – perhaps it was disguised – for the tall narrow characters were sloped backward; and with the self-inflicted suspense which we so often see practised in such cases, he puzzled over the inscription for a full minute before he broke the seal. When he did so, he read the following words, written in the same hand:

> Mr Barton, late captain of the *Dolphin*, is warned of *danger*. He will do wisely to avoid – Street – (here the locality of his last night's adventure was named) – if he walks there as usual, he will meet with something bad. Let him take warning, once for all, for he has good reason to dread – THE WATCHER.

Captain Barton read and re-read this strange effusion; in every light and in every direction he turned it over and over. He examined the paper on which it was written, and closely scrutinised the handwriting. Defeated here, he turned to the seal; it was nothing but a patch of wax, upon which the accidental impression of a coarse thumb was imperfectly visible. There was not the slightest mark, no clue or indication of any kind, to lead him to even a guess as to its possible origin. The writers object seemed a friendly one, and yet he subscribed himself as one whom he had 'good reason to dread'. Altogether, the letter, its author, and its real purpose, were to him an inexplicable puzzle, and one, moreover, unpleasantly suggestive, in his mind, of associations connected with the last night's adventure.

In obedience to some feeling – perhaps of pride – Mr Barton did not communicate, even to his intended bride, the occurrences which we have just detailed. Trifling as they might appear, they had in reality most disagreeably affected his imagination, and he cared not to disclose, even to the young lady in question, what she might possibly look upon as evidences of weakness. The letter might very well be but a hoax, and the mysterious footfall but a delusion of his fancy. But although he affected to treat the whole affair as unworthy of a thought, it yet haunted him pertinaciously, tormenting him with perplexing doubts, and depressing him with undefined apprehensions. Certain it is, that for a considerable time afterwards he carefully avoided the street indicated in the letter as the scene of danger.

It was not until about a week after the receipt of the letter which I have transcribed, that anything further occurred to remind Captain Barton of its contents, or to counteract the gradual disappearance from his mind of the disagreeable impressions which he had then received. He was returning one night, after the interval I have stated, from the theatre, which was then situated in Crow Street, and having there handed Miss Montague and Lady Rochdale into their carriage, he loitered for some time with two or three acquaintances. With these, however, he parted close to the College, and pursued his way alone. It was now about one o'clock, and the streets were quite deserted. During the whole of his walk with the companions from whom he had just parted, he had been at times painfully aware of the sound of steps, as it seemed, dogging them on their way. Once or twice he had looked back, in the uneasy anticipation that he was again about to experience the same mysterious annoyances which had so much disconcerted him a week before, and earnestly hoping that he might *see* some form from whom the sounds might naturally proceed. But the street was deserted; no form was visible. Proceeding now quite alone upon his homeward way, he grew really nervous and uncomfortable, as he became sensible, with increased distinctness, of the well-known and now absolutely dreaded sounds.

By the side of the dead wall which bounded the College Park, the sounds followed, recommencing almost simultaneously with his own steps. The same unequal pace, sometimes slow, sometimes, for a score yards or so, quickened to a run, was audible from behind him. Again and again he turned, quickly and stealthily he glanced over his shoulder almost at every half-dozen steps; but no one was visible. The horrors of this intangible and unseen persecution became gradually all but intolerable; and when at last he reached his home his nerves were strung to such a pitch of excitement that he could not rest, and did not attempt even to lie down until after the daylight had broken.

He was awakened by a knock at his chamber-door, and his servant entering, handed him several letters which had just been received by the early post. One among them instantly arrested his attention; a single glance at the direction aroused him thoroughly. He at once recognised its character, and read as follows:

> You may as well think, Captain Barton, to escape from your own shadow as from me; do what you may, I will see you as often as I please, and you shall see me, for I do not want to hide myself, as you fancy. Do not let it trouble your rest, Captain Barton; for, with a *good conscience*, what need you fear from the eye of – THE WATCHER?

It is scarcely necessary to dwell upon the feelings elicited by a perusal of this strange communication. Captain Barton was observed to be unusually absent and out of spirits for several days afterwards; but no one divined the cause. Whatever he might think as to the phantom steps which followed him, there could be no possible illusion about the letters he had received; and, to say the least of it, their immediate sequence upon the mysterious sounds which had haunted him was an odd coincidence. The whole circumstance, in his own mind, was vaguely and instinctively connected with certain passages in his past life, which, of all others, he hated to remember.

It so happened that just about this time, in addition to his approaching nuptials, Captain Barton had fortunately, perhaps, for himself, some business of an engrossing kind connected with the adjustment of a large and long-litigated claim upon certain properties. The hurry and excitement of business had its natural effect in gradually dispelling the marked gloom which had for a time occasionally oppressed him, and in a little while his spirits had entirely resumed their accustomed tone.

During all this period, however, he was occasionally dismayed by indistinct and half-heard repetitions of the same annoyance, and that in lonely places, in the day time as well as after nightfall. These renewals of the strange impressions from which he had suffered so much were, however, desultory and faint, insomuch that often he really could not, to his own satisfaction, distinguish between them and the mere suggestions of an excited imagination. One evening he walked down to the House of Commons with a Mr Norcott, a Member. As they walked down together he was observed to become absent and silent, and to a degree so marked as scarcely to consist with good breeding; and this, in one who was obviously in all his habits so perfectly a gentleman, seemed to argue the pressure of some urgent and absorbing anxiety. It was afterwards known that, during the whole of that walk, he had heard the well-known footsteps dogging him as he proceeded. This, however, was the last time he suffered from this phase of the persecution of which he was already the anxious victim. A new and a very different one was about to be presented.

Of the new series of impressions which were afterwards gradually to work out his destiny, that evening disclosed the first; and but for its relation to the train of events which followed, the incident would scarcely have been remembered by anyone. As they were walking in at the passage, a man (of whom his friend could afterwards remember only that he was short in stature, looked like a foreigner, and wore a kind of travelling-cap) walked very rapidly, and, as if under some fierce excitement, directly towards them, muttering to himself fast and vehemently the while. This odd-looking person proceeded straight toward Barton, who was foremost, and halted, regarding him for a moment or two with a look of menace and fury almost maniacal; and then turning about as abruptly, he walked before them at the same agitated pace, and disappeared by a side passage. Norcott distinctly remembered being a good deal shocked at the countenance and bearing of this man, which indeed irresistibly impressed him with an undefined sense of danger, such as he never felt before or since from the presence of anything human; but these sensations were far from amounting to anything so disconcerting as to flurry or excite him – he had seen only a singularly evil countenance, agitated, as it seemed, with the excitement of madness. He was absolutely astonished, however, at the effect of this apparition upon Captain Barton. He knew him to be a man of proved courage and coolness in real danger, a circumstance which made his conduct upon this occasion the more conspicuously odd. He recoiled a step or two as the stranger advanced, and clutched his companions arm in silence, with a spasm of agony or terror; and then, as the figure disappeared, shoving him roughly back, he followed it for a few paces, stopped in great disorder, and sat down upon a form. A countenance more ghastly and haggard it was impossible to fancy.

'For God's sake, Barton, what is the matter?' said Norcott, really alarmed at his friend's appearance. 'You're not hurt, are you? nor unwell? What is it?'

'What did he say? I did not hear it. What was it?' asked Barton, wholly disregarding the question.

'Tut, tut, nonsense!' said Norcott, greatly surprised; 'who cares what the fellow said? You are unwell, Barton, decidedly unwell; let me call a coach.'

'Unwell! Yes, no, not exactly unwell,' he said, evidently making an effort to recover his self-possession; 'but, to say the truth, I am fatigued, a little overworked, and perhaps over anxious. You know I have been in Chancery, and the winding up of a suit is always a nervous affair. I have felt uncomfortable all this evening; but I am better now. Come, come, shall we go on?'

'No, no. Take my advice, Barton, and go home; you really do need rest; you are looking absolutely ill. I really do insist on your allowing me to see you home,' replied his companion.

It was obvious that Barton was not himself disinclined to be persuaded. He accordingly took his leave, politely declining his friend's offered escort. Notwithstanding the few commonplace regrets which Norcott had expressed, it was plain that he was just as little deceived as Barton himself by the extempore plea of illness with which he had accounted for the strange exhibition, and that he even then suspected some lurking mystery in the matter.

Norcott called next day at Bartons lodgings, to enquire for him, and learned from the servant that he had not left his room since his return the night before; but that he was not seriously indisposed, and hoped to be out again in a few days. That evening he sent for Dr Richards, then in large and fashionable practice in Dublin, and their interview was, it is said, an odd one.

He entered into a detail of his own symptoms in an abstracted and desultory kind of way, which seemed to argue a strange want of interest in his own cure, and, at all events, made it manifest that there was some topic engaging his mind of more engrossing importance than his present ailment. He complained of occasional palpitations, and headache. Dr Richards asked him, among other questions, whether there was any irritating circumstance or anxiety to account for it. This he denied quickly and peevishly; and the physician thereupon declared his opinion, that there was nothing amiss except some slight derangement of the digestion, for which he accordingly wrote a prescription, and was about to withdraw, when Mr Barton, with the air of a man who suddenly recollects a topic which had nearly escaped him, recalled him.

'I beg your pardon, doctor, but I had really almost forgot; will you permit me to ask you two or three medical questions? – rather odd ones, perhaps, but as a wager depends upon their solution, you will, I hope, excuse my unreasonableness.'

The physician readily undertook to satisfy the enquirer.

Barton seemed to have some difficulty about opening the proposed interrogatories, for he was silent for a minute, then walked to his bookcase and returned as he had gone; at last he sat down, and said: 'You'll think them very childish questions, but I can't recover my wager without a decision; so I must put them. I want to know first about lockjaw. If a man actually has had that complaint, and appears to have died of it – so that in fact a physician of average skill pronounces him actually dead – may he, after all, recover?'

Dr Richards smiled, and shook his head.

'But – but a blunder may be made,' resumed Barton. 'Suppose an ignorant pretender to medical skill; may *he* be so deceived by any stage of the complaint, as to mistake what is only a part of the progress of the disease, for death itself?'

'No one who had ever seen death,' answered he, 'could mistake it in the case of lockjaw.'

Barton mused for a few minutes. 'I am going to ask you a question, perhaps still more childish; but first tell me, are not the regulations of foreign hospitals, such as those of, let us say, Lisbon, very lax and bungling? May not all kinds of blunders and slips occur in their entries of names, and so forth?'

Dr Richards professed his inability to answer that query.

'Well, then, doctor, here is the last of my questions. You will probably laugh at it; but it must out nevertheless. Is there any disease, in all the range of human maladies, which would have the effect of perceptibly contracting the stature, and the whole frame – causing the man to shrink in all his proportions, and yet to preserve his exact resemblance to himself in every particular – with the one exception, his height and bulk; *any* disease, mark, no matter how rare, how little believed in, generally, which could possibly result in producing such an effect?'

The physician replied with a smile, and a very decided negative.

'Tell me, then,' said Barton, abruptly, 'if a man be in reasonable fear of assault from a lunatic who is at large, can he not procure a warrant for his arrest and detention?'

'Really, that is more a lawyer's question than one in my way,' replied Dr Richards; 'but I believe, on applying to a magistrate, such a course would be directed.'

The physician then took his leave; but, just as he reached the hall-door, remembered that he had left his cane upstairs, and returned. His reappearance was awkward, for a piece of paper, which he recognised as his own prescription, was slowly burning upon the fire, and Barton sitting close by with an expression of settled gloom and dismay. Dr Richards had too much tact to appear to observe what presented itself; but he had seen quite enough to assure him that the mind, and not the body, of Captain Barton was in reality the seat of his sufferings.

A few days afterwards, the following advertisement appeared in the Dublin newspapers:

> If Sylvester Yelland, formerly a foremast man on board his Majesty's frigate *Dolphin*, or his nearest of kin, will apply to Mr Robery Smith, solicitor, at his office, Dame Street, he or they may hear of something greatly to his or their advantage. Admission may be had at any hour up to twelve o'clock at night for the next fortnight, should parties desire to avoid observation; and the strictest secrecy, as to all communications intended to be confidential, shall be honourably observed.

The *Dolphin*, as we have mentioned, was the vessel which Captain Barton had commanded; and this circumstance, connected with the extraordinary exertions made by the circulation of handbills, etc., as well as by repeated advertisements, to secure for this strange notice the utmost possible publicity, suggested to Dr Richards the idea that Captain Barton's extreme uneasiness was somehow connected with the individual to whom the advertisement was addressed, and he himself the author of it. This, however, it is needless to add, was no more than a conjecture. No information whatsoever, as to the real purpose of the advertisement itself, was divulged by the agent, nor yet any hint as to who his employer might be.

Mr Barton, although he had latterly begun to earn for himself the character of a hypochondriac, was yet very far from deserving it.

Though by no means lively, he had yet, naturally, what are termed 'even spirits,' and was not subject to continual depressions. He soon, therefore, began to return to his former habits; and one of the earliest symptoms of this healthier tone of spirits was his appearing at a grand dinner of the Freemasons, of which worthy fraternity he was himself a brother. Barton, who had been at first gloomy and abstracted, drank much more freely than was his wont – possibly with the purpose of dispelling his own secret anxieties – and under the influence of good wine, and pleasant company, became gradually (unlike his usual self) talkative, and even noisy. It was under this unwonted excitement that he left his company at about half-past ten o'clock; and as conviviality is a strong incentive to gallantry, it occurred to him to proceed forthwith to Lady Rochdale's, and pass the remainder of the evening with her and his destined bride.

Accordingly, he was soon at — Street, and chatting gaily with the ladies. It is not to be supposed that Captain Barton had exceeded the limits which propriety prescribes to good fellowship; he had merely taken enough of wine to raise his spirits, without, however, in the least degree unsteadying his mind, or affecting his manners. With this undue elevation of spirits had supervened an entire oblivion or contempt of those undefined apprehensions which had for so long weighed upon his mind, and to a certain extent estranged him from society; but as the night wore away, and his artificial gaiety began to flag, these painful feelings gradually intruded themselves again, and he grew abstracted and anxious as heretofore. He took his leave at length, with an unpleasant foreboding of some coming mischief, and with a mind haunted with a thousand mysterious apprehensions, such as, even while he acutely felt their pressure, he, nevertheless, inwardly strove, or affected to contemn.

It was his proud defiance of what he considered to be his own weakness which prompted him upon this occasion to the course which brought about the adventure which we are now about to relate. Mr Barton might have easily called a coach, but he was conscious that his strong inclination to do so proceeded from no cause other than what he desperately persisted in representing to himself to be his own superstitious tremors. He might also have returned home by a rout different from that against which he had been warned by his mysterious correspondent; but for the same reason he dismissed this idea also, and with a dogged and half desperate resolution to force matters to a crisis of some kind, to see if there were any reality in the causes of his former suffering, and if not, satisfactorily to bring their delusiveness to the proof, he determined to follow precisely the course which he had trodden upon the night so painfully memorable in his own mind as that on which his strange persecution had commenced. Though, sooth to say, the pilot who for the first time steers his vessel under the muzzles of a hostile battery never felt his resolution more severely tasked than did Captain Barton, as he breathlessly pursued this solitary path; a path which, in spite of every effort of scepticism and reason, he felt to be, as respected *him*, infested by a malignant influence.

He pursued his way steadily and rapidly, scarcely breathing from intensity of suspense; he, however, was troubled by no renewal of the dreaded footsteps, and was beginning to feel a return of confidence, as, more than three-fourths of the way being accomplished with impunity, he approached the long line of twinkling oil lamps which indicated the frequented streets. This feeling of self-congratulation was, however, but momentary. The report of a musket at some two hundred yards behind him, and the whistle of a bullet close to his head, disagreeably and startlingly dispelled it. His first impulse was to retrace his steps in pursuit of the assassin; but the road on either side was, as we have said, embarrassed by the foundations of a street, beyond which extended waste fields, full of rubbish and neglected lime and brick kilns, and all now as utterly silent as though no sound had ever disturbed their dark and unsightly solitude. The futility of attempting, single-handed, under such circumstances, a search for the murderer, was apparent, especially as no further sound whatever was audible to direct his pursuit.

With the tumultuous sensations of one whose life had just been exposed to a murderous attempt, and whose escape has been the narrowest possible, Captain Barton turned, and without, however, quickening his pace actually to a run, hurriedly pursued his way. He had turned, as we have said, after a pause of a few seconds, and had just commenced his rapid retreat, when on a sudden he met the well-remembered little man in the fur cap. The encounter was but momentary. The figure was walking at the same exaggerated pace, and with the same strange air of menace as before; and as it passed him, he thought he heard it say, in a furious whisper, 'Still alive, still alive!'

The state of Mr Barton's spirits began now to work a corresponding alteration in his health and looks, and to such a degree that it was impossible that the change should escape general remark. For some reasons, known but to himself, he took no step whatsoever to bring the attempt upon his life, which he had so narrowly escaped,under the notice of the authorities; on the contrary, he kept it jealously to himself; and itwas not for many weeks after the occurrence that he mentioned it, and then in strict confidence to a gentleman, the torments of his mind having at last compelled him to consult a friend.

Spite of his blue devils, however, poor Barton, having no satis-factory reason to render to the public for any undue remissness in the attentions which his relation to Miss Montague required, was obliged to exert himself, and present to the world a confident and cheerful bearing. The true source of his sufferings, and every circum-stance connected with them, he guarded with a reserve so jealous, that it seemed dictated by at least a suspicion that the origin of his strange persecution was known to himself, and that it was of a nature which, upon his own account, he could not or dare not disclose.

The mind thus turned in upon itself, and constantly occupied with a haunting anxiety which it dared not reveal, or confide to any human breast, became daily more excited; and, of course, more vividly impressible, by a system of attack which operated through the nervous system; and in this state he was destined to sustain, with increasing frequency, the stealthy visitations of that apparition, which from the first had seemed to possess so unearthly and terrible a hold upon his imagination.

*   *   *

It was about this time that Captain Barton called upon the then celebrated preacher, Dr Macklin, with whom he had a slight acquaint-ance; and an extraordinary conversation ensued. The divine was seated in his chambers in college, surrounded with works upon his favourite pursuit and deep in theology, when Barton was announced. There was something at once embarrassed and excited in his manner, which, along with his wan and haggard countenance, impressed the student with the unpleasant consciousness that his visitor must have recently suffered terribly indeed to account for an alteration so striking, so shocking.

After the usual interchange of polite greeting, and a few common-place remarks, Captain Barton, who obviously perceived the surprise which his visit had excited, and which Dr Macklin was unable wholly to conceal, interrupted a brief pause by remarking – 'This is a strange call, Dr Macklin, perhaps scarcely warranted by an acquaintance so slight as mine with you. I should not, under ordinary circumstances, have ventured to disturb you, but my visit is neither an idle nor impertinent intrusion. I am sure you will not so account it, when – '

Dr Macklin interrupted him with assurances, such as good breeding suggested, and Barton resumed: 'I am come to task your patience by asking your advice. When I say your patience, I might, indeed, say more; I might have said your humanity, your compassion; for I have been, and am a great sufferer.'

'My dear sir,' replied the churchman, 'it will, indeed, afford me infinite gratification if I can give you comfort in any distress of mind, but – but – '

'I know what you would say,' resumed Barton, quickly. 'I am an unbeliever, and, therefore, incapable of deriving help from religion, but don't take that for granted. At least you must not assume that, however unsettled my convictions may be, I do not feel a deep, a very deep, interest in the subject. Circumstances have lately forced it upon my attention in such a way as to compel me to review the whole question in a more candid and teachable spirit, I believe, than I ever studied it in before.'

'Your difficulties, I take it for granted, refer to the evidences of revelation,' suggested the clergyman.

'Why – no – yes; in fact I am ashamed to say I have not considered even my objections sufficiently to state them connectedly but – but there is one subject on which I feel a peculiar interest.'

He paused again, and Dr Macklin pressed him to proceed.

'The fact is,' said Barton, 'whatever may be my uncertainty as to the authenticity of what we are taught to call revelation, of one fact I am deeply and horribly convinced: that there does exist beyond this a spiritual world – a system whose workings are generally in mercy hidden from us – a system which may be, and which is sometimes, partially and terribly revealed. I am sure, I know,' continued Barton, with increasing excitement, 'there is a God – a dreadful God – and that retribution follows guilt. In ways, the most mysterious and stupendous; by agencies, the most inexplicable and terrific; there is a spiritual system – great Heavens, how frightfully I have been convinced – a system malignant, and inexorable, and omnipotent, under whose persecutions I am, and have been, suffering the torments of the damned! – yes, sir – yes – the fires and frenzy of hell'

As Barton continued, his agitation became so vehement that the divine was shocked and even alarmed. The wild and excited rapidity with which he spoke, and, above all, the indefinable horror which stamped his features, afforded a contrast to his ordinary cool and unimpassioned self-possession, striking and painful in the last degree.

'My dear sir,' said Dr Macklin, after a brief pause, 'I fear you have been suffering much, indeed; but I venture to predict that the depression under which you labour will be found to originate in purely physical causes, and that with a change of air and the aid of a few tonics, your spirits will return, and the tone of your mind be once more cheerful and tranquil as heretofore. There was, after all, more truth than we are quite willing to admit in the classic theories which assigned the undue predominance of any one affection of the mind to the undue action or torpidity of one or other of our bodily organs. Believe me, that a little attention to diet, exercise, and the other essentials of health, under competent direction, will make you as much yourself as you can wish.'

'Dr Macklin,' said Barton, with something like a shudder, 'I *cannot* delude myself with such a hope. I have no hope to cling to but one, and that is, that by some other spiritual agency more potent than that which tortures me, *it* may be combated, and I delivered. If this may not be, I am lost – now and for ever lost.'

'But, Mr Barton, you must remember,' urged his companion, 'that others have suffered as you have done, and – '

'No, no, no,' interrupted he with irritability; 'no, sir, I am not a credulous – far from a superstitious man. I have been, perhaps, too much the reverse – too sceptical, too slow of belief; but unless I were one whom no amount of evidence could convince, unless I were to condemn the repeated, the *perpetual* evidence of my own senses, I am now – now at last constrained to believe I have no escape from the conviction, the overwhelming certainty, that I am haunted and dogged, go where I may, by – by a Demon.'

There was an almost preternatural energy of horror in Barton's face, as, with its damp and deathlike lineaments turned towards his companion, he thus delivered himself.

'God help you, my poor friend' said Dr Macklin, much shocked. 'God help you for, indeed, you *are* a sufferer, however your sufferings may have been caused.'

'Ay, ay, God help me,' echoed Barton sternly; 'but *will* He help me? will He help me?'

'Pray to Him; pray in an humble and trusting spirit,' said he.

'Pray, pray,' echoed he again; 'I can't pray; I could as easily move a mountain by an effort of my will. I have not belief enough to pray; there is something within me that will not pray. You prescribe impossibilities – literal impossibilities.'

'You will not find it so, if you will but try,' said Dr Macklin.

'Try! I *have* tried, and the attempt only fills me with confusion and terror. I have tried in vain, and more than in vain. The awful, unutterable idea of eternity and infinity oppresses and maddens my brain, whenever my mind approaches the contemplation of the Creator I recoil from the effort, scared, confounded, terrified. I tell you, Dr Macklin, if I am to be saved, it must be by other means. The idea of the Creator is to me intolerable; my mind cannot support it.'

'Say, then, my dear sir,' urged he, 'say how you would have me serve you. What you would learn of me. What can I do or say to relieve you?'

'Listen to me first,' replied Captain Barton, with a subdued air, and an evident effort to suppress his excitement; 'listen to me while I detail the circumstances of the terrible persecution under which my life has become all but intolerable – a persecution which has made me fear *death* and the world beyond the grave as much as I have grown to hate existence.'

Barton then proceeded to relate the circumstances which we have already detailed, and then continued: 'This has now become habitual – an accustomed thing. I do not mean the actual seeing him in the flesh; thank God, *that* at least is not permitted daily Thank God, from the unutterable horrors of that visitation I have been mercifully allowed intervals of repose, though none of security; but from the consciousness that a malignant spirit is following and watching me wherever I go, I have never, for a single instant, a temporary respite: I am pursued with blasphemies, cries of despair, and appalling hatred; I hear those dreadful sounds called after me as I turn the corners of streets; they come in the night-time while I sit in my chamber alone; they haunt me everywhere, charging me with hideous crimes, and – great God – threatening me with coming vengeance and eternal misery! Hush do you hear *that?*' he cried, with a horrible smile of triumph. 'There – there, will that convince you?'

The clergyman felt the chillness of horror irresistibly steal over him, while, during the wail of a sudden gust of wind, he heard, or fancied he heard, the half articulate sounds of rage and derision mingling in their sough.

'Well, what do you think of *that?*' at length Barton cried, drawing a long breath through his teeth

'I hear the wind,' said Dr Macklin; 'what should I think of it? What is there remarkable about it?'

'The prince of the powers of the air,' muttered Barton, with a shudder.

'Tut, tut my dear sir!' said the student, with an effort to reassure himself; for though it was broad daylight, there was nevertheless something disagreeably contagious in the nervous excitement under which his visitor so obviously suffered 'You must not give way to those wild fancies: you must resist those impulses of the imagination.'

'Ay, ay; "resist the devil, and he will flee from thee," ' said Barton, in the same tone; 'but *how* resist him? Ay, there it is: there is the rub. What – *what* am I to do? What *can* I do?'

'My dear sir, this is fancy,' said the man of folios 'you are your own tormentor.'

'No, no, sir; fancy has no part in it,' answered Barton, somewhat sternly. 'Fancy, forsooth! Was it that made *you*, as well as me, hear, but this moment, those appalling accents of hell? Fancy, indeed! No, no.'

'But you have seen this person frequently,' said the ecclesiastic; 'why have you not accosted or secured him? Is it not somewhat precipitate, to say no more, to assume, as you have done, the existence of preternatural agency, when, after all, everything may be easily accountable, if only proper means were taken to sift the matter.'

'There are circumstances connected with this – this *appearance*,' said Barton, 'which it were needless to disclose, but which to *me* are proofs of its horrible and unearthly nature. I know that the being who haunts me is not *man*. I say I *know* this; I could prove it to your own conviction.' He paused for a minute, and then added, 'And as to accosting it, I dare not – I could not. When I see it I am powerless; I stand in the gaze of death, in the triumphant presence of preter-human power and malignity; my strength, and faculties, and memory all forsake me. Oh, God! I fear, sir, you know not what you speak of. Mercy, mercy heaven have pity on me.'

He leaned his elbow on the table, and passed his hand across his eyes, as if to exclude some image of horror, muttering the last words of the sentence he had just concluded, again and again.

'Dr Macklin,' he said, abruptly raising himself, and looking full upon the clergyman with an imploring eye, 'I know you will do for me whatever may be done. You know now fully the circumstances and the nature of the mysterious agency of which I am the victim. I tell you I cannot help myself; I cannot hope to escape; I am utterly passive. I conjure you, then, to weigh my case well, and if anything may be done for me by vicarious supplication, by the intercession of the good, or by any aid or influence whatsoever, I implore of you, I adjure you in the name of the Most High, give me the benefit of that influence, deliver me from the body of this death! Strive for me; pity me! I know you will; you cannot refuse this; it is the purpose and object of my visit. Send me away with some hope, however little – some faint hope of ultimate deliverance, and I will nerve myself to endure, from hour to hour, the hideous dream into which my existence is transformed.'

Dr Macklin assured him that all he could do was to pray earnestly for him, and that so much he would not fail to do. They parted with a hurried and melancholy valediction. Barton hastened to the carriage which awaited him at the door, drew the blinds, and drove away, while Dr Macklin returned to his chamber, to ruminate at leisure upon the strange interview which had just interrupted his studies.

It was not to be expected that Captain Barton's changed and eccentric habits should long escape remark and discussion. Various were the theories suggested to account for it. Some attributed the alteration to the pressure of secret pecuniary embarrassments; others to a repugnance to fulfil an engagement into which he was presumed to have too precipitately entered; and others, again, to the supposed incipiency of mental disease, which latter, indeed, was the most plausible, as well as the most generally received, of the hypotheses circulated in the gossip of the day.

From the very commencement of this change, at first so gradual in its advances, Miss Montague had, of course, been aware of it. The intimacy involved in their peculiar relation, as well as the near interest which it inspired, afforded, in her case, alike opportunity and motive for the successful exercise of that keen and penetrating observation peculiar to the sex. His visits became, at length, so interrupted, and his manner, while they lasted, so abstracted, strange, and agitated, that Lady Rochdale, after hinting her anxiety and her suspicions more than once, at length distinctly stated her anxiety, and pressed for an explanation. The explanation was given, and although its nature at first relieved the worst solicitudes of the old lady and her niece, yet the circumstances which attended it, and the really dreadful consequences which it obviously threatened as regarded the spirits, and, indeed, the reason, of the now wretched man who made the strange declaration, were enough, upon a little reflection, to fill their minds with perturbation and alarm.

General Montague, the young lady's father, at length arrived. He had himself slightly known Barton, some ten or twelve years previously, and being aware of his fortune and connections, was disposed to regard him as an unexceptionable and indeed a most desirable match for his daughter. He laughed at the story of Barton's supernatural visitations, and lost not a moment in calling upon his intended son-in-law.

'My dear Barton,' he continued gaily, after a little conversation, 'my sister tells me that you are a victim to blue devils in quite a new and original shape.'

Barton changed countenance, and sighed profoundly.

'Come, come; I protest this will never do,' continued the general; 'you are more like a man on his way to the gallows than to the altar. These devils have made quite a saint of you.'

Barton made an effort to change the conversation.

'No, no, it won't do,' said his visitor, laughing; 'I am resolved to say out what I have to say about this magnificent mock mystery of yours. Come, you must not be angry; but, really, it is too bad to see you, at your time of life, absolutely frightened into good behaviour, like a naughty child, by a bugaboo, and, as far as I can learn, a very particularly contemptible one. Seriously, though, my dear Barton, I have been a good deal annoyed at what they tell me; but, at the same time, thoroughly convinced that there is nothing in the matter that may not be cleared up, with just a little attention and management, within a week at furthest.'

'Ah, general, you do not know – ' he began.

'Yes, but I do know quite enough to warrant my confidence,' interrupted the soldier. 'I know that all your annoyance proceeds from the occasional appearance of a certain little man in a cap and a greatcoat, with a red vest and bad countenance, who follows you about, and pops upon you at the corners of lanes, and throws you into ague fits. Now, my dear fellow, I'll make it my business to *catch* this mischievous little mountebank, and either beat him into a jelly with my own hands, or have him whipped through the town at the cart's tail.'

'If *you* knew what I know,' said Barton, with gloomy agitation, 'you would speak very differently. Don't imagine that I am so weak and foolish as to assume, without proof the most overwhelming, the conclusion to which I have been forced. The proofs are here, locked up here.' As he spoke, he tapped upon his breast, and with an anxious sigh continued to walk up and down the room.

'Well, well, Barton,' said his visitor, 'I'll wager a rump and a dozen I collar the ghost, and convince yourself before many days are over.'

He was running on in the same strain when he was suddenly arrested, and not a little shocked, by observing Barton, who had approached the window, stagger slowly back, like one who had received a stunning blow – his arm feebly extended towards the street, his face and his very lips white as ashes – while he uttered, 'There – there – there!'

General Montague started mechanically to his feet, and, from the window of the drawing-room, saw a figure corresponding, as well as his hurry would permit him to discern, with the description of the person whose appearance so constantly and dreadfully disturbed the repose of his friend. The figure was just turning from the rails of the area upon which it had been leaning, and without waiting to see more, the old gentleman snatched his cane and hat, and rushed down the stairs and into the street, in the furious hope of securing the person, and punishing the audacity of the mysterious stranger. He looked around him, but in vain, for any trace of the form he had himself distinctly beheld. He ran breathlessly to the nearest corner, expecting to see from thence the retreating figure, but no such form was visible. Back and forward, from crossing to crossing, he ran at fault, and it was not until the curious gaze and laughing countenances of the passers-by reminded him of the absurdity of his pursuit, that he checked his hurried pace, lowered his walking-cane from the menacing altitude which he had mechanically given it, adjusted his hat, and walked composedly back again, inwardly vexed and flurried. He found Barton pale and trembling in every joint; they both remained silent, though under emotions very different. At last Barton whispered, 'You saw it?'

'It! – him – someone – you mean – to be sure I did,' replied Montague, testily. 'But where is the good or the harm of seeing him? The fellow runs like a lamplighter. I wanted to *catch* him, but he had stolen away before I could reach the hall door. However, it is no great matter; next time, I dare say, I'll do better; and, egad, if I once come within reach of him. I'll introduce his shoulders to the weight of my cane, in a way to make him cry *peccavi*.'

Notwithstanding General Montague's undertakings and exhortations, however, Barton continued to suffer from the selfsame unexplained cause. Go how, when, or where he would. He was still constantly dogged or confronted by the hateful being who had established over him so dreadful and mysterious an influence; nowhere, and at no time, was he secure against the odious appearance which haunted him with such diabolical perseverance. His depression, misery, and excitement became more settled and alarming every day, and the mental agonies that ceaselessly preyed upon him began at last so sensibly to affect his general health, that Lady Rochdale and General Montague succeeded (without, indeed, much difficulty) in persuading him to try a short tour on the Continent, in the hope that an entire change of scene would, at all events, have the effect of breaking through the influences of local association, which the more sceptical of his friends assumed to be by no means inoperative in suggesting and perpetuating what they conceived to be a mere form of nervous illusion. General Montague, moreover, was persuaded that the figure which haunted his intended son-in-law was by no means the creation of his own imagination, but, on the contrary, a substantial form of flesh and blood, animated by a spiteful and obstinate resolution, perhaps with some murderous object in perspective, to watch and follow the unfortunate gentleman. Even this hypothesis was not a very pleasant one; yet it was plain that if Barton could once be convinced that there was nothing preternatural in the phenomenon, which he had hitherto regarded in that light, the affair would lose all its terrors in his eyes, and wholly cease to exercise upon his health and spirits the baneful influence which it had hitherto done. He therefore reasoned, that if the annoyance were actually escaped from by mere change of scene, it obviously could not have originated in any supernatural agency.

Yielding to their persuasions, Barton left Dublin for England, accompanied by General Montague. They posted rapidly to London, and thence to Dover, whence they took the packet with a fair wind for Calais. The general's confidence in the result of the expedition on Barton's spirits had risen day by day since their departure from the shores of Ireland; for, to the inexpressible relief and delight of the latter, he had not, since then, so much as even once fancied a repetition of those impressions which had, when at home, drawn him gradually down to the very abyss of horror and despair. This exemption from what he had begun to regard as the inevitable condition of his existence, and the sense of security which began to pervade his mind, were inexpressibly delightful; and in the exultation of what he considered his deliverance, he indulged in a thousand happy anticipations for a future into which so lately he had hardly dared to look. In short, both he and his companion secretly congratulated themselves upon the termination of that persecution which had been to its immediate victim a source of such unspeakable agony.

It was a beautiful day, and a crowd of idlers stood upon the jetty to receive the packet, and enjoy the bustle of the new arrivals. Montague walked a few paces in advance of his friend, and as he made his way through the crowd, a little man touched his arm, and said to him, in a broad provincial *patois*: 'Monsieur is walking too fast; he will lose his sick comrade in the throng, for, by my faith, the poor gentleman seems to be fainting.'

Montague turned quickly, and observed that Barton did indeed look deadly pale. He hastened to his side.

'My poor fellow, are you ill?' he asked anxiously.

The question was unheeded, and twice repeated, ere Barton stammered: 'I saw him – by —, I saw him!'

'*Him*! – who? – where? – when did you see him? – where is he?' cried Montague, looking around him.

'I saw him – but he is gone,' repeated Barton, faintly.

'But where – where? For God's sake, speak,' urged Montague, vehemently.

'It is but this moment – *here*,' said he.

'But what did he look like? – what had he on? – what did he wear? – quick, quick,' urged his excited companion, ready to dart among the crowd, and collar the delinquent on the spot.

'He touched your arm – he spoke to you – he pointed to me. God be merciful to me, there is no escape!' said Barton, in the low, subdued tones of intense despair.

Montague had already bustled away in all the flurry of mingled hope and indignation; but though the singular *personnel* of the stranger who had accosted him was vividly and perfectly impressed upon his recollection, he failed to discover among the crowd even the slightest resemblance to him. After a fruitless search, in which he enlisted the services of several of the bystanders, who aided all the more zealously as they believed he had been robbed, he at length, out of breath and baffled, gave over the attempt.

'Ah, my friend, it won't do,' said Barton, with the faint voice and bewildered, ghastly look of one who had been stunned by some mortal shock; 'there is no use in contending with it; whatever it is, the dreadful association between me and it is now established; I shall never escape – never, never!'

'Nonsense, nonsense, my dear fellow; don't talk so,' said Montague, with something at once of irritation and dismay; 'you must not; never mind, I say – never mind, we'll jockey the scoundrel yet.'

It was, however, but lost labour to endeavour henceforward to inspire Barton with one ray of hope; he became utterly desponding. This intangible and, as it seemed, utterly inadequate influence was fast destroying his energies of intellect, character, and health. His first object was now to return to Ireland, there, as he believed, and now almost hoped, speedily to die.

To Ireland, accordingly, he came, and one of the first faces he saw upon the shore was again that of his implacable and dreaded persecutor. Barton seemed at last to have lost not only all enjoyment and every hope in existence, but all independence of will besides. He now submitted himself passively to the management of the friends most nearly interested in his welfare. With the apathy of entire despair, he implicitly assented to whatever measures they suggested and advised; and, as a last resource, it was determined to remove him to a house of Lady Rochdale's in the neighbourhood of Clontarf, where, with the advice of his medical attendant (who persisted in his opinion that the whole train of impressions resulted merely from some nervous derangement) it was resolved that he was to confine himself strictly to the house, and to make use only of those apart-ments which commanded a view of an enclosed yard, the gates of which were to be kept jealously locked. These precautions would at least secure him against the casual appearance of any living form which his excited imagination might possibly confound with the spectre which, as it was contended, his fancy recognised in every figure that bore even a distant or general resemblance to the traits with which he had at first invested it. A month or six weeks' absolute seclusion under these conditions, it was hoped, might, by interrupting the series of these terrible impressions, gradually dispel the predisposing apprehension, and effectually break up the associations which had confirmed the supposed disease, and rendered recovery hopeless. Cheerful society and that of his friends was to be constantly supplied, and on the whole, very sanguine expectations were indulged in, that under this treatment the obstinate hypochondria of the patient might at length give way.

Accompanied, therefore, by Lady Rochdale, General Montague, and his daughter – his own affianced bride – poor Barton, himself never daring to cherish a hope of his ultimate emancipation from the strange horrors under which his life was literally wasting away, took possession of the apartments whose situation protected him against the dreadful intrusions from which he shrank with such unutterable terror.

After a little time, a steady persistence in this system began to manifest its results in a very marked though gradual improvement alike in the health and spirits of the invalid. Not, indeed, that anything at all approaching to complete recovery was yet discernible. On the contrary, to those who had not seen him since the commencement of his strange sufferings, such an alteration would have been apparent as might well have shocked them. The improvement, however, such as it was, was welcomed with gratitude and delight, especially by the poor young lady, whom her attachment to him, as well as her now singularly painful position, consequent on his mysterious and protracted illness, rendered an object of pity scarcely one degree less to be commiserated than himself.

A week passed – a fortnight – a month – and yet no recurrence of the hated visitation had agitated and terrified him as before. The treatment had, so far, been followed by complete success. The chain of association had been broken. The constant pressure upon the over-tasked spirits had been removed, and, under these comparatively favourable circumstances, the sense of social community with the world about him, and something of human interest, if not of enjoyment, began to reanimate his mind.

It was about this time that Lady Rochdale, who, like most old ladies of the day, was deep in family receipts, and a great pretender to medical science, being engaged in the concoction of certain unpalatable mixtures of marvellous virtue, despatched her own maid to the kitchen garden with a list of herbs which were there to be carefully culled and brought back to her for the purpose stated. The hand-maiden, however, returned with her task scarce half-completed, and a good deal flurried and alarmed. Her mode for accounting for her precipitate retreat and evident agitation was odd, and to the old lady unpleasantly startling.

It appeared that she had repaired to the kitchen garden, pursuant to her mistress's directions, and had there begun to make the specified selection among the rank and neglected herbs which crowded one corner of the enclosure, and while engaged in this pleasant labour she carelessly sang a fragment of an old song, as she said, 'to keep herself company.' She was, however, interrupted by a sort of mocking echo of the air she was singing; and looking up, she saw through the old thorn hedge, which surrounded the garden, a singularly ill-looking, little man, whose countenance wore the stamp of menace and malignity, standing close to her at the other side of the hawthorn screen. She described herself as utterly unable to move or speak, while he charged her with a message for Captain Barton, the substance of which she distinctly remembered to have been to the effect that he, Captain Barton, must come abroad as usual, and show himself to his friends out of doors, or else prepare for a visit in his own chamber. On concluding this brief message, the stranger had, with a threatening air, got down into the outer ditch, and seizing the hawthorn stems in his hands, seemed on the point of climbing through the fence, a feat which might have been accomplished without much difficulty. Without, of course, awaiting this result, the girl, throwing down her treasures of thyme and rosemary, had turned and run, with the swiftness of terror, to the house. Lady Rochdale commanded her, on pain of instant dismissal, to observe an absolute silence respecting all that portion of the incident which related to Captain Barton; and, at the same time, directed instant search to be made by her men in the garden and fields adjacent. This measure, however, was attended with the usual unsuccess, and filled with fearful and indefinable misgivings, Lady Rochdale communicated the incident to her brother. The story, however, until long afterwards, went no further, and of course it was jealously guarded from Barton, who continued to mend, though slowly and imperfectly.

Barton now began to walk occasionally in the courtyard which we have mentioned, and which, being surrounded by a high wall, commanded no view beyond its own extent. Here he, therefore, considered himself perfectly secure; and, but for a careless violation of orders by one of the grooms, he might have enjoyed, at least for some time longer, his much-prized immunity. Opening upon the public road, this yard was entered by a wooden gate, with a wicket in it, which was further defended by an iron gate upon the outside. Strict orders had been given to keep them carefully locked; but, in spite of these, it had happened that one day, as Barton was slowly pacing this narrow enclosure, in his accustomed walk, and reaching the further extremity, was turning to retrace his steps, he saw the boarded wicket ajar, and the face of his tormentor immovably looking at him through the iron bars. For a few seconds he stood riveted to the earth, breathless and bloodless, in the fascination of that dreaded gaze, and then fell helplessly upon the pavement.

There was he found a few minutes afterwards, and conveyed to his room, the apartment which he was never afterwards to leave alive. Henceforward, a marked and unaccountable change was observable in the tone of his mind. Captain Barton was now no longer the excited and despairing man he had been before; a strange alteration had passed upon him, an unearthly tranquillity reigned in his mind; it was the anticipated stillness of the grave.

'Montague, my friend, this struggle is nearly ended now,' he said, tranquilly, but with a look of fixed and fearful awe. 'I have, at last, some comfort from that world of spirits, from which my *punishment* has come. I know now that my sufferings will be soon over.'

Montague pressed him to speak on.

'Yes,' said he, in a softened voice, 'my punishment is nearly ended. From sorrow perhaps I shall never, in time or eternity, escape; but my *agony* is almost over. Comfort has been revealed to me, and what remains of my allotted struggle I will bear with submission, even with hope.'

'I am glad to hear you speak so tranquilly, my dear fellow,' said Montague; 'peace and cheerfulness of mind are all you need to make you what you were.'

'No, no, I never can be that,' said he, mournfully. 'I am no longer fit for life. I am soon to die: I do not shrink from death as I did. I am to see *him* but once again, and then all is ended.'

'He said so, then?' suggested Montague.

'*He*?' No, no; good tidings could scarcely come through him; and these were good and welcome and they came so solemnly and sweetly, with unutterable love and melancholy, such as I could not, without saying more than is needful or fitting, of other long-past scenes and persons, fully explain to you.' As Barton said this he shed tears.

'Come, come,' said Montague, mistaking the source of his emotions, 'you must not give way. What is it, after all, but a pack of dreams and nonsense; or, at worst, the practices of a scheming rascal that enjoys his power of playing upon your nerves, and loves to exert it; a sneaking vagabond that owes you a grudge, and pays it off this way, not daring to try a more manly one.'

'A grudge, indeed, he owes me; you say rightly,' said Barton, with a sullen shudder; 'a grudge as you call it. Oh, God! when the justice of heaven permits the Evil One to carry out a scheme of vengeance, when its execution is committed to the lost and frightful victim of sin, who owes his own ruin to the man, the very man, whom he is commissioned to pursue; then, indeed, the torments and terrors of hell are anticipated on earth. But heaven has dealt mercifully with me: hope has opened to me at last; and if death could come without the dreadful sight I am doomed to see, I would gladly close my eyes this moment upon the world. But though death is welcome, I shrink with an agony you cannot understand; a maddening agony, an actual frenzy of terror, from the last encounter with that – that demon, who has drawn me thus to the verge of the chasm, and who is himself to plunge me down. I am to see him again, once more, but under circumstances unutterably more terrific than ever.'

As Barton thus spoke, he trembled so violently that Montague was really alarmed at the extremity of his sudden agitation, and hastened to lead him back to the topic which had before seemed to exert so tranquillising an effect upon his mind.

'It was not a dream,' he said, after a time; 'I was in a different state, I felt differently and strangely; and yet it was all as real, as clear and vivid, as what I now see and hear; it was a reality.'

'And what *did* you see and hear?' urged his companion.

'When I awakened from the swoon I fell into on seeing *him*,' said Barton, continuing, as if he had not heard the question, 'it was slowly, very slowly; I was reclining by the margin of a broad lake, surrounded by misty hills, and a soft, melancholy, rose-coloured light illuminated it all. It was indescribably sad and lonely, and yet more beautiful than any earthly scene. My head was leaning on the lap of a girl, and she was singing a strange and wondrous song, that told, I known not how, whether by words or harmony, of all my life, all that is past, and all that is still to come. And with the song the old feelings that I thought had perished within me came back, and tears flowed from my eyes, partly for the song and its mysterious beauty, and partly for the unearthly sweetness of her voice; yet I know the voice, oh! how well; and I was spellbound as I listened and looked at the strange and solitary scene, without stirring, almost without breathing, and, alas, alas! alas! without turning my eyes toward the face that I knew was near me, so sweetly powerful was the enchantment that held me. And so, slowly and softly, the song and scene grew fainter, and ever fainter, to my senses, till all was dark and still again. And then I wakened to this world, as you saw, comforted, for I knew that I was forgiven much.' Barton wept again long and bitterly.

From this time, as we have said, the prevailing tone of his mind was one of profound and tranquil melancholy. This, however, was not without its interruptions. He was thoroughly impressed with the conviction that he was to experience another and a final visitation, illimitably transcending in horror all he had before experienced. From this anticipated and unknown agony he often shrunk in such paroxysms of abject terror and distraction, as filled the whole household with dismay and superstitious panic. Even those among them who affected to discredit the supposition of preternatural agency in the matter, were often in their secret souls visited during the darkness and solitude of night with qualms and apprehensions which they would not have readily confessed; and none of them attempted to dissuade Barton from the resolution on which he now systematically acted, of shutting himself up in his own apartment. The window-blinds of this room were kept jealously down; and his own man was seldom out of his presence, day or night, his bed being placed in the same chamber.

This man was an attached and respectable servant; and his duties, in addition to those ordinarily imposed upon *valets*, but which Barton's independent habits generally dispensed with, were to attend carefully to the simple precautions by means of which his master hoped to exclude the dreaded intrusion of the 'Watcher,' as the strange letter he had at first received had designated his persecutor. And, in addition to attending to these arrangements, which consisted merely in anticipating the possibility of his master's being, through any unscreened window or opened door, exposed to the dreaded influence, the valet was never to suffer him to be for one moment alone: total solitude, even for a minute, had become to him now almost as intolerable as the idea of going abroad into the public ways; it was an instinctive anticipation of what was coming.

It is needless to say, that, under these mysterious and horrible circumstances, no steps were taken toward the fulfilment of that engagement into which he had entered. There was quite disparity enough in point of years, and indeed of habits, between the young lady and Captain Barton, to have precluded anything like very vehement or romantic attachment on her part. Though grieved and anxious, therefore, she was very far from being heart-broken; a circumstance which, for the sentimental purposes of our tale, is much to be deplored. But truth must be told, especially in a narrative whose chief, if not only, pretensions to interest consist in a rigid adherence to facts, or what are so reported to have been.

Miss Montague, nevertheless, devoted much of her time to a patient but fruitless attempt to cheer the unhappy invalid. She read for him, and conversed with him; but it was apparent that whatever exertions he made, the endeavour to escape from the one constant and ever-present fear that preyed upon him was utterly and miserably unavailing.

Young ladies, as all the world knows, are much given to the cultivation of pets; and among those who shared the favour of Miss Montague was a fine old owl, which the gardener, who caught him napping among the ivy of a ruined stable, had dutifully presented to that young lady.

The caprice which regulates such preferences was manifested in the extravagant favour with which this grim and ill-favoured bird was at once distinguished by his mistress; and, trifling as this whimsical circumstance may seem, I am forced to mention it, inasmuch as it is connected, oddly enough, with the concluding scene of the story. Barton, so far from sharing in this liking for the new favourite, regarded it from the first with an antipathy as violent as it was utterly unaccountable. Its very vicinity was insupportable to him. He seemed to hate and dread it with a vehemence absolutely laughable, and to those who have never witnessed the exhibition of antipathies of this kind, his dread would seem all but incredible.

With these few words of preliminary explanation, I shall proceed to state the particulars of the last scene in this strange series of incidents. It was almost two o'clock one winter's night, and Barton was, as usual at that hour, in his bed; the servant we have mentioned occupied a smaller bed in the same room, and a candle was burning. The man was on a sudden aroused by his master, who said: 'I can't get it out of my head that that accursed bird has escaped somehow, and is lurking in some corner of the room. I have been dreaming of him. Get up, Smith, and look about; search for him. Such hateful dreams!'

The servant rose, and examined the chamber, and while engaged in so doing, he heard the well-known sound, more like a long-drawn gasp than a hiss, with which these birds from their secret haunts affright the quiet of the night. This ghostly indication of its proximity, for the sound proceeded from the passage upon which Barton's chamber-door opened, determined the search of the servant, who, opening the door, proceeded a step or two forward for the purpose of driving the bird away. He had, however, hardly entered the lobby, when the door behind him slowly swung to under the impulse, as it seemed, of some gentle current of air; but as immediately over the door there was a kind of window, intended in the daytime to aid in lighting the passage, and through which the rays of the candle were then issuing, the valet could see quite enough for his purpose. As he advanced he heard his master (who, lying in a well-curtained bed had not, as it seemed, perceived his exit from the room) call him by name, and direct him to place the candle on the table by his bed. The servant, who was now some way in the long passage, did not like to raise his voice for the purpose of replying, lest he should startle the sleeping inmates of the house, began to walk hurriedly and softly back again, when, to his amazement, he heard a voice in the interior of the chamber answering calmly, and the man actually saw, through the window which over-topped the door, that the light was slowly shifting, as if carried across the chamber in answer to his master's call. Palsied by a feeling akin to terror, yet not unmingled with a horrible curiosity, he stood breathless and listening at the threshold, unable to summon resolution to push open the door and enter. Then came a rustling of the curtains, and a sound like that of one who in a low voice hushes a child to rest, in the midst of which he heard Barton say, in a tone of stifled horror – 'Oh, God – oh, my God!' and repeat the same exclamation several times. Then ensued a silence, which again was broken by the same strange soothing sound; and at last there burst forth, in one swelling peal, a yell of agony so appalling and hideous, that, under some impulse of ungovernable horror, the man rushed to the door, and with his whole strength strove to force it open. Whether it was that, in his agitation, he had himself but imperfectly turned the handle, or that the door was really secured upon the inside, he failed to effect an entrance; and as he tugged and pushed, yell after yell rang louder and wilder through the chamber, accompanied all the while by the same hushing sounds. Actually freezing with terror, and scarce knowing what he did, the man turned and ran down the passage, wringing his hands in the extremity of horror and irresolution. At the stair-head he was encountered by General Montague, scared and eager, and just as they met the fearful sounds had ceased.

'What is it? – who – where is your master?' said Montague, with the incoherence of extreme agitation. 'Has anything – for God's sake, is anything wrong?'

'Lord have mercy on us, it's all over,' said the man, staring wildly towards his master's chamber. 'He's dead, sir; I'm sure he's dead.'

Without waiting for enquiry or explanation, Montague, closely followed by the servant, hurried to the chamber-door, turned the handle, and pushed it open. As the door yielded to his pressure, the ill-omened bird of which the servant had been in search, uttering its spectral warning, started suddenly from the far side of the bed, and flying through the doorway close over their heads, and extinguishing, in its passage, the candle which Montague carried, crashed through the skylight that overlooked the lobby, and sailed away into the darkness of the outer space.

'There it is, God bless us!' whispered the man, after a breathless pause.

'Curse that bird!' muttered the general, startled by the suddenness of the apparition, and unable to conceal his discomposure.

'The candle was moved,' said the man, after another breathless pause; 'see, they put it by the bed!'

'Draw the curtains, fellow, and don't stand gaping there,' whispered Montague, sternly.

The man hesitated.

'Hold this, then,' said Montague, impatiently, thrusting the candle-stick into the servant's hand; and himself advancing to the bedside, he drew the curtains apart. The light of the candle, which was still burning at the bedside, fell upon a figure huddled together, and half upright, at the head of the bed. It seemed as though it had shrunk back as far as the solid panelling would allow, and the hands were still clutched in the bedclothes.

'Barton, Barton, Barton!' cried the general, with a strange mixture of awe and vehemence.

He took the candle, and held it so that it shone full upon his face. The features were fixed, stern and white; the jaw was fallen, and the sightless eyes, still open, gazed vacantly forward toward the front of the bed.

'God Almighty, he's dead!' muttered the general, as he looked upon this fearful spectacle. They both continued to gaze upon it in silence for a minute or more. 'And cold, too,' said Montague, withdrawing his hand from that of the dead man.

'And see, see; may I never have life, sir,' added the man, after another pause, with a shudder, 'but there was something else on the bed with him! Look there – look there; see that, sir!'

As the man thus spoke, he pointed to a deep indenture, as if caused by a heavy pressure, near the foot of the bed.

Montague was silent.

'Come, sir, come away, for God's sake!' whispered the man, drawing close up to him, and holding fast by his arm while he glanced fearfully round; 'what good can be done here now? – come away, for God's sake!'

At this moment they heard the steps of more than one approaching, and Montague, hastily desiring the servant to arrest their progress, endeavoured to loose the rigid grip with which the fingers of the dead man were clutched in the bedclothes, and drew, as well as he was able, the awful figure into a reclining posture. Then closing the curtains carefully upon it, he hastened himself to meet those who were approaching.

*   *   *

It is needless to follow the personages so slightly connected with this narrative into the events of their after lives; it is enough for us to remark that no clue to the solution of these mysterious occurrences was ever afterwards discovered; and so long an interval having now passed, it is scarcely to be expected that time can throw any new light upon their inexplicable obscurity. Until the secrets of the earth shall be no longer hidden, these transactions must remain shrouded in mystery.

The only occurrence in Captain Barton's former life to which reference was ever made, as having any possible connection with the sufferings with which his existence closed, and which he himself seemed to regard as working out a retribution for some grievous sin of his past life, was a circumstance which not for several years after his death was brought to light. The nature of this disclosure was painful to his relatives and discreditable to his memory.

It appeared, then, that some eight years before Captain Barton's final return to Dublin, he had formed, in the town of Plymouth, a guilty attachment, the object of which was the daughter of one of the ship's crew under his command. The father had visited the frailty of his unhappy child with extreme harshness, and even brutality, and it was said that she had died heart-broken. Presuming upon Barton's implication in her guilt, this man had conducted himself towards him with marked insolence, and Barton resented this – and what he resented with still more exasperated bitterness, his treatment of the unfortunate girl – by a systematic exercise of those terrible and arbitrary severities with which the regulations of the navy arm those who are responsible for its discipline. The man had at length made his escape, while the vessel was in port at Lisbon, but died, as it was said, in an hospital in that town, of the wounds inflicted in one of his recent and sanguinary punishments.

Whether these circumstances in reality bear or not upon the occurrences of Barton's afterlife, it is of course impossible to say. It seems, however, more than probable that they were, at least in his own mind, closely associated with them. But however the truth may be as to the origin and motives of this mysterious persecution, there can be no doubt that, with respect to the agencies by which it was accomplished, absolute and impenetrable mystery is like to prevail until the day of doom.

The Spectre Lovers

SHERIDAN LE FANU

There lived some fifteen years since in a small and ruinous house, little better than a hovel, an old woman who was reported to have considerably exceeded her eightieth year, and who rejoiced in the name of Alice, or popularly, Ally Moran. Her society was not much courted, for she was neither rich, nor, as the reader may suppose, beautiful. In addition to a lean cur and cat she had one human companion, her grandson, Peter Brien, whom, with laudable good-nature, she had supported from the period of his orphanage down to that of my story, which finds him in his twentieth year. Peter was a good-natured slob of a fellow much more addicted to wrestling, dancing, and lovemaking, than to hard work, and fonder of whiskey punch than good advice. His grandmother had a high opinion of his accomplishments, which indeed was but natural, and also of his genius, for Peter had of late years begun to apply his mind to politics; and as it was plain that he had a mortal hatred of honest labour, his grandmother predicted, like a true fortune-teller, that he was born to marry an heiress, and Peter himself (who had no mind to forego his freedom even on such terms) that he was destined to find a pot of gold. Upon one point both agreed, that being unfitted by the peculiar bias of his genius for work, he was to acquire the immense fortune to which his merits entitled him by means of a pure run of good luck. This solution of Peter's future had the double effect of reconciling both himself and his grandmother to his idle courses, and also of maintaining that even flow of hilarious spirits which made him everywhere welcome, and which was in truth the natural result of his consciousness of approaching affluence.

It happened one night that Peter had enjoyed himself to a very late hour with two or three choice spirits near Palmerstown. They had talked politics and love, sung songs, and told stories, and, above all, had swallowed, in the chastened disguise of punch, at least a pint of good whiskey, every man.

It was considerably past one o'clock when Peter bid his companions goodbye, with a sigh and a hiccough, and lighting his pipe set forth on his solitary homeward way.

The bridge of Chapelizod was pretty nearly the midway point of his night march, and from one cause or another his progress was rather slow, and it was past two o'clock by the time he found himself leaning over its old battlements, and looking up the river, over whose winding current and wooded banks the soft moonlight was falling.

The cold breeze that blew lightly down the stream was grateful to him. It cooled his throbbing head, and he drank it in at his hot lips. The scene, too, had, without his being well sensible of it, a secret fascination. The village was sunk in the profoundest slumber, not a mortal stirring, not a sound afloat, a soft haze covered it all, and the fairy moonlight hovered over the entire landscape.

In a state between rumination and rapture, Peter continued to lean over the battlements of the old bridge, and as he did so he saw, or fancied he saw, emerging one after another along the river bank in the little gardens and enclosures in the rear of the street of Chapelizod, the queerest little whitewashed huts and cabins he had ever seen there before. They had not been there that evening when he passed the bridge on the way to his merry tryst. But the most remarkable thing about it was the odd way in which these quaint little cabins showed themselves. First he saw one or two of them just with the corner of his eye, and when he looked full at them, strange to say, they faded away and disappeared. Then another and another came in view, but all in the same coy way, just appearing and gone again before he could well fix his gaze upon them; in a little while, however, they began to bear a fuller gaze, and he found, as it seemed to himself, that he was able by an effort of attention to fix the vision for a longer and a longer time, and when they waxed faint and nearly vanished, he had the power of recalling them into light and substance, until at last their vacillating indistinctness became less and less, and they assumed a permanent place in the moonlit landscape.

'Be the hokey,' said Peter, lost in amazement, and dropping his pipe into the river unconsciously, 'them is the quarist bits iv mud cabins I ever seen, growing up like musharoons in the dew of an evening, and poppin' up here and down again there, and up again in another place, like so many white rabbits in a warren; and there they stand at last as firm and fast as if they were there from the Deluge; bedad it's enough to make a man a'most believe in the fairies.'

This latter was a large concession from Peter, who was a bit of a free-thinker, and spoke contemptuously in his ordinary conversation of that class of agencies.

Having treated himself to a long last stare at these mysterious fabrics, Peter prepared to pursue his homeward way; having crossed the bridge and passed the mill, he arrived at the corner of the main street of the little town, and casting a careless look up the Dublin road, his eye was arrested by a most unexpected spectacle.

This was no other than a column of foot-soldiers, marching with perfect regularity towards the village, and headed by an officer on horseback. They were at the far side of the turnpike, which was closed; but much to his perplexity he perceived that they marched on through it without appearing to sustain the least check from that barrier.

On they came at a slow march; and what was most singular in the matter was that they were drawing several cannons along with them; some held ropes, others spoked the wheels, and others again marched in front of the guns and behind them, with muskets shouldered, giving a stately character of parade and regularity to this, as it seemed to Peter, most unmilitary procedure.

It was owning either to some temporary defect in Peter's vision, or to some illusion attendant upon mist and moonlight, or perhaps to some other cause, that the whole procession had a certain waving and vapoury character which perplexed and tasked his eyes not a little. It was like the pictured pageant of a phantasmagoria reflected upon smoke. It was as if every breath disturbed it; sometimes it was blurred, sometimes obliterated; now here, now there. Sometimes, while the upper part was quite distinct, the legs of the column would nearly fade away or vanish outright, and then again they would come out into clear relief, marching on with measured tread, while the cocked hats and shoulders grew, as it were, transparent, and all but disappeared.

Notwithstanding these strange optical fluctuations however, the column continued steadily to advance. Peter crossed the street from the corner near the old bridge, running on tiptoe, and with his body stooped to avoid observation, and took up a position upon the raised footpath in the shadow of the houses, where, as the soldiers kept the middle of the road, he calculated that he might, himself undetected, see them distinctly enough as they passed.

'What the div—, what on airth,' he muttered, checking the irreligious ejaculation with which he was about to start, for certain queer misgivings were hovering about his heart, notwithstanding the factitious courage of the whiskey bottle. 'What on airth is the manin' of all this? Is it the French that's landed at last to give us a hand and help us in airnest to this blessed repale? If it is not them, I simply ask who the d—l, I mane who on airth are they, for such sogers as them I never seen before in my born days?'

By this time the foremost of them were quite near, and truth to say they were the queerest soldiers he had ever seen in the course of his life. They wore long gaiters and leather breeches, three-cornered hats, bound with silver lace, long blue coats, with scarlet facings and linings, which latter were shown by a fastening which held together the two opposite corners of the skirt behind; and in front the breasts were in like manner connected at a single point, where and below which they sloped back, disclosing a long-flapped waistcoat of snowy whiteness; they had very large, long cross-belts, and wore enormous pouches of white leather hung extraordinarily low, and on each of which a little silver star was glittering. But what struck him as most grotesque and outlandish in their costume was their extraordinary display of shirt-frill in front, and of ruffle about their wrists, and the strange manner in which their hair was frizzled out and powdered under their hats, and clubbed up into great rolls behind. But one of the party was mounted. He rode a tall white horse with high action and arching neck; he had a snow-white feather in his three-cornered hat, and his coat was shimmering all over with a profusion of silver lace. From these circumstances Peter concluded that he must be the commander of the detachment, and examined him as he passed attentively. He was a slight, tall man, whose legs did not half fill his leather breeches, and he appeared to be at the wrong side of sixty. He had a shrunken, weather-beaten, mulberry-coloured face, carried a large black patch over one eye, and turned neither to the right nor to the left, but rode on at the head of his men, with a grim, military inflexibility.

The countenances of these soldiers, officers as well as men, seemed all full of trouble, and, so to speak, scared and wild. He watched in vain for a single contented or comely face. They had, one and all, a melancholy and hang-dog look; and as they passed by, Peter fancied that the air grew cold and thrilling.

He had seated himself upon a stone bench, from which, staring with all his might, he gazed upon the grotesque and noiseless procession as it filed by him. Noiseless it was; he could neither hear the jingle of accoutrements, the tread of feet, nor the rumble of the wheels; and when the old colonel turned his horse a little, and made as though he were giving the word of command, and a trumpeter, with a swollen blue nose and white feather fringe round his hat, who was walking beside him, turned about and put his bugle to his lips, still Peter heard nothing, although it was plain the sound had reached the soldiers, for they instantly changed their front to three abreast.

'Botheration!' muttered Peter, 'is it deaf I'm growing?'

But that could not be, for he heard the sighing of the breeze and the rush of the neighbouring Liffey plain enough.

'Well,' said he, in the same cautious key, 'by the piper, this bangs Banagher fairly! It's either the Frinch army that's in it, come to take the town iv Chapelizod by surprise, an' makin' no noise for feard iv wakenin' the inhabitants; or else it's – it's – what it's – somethin' else. But, tundher-an-ouns, what's gone wid Fitzpatrick's shop across the way?'

The brown, dingy stone building at the opposite side of the street looked newer and cleaner that he had been used to see it; the front door of it stood open, and a sentry, in the same grotesque uniform, with shouldered musket, was pacing noiselessly to and fro before it. At the angle of this building, in like manner, a wide gate (of which Peter had no recollection whatever) stood open, before which, also, a similar sentry was gliding, and into this gateway the whole column gradually passed, and Peter finally lost sight of it.

'I'm not asleep; I'm not dhramin',' said he, rubbing his eyes, and stamping slightly on the pavement, to assure himself that he was wide awake. 'It is a quare business, whatever it is; an' it's not alone that, but everything about the town looks strange to me. There's Tresham's house new painted, bedad, an' them flowers in the windies! An' Delany's house, too, that had not a whole pane of glass in it this morning, and scarce a slate on the roof of it! It is not possible it's what it's dhrunk I am. Sure there's the big tree, and not a leaf of it changed since I passed, and the stars overhead, all night. I don't think it is in my eyes it is.'

And so looking about him, and every moment finding or fancying new food for wonder, he walked along the pavement, intending, without further delay, to make his way home.

But his adventures for the night were not concluded. He had nearly reached the angle of the short lane that leads up to the church, when for the first time he perceived that an officer, in the uniform he had just seen, was walking before, only a few yards in advance of him.

The officer was walking along at an easy, swinging gait, and carried his sword under his arm, and was looking down on the pavement with an air of reverie.

In the very fact that he seemed unconscious of Peter's presence, and disposed to keep his reflections to himself, there was something reassuring. Besides, the reader must please to remember that our hero had a *quantum sufficit* of good punch before his adventure commenced, and was thus fortified against those qualms and terrors under which, in a more reasonable state of mind, he might not impossibly have sunk.

The idea of the French invasion revived in full power in Peter's fuddled imagination, as he pursued the nonchalant swagger of the officer.

'Be the powers iv Moll Kelly, I'll ax him what it is,' said Peter, with a sudden accession of rashness. 'He may tell me or not, as he plases, but he can't be offinded, anyhow.'

With this reflection having inspired himself, Peter cleared his voice and began: 'Captain!' said he, 'I ax your pardon, captain, an' maybe you'd be so condescindin' to my ignorance as to tell me, if it's plasin' to yer honour, whether your honour is not a Frinchman, if it's plasin' to you.'

This he asked, not thinking that, had it been as he suspected, not one word of his question in all probability would have been intelligible to the person he addressed. He was, however, understood, for the officer answered him in English, at the same time slackening his pace and moving a little to the side of the pathway, as if to invite his interrogator to take his place beside him.

'No; I am an Irishman,' he answered.

'I humbly thank you honour,' said Peter, drawing nearer – for the affability and the nativity of the officer encouraged him – 'but maybe your honour is in the service of the King of France?'

'I serve the same King as you do,' he answered, with a sorrowful significance which Peter did not comprehend at the time, and, interrogating in turn, he asked, 'But what calls you forth at this hour of the day?'

'The *day*, your honour! – the night, you mane.'

'It was always our way to turn night into day, and we keep to it still,' remarked the soldier. 'But, no matter, come up here to my

house; I have a job for you, if you wish to earn some money easily. I
live here.'

As he said this, he beckoned authoritatively to Peter, who followed
almost mechanically at his heels, and they turned up a little lane
near the old Roman Catholic chapel, at the end of which stood, in
Peter's time, the ruins of a tall, stonebuilt house.

Like everything else in the town, it had suffered a metamorphosis.
The stained and ragged walls were now erect, perfect, and covered
with pebble-dash; windowpanes glittered coldly in every window;
the green hall-door had a bright brass knocker on it. Peter did not
know whether to believe his previous or his present impressions;
seeing is believing, and Peter could not dispute the reality of the
scene. All the records of his memory seemed but the images of a
tipsy dream. In a trance of astonishment and perplexity, therefore,
he submitted himself to the chances of his adventure.

The door opened, the officer beckoned with a melancholy air of
authority to Peter, and entered. Our hero followed him into a sort
of hall, which was very dark, but he was guided by the steps of the
soldier, and, in silence, they ascended the stairs. The moonlight,
which shone in at the lobbies, showed an old, dark wainscoting, and
a heavy oak banister. They passed by closed doors at different
landing-places, but all was dark and silent as, indeed, became that
late hour of the night.

Now they ascended to the topmost floor. The captain paused for a
minute at the nearest door, and, with a heavy groan, pushing it
open, entered the room. Peter remained at the threshold. A slight
female form in a sort of loose white robe, and with a great deal of
dark hair hanging loosely about her, was standing in the middle of
the floor, with her back towards them.

The soldier stopped short before he reached her, and said, in a
voice of great anguish, 'Still the same, sweet bird – sweet bird! still
the same.' Whereupon, she turned suddenly and threw her arms
about the neck of the officer, with a gesture of fondness and despair,
and her frame was agitated as if by a burst of sobs. He held her
close to his breast in silence; and honest Peter felt a strange terror
creep over him, as he witnessed these mysterious sorrows and
endearments.

'Tonight, tonight – and then ten years more – ten long years –
another ten years.'

The officer and the lady seemed to speak these words together:

here voice mingled with his in a musical and fearful wail, like a distant summer wind, in the dead hour of night wandering through ruins. Then he heard the officer say alone, in a voice of anguish: 'Upon me be it all, for ever, sweet birdie, upon me.'

And again they seemed to mourn together in the same soft and desolate wail, like sounds of grief heard from a great distance.

Peter was thrilled with horror, but he was also under a strange fascination; and an intense and dreadful curiosity held him fast.

The moon was shining obliquely into the room, and through the window Peter saw the familiar slopes of the Park, sleeping mistily under its shimmer. He could also see the furniture of the room with tolerable distinctness – the old balloon-backed chairs, a four-post bed in a sort of recess and a rack against the wall, from which hung some military clothes and accoutrements; and the sight of all these homely objects reassured him somewhat, and he could not help feeling unspeakably curious to see the face of the girl whose long hair was streaming over the officer's epaulet.

Peter, accordingly, coughed, at first slightly, and afterward more loudly, to recall her from her reverie of grief: and, apparently, he succeeded; for she turned round, as did her companion, and both, standing hand in hand, gazed upon him fixedly. He thought he had never seen such large, strange eyes in all his life; and their gaze seemed to chill the very air around him, and arrest the pulses of his heart. An eternity of misery and remorse was in the shadowy faces that looked upon him.

If Peter had taken less whiskey by a single thimbleful, it is probable that he would have lost heart altogether before these figures, which seemed every moment to assume a more marked and fearful, though hardly definable, contrast to ordinary human shapes.

'What is it you want with me?' he stammered.

'To bring my lost treasure to the churchyard,' replied the lady, in a silvery voice of more than mortal desolation.

The word 'treasure' revived the resolution of Peter, although a cold sweat was covering him, and his hair was bristling with horror; he believed, however, that he was on the brink of fortune, if he could but command nerve to brave the interview to its close.

'And where,' he gasped, 'is it hid – where will I find it?'

They both pointed to the sill of the window, through which the moon was shining at the far end of the room, and the soldier said: 'Under that stone.'

Peter drew a long breath, and wiped the cold dew from his face, preparatory to passing to the window, where he expected to secure the reward of his protracted terrors. But looking steadfastly at the window, he saw the faint image of a new-born child sitting upon the sill in the moonlight, with its little arms stretched toward him, and a smile so heavenly as he never beheld before.

At sight of this, strange to say, his heart entirely failed him; he looked on the figures that stood near, and beheld them gazing on the infantine form with a smile so guilty and distorted, that he felt as if he were entering alive among the scenery of hell, and shuddering, he cried in an irrepressible agony of horror: 'I'll have nothing to say with you, and nothing to do with you: I don't know what yez are or what yez want iv me, but let me go this minute, every one of yez, in the name of God.'

With these words there came a strange rumbling and sighing about Peter's ears; he lost sight of everything, and felt that peculiar and not unpleasant sensation of falling softly, that sometimes supervenes in sleep, ending in a dull shock. After that he had neither dream nor consciousness till he wakened, chill and stiff, stretched between two piles of old rubbish, among the black and roofless walls of the ruined house.

We need hardly mention that the village had put on its wonted air of neglect and decay, or that Peter looked around him in vain for traces of those novelties which had so puzzled and distracted him upon the previous night.

'Ay, ay,' said his grandmother, removing her pipe, as he ended his description of the view from the bridge, 'sure enough I remember myself, when I was a slip of a girl, these little white cabins among the gardens by the river side. The artillery sogers that was married, or had not room in the barracks, used to be in them, but they're all gone long ago.'

'The Lord be merciful to us!' she resumed, when he had described the military procession, 'it's often I seen the regiment marchin' into the town, jist as you saw it last night, acushla. Oh, voch, but it makes my heart sore to think iv them days; they were pleasant times, sure enough; but is not it terrible, *avick* [my son], to think it's what it was the ghost of the regiment you seen? The Lord betune us an' harm, for it was nothing else, as sure as I'm sittin' here.'

When he mentioned the peculiar physiognomy and figure of the old officer who rode at the head of the regiment: '*That*,' said the old crone, dogmatically, 'was ould Colonel Grimshaw, the Lord presarve us! he's buried in the churchyard iv Chapelizod, and well I remember him, when I was a young thing, an' a cross ould floggin' fellow he was wid the men, an' a devil's boy among the girls – rest his soul!'

'Amen!' said Peter; 'it's often I read his tombstone myself; but he's a long time dead.'

'Sure, I tell you he died when I was no more nor a slip iv a girl – the Lord betune us and harm!'

'I'm afeard it is what I'm not long for this world myself, afther seeing such as that,' said Peter, fearfully.

'Nonsinse, avourneen,' retorted his grandmother, indignantly, though she had herself misgivings on the subject; 'sure there was Phil Doolan, the ferryman, that seen black Ann Scanlan in his own boat, and what harm ever kem of it?'

Peter proceeded with his narrative, but when he came to the description of the house, in which his adventure had had so sinister a conclusion, the old woman was at fault.

'I know the house and the ould walls well, an' I can remember the time there was a roof on it, and the doors an' windows in it, but it had a bad name about being haunted, but by who, or for what, I forget entirely.'

'Did you ever hear was there gold or silver there?' he enquired.

'No, no, avick, don't be thinking about the likes; take a fool's advice, and never go next or near them ugly black walls again the longest day you have to live; an' I'd take my davy, it's what it's the same word the priest himself I'd be afther sayin' to you if you wor to ax his raverence consarnin' it, for it's plain to be seen it was nothing good you seen there, and there's neither luck nor grace about it.'

Peter's adventure made no little noise in the neighbourhood, as the reader may well suppose; and a few evenings after it, being on an errand to old Major Vandeleur, who lived in a snug old-fashioned house, close by the river, under a perfect bower of ancient trees, he was called on to relate the story in the parlour.

The Major was, as I have said, on old man; he was small, lean, and upright, with a mahogany complexion, and a wooden inflexibility of face; he was a man, besides, of few words, and if *he* was old, it follows plainly that his mother was older still. Nobody could guess or tell *how* old, but it was admitted that her own generation had long passed away, and that she had not a competitor left. She had French blood in her veins, and although she did not retain her charms quite so well as Niñon de l'Enclos, she was in full possession of all her mental activity, and talked quite enough for herself and the Major.

'So, Peter,' she said, 'you have seen the dear old Royal Irish again in the streets of Chapelizod. Make him a tumbler of punch, Frank; and Peter, sit down, and while you take it let us have the story.'

Peter accordingly, seated near the door, with a tumbler of the nectarian stimulant steaming beside him, proceeded with marvellous courage, considering they had no light but the uncertain glare of the fire, to relate with minute particularity his awful adventure. The old lady listened at first with a smile of good-natured incredulity; her cross-examination touching the drinking-bout at Palmerstown had been teasing, but as the narrative proceeded she became attentive, and at length absorbed, and once or twice she uttered ejaculations of pity or awe. When it was over, the old lady looked with a somewhat sad and stern abstraction on the table, patting her cat assiduously meanwhile, and then suddenly looking upon her son, the Major, she said: 'Frank, as sure as I live he has seen the wicked Captain Devereux.'

The Major uttered an inarticulate expression of wonder.

'The house was precisely that he has described. I have told you the story often, as I heard it from your dear grandmother, about the poor young lady he ruined, and the dreadful suspicion about the little baby. *She*, poor thing, died in that house heartbroken, and you know he was shot shortly after in a duel.'

This was the only light that Peter ever received respecting his adventure. It was supposed, however, that he still clung to the hope that treasure of some sort was hidden about the old house, for he was often seen lurking about its walls, and at last his fate overtook him, poor fellow, in the pursuit; for climbing near the summit one day, his holding gave way, and he fell upon the hard uneven ground, fracturing a leg and a rib, and after a short interval died, and he, like the other heroes, lies buried in the little churchyard of Chapelizod.

An Account of Some Strange
Disturbances in Aungier Street

SHERIDAN LE FANU

It is not worth telling, this story of mine – at least, not worth writing. Told, indeed, as I have sometimes been called upon to tell it, to a circle of intelligent and eager faces, lighted up by a good after-dinner fire on a winter's evening, with a cold wind rising and wailing outside, and all snug and cosy within, it has gone off – though I say it, who should not – indifferent well. But it is a venture to do as you would have me. Pen, ink, and paper are cold vehicles for the marvellous, and a 'reader' decidedly a more critical animal than a 'listener.' If, however, you can induce your friends to read it after nightfall, and when the fireside talk has run for a while on thrilling tales of shapeless terror; in short, if you will secure me the *mollia tempora fandi*, I will go to my work, and say my say, with better heart. Well, then, these conditions presupposed, I shall waste no more words, but tell you simply how it all happened.

My cousin (Tom Ludlow) and I studied medicine together. I think he would have succeeded, had he stuck to the profession; but he preferred the Church, poor fellow, and died early, a sacrifice to contagion, contracted in the noble discharge of his duties. For my present purpose, I say enough of his character when I mention that he was of a sedate but frank and cheerful nature; very exact in his observance of truth, and not by any means like myself – of an excitable or nervous temperament.

My Uncle Ludlow – Tom's father – while we were attending lectures, purchased three or four old houses in Aungier Street, one of which was unoccupied. *He* resided in the country, and Tom proposed that we should take up our abode in the untenanted house, so long as it should continue unlet; a move which would accomplish the double end of settling us nearer alike to our lecture-rooms and to our amusements, and of relieving us from the weekly charge of rent for our lodgings.

Our furniture was very scant – our whole equipage remarkably modest and primitive; and, in short, our arrangements pretty nearly as simple as those of a bivouac. Our new plan was, therefore, executed almost as soon as conceived. The front drawing-room was our sitting-room. I had the bedroom over it, and Tom the back bedroom on the same floor, which nothing could have induced me to occupy.

The house, to begin with, was a very old one. It had been, I believe, newly fronted about fifty years before; but with this exception, it had nothing modern about it. The agent who bought it and looked into the titles for my uncle, told me that it was sold, along with much other forfeited property, at Chichester House, I think, in 1702; and had belonged to Sir Thomas Hacket, who was Lord Mayor of Dublin in James II's time. How old it was *then*, I can't say; but, at all events, it had seen years and changes enough to have contracted all that mysterious and saddened air, at once exciting and depressing, which belongs to most old mansions.

There had been very little done in the way of modernising details; and, perhaps, it was better so; for there was something queer and bygone in the very walls and ceilings – in the shape of doors and windows – in the odd diagonal site of the chimney-pieces – in the beams and ponderous cornices – not to mention the singular solidity of all the woodwork, from the bannisters to the window-frames, which hopelessly defied disguise, and would have emphatically proclaimed their antiquity through any conceivable amount of modern finery and varnish.

An effort had, indeed, been made, to the extent of papering the drawing-rooms; but somehow, the paper looked raw and out of keeping; and the old woman, who kept a little dirt-pie of a shop in the lane, and whose daughter – a girl of two and fifty – was our solitary handmaid, coming in at sunrise, and chastely receding again as soon as she had made all ready for tea in our state apartment; – this woman, I say, remembered it, when old Judge Horrocks (who, having earned the reputation of a particularly 'hanging judge,' ended by hanging himself, as the coroner's jury found, under an impulse of 'temporary insanity,' with a child's skipping-rope, over the massive old bannisters) resided there, entertaining good company, with fine venison and rare old port. In those halcyon days, the drawing-rooms were hung with gilded leather, and, I dare say, cut a good figure, for they were really spacious rooms.

The bedrooms were wainscoted, but the front one was not gloomy;

and in it the cosiness of antiquity quite overcame its sombre associations. But the back bedroom, with its two queerly-placed melancholy windows, staring vacantly at the foot of the bed, and with the shadowy recess to be found in most old houses in Dublin, like a large ghostly closet, which, from congeniality of temperament, had amalgamated with the bedchamber, and dissolved the partition. At night-time, this 'alcove' – as our 'maid' was wont to call it – had, in my eyes, a specially sinister and suggestive character. Tom's distant and solitary candle glimmered vainly into its darkness. *There* it was always overlooking him – always itself impenetrable. But this was only part of the effect. The whole room was, I can't tell how, repulsive to me. There was, I suppose, in its proportions and features, a latent discord – a certain mysterious and indescribable relation, which jarred indistinctly upon some secret sense of the fitting and the safe, and raised indefinable suspicions and apprehensions of the imagination. On the whole, as I began by saying, nothing could have induced me to pass a night alone in it.

I had never pretended to conceal from poor Tom my superstitious weakness; and he, on the other hand, most unaffectedly ridiculed my tremors. The sceptic was, however, destined to receive a lesson, as you shall hear.

We had not been very long in occupation of our respective dormitories, when I began to complain of uneasy nights and disturbed sleep. I was, I suppose, the more impatient under this annoyance, as I was usually a sound sleeper, and by no means prone to nightmares. It was now, however, my destiny, instead of enjoying my customary repose, every night to 'sup full of horrors'. After a preliminary course of disagreeable and frightful dreams, my troubles took a definite form, and the same vision, without an appreciable variation in a single detail, visited me at least (on an average) every second night in the week.

Now, this dream, nightmare, or infernal illusion – which you please – of which I was the miserable sport, was on this wise – I saw, or thought I saw, with the most abominable distinctness, although at the time in profound darkness, every article of furniture and accidental arrangement of the chamber in which I lay. This, as you know, is incidental to ordinary nightmare. Well, while in this clair-voyant condition, which seemed but the lighting up of the theatre in which was to be exhibited the monotonous tableau of horror, which made my nights insupportable, my attention invariably became, I know not why, fixed upon the windows opposite the foot of my bed; and, uniformly with the same effect, a sense of dreadful anticipation always took slow but sure possession of me. I became somehow conscious of a sort of horrid but undefined preparation going forward in some unknown quarter, and by some unknown agency, for my torment; and, after an interval, which always seemed to me of the same length, a picture suddenly flew up to the window, where it remained fixed, as if by an electrical attraction, and my discipline of horror then commenced, to last perhaps for hours. The picture thus mysteriously glued to the window-panes, was the portrait of an old man, in a crimson flowered silk dressing-gown, the folds of which I could now describe, with a countenance embodying a strange mixture of intellect, sensuality, and power, but withal sinister and full of malignant omen. His nose was hooked, like the beak of a vulture; his eyes large, grey, and prominent, and lighted up with a more than mortal cruelty and coldness. These features were sur-mounted by a crimson velvet cap, the hair that peeped from under which was white with age, while the eyebrows retained their original blackness. Well I remember every line, hue, and shadow of that stony countenance, and well I may! The gaze of this hellish visage was fixed upon me, and mine returned it with the inexplicable fascination of nightmare, for what appeared to me to be hours of agony. At last – 'The cock he crew, away then flew', the fiend who had enslaved me through the awful watches of the night; and, harassed and nervous, I rose to the duties of the day.

I had – I can't say exactly why, but it may have been from the exquisite anguish and profound impressions of unearthly horror, with which this strange phantasmagoria was associated – an insur-mountable antipathy to describing the exact nature of my nightly troubles to my friend and comrade. Generally, however, I told him that I was haunted by abominable dreams; and, true to the imputed materialism of medicine, we put our heads together to dispel my horrors, not by exorcism, but by a tonic.

I will do this tonic justice, and frankly admit that the accursed portrait began to intermit its visits under its influence. What of that? Was this singular apparition – as full of character as of terror – therefore the creature of my fancy, or the invention of my poor stomach? Was it, in short, *subjective* (to borrow the technical slang of the day) and not the palpable aggression and intrusion of an external agent? That, good friend, as we will both admit, by no means follows.

The evil spirit, who enthralled my senses in the shape of that portrait, may have been just as near me, just as energetic, just as malignant, though I saw him not. What means the whole moral code of revealed religion regarding the due keeping of our own bodies, soberness, temperance, etc.? here is an obvious connection between the material and the invisible; the healthy tone of the system, and its unimpaired energy, may, for aught we can tell, guard us against influences which would otherwise render life itself terrific. The mesmerist and the electro-biologist will fail upon an average with nine patients out of ten – so may the evil spirit. Special conditions of the corporeal system are indispensable to the production of certain spiritual phenomena. The operation succeeds sometimes – sometimes fails – that is all.

I found afterwards that my would-be sceptical companion had his troubles too. But of these I knew nothing yet. One night, for a wonder, I was sleeping soundly, when I was roused by a step on the lobby outside my room, followed by the loud clang of what turned out to be a large brass candlestick, flung with all his force by poor Tom Ludlow over the banisters, and rattling with a rebound down the second flight of stairs; and almost concurrently with this, Tom burst open my door, and bounced into my room backwards, in a state of extraordinary agitation.

I had jumped out of bed and clutched him by the arm before I had any distinct idea of my own whereabouts. There we were – in our shirts – standing before the open door – staring through the great old banister opposite, at the lobby window, through which the sickly light of a clouded moon was gleaming.

'What's the matter, Tom? What's the matter with you? What the devil's the matter with you, Tom?' I demanded shaking him with nervous impatience.

He took a long breath before he answered me, and then it was not very coherently.

'It's nothing, nothing at all – did I speak? – what did I say? – where's the candle, Richard? It's dark; I – I had a candle!'

'Yes, dark enough,' I said; 'but what's the matter? – what is it? – why don't you speak, Tom? – have you lost your wits? – what is the matter?'

'The matter? – oh, it is all over. It must have been a dream – nothing at all but a dream – don't you think so? It could not be anything more than a dream.'

'Of *course*,' said I, feeling uncommonly nervous, 'it *was* a dream.'

'I thought,' he said, 'there was a man in my room, and – and I jumped out of bed; and – and – where's the candle?'

'In your room, most likely,' I said, 'shall I go and bring it?'

'No; stay here – don't go; it's no matter – don't, I tell you; it was all a dream. Bolt the door, Dick; I'll stay here with you – I feel nervous. So, Dick, like a good fellow, light your candle and open the window – I am in a *shocking state*.'

I did as he asked me, and robing himself like Granuaile in one of my blankets, he seated himself close beside my bed.

Everybody knows how contagious is fear of all sorts, but more especially that particular kind of fear under which poor Tom was at that moment labouring. I would not have heard, nor I believe would he have recapitulated, just at that moment, for half the world, the details of the hideous vision which had so unmanned him.

'Don't mind telling me anything about your nonsensical dream, Tom,' said I, affecting contempt, really in a panic; 'let us talk about something else; but it is quite plain that this dirty old house disagrees with us both, and hang me if I stay here any longer, to be pestered with indigestion and – and – bad nights, so we may as well look out for lodgings – don't you think so? – at once.'

Tom agreed, and, after an interval, said – 'I have been thinking, Richard, that it is a long time since I saw my father, and I have made up my mind to go down tomorrow and return in a day or two, and you can take rooms for us in the meantime.'

I fancied that this resolution, obviously the result of the vision which had so profoundly scared him, would probably vanish next morning with the damps and shadows of night. But I was mistaken. Off went Tom at peep of day to the country, having agreed that so soon as I had secured suitable lodgings, I was to recall him by letter from his visit to my Uncle Ludlow.

Now, anxious as I was to change my quarters, it so happened, owing to a series of petty procrastinations and accidents, that nearly a week elapsed before my bargain was made and my letter of recall on the wing to Tom; and, in the meantime, a trifling adventure or two had occurred to your humble servant, which, absurd as they now appear, diminished by distance, did certainly at the time serve to whet my appetite for change considerably.

A night or two after the departure of my comrade, I was sitting by my bedroom fire, the door locked, and the ingredients of a tumbler of hot whisky-punch upon the crazy spider-table; for, as the best mode of keeping the

> Black spirits and white,
> Blue spirits and grey,

with which I was environed, at bay, I had adopted the practice recommended by the wisdom of my ancestors, and 'kept my spirits up by pouring spirits down.' I had thrown aside my volume of Anatomy, and was treating myself by way of a tonic, preparatory to my punch and bed, to half a dozen pages of the *Spectator*, when I heard a step on the flight of stairs descending from the attics. It was two o'clock, and the streets were as silent as a churchyard – the sounds were, therefore, perfectly distinct. There was a slow, heavy tread, characterised by the emphasis and deliberation of age, descending by the narrow staircase from above; and, what made the sound more singular, it was plain that the feet which produced it were perfectly bare, measuring the descent with something between a pound and a flop, very ugly to hear.

I knew quite well that my attendant had gone away many hours before, and that nobody but myself had any business in the house. It was quite plain also that the person who was coming downstairs had no intention whatever of concealing his movements; but, on the contrary, appeared disposed to make even more noise, and proceed more deliberately, than was at all necessary. When the step reached the foot of the stairs outside my room, it seemed to stop; and I expected every moment to see my door open spontaneously, and give admission to the original of my detested portrait. I was, however, relieved in a few seconds by hearing the descent renewed, just in the same manner, upon the staircase leading down to the drawing-rooms, and thence, after another pause, down the next flight, and so on to the hall, whence I heard no more.

Now, by the time the sound had ceased, I was wound up, as they say, to a very unpleasant pitch of excitement. I listened, but there was not a stir. I screwed up my courage to a decisive experiment – opened my door, and in a stentorian voice bawled over the banisters, 'Who's there?' There was no answer but the ringing of my own voice through the empty old house, – no renewal of the movement; nothing, in short, to give my unpleasant sensations a definite direction. There is, I think, something most disagreeably disenchanting in the sound of one's own voice under such circumstances, exerted in solitude, and in vain. It redoubled my sense of isolation and my misgivings increased on perceiving that the door, which I certainly thought I had left open, was closed behind me; in a vague alarm, lest my retreat should be cut off, I got again into my room as quickly as I could, where I remained in a state of imaginary blockade, and very uncomfortable indeed, till morning.

Next night brought no return of my barefooted fellow-lodger; but the night following, being in my bed, and in the dark – somewhere, I suppose, about the same hour as before, I distinctly heard the old fellow again descending from the garrets.

This time I had had my punch, and the *morale* of the garrison was consequently excellent. I jumped out of bed, clutched the poker as I passed the expiring fire, and in a moment was upon the lobby. The sound had ceased by this time – the dark and chill were discouraging; and, guess my horror, when I saw, or thought I saw, a black monster, whether in the shape of a man or a bear I could not say, standing, with its back to the wall, on the lobby, facing me, with a pair of great greenish eyes shining dimly out. Now, I must be frank, and confess that the cupboard which displayed our plates and cups stood just there, though at the moment I did not recollect it. At the same time I must honestly say, that making every allowance for an excited imagination, I never could satisfy myself that I was made the dupe of my own fancy in this matter; for this apparition, after one or two shiftings of shape, as if in the act of incipient transformation, began, as it seemed on second thoughts, to advance upon me in its original form. From an instinct of terror rather than of courage, I hurled the poker, with all my force, at its head; and to the music of a horrid crash made my way into my room, and double-locked the door. Then, in a minute more, I heard the horrid bare feet walk down the stairs, till the sound ceased in the hall, as on the former occasion.

If the apparition of the night before was an ocular delusion of my fancy sporting with the dark outlines of our cupboard, and if its horrid eyes were nothing but a pair of inverted teacups, I had, at all events, the satisfaction of having launched the poker with admirable effect, and in true 'fancy' phrase, 'knocked its two daylights into one', as the commingled fragments of my tea-service testified. I did my best to gather comfort and courage from these evidences; but it would not do. And then what could I say of those horrid bare feet, and the regular tramp, tramp, tramp, which measured the distance of the entire staircase through the solitude of my haunted dwelling, and at an hour when no good influence was stirring? Confound it! – the whole affair was abominable. I was out of spirits, and dreaded the approach of night.

It came, ushered ominously in with a thunderstorm and dull torrents of depressing rain. Earlier than usual the streets grew silent; and by twelve o'clock nothing but the comfortless pattering of the rain was to be heard.

I made myself as snug as I could. I lighted *two* candles instead of one. I forswore bed, and held myself in readiness for a sally, candle in hand; for, *coute qui coute*, I was resolved to *see* the being, if visible at all, who troubled the nightly stillness of my mansion. I was fidgetty and nervous and, tried in vain to interest myself with my books. I walked up and down my room, whistling in turn martial and hilarious music, and listening ever and anon for the dreaded noise. I sate down and stared at the square label on the solemn and reserved-looking black bottle, until 'Flanagan & Co.'s Best Old Malt Whisky' grew into a sort of subdued accompaniment to all the fantastic and horrible speculations which chased one another through my brain.

Silence, meanwhile, grew more silent, and darkness darker. I listened in vain for the rumble of a vehicle, or the dull clamour of a distant row. There was nothing but the sound of a rising wind, which had succeeded the thunderstorm that had travelled over the Dublin mountains quite out of hearing. In the middle of this great city I began to feel myself alone with nature, and Heaven knows what beside. My courage was ebbing. Punch, however, which makes beasts of so many, made a man of me again – just in time to hear with tolerable nerve and firmness the lumpy, flabby, naked feet deliberately descending the stairs again.

I took a candle, not without a tremor. As I crossed the floor I tried to extemporise a prayer, but stopped short to listen, and never finished it. The steps continued. I confess I hesitated for some seconds at the door before I took heart of grace and opened it. When I peeped out the lobby was perfectly empty – there was no monster standing on the staircase; and as the detested sound ceased, I was reassured enough to venture forward nearly to the banisters. Horror of horrors! within a stair or two beneath the spot where I stood the unearthly tread smote the floor. My eye caught something in motion; it was about the size of Goliah's foot – it was grey, heavy, and flapped with a dead weight from one step to another. As I am alive, it was the most monstrous grey rat I ever beheld or imagined.

Shakespeare says – 'Some men there are cannot abide a gaping pig, and some that are mad if they behold a cat.' I went well-nigh out of my wits when I beheld this *rat*; for, laugh at me as you may, it fixed upon me, I thought, a perfectly human expression of malice; and, as it shuffled about and looked up into my face almost from between my feet, I saw, I could swear it – I felt it then, and know it now, the infernal gaze and the accursed countenance of my old friend in the portrait, transfused into the visage of the bloated vermin before me.

I bounced into my room again with a feeling of loathing and horror I cannot describe, and locked and bolted my door as if a lion had been at the other side. D—n him or *it*; curse the portrait and its original! I felt in my soul that the rat – yes, the *rat*, the rat I had just seen, was that evil being in masquerade, and rambling through the house upon some infernal night lark.

Next morning I was early trudging through the miry streets; and, among other transactions, posted a peremptory note recalling Tom. On my return, however, I found a note from my absent 'chum,' announcing his intended return next day. I was doubly rejoiced at this, because I had succeeded in getting rooms; and because the change of scene and return of my comrade were rendered specially pleasant by the last night's half ridiculous half horrible adventure.

I slept extemporaneously in my new quarters in Digges' Street that night, and next morning returned for breakfast to the haunted mansion, where I was certain Tom would call immediately on his arrival.

I was quite right – he came; and almost his first question referred to the primary object of our change of residence.

'Thank God,' he said with genuine fervour, on hearing that all was arranged. 'On *your* account I am delighted. As to myself, I assure you that no earthly consideration could have induced me ever again to pass a night in this disastrous old house.'

'Confound the house!' I ejaculated, with a genuine mixture of fear and detestation, 'we have not had a pleasant hour since we came to live here'; and so I went on, and related incidentally my adventure with the plethoric old rat.

'Well, if that were *all*,' said my cousin, affecting to make light of the matter, 'I don't think I should have minded it very much.'

'Ay, but its eye – its countenance, my dear Tom,' – urged I; 'if you had seen that, *you* would have felt it might be *anything* but what it seemed.'

'I inclined to think the best conjurer in such a case would be an able-bodied cat,' he said, with a provoking chuckle.

'But let us hear your own adventure,' I said tartly.

At this challenge he looked uneasily round him. I had poked up a very unpleasant recollection.

'You shall hear it, Dick; I'll tell it to you,' he said. 'Begad, sir, I should feel quite queer, though, telling it *here*, though we are too strong a body for ghosts to meddle with just now.'

Though he spoke this like a joke, I think it was serious calculation. Our Hebe was in a corner of the room, packing our cracked delft tea and dinner-services in a basket. She soon suspended operations, and with mouth and eyes wide open became an absorbed listener. Tom's experiences were told nearly in these words: 'I saw it three times, Dick – three distinct times; and I am perfectly certain it meant me some infernal harm. I was, I say, in danger – in *extreme* danger; for, if nothing else had happened, my reason would most certainly have failed me, unless I had escaped so soon. Thank God. I *did* escape.

'The first night of this hateful disturbance, I was lying in the attitude of sleep, in that lumbering old bed. I hate to think of it. I was really wide awake, though I had put out my candle, and was lying as quietly as if I had been asleep; and although accidentally restless, my thoughts were running in a cheerful and agreeable channel.

'I think it must have been two o'clock at least when I thought I heard a sound in that – that odious dark recess at the far end of the bedroom. It was as if someone was drawing a piece of cord slowly along the floor, lifting it up, and dropping it softly down again in coils. I sate up once or twice in my bed, but could see nothing, so I concluded it must be mice in the wainscot. I felt no emotion graver than curiosity, and after a few minutes ceased to observe it.

'While lying in this state, strange to say, without at first a suspicion of anything supernatural, on a sudden I saw an old man, rather stout and square, in a sort of roan-red dressing-gown, and with a black cap on his head, moving stiffly and slowly in a diagonal direction, from the recess, across the floor of the bedroom, passing my bed at the foot, and entering the lumber-closet at the left. He had something under his arm; his head hung a little at one side; and, merciful God! when I saw his face.'

Tom stopped for a while, and then said: 'That awful countenance, which living or dying I never can forget, disclosed what he was.

Without turning to the right or left, he passed beside me, and entered the closet by the bed's head.

'While this fearful and indescribable type of death and guilt was passing, I felt that I had no more power to speak or stir than if I had been myself a corpse. For hours after it had disappeared, I was too terrified and weak to move. As soon as daylight came, I took courage, and examined the room, and especially the course which the frightful intruder had seemed to take, but there was not a vestige to indicate anybody's having passed there; no sign of any disturbing agency visible among the lumber that strewed the floor of the closet.

'I now began to recover a little. I was fagged and exhausted, and at last, overpowered by a feverish sleep. I came down late; and finding you out of spirits, on account of your dreams about the portrait, whose *original* I am now certain disclosed himself to me, I did not care to talk about the infernal vision. In fact, I was trying to persuade myself that the whole thing was an illusion, and I did not like to revive in their intensity the hated impressions of the past night – or, to risk the constancy of my scepticism, by recounting the tale of my sufferings.

'It required some nerve, I can tell you, to go to my haunted chamber next night, and lie down quietly in the same bed,' continued Tom. 'I did so with a degree of trepidation, which, I am not ashamed to say, a very little matter would have sufficed to stimulate to downright panic. This night, however, passed off quietly enough, as also the next; and so too did two or three more. I grew more confident, and began to fancy that I believed in the theories of spectral illusions, with which I had at first vainly tried to impose upon my convictions.

'The apparition had been, indeed, altogether anomalous. It had crossed the room without any recognition of my presence: I had not disturbed *it*, and *it* had no mission to *me*. What, then, was the imaginable use of its crossing the room in a visible shape at all? Of course it might have *been* in the closet instead of *going* there, as easily as it introduced itself into the recess without entering the chamber in a shape discernible by the senses. Besides, how the deuce *had* I seen it? It was a dark night; I had no candle; there was no fire; and yet I saw it as distinctly, in colouring and outline, as ever I beheld human form! A cataleptic dream would explain it all; and I was determined that a dream it should be.

'One of the most remarkable phenomena connected with the

practice of mendacity is the vast number of deliberate lies we tell ourselves, whom, of all persons, we can least expect to deceive. In all this, I need hardly tell you, Dick, I was simply lying to myself, and did not believe one word of the wretched humbug. Yet I went on, as men will do, like persevering charlatans and impostors, who tire people into credulity by the mere force of reiteration; so I hoped to win myself over at last to a comfortable scepticism about the ghost.

'He had not appeared a second time – that certainly was a comfort; and what, after all, did I care for him, and his queer old toggery and strange looks? Not a fig! I was nothing the worse for having seen him, and a good story the better. So I tumbled into bed, put out my candle, and, cheered by a loud drunken quarrel in the back lane, went fast asleep.

'From this deep slumber I awoke with a start. I knew I had had a horrible dream; but what it was I could not remember. My heart was thumping furiously; I felt bewildered and feverish; I sate up in the bed and looked about the room. A broad flood of moonlight came in through the curtainless window; everything was as I had last seen it; and though the domestic squabble in the back lane was, unhappily for me, allayed, I yet could hear a pleasant fellow singing, on his way home, the then popular comic ditty called, "Murphy Delany". Taking advantage of this diversion I lay down again, with my face towards the fireplace, and closing my eyes, did my best to think of nothing else but the song, which was every moment growing fainter in the distance:

> 'Twas Murphy Delany, so funny and frisky,
>   Stepped into a shebeen shop to get his skin full;
> He reeled out again pretty well lined with whiskey,
>   As fresh as a shamrock, as blind as a bull.

'The singer, whose condition I dare say resembled that of his hero, was soon too far off to regale my ears any more; and as his music died away, I myself sank into a doze, neither sound nor refreshing. Somehow the song had got into my head, and I went meandering on through the adventures of my respectable fellow-countryman, who, on emerging from the "shebeen shop," fell into a river, from which he was fished up to be "sat upon" by a coroner's jury, who having learned from a "horse-doctor" that he was "dead as a doornail, so there was an end," returned their verdict accordingly, just as he returned to his senses, when an angry altercation and a

pitched battle between the body and the coroner winds up the lay
with due spirit and pleasantry.

'Through this ballad I continued with a weary monotony to plod,
down to the very last line, and then *da capo*, and so on, in my
uncomfortable half sleep, for how long, I can't conjecture. I found
myself at last, however, muttering, "*dead* as a doornail, so there was
an end"; and something like another voice within me, seemed to say,
very faintly, but sharply, "dead! dead! *dead!* and may the Lord have
mercy on your soul!" and instantaneously I was wide awake, and
staring right before me from the pillow.

'Now – will you believe it, Dick? – I saw the same accursed figure
standing full front, and gazing at me with its stony and fiendish
countenance, not two yards from the bedside.'

Tom stopped here, and wiped the perspiration from his face. I
felt very queer. The girl was as pale as Tom; and, assembled as we
were in the very scene of these adventures, we were all, I dare say,
equally grateful for the clear daylight and the resuming bustle out
of doors.

'For about three seconds only I saw it plainly; then it grew
indistinct; but, for a long time, there was something like a column of
dark vapour where it had been standing, between me and the wall;
and I felt sure that he was still there. After a good while, this
appearance went too. I took my clothes downstairs to the hall, and
dressed there, with the door half open; then went out into the street,
and walked about the town till morning when I came back, in a
miserable state of nervousness and exhaustion. I was such a fool,
Dick, as to be ashamed to tell you how I came to be so upset. I
thought you would laugh at me; especially as I had always talked
philosophy, and treated your ghosts with contempt. I concluded you
would give me no quarter; and so kept my tale of horror to myself.

'Now, Dick, you will hardly believe me, when I assure you, that
for many nights after this last experience, I did not go to my room at
all. I used to sit up for a while in the drawing-room after you had
gone up to your bed; and then steal down softly to the hall-door, let
myself out, and sit in the "Robin Hood" tavern until the last guest
went off; and then I got through the night like a sentry, pacing the
streets till morning.

'For more than a week I never slept in bed. I sometimes had a
snooze on a form in the "Robin Hood", and sometimes a nap in a
chair during the day; but regular sleep I had absolutely none.

'I was quite resolved that we should get into another house; but I could not bring myself to tell you the reason, and I somehow put it off from day to day, although my life was, during every hour of this procrastination, rendered as miserable as that of a felon with the constables on his track. I was growing absolutely ill from this wretched mode of life.

'One afternoon I determined to enjoy an hour's sleep upon your bed. I hated mine; so that I had never, except in a stealthy visit every day to unmake it, lest Martha should discover the secret of my nightly absence, entered the ill-omened chamber.

'As ill-luck would have it, you had locked your bedroom, and taken away the key. I went into my own to unsettle the bedclothes, as usual, and give the bed the appearance of having been slept in. Now, a variety of circumstances concurred to bring about the dreadful scene through which I was that night to pass. In the first place, I was literally overpowered with fatigue, and longing for sleep; in the next place, the effect of this extreme exhaustion upon my nerves resembled that of a narcotic, and rendered me less susceptible than, perhaps I should in any other condition have been, of the exciting fears which had become habitual to me. Then again, a little bit of the window was open, a pleasant freshness pervaded the room, and, to crown all, the cheerful sun of day was making the room quite pleasant. What was to prevent my enjoying an hour's nap *here*? The whole air was resonant with the cheerful hum of life, and the broad matter-of-fact light of day filled every corner of the room.

'I yielded – stifling my qualms – to the almost overpowering temptation; and merely throwing off my coat, and loosening my cravat, I lay down, limiting myself to *half* an hour's doze in the unwonted enjoyment of a feather bed, a coverlet, and a bolster.

'It was horribly insidious; and the demon, no doubt, marked my infatuated preparations. Dolt that I was, I fancied, with mind and body worn out for want of sleep, and an arrear of a full week's rest to my credit, that such measure as *half* an hour's sleep, in such a situation, was possible. My sleep was deathlike, long, and dreamless.

'Without a start or fearful sensation of any kind, I waked gently, but completely. It was, as you have good reason to remember, long past midnight – I believe, about two o'clock. When sleep has been deep and long enough to satisfy nature thoroughly, one often wakens in this way, suddenly, tranquilly, and completely.

'There was a figure seated in that lumbering, old sofa-chair, near the fireplace. Its back was rather towards me, but I could not be mistaken; it turned slowly round, and, merciful heavens! there was the stony face, with its infernal lineaments of malignity and despair, gloating on me. There was now no doubt as to its consciousness of my presence, and the hellish malice with which it was animated, for it arose, and drew close to the bedside. There was a rope about its neck, and the other end, coiled up, it held stiffly in its hand.

'My good angel nerved me for this horrible crisis. I remained for some seconds transfixed by the gaze of this tremendous phantom. He came close to the bed, and appeared on the point of mounting upon it. The next instant I was upon the floor at the far side, and in a moment more was, I don't know how, upon the lobby.

'But the spell was not yet broken; the valley of the shadow of death was not yet traversed. The abhorred phantom was before me there; it was standing near the banisters, stooping a little, and with one end of the rope round its own neck, was poising a noose at the other, as if to throw over mine; and while engaged in this baleful pantomime, it wore a smile so sensual, so unspeakably dreadful, that my senses were nearly overpowered. I saw and remember nothing more, until I found myself in your room.

'I had a wonderful escape, Dick – there is no disputing *that* – an escape for which, while I live, I shall bless the mercy of heaven. No one can conceive or imagine what it is for flesh and blood to stand in the presence of such a thing, but one who has had the terrific experience. Dick, Dick, a shadow has passed over me – a chill has crossed my blood and marrow, and I will never be the same again – never, Dick – never!'

Our handmaid, a mature girl of two-and-fifty, as I have said, stayed her hand, as Tom's story proceeded, and by little and little drew near to us, with open mouth, and her brows contracted over her little, beady black eyes, till stealing a glance over her shoulder now and then, she established herself close behind us. During the relation, she had made various earnest comments, in an undertone; but these and her ejaculations, for the sake of brevity and simplicity, I have omitted in my narration.

'It's often I heard tell of it,' she now said, 'but I never believed it rightly till now – though, indeed, why should not I? Does not my mother, down there in the lane, know quare stories, God bless us, beyant telling about it? But you ought not to have slept in the back bedroom. She was loath to let me be going in and out of that room even in the day time, let alone for any Christian to spend the night in it; for sure she says it was his own bedroom.'

'*Whose* own bedroom?' we asked, in a breath.

'Why, *his* – the ould Judge's – Judge Horrock's, to be sure, God rest his sowl'; and she looked fearfully round.

'Amen!' I muttered. 'But did he die there?'

'Die there! No, not quite *there*,' she said. 'Shure, was not it over the bannisters he hung himself, the ould sinner, God be merciful to us all? and was not it in the alcove they found the handles of the skipping-rope cut off, and the knife where he was settling the cord, God bless us, to hang himself with? It was his housekeeper's daughter owned the rope, my mother often told me, and the child never throve after, and used to be starting up out of her sleep, and screeching in the night time, wid dhrames and frights that cum an her; and they said how it was the speerit of the ould Judge that was tormentin' her; and she used to be roaring and yelling out to hould back the big ould fellow with the crooked neck; and then she'd screech "Oh, the master! the master! he's stampin' at me, and beckoning to me! Mother, darling, don't let me go!" And so the poor crathure died at last, and the docthers said it was wather on the brain, for it was all they could say.'

'How long ago was all this?' I asked.

'Oh, then, how would I know?' she answered. 'But it must be a wondherful long time ago, for the housekeeper was an ould woman, with a pipe in her mouth, and not a tooth left, and better nor eighty years ould when my mother was first married; and they said she was a rale buxom, fine-dressed woman when the ould Judge come to his end; an', indeed, my mother's not far from eighty years ould herself this day; and what made it worse for the unnatural ould villain, God rest his soul, to frighten the little girl out of the world the way he did, was what was mostly thought and believed by everyone. My mother says how the poor little crathure was his own child; for he was by all accounts an ould villain every way, an' the hangin'est judge that ever was known in Ireland's ground.'

'From what you said about the danger of sleeping in that bed-room,' said I, 'I suppose there were stories about the ghost having appeared there to others.'

'Well, there *was* things said – quare things, surely,' she answered, as it seemed, with some reluctance. 'And why would not there? Sure was it not up in that same room he slept for more than twenty years? and was it not in the *alcove* he got the rope ready that done his own business at last, the way he done many a betther man's in his lifetime? – and was not the body lying in the same bed after death, and put in the coffin there, too, and carried out to his grave from it in Pether's churchyard, after the coroner was done? But there was quare stories – my mother has them all – about how one Nicholas Spaight got into trouble on the head of it.'

'And what did they say of this Nicholas Spaight?' I asked.

'Oh, for that matther, it's soon told,' she answered.

And she certainly did relate a very strange story, which so piqued my curiosity, that I took occasion to visit the ancient lady, her mother, from whom I learned many very curious particulars. Indeed, I am tempted to tell the tale, but my fingers are weary, and I must defer it. But if you wish to hear it another time, I shall do my best.

When we had heard the strange tale I have *not* told you, we put one or two further questions to her about the alleged spectral visitations, to which the house had, ever since the death of the wicked old Judge, been subjected.

'No one ever had luck in it,' she told us. 'There was always cross accidents, sudden deaths, and short times in it. The first that tuck it was a family – I forget their name – but at any rate there was two young ladies and their papa. He was about sixty, and a stout healthy gentleman as you'd wish to see at that age. Well, he slept in that unlucky back bedroom; and, God between us an' harm! sure enough he was found dead one morning, half out of the bed, with his head as black as a sloe, and swelled like a puddin', hanging down near the floor. It was a fit, they said. He was as dead as a mackerel, and so *he* could not say what it was; but the ould people was all sure that it was nothing at all but the ould Judge, God bless us! that frightened him out of his senses and his life together.

'Some time after there was a rich old maiden lady took the house. I don't know which room *she* slept in, but she lived alone; and at any rate, one morning, the servants going down early to their work, found her sitting on the passage-stairs, shivering and talkin' to herself, quite mad; and never a word more could any of *them* or her friends get from her ever afterwards but, "Don't ask me to go, for I promised to wait for him." They never made out from her who it was she meant by *him*, but of course those that knew all about the ould house were at no loss for the meaning of all that happened to her.

'Then afterwards, when the house was let out in lodgings, there was Micky Byrne that took the same room, with his wife and three little children; and sure I heard Mrs Byrne myself telling how the children used to be lifted up in the bed at night, she could not see by what mains; and how they were starting and screeching every hour, just all as one as the housekeeper's little girl that died, till at last one night poor Micky had a dhrop in him, the way he used now and again; and what do you think in the middle of the night he thought he heard a noise on the stairs, and being in liquor, nothing less id do him but out he must go himself to see what was wrong. Well, after that, all she ever heard of him was himself sayin', "Oh, God!" and a tumble that shook the very house; and there, sure enough, he was lying on the lower stairs, under the lobby, with his neck smashed double undher him, where he was flung over the banisters.'

Then the handmaiden added: 'I'll go down to the lane, and send up Joe Gavvey to pack up the rest of the taythings, and bring all the things across to your new lodgings.'

And so we all sallied out together, each of us breathing more freely, I have no doubt, as we crossed that ill-omened threshold for the last time.

Now, I may add thus much, in compliance with the immemorial usage of the realm of fiction, which sees the hero not only through his adventures, but fairly out of the world. You must have perceived that what the flesh, blood, and bone hero of romance proper is to the regular compounder of fiction, this old house of brick, wood, and mortar is to the humble recorder of this true tale. I, therefore, relate, as in duty bound, the catastrophe which ultimately befell it, which was simply this – that about two years subsequently to my story it was taken by a quack doctor, who called himself Baron Duhlstoerf, and filled the parlour windows with bottles of indescribable horrors preserved in brandy, and the newspapers with the usual grandiloquent and mendacious advertisements. This gentleman among his virtues did not reckon sobriety, and one night, being overcome with much wine, he set fire to his bed curtains, partially burned himself, and totally consumed the house. It was afterwards rebuilt, and for a time an undertaker established himself in the premises.

I have now told you my own and Tom's adventures, together with some valuable collateral particulars; and having acquitted myself of my engagement, I wish you a very good night, and pleasant dreams.

Passage in the Secret History of an Irish Countess

SHERIDAN LE FANU

The following paper is written in a female hand, and was no doubt communicated to my much regretted friend by the lady whose early history it serves to illustrate, the Countess D—. She is no more – she long since died, a childless and a widowed wife, and, as her letter sadly predicts, none survive to whom the publication of this narrative can prove 'injurious, or even painful'. Strange! two powerful and wealthy families, that in which she was born, and that into which she had married, are utterly extinct.

To those who know anything of the history of Irish families, as they were less than a century ago, the facts which immediately follow will at once suggest the names of the principal actors; and to others their publication would be useless – to us, possibly, if not probably injurious. I have therefore altered such of the names as might, if stated, get us into difficulty; others, belonging to minor characters in the strange story, I have left untouched.

MY DEAR FRIEND – You have asked me to furnish you with a detail of the strange events which marked my early history, and I have, without hesitation, applied myself to the task, knowing that, while I live, a kind consideration for my feelings will prevent you giving publicity to the statement; and conscious that, when I am no more, there will not survive one to whom the narrative can prove injurious, or even painful.

My mother died when I was quite an infant, and of her I have no recollection, even the faintest. By her death, my education and habits were left solely to the guidance of my surviving parent; and, so far as a stern attention to my religious instruction, and an active anxiety evinced by his procuring for me the best masters to perfect me in those accomplishments which my station and wealth might seem to require, could avail, he amply discharged the task.

My father was what is called an oddity, and his treatment of me, though uniformly kind, flowed less from affection and tenderness than from a sense of obligation and duty. Indeed, I seldom even spoke to him except at meal-times, and then his manner was silent and abrupt; his leisure hours, which were many, were passed either in his study or in solitary walks; in short, he seemed to take no further interest in my happiness or improvement than a conscientious regard to the discharge of his own duty would seem to claim.

Shortly before my birth, a circumstance had occurred which had contributed much to form and to confirm my father's secluded habits – it was the fact that a suspicion of murder had fallen upon his younger brother, a suspicion not sufficiently definite to lead to an indictment, yet strong enough to ruin him in public opinion.

This disgraceful and dreadful doubt cast upon the family name my father felt deeply and bitterly, and not the less so that he himself was thoroughly convinced of his brother's innocence. The sincerity and strength of this impression he shortly afterwards proved in a manner which produced the dark events which follow. Before, however, I enter upon the statement of them, I ought to relate the circumstances which had awakened the suspicion inasmuch as they are in themselves somewhat curious, and, in their effects, most intimately connected with my after history.

My uncle, Sir Arthur T—n, was a gay and extravagant man, and, among other vices, was ruinously addicted to gambling; this unfortunate propensity, even after his fortune had suffered so severely as to render inevitable a reduction in his expenses by no means inconsiderable, nevertheless continued to actuate him, almost to the exclusion of all other pursuits. He was a proud, or rather a vain man, and could not bear to make the diminution of his income a matter of gratulation and triumph to those with whom he had hitherto competed; and the consequence was that he frequented no longer the expensive haunts of dissipation, and retired from the gay world, leaving his coterie to discover his reasons as best they might.

He did not, however, forego his favourite vice, for, though he could not worship his divinity in the costly temples where it was formerly his wont to take his stand, yet he found it very possible to bring about him a sufficient number of the votaries of chance to answer all his ends. The consequence was that Carrickleigh, which was the name of my uncle's residence, was never without one or more of such reckless visitors.

It happened that upon one occasion he was visited by one Hugh

Tisdall – a gentleman of loose habits but of considerable wealth – who had, in early youth, travelled with my uncle upon the Continent. The period of his visit was winter, and, consequently, the house was nearly deserted except by its regular inmates; Mr Tisdall was therefore highly acceptable, particularly as my uncle was aware that his visitor's tastes accorded exactly with his own.

Both parties seemed determined to avail themselves of their suitability during the brief stay which Mr Tisdall had promised; the consequence was that they shut themselves up in Sir Arthur's private room for nearly all the day and the greater part of the night, during the space of nearly a week. At the end of this period the servant having one morning, as usual, knocked at Mr Tisdall's bedroom door repeatedly, received no answer, and, upon attempting to enter, found that it was locked. This appeared suspicious, and the inmates of the house having been alarmed, the door was forced open, and, on proceeding to the bed, they found the body of its occupant perfectly lifeless, and hanging halfway out, the head downwards, and near the floor. One deep wound had been inflicted upon the temple, apparently with some blunt instrument, which had penetrated the brain; and another blow less effective, probably the first aimed, had grazed the head, removing some of the scalp, but leaving the skull untouched. The door had been double-locked upon the inside, in evidence of which the key still lay where it had been placed in the lock.

The window, though not secured on the interior, was closed – a circumstance not a little puzzling, as it afforded the only other mode of escape from the room; it looked out, too, upon a kind of courtyard, round which the old buildings stood, formerly accessible by a narrow doorway and passage lying in the oldest side of the quadrangle, but which had since been built up, so as to preclude all ingress or egress. The room was also upon the second storey, and the height of the window considerable. Near the bed were found a pair of razors belonging to the murdered man, one of them upon the ground and both of them open. The weapon which had inflicted the mortal wound was not to be found in the room, nor were any footsteps or other traces of the murderer discoverable.

At the suggestion of Sir Arthur himself, a coroner was instantly summoned to attend, and an inquest was held; nothing, however, in any degree conclusive was elicited. The walls, ceiling, and floor of the room were carefully examined, in order to ascertain whether they contained a trap-door or other concealed mode of entrance – but no such thing appeared.

Such was the minuteness of investigation employed that although the grate had contained a large fire during the night, they proceeded to examine even the very chimney, in order to discover whether escape by it were possible; but this attempt, too, was fruitless, for the chimney, built in the old fashion, rose in a perfectly perpendicular line from the hearth to a height of nearly fourteen feet above the roof, affording in its interior scarcely the possibility of ascent, the flue being smoothly plastered, and sloping towards the top like an inverted funnel. Even if the summit of the chimney were attained, it promised, owing to its great height, but a precarious descent upon the sharp and steep-ridged roof. The ashes, too, which lay in the grate, and the soot, as far as it could be seen, were undisturbed, a circumstance almost conclusive.

Sir Arthur was of course examined; his evidence was given with a clearness and unreserve which seemed calculated to silence all suspicion. He stated that up to the day and night immediately preceding the catastrophe, he had lost to a heavy amount, but that, at their last sitting, he had not only won back his original loss, but upwards of four thousand pounds in addition; in evidence of which he produced an acknowledgment of debt to that amount in the handwriting of the deceased, and bearing the date of the fatal night. He had mentioned the circumstance to his lady, and in presence of some of the domestics; which statement was supported by their respective evidence.

One of the jury shrewdly observed that the circumstance of Mr Tisdall's having sustained so heavy a loss might have suggested to some ill-minded persons, accidentally hearing it, the plan of robbing him, after having murdered him, in such a manner as might make it appear that he had committed suicide; a supposition which was strongly supported by the razors having been found thus displaced, and removed from their case. Two persons had probably been engaged in the attempt, one watching by the sleeping man, and ready to strike him in case of his awakening suddenly, while the other was procuring the razors and employed in inflicting the fatal gash so as to make it appear to have been the act of the murdered man himself. It was said that while the juror was making this suggestion Sir Arthur changed colour.

Nothing, however, like legal evidence appeared against him, and the consequence was that the verdict was found against a person or persons unknown; and for some time the matter was suffered to rest, until, after about five months, my father received a letter from a person signing himself Andrew Collis, and representing himself to be the cousin of the deceased. This letter stated that Sir Arthur was likely to incur not merely suspicion, but personal risk, unless he could account for certain circumstances connected with the recent murder, and contained a copy of a letter written by the deceased, and bearing date – the day of the week, and of the month – upon the night the deed of blood had been perpetrated. Tisdall's note ran as follows:

DEAR COLLIS – I have had sharp work with Sir Arthur; he tried some of his stale tricks, but soon found that *I* was Yorkshire too; it would not do – you understand me. We went to the work like good ones, head, heart and soul; and, in fact, since I came here, I have lost no time. I am rather fagged, but I am sure to be well paid for my hardship I never want sleep so long as I can have the music of a dice-box, and wherewithal to pay the piper. As I told you, he tried some of his queer turns, but I foiled him like a man, and, in return, gave him more than he could relish of the genuine *dead knowledge*.

In short, I have plucked the old baronet as never baronet was plucked before; I have scarce left him the stump of a quill; I have got promissory notes in his hand to the amount of – if you like round numbers, say, thirty thousand pounds, safely deposited in my portable strong-box, alias double-clasped pocket-book. I leave this ruinous old rat-hole early on tomorrow, for two reasons – first, I do not want to play with Sir Arthur deeper than I think his security, that is, his money, or his money's worth, would warrant; and, secondly, because I am safer a hundred miles from Sir Arthur than in the house with him. Look you, my worthy, I tell you this between ourselves – I may be wrong, but, by G—, I am as sure as that I am now living, that Sir A— attempted to poison me last night. So much for old friendship on both sides!

When I won the last stake, a heavy one enough, my friend leant his forehead upon his hands, and you'll laugh when I tell you that his head literally smoked like a hot dumpling. I do not know whether his agitation was produced by the plan which he had against me, or by his having lost so heavily – though it must be allowed that he had reason to be a little funked, whichever way his thoughts went; but he pulled the bell, and ordered two bottles of champagne. While the fellow was bringing them he drew out a promissory note to the full amount, which he signed, and, as the man came in with the bottles and glasses, he desired him to be off; he filled out a glass for me, and, while he thought my eyes were off, for I was putting up his note at the time, he dropped something slyly into it, no doubt to sweeten it; but I saw it all, and when he handed it to me, I said, with an emphasis which he might or might not understand: 'There is some sediment in this; I'll not drink it.'

'Is there?' said he, and at the same time snatched it from my hand and threw it into the fire. What do you think of that? have I not a tender chicken to manage? Win or lose, I will not play beyond five thousand tonight, and tomorrow sees me safe out of the reach of Sir Arthur's champagne. So, all things considered, I think you must allow that you are not the last who have found a knowing boy in

Yours to command,

HUGH TISDALL

Of the authenticity of this document I never heard my father express a doubt; and I am satisfied that, owing to his strong conviction in favour of his brother, he would not have admitted it without sufficient enquiry, inasmuch as it tended to confirm the suspicions which already existed to his prejudice.

Now, the only point in this letter which made strongly against my uncle was the mention of the 'double-clasped pocketbook' as the receptacle of the papers likely to involve him, for this pocketbook was not forthcoming, nor anywhere to be found, nor had any papers referring to his gaming transactions been found upon the dead man. However, whatever might have been the original intention of this Collis, neither my uncle nor my father ever heard more of him; but he published the letter in Faulkner's Newspaper, which was shortly afterwards made the vehicle of a much more mysterious attack. The passage in that periodical to which I allude appeared about four years afterwards, and while the fatal occurrence was still fresh in public recollection. It commenced by a rambling preface, stating that 'a *certain person* whom *certain* persons thought to be dead, was not so, but living, and in full possession of his memory, and moreover ready and able to make *great* delinquents tremble.' It then went on to describe the murder, without, however, mentioning names; and in doing so, it entered into minute and circumstantial particulars of which none by an *eye-witness* could have been possessed, and by implications almost too unequivocal to be regarded in the light of insinuation, to involve the '*titled gambler*' in the guilt of the transaction.

My father at once urged Sir Arthur to proceed against the paper in an action of libel; but he would not hear of it, nor consent to my father's taking any legal steps whatever in the matter. My father, however, wrote in a threatening tone to Faulkner, demanding a surrender of the author of the obnoxious article. The answer to this application is still in my possession, and is penned in an apologetic tone: it states that the manuscript had been handed in, paid for, and inserted as an advertisement, without sufficient enquiry, or any knowledge as to whom it referred.

No step, however, was taken to clear my uncle's character in the judgment of the public; and as he immediately sold a small property, the application of the proceeds of which was known to none, he was said to have disposed of it to enable himself to buy off the threatened information. However the truth might have been, it is certain that no charges respecting the mysterious murder were afterwards publicly made against my uncle, and, as far as external disturbances were concerned, he enjoyed henceforward perfect security and quiet.

A deep and lasting impression, however, had been made upon the public mind, and Sir Arthur T—n was no longer visited or noticed by the gentry and aristocracy of the county, whose attention and courtesies he had hitherto received. He accordingly affected to despise these enjoyments which he could not procure, and shunned even that society which he might have commanded.

This is all that I need recapitulate of my uncle's history, and I now recur to my own. Although my father had never, within my recollection, visited, or been visited by, my uncle, each being of sedentary, procrastinating, and secluded habits, and their respective residences being very far apart – the one lying in the county of Galway, the other in that of Cork – he was strongly attached to his brother, and evinced his affection by an active correspondence, and by deeply and proudly resenting that neglect which had marked Sir Arthur as unfit to mix in society.

When I was about eighteen years of age, my father, whose health had been gradually declining, died, leaving me in heart wretched and desolate, and, owing to his previous seclusion, with few acquaintances, and almost no friends.

The provisions of his will were curious, and when I had sufficiently come to myself to listen to or comprehend them, surprised me not a little: all his vast property was left to me, and to the heirs of my body, for ever; and, in default of such heirs, it was to go after my death to my uncle, Sir Arthur, without any entail.

At the same time, the will appointed him my guardian, desiring that I might be received within his house, and reside with his family, and under his care, during the term of my minority; and in consideration of the increased expense consequent upon such an arrangement, a handsome annuity was allotted to him during the term of my proposed residence.

The object of this last provision I at once understood: my father desired, by making it the direct, apparent interest of Sir Arthur that I should die without issue, while at the same time placing me wholly in his power, to prove to the world how great and unshaken was his confidence in his brother's innocence and honour, and also to afford him an opportunity of showing that this mark of confidence was not unworthily bestowed.

It was a strange, perhaps an idle scheme; but as I had been always brought up in the habit of considering my uncle as a deeply-injured man, and had been taught, almost as a part of my religion, to regard him as the very soul of honour, I felt no further uneasiness respecting the arrangement than that likely to result to a timid girl of secluded habits from the immediate prospect of taking up her abode for the first time in her life among total strangers. Previous to leaving my home, which I felt I should do with a heavy heart, I received a most tender and affectionate letter from my uncle, calculated, if anything could do so, to remove the bitterness of parting from scenes familiar and dear from my earliest childhood, and in some degree to reconcile me to the change.

It was during a fine autumn that I approached the old domain of Carrickleigh. I shall not soon forget the impression of sadness and of gloom which all that I saw produced upon my mind; the sunbeams were falling with a rich and melancholy tint upon the fine old trees, which stood in lordly groups, casting their long, sweeping shadows over rock and sward. There was an air of desolation and decay about the spot, which amounted almost to desolation; the symptoms of this increased in number as we approached the building itself, near which the ground had been originally more artificially and carefully cultivated than elsewhere, and the neglect consequently more immediately and strikingly betrayed itself.

As we proceeded, the road wound near the beds of what had been formerly two fishponds – now nothing more than stagnant swamps, overgrown with rank weeds, and here and there encroached upon by the straggling underwood. The avenue itself was much broken, and in many places the stones were almost concealed by grass and nettles; the loose stone walls which had here and there intersected the broad park were, in many places, broken down, so as no longer to answer their original purpose as fences; piers were now and then to be seen, but the gates were gone. And, to add to the general air of dilapidation, some huge trunks were lying scattered through the venerable old trees, either the work of the winter storms, or perhaps the victims of some extensive but desultory scheme of denudation, which the projector had not capital or perseverance to carry into full effect.

After the carriage had travelled a mile of this avenue, we reached the summit of rather an abrupt eminence, one of the many which added to the picturesqueness, if not to the convenience of this rude passage. From the top of this ridge the grey walls of Carrickleigh were visible, rising at a small distance in front, and darkened by the hoary wood which crowded around them. It was a quadrangular building of considerable extent, and the front which lay towards us, and in which the great entrance was placed, bore unequivocal marks of antiquity; the timeworn, solemn aspect of the old building, the ruinous and deserted appearance of the whole place, and the associations which connected it with a dark page in the history of my family, combined to depress spirits already predisposed for the reception of sombre and dejecting impressions.

When the carriage drew up in the grass-grown courtyard before the hall door, two lazy-looking men, whose appearance well accorded with that of the place which they tenanted, alarmed by the obstreperous barking of a great chained dog, ran out from some half-ruinous out-houses, and took charge of the horses; the hall door stood open, and I entered a gloomy and imperfectly lighted apartment, and found no one within. However, I had not long to wait in this awkward predicament, for before my luggage had been deposited in the house – indeed, before I had well removed my cloak and other wraps, so as to enable me to look around – a young girl ran lightly into the hall, and kissing me heartily, and somewhat boisterously, exclaimed: 'My dear cousin, my dear Margaret, I am so delighted, so out of breath. We did not expect you till ten o'clock; my father is somewhere about the place; he must be close at hand. James, Corney – run out and tell your master – my brother is seldom at home, at least at any reasonable hour – you must be so tired, so fatigued, let me show you to your room. See that Lady Margaret's luggage is all brought up, you must lie down and rest yourself. Deborah, bring some coffee – Up these stairs! We are so delighted to see you, you cannot think how lonely I have been. How steep these stairs are, are they not? I am so glad you are come; I could hardly bring myself to believe that you were really coming; how good of you, dear Lady Margaret.'

There was real good nature and delight in my cousin's greeting, and a kind of constitutional confidence of manner which placed me at once at ease, and made me feel immediately upon terms of intimacy with her. The room into which she ushered me, although partaking in the general air of decay which pervaded the mansion and all about it, had nevertheless been fitted up with evident attention to comfort, and even with some dingy attempt at luxury; but what pleased me most was that it opened, by a second door, upon a lobby which communicated with my fair cousin's apartment; a circumstances which divested the room, in my eyes, of the air of solitude and sadness which would otherwise have characterised it, to a degree almost painful to one so dejected in spirits as I was.

After such arrangements as I found necessary were completed, we both went down to the parlour, a large wainscoted room, hung round with grim old portraits, and, as I was not sorry to see, containing in its ample grate a large and cheerful fire. Here my cousin had leisure to talk more at ease; and from her I learned something of the manners and the habits of the two remaining members of her family, whom I had not yet seen.

On my arrival I had known nothing of the family among whom I was come to reside, except that it consisted of three individuals, my uncle, and his son and daughter, Lady T—n having been long dead. In addition to this very scanty stock of information, I shortly learned from my communicative companion that my uncle was, as I had suspected, completely reserved in his habits, and besides that, having been so far back as she could well recollect, always rather strict (as reformed rakes frequently become), he had latterly been growing more gloomily and sternly religious than heretofore.

Her account of her brother was far less favourable, though she did not say anything directly to his disadvantage. From all that I could gather from her, I was led to suppose that he was a specimen of the idle, coarse-mannered, profligate, low-minded 'squirearchy' – a result which might naturally have flowed from the circumstance of his being, as it were, outlawed from society, and driven for companionship to grades below his own; enjoying, too, the dangerous prerogative of spending much money.

However, you may easily suppose that I found nothing in my cousin's communication fully to bear me out in so very decided a conclusion.

I awaited the arrival of my uncle, which was every moment to be expected, with feelings half of alarm, half of curiosity – a sensation which I have often since experienced, though to a less degree, when upon the point of standing for the first time in the presence of one of whom I have long been in the habit of hearing or thinking with interest.

It was, therefore, with some little perturbation that I heard, first a light bustle at the outer door, then a slow step traverse the hall, and finally witnessed the door open, and my uncle enter the room. He was a striking-looking man; from peculiarities both of person and of garb, the whole effect of his appearance amounted to extreme singularity. He was tall, and when young his figure must have been strikingly elegant; as it was, however, its effect was marred by a very decided stoop. His dress was of a sober colour, and in fashion anterior to anything which I could remember. It was, however, handsome, and by no means carelessly put on. But what completed the singularity of his appearance was his uncut white hair, which hung in long, but not at all neglected curls, even so far as his shoulders, and which combined with his regularly classic features and fine dark eyes, to bestow upon him an air of venerable dignity and pride which I have never seen equalled elsewhere. I rose as he entered, and met him about the middle of the room; he kissed my cheek and both my hands, saying: 'You are most welcome, dear child, as welcome as the command of this poor place and all that it contains can make you. I am most rejoiced to see you – truly rejoiced. I trust that you are not much fatigued – pray be seated again.' He led me to my chair, and continued: 'I am glad to perceive you have made acquaintance with Emily already; I see, in your being thus brought together, the foundation of a lasting friendship. You are both innocent, and both young. God bless you – God bless you, and make you all that I could wish!'

He raised his eyes, and remained for a few moments silent, as if in secret prayer. I felt that it was impossible that this man, with feelings so quick, so warm, so tender, could be the wretch that public opinion had represented him to be. I was more than ever convinced of his innocence.

His manner was, or appeared to me, most fascinating; there was a mingled kindness and courtesy in it which seemed to speak bene-volence itself. It was a manner which I felt cold art could never have taught; it owed most of its charm to its appearing to emanate directly from the heart; it must be a genuine index of the owner's mind. So I thought.

My uncle having given me fully to understand that I was most welcome, and might command whatever was his own, pressed me to take some refreshment; and on my refusing, he observed that previously to bidding me good-night, he had one duty further to perform, one in whose observance he was convinced I would cheerfully acquiesce.

He then proceeded to read a chapter from the Bible; after which he took his leave with the same affectionate kindness with which he had greeted me, having repeated his desire that I should consider everything in his house as altogether at my disposal. It is needless to say that I was much pleased with my uncle – it was impossible to avoid being so; and I could not help saying to myself, if such a man as this is not safe from the assaults of slander, who is? I felt much happier than I had done since my father's death, and enjoyed that night the first refreshing sleep which had visited me since that event.

My curiosity respecting my male cousin did not long remain unsatisfied – he appeared the next day at dinner. His manners, though not so coarse as I had expected, were exceedingly disagreeable; there was an assurance and a forwardness for which I was not prepared; there was less of the vulgarity of manner, and almost more of that of the mind, than I had anticipated. I felt quite uncomfortable in his presence; there was just that confidence in his look and tone which would read encouragement even in mere toleration; and I felt more disgusted and annoyed at the coarse and extravagant compliments which he was pleased from time to time to pay me, than perhaps the extent of the atrocity might fully have warranted. It was, however, one consolation that he did not often appear, being much engrossed by pursuits about which I neither knew nor cared anything; but when he did appear, his attentions, either with a view to his amusement or to some more serious advantage, were so obviously and perseveringly directed to me, that young and inexperienced as I was, even *I* could not be ignorant of his preference. I felt more provoked by this odious persecution than I can express, and discouraged him with so much vigour, that I employed even rudeness to convince him his assiduities were unwelcome; but all in vain.

This had gone on for nearly a twelvemonth, to my infinite annoyance, when one day as I was sitting at some needlework with my companion Emily, as was my habit, in the parlour, the door opened, and my cousin Edward entered the room. There was something, I thought, odd in his manner; a kind of struggle between shame and impudence – a kind of flurry and ambiguity which made him appear, if possible, more than ordinarily disagreeable.

'Your servant, ladies,' he said, seating himself at the same time; 'sorry to spoil your tête-à-tête, but never mind! I'll only take Emily's place for a minute or two; and then we part for a while, fair cousin. Emily, my father wants you in the corner turret. No shilly-shally; he's in a hurry.' She hesitated. 'Be off – tramp, march!' he exclaimed, in a tone which the poor girl dared not disobey.

She left the room, and Edward followed her to the door. He stood there for a minute or two, as if reflecting what he should say, perhaps satisfying himself that no one was within hearing in the hall.

At length he turned about, having closed the door, as if carelessly, with his foot; and advancing slowly, as if in deep thought, he took his seat at the side of the table opposite to mine.

There was a brief interval of silence, after which he said: 'I imagine that you have a shrewd suspicion of the object of my early visit; but I suppose I must go into particulars. Must I?'

'I have no conception,' I replied, 'what your object may be.'

'Well, well,' said he, becoming more at his ease as he proceeded, 'it may be told in a few words. You know that it is totally impossible – quite out of the question – that an offhand young fellow like me, and a good-looking girl like yourself, could meet continually, as you and I have done, without an attachment – a liking growing up on one side or other; in short, I think I have let you know as plain as if I spoke it, that I have been in love with you almost from the first time I saw you.'

He paused; but I was too much horrified to speak. He interpreted my silence favourably.

'I can tell you,' he continued, 'I'm reckoned rather hard to please, and very hard to *hit*. I can't say when I was taken with a girl before; so you see fortune reserved me – '

Here the odious wretch wound his arm round my waist. The action at once restored me to utterance, and with the most indignant vehemence I released myself from his hold, and at the same time said: 'I have not been insensible, sir, of your most disagreeable attentions – they have long been a source of much annoyance to me; and you must be aware that I have marked my disapprobation – my disgust – as unequivocally as I possibly could, without actual indelicacy.'

I paused, almost out of breath from the rapidity with which I had spoken; and, without giving him time to renew the conversation, I hastily quitted the room, leaving him in a paroxysm of rage and mortification.

As I ascended the stairs, I heard him open the parlour-door with violence, and take two or three rapid strides in the direction in which I was moving. I was now much frightened, and ran the whole way until I reached my room; and having locked the door, I listened breathlessly, but heard no sound. This relieved me for the present; but so much had I been overcome by the agitation and annoyance attendant upon the scene which I had just gone through, that when Emily knocked at my door, I was weeping in strong hysterics.

You will readily conceive my distress, when you reflect upon my strong dislike to my cousin Edward, combined with my youth and extreme inexperience. Any proposal of such a nature must have agitated me; but that it should have come from the man whom of all others I most loathed and abhorred, and to whom I had, as clearly as manner could do it, expressed the state of my feelings, was almost too overwhelming to be borne. It was a calamity, too, in which I could not claim the sympathy of my cousin Emily, which had always been extended to me in my minor grievances. Still I hoped that it might not be unattended with good; for I thought that one inevitable and most welcome consequence would result from this painful *eclaircissement*, in the discontinuance of my cousin's odious persecution.

When I arose next morning, it was with the fervent hope that I might never again behold the face, or even hear the name, of my cousin Edward but such a consummation, though devoutly to be wished, was hardly likely to occur. The painful impressions of yesterday were too vivid to be at once erased; and I could not help feeling some dim foreboding of coming annoyance and evil.

To expect on my suitor's part anything like delicacy or consideration for me was out of the question. I saw that he had set his heart upon my property, and that he was not likely easily to forego such an acquisition – possessing what might have been considered opportunities and facilities almost to compel my compliance.

I now keenly felt the unreasonableness of my father's conduct in placing me to reside with a family of all whose members, with one exception, he was wholly ignorant, and I bitterly felt the helplessness of my situation. I determined, however, in case of my cousin's persevering in his addresses, to lay all the particulars before my uncle (although he had never in kindness or intimacy gone a step beyond our first interview), and to throw myself upon his hospitality and his sense of honour for protection against a repetition of such scenes.

My cousin's conduct may appear to have been an inadequate cause for such serious uneasiness; but my alarm was caused neither by his acts nor words, but entirely by his manner, which was strange and even intimidating to excess. At the beginning of yesterday's interview there was a sort of bullying swagger in his air, which towards the close gave place to the brutal vehemence of an undisguised ruffian – a transition which had tempted me into a belief that he might seek even forcibly to extort from me a consent to his wishes, or by means still more horrible, of which I scarcely dared to trust myself to think, to possess himself of my property.

I was early next day summoned to attend my uncle in his private room, which lay in a corner turret of the old building; and thither I accordingly went, wondering all the way what this unusual measure might prelude. When I entered the room, he did not rise in his usual courteous way to greet me, but simply pointed to a chair opposite to his own. This boded nothing agreeable. I sat down, however, silently waiting until he should open the conversation.

'Lady Margaret,' at length he said, in a tone of greater sternness than I had thought him capable of using, 'I have hitherto spoken to you as a friend, but I have not forgotten that I am also your guardian, and that my authority as such gives me a right to control your conduct. I shall put a question to you, and I expect and will demand a plain, direct answer. Have I rightly been informed that you have contemptuously rejected the suit and hand of my son Edward?'

I stammered forth with a good deal of trepidation: 'I believe – that is, I have, sir, rejected my cousin's proposals; and my coldness and discouragement might have convinced him that I had determined to do so.'

'Madam,' replied he, with suppressed, but, as it appeared to me, intense anger, 'I have lived long enough to know that coldness and discouragement, and such terms, form the common cant of a worthless coquette. You know to the full, as well as I, that *coldness and discouragement* may be so exhibited as to convince their object that he is neither distasteful nor indifferent to the person who wears this manner. You know, too, none better, that an affected neglect, when skilfully managed, is among the most formidable of the engines which artful beauty can employ. I tell you, madam, that having, without one word spoken in discouragement, permitted my son's most marked attentions for a twelvemonth or more, you have no right to dismiss him with no further explanation than demurely telling him that you had always looked coldly upon him; and neither your wealth nor your *ladyship*' (there was an emphasis of scorn on the word, which would have become Sir Giles Overreach himself) 'can warrant you in treating with contempt the affectionate regard of an honest heart.'

I was too much shocked at this undisguised attempt to bully me into an acquiescence in the interested and unprincipled plan for their own aggrandisement, which I now perceived my uncle and his son to have deliberately entered into, at once to find strength or collectedness to frame an answer to what he had said. At length I replied, with some firmness: 'In all that you have just now said, sir, you have grossly misstated my conduct and motives. Your information must have been most incorrect as far as it regards my conduct towards my cousin; my manner towards him could have conveyed nothing but dislike; and if anything could have added to the strong aversion which I have long felt towards him, it would be his attempting thus to trick and frighten me into a marriage which he knows to be revolting to me, and which is sought by him only as a means for securing to himself whatever property is mine.'

As I said this, I fixed my eyes upon those of my uncle, but he was too old in the world's ways to falter beneath the gaze of more searching eyes than mine; he simply said: 'Are you acquainted with the provisions of your father's will?'

I answered in the affirmative; and he continued: 'Then you must be aware that if my son Edward were – which God forbid – the unprincipled, reckless man you pretend to think him' – (here he spoke very slowly, as if he intended that every word which escaped him should be registered in my memory, while at the same time the expression of his countenance underwent a gradual but horrible change and the eyes which he fixed upon me became so darkly vivid, that I almost lost sight of everything else) – 'if he were what you have described him, think you, girl, he could find no briefer means than wedding contracts to gain his ends? 'twas but to gripe your slender neck until the breath had stopped, and lands, and lakes, and all were his.'

I stood staring at him for many minutes after he had ceased to speak, fascinated by the terrible serpent-like gaze, until he continued with a welcome change of countenance: 'I will not speak again to you upon this topic until one month has passed. You shall have time to consider the relative advantages of the two courses which are open to you. I should be sorry to hurry you to a decision. I am satisfied with having stated my feelings upon the subject, and pointed out to you the path of duty. Remember this day month – not one word sooner.'

He then rose, and I left the room, much agitated and exhausted.

This interview, all the circumstances attending it, but most par-ticularly the formidable expression of my uncle's countenance while he talked, though hypothetically, of murder, combined to arouse all my worst suspicions of him. I dreaded to look upon the face that had so recently worn the appalling livery of guilt and malignity. I regarded it with the mingled fear and loathing with which one looks upon an object which has tortured them in a nightmare.

In a few days after the interview, the particulars of which I have just related, I found a note upon my toilet-table, and on opening it I read as follows:

My dear Lady Margaret – You will be perhaps surprised to see a strange face in your room today. I have dismissed your Irish maid, and secured a French one to wait upon you – a step rendered necessary by my proposing shortly to visit the Continent, with all my family.

Your faithful guardian,

ARTHUR T—N

On enquiry, I found that my faithful attendant was actually gone, and far on her way to the town of Galway; and in her stead there appeared a tall, raw-boned, ill-looking, elderly Frenchwoman, whose sullen and presuming manners seemed to imply that her vocation had never before been that of a lady's maid. I could not help regarding her as a creature of my uncle's, and therefore to be dreaded, even had she been in no other way suspicious.

Days and weeks passed away without any, even a momentary doubt upon my part, as to the course to be pursued by me. The allotted period had at length elapsed; the day arrived on which I was to communicate my decision to my uncle. Although my resolution had never for a moment wavered, I could not shake off the dread of the approaching colloquy; and my heart sank within me as I heard the expected summons.

I had not seen my cousin Edward since the occurrence of the grand *eclaircissement*; he must have studiously avoided me – I suppose from policy, it could not have been from delicacy. I was prepared for a terrific burst of fury from my uncle, as soon as I should make known my determination; and I not unreasonably feared that some act of violence or of intimidation would next be resorted to.

Filled with these dreary forebodings, I fearfully opened the study door, and the next minute I stood in my uncle's presence. He received me with a politeness which I dreaded, as arguing a favourable anticipation respecting the answer which I was to give; and after some slight delay, he began by saying: 'It will be a relief to both of us, I believe, to bring this conversation as soon as possible to an issue. You will excuse me, then, my dear niece, for speaking with an abruptness which, under other circumstances, would be unpardonable. You have, I am certain, given the subject of our last interview fair and serious consideration; and I trust that you are now prepared with candour to lay your answer before me. A few words will suffice – we perfectly understand one another.'

He paused, and I, though feeling that I stood upon a mine which might in an instant explode, nevertheless answered with perfect composure: 'I must now, sir, make the same reply which I did upon the last occasion, and I reiterate the declaration which I then made, than I never can nor will, while life and reason remain, consent to a union with my cousin Edward.'

This announcement wrought no apparent change in Sir Arthur, except that he became deadly, almost lividly pale. He seemed lost in dark thought for a minute, and then with a slight effort said: 'You have answered me honestly and directly; and you say your resolution is unchangeable. Well, would it had been otherwise – would it had been otherwise; but be it as it is, I am satisfied.'

He gave me his hand – it was cold and damp as death; under an assumed calmness, it was evident that he was fearfully agitated. He continued to hold my hand with an almost painful pressure, while, as if unconsciously, seeming to forget my presence, he muttered: 'Strange, strange, strange, indeed! fatuity, helpless fatuity!' there was here a long pause. 'Madness indeed to strain a cable that is rotten to the very heart – it must break – and then – all goes.'

There was again a pause of some minutes, after which, suddenly changing his voice and manner to one of wakeful alacrity, he exclaimed: 'Margaret, my son Edward shall plague you no more. He leaves this country on tomorrow for France – he shall speak no more upon this subject – never, never more – whatever events depended upon your answer must now take their own course; but, as for this fruitless proposal, it has been tried enough; it can be repeated no more.'

At these words he coldly suffered my hand to drop, as if to express his total abandonment of all his projected schemes of alliance; and certainly the action, with the accompanying words, produced upon my mind a more solemn and depressing effect than I believed possible to have been caused by the course which I had determined to pursue; it struck upon my heart with an awe and heaviness which *will* accompany the accomplishment of an important and irrevocable act, even though no doubt or scruple remains to make it possible that the agent should wish it undone.

'Well,' said my uncle, after a little time, 'we now cease to speak upon this topic, never to resume it again. Remember you shall have no further uneasiness from Edward; he leaves Ireland for France on tomorrow; this will be a relief to you. May I depend upon your honour that no word touching the subject of this interview shall ever escape you?'

I gave him the desired assurance; he said: 'It is well – I am satisfied;

we have nothing more, I believe, to say, and my presence must be a restraint upon you, I shall therefore bid you farewell.'

I then left the apartment, scarcely knowing what to think of the strange interview which had just taken place.

On the next day my uncle took occasion to tell me that Edward had actually sailed, if his intention had not been interfered with by adverse circumstances; and two days subsequently he actually produced a letter from his son, written, as it said, on board, and despatched while the ship was getting under weigh. This was a great satisfaction to me and as being likely to prove so, it was no doubt communicated to me by Sir Arthur.

During all this trying period, I had found infinite consolation in the society and sympathy of my dear cousin Emily. I never in afterlife formed a friendship so close, so fervent, and upon which, in all its progress, I could look back with feelings of such unalloyed pleasure, upon whose termination I must ever dwell with so deep, yet so unembittered regret. In cheerful converse with her I soon recovered my spirits considerably, and passed my time agreeably enough, although still in the strictest seclusion.

Matters went on sufficiently smooth, although I could not help sometimes feeling a momentary, but horrible uncertainty respecting my uncle's character; which was not altogether unwarranted by the circumstances of the two trying interviews whose particulars I have just detailed. The unpleasant impression which these conferences were calculated to leave upon my mind was fast wearing away, when there occurred a circumstance, slight indeed in itself, but calculated irresistibly to awaken all my worst suspicions, and to overwhelm me again with anxiety and terror.

I had one day left the house with my cousin Emily, in order to take a ramble of considerable length, for the purpose of sketching some favourite views, and we had walked about half a mile, when I perceived that we had forgotten our drawing materials, the absence of which would have defeated the object of our walk. Laughing at our own thoughtlessness, we returned to the house, and leaving Emily without, I ran upstairs to procure the drawing-books and pencils, which lay in my bedroom.

As I ran up the stairs I was met by the tall, ill-looking French-woman, evidently a good deal flurried.

'Que veut, madame?' said she, with a more decided effort to be polite than I had ever known her make before.

'No, no – no matter,' said I, hastily running by her in the direction of my room.

'Madame,' cried she, in a high key, 'restez ici, s'il vous plait; votre chambre n'est pas faite – your room is not ready for your reception yet.'

I continued to move on without heeding her. She was some way behind me, and feeling that she could not otherwise prevent my entrance, for I was now upon the very lobby, she made a desperate attempt to seize hold of my person: she succeeded in grasping the end of my shawl, which she drew from my shoulders; but slipping at the same time upon the polished oak floor, she fell at full length upon the boards.

A little frightened as well as angry at the rudeness of this strange woman, I hastily pushed open the door of my room, at which I now stood, in order to escape from her; but great was my amazement on entering to find the apartment occupied.

The window was open, and beside it stood two male figures; they appeared to be examining the fastenings of the casement, and their backs were turned towards the door. One of them was my uncle; they both turned on my entrance, as if startled. The stranger was booted and cloaked, and wore a heavy broad-leafed hat over his brows. He turned but for a moment, and averted his face; but I had seen enough to convince me that he was no other than my cousin Edward. My uncle had some iron instrument in his hand, which he hastily concealed behind his back; and, coming towards me, said something as if in an explanatory tone; but I was too much shocked and confounded to understand what it might be. He said something about 'repairs – window-frames – cold, and safety.'

I did not wait, however, to ask or to receive explanations, but hastily left the room. As I went down the stairs I thought I heard the voice of the French woman in all the shrill volubility of excuse, which was met, however, by suppressed but vehement imprecations, or what seemed to me to be such, in which the voice of my cousin Edward distinctly mingled.

I joined my cousin Emily quite out of breath. I need not say that my head was too full of other things to think much of drawing for that day. I imparted to her frankly the cause of my alarms, but at the same time as gently as I could; and with tears she promised vigilance, and devotion, and love. I never had reason for a moment to repent the unreserved confidence which I then reposed in her. She was no less surprised than I at the unexpected appearance of her brother, whose departure for France neither of us had for a moment doubted, but which was now proved by his actual presence to be nothing more than an imposture, practised, I feared, for no good end.

The situation in which I had found my uncle had removed completely all my doubts as to his designs. I magnified suspicions into certainties, and dreaded night after night that I should be murdered in my bed. The nervousness produced by sleepless nights and days of anxious fears increased the horrors of my situation to such a degree, that I at length wrote a letter to a Mr Jefferies, an old and faithful friend of my father's, and perfectly acquainted with all his affairs, praying him, for God's sake, to relieve me from my present terrible situation, and communicating without reserve the nature and grounds of my suspicions.

This letter I kept sealed and directed for two or three days always about my person – for discovery would have been ruinous – in expectation of an opportunity which might be safely trusted, whereby to have it placed in the post-office. As neither Emily nor I was permitted to pass beyond the precincts of the demesne itself, which was surrounded by high walls formed of dry stone, the difficulty of procuring such an opportunity was greatly enhanced.

At this time Emily had a short conversation with her father, which she reported to me instantly.

After some indifferent matter, he had asked her whether she and I were upon good terms, and whether I was unreserved in my disposition. She answered in the affirmative; and he then enquired whether I had been much surprised to find him in my chamber on the other day. She answered that I had been both surprised and amused.

'And what did she think of George Wilson's appearance?'

'Who?' enquired she.

'Oh, the architect,' he answered, 'who is to contract for the repairs of the house; he is accounted a handsome fellow.'

'She could not see his face,' said Emily, 'and she was in such a hurry to escape that she scarcely noticed him.'

Sir Arthur appeared satisfied, and the conversation ended.

This slight conversation, repeated accurately to me by Emily, had the effect of confirming, if indeed anything was required to do so, all that I had before believed as to Edward's actual presence; and I naturally became, if possible, more anxious than ever to despatch the letter to Mr Jefferies. An opportunity at length occurred.

As Emily and I were walking one day near the gate of the demesne, a man from the village happened to be passing down the avenue from the house; the spot was secluded, and as this person was not connected by service with those whose observation I dreaded, I committed the letter to his keeping, with strict injunctions that he should put it without delay into the receiver of the town post-office; at the same time I added a suitable gratuity, and the man, having made many protestations of punctuality, was soon out of sight.

He was hardly gone when I began to doubt my discretion in having trusted this person; but I had no better or safer means of despatching the letter, and I was not warranted in suspecting him of such wanton dishonesty as an inclination to tamper with it; but I could not be quite satisfied of its safety until I had received an answer, which could not arrive for a few days. Before I did, however, an event occurred which a little surprised me.

I was sitting in my bedroom early in the day, reading by myself, when I heard a knock at the door.

'Come in,' said I; and my uncle entered the room.

'Will you excuse me?' said he. 'I sought you in the parlour, and thence I have come here. I desire to say a word with you. I trust that you have hitherto found my conduct to you such as that of a guardian towards his ward should be.'

I dared not withhold my assent.

'And,' he continued, 'I trust that you have not found me harsh or unjust, and that you have perceived, my dear niece, that I have sought to make this poor place as agreeable to you as may be.'

I assented again; and he put his hand in his pocket, whence he drew a folded paper, and dashing it upon the table with startling emphasis, he said: 'Did you write that letter?'

The sudden and fearful alteration of his voice, manner, and face, but, more than all, the unexpected production of my letter to Mr Jefferies, which I at once recognised, so confounded and terrified me that I felt almost choking.

I could not utter a word.

'Did you write that letter?' he repeated, with slow and intense emphasis. 'You did, liar and hypocrite! You dared to write this foul and infamous libel; but it shall be your last. Men will universally believe you mad, if I choose to call for an enquiry. I can make you appear so. The suspicions expressed in this letter are the hallucinations and alarms of moping lunacy. I have defeated your first attempt, madam; and by the holy God, if ever you make another, chains, straw, darkness, and the keeper's whip shall be your lasting portion!'

With these astounding words he left the room, leaving me almost fainting.

I was now almost reduced to despair; my last cast had failed; I had no course left but that of eloping secretly from the castle and placing myself under the protection of the nearest magistrate. I felt if this were not done, and speedily, that I should be *murdered*.

No one, from mere description, can have an idea of the unmitigated horror of my situation – a helpless, weak, inexperienced girl, placed under the power and wholly at the mercy of evil men, and feeling that she had it not in her power to escape for a moment from the malignant influences under which she was probably fated to fall; and with a consciousness that if violence, if murder were designed, her dying shriek would be lost in void space; no human being would be near to aid her, no human interposition could deliver her.

I had seen Edward but once during his visit, and, as I did not meet with him again, I began to think that he must have taken his departure – a conviction which was to a certain degree satisfactory, as I regarded his absence is indicating the removal of immediate danger.

Emily also arrived circuitously at the same conclusion, and not without good grounds, for she managed indirectly to learn that Edward's black horse had actually been for a day and part of a night in the castle stables, just at the time of her brother's supposed visit. The horse had gone and, as she argued, the rider must have departed with it.

This point being so far settled, I felt a little less uncomfortable; when, being one day alone in my bedroom, I happened to look out from the window, and, to my unutterable horror, I beheld, peering through an opposite casement, my cousin Edward's face. Had I seen the evil one himself in bodily shape, I could not have experienced a more sickening revulsion.

I was too much appalled to move at once from the window, but I did so soon enough to avoid his eye. He was looking fixedly into the narrow quadrangle upon which the window opened. I shrank back unperceived, to pass the rest of the day in terror and despair. I went to my room early that night, but I was too miserable to sleep.

At about twelve o'clock, feeling very nervous, I determined to call my cousin Emily, who slept, you will remember, in the next room, which communicated with mine by a second door. By this private entrance I found my way into her chamber, and without difficulty persuaded her to return to my room and sleep with me. We accordingly lay down together, she undressed, and I with my clothes on, for I was every moment walking up and down the room, and felt too nervous and miserable to think of rest or comfort.

Emily was soon fast asleep, and I lay awake, fervently longing for the first pale gleam of morning; reckoning every stroke of the old clock with an impatience which made every hour appear like six.

It must have been about one o'clock when I thought I heard a slight noise at the partition-door between Emily's room and mine, as if caused by somebody turning the key in the lock. I held my breath, and the same sound was repeated at the second door of my room – that which opened upon the lobby – the sound was here distinctly caused by the revolution of the bolt in the lock, and it was followed by a slight pressure upon the door itself, as if to ascertain the security of the lock.

The person, whoever it might be, was probably satisfied, for I heard the old boards of the lobby creak and strain, as if under the weight of somebody moving cautiously over them. My sense of hearing became unnaturally, almost painfully acute. I suppose my imagination added distinctness to sounds vague in themselves. I thought that I could actually hear the breathing of the person who was slowly returning down the lobby. At the head of the staircase there appeared to occur a pause; and I could distinctly hear two or three sentences hastily whispered; the steps then descended the stairs with apparently less caution. I now ventured to walk quickly and lightly to the lobby door, and attempted to open it; it was indeed fast locked upon the outside, as was also the other.

I now felt that the dreadful hour was come; but one desperate expedient remained – it was to awaken Emily, and by our united strength to attempt to force the partition-door, which was slighter than the other, and through this to pass to the lower part of the house, whence it might be possible to escape to the grounds, and forth to the village.

I returned to the bedside and shook Emily, but in vain. Nothing that I could do availed to produce from her more than a few incoherent words – it was a deathlike sleep. She had certainly drunk of some narcotic, as had I probably also, spite of all the caution with which I had examined everything presented to us to eat or drink.

I now attempted, with as little noise as possible, to force first one door, then the other; but all in vain. I believe no strength could have effected my object, for both doors opened inwards. I therefore collected whatever movables I could carry thither, and piled them against the doors, so as to assist me in whatever attempts I should make to resist the entrance of those without. I then returned to the bed and endeavoured again, but fruitlessly, to awaken my cousin. It was not sleep, it was torpor, lethargy, death. I knelt down and prayed with an agony of earnestness; and then seating myself upon the bed, I awaited my fate with a kind of terrible tranquillity.

I heard a faint clanking sound from the narrow court which I have already mentioned, as if caused by the scraping of some iron instrument against stones or rubbish. I at first determined not to disturb the calmness which I now felt by uselessly watching the proceedings of those who sought my life; but as the sounds continued, the horrible curiosity which I felt overcame every other emotion, and I determined, at all hazards, to gratify it. I therefore crawled upon my knees to the window, so as to let the smallest portion of my head appear above the sill.

The moon was shining with an uncertain radiance upon the antique grey buildings, and obliquely upon the narrow court beneath, one side of which was therefore clearly illuminated, while the other was lost in obscurity; the sharp outlines of the old gables, with their nodding clusters of ivy, being at first alone visible.

Whoever or whatever occasioned the noise which had excited my curiosity, was concealed under the shadow of the dark side of the quadrangle. I placed my hand over my eyes to shade them from the moonlight, which was so bright as to be almost dazzling, and, peering into the darkness, I first dimly, but afterwards gradually almost with full distinctness, beheld the form of a man engaged in digging what appeared to be a rude hole close under the wall. Some implements, probably a shovel and pickaxe, lay beside him, and to these he every now and then applied himself as the nature of the ground required. He pursued his task rapidly, and with as little noise as possible.

'So,' thought I, as, shovelful after shovelful, the dislodged rubbish mounted into a heap, 'they are digging the grave in which, before two hours pass, I must lie, a cold, mangled corpse. I am *theirs* – I cannot escape.'

I felt as if my reason was leaving me. I started to my feet, and in mere despair I applied myself again to each of the two doors alternately. I strained every nerve and sinew, but I might as well have attempted, with my single strength, to force the building itself from its foundation. I threw myself madly upon the ground, and clasped my hands over my eyes as if to shut out the horrible images which crowded upon me.

The paroxysm passed away. I prayed once more, with the bitter, agonised fervour of one who feels that the hour of death is present and inevitable. When I arose, I went once more to the window and looked out, just in time to see a shadowy figure glide stealthily along the wall. The task was finished. The catastrophe of the tragedy must soon be accomplished.

I determined now to defend my life to the last; and that I might be able to do so with some effect, I searched the room for something which might serve as a weapon; but either through accident, or from an anticipation of such a possibility, everything which might have been made available for such a purpose had been carefully removed. I must then die tamely, and without an effort to defend myself.

A thought suddenly struck me – might it not be possible to escape through the door, which the assassin must open in order to enter the room? I resolved to make the attempt. I felt assured that the door through which ingress to the room would be effected was that which opened upon the lobby. It was the more direct way, besides being, for obvious reasons, less liable to interruption than the other. I resolved, then, to place myself behind a projection of the wall, whose shadow would serve fully to conceal me, and when the door should be opened, and before they should have discovered the identity of the occupant of the bed, to creep noiselessly from the room, and then to trust to Providence for escape.

In order to facilitate this scheme, I removed all the lumber which I had heaped against the door; and I had nearly completed my arrangements, when I perceived the room suddenly darkened by the close approach of some shadowy object to the window. On turning my eyes in that direction, I observed at the top of the casement, as if suspended from above, first the feet, then the legs, then the body, and at length the whole figure of a man present himself. It was Edward T—n.

He appeared to be guiding his descent so as to bring his feet upon the centre of the stone block which occupied the lower part of the window; and, having secured his footing upon this, he kneeled down and began to gaze into the room. As the moon was gleaming into the chamber, and the bed curtains were drawn, he was able to distinguish the bed itself and its contents. He appeared satisfied with his scrutiny, for he looked up and made a sign with his hand, upon which the rope by which his descent had been effected was slackened from above, and he proceeded to disengage it from his waist; this accomplished, he applied his hands to the window-frame, which must have been ingeniously contrived for the purpose, for, with apparently no resistance, the whole frame, containing casement and all, slipped from its position in the wall, and was by him lowered into the room.

The cold night wind waved the bed-curtains, and he paused for a moment; all was still again, and he stepped in upon the floor of the room. He held in his hand what appeared to be a steel instrument, shaped something like a hammer, but larger and sharper at the extremities. This he held rather behind him, while, with three long, tiptoe strides, he brought himself to the bedside.

I felt that the discovery must now be made, and held my breath in momentary expectation of the execration in which he would vent his surprise and disappointment. I closed my eyes – there was a pause, but it was a short one. I heard two dull blows, given in rapid succession: a quivering sigh, and the long-drawn, heavy breathing of the sleeper was for ever suspended. I unclosed my eyes, and saw the murderer fling the quilt across the head of his victim: he then, with the instrument of death still in his hand, proceeded to the lobby door, upon which he tapped sharply twice or thrice. A quick step was then heard approaching, and a voice whispered something from without. Edward answered, with a kind of chuckle, 'Her ladyship is past complaining; unlock the door, in the devil's name, unless you're afraid to come in, and help me to lift the body out of the window.'

The key was turned in the lock – the door opened, and my uncle entered the room.

I have told you already that I had placed myself under the shade of a projection of the wall, close to the door. I had instinctively shrunk down, cowering towards the ground, on the entrance of Edward through the window. When my uncle entered the room, he and his son both stood so very close to me that his hand was every moment upon the point of touching my face. I held my breath, and remained motionless as death.

'You had no interruption from the next room?' said my uncle.

'No,' was the brief reply.

'Secure the jewels, Ned; the French harpy must not lay her claws upon them. You're a steady hand, by G—! not much blood – eh?'

'Not twenty drops,' replied his son, 'and those on the quilt.'

'I'm glad it's over,' whispered my uncle again. 'We must lift the – the *thing* through the window and lay the rubbish over it.'

They then turned to the bedside, and, winding the bedclothes round the body, carried it between them slowly to the window, and, exchanging a few brief words with someone below, they shoved it over the window-sill, and I heard it fall heavily on the ground underneath.

'I'll take the jewels,' said my uncle; 'there are two caskets in the lower drawer.'

He proceeded, with an accuracy which, had I been more at ease, would have furnished me with matter of astonishment, to lay his hand upon the very spot where my jewels lay; and having possessed himself of them, he called to his son: 'Is the rope made fast above?'

'I'm not a fool – to be sure it is,' replied he.

They then lowered themselves from the window. I now rose lightly and cautiously, scarcely daring to breathe, from my place of conceal-ment, and was creeping towards the door, when I heard my cousin's voice, in a sharp whisper, exclaim: 'Scramble up again! G—d d—n you, you've forgot to lock the room-door!' and I perceived, by the straining of the rope which hung from above, that the mandate was instantly obeyed.

Not a second was to be lost. I passed through the door, which was only closed, and moved as rapidly as I could, consistently with stillness, along the lobby. Before I had gone many yards, I heard the door through which I had just passed double-locked on the inside. I glided down the stairs in terror, lest, at every corner, I should meet the murderer or one of his accomplices.

I reached the hall, and listened for a moment, to ascertain whether all was silent around; no sound was audible. The parlour windows opened on the park, and through one of them I might, I thought, easily effect my escape. Accordingly, I hastily entered; but, to my consternation, a candle was burning in the room, and by its light I saw a figure seated at the dinner-table, upon which lay glasses, bottles, and the other accompaniments of a drinking-party. Two or three chairs were placed about the table irregularly, as if hastily abandoned by their occupants.

A single glance satisfied me that the figure was that of my French attendant. She was fast asleep, having probably drunk deeply. There was something malignant and ghastly in the calmness of this bad woman's features, dimly illuminated as they were by the flickering blaze of the candle. A knife lay upon the table, and the terrible thought struck me – 'Should I kill this sleeping accomplice, and thus secure my retreat?'

Nothing could be easier – it was but to draw the blade across her throat – the work of a second. An instant's pause, however, corrected me. 'No,' thought I, 'the God who has conducted me thus far through the valley of the shadow of death, will not abandon me now. I will fall into their hands, or I will escape hence, but it shall be free from the stain of blood. His will be done!'

I felt a confidence arising from this reflection, an assurance of protection which I cannot describe. There was no other means of escape, so I advanced, with a firm step and collected mind, to the window. I noiselessly withdrew the bars and unclosed the shutters – I pushed open the casement, and, without waiting to look behind me, I ran with my utmost speed, scarcely feeling the ground under me, down the avenue, taking care to keep upon the grass which bordered it.

I did not for a moment slacken my speed, and I had now gained the centre point between the park-gate and the mansion-house. Here the avenue made a wider circuit, and in order to avoid delay, I directed my way across the smooth sward round which the pathway wound, intending, at the opposite side of the flat, at a point which I distinguished by a group of old birch trees, to enter again upon the beaten track, which was from thence tolerably direct to the gate.

I had, with my utmost speed, got about halfway across this broad flat, when the rapid treading of a horse's hoofs struck upon my ear. My heart swelled in my bosom as though I would smother. The clattering of galloping hoofs approached – I was pursued – they were now upon the sward on which I was running – there was not a bush or a bramble to shelter me – and, as if to render escape altogether desperate, the moon, which had hitherto been obscured, at this moment shone forth with a broad clear light, which made every object distinctly visible.

The sounds were now close behind me. I felt my knees bending under me, with the sensation which torments one in dreams. I reeled – I stumbled – I fell – and at the same instant the cause of my alarm wheeled past me at full gallop. It was one of the young fillies which pastured loose about the park, whose frolics had thus all but maddened me with terror. I scrambled to my feet, and rushed on with weak but rapid steps, my sportive companion still galloping round and round me with many a frisk and fling, until, at length, more dead than alive, I reached the avenue-gate, and crossed the stile, I scarce knew how.

I ran through the village, in which all was silent as the grave, until my progress was arrested by the hoarse voice of a sentinel, who cried, 'Who goes there?' I felt that I was now safe. I turned in the direction of the voice, and fell fainting at the soldier's feet. When I came to myself, I was sitting in a miserable hovel, surrounded by strange faces, all bespeaking curiosity and compassion.

Many soldiers were in it also: indeed, as I afterwards found, it was employed as a guardroom by a detachment of troops quartered for that night in the town. In a few words I informed their officer of the circumstances which had occurred, describing also the appearance of the persons engaged in the murder; and he, without loss of time, proceeded to the mansion-house of Carrickleigh, taking with him a party of his men. But the villains had discovered their mistake, and had effected their escape before the arrival of the military.

The Frenchwoman was, however, arrested in the neighbourhood upon the next day. She was tried and condemned upon the ensuing assizes; and previous to her execution, confessed that '*she had a hand in making Hugh Tisdall's bed.*' She had been a housekeeper in the castle at the time, and a kind of *chère amie* of my uncle's. She was, in reality, able to speak English like a native, but had exclusively used the French language, I suppose, to facilitate her disguise. She died the same hardened wretch she had lived, confessing her crimes only, as she alleged, that her doing so might involve Sir Arthur T—n, the great author of her guilt and misery, and whom she now regarded with unmitigated detestation.

With the particulars of Sir Arthur's and his son's escape, as far as they are known, you are acquainted. You are also in possession of their after fate – the terrible, the tremendous retribution which, after long delays of many years, finally overtook and crushed them. Wonderful and inscrutable are the dealings of God with His creatures.

Deep and fervent as must always be my gratitude to Heaven for my deliverance, effected by a chain of providential occurrences, the failing of a single link of which must have ensured my destruction, I was long before I could look back upon it with other feelings than those of bitterness, almost of agony. The only being that had ever really loved me, my nearest and dearest friend, ever ready to sympathise, to counsel, and to assist – the gayest, the gentlest, the warmest heart; the only creature on earth that cared for me – *her* life had been the price of my deliverance; and I then uttered the wish, which no event of my long and sorrowful life has taught me to recall, that she had been spared, and that, in her stead, *I* were mouldering in the grave, forgotten and at rest.

Strange Event in the Life of Schalken the Painter

SHERIDAN LE FANU

You will no doubt be surprised, my dear friend, at the subject of the following narrative. What had I to do with Schalken, or Schalken with me? He had returned to his native land, and was probably dead and buried before I was born; I never visited Holland, nor spoke with a native of that country. So much I believe you already know. I must, then, give you my authority, and state to you frankly the ground upon which rests the credibility of the strange story which I am about to lay before you.

I was acquainted, in my early days, with a Captain Vandael, whose father had served King William in the Low Countries, and also in my own unhappy land during the Irish campaigns. I know not how it happened that I liked this man's society, spite of his politics and religion: but so it was; and it was by means of the free intercourse to which our intimacy gives rise that I became possessed of the curious tale which you are about to hear.

I had often been struck, while visiting Vandael, by a remarkable picture, in which, though no *connoisseur* myself, I could not fail to discern some very strong peculiarities, particularly in the distribution of light and shade, as also a certain oddity in the design itself, which interested my curiosity. It represented the interior of what might be a chamber in some antique religious building – the foreground was occupied by a female figure, arrayed in a species of white robe, part of which was arranged so as to form a veil. The dress, however, was not strictly that of any religious order. In its hand the figure bore a lamp, by whose light alone the form and face were illuminated; the features were marked by an arch smile, such as pretty women wear when engaged in successfully practising some roguish trick; in the background, and (excepting where the dim red light of an expiring fire serves to define the form) totally in the shade, stood the figure of a man equipped in the old fashion, with doublet and so forth, in an attitude of alarm, his hand being placed upon the hilt of his sword, which he appeared to be in the act of drawing.

'There are some pictures,' said I to my friend, 'which impress one, I know not how, with a conviction that they represent not the mere ideal shapes and combinations which have floated through the imagination of the artist, but scenes, faces, and situations which have actually existed. When I look upon that picture, something assures me that I behold the representation of a reality.'

Vandael smiled, and, fixing his eyes upon the painting musingly, he said: 'Your fancy has not deceived you, my good friend, for that picture is the record, and I believe a faithful one, of a remarkable and mysterious occurrence. It was painted by Schalken, and contains, in the face of the female figure which occupies the most prominent place in the design, an accurate portrait of Rose Velderkaust, the niece of Gerard Douw, the first and, I believe, the only love of Godfrey Schalken. My father knew the painter well, and from Schalken himself he learned the story of the mysterious drama, one scene of which the picture has embodied. This painting, which is accounted a fine specimen of Schalken's style, was bequeathed to my father by the artist's will, and, as you have observed, is a very striking and interesting production.'

I had only to request Vandael to tell the story of the painting in order to be gratified; and thus it is that I am enabled to submit to you a faithful recital of what I heard myself, leaving you to reject or to allow the evidence upon which the truth of the tradition depends – with this one assurance, that Schalken was an honest, blunt Dutchman, and, I believe, wholly incapable of committing a flight of imagination; and further, that Vandael, from whom I heard the story, appeared firmly convinced of its truth.

There are few forms upon which the mantle of mystery and romance could seem to hang more ungracefully than upon that of the uncouth and clownish Schalken – the Dutch boor – the rude and dogged, but most cunning worker in oils, whose pieces delight the initiated of the present day almost as much as his manner disgusted the refined of his own; and yet this man, so rude, so dogged, so slovenly, I had almost said so savage in mien and manner, during his after successes, had been selected by the capricious goddess, in his early life, to figure as the hero of a romance by no means devoid of interest or of mystery.

Who can tell how meet he may have been in his young days to

play the part of the lover or of the hero? who can say that in early life he had been the same harsh, unlicked, and rugged boor that, in his maturer age, he proved? or how far the neglected rudeness which afterwards marked his air, and garb, and manners, may not have been the growth of that reckless apathy not unfrequently produced by bitter misfortunes and disappointments in early life?

These questions can never now be answered.

We must content ourselves, then, with a plain statement of facts, leaving matters of speculation to those who like them.

When Schalken studied under the immortal Gerard Douw, he was a young man; and in spite of the phlegmatic constitution and excitable manner which he shared, we believe, with his countrymen, he was not incapable of deep and vivid impressions, for it is an established fact that the young painter looked with considerable interest upon the beautiful niece of his wealthy master.

Rose Velderkaust was very young, having, at the period of which we speak, not yet attained her seventeenth year; and, if tradition speaks truth, she possessed all the soft dimpling charms of the fair, light-haired Flemish maidens. Schalken had not studied long in the school of Gerard Douw when he felt this interest deepening into something of a keener and intenser feeling than was quite consistent with the tranquillity of his honest Dutch heart; and at the same time he perceived, or thought he perceived, flattering symptoms of a reciprocal attachment, and this was quite sufficient to determine whatever indecision he might have heretofore experienced, and to lead him to devote exclusively to her every hope and feeling of his heart. In short, he was as much in love as a Dutchman could be. He was not long in making his passion known to the pretty maiden herself, and his declaration was followed by a corresponding con-fession upon her part.

Schalken, howbeit, was a poor man, and he possessed no counter-balancing advantages of birth or position to induce the old man to consent to a union which must involve his niece and ward in the strugglings and difficulties of a young and nearly friendless artist. He was, therefore, to wait until time had furnished him with opportunity, and accident with success; and then, if his labours were found sufficiently lucrative, it was to be hoped that his proposals might at least be listened to by her jealous guardian. Months passed away, and, cheered by the smiles of the little Rose, Schalken's labours were redoubled, and with such effect and improvement as reasonably to promise the realisation of his hopes, and no contemptible eminence in his art, before many years should have elapsed.

The even course of this cheering prosperity was, unfortunately, destined to experience a sudden and formidable interruption, and that, too, in a manner so strange and mysterious as to baffle all investigation, and throw upon the events themselves a shadow of almost supernatural horror.

Schalken had one evening remained in the master's studio considerably longer than his more volatile companions, who had gladly availed themselves of the excuse which the dusk of evening afforded to withdraw from their several tasks, in order to finish a day of labour in the jollity and conviviality of the tavern.

But Schalken worked for improvement, or rather for love. Besides, he was now engaged merely in sketching a design, an operation which, unlike that of colouring, might be continued as long as there was light sufficient to distinguish between canvas and charcoal. He had not then, nor, indeed, until long after, discovered the peculiar powers of his pencil; and he was engaged in composing a group of extremely roguish-looking and grotesque imps and demons, who were inflicting various ingenious torments upon a perspiring and pot-bellied St Anthony, who reclined in the midst of them, apparently in the last stage of drunkenness.

The young artist, however, though incapable of executing, or even of appreciating, anything of true sublimity, had nevertheless discernment enough to prevent his being by any means satisfied with his work; and many were the patient erasures and corrections which the limbs and features of saint and devil underwent, yet all without producing in their new arrangement anything of improvement or increased effect.

The large, old-fashioned room was silent, and, with the exception of himself, quite deserted by its usual inmates. An hour had passed – nearly two – without any improved result. Daylight had already declined, and twilight was fast giving way to the darkness of night. The patience of the young man was exhausted, and he stood before his unfinished production, absorbed in no very pleasing ruminations, one hand buried in the folds of his long dark hair, and the other holding the piece of charcoal which had so ill executed its office, and which he now rubbed, without much regard to the sable streaks which it produced, with irritable pressure upon his ample Flemish inexpressibles.

'Pshaw!' said the young man aloud, 'would that picture, devils, saint, and all, were where they should be – in hell!'

A short, sudden laugh, uttered startlingly close to his ear, instantly responded to the ejaculation.

The artist turned sharply round, and now for the first time became aware that his labours had been overlooked by a stranger.

Within about a yard and a half, and rather behind him, there stood what was, or appeared to be, the figure of an elderly man: he wore a short cloak, and broad-brimmed hat with a conical crown, and in his hand, which was protected with a heavy, gauntlet-shaped glove, he carried a long ebony walking-stick, surmounted with what appeared, as it glittered dimly in the twilight to be a massive head of gold; and upon his breast, through the folds of the cloak, there shone the links of a rich chain of the same metal.

The room was so obscure that nothing further of the appearance of the figure could be ascertained, and the face was altogether overshadowed by the heavy flap of the beaver which overhung it, so that no feature could be clearly discerned. A quantity of dark hair escaped from beneath this sombre hat, a circumstance which, connected with the firm, upright carriage of the intruder, proved that his years could not exceed threescore or thereabouts.

There was an air of gravity and importance about the garb of this person, and something indescribably odd – I might say awful – in the perfect, stonelike movelessness of the figure, that effectually checked the testy comment which had at once risen to the lips of the irritated artist. He therefore, as soon as he had sufficiently recovered the surprise, asked the stranger, civilly, to be seated, and desired to know if he had any message to leave for his master.

'Tell Gerard Douw,' said the unknown, without altering his attitude in the smallest degree, 'that Mynher Vanderhausen, of Rotterdam, desires to speak with him tomorrow evening at this hour, and, if he please, in this room, upon matters of weight; that is all. Good-night.'

The stranger, having finished this message, turned abruptly, and, with a quick but silent step quitted the room before Schalken had time to say a word in reply.

The young man felt a curiosity to see in what direction the burgher of Rotterdam would turn on quitting the studio, and for that purpose he went directly to the window which commanded the door.

A lobby of considerable extent intervened between the inner door of the painter's room and the street entrance, so that Schalken occupied the post of observation before the old man could possibly have reached the street.

He watched in vain, however. There was no other mode of exit.

Had the old man vanished, or was he lurking about the recesses of the lobby for some bad purpose? This last suggestion filled the mind of Schalken with a vague horror, which was so unaccountably intense as to make him alike afraid to remain in the room alone and reluctant to pass through the lobby.

However, with an effort which appeared very disproportioned to the occasion, he summoned resolution to leave the room, and, having double-locked the door, and thrust the key in his pocket, without looking at the right or left, he traversed the passage which had so recently, perhaps still, contained the person of his mysterious visitant, scarcely venturing to breathe till he had arrived in the open street.

'Mynher Vanderhausen,' said Gerard Douw, within himself, as the appointed hour approached; 'Mynher Vanderhausen, of Rotterdam! I never heard of the man till yesterday. What can he want of me? A portrait, perhaps, to be painted; or a younger son or a poor relation to be apprenticed; or a collection to be valued; or – pshaw! there's no one in Rotterdam to leave me a legacy. Well, whatever the business may be, we shall soon know it all.'

It was now the close of day, and every easel, except that of Schalken, was deserted. Gerard Douw was pacing the apartment with the restless step of impatient expectation, every now and then humming a passage from a piece of music which he was himself composing for, though no great proficient, he admired the art; sometimes pausing to glance over the work of one of his absent pupils, but more frequently placing himself at the window, from whence he might observe the passengers who threaded the obscure by-street in which his studio was placed.

'Said you not, Godfrey,' exclaimed Douw, after a long and fruitless gaze from his post of observation, and turning to Schalken – 'said you not the hour of appointment was at about seven by the clock of the Stadhouse?'

'It had just told seven when I first saw him, sir,' answered the student.

'The hour is close at hand, then,' said the master, consulting a horologe as large and as round as a full-grown orange. 'Mynher Vanderhausen, from Rotterdam – is it not so?'

'Such was the name.'

'And an elderly man, richly clad?' continued Douw.

'As well as I might see,' replied his pupil. 'He could not be young, nor yet very old neither, and his dress was rich and grave, as might become a citizen of wealth and consideration.'

At this moment the sonorous boom of the Stadhouse clock told, stroke after stroke, the hour of seven; the eyes of both master and student were directed to the door; and it was not until the last peal of the old bell had ceased to vibrate, that Douw exclaimed: 'So, so; we shall have his worship presently – that is, if he means to keep his hour; if not, thou mayst wait for him, Godfrey, if you court the acquaintance of a capricious burgomaster. As for me, I think our old Leyden contains a sufficiency of such commodities, without an importation from Rotterdam.'

Schalken laughed, as in duty bound; and, after a pause of some minutes, Douw suddenly exclaimed: 'What if it should all prove a jest, a piece of mummery got up by Vankarp, or some such worthy! I wish you had run all risks, and cudgelled the old burgomaster, stadholder, or whatever else he may be, soundly. I would wager a dozen of Rhenish, his worship would have pleaded old acquaintance before the third application.'

'Here he comes, sir,' said Schalken, in a low, admonitory tone; and instantly, upon turning towards the door, Gerard Douw observed the same figure which had, on the day before, so unexpectedly greeted the vision of his pupil Schalken.

There was something in the air and mien of the figure which at once satisfied the painter that there was no mummery in the case, and that he really stood in the presence of a man of worship; and so, without hesitation, he doffed his cap, and courteously saluting the stranger, requested him to be seated.

The visitor waved his hand slightly, as if in acknowledgment of the courtesy, but remained standing.

'I have the honour to see Mynher Vanderhausen, of Rotterdam?' said Gerard Douw.

'The same,' was the laconic reply.

'I understood your worship desires to speak with me,' continued Douw, 'and I am here by appointment to wait your commands.'

'Is that a man of trust?' said Vanderhausen, turning towards Schalken, who stood at a little distance behind his master.

'Certainly,' replied Gerard.

'Then let him take this box and get the nearest jeweller or gold-smith to value its contents, and let him return hither with a certificate of the valuation.'

At the same time he placed a small case, about nine inches square, in the hands of Gerard Douw, who was as much amazed at its weight as at the strange abruptness with which it was handed to him.

In accordance with the wishes of the stranger, he delivered it into the hands of Schalken, and repeating *his* directions, despatched him upon the mission.

Schalken disposed his precious charge securely beneath the folds of his cloak, and rapidly traversing two or three narrow streets, he stopped at a corner house, the lower part of which was then occupied by the shop of Jewish goldsmith.

Schalken entered the shop, and calling the little Hebrew into the obscurity of its back recesses, he proceeded to lay before him Van-derhausen's packet.

On being examined by the light of a lamp, it appeared entirely cased with lead, the outer surface of which was much scraped and soiled, and nearly white with age. This was with difficulty partially removed, and disclosed beneath a box of some dark and singularly hard wood; this, too, was forced, and after the removal of two or three folds of linen, its contents proved to be a mass of golden ingots, close packed, and, as the Jew declared, of the most perfect quality.

Every ingot underwent the scrutiny of the little Jew, who seemed to feel an epicurean delight in touching and testing these morsels of the glorious metal; and each one of them was replaced in the box with the exclamation: '*Mein Gott*, how very perfect! not one grain of alloy – beautiful, beautiful!'

The task was at length finished, and the Jew certified under his hand that the value of the ingots submitted to his examination amounted to many thousand rix-dollars.

With the desired document in his bosom, and the rich box of gold carefully pressed under his arm, and concealed by his cloak, he retraced his way, and, entering the studio, found his master and the stranger in close conference.

Schalken had no sooner left the room, in order to execute the commission he had taken in charge, than Vanderhausen addressed Gerard Douw in the following terms: 'I may not tarry with you tonight more than a few minutes, and so I shall briefly tell you the matter upon which I come. You visited the town of Rotterdam some four months ago, and then I saw in the church of : Lawrence your niece, Rose Velderkaust. I desire to marry her, and if I satisfy you as to the fact that I am very wealthy – more wealthy than any husband you could dream of for her – I expect that you will forward my views to the utmost of your authority. If you approve my proposal, you must close with it at once, for I cannot command time enough to wait for calculations and delays.'

Gerard Douw was, perhaps, as much astonished as anyone could be by the very unexpected nature of Mynher Vanderhausen's communication; but he did not give vent to any unseemly expression of surprise. In addition to the motives supplied by prudence and politeness, the painter experienced a kind of chill and oppressive sensation – a feeling like that which is supposed to affect a man who is placed unconsciously in immediate contact with something to which he has a natural antipathy – an undefined horror and dread – while standing in the presence of the eccentric stranger, which made him very unwilling to say anything that might reasonably prove offensive.

'I have no doubt,' said Gerard, after two or three prefatory hems, 'that the connection which you propose would prove alike advantageous and honourable to my niece; but you must be aware that she has a will of her own, and may not acquiesce in what *we* may design for her advantage.'

'Do not seek to deceive me, Sir Painter,' said Vanderhausen; 'you are her guardian – she is your ward. She is mine if *you* like to make her so.'

The man of Rotterdam moved forward a little as he spoke, and Gerard Douw, he scarce knew why, inwardly prayed for the speedy return of Schalken.

'I desire,' said the mysterious gentleman, 'to place in your hands at once an evidence of my wealth, and a security for my liberal dealing with your niece. The lad will return in a minute or two with a sum in value five times the fortune which she has a right to expect from a husband. This shall lie in your hands, together with her dowry, and you may apply the united sum as suits her interest best; it shall be all exclusively hers while she lives. Is that liberal?'

Douw assented, and inwardly thought that fortune had been extraordinarily kind to his niece. The stranger, he deemed, must be most wealthy and generous, and such an offer was not to be despised, though made by a humourist, and one of no very prepossessing presence.

Rose had no very high pretensions, for she was almost without dowry; indeed, altogether so, excepting so far as the deficiency had been supplied by the generosity of her uncle. Neither had she any right to raise any scruples against the match on the score of birth, for her own origin was by no means elevated; and as to other objections, Gerard resolved, and, indeed, by the usages of the time was warranted in resolving, not to listen to them for a moment.

'Sir,' said he, addressing the stranger, 'your offer is most liberal, and whatever hesitation I may feel in closing with it immediately, arises solely from my not having the honour of knowing anything of your family or station. Upon these points you can, of course, satisfy me without difficulty?'

'As to my respectability,' said the stranger, drily, 'you must take that for granted at present; pester me with no enquiries; you can discover nothing more about me than I choose to make known. You shall have sufficient security for my respectability – my word, if you are honourable: if you are sordid, my gold.'

'A testy old gentleman,' thought Douw; 'he must have his own way. But, all things considered, I am justified in giving my niece to him. Were she my own daughter, I would do the like by her. I will not pledge myself unnecessarily, however.'

'You will not pledge yourself unnecessarily,' said Vanderhausen, strangely uttering the very words which had just floated through the mind of his companion; 'but you will do so if it *is* necessary, I presume; and I will show you that I consider it indispensable. If the gold I mean to leave in your hands satisfies you, and if you desire that my proposal shall not be at once withdrawn, you must, before I leave this room, write your name to this engagement.'

Having thus spoken, he placed a paper in the hands of Gerard, the contents of which expressed an engagement entered into by Gerard Douw, to give to Wilken Vanderhausen, of Rotterdam, in marriage, Rose Velderkaust, and so forth, within one week of the date hereof.

While the painter was employed in reading this covenant, Schalken, as we have stated, entered the studio, and having delivered the box and the valuation of the Jew into the hands of the stranger, he was about to retire, when Vanderhausen called to him to wait; and, presenting the case and the certificate to Gerard Douw, he waited in silence until he had satisfied himself by an inspection of both as to the value of the pledge left in his hands. At length he said: 'Are you content?'

The painter said 'he would fain have another day to consider.'

'Not an hour,' said the suitor, coolly.

'Well, then,' said Douw, 'I am content; it is a bargain.'

'Then sign at once,' said Vanderhausen; 'I am weary.'

At the same time he produced a small case of writing materials, and Gerard signed the important document.

'Let this youth witness the covenant,' said the old man; and Godfrey Schalken unconsciously signed the instrument which bestowed upon another that hand which he had so long regarded as the object and reward of all his labours.

The compact being thus completed, the strange visitor folded up the paper, and stowed it safely in an inner pocket.

'I will visit you tomorrow night, at nine of the clock, at your house, Gerard Douw, and will see the subject of our contract. Farewell.' And so saying, Wilken Vanderhausen moved stiffly, but rapidly out of the room.

Schalken, eager to resolve his doubts, had placed himself by the window in order to watch the street entrance; but the experiment served only to support his suspicions, for the old man did not issue from the door. This was very strange, very odd, very fearful. He and his master returned together, and talked but little on the way, for each had his own subjects of reflection, of anxiety, and of hope.

Schalken, however, did not know the ruin which threatened his cherished schemes.

Gerard Douw knew nothing of the attachment which had sprung up between his pupil and his niece; and even if he had, it is doubtful whether he would have regarded its existence as any serious obstruction to the wishes of Mynher Vanderhausen.

Marriages were then and there matters of traffic and calculation; and it would have appeared as absurd in the eyes of the guardian to make a mutual attachment an essential element in a contract of marriage, as it would have been to draw up his bonds and receipts in the language of chivalrous romance.

The painter, however, did not communicate to his niece the important step which he had taken in her behalf, and his resolution arose not from any anticipation of opposition on her part, but solely from a ludicrous consciousness that if his ward were, as she very naturally might do, to ask him to describe the appearance of the bridegroom whom he destined for her, he would be forced to confess that he had not seen his face, and, if called upon, would find it impossible to identify him.

Upon the next day, Gerard Douw having dined, called his niece to him, and having scanned her person with an air of satisfaction, he took her hand, and looking upon her pretty, innocent face with a smile of kindness, he said: 'Rose, my girl, that face of yours will make your fortune.' Rose blushed and smiled. 'Such faces and such tempers seldom go together, and, when they do, the compound is a love-potion which few heads or hearts can resist. Trust me, thou wilt soon be a bride, girl. But this is trifling, and I am pressed for time, so make ready the large room by eight o'clock tonight, and give directions for supper at nine. I expect a friend tonight; and observe me, child, do thou trick thyself out handsomely. I would not have him think us poor or sluttish.'

With these words he left the chamber, and took his way to the room to which we have already had occasion to introduce our readers – that in which his pupils worked.

When the evening closed in, Gerard called Schalken, who was about to take his departure to his obscure and comfortless lodgings, and asked him to come home and sup with Rose and Vanderhausen.

The invitation was of course accepted, and Gerard Douw and his pupil soon found themselves in the handsome and somewhat antique-looking room which had been prepared for the reception of the stranger.

A cheerful wood-fire blazed in the capacious hearth; a little at one side an old-fashioned table, with richly-carved legs, was placed – destined, no doubt, to receive the supper, for which preparations were going forward; and ranged with exact regularity stood the tall-backed chairs whose ungracefulness was more than counterbalanced by their comfort.

The little party, consisting of Rose, her uncle, and the artist, awaited the arrival of the expected visitor with considerable impatience.

Nine o'clock at length came, and with it a summons at the street-door, which, being speedily answered, was followed by a slow and emphatic tread upon the staircase; the steps moved heavily across the lobby, the door of the room in which the party which we have described were assembled slowly opened, and there entered a figure which startled, almost appalled, the phlegmatic Dutchmen, and nearly made Rose scream with affright; it was the form, and arrayed in the garb, of Mynher Vanderhausen; the air, the gait, the height was the same, but the features had never been seen by any of the party before.

The stranger stopped at the door of the room, and displayed his

form and face completely. He wore a dark coloured cloth cloak, which
was short and full, not falling quite to the knees; his legs were cased in
dark purple silk stockings, and his shoes were adorned with roses of
the same colour. The opening of the cloak in front showed the
undersuit to consist of some very dark, perhaps sable material, and his
hands were enclosed in a pair of heavy leather gloves which ran up
considerably above the wrist, in the manner of a gauntlet. In one
hand he carried his walking-stick and his hat, which he had removed,
and the other hung heavily by his side. A quantity of grizzled hair
descended in long tresses from his head, and its folds rested upon the
plaits of a stiff ruff, which effectually concealed his neck.

So far all was well; but the face! – all the flesh of the face was
coloured with the bluish leaden hue which is sometimes produced
by the operation of metallic medicines administered in excessive
quantities; the eyes were enormous, and the white appeared both
above and below the iris, which gave to them an expression of
insanity, which was heightened by their glassy fixedness; the nose
was well enough, but the mouth was writhed considerably to one
side, where it opened in order to give egress to two long, discoloured
fangs, which projected from the upper jaw, far below the lower lip;
the hue of the lips themselves bore the usual relation to that of the
face, and was consequently nearly black. The character of the face
was malignant, even satanic, to the last degree; and, indeed, such a
combination of horror could hardly be accounted for, except by
supposing the corpse of some atrocious malefactor, which had long
hung blackening upon the gibbet, to have at length become the
habitation of a demon – the frightful sport of satanic possession.

It was remarkable that the worshipful stranger suffered as little as
possible of his flesh to appear, and that during his visit he did not
once remove his gloves.

Having stood for some moments at the door, Gerard Douw at
length found breath and collectedness to bid him welcome, and,
with a mute inclination of the head, the stranger stepped forward
into the room.

There was something indescribably odd, even horrible about all his
motions, something undefinable, something unnatural, unhuman – it
was as if the limbs were guided and directed by a spirit unused to the
management of bodily machinery.

The stranger said hardly anything during his visit, which did not
exceed half an hour; and the host himself could scarcely muster

courage enough to utter the few necessary salutations and courtesies: and, indeed, such was the nervous terror which the presence of Vanderhausen inspired, that very little would have made all his entertainers fly bellowing from the room.

They had not so far lost all self-possession, however, as to fail to observe two strange peculiarities of their visitor.

During his stay he did not once suffer his eyelids to close, nor even to move in the slightest degree; and further, there was deathlike stillness in his whole person, owing to the total absence of the heaving motion of the chest caused by the process of respiration.

These two peculiarities, though when told they may appear trifling, produced a very striking and unpleasant effect when seen and observed. Vanderhausen at length relieved the painter of Leyden of his inauspicious presence; and with no small gratification the little party heard the street door close after him.

'Dear uncle,' said Rose, 'what a frightful man! I would not see him again for the wealth of the States!'

'Tush, foolish girl!' said Douw, whose sensations were anything but comfortable. 'A man may be as ugly as the devil, and yet if his heart and actions are good, he is worth all the pretty-faced, perfumed puppies that walk the Mall. Rose, my girl, it is very true he has not thy pretty face, but I know him to be wealthy and liberal; and were he ten times more ugly – '

'Which is inconceivable,' observed Rose.

'These two virtues would be sufficient,' continued her uncle, 'to counterbalance all his deformity; and if not of power sufficient actually to alter the shape of the features, at least of efficacy enough to prevent one thinking them amiss.'

'Do you know, uncle,' said Rose, 'when I saw him standing at the door, I could not get it out of my head that I saw the old, painted, wooden figure that used to frighten me so much in the church of St Laurence at Rotterdam.'

Gerard laughed, though he could not help inwardly acknowledging the justness of the comparison. He was resolved, however, as far as he could, to check his niece's inclination to ridicule the ugliness of her intended bridegroom, although he was not a little pleased to observe that she appeared totally exempt from that mysterious dread of the stranger, which, he could not disguise it from himself, considerably affected him, as it also did his pupil Godfrey Schalken.

Early on the next day there arrived from various quarters of the town, rich presents of silks, velvets, jewellery, and so forth, for Rose; and also a packet directed to Gerard Douw, which, on being opened, was found to contain a contract of marriage, formally drawn up, between Wilken Vanderhausen of the Boom-quay, in Rotterdam, and Rose Velderkaust of Leyden, niece to Gerard Douw, master in the art of painting, also of the same city; and containing engagements on the part of Vanderhausen to make settlements upon his bride far more splendid than he had before led her guardian to believe likely, and which were to be secured to her use in the most unexceptionable manner possible – the money being placed in the hands of Gerard Douw himself.

I have no sentimental scenes to describe, no cruelty of guardians or magnanimity of wards, or agonies of lovers. The record I have to make is one of sordidness, levity, and interest. In less than a week after the first interview which we have just described, the contract of marriage was fulfilled, and Schalken saw the prize which he would have risked anything to secure, carried off triumphantly by his formidable rival.

For two or three days he absented himself from the school; he then returned and worked, if with less cheerfulness, with far more dogged resolution than before; the dream of love had given place to that of ambition.

Months passed away, and, contrary to his expectation, and, indeed, to the direct promise of the parties, Gerard Douw heard nothing of his niece or her worshipful spouse. The interest of the money, which was to have been demanded in quarterly sums, lay unclaimed in his hands. He began to grow extremely uneasy.

Mynher Vanderhausen's direction in Rotterdam he was fully possessed of. After some irresolution he finally determined to journey thither – a trifling undertaking, and easily accomplished – and thus to satisfy himself of the safety and comfort of his ward, for whom he entertained an honest and strong affection.

His search was in vain, however. No one in Rotterdam had ever heard of Mynher Vanderhausen.

Gerard Douw left not a house in the Boom-quay untried; but all in vain. No one could give him any information whatever touching the object of his enquiry; and he was obliged to return to Leyden, nothing wiser than when he had left it.

On his arrival he hastened to the establishment from which

Vanderhausen had hired the lumbering, though, considering the times, most luxurious vehicle which the bridal party had employed to convey them to Rotterdam. From the driver of this machine he learned, that having proceeded by slow stages, they had late in the evening approached Rotterdam; but that before they entered the city, and while yet nearly a mile from it, a small party of men, soberly clad, and after the old fashion, with peaked beards and moustaches, standing in the centre of the road, obstructed the further progress of the carriage. The driver reined in his horses, much fearing, from the obscurity of the hour, and the loneliness of the road, that some mischief was intended.

His fears were, however, somewhat allayed by his observing that these strange men carried a large litter, of an antique shape, and which they immediately set down upon the pavement, whereupon the bridegroom, having opened the coach-door from within, descended, and having assisted his bride to do likewise, led her, weeping bitterly and wringing her hands, to the litter, which they both entered. It was then raised by the men who surrounded it, and speedily carried towards the city, and before it had proceeded many yards the darkness concealed it from the view of the Dutch chariot.

In the inside of the vehicle he found a purse, whose contents more than thrice paid the hire of the carriage and man. He saw and could tell nothing more of Mynher Vanderhausen and his beautiful lady. This mystery was a source of deep anxiety and almost of grief to Gerard Douw.

There was evidently fraud in the dealing of Vanderhausen with him, though for what purpose committed he could not imagine. He greatly doubted how far it was possible for a man possessing in his countenance so strong an evidence of the presence of the most demoniac feelings to be in reality anything but a villain; and every day that passed without his hearing from or of his niece, instead of inducing him to forget his fears, tended more and more to intensify them.

The loss of his niece's cheerful society tended also to depress his spirits; and in order to dispel this despondency, which often crept upon his mind after his daily employment was over, he was wont frequently to prevail upon Schalken to accompany him home, and by his presence to dispel, in some degree, the gloom of his otherwise solitary supper.

One evening, the painter and his pupil were sitting by the fire, having accomplished a comfortable supper. They had yielded to that silent pensiveness sometimes induced by the process of digestion, when their reflections were disturbed by a loud sound at the street-door, as if occasioned by some person rushing forcibly and repeatedly against it. A domestic had run without delay to ascertain the cause of the disturbance, and they heard him twice or thrice interrogate the applicant for admission, but without producing an answer or any cessation of the sounds.

They heard him then open the hall door, and immediately there followed a light and rapid tread upon the staircase. Schalken laid his hand on his sword, and advanced towards the door. It opened before he reached it, and Rose rushed into the room. She looked wild and haggard, and pale with exhaustion and terror; but her dress surprised them as much even as her unexpected appearance. It consisted of a kind of white woollen wrapper, made close about the neck, and descending to the very ground. It was much deranged and travel-soiled. The poor creature had hardly entered the chamber when she fell senseless on the floor. With some difficulty they succeeded in reviving her, and on recovering her senses she instantly exclaimed, in a tone of eager, terrified impatience: 'Wine, wine, quickly, or I'm lost!'

Much alarmed at the strange agitation in which the call was made, they at once administered to her wishes, and she drank some wine with a haste and eagerness which surprised him. She had hardly swallowed it, when she exclaimed with the same urgency: 'Food, food, at once, or I perish!'

A considerable fragment of a roast joint was upon the table, and Schalken immediately proceeded to cut some, but he was anticipated; for no sooner had she become aware of its presence than she darted at it with the rapacity of a vulture, and, seizing it in her hands, she tore off the flesh with her teeth and swallowed it.

When the paroxysm of hunger had been a little appeased, she appeared suddenly to become aware how strange her conduct had been, or it may have been that other more agitating thoughts recurred to her mind, for she began to weep bitterly, and to wring her hands.

'Oh! send for a minister of God,' said she; 'I am not safe till he comes; send for him speedily.'

Gerard Douw despatched a messenger instantly, and prevailed on his niece to allow him to surrender his bedchamber to her use; he also persuaded her to retire to it at once and to rest; her consent was extorted upon the condition that they would not leave her for a moment.

'Oh that the holy man were here!' she said; 'he can deliver me. The dead and the living can never be one – God has forbidden it.'

With these mysterious words she surrendered herself to their guidance, and they proceeded to the chamber which Gerard Douw had assigned to her use.

'Do not – do not leave me for a moment,' said she. 'I am lost for ever if you do.'

Gerard Douw's chamber was approached through a spacious apartment, which they were now about to enter. Gerard Douw and Schalken each carried a wax candle, so that sufficient degree of light was cast upon all surrounding objects. They were now entering the large chamber, which, as I have said, communicated with Douw's apartment, when Rose suddenly stopped, and, in a whisper which seemed to thrill with horror, she said: 'O God! he is here – he is here! See, see – there he goes!'

She pointed towards the door of the inner room, and Schalken thought he saw a shadowy and ill-defined form gliding into that apartment. He drew his sword, and raising the candle so as to throw its light with increased distinctness upon the objects in the room, he entered the chamber into which the figure had glided. No figure was there – nothing but the furniture which belonged to the room, and yet he could not be deceived as to the fact that something had moved before them into the chamber.

A sickening dread came upon him, and the cold perspiration broke out in heavy drops upon his forehead; nor was he more composed when he heard the increased urgency, the agony of entreaty, with which Rose implored them not to leave her for a moment.

'I saw him,' said she. 'He's here! I cannot be deceived – I know him. He's by me – he's with me – he's in the room. Then, for God's sake, as you would save, do not stir from beside me!'

They at length prevailed upon her to lie down upon the bed, where she continued to urge them to stay by her. She frequently uttered incoherent sentences, repeating again and again, 'The dead and the living cannot be one – God has forbidden it!' and then again, 'Rest to the wakeful – sleep to the sleepwalkers.'

These and such mysterious and broken sentences she continued to utter until the clergyman arrived.

Gerard Douw began to fear, naturally enough, that the poor girl, owing to terror or ill-treatment, had become deranged; and he half suspected, by the suddenness of her appearance, and the unseasonableness of the hour, and, above all, from the wildness and terror of her manner, that she had made her escape from some place of confinement for lunatics, and was in immediate fear of pursuit. He resolved to summon medical advice as soon as the mind of his niece had been in some measure set at rest by the offices of the clergyman whose attendance she had so earnestly desired; and until this object had been attained, he did not venture to put any questions to her, which might possibly, by reviving painful or horrible recollections, increase her agitation.

The clergyman soon arrived – a man of ascetic countenance – and venerable age – one whom Gerard Douw respected much, forasmuch as he was a veteran polemic, though one, perhaps, more dreaded as a combatant than beloved as a Christian – of pure morality, subtle brain, and frozen heart. He entered the chamber which communicated with that in which Rose reclined, and immediately on his arrival she requested him to pray for her, as for one who lay in the hands of Satan, and who could hope for deliverance only from Heaven.

That our readers may distinctly understand all the circumstances of the event which we were about imperfectly to describe, it is necessary to state the relative positions of the parties who were engaged in it. The old clergyman and Schalken were in the anteroom of which we have already spoken; Rose lay in the inner chamber, the door of which was open; and by the side of the bed, at her urgent desire, stood her guardian; a candle burned in the bedchamber, and three were lighted in the outer apartment.

The old man now cleared his voice, as if about to commence; but before he had time to begin, a sudden gust of air blew out the candle which served to illuminate the room in which the poor girl lay, and she with hurried alarm, exclaimed: 'Godfrey, bring in another candle; the darkness is unsafe.'

Gerard Douw, forgetting for the moment her repeated injunctions in the immediate impulse, stepped from the bedchamber into the other, in order to supply what she desired.

'O God! do not go, dear uncle!' shrieked the unhappy girl; and at the same time she sprang from the bed and darted after him, in order, by her grasp, to detain him.

But the warning came too late, for scarcely had he passed the threshold, and hardly had his niece had time to utter the startling exclamation, when the door which divided the two rooms closed violently after him, as if swung to by a strong blast of wind.

Schalken and he both rushed to the door, but their united and desperate efforts could not avail so much as to shake it.

Shriek after shriek burst from the inner chamber, with all the piercing loudness of despairing terror. Schalken and Douw applied every energy and strained every nerve to force open the door; but all in vain.

There was no sound of struggling from within, but the screams seemed to increase in loudness, and at the same time they heard the bolts of the latticed window withdrawn, and the window itself grated upon the sill as if thrown open.

One last shriek, so long and piercing and agonised as to be scarcely human, swelled from the room, and suddenly there followed a death-like silence.

A light step was heard crossing the floor, as if from the bed to the window; and almost at the same instant the door gave way, and yielding to the pressure of the external applicants, they were nearly precipitated into the room. It was empty. The window was open, and Schalken sprang to a chair and gazed out upon the street and at the canal below. He saw no form, but he beheld, or thought he beheld, the waters of the broad canal beneath settling ring after ring in heavy circular ripples, as if a moment before disturbed by the immersion of some large and heavy mass.

No trace of Rose was ever after discovered, nor was anything certain respecting her mysterious wooer detected or even suspected; no clue whereby to trace the intricacies of the labyrinth, and to arrive at a distinct conclusion was to be found. But an incident occurred, which, though it will not be received by our rational readers as at all approaching to evidence upon the matter, nevertheless produced a strong and a lasting impression upon the mind of Schalken.

Many years after the events which we had detailed, Schalken, then remotely situated, received an intimation of his father's death, and of his intended burial upon a fixed day in the church of Rotterdam. It was necessary that a very considerable journey should be performed by the funeral procession, which, as it will readily be believed, was not very numerously attended. Schalken with difficulty arrived in Rotterdam late in the day upon which the funeral was appointed to take place. The procession had not then arrived. Evening closed in, and still it did not appear.

Schalken strolled down to the church – he found it open; notice of the arrival of the funeral had been given, and the vault in which the body was to be laid had been opened. The official who corresponds to our sexton, on seeing a well-dressed gentleman, whose object was to attend the expected funeral, pacing the aisle of the church, hospitably invited him to share with him the comforts of a blazing wood fire, which as was his custom in winter time upon such occasions, he had kindled on the hearth of a chamber which communicated by a flight of steps with the vault below.

In this chamber Schalken and his entertainer seated themselves; and the sexton, after some fruitless attempts to engage his guest in conversation, was obliged to apply himself to his tobacco-pipe and can to solace his solitude.

In spite of his grief and cares, the fatigues of a rapid journey of nearly forty hours gradually overcame the mind and body of Godfrey Schalken, and he sank into a deep sleep, from which he was awakened by someone shaking him gently by the shoulder. He first thought that the old sexton had called him, but *he* was no longer in the room.

He roused himself, and as soon as he could clearly see what was around him, he perceived a female form, clothed in a kind of light robe of muslin, part of which was so disposed as to act as a veil, and in her hand she carried a lamp. She was moving rather away from him, and towards the flight of steps which conducted towards the vaults.

Schalken felt a vague alarm at the sight of this figure, and at the same time an irresistible impulse to follow its guidance. He followed it towards the vaults, but when it reached the head of the stairs, he paused; the figure paused also, and turning gently round, displayed, by the light of the lamp it carried, the face and features of his first love, Rose Velderkaust. There was nothing horrible, or even sad, in the countenance. On the contrary, it wore the same arch smile which used to enchant the artist long before in his happy days.

A feeling of awe and of interest, too intense to be resisted, prompted him to follow the spectre, if spectre it were. She descended the stairs – he followed; and, turning to the left, through a narrow passage she led him, to his infinite surprise, into what appeared to be an old-fashioned Dutch apartment, such as the pictures of Gerard Douw have served to immortalise.

Abundance of costly antique furniture was disposed about the room, and in one corner stood a four-post bed, with heavy black cloth curtains around it. The figure frequently turned towards him with the same arch smile; and when she came to the side of the bed, she drew the curtains, and by the light of the lamp which she held towards its contents, she disclosed to the horror-stricken painter, sitting bolt upright in the bed, the livid and demoniac form of Vanderhausen. Schalken had hardly seen him when he fell senseless upon the floor, where he lay until discovered, on the next morning, by persons employed in closing the passages into the vaults. He was lying in a cell of considerable size, which had not been disturbed for a long time, and he had fallen beside a large coffin which was supported upon small stone pillars, a security against the attacks of vermin.

To his dying day Schalken was satisfied of the reality of the vision which he had witnessed, and he has left behind him a curious evidence of the impression which it wrought upon his fancy, in a painting executed shortly after the event we have narrated, and which is valuable as exhibiting not only the peculiarities which have made Schalken's pictures sought after, but even more so as presenting a portrait, as close and faithful as one taken from memory can be, of his early love, Rose Velderkaust, whose mysterious fate must ever remain matter of speculation.

The picture represents a chamber of antique masonry, such as might be found in most old cathedrals, and is lighted faintly by a lamp carried in the hand of a female figure, such as we have above attempted to describe; and in the background, and to the left of him who examines the painting, there stands the form of a man apparently aroused from sleep, and by his attitude, his hand being laid upon his sword, exhibiting considerable alarm; this last figure is illuminated only by the expiring glare of a wood or charcoal fire.

The whole production exhibits a beautiful specimen of that artful and singular distribution of light and shade which has rendered the name of Schalken immortal among the artists of his country. This tale is traditionary, and the reader will easily perceive, by our studiously omitting to heighten many points of the narrative, when a little additional colouring might have added effect to the recital, that we have desired to lay before him, not a figment of the brain, but a curious tradition connected with, and belonging to, the biography of a famous artist.

The Fortunes of Sir Robert Ardagh

SHERIDAN LE FANU

In the south of Ireland, and on the borders of the country of Limerick, there lies a district of two or three miles in length, which is rendered interesting by the fact that it is one of the very few spots throughout this country in which some vestiges of aboriginal forests still remain. It has little or none of the lordly character of the American forest, for the axe has felled its oldest and its grandest trees; but in the close wood which survives live all the wild and pleasing peculiarities of nature: its complete irregularity, its vistas, in whose perspective the quiet cattle are browsing; its refreshing glades, where the grey rocks arise from amid the nodding fern; the silvery shafts of the old birch trees; the knotted trunks of the hoary oak, the grotesque but graceful branches which never shed their honours under the tyrant pruning-hook the soft green sward; the chequered light and shade; the wild luxuriant weeds; the lichen and the moss – all are beautiful alike in the green freshness of spring or in the sadness and sere of autumn. Their beauty is of that kind which makes the heart full with joy – appealing to the affections with a power which belongs to nature only. This wood runs up, from below the base, to the ridge of a long line of irregular hills, having perhaps, in primitive times, formed but the skirting of some mighty forest which occupied the level below. But now, alas! whither have we drifted? whither has the tide of civilisation borne us? It has passed over a land unprepared for it – it has left nakedness behind it; we have lost our forests, but our marauders remain; we have destroyed all that is picturesque, while we have retained everything that is revolting in barbarism.

Through the midst of this woodland there runs a deep gully or glen, where the stillness of the scene is broken in upon by the brawling of a mountain-stream, which, however, in the winter season, swells into a rapid and formidable torrent. There is one point at which the glen becomes extremely deep and narrow; the sides descend to the depth of some hundred feet, and are so steep as to be nearly perpendicular. The wild trees which have taken root in the crannies and chasms of the rock are so intersected and entangled, that one can with difficulty catch a glimpse of the stream which wheels, flashes, and foams below, as if exulting in the surrounding silence and solitude.

This spot was not unwisely chosen, as a point of no ordinary strength, for the erection of a massive square tower or keep, one side of which rises as if in continuation of the precipitous cliff on which it is based. Originally, the only mode of ingress was by a narrow portal in the very wall which overtopped the precipice, opening upon a ledge of rock which afforded a precarious pathway, cautiously intersected, however, by a deep trench cut out with great labour in the living rock; so that, in its pristine state, and before the introduction of artillery into the art of war, this tower might have been pronounced, and that not presumptuously, impregnable.

The progress of improvement and the increasing security of the times had, however, tempted its successive proprietors, if not to adorn, at least to enlarge their premises, and about the middle of the last century, when the castle was last inhabited, the original square tower formed but a small part of the edifice.

The castle, and a wide tract of the surrounding country, had from time immemorial belonged to a family which, for distinctness, we shall call by the name of Ardagh; and owing to the associations which, in Ireland, almost always attach to scenes which have long witnessed alike the exercise of stern feudal authority, and of that savage hospitality which distinguished the good old times, this building has become the subject and the scene of many wild and extraordinary traditions. One of them I have been enabled, by a personal acquaintance with an eye-witness of the events, to trace to its origin and yet it is hard to say whether the events which I am about to record appear more strange and improbable as seen through the distorting medium of tradition, or in the appalling dimness of uncertainty which surrounds the reality.

Tradition says that, sometime in the last century, Sir Robert Ardagh, a young man, and the last heir of that family, went abroad and served in foreign armies and that, having acquired considerable honour and emolument, he settled at Castle Ardagh, the building we have just now attempted to describe. He was what the country people call a *dark* man that is, he was considered morose, reserved, and ill-tempered and, as it was supposed from the utter solitude of his life, was upon no terms of cordiality with the other members of his family.

The only occasion upon which he broke through the solitary monotony of his life was during the continuance of the racing season, and immediately subsequent to it; at which time he was to be seen among the busiest upon the course, betting deeply and unhesitatingly, and invariably with success. Sir Robert was, however, too well known as a man of honour, and of too high a family, to be suspected of any unfair dealing. He was, moreover, a soldier, and a man of intrepid as well as of a haughty character and no one cared to hazard a surmise, the consequences of which would be felt most probably by its originator only.

Gossip, however, was not silent; it was remarked that Sir Robert never appeared at the race-ground, which was the only place of public resort which he frequented, except in company with a certain strange-looking person, who was never seen elsewhere, or under other circumstances. It was remarked, too, that this man, whose relation to Sir Robert was never distinctly ascertained, was the only person to whom he seemed to speak unnecessarily; it was observed that while with the country gentry he exchanged no further communication than what was unavoidable in arranging his sporting transactions, with this person he would converse earnestly and frequently. Tradition asserts that, to enhance the curiosity which this unaccountable and exclusive preference excited, the stranger possessed some striking and unpleasant peculiarities of person and of garb – though it is not stated, however, what these were – but they, in conjunction with Sir Robert's secluded habits and extraordinary run of luck – a success which was supposed to result from the suggestions and immediate advice of the unknown – were sufficient to warrant report in pronouncing that there was something *queer* in the wind, and in surmising that Sir Robert was playing a fearful and a hazardous game, and that, in short, his strange companion was little better than the Devil himself.

Years rolled quietly away, and nothing very novel occurred in the arrangements of Castle Ardagh, excepting that Sir Robert parted with his odd companion, but as nobody could tell whence he came, so nobody could say whither he had gone. Sir Robert's habits, however, underwent no consequent change; he continued regularly to frequent the race meetings, without mixing at all in the convivialities of the gentry, and immediately afterwards to relapse into the secluded monotony of his ordinary life.

It was said that he had accumulated vast sums of money – and, as his bets were always successful and always large, such must have been the case. He did not suffer the acquisition of wealth, however, to influence his hospitality or his housekeeping – he neither purchased land, nor extended his establishment and his mode of enjoying his money must have been altogether that of the miser – consisting merely in the pleasure of touching and telling his gold, and in the consciousness of wealth.

Sir Robert's temper, so far from improving, became more than ever gloomy and morose. He sometimes carried the indulgence of his evil dispositions to such a height that it bordered upon insanity. During these paroxysms he would neither eat, drink, nor sleep. On such occasions he insisted on perfect privacy, even from the intrusion of his most trusted servants; his voice was frequently heard, sometimes in earnest supplication, sometimes raised, as if in loud and angry altercation with some unknown visitant. Sometimes he would for hours together walk to and fro throughout the long oak-wainscoted apartment which he generally occupied, with wild gesticulations and agitated pace, in the manner of one who has been roused to a state of unnatural excitement by some sudden and appalling intimation.

These paroxysms of apparent lunacy were so frightful, that during their continuance even his oldest and most faithful domestics dared not approach him; consequently his hours of agony were never intruded upon, and the mysterious causes of his sufferings appeared likely to remain hidden for ever.

On one occasion a fit of this kind continued for an unusual time; the ordinary term of their duration – about two days – had been long past, and the old servant who generally waited upon Sir Robert after these visitations, having in vain listened for the well-known tinkle of his master's hand bell, began to feel extremely anxious; he feared that his master might have died from sheer exhaustion, or perhaps put an end to his on existence during his miserable depression. These fears at length became so strong, that having in vain urged some of his brother servants to accompany him, he determined to go up alone, and himself see whether any accident had befallen Sir Robert.

He traversed the several passages which conducted from the new to the more ancient parts of the mansion, and having arrived in the old hall of the castle, the utter silence of the hour – for it was very late in the night – the idea of the nature of the enterprise in which he was engaging himself, a sensation of remoteness from anything like human companionship, but, more than all, the vivid but undefined anticipation of something horrible, came upon him with such oppressive weight that he hesitated as to whether he should proceed. Real uneasiness, however, respecting the fate of his master, for who he felt that kind of attachment which the force of habitual intercourse not unfrequently engenders respecting objects not in themselves amiable, and also a latent unwillingness to expose his weakness to the ridicule of his fellow-servants, combined to over-come his reluctance; and he had just placed his foot upon the first step of the staircase which conducted his master's chamber, when his attention was arrested by low but distinct knocking at the hall-door. Not, perhaps, very sorry at finding thus an excuse even for deferring his intended expedition, he placed the candle upon a stone block which lay in the hall and approached the door, uncertain whether his ears had not deceived him. This doubt was justified by the circumstance that the hall entrance had been for nearly fifty years disused as a mode of ingress to the castle. The situation of this gate also, which we have endeavoured to describe, opening upon a narrow ledge of rock which overhangs a perilous cliff, rendered it at all times, but particularly at night, a dangerous entrance. This shelving platform of rock, which formed the only avenue to the door, was divided, as I have already stated, by a broad chasm, the planks across which had long disappeared, by decay or otherwise; so that it seemed at least highly improbable that any man could have found his way across the passage in safety to the door, more particularly on a night like this, of singular darkness. The old man, therefore, listened attentively, to ascertain whether the first application should be followed by another. He had not long to wait. The same low but singularly distinct knocking was repeated; so low that it seemed as if the applicant had employed no harder or heavier instrument than his hand, and yet, despite the immense thickness of the door, with such strength that the sound was distinctly audible.

The knock was repeated a third time, without any increase of loudness; and the old man, obeying an impulse for which to his dying hour he could never account, proceeded to remove, one by one, the three great oaken bars which secured the door. Time and damp had effectually corroded the iron chambers of the lock, so that it afforded little resistance. With some effort, as he believed, assisted from without, the old servant succeeded in opening the door; and a low, square-built figure, apparently that of a man wrapped in a large black cloak, entered the hall. The servant could not see much of this visitor with any distinctness; his dress appeared foreign, the skirt of his ample cloak was thrown over one shoulder; he wore a large felt hat, with a very heavy leaf, from under which escaped what appeared to be a mass of long sooty-black hair his feet were cased in heavy riding-boots. Such were the few particulars which the servant had time and light to observe. The stranger desired him to let his master know instantly that a friend had come, by appointment, to settle some business with him. The servant hesitated, but a slight motion on the part of his visitor, as if to possess himself of the candle, determined him; so, taking it in his hand, he ascended the castle stairs, leaving the guest in the hall.

On reaching the apartment which opened upon the oak chamber he was surprised to observe the door of that room partly open, and the room itself lit up. He paused, but there was no sound; he looked in, and saw Sir Robert, his head and the upper part of his body reclining on a table, upon which two candles burned; his arms were stretched forward on either side, and perfectly motionless; it appeared that, having been sitting at the table, he had thus sunk forward, either dead or in a swoon. There was no sound of breathing; all was silent, except the sharp ticking of a watch, which lay beside the lamp. The servant coughed twice or thrice, but with no effect; his fears now almost amounted to certainty, and he was approaching the table on which his master partly lay, to satisfy himself of his death, when Sir Robert slowly raised his head, and, throwing himself back in his chair, fixed his eyes in a ghastly and uncertain gaze upon his attendant. At length he said, slowly and painfully, as if he dreaded the answer: 'In God's name, what are you?'

'Sir,' said the servant, 'a strange gentleman wants to see you below.'

At this intimation Sir Robert, starting to his feet and tossing his arms wildly upwards, uttered a shriek of such appalling and despairing terror that it was almost too fearful for human endurance; and long after the sound had ceased it seemed to the terrified imagination of the old servant to roll through the deserted passages in bursts of unnatural laughter. After a few moments Sir Robert said: 'Can't you send him away? Why does he come so soon? O Merciful Powers! let him leave me for an hour; a little time. I can't see him now; try to get him away. You see I can't go down now I have not strength. O God! O God! let him come back in an hour it is not long to wait. He cannot lose anything by it; nothing, nothing, nothing. Tell him that! Say anything to him.'

The servant went down. In his own words, he did not feel the stairs under him till he got to the hall. The figure stood exactly as he had left it. He delivered his master's message as coherently as he could. The stranger replied in a careless tone: 'If Sir Robert will not come down to me; I must go up to him.'

The man returned, and to his surprise he found his master much more composed in manner. He listened to the message, and though the cold perspiration rose in drops upon his forehead faster than he could wipe it away, his manner had lost the dreadful agitation which had marked it before. He rose feebly, and casting a last look of agony behind him, passed from the room to the lobby, where he signed to his attendant not to follow him. The man moved as far as the head of the staircase, from whence he had a tolerably distinct view of the hall, which was imperfectly lighted by the candle he had left there.

He saw his master reel, rather than walk, down the stairs, clinging all the way to the banisters. He walked on, as if about to sink every moment from weakness. The figure advanced as if to meet him, and in passing struck down the light. The servant could see no more; but there was a sound of struggling, renewed at intervals with silent but fearful energy. It was evident, however, that the parties were approaching the door, for he heard the solid oak sound twice or thrice, as the feet of the combatants, in shuffling hither and thither over the floor, struck upon it. After a slight pause, he heard the door thrown open with such violence that the leaf seemed to strike the side-wall of the hall, for it was so dark without that this could only be surmised by the sound. The struggle was renewed with an agony and intenseness of energy that betrayed itself in deep-drawn gasps. One desperate effort, which terminated in the breaking of some part of the door, producing a sound as if the doorpost was wrenched from its position, was followed by another wrestle, evidently upon the narrow ledge which ran outside the door, overtopping the precipice. This proved to be the final struggle; it was followed by a crashing sound as if some heavy body had fallen over, and was rushing down the precipice through the light boughs that crossed near the top. All then became still as the grave, except when the moan of the night-wind sighed up the wooded glen.

The old servant had not nerve to return through the hall, and to him the darkness seemed all but endless; but morning at length came, and with it the disclosure of the events of the night. Near the door, upon the ground, lay Sir Robert's sword-belt, which had given way in the scuffle. A huge splinter from the massive doorpost had been wrenched off by an almost superhuman effort – one which nothing but the gripe of a despairing man could have severed – and on the rocks outside were left the marks of the slipping and sliding of feet.

At the foot of the precipice, not immediately under the castle, but dragged some way up the glen, were found the remains of Sir Robert, with hardly a vestige of a limb or feature left distinguishable. The right hand, however, was uninjured, and in its fingers were clutched, with the fixedness of death, a long lock of coarse sooty hair – the only direct circumstantial evidence of the presence of a second person.

The Dream

SHERIDAN LE FANU

Dreams! What age, or what country of the world, has not felt and acknowledged the mystery of their origin and end? I have thought not a little upon the subject, seeing it is one which has been often forced upon my attention, and sometimes strangely enough; and yet I have never arrived at anything which at all appeared a satis-factory conclusion. It does appear that a mental phenomenon so extraordinary cannot be wholly without its use. We know, indeed, that in the olden times it has been made the organ of communic-ation between the Deity and His creatures; and when a dream produces upon a mind, to all appearance hopelessly reprobate and depraved, an effect so powerful and so lasting as to break down the inveterate habits, and to reform the life of an abandoned sinner, we see in the result, in the reformation of morals which appeared incorrigible, in the reclamation of a human soul which seemed to be irretrievably lost, something more than could be produced by a mere chimera of the slumbering fancy, something more than could arise from the capricious images of a terrified imagination. And while Reason rejects as absurd the superstition which will read a prophecy in every dream, she may, without violence to herself, recognise, even in the wildest and most incongruous of the wanderings of a slumbering intellect, the evidences and the fragments of a language which may be spoken, which *has* been spoken, to terrify, to warn and to command. We have reason to believe too, by the promptness of action which in the age of the prophets followed all intimations of this kind, and by the strength of con-viction and strange permanence of the effects resulting from certain dreams in latter times – which effects we ourselves may have witnessed – that when this medium of communication has been employed by the Deity, the evidences of His presence have been unequivocal. My thoughts were directed to this subject in a manner to leave a lasting impression upon my mind, by the events which I shall now relate, the statement of which, however extraordinary, is nevertheless accurate.

About the year 17—, having been appointed to the living of C—, I rented a small house in the town which bears the same name: one morning in the month of November, I was awakened before my usual time by my servant, who bustled into my bedroom for the purpose of announcing a sick call. As the Catholic Church holds her last rites to be totally indispensable to the safety of the departing sinner, no conscientious clergyman can afford a moment's unnecessary delay, and in little more than five minutes I stood ready, cloaked and booted for the road, in the small front parlour in which the messenger, who was to act as my guide, awaited my coming. I found a poor little girl crying piteously near the door, and after some slight difficulty I ascertained that her father was either dead or just dying.

'And what may be your father's name, my poor child?' said I. She held down her head as if ashamed. I repeated the question, and the wretched little creature burst into floods of tears still more bitter than she had shed before. At length, almost angered by conduct which appeared to me so unreasonable, I began to lose patience, and I said rather harshly: 'If you will not tell me the name of the person to whom you would lead me, your silence can arise from no good motive, and I might be justified in refusing to go with you at all.'

'Oh, don't say that – don't say that!' cried she. 'Oh, sir, it was that I was afeard of when I would not tell you – I was afeard, when you heard his name, you would not come with me; but it is no use hidin' it now – it's Pat Connell, the carpenter, your honour.'

She looked in my face with the most earnest anxiety, as if her very existence depended upon what she should read there. I relieved the child at once. The name, indeed, was most unpleasantly familiar to me; but, however fruitless my visits and advice might have been at another time, the present was too fearful an occasion to suffer my doubts of their utility, or my reluctance to re-attempting what appeared a hopeless task, to weigh even against the lightest chance that a consciousness of his imminent danger might produce in him a more docile and tractable disposition. Accordingly I told the child to lead the way, and followed her in silence. She hurried rapidly through the long narrow street which forms the great thoroughfare of the town. The darkness of the hour, rendered still deeper by the close approach of the old-fashioned houses, which lowered in tall obscurity on either side of the way; the damp, dreary chill which renders the advance of morning peculiarly cheerless, combined with the object of my walk – to visit the deathbed of a presumptuous sinner, to endeavour, almost against my own conviction, to infuse a hope into the heart of a dying reprobate – a drunkard but too probably perishing under the consequences of some mad fit of intoxication; all these circumstances served to enhance the gloom and solemnity of my feelings, as I silently followed my little guide, who with quick steps traversed the uneven pavement of the Main Street. After a walk of about five minutes, she turned off into a narrow lane, of that obscure and comfortless class which is to be found in almost all small old-fashioned towns, chill, without ventilation, reeking with all manner of offensive effluvia, and lined by dingy, smoky, sickly and pent-up buildings, frequently not only in a wretched but in a dangerous condition.

'Your father has changed his abode since I last visited him, and, I am afraid, much for the worse,' said I.

'Indeed he has, sir; but we must not complain,' replied she. 'We have to thank God that we have lodging and food, though it's poor enough, it is, your honour.'

Poor child! thought I. How many an older head might learn wisdom from thee – how many a luxurious philosopher, who is skilled to preach but not to suffer, might not thy patient words put to the blush! The manner and language of my companion were alike above her years and station; and, indeed, in all cases in which the cares and sorrows of life have anticipated their usual date, and have fallen, as they sometimes do, with melancholy prematurity to the lot of childhood, I have observed the result to have proved uniformly the same. A young mind, to which joy and indulgence have been strangers, and to which suffering and self-denial have been familiarised from the first, acquires a solidity and an elevation which no other discipline could have bestowed, and which, in the present case, communicated a striking but mournful peculiarity to the manners, even to the voice, of the child. We paused before a narrow, crazy door, which she opened by means of a latch, and we forthwith began to ascend the steep and broken stairs which led to the sick man's room.

As we mounted flight after flight towards the garret-floor, I heard more and more distinctly the hurried talking of many voices. I could also distinguish the low sobbing of a female. On arriving upon the uppermost lobby, these sounds became fully audible.

'This way, your honour,' said my little conductress; at the same time, pushing open a door of patched and half-rotten plank, she admitted me into the squalid chamber of death and misery. But one candle, held in the fingers of a scared and haggard-looking child, was burning in the room, and that so dim that all was twilight or darkness except within its immediate influence. The general obscurity, however, served to throw into prominent and startling relief the deathbed and its occupant. The light fell with horrible clearness upon the blue and swollen features of the drunkard. I did not think it possible that a human countenance could look so terrific. The lips were black and drawn apart; the teeth were firmly set; the eyes a little unclosed, and nothing but the whites appearing. Every feature was fixed and livid, and the whole face wore a ghastly and rigid expression of despairing terror such as I never saw equalled. His hands were crossed upon his breast, and firmly clenched while, as if to add to the corpse-like effect of the whole, some white cloths, dipped in water, were wound about the forehead and temples.

As soon as I could remove my eyes from this horrible spectacle, I observed my friend Dr D—, one of the most humane of a humane profession, standing by the bedside. He had been attempting, but unsuccessfully, to bleed the patient, and had now applied his finger to the pulse.

'Is there any hope?' I enquired in a whisper.

A shake of the head was the reply. There was a pause, while he continued to hold the wrist; but he waited in vain for the throb of life – it was not there: and when he let go the hand, it fell stiffly back into its former position upon the other.

'The man is dead,' said the physician, as he turned from the bed where the terrible figure lay.

Dead! thought I, scarcely venturing to look upon the tremendous and revolting spectacle. Dead! without an hour for repentance, even a moment for reflection. Dead! without the rites which even the best should have. Was there a hope for him? The glaring eyeball, the grinning mouth, the distorted brow – that unutterable look in which a painter would have sought to embody the fixed despair of the nethermost hell – These were my answer.

The poor wife sat at a little distance, crying as if her heart would break – the younger children clustered round the bed, looking with wondering curiosity upon the form of death, never seen before.

When the first tumult of uncontrollable sorrow had passed away, availing myself of the solemnity and impressiveness of the scene, I desired the heart-stricken family to accompany me in prayer, and all knelt down while I solemnly and fervently repeated some of those prayers which appeared most applicable to the occasion. I employed myself thus in a manner which I trusted was not unprofitable, at least to the living, for about ten minutes; and having accomplished my task, I was the first to arise.

I looked upon the poor, sobbing, helpless creatures who knelt so humbly around me, and my heart bled for them. With a natural transition I turned my eyes from them to the bed in which the body lay; and, great God! what was the revulsion, the horror which I experienced on seeing the corpse-like, terrific thing seated half upright before me. The white cloths which had been wound about the head had now partly slipped from their position, and were hanging in grotesque festoons about the face and shoulders, while the distorted eyes leered from amid them: 'A sight to dream of, not to tell.'

I stood actually riveted to the spot. The figure nodded its head and lifted its arm, I thought, with a menacing gesture. A thousand confused and horrible thoughts at once rushed upon my mind. I had often read that the body of a presumptuous sinner, who, during life, had been the willing creature of every satanic impulse, had been known, after the human tenant had deserted it, to become the horrible sport of demoniac possession.

I was roused by the piercing scream of the mother, who now, for the first time perceived the change which had taken place. She rushed towards the bed, but, stunned by the shock and overcome by the conflict of violent emotions, before she reached it she fell prostrate upon the floor.

I am perfectly convinced that had I not been startled from the torpidity of horror in which I was bound by some powerful and arousing stimulant, I should have gazed upon this unearthly apparition until I had fairly lost my senses. As it was, however, the spell was broken – superstition gave way to reason: the man whom all believed to have been actually dead was living!

Dr D— was instantly standing by the bedside, and upon examination he found that a sudden and copious flow of blood had taken place from the wound which the lancet had left; and this, no doubt, had effected his sudden and almost preternatural restoration to an existence from which all thought he had been for ever removed. The man was still speechless, but he seemed to understand the physician when he forbade his repeating the painful and fruitless attempts which he made to articulate, and he at once resigned himself quietly into his hands.

I left the patient with leeches upon his temples, and bleeding freely, apparently with little of the drowsiness which accompanies, apoplexy. Indeed, Dr D— told me that he had never before witnessed a seizure which seemed to combine the symptoms of so many kinds, and yet which belonged to none of the recognised classes; it certainly was not apoplexy, catalepsy, nor *delirium tremens*, and yet it seemed, in some degree, to partake of the properties of all. It was strange, but stranger things are coming.

During two or three days Dr D— would not allow his patient to converse in a manner which could excite or exhaust him, with anyone; he suffered him merely as briefly as possible to express his immediate wants. And it was not until the fourth day after my early visit, the particulars of which I have just detailed, that it was thought expedient that I should see him, and then only because it appeared that his extreme importunity and impatience to meet me were likely to retard his recovery more than the mere exhaustion attendant upon a short conversation could possibly do. Perhaps, too, my friend entertained some hope that if by holy confession his patient's bosom were eased of the perilous stuff which no doubt oppressed it, his recovery would be more assured and rapid. It was then, as I have said, upon the fourth day after my first professional call, that I found myself once more in the dreary chamber of want and sickness.

The man was in bed, and appeared low and restless. On my entering the room he raised himself in the bed, and muttered, twice or thrice,

'Thank God! thank God!'

I signed to those of his family who stood by to leave the room, and took a chair beside the bed. So soon as we were alone, he said, rather doggedly: 'There's no use in telling me of the sinfulness of bad ways – I know it all. I know where they lead to – I have seen everything about it with my own eyesight, as plain as I see you.' He rolled himself in the bed, as if to hide his face in the clothes; and then suddenly raising himself, he exclaimed with startling vehemence, 'Look, sir! there is no use in mincing the matter: I'm blasted with the fires of hell; I have been in hell. What do you think of that? In hell – I'm lost for ever – I have not a chance. I am damned already – damned – damned!'

The end of this sentence he actually shouted. His vehemence was perfectly terrific; he threw himself back, and laughed, and sobbed hysterically. I poured some water into a teacup, and gave it to him. After he had swallowed it, I told him if he had anything to communicate, to do so as briefly as he could, and in a manner as little agitating to himself as possible; threatening at the same time, though I had no intention of doing so, to leave him at once in case he again gave way to such passionate excitement.

'It's only foolishness,' he continued, 'for me to try to thank you for coming to such a villain as myself at all. It's no use for me to wish good to you, or to bless you; for such as me has no blessings to give.'

I told him that I had but done my duty, and urged him to proceed to the matter which weighed upon his mind. He then spoke nearly as follows: 'I came in drunk on Friday night last, and got to my bed here; I don't remember how. Sometime in the night it seemed to me I wakened, and feeling uneasy in myself, I got up out of the bed. I wanted the fresh air; but I would not make a noise to open the window, for fear I'd waken the crathurs. It was very dark and trouble-some to find the door but at last I did get it, and I groped my way out, and went down as easy as I could. I felt quite sober, and I counted the steps one after another, as I was going down, that I might not stumble at the bottom.

'When I came to the first landing-place – God be about us always! – the floor of it sunk under me, and I went down – down – down, till the senses almost left me. I do not know how long I was falling, but it seemed to me a great while. When I came rightly to myself at last, I was sitting near the top of a great table; and I could not see the end of it, if it had any, it was so far off. And there was men beyond reckoning sitting down all along by it, at each side, as far as I could see at all. I did not know at first was it in the open air; but there was a close smothering feel in it that was not natural. And there was a kind of light that my eyesight never saw before, red and unsteady; and I did not see for a long time where it was coming from, until I looked straight up, and then I seen that it came from great balls of blood-coloured fire that were rolling high overhead with a sort of rushing, trembling sound, and I perceived that they shone on the ribs of a great roof of rock that was arched overhead instead of the sky. When I seen this, scarce knowing what I did, I got up, and I said, "I have no right to be here; I must go." And the man that was sitting at my left hand only smiled, and said, "Sit down again; you can *never* leave this place." And his voice was weaker than any child's voice I ever heard and when he was done speaking he smiled again.

'Then I spoke out very loud and bold, and I said, "In the name of God, let me out of this bad place." And there was a great man that I did not see before, sitting at the end of the table that I was near; and he was taller than twelve men, and his face was very proud and terrible to look at. And he stood up and stretched out his hand before him; and when he stood up, all that was there, great and small, bowed down with a sighing sound; and a dread came on my heart, and he looked at me, and I could not speak. I felt I was his own, to do what he liked with, for I knew at once who he was; and he said, "If you promise to return, you may depart for a season; and the voice he spoke with was terrible and mournful, and the echoes of it went rolling and swelling down the endless cave, and mixing with the trembling of the fire overhead; so that when he sat down there was a sound after him, all through the place, like the roaring of a furnace. And I said, with all the strength I had, 'I promise to come back – in God's name let me go!"

'And with that I lost the sight and the hearing of all that was there, and when my senses came to me again, I was sitting in the bed with the blood all over me, and you and the rest praying around the room.'

Here he paused, and wiped away the chill drops which hung upon his forehead.

I remained silent for some moments. The vision which he had just described struck my imagination not a little, for this was long before Vathek and the 'Hall of Eblis' had delighted the world; and the description which he gave had, as I received it, all the attractions of novelty beside the impressiveness which always belongs to the narration of an *eyewitness*, whether in the body or in the spirit, of the scenes which he describes. There was something, too, in the stern horror with which the man related these things, and in the incongruity of his description with the vulgarly received notions of the great place of punishment, and of its presiding spirit, which struck my mind with awe, almost with fear. At length he said, with an expression of horrible, imploring earnestness, which I shall never forget: 'Well, sir, is there any hope; is there any chance at all? or is my soul pledged and promised away for ever? is it gone out of my power? must I go back to the place?'

In answering him, I had no easy task to perform; for however clear might be my internal conviction of the groundlessness of his fears, and however strong my scepticism respecting the reality of what he had described, I nevertheless felt that his impression to the contrary, and his humility and terror resulting from it, might be made available as no mean engines in the work of his conversation from profligacy, and of his restoration to decent habits and to religious feeling.

I therefore told him that he was to regard his dream rather in the light of a warning than in that of a prophecy; that our salvation depended not upon the word or deed of a moment, but upon the habits of a life; that if he at once discarded his idle companions and evil habits, and firmly adhered to a sober, industrious, and religious course of life, the powers of darkness might claim his soul in vain, for that there were higher and firmer pledges than human tongue could utter, which promised salvation to him who should repent and lead a new life.

I left him much comforted, and with a promise to return upon the next day. I did so, and found him much more cheerful, and without any remains of the dogged sullenness which I suppose had arisen from his despair. His promises of amendment were given in that tone of deliberate earnestness which belongs to deep and solemn determination and it was with no small delight that I observed, after repeated visits, that his good resolutions, so far from failing, did but gather strength by time; and when I saw that man shake off the idle and debauched companions whose society had for years formed alike his amusement and his ruin, and revive his long-discarded habits of industry and sobriety, I said within myself, There is something more in all this than the operation of an idle dream.

One day, some time after his perfect restoration to health, I was surprised, on ascending the stairs for the purpose of visiting this man, to find him busily employed in nailing down some planks upon the landing-place, through which, at the commencement of his mysterious vision, it seemed to him that he had sunk. I perceived at once that he was strengthening the floor with a view to securing himself against such a catastrophe, and could scarcely forbear a smile as I bid 'God bless his work.'

He perceived my thoughts, I suppose, for he immediately said: 'I can never pass over that floor without trembling. I'd leave this house if I could, but I can't find another lodging in the town so cheap, and I'll not take a better till I've paid off all my debts, please God; but I could not be easy in my mind till I made it as safe as I could. You'll hardly believe me, your honour, that while I'm working, maybe a mile away, my heart is in a flutter the whole way back, with the bare thoughts of the two little steps I have to walk upon this bit of a floor. So it's no wonder, sir, I'd try to make it sound and firm with any idle timber I have.'

I applauded his resolution to pay off his debts, and the steadiness with which he perused his plans of conscientious economy, and passed on.

Many months elapsed, and still there appeared no alteration in his resolutions of amendment. He was a good workman, and with his better habits he recovered his former extensive and profitable employment. Everything seemed to promise comfort and respectability. I have little more to add, and that shall be told quickly. I had one evening met Pat Connell, as he returned from his work, and as usual, after a mutual, and on his side respectful salutation, I spoke a few words of encouragement and approval. I left him industrious, active, healthy – when next I saw him, not three days after, he was a corpse.

The circumstances which marked the event of his death were somewhat strange – I might say fearful. The unfortunate man had accidentally met an old friend just returned, after a long absence; and in a moment of excitement, forgetting everything in the warmth of his joy, he yielded to his urgent invitation to accompany him into a public-house, which lay close by the spot where the encounter had taken place. Connell, however, previously to entering the room, had announced his determination to take nothing more than the strictest temperance would warrant.

But oh! who can describe the inveterate tenacity with which a drunkard's habits cling to him through life? He may repent, he may reform, he may look with actual abhorrence upon his past profligacy; but amid all this reformation and compunction, who can tell the moment in which the base and ruinous propensity may not recur, triumphing over resolution, remorse, shame, everything, and prostrating its victim once more in all that is destructive and revolting in that fatal vice?

The wretched man left the place in a state of utter intoxication. He was brought home nearly insensible, and placed in his bed. The younger part of the family retired to rest much after their usual hour; but the poor wife remained up sitting by the fire, too much grieved and shocked at the occurrence of what she had so little expected, to settle to rest. Fatigue, however, at length overcame her, and she sank gradually into an uneasy slumber. She could not tell how long she had remained in this state; but when she awakened, and immediately on opening her eyes, she perceived by the faint red light of the smouldering turf embers, two persons, one of whom she recognised as her husband, noiselessly gliding out of the room.

'Pat, darling, where are you going?' said she.

There was no answer – the door closed after them but in a moment she was startled and terrified by a loud and heavy crash, as if some ponderous body had been hurled down the stair.

Much alarmed, she started up, and going to the head of the staircase, she called repeatedly upon her husband, but in vain.

She returned to the room, and with the assistance of her daughter, whom I had occasion to mention before, she succeeded in finding and lighting a candle, with which she hurried again to the head of the staircase.

At the bottom lay what seemed to be a bundle of clothes, heaped together, motionless, lifeless – it was her husband. In going down the stairs, for what purpose can never now be known, he had fallen helplessly and violently to the bottom, and coming head foremost, the spine of the neck had been dislocated by the shock, and instant death must have ensued.

The body lay upon that landing-place to which his dream had referred.

It is scarcely worth endeavouring to clear up a single point in a narrative where all is mystery; yet I could not help suspecting that the second figure which had been seen in the room by Connell's wife on the night of his death might have been no other than his own shadow.

I suggested this solution of the difficulty; but she told me that the unknown person had been considerably in advance of her husband, and on reaching the door, had turned back as if to communicate something to his companion.

It was, then, a mystery.

Was the dream verified? – whither had the disembodied spirit sped? who can say? We know not. But I left the house of death that day in a state of horror which I could not describe. It seemed to me that I was scarce awake. I heard and saw everything as if under the spell of a nightmare. The coincidence was terrible.

A Chapter in the History of a Tyrone Family

SHERIDAN LE FANU

In the following narrative I have endeavoured to give as nearly as possible the *ipsissima verba* of the valued friend from whom I received it, conscious that any aberration from *her* mode of telling the tale of her own life would at once impair its accuracy and its effect.

Would that, with her words, I could also bring before you her animated gesture, the expressive countenance, the solemn and thrilling air and accent with which she related the dark passages in her strange story; and, above all, that I could communicate the impressive consciousness that the narrator had seen with her own eyes, and personally acted in the scenes which she described. These accompaniments, taken with the additional circumstance that she who told the tale was one far too deeply and sadly impressed with religious principle to misrepresent or fabricate what she repeated as fact, gave to the tale a depth of interest which the recording of the events themselves could hardly have produced.

I became acquainted with the lady from whose lips I heard this narrative nearly twenty years since, and the story struck my fancy so much that I committed it to paper while it was still fresh in my mind; and should its perusal afford you entertainment for a listless half-hour, my labour shall not have been bestowed in vain.

I find that I have taken the story down as she told it, in the first person, and perhaps this is as it should be.

She began as follows: My maiden name was Richardson, the designation of a family of some distinction in the county of Tyrone. I was the younger of two daughters, and we were the only children. There was a difference in our ages of nearly six years, so that I did not, in my childhood, enjoy that close companionship which sisterhood, in other circumstances, necessarily involves; and while I was still a child, my sister was married.

The person upon whom she bestowed her hand was a Mr Carew, a gentleman of property and consideration in the north of England.

I remember well the eventful day of the wedding; the thronging carriages, the noisy menials, the loud laughter, the merry faces, and the gay dresses. Such sights were then new to me, and harmonised ill with the sorrowful feelings with which I regarded the event which was to separate me from a sister whose tenderness alone had hitherto more than supplied all that I wanted in my mother's affection.

The day soon arrived which was to remove the happy couple from Ashtown House. The carriage stood at the hall-door, and my poor sister kissed me again and again, telling me that I should see her soon.

The carriage drove away, and I gazed after it until my eyes filled with tears, and, returning slowly to my chamber, I wept more bitterly and, so to speak, more desolately, than ever I had wept before.

My father had never seemed to love or to take an interest in me. He had desired a son, and I think he never thoroughly forgave me my unfortunate sex.

My having come into the world at all as his child he regarded as a kind of fraudulent intrusion; and as his antipathy to me had its origin in an imperfection of mine too radical for removal, I never even hoped to stand high in his good graces.

My mother was, I dare say, as fond of me as she was of anyone; but she was a woman of a masculine and a worldly cast of mind. She had no tenderness or sympathy for the weaknesses, or even for the affections, of woman's nature, and her demeanour towards me was peremptory, and often even harsh.

It is not to be supposed, then, that I found in the society of my parents much to supply the loss of my sister. About a year after her marriage, we received letters from Mr Carew, containing accounts of my sister's health, which, though not actually alarming, were calculated to make us seriously uneasy. The symptoms most dwelt upon were loss of appetite, and a cough.

The letters concluded by intimating that he would avail himself of my father and mother's repeated invitation to spend some time at Ashtown, particularly as the physician who had been consulted as to my sister's health had strongly advised a removal to her native air.

There were added repeated assurances that nothing serious was apprehended, as it was supposed that a deranged state of the liver was the only source of the symptoms which at first had seemed to intimate consumption.

In accordance with this announcement, my sister and Mr Carew arrived in Dublin, where one of my father's carriages awaited them, in readiness to start upon whatever day or hour they might choose for their departure.

It was arranged that Mr Carew was, as soon as the day upon which they were to leave Dublin was definitely fixed, to write to my father, who intended that the two last stages should be performed by his own horses, upon whose speed and safety far more reliance might be placed than upon those of the ordinary post-horses, which were at that time, almost without exception, of the very worst order. The journey, one of about ninety miles, was to be divided; the larger portion being reserved for the second day.

On Sunday a letter reached us, stating that the party would leave Dublin on Monday, and in due course reach Ashtown upon Tuesday evening.

Tuesday came: the evening closed in, and yet no carriage: darkness came on, and still no sign of our expected visitors.

Hour after hour passed away, and it was now past twelve; the night was remarkably calm, scarce a breath stirring, so that any sound, such as that produced by the rapid movement of a vehicle, would have been audible at a considerable distance. For some such sound I was feverishly listening.

It was, however, my father's rule to close the house at nightfall, and the window-shutters being fastened, I was unable to reconnoitre the avenue as I would have wished. It was nearly one o'clock, and we began almost to despair of seeing them upon that night, when I thought I distinguished the sound of wheels, but so remote and faint as to make me at first very uncertain. The noise approached; it became louder and clearer; it stopped for a moment.

I now heard the shrill screaming of the rusty iron, as the avenue gate revolved on its hinges; again came the sound of wheels in rapid motion.

'It is they,' said I, starting up 'the carriage is in the avenue.'

We all stood for a few moments breathlessly listening. On thundered the vehicle with the speed of the whirlwind; crack went the whip, and clatter went the wheels, as it rattled over the uneven pavement of the court. A general and furious barking from all the dogs about the house hailed its arrival.

We hurried to the hall in time to hear the steps let down with the sharp clanging noise peculiar to the operation, and the hum of voices exerted in the bustle of arrival. The hall door was now thrown open, and we all stepped forth to greet our visitors.

The court was perfectly empty; the moon was shining broadly and brightly upon all around; nothing was to be seen but the tall trees with their long spectral shadows, now wet with the dews of midnight.

We stood gazing from right to left as if suddenly awakened from a dream; the dogs walked suspiciously, growling and snuffling about the court, and by totally and suddenly ceasing their former loud barking, expressed the predominance of fear.

We stared one upon another in perplexity and dismay, and I think I never beheld more pale faces assembled. By my father's directions, we looked about to find anything which might indicate or account for the noise which we had heard; but no such thing was to be seen – even the mire which lay upon the avenue was undisturbed. We returned to the house, more panic-stricken than I can describe.

On the next day, we learned by a messenger, who had ridden hard the greater part of the night, that my sister was dead On Sunday evening she had retired to bed rather unwell, and on Monday her indisposition declared itself unequivocally to be malignant fever. She became hourly worse, and, on Tuesday night, a little after midnight, she expired.

I mention this circumstance, because it was one upon which a thousand wild and fantastical reports were founded, though one would have thought that the truth scarcely required to be improved upon; and again, because it produced a strong and lasting effect upon my spirits, and indeed, I am inclined to think, upon my character.

I was, for several years after this occurrence, long after the violence of my grief subsided, so wretchedly low-spirited and nervous, that I could scarcely be said to live; and during this time, habits of indecision, arising out of a listless acquiescence in the will of others, a fear of encountering even the slightest opposition, and a disposition to shrink from what are commonly called amusements, grew upon me so strongly, that I have scarcely even yet altogether overcome them.

We saw nothing more of Mr Carew. He returned to England as soon as the melancholy rites attendant upon the event which I have just mentioned were performed; and not being altogether inconsolable, he married again within two years; after which, owing to the remoteness of our relative situations, and other circumstances, we gradually lost sight of him.

I was now an only child; and, as my elder sister had died without issue, it was evident that, in the ordinary course of things, my father's property, which was altogether in his power, would go to me; and the consequence was, that before I was fourteen, Ashtown House was besieged by a host of suitors. However, whether it was that I was too young, or that none of the aspirants to my hand stood sufficiently high in rank or wealth, I was suffered by both parents to do exactly as I pleased; and well was it for me, as I afterwards found, that fortune, or rather Providence, had so ordained it, that I had not suffered my affections to become in any degree engaged, for my mother would never have suffered any silly fancy of mine, as she was in the habit of styling an attachment, to stand in the way of her ambitious views – views which she was determined to carry into effect in defiance of every obstacle, and in order to accomplish which she would not have hesitated to sacrifice anything so unreasonable and contemptible as a girlish passion.

When I reached the age of sixteen, my mother's plans began to develop themselves; and, at her suggestion, we moved to Dublin to sojourn for the winter, in order that no time might be lost in disposing of me to the best advantage.

I had been too long accustomed to consider myself as of no importance whatever, to believe for a moment that I was in reality the cause of all the bustle and preparation which surrounded me; and being thus relieved from the pain which a consciousness of my real situation would have inflicted, I journeyed towards the capital with a feeling of total indifference.

My father's wealth and connection had established him in the best society, and consequently, upon our arrival in the metropolis, we commanded whatever enjoyment or advantages its gaieties afforded.

The tumult and novelty of the scenes in which I was involved did not fail considerably to amuse me, and my mind gradually recovered its tone, which was naturally cheerful.

It was almost immediately known and reported that I was an heiress, and of course my attractions were pretty generally acknowledged.

Among the many gentlemen whom it was my fortune to please, one, ere long, established himself in my mother's good graces, to the exclusion of all less important aspirants. However, I had not understood or even remarked his attentions, nor in the slightest degree suspected his or my mother's plans respecting me, when I was made aware of them rather abruptly by my mother herself.

We had attended a splendid ball, given by Lord M— at his residence in Stephen's Green, and I was, with the assistance of my waiting-maid, employed in rapidly divesting myself of the rich ornaments which, in profuseness and value, could scarcely have found their equals in any private family in Ireland.

I had thrown myself into a lounging-chair beside the fire, listless and exhausted after the fatigues of the evening, when I was aroused from the reverie into which I had fallen by the sound of footsteps approaching my chamber, and my mother entered.

'Fanny, my dear,' said she, in her softest tone, 'I wish to say a word or two with you before I go to rest. You are not fatigued, love, I hope?'

'No, no, madam, I thank you,' said I, rising at the same time from my seat, with the formal respect so little practised now.

'Sit down, my dear,' said she, placing herself upon a chair beside me; 'I must chat with you for a quarter of an hour or so. Saunders' (to the maid), 'you may leave the room; do not close the room door, but shut that of the lobby.'

This precaution against curious ears having been taken as directed, my mother proceeded: 'You have observed, I should suppose, my dearest Fanny – indeed, you *must* have observed Lord Glenfallen's marked attentions to you?'

'I assure you, madam – ' I began.

'Well, well, that is all right,' interrupted my mother. 'Of course, you must be modest upon the matter; but listen to me for a few moments, my love, and I will prove to your satisfaction that your modesty is quite unnecessary in this case. You have done better than we could have hoped, at least, so very soon. Lord Glenfallen is in love with you. I give you joy of your conquest;' and, saying this, my mother kissed my forehead.

'In love with me!' I exclaimed in unfeigned astonishment.

'Yes, in love with you,' repeated my mother; 'devotedly, distractedly in love with you. Why, my dear, what is there wonderful in it? Look in the glass, and look at these,' she continued, pointing, with a smile, to the jewels which I had just removed from my person, and which now lay in a glittering heap upon the table.

'May there not – ' said I, hesitating between confusion and real alarm, 'is it not possible that some mistake may be at the bottom of all this?'

'Mistake, dearest! none,' said my mother. 'None; none in the world. Judge for yourself; read this, my love.' And she placed in my hand a letter, addressed to herself, the seal of which was broken. I read it through with no small surprise. After some very fine complimentary flourishes upon my beauty and perfections, as also upon the antiquity and high reputation of our family, it went on to make a formal proposal of marriage, to be communicated or not to me at present, as my mother should deem expedient; and the letter wound up by a request that the writer might be permitted, upon our return to Ashtown House, which was soon to take place, as the spring was now tolerably advanced, to visit us for a few days, in case his suit was approved.

'Well, well, my dear,' said my mother, impatiently; 'do you know who Lord Glenfallen is?'

'I do, madam,' said I, rather timidly; for I dreaded an altercation with my mother.

'Well, dear, and what frightens you?' continued she. 'Are you afraid of a title? What has he done to alarm you? He is neither old nor ugly.'

I was silent, though I might have said, 'He is neither young nor handsome.'

'My dear Fanny,' continued my mother, 'in sober seriousness, you have been most fortunate in engaging the affections of a nobleman such as Lord Glenfallen, young and wealthy, with first-rate – yes, acknowledged *first-rate* abilities, and of a family whose influence is not exceeded by that of any in Ireland. Of course, you see the offer in the same light that I do – indeed, I think you *must*.'

This was uttered in no very dubious tone. I was so much astonished by the suddenness of the whole communication, that I literally did not know what to say.

'You are not in love?' said my mother, turning sharply, and fixing her dark eyes upon me with severe scrutiny.

'No, madam,' said I, promptly horrified – what young lady would not have been? – at such a query.

'I'm glad to hear it,' said my mother, drily. 'Once, nearly twenty years ago, a friend of mine consulted me as to how he should deal with a daughter who had made what they call a love-match – beggared herself, and disgraced her family; and I said, without hesitation, take no care for her, but cast her off. Such punishment I awarded for an offence committed against the reputation of a family not my own; and what I advised respecting the child of another, with full as small compunction I would *do* with mine. I cannot conceive anything more unreasonable or intolerable than that the fortune and the character of a family should be marred by the idle caprices of a girl.'

She spoke this with great severity, and paused as if she expected some observation from me.

I, however, said nothing.

'But I need not explain to you, my dear Fanny,' she continued, 'my views upon this subject; you have always known them well, and I have never yet had reason to believe you are likely to offend me voluntarily, or to abuse or neglect any of those advantages which reason and duty tell you should be improved. Come hither, my dear; kiss me, and do not look so frightened. Well, now, about this letter – you need not answer it yet; of course, you must be allowed time to make up your mind. In the meantime, I will write to his lordship to give him my permission to visit us at Ashtown. Good-night, my love.'

And thus ended one of the most disagreeable, not to say astounding, conversations I had ever had. It would not be easy to describe exactly what were my feelings towards Lord Glenfallen; – whatever might have been my mother's suspicions, my heart was perfectly disengaged – and hitherto, although I had not been made in the slightest degree acquainted with his real views, I had liked him very much as an agreeable, well-informed man, whom I was always glad to meet in society. He had served in the navy in early life, and the polish which his manners received in his after intercourse with courts and cities had not served to obliterate that frankness of manner which belongs proverbially to the sailor.

Whether this apparent candour went deeper than the outward bearing, I was yet to learn. However, there was no doubt that, as far as I had seen of Lord Glenfallen, he was, though perhaps not so young as might have been desired in a lover, a singularly pleasing man; and whatever feeling unfavourable to him had found its way into my mind, arose altogether from the dread, not an unreasonable one, that constraint might be practised upon my inclinations. I reflected, however, that Lord Glenfallen was a wealthy man, and one highly thought of; and although I could never expect to love him in the romantic sense of the term, yet I had no doubt but that, all things considered, I might be more happy with him than I could hope to be at home.

When next I met him it was with no small embarrassment; his tact and good breeding, however, soon reassured me, and effectually prevented my awkwardness being remarked upon. And I had the satisfaction of leaving Dublin for the country with the full conviction that nobody, not even those most intimate with me, even suspected the fact of Lord Glenfallen's having made me a formal proposal.

This was to me a very serious subject of self-gratification, for, besides my instinctive dread of becoming the topic of the speculations of gossip, I felt that if the situation which I occupied in relation to him were made publicly known, I should stand committed in a manner which would scarcely leave me the power of retraction.

The period at which Lord Glenfallen had arranged to visit Ashtown House was now fast approaching, and it became my mother's wish to form me thoroughly to her will, and to obtain my consent to the proposed marriage before his arrival, so that all things might proceed smoothly, without apparent opposition or objection upon my part. Whatever objections, therefore, I had entertained were to be subdued; whatever disposition to resistance I had exhibited or had been supposed to feel, were to be completely eradicated before he made his appearance; and my mother addressed herself to the task with a decision and energy against which even the barriers her imagination had created could hardly have stood.

If she had, however, expected any determined opposition from me, she was agreeably disappointed. My heart was perfectly free, and all my feelings of liking and preference were in favour of Lord Glenfallen; and I well knew that in case I refused to dispose of myself as I was desired, my mother had alike the power and the will to render my existence as utterly miserable as even the most ill-assorted marriage could possibly have made it.

You will remember, my good friend, that I was very young and very completely under the control of my parents, both of whom, my mother particularly, were unscrupulously determined in matters of this kind, and willing, when voluntary obedience on the part of those within their power was withheld, to compel a forced acquiescence by an unsparing use of all the engines of the most stern and rigorous domestic discipline.

All these combined, not unnaturally induced me to resolve upon yielding at once, and without useless opposition, to what appeared almost to be my fate.

The appointed time was come, and my now accepted suitor arrived; he was in high spirits, and, if possible, more entertaining than ever.

I was not, however, quite in the mood to enjoy his sprightliness; but whatever I wanted in gaiety was amply made up in the triumphant and gracious good-humour of my mother, whose smiles of bene-volence and exultation were showered around as bountifully as the summer sunshine.

I will not weary you with unnecessary details. Let it suffice to say, that I was married to Lord Glenfallen with all the attendant pomp and circumstance of wealth, rank, and grandeur. According to the usage of the times, now humanely reformed, the ceremony was made, until long past midnight, the season of wild, uproarious, and promiscuous feasting and revelry.

Of all this I have a painfully vivid recollection, and particularly of the little annoyances inflicted upon me by the dull and coarse jokes of the wits and wags who abound in all such places, and upon all such occasions.

I was not sorry when, after a few days, Lord Glenfallen's carriage appeared at the door to convey us both from Ashtown for any change would have been a relief from the irksomeness of ceremonial and formality which the visits received in honour of my newly-acquired titles hourly entailed upon me.

It was arranged that we were to proceed to Cahergillagh, one of the Glenfallen estates, lying, however, in a southern county; so that, owing to the difficulty of the roads at the time; a tedious journey of three days intervened.

I set forth with my noble companion, followed by the regrets of some, and by the envy of many; though God knows I little deserved the latter. The three days of travel were now almost spent, when passing the brow of a wild heathy hill, the domain of Cahergillagh opened suddenly upon our view.

It formed a striking and a beautiful scene. A lake of considerable extent stretching away towards the west, and reflecting from its broad, smooth waters the rich glow of the setting sun, was overhung by steep hills, covered by a rich mantle of velvet sward, broken here and there by the grey front of some old rock, and exhibiting on their shelving sides and on their slopes and hollows every variety of light and shade. A thick wood of dwarf oak, birch, and hazel skirted these hills, and clothed the shores of the lake, running out in rich luxuriance upon every promontory, and spreading upward considerably upon the side of the hills.

'There lies the enchanted castle,' said Lord Glenfallen, pointing towards a considerable level space intervening between two of the picturesque hills which rose dimly around the lake.

This little plain was chiefly occupied by the same low, wild wood which covered the other parts of the domain; but towards the centre, a mass of taller and statelier forest trees stood darkly grouped together, and among them stood an ancient square tower, with many buildings of a humbler character, forming together the manor-house, or, as it was more usually called, the Court of Cahergillagh.

As we approached the level upon which the mansion stood, the winding road gave us many glimpses of the timeworn castle and its surrounding buildings; and seen as it was through the long vistas of the fine old trees, and with the rich glow of evening upon it, I have seldom beheld an object more picturesquely striking.

I was glad to perceive, too, that here and there the blue curling smoke ascended from stacks of chimneys now hidden by the rich, dark ivy which, in a great measure, covered the building. Other indications of comfort made themselves manifest as we approached; and indeed, though the place was evidently one of considerable antiquity, it had nothing whatever of the gloom of decay about it.

'You must not, my love,' said Lord Glenfallen, 'imagine this place worse than it is. I have no taste for antiquity – at least I should not choose a house to reside in because it is old. Indeed, I do not recollect that I was even so romantic as to overcome my aversion to rats and rheumatism, those faithful attendants upon your noble relics of feudalism; and I much prefer a snug, modern, unmysterious bedroom, with well-aired sheets, to the waving tapestry, mildewed cushions, and all the other interesting appliances of romance. However, though I cannot promise you all the discomfort generally belonging to an old castle, you will find legends and ghostly lore enough to claim your respect; and if old Martha be still to the fore, as I trust she is, you will soon have a supernatural and appropriate anecdote for every closet and corner of the mansion. But here we are – so, without more ado, welcome to Cahergillagh!'

We now entered the hall of the castle, and while the domestics were employed in conveying our trunks and other luggage which we had brought with us for immediate use, to the apartments which Lord Glenfallen had selected for himself and me, I went with him into a spacious sitting-room, wainscoted with finely-polished black oak, and hung round with the portraits of various worthies of the Glenfallen family.

This room looked out upon an extensive level covered with the softest green sward, and irregularly bounded by the wild wood I have before mentioned, through the leafy arcade formed by whose boughs and trunks the level beams of the setting sun were pouring. In the distance a group of dairymaids were plying their task, which they accompanied throughout with snatches of Irish songs which, mellowed by the distance, floated not unpleasingly to the ear; and beside them sat or lay, with all the grave importance of conscious protection, six or seven large dogs of various kinds. Farther in the distance, and through the cloisters of the arching wood, two or three ragged urchins were employed in driving such stray kine as had wandered farther than the rest to join their fellows.

As I looked upon the scene which I have described, a feeling of tranquillity and happiness came upon me, which I have never experienced in so strong a degree; and so strange to me was the sensation that my eyes filled with tears.

Lord Glenfallen mistook the cause of my emotion, and taking me kindly and tenderly by the hand, he said: 'Do not suppose, my love, that it is my intention to *settle* here. Whenever you desire to leave this, you have only to let me know your wish, and it shall be complied with; so I must entreat of you not to suffer any circumstances which I can control to give you one moment's uneasiness. But here is old Martha; you must be introduced to her, one of the heirlooms of our family.'

A hale, good-humoured, erect old woman was Martha, and an agreeable contrast to the grim, decrepid hag which my fancy had conjured up, as the depository of all the horrible tales in which I doubted not this old place was most fruitful.

She welcomed me and her master with a profusion of gratulations, alternately kissing our hands and apologising for the liberty; until at length Lord Glenfallen put an end to this somewhat fatiguing ceremonial by requesting her to conduct me to my chamber, if it were prepared for my reception.

I followed Martha up an old-fashioned oak staircase into a long, dim passage, at the end of which lay the door which communicated with the apartments which had been selected for our use; here the old woman stopped, and respectfully requested me to proceed.

I accordingly opened the door, and was about to enter, when something like a mass of black tapestry, as it appeared, disturbed by my sudden approach, fell from above the door, so as completely to screen the aperture; the startling unexpectedness of the occurrence, and the rustling noise which the drapery made in its descent, caused me involuntarily to step two or three paces backward. I turned, smiling and half-ashamed, to the old servant, and said: 'You see what a coward I am.'

The woman looked puzzled, and, without saying any more, I was about to draw aside the curtain and enter the room, when, upon turning to do so, I was surprised to find that nothing whatever interposed to obstruct the passage.

I went into the room, followed by the servant-woman, and was amazed to find that it, like the one below, was wainscoted, and that nothing like drapery was to be found near the door.

'Where is it?' said I; 'what has become of it?'

'What does your ladyship wish to know?' said the old woman.

'Where is the black curtain that fell across the door, when I attempted first to come to my chamber?' answered I.

'The cross of Christ about us!' said the old woman, turning suddenly pale.

'What is the matter, my good friend?' said I; 'you seem frightened.'

'Oh no your ladyship,' said the old woman, endeavouring to conceal her agitation; but in vain, for tottering towards a chair, she sank into it, looking so deadly pale and horror-struck that I thought every moment she would faint.

'Merciful God, keep us from harm and danger!' muttered she at length.

'What can have terrified you so?' said I, beginning to fear that she had seen something more than had met my eye. 'You appear ill, my poor woman!'

'Nothing, nothing, my lady,' said she. 'I beg your ladyship's pardon for making so bold. May the great God defend us from misfortune!'

'Martha,' said I, 'something has frightened you very much, and I insist on knowing what it is; your keeping me in the dark upon the subject will make me much more uneasy than anything you could tell me. I desire you, therefore, to let me know what agitates you; I command you to tell me.'

'Your ladyship said you saw a black curtain falling across the door when you were coming into the room,' said the old woman.

'I did,' said I; 'but though the whole thing appears somewhat strange, I cannot see anything in the matter to agitate you so excessively.'

'It's for no good you saw that, my lady,' said the crone; 'something terrible is coming. It's a sign, my lady – a sign that never fails.'

'Explain, explain what you mean, my good woman,' said I, in spite of myself, catching more than I could account for, of her super-stitious terror.

'Whenever something – something *bad* is going to happen to the Glenfallen family, someone that belongs to them sees a black hand-kerchief or curtain just waved or falling before their faces. I saw it myself,' continued she, lowering her voice, 'when I was only a little girl, and I'll never forget it. I often heard of it before, though I never saw it till then, nor since, praised be God. But I was going into Lady Jane's room to waken her in the morning; and sure enough when I got first to the bed and began to draw the curtain, something dark was waved across the division, but only for a moment; and when I saw rightly into the bed, there she was lying cold and dead, God be merciful to me! So, my lady, there is small blame to me to be daunted when anyone of the family sees it for it's many the story I heard of it, though I saw it but once.'

I was not of a superstitious turn of mind, yet I could not resist a feeling of awe very nearly allied to the fear which my companion had so unreservedly expressed; and when you consider my situation, the loneliness, antiquity, and gloom of the place, you will allow that the weakness was not without excuse.

In spite of old Martha's boding predictions, however, time flowed on in an unruffled course. One little incident, however, though trifling in itself, I must relate, as it serves to make what follows more intelligible.

Upon the day after my arrival, Lord Glenfallen of course desired to make me acquainted with the house and domain; and accordingly we set forth upon our ramble. When returning, he became for some time silent and moody, a state so unusual with him as considerably to excite my surprise.

I endeavoured by observations and questions to arouse him – but in vain. At length, as we approached the house, he said, as if speaking to himself: ' 'Twere madness – madness – madness,' repeating the words bitterly; 'sure and speedy ruin.'

There was here a long pause; and at length, turning sharply

towards me, in a tone very unlike that in which he had hither- to addressed me, he said: 'Do you think it possible that a woman can keep a secret?'

'I am sure,' said I, 'that women are very much belied upon the score of talkativeness, and that I may answer your question with the same directness with which you put it – I reply that I *do* think a woman can keep a secret.'

'But I do not,' said he, drily.

We walked on in silence for a time. I was much astonished at his unwonted abruptness – I had almost said rudeness.

After a considerable pause he seemed to recollect himself, and with an effort resuming his sprightly manner, he said: 'Well, well, the next thing to keeping a secret well is not to desire to possess one; talkativeness and curiosity generally go together. Now I shall make test of you, in the first place, respecting the latter of these qualities. I shall be your *Bluebeard* – tush, why do I trifle thus? Listen to me, my dear Fanny; I speak now in solemn earnest. What I desire is intimately, inseparably connected with your happiness and honour as well as my own; and your compliance with my request will not be difficult. It will impose upon you a very trifling restraint during your sojourn here, which certain events which have occurred since our arrival have determined me shall not be a long one. You must promise me, upon your sacred honour, that you will visit *only* that part of the castle which can be reached from the front entrance, leaving the back entrance and the part of the building commanded immediately by it to the menials, as also the small garden whose high wall you see yonder; and never at any time seek to pry or peep into them, nor to open the door which communicates from the front part of the house through the corridor with the back. I do not urge this in jest or in caprice, but from a solemn conviction that danger and mischief will be the certain consequences of your not observing what I prescribe. I cannot explain myself further at present. Promise me, then, these things, as you hope for peace here and for mercy hereafter.'

I did make the promise as desired; and he appeared relieved; his manner recovered all its gaiety and elasticity: but the recollection of the strange scene which I have just described dwelt painfully upon my mind.

More than a month passed away without any occurrence worth recording; but I was not destined to leave Cahergillagh without further adventure. One day, intending to enjoy the pleasant sunshine in a ramble through the woods, I ran up to my room to procure my hat and cloak. Upon entering the chamber I was surprised and somewhat startled to find it occupied. Beside the fireplace, and nearly opposite the door, seated in a large, old-fashioned elbow-chair, was placed the figure of a lady. She appeared to be nearer fifty than forty, and was dressed suitably to her age, in a handsome suit of flowered silk; she had a profusion of trinkets and jewellery about her person, and many rings upon her fingers. But although very rich, her dress was not gaudy or in ill taste. But what was remarkable in the lady was, that although her features were handsome, and upon the whole pleasing, the pupil of each eye was dimmed with the whiteness of cataract, and she was evidently stone-blind. I was for some seconds so surprised at this unaccountable apparition, that I could not find words to address her.

'Madam,' said I, 'there must be some mistake here – this is my bedchamber.'

'Marry come up,' said the lady, sharply; '*your* chamber! Where is Lord Glenfallen?'

'He is below, madam,' replied I; 'and I am convinced he will be not a little surprised to find you here.'

'I do not think he will,' said she, 'with your good leave; talk of what you know something about. Tell him I want him. Why does the minx dilly-dally so?'

In spite of the awe which this grim lady inspired, there was something in her air of confident superiority which, when I considered our relative situations, was not a little irritating.

'Do you know, madam, to whom you speak?' said I.

'I neither know nor care,' said she; 'but I presume that you are someone about the house, so again I desire you, if you wish to continue here, to bring your master hither forthwith.'

'I must tell you, madam,' said I, 'that I am Lady Glenfallen.'

'What's that?' said the stranger, rapidly.

'I say, madam,' I repeated, approaching her that I might be more distinctly heard, 'that I am Lady Glenfallen.'

'It's a lie, you trull!' cried she, in an accent which made me start, and at the same time, springing forward, she seized me in her grasp, and shook me violently, repeating, 'It's a lie – it's a lie!' with a rapidity and vehemence which swelled every vain of her face. The violence of her action, and the fury which convulsed her face, effectually terrified me, and disengaged myself from her grasp, I screamed as loud as I could for help. The blind woman continued to pour out a torrent of abuse upon me, foaming at the mouth with rage, and impotently shaking her clenched fist towards me.

I heard Lord Glenfallen's step upon the stairs, and I instantly ran out; as I passed him I perceived that he was deadly pale, and just caught the words: 'I hope that demon has not hurt you?'

I made some answer, I forget what, and he entered the chamber, the door of which he locked upon the inside. What passed within I know not; but I heard the voices of the two speakers raise in loud and angry altercation.

I thought I heard the shrill accents of the woman repeat the words, 'Let her look to herself;' but I could not be quite sure. This short sentence, however, was, to my alarmed imagination, pregnant with fearful meaning.

The storm at length subsided, though not until after a conference of more than two long hours. Lord Glenfallen then returned, pale and agitated.

'That unfortunate woman,' said he, 'is out of her mind. I dare say she treated you to some of her ravings; but you need not dread any further interruption from her: I have brought her so far to reason. She did not hurt you, I trust.'

'No, no,' said I; 'but she terrified me beyond measure.'

'Well,' said he, 'she is likely to behave better for the future; and I dare swear that neither you nor she would desire, after what has passed, to meet again.'

This occurrence, so startling and unpleasant, so involved in mystery, and giving rise to so many painful surmises, afforded me no very agreeable food for rumination.

All attempts on my part to arrive at the truth were baffled; Lord Glenfallen evaded all my enquiries, and at length peremptorily forbade any further allusion to the matter. I was thus obliged to rest satisfied with what I had actually seen, and to trust to time to resolve the perplexities in which the whole transaction had involved me.

Lord Glenfallen's temper and spirits gradually underwent a complete and most painful change; he became silent and abstracted, his manner to me was abrupt and often harsh, some grievous anxiety seemed ever present to his mind; and under its influence his spirits sank and his temper became soured.

I soon perceived that his gaiety was rather that which the stir and excitement of society produce, than the result of a healthy habit of mind; every day confirmed me in the opinion, that the considerate good-nature which I had so much admired in him was little more than a mere manner; and to my infinite grief and surprise, the gay, kind, open-hearted nobleman who had for months followed and flattered me, was rapidly assuming the form of a gloomy, morose, and singularly selfish man. This was a bitter discovery, and I strove to conceal it from myself as long as I could; but the truth was not to be denied, and I was forced to believe that my husband no longer loved me, and that he was at little pains to conceal the alteration in his sentiments.

One morning after breakfast, Lord Glenfallen had been for some time walking silently up and down the room, buried in his moody reflections, when pausing suddenly, and turning towards me, he exclaimed: 'I have it – I have it! We must go abroad, and stay there too; and if that does not answer, why – why, we must try some more effectual expedient. Lady Glenfallen, I have become involved in heavy embarrassments. A wife, you know, must share the fortunes of her husband, for better for worse; but I will waive my right if you prefer remaining here – here at Cahergillagh. For I would not have you seen elsewhere without the state to which your rank entitles you; besides, it would break your poor mother's heart,' he added, with sneering gravity. 'So make up your mind – Cahergillagh or France. I will start if possible in a week, so determine between this and then.'

He left the room, and in a few moments I saw him ride past the window, followed by a mounted servant. He had directed a domestic to inform me that he should not be back until the next day.

I was in very great doubt as to what course of conduct I should pursue as to accompanying him in the continental tour so suddenly determined upon. I felt that it would be a hazard too great to encounter; for at Cahergillagh I had always the consciousness to sustain me, that if his temper at any time led him into violent or unwarrantable treatment of me, I had a remedy within reach, in the protection and support of my own family, from all useful and effective communication with whom, if once in France, I should be entirely debarred.

As to remaining at Cahergillagh in solitude, and, for aught I knew, exposed to hidden dangers, it appeared to me scarcely less objectionable than the former proposition; and yet I feared that with one or other I must comply, unless I was prepared to come to an actual breach with Lord Glenfallen. Full of these unpleasing doubts and perplexities, I retired to rest.

I was wakened, after having slept uneasily for some hours, by some person shaking me rudely by the shoulder; a small lamp burned in my room, and by its light, to my horror and amazement, I discovered that my visitant was the selfsame blind old lady who had so terrified me a few weeks before.

I started up in the bed, with a view to ring the bell, and alarm the domestics; but she instantly anticipated me by saying: 'Do not be frightened, silly girl! If I had wished to harm you, I could have done it while you were sleeping; I need not have wakened you. Listen to me, now, attentively and fearlessly, for what I have to say interests you to the full as much as it does me. Tell me here, in the presence of God, did Lord Glenfallen marry you – *actually marry* you? Speak the truth, woman.'

'As surely as I live and speak,' I replied, 'did Lord Glenfallen marry me, in presence of more than a hundred witnesses.'

'Well,' continued she, 'he should have told you *then*, before you married him, that he had a wife living – that I am his wife. I feel you tremble – tush! do not be frightened. I do not mean to harm you. Mark me now – you are *not* his wife. When I make my story known you will be so neither in the eye of God nor of man. You must leave this house upon tomorrow. Let the world know that your husband has another wife living; go you into retirement, and leave him to justice, which will surely overtake him. If you remain in this house after tomorrow, you will reap the bitter fruits of your sin.'

So saying, she quitted the room, leaving me very little disposed to sleep.

Here was food for my very worst and most terrible suspicions; still there was not enough to remove all doubt. I had no proof of the truth of this woman's statement.

Taken by itself, there was nothing to induce me to attach weight to it; but when I viewed it in connection with the extraordinary mystery of some of Lord Glenfallen's proceedings, his strange anxiety to exclude me from certain portions of the mansion, doubtless lest I should encounter this person – the strong influence, nay, command which she possessed over him, a circumstance clearly established by the very fact of her residing in the very place where, of all others, he should least have desired to find her – her thus acting, and continuing to act in direct contradiction to his wishes; when, I say, I viewed her disclosure in connection with all these circumstances, I could not help feeling that there was at least a fearful verisimilitude in the allegations which she had made.

Still I was not satisfied, nor nearly so. Young minds have a reluctance almost insurmountable to believing, upon anything short of unquestionable proof, the existence of premeditated guilt in anyone whom they have ever trusted; and in support of this feeling I was assured that if the assertion of Lord Glenfallen, which nothing in this woman's manner had led me to disbelieve, were true, namely that her mind was unsound, the whole fabric of my doubts and fears must fall to the ground.

I determined to state to Lord Glenfallen freely and accurately the substance of the communication which I had just heard, and in his words and looks to seek for its proof or refutation. Full of these thoughts, I remained wakeful and excited all night, every moment fancying that I heard the step or saw the figure of my recent visitor, towards whom I felt a species of horror and dread which I can hardly describe.

There was something in her face, though her features had evidently been handsome, and were not, at first sight, unpleasing, which, upon a nearer inspection, seemed to indicate the habitual prevalence and indulgence of evil passions, and a power of expressing mere animal anger with an intenseness that I have seldom seen equalled, and to which an almost unearthly effect was given by the convulsive quivering of the sightless eyes.

You may easily suppose that it was no very pleasing reflection to me to consider that, whenever caprice might induce her to return, I was within the reach of this violent and, for aught I knew, insane woman, who had, upon that very night, spoken to me in a tone of menace, of which her mere words, divested of the manner and look with which she uttered them, can convey but a faint idea.

Will you believe me when I tell you that I was actually afraid to leave my bed in order to secure the door, lest I should again encounter the dreadful object lurking in some corner or peeping from behind the window-curtains, so very a child was I in my fears?

The morning came, and with it Lord Glenfallen. I knew not, and indeed I cared not, where he might have been; my thoughts were wholly engrossed by the terrible fears and suspicions which my last night's conference had suggested to me. He was, as usual, gloomy and abstracted, and I feared in no very fitting mood to hear what I had to say with patience, whether the charges were true or false.

I was, however, determined not to suffer the opportunity to pass, or Lord Glenfallen to leave the room, until, at all hazards, I had unburdened my mind.

'My lord,' said I, after a long silence, summoning up all my firmness, 'my lord, I wish to say a few words to you upon a matter of very great importance, of very deep concernment to you and to me.'

I fixed my eyes upon him to discern, if possible, whether the announcement caused him any uneasiness; but no symptom of any such feeling was perceptible.

'Well, my dear,' said he, 'this is no doubt a very grave preface, and portends, I have no doubt, something extraordinary. Pray let us have it without more ado.'

He took a chair, and seated himself nearly opposite to me.

'My lord,' said I, 'I have seen the person who alarmed me so much a short time since, the blind lady, again, upon last night.' His face, upon which my eyes were fixed, turned pale; he hesitated for a moment, and then said: 'And did you, pray, madam, so totally forget or spurn my express command, as to enter that portion of the house from which your promise, I might say your oath, excluded you? Answer me that!' he added fiercely.

'My lord,' said I, 'I have neither forgotten your *commands*, since such they were, nor disobeyed them. I was, last night, wakened from my sleep, as I lay in my own chamber, and accosted by the person whom I have mentioned. How she found access to the room I cannot pretend to say.'

'Ha! this must be looked to,' said he, half reflectively. 'And pray,' added he quickly, while in turn he fixed his eyes upon me, 'what did this person say? since some comment upon her communication forms, no doubt, the sequel to your preface.'

'Your lordship is not mistaken,' said I; 'her statement was so extraordinary that I could not think of withholding it from you. She told me, my lord, that you had a wife living at the time you married me, and that she was that wife.'

Lord Glenfallen became ashy pale, almost livid; he made two or three efforts to clear his voice to speak, but in vain, and turning suddenly from me, he walked to the window. The horror and dismay which, in the olden time, overwhelmed the woman of Endor when her spells unexpectedly conjured the dead into her presence, were but types of what I felt when thus presented with what appeared to be almost unequivocal evidence of the guilt whose existence I had before so strongly doubted.

There was a silence of some moments, during which it were hard to conjecture whether I or my companion suffered most.

Lord Glenfallen soon recovered his self-command; he returned to the table, again sat down, and said: 'What you have told me has so astonished me, has unfolded such a tissue of motiveless guilt, and in a quarter from which I had so little reason to look for ingratitude or treachery, that your announcement almost deprived me of speech; the person in question, however, has one excuse, her mind is, as I told you before, unsettled. You should have remembered that, and hesitated to receive as unexceptionable evidence against the honour of your husband, the ravings of a lunatic. I now tell you that this is the last time I shall speak to you upon this subject, and, in the presence of the God who is to judge me, and as I hope for mercy in the day of judgment, I swear that the charge thus brought against me is utterly false, unfounded, and ridiculous. I defy the world in any point to taint my honour; and, as I have never taken the opinion of madmen touching your character or morals, I think it but fair to require that you will evince a like tenderness for me; and now, once for all, never again dare to repeat to me your insulting suspicions, or the clumsy and infamous calumnies of fools. I shall instantly let the worthy lady who contrived this somewhat original device understand fully my opinion upon the matter. Good morning.'

And with these words he left me again in doubt, and involved in all the horrors of the most agonising suspense.

I had reason to think that Lord Glenfallen wreaked his vengeance upon the author of the strange story which I had heard, with a violence which was not satisfied with mere words for old Martha, with whom I was a great favourite, while attending me in my room, told me that she feared her master had ill-used the poor blind Dutchwoman, for that she had heard her scream as if the very life were leaving her, but added a request that I should not speak of what she had told me to anyone, particularly to the master.

'How do you know that she is a Dutchwoman?' enquired I, anxious to learn anything whatever that might throw a light upon the history of this person, who seemed to have resolved to mix herself up in my fortunes.

'Why, my lady,' answered Martha, 'the master often calls her the Dutch hag, and other names you would not like to hear, and I am sure she is neither English nor Irish; for, whenever they talk together, they speak some queer foreign lingo, and fast enough, I'll be bound. But I ought not to talk about her at all; it might be as much as my place is worth to mention her, only you saw her first yourself, so there can be no great harm in speaking of her now.'

'How long has this lady been here?' continued I.

'She came early on the morning after your ladyship's arrival,' answered she; 'but do not ask me any more, for the master would think nothing of turning me out of doors for daring to speak of her at all, much less to *you*, my lady.'

I did not like to press the poor woman further, for her reluctance to speak on this topic was evident and strong.

You will readily believe that upon the very slight grounds which my information afforded, contradicted as it was by the solemn oath of my husband, and derived from what was, at best, a very questionable source, I could not take any very decisive measures whatever; and as to the menace of the strange woman who had thus unaccountably twice intruded herself into my chamber, although, at the moment, it occasioned me some uneasiness, it was not, even in my eyes, sufficiently formidable to induce my departure from Cahergillagh.

A few nights after the scene which I have just mentioned, Lord Glenfallen having, as usual, retired early to his study, I was left alone in the parlour to amuse myself as best I might.

It was not strange that my thoughts should often recur to the agitating scenes in which I had recently taken a part.

The subject of my reflections, the solitude, the silence, and the lateness of the hour, as also the depression of spirits to which I had of late been a constant prey, tended to produce that nervous excitement which places us wholly at the mercy of the imagination.

In order to calm my spirits I was endeavouring to direct my thoughts into some more pleasing channel, when I heard, or thought I heard, uttered within a few yards of me, in an odd, half-sneering tone, the words: 'There is blood upon your ladyship's throat.'

So vivid was the impression that I started to my feet, and involuntarily placed my hand upon my neck.

I looked around the room for the speaker, but in vain.

I went then to the room-door, which I opened, and peered into the passage, nearly faint with horror lest some leering shapeless thing should greet me upon the threshold.

When I had gazed long enough to assure myself that no strange object was within sight,

'I have been too much of a rake lately; I am racking out my nerves,' said I, speaking aloud, with a view to reassure myself.

I rang the bell, and, attended by old Martha, I retired for the night.

While the servant was – as was her custom – arranging the lamp which I have already stated always burned during the night in my chamber, I was employed in undressing, and, in doing so, I had recourse to a large looking-glass which occupied a considerable portion of the wall in which it was fixed, rising from the ground to a height of about six feet; this mirror filled the space of a large panel in the wainscoting opposite the foot of the bed.

I had hardly been before it for the lapse of a minute when something like a black pall was slowly waved between me and it.

'Oh, God! there it is,' I exclaimed, wildly. 'I have seen it again, Martha – the black cloth.'

'God be merciful to us, then!' answered she, tremulously crossing herself. 'Some misfortune is over us.'

'No, no, Martha,' said I, almost instantly recovering my collectedness; for, although of a nervous temperament, I had never been superstitious. 'I do not believe in omens. You know I saw, or fancied I saw, this thing before, and nothing followed.'

'The Dutch lady came the next morning,' replied she.

'But surely her coming scarcely deserved such a dreadful warning,' I replied.

'She is a strange woman, my lady,' said Martha; 'and she is not *gone* yet – mark my words.'

'Well, well, Martha,' said I, 'I have not wit enough to change your opinions, nor inclination to alter mine; so I will talk no more of the matter. Good-night,' and so I was left to my reflections.

After lying for about an hour awake, I at length fell into a kind of doze; but my imagination was very busy, for I was startled from this unrefreshing sleep by fancying that I heard a voice close to my face exclaim as before: 'There is blood upon your ladyship's throat.'

The words were instantly followed by a loud burst of laughter.

Quaking with horror, I awakened, and heard my husband enter the room. Even this was a relief.

Scared as I was, however, by the tricks which my imagination had played me, I preferred remaining silent, and pretending to sleep, to attempting to engage my husband in conversation, for I well knew that his mood was such, that his words would not, in all probability, convey anything that had not better be unsaid and unheard.

Lord Glenfallen went into his dressing-room, which lay upon the right-hand side of the bed. The door lying open, I could see him by himself, at full length upon a sofa, and, in about half an hour, I became aware, by his deep and regularly drawn respiration, that he was fast asleep.

When slumber refuses to visit one, there is something peculiarly irritating, not to the temper, but to the nerves, in the consciousness that someone is in your immediate presence, actually enjoying the boon which you are seeking in vain; at least, I have always found it so, and never more than upon the present occasion.

A thousand annoying imaginations harassed and excited me; every object which I looked upon, though ever so familiar, seemed to have acquired a strange phantomlike character, the varying shadows thrown by the flickering of the lamplight seemed shaping themselves into grotesque and unearthly forms, and whenever my eyes wandered to the sleeping figure of my husband, his features appeared to undergo the strangest and most demoniacal contortions.

Hour after hour was told by the old clock, and each succeeding one found me, if possible, less inclined to sleep than its predecessor.

It was now considerably past three; my eyes, in their involuntary wanderings, happened to alight upon the large mirror which was, as I have said, fixed in the wall opposite the foot of the bed. A view of it was commanded from where I lay, through the curtains. As I gazed fixedly upon it, I thought I perceived the broad sheet of glass shifting its position in relation to the bed; I riveted my eyes upon it with intense scrutiny; it was no deception, the mirror, as if acting of its own impulse, moved slowly aside, and disclosed a dark aperture in the wall, nearly as large as an ordinary door; a figure evidently stood in this, but the light was too dim to define it accurately.

It stepped cautiously into the chamber, and with so little noise, that had I not actually seen it, I do not think I should have been aware of its presence. It was arrayed in a kind of woollen nightdress, and a white handkerchief or cloth was bound tightly about the head; I had no difficulty, spite of the strangeness of the attire, in recognising the blind woman whom I so much dreaded.

She stooped down, bringing her head nearly to the ground, and in that attitude she remained motionless for some moments, no doubt in order to ascertain if any suspicious sounds were stirring.

She was apparently satisfied by her observations, for she immediately recommended her silent progress towards a ponderous mahogany dressing-table of my husband's. When she had reached it, she paused again, and appeared to listen attentively for some minutes; she then noiselessly opened one of the drawers, from which, having groped for some time, she took something, which I soon perceived to be a case of razors. She opened it, and tried the edge of each of the two instruments upon the skin of her hand; she quickly selected one, which she fixed firmly in her grasp. She now stooped down as before, and having listened for a time, she, with the hand that was disengaged, groped her way into the dressing-room where Lord Glenfallen lay fast asleep.

I was fixed as if in the tremendous spell of a nightmare. I could not stir even a finger; I could not lift my voice; I could not even breathe; and though I expected every moment to see the sleeping man murdered, I could not even close my eyes to shut out the horrible spectacle which I had not the power to avert.

I saw the woman approach the sleeping figure, she laid the unoccupied hand lightly along his clothes, and having thus ascertained his identity, she, after a brief interval, turned back and again entered my chamber; here she bent down again to listen.

I had now not a doubt but that the razor was intended for my throat; yet the terrific fascination which had locked all my powers so long, still continued to bind me fast.

I felt that my life depended upon the slightest ordinary exertion, and yet I could not stir one joint from the position in which I lay, nor even make noise enough to waken Lord Glenfallen.

The murderous woman now, with long, silent steps, approached the bed; my very heart seemed turning to ice; her left hand, that which was disengaged, was upon the pillow; she gradually slid it forward towards my head, and in an instant, with the speed of lightning, it was clutched in my hair, while, with the other hand, she dashed the razor at my throat.

A slight inaccuracy saved me from instant death; the blow fell short, the point of the razor grazing my throat. In a moment, I know not how, I found myself at the other side of the bed, uttering shriek after shriek; the wretch was however determined, if possible, to murder me.

Scrambling along by the curtains, she rushed round the bed towards me; I seized the handle of the door to make my escape. It was, however, fastened. At all events, I could not open it. From the mere instinct of recoiling terror, I shrunk back into a corner. She was now within a yard of me. Her hand was upon my face.

I closed my eyes fast, expecting never to open them again, when a blow, inflicted from behind by a strong arm, stretched the monster senseless at my feet. At the same moment the door opened, and several domestics, alarmed by my cries, entered the apartment.

I do not recollect what followed, for I fainted. One swoon succeeded another, so long and deathlike, that my life was considered very doubtful.

At about ten o'clock however, I sank into a deep and refreshing sleep, from which I was awakened at about two, that I might swear my deposition before a magistrate, who attended for that purpose.

I accordingly did so, as did also Lord Glenfallen, and the woman was fully committed to stand her trial at the ensuing assizes.

I shall never forget the scene which the examination of the blind woman and of the other parties afforded.

She was brought into the room in the custody of two servants. She wore a kind of flannel wrapper, which had not been changed since the night before. It was torn and soiled, and here and there smeared with blood, which had flowed in large quantities from a wound in her head. The white handkerchief had fallen off in the scuffle, and her grizzled hair fell in masses about her wild and deadly pale countenance.

She appeared perfectly composed, however, and the only regret she expressed throughout, was at not having succeeded in her attempt, the object of which she did not pretend to conceal.

On being asked her name, she called herself the Countess Glenfallen, and refused to give any other title.

'The woman's name is Flora Van-Kemp,' said Lord Glenfallen.

'It *was*, it *was*, you perjured traitor and cheat!' screamed the woman; and then there followed a volley of words in some foreign language. 'Is there a magistrate here?' she resumed; 'I am Lord Glenfallen's wife – I'll prove it – write down my words. I am willing to be hanged or burned, so *he* meets his deserts. I did try to kill that doll of his; but it was he who put it into my head to do it – two wives were too many; I was to murder her, or she was to hang me: listen to all I have to say.'

Here Lord Glenfallen interrupted.

'I think, sir,' said he, addressing the magistrate 'that we had better proceed to business; this unhappy woman's furious recriminations but waste our time. If she refuses to answer your questions, you had better, I presume, take my depositions.'

'And are you going to swear away my life, you black-perjured murderer?' shrieked the woman. 'Sir, sir, sir, you must hear me,' she continued, addressing the magistrate; 'I can convict him – he bid me murder that girl, and then, when I failed, he came behind me, and struck me down, and now he wants to swear away my life. Take down all I say.'

'If it is your intention,' said the magistrate, 'to confess the crime with which you stand charged, you may, upon producing sufficient evidence, criminate whom you please.'

'Evidence! – I have no evidence but myself,' said the woman. 'I will swear it all – write down my testimony – write it down, I say – we shall hang side by side, my brave lord – all your own handy-work, my gentle husband!'

This was followed by a low, insolent, and sneering laugh, which, from one in her situation, was sufficiently horrible.

'I will not at present hear anything,' replied he, 'but distinct answers to the questions which I shall put to you upon this matter.'

'Then you shall hear nothing,' replied she sullenly, and no inducement or intimidation could bring her to speak again.

Lord Glenfallen's deposition and mine were then given, as also those of the servants who had entered the room at the moment of my rescue.

The magistrate then intimated that she was committed, and must proceed directly to gaol, whither she was brought in a carriage of Lord Glenfallen's, for his lordship was naturally by no means indifferent to the effect which her vehement accusations against himself might produce, if uttered before every chance hearer whom she might meet with between Cahergillagh and the place of confinement whither she was despatched.

During the time which intervened between the committal and the trial of the prisoner, Lord Glenfallen seemed to suffer agonies of mind which baffled all description; he hardly ever slept, and when he did, his slumbers seemed but the instruments of new tortures, and his waking hours were, if possible exceeded in intensity of terror by the dreams which disturbed his sleep.

Lord Glenfallen rested, if to lie in the mere attitude of repose were to do so, in his dressing-room, and thus I had an opportunity of witnessing, far oftener than I wished it, the fearful workings of his mind. His agony often broke out into such fearful paroxysms that delirium and total loss of reason appeared to be impending. He frequently spoke of flying from the country, and bringing with him all the witnesses of the appalling scene upon which the prosecution was founded; then, again, he would fiercely lament that the blow which he had inflicted had not ended at all.

The assizes arrived, however, and upon the day appointed Lord Glenfallen and I attended in order to give our evidence.

The cause was called on, and the prisoner appeared at the bar.

Great curiosity and interest were felt respecting the trial, so that the court was crowded to excess.

The prisoner, however, without appearing to take the trouble of listening to the indictment, pleaded guilty, and no representations on the part of the court availed to induce her to retract her plea.

After much time had been wasted in a fruitless attempt to prevail upon her to reconsider her words, the court proceeded, according to the usual form, to pass sentence.

This having been done, the prisoner was about to be removed, when she said, in a low, distinct voice: 'A word – a word, my lord! – Is Lord Glenfallen here in the court?'

On being told that he was, she raised her voice to a tone of loud menace, and continued: 'Hardress, Earl of Glenfallen, I accuse you here in this court of justice of two crimes – first, that you married a second wife while the first was living; and again, that you prompted me to the murder, for attempting which I am to die. Secure him – chain him – bring him here!'

There was a laugh through the court at these words, which were naturally treated by the judge as a violent extemporary recrimination, and the woman was desired to be silent.

'You won't take him, then?' she said; 'you won't try him? You'll let him go free?'

It was intimated by the court that he would certainly be allowed 'to go free,' and she was ordered again to be removed.

Before, however, the mandate was executed, she threw her arms wildly into the air, and uttered one piercing shriek so full of preternatural rage and despair, that it might fitly have ushered a soul into those realms where hope can come no more.

The sound still rang in my ears, months after the voice that had uttered it was for ever silent.

The wretched woman was executed in accordance with the sentence which had been pronounced.

For some time after this event, Lord Glenfallen appeared, if possible, to suffer more than he had done before, and altogether his language, which often amounted to half confessions of the guilt imputed to him, and all the circumstances connected with the late occurrences, formed a mass of evidence so convincing that I wrote to my father, detailing the grounds of my fears, and imploring him to come to Cahergillagh without delay, in order to remove me from my husband's control, previously to taking legal steps for a final separation.

Circumstanced as I was, my existence was little short of intolerable, for, besides the fearful suspicions which attached to my husband, I plainly perceived that if Lord Glenfallen were not relieved, and that speedily, insanity must supervene. I therefore expected my father's arrival, or at least a letter to announce it, with indescribable impatience.

About a week after the execution had taken place, Lord Glenfallen one morning met me with an unusually sprightly air.

'Fanny,' said he, 'I have it now for the first time in my power to explain to your satisfaction everything which has hitherto appeared suspicious or mysterious in my conduct. After breakfast come with me to my study, and I shall, I hope, make all things clear.'

This invitation afforded me more real pleasure than I had experienced for months. Something had certainly occurred to tranquillise my husband's mind in no ordinary degree, and I thought it by no means impossible that he would, in the proposed interview, prove himself the most injured and innocent of men.

Full of this hope, I repaired to his study at the appointed hour. He was writing busily when I entered the room, and just raising his eyes, he requested me to be seated.

I took a chair as he desired, and remained silently awaiting his leisure, while he finished, folded, directed, and sealed his letter. Laying it then upon the table with the address downward, he said,

'My dearest Fanny, I know I must have appeared very strange to you and very unkind – often even cruel. Before the end of this week I will show you the necessity of my conduct – how impossible it was that I should have seemed otherwise. I am conscious that many acts of mine must have inevitably given rise to painful suspicions – suspicions which, indeed, upon one occasion, you very properly communicated to me. I have got two letters from a quarter which commands respect, containing information as to the course by which I may be enabled to prove the negative of all the crimes which even the most credulous suspicion could lay to my charge. I expected a third by this morning's post, containing documents which will set the matter for ever at rest, but owing, no doubt, to some neglect, or perhaps to some difficulty in collecting the papers, some inevitable delay, it has not come to hand this morning, according to my expectation. I was finishing one to the very same quarter when you came in, and if a sound rousing be worth anything, I think I shall have a special messenger before two days have passed. I have been anxiously considering with myself, as to whether I had better imperfectly clear up your doubts by submitting to your inspection the two letters which I have already received, or wait till I can triumphantly vindicate myself by the production of the documents which I have already mentioned, and I have, I think, not unnaturally decided upon the latter course. However, there is a person in the next room whose testimony is not without its value – excuse me for one moment.'

So saying, he arose and went to the door of a closet which opened from the study; this he unlocked, and half opening the door, he said, 'It is only I,' and then slipped into the room, and carefully closed and locked the door behind him.

I immediately heard his voice in animated conversation. My curiosity upon the subject of the letter was naturally great, so, smothering any little scruples which I might have felt, I resolved to look at the address of the letter which lay, as my husband had left it, with its face upon the table. I accordingly drew it over to me, and turned up the direction.

For two or three moments I could scarce believe my eyes, but there could be no mistake – in large characters were traced the words. 'To the Archangel Gabriel in Heaven.'

I had scarcely returned the letter to its original position, and in some degree recovered the shock which this unequivocal proof of insanity produced, when the closet door was unlocked, and Lord Glenfallen re-entered the study, carefully closing and locking the door again upon the outside.

'Whom have you there?' enquired I, making a strong effort to appear calm.

'Perhaps,' said he, musingly, 'you might have some objection to seeing her, at least for a time.'

'Who is it?' repeated I.

'Why,' said he, 'I see no use in hiding it – the blind Dutch-woman. I have been with her the whole morning. She is very anxious to get out of that closet; but you know she is odd, she is scarcely to be trusted.'

A heavy gust of wind shook the door at this moment with a sound as if something more substantial were pushing against it.

'Ha, ha, ha! – do you hear her?' said he, with an obstreperous burst of laughter.

The wind died away in a long howl, and Lord Glenfallen, suddenly checking his merriment, shrugged his shoulders, and muttered: 'Poor devil, she has been hardly used.'

'We had better not tease her at present with questions,' said I, in as unconcerned a tone as I could assume, although I felt every moment as if I should faint.

'Humph! may be so,' said he. 'Well, come back in an hour or two, or when you please, and you will find us here.'

He again unlocked the door, and entered with the same pre-cautions which he had adopted before, locking the door upon the inside; and as I hurried from the room, I heard his voice again exerted as if in eager parley.

I can hardly describe my emotions; my hopes had been raised to the highest, and now, in an instant, all was gone; the dreadful consummation was accomplished – the fearful retribution had fallen upon the guilty man – the mind was destroyed, the power to repent was gone.

The agony of the hours which followed what I would still call my awful interview with Lord Glenfallen, I cannot describe; my solitude was, however, broken in upon by Martha, who came to inform me of the arrival of a gentleman, who expected me in the parlour.

I accordingly descended, and, to my great joy, found my father seated by the fire.

This expedition upon his part was easily accounted for: my communications had touched the honour of the family. I speedily informed him of the dreadful malady which had fallen upon the wretched man.

My father suggested the necessity of placing some person to watch him, to prevent his injuring himself or others.

I rang the bell, and desired that one Edward Cooke, an attached servant of the family, should be sent to me.

I told him distinctly and briefly the nature of the service required of him, and, attended by him, my father and I proceeded at once to the study. The door of the inner room was still closed, and everything in the outer chamber remained in the same order in which I had left it.

We then advanced to the closet-door, at which we knocked, but without receiving any answer.

We next tried to open the door, but in vain; it was locked upon the inside. We knocked more loudly, but in vain.

Seriously alarmed, I desired the servant to force the door, which was, after several violent efforts, accomplished, and we entered the closet.

Lord Glenfallen was lying on his face upon a sofa.

'Hush!' said I; 'he is asleep.' We paused for a moment.

'He is too still for that,' said my father.

We all of us felt a strong reluctance to approach the figure.

'Edward,' said I, 'try whether your master sleeps.'

The servant approached the sofa where Lord Glenfallen lay. He leant his ear towards the head of the recumbent figure, to ascertain whether the sound of breathing was audible. He turned towards us, and said: 'My lady, you had best not wait here; I am sure he is dead!'

'Let me see the face,' said I, terribly agitated; 'you *may* be mistaken.'

The man then, in obedience to my command, turned the body round, and, gracious God! what a sight met my view.

The whole breast of the shirt, with its lace frill, was drenched with his blood, as was the couch underneath the spot where he lay.

The head hung back, as it seemed, almost severed from the body by a frightful gash, which yawned across the throat. The razor which had inflicted the wound was found under his body.

All, then, was over; I was never to learn the history in whose termination I had been so deeply and so tragically involved.

The severe discipline which my mind had undergone was not bestowed in vain. I directed my thoughts and my hopes to that place where there is no more sin, nor danger, nor sorrow.

Thus ends a brief tale whose prominent incidents many will recognise as having marked the history of a distinguished family; and though it refers to a somewhat distant date, we shall be found not to have taken, upon that account, any liberties with the facts.

Narrative of the Ghost of a Hand

LE FANU

I'm sure she believed every word she related, for old Sally was veracious. But all this was worth just so much as such talk commonly is – marvels, fabulae, what our ancestors called winter's tales – which gathered details from every narrator, and dilated in the act of narration. Still it was not quite for nothing that the house was held to be haunted. Under all this smoke there smouldered just a little spark of truth – an authenticated mystery, for the solution of which some of my readers may possibly suggest a theory, though I confess I can't.

Miss Rebecca Chattesworth, in a letter dated late in the autumn of 1753, gives a minute and curious relation of occurrences in the Tiled House, which, it is plain, although at starting she protests against all such fooleries, she has heard with a peculiar sort of interest, and relates it certainly with an awful sort of particularity.

I was for printing the entire letter, which is really very singular as well as characteristic. But my publisher meets me with his *veto*; and I believe he is right. The worthy old lady's letter *is*, perhaps, too long; and I must rest content with a few hungry notes of its tenor.

That year, and somewhere about the 24 October, there broke out a strange dispute between Mr Alderman Harper, of High Street, Dublin, and my Lord Castlemallard, who, in virtue of his cousinship to the young heir's mother, had undertaken for him the management of the tiny estate on which the Tiled or Tyled House – for I find it spelt both ways – stood.

This Alderman Harper had agreed for a lease of the house for his daughter, who was married to a gentleman named Prosser. He furnished it, and put up hangings, and otherwise went to considerable expense. Mr and Mrs Prosser came there sometime in June, and after having parted with a good many servants in the interval, she made up her mind that she could not live in the house, and her father waited on Lord Castlemallard, and told him plainly that he would not take out the lease because the house was subjected to annoyances which he could not explain. In plain terms, he said it was haunted, and that no servants would live there more than a few weeks, and that after what his son-in-law's family had suffered there, not only should he be excused from taking a lease of it, but that the house itself ought to be pulled down as a nuisance and the habitual haunt of something worse than human malefactors.

Lord Castlemallard filed a bill in the Equity side of the Exchequer to compel Mr Alderman Harper to perform his contract, by taking out the lease. But the Alderman drew an answer, supported by no less than seven long affidavits, copies of all which were furnished to his lordship, and with the desired effect; for rather than compel him to place them upon the file of the court, his lordship struck, and consented to release him.

I am sorry the cause did not proceed at least far enough to place upon the files of the court the very authentic and unaccountable story which Miss Rebecca relates.

The annoyances described did not begin till the end of August, when, one evening, Mrs Prosser, quite alone, was sitting in the twilight at the back-parlour window, which was open, looking out into the orchard, and plainly saw a hand stealthily placed upon the stone window-sill outside, as if by someone beneath the window, at her right side, intending to climb up. There was nothing but the hand, which was rather short but handsomely formed, and white and plump, laid on the edge of the window-sill; and it was not a very young hand, but one aged somewhere about forty, as she conjectured. It was only a few weeks before that the horrible robbery at Clondalkin had taken place, and the lady fancied that the hand was that of one of the miscreants who was now about to scale the windows of the Tiled House. She uttered a loud scream and an ejaculation of terror, and at the same moment the hand was quietly withdrawn.

Search was made in the orchard, but no indications were found of any person's having been under the window, beneath which, ranged along the wall, stood a great column of flower-pots, which it seemed must have prevented anyone's coming within reach of it.

The same night there came a hasty tapping, every now and then, at the window of the kitchen. The women grew frightened, and the servant-man, taking firearms with him, opened the back-door, but discovered nothing. As he shut it, however, he said, 'a thump came on it', and a pressure as of somebody striving to force his way in, which frightened him; and though the tapping went on upon the kitchen window panes, he made no further explorations.

About six o'clock on the Saturday evening following, the cook, 'an honest, sober woman, now aged nigh sixty years', being alone in the kitchen, saw, on looking up, it is supposed, the same fat but aristo-cratic-looking hand, laid with its palm against the glass, near the side of the window, and this time moving slowly up and down, pressed all the while against the glass, as if feeling carefully for some inequality in its surface. She cried out, and said something like a prayer on seeing it. But it was not withdrawn for several seconds after.

After this, for a great many nights, there came at first a low, and afterwards an angry rapping, as it seemed with a set of clenched knuckles at the back-door. And the servant-man would not open it, but called to know who was there; and there came no answer, only a sound as if the palm of the hand was placed against it, and drawn slowly from side to side with a sort of soft, groping motion.

All this time, sitting in the back parlour, which, for the time, they used as a drawing-room, Mr and Mrs Prosser were disturbed by rappings at the window, sometimes very low and furtive, like a clandestine signal, and at others sudden, and so loud as to threaten the breaking of the pane.

This was all at the back of the house, which looked upon the orchard as you know. But on a Tuesday night, at about half-past nine, there came precisely the same rapping at the hall-door, and it went on, to the great annoyance of the master and terror of his wife, at intervals, for nearly two hours.

After this, for several days and nights, they had no annoyance whatsoever, and began to think that the nuisance had expended itself. But on the night of 13 September, Jane Easterbrook, an English maid, having gone into the pantry for the small silver bowl in which her mistress's posset was served, happening to look up at the little window of only four panes, observed through an auger-hole which was drilled through the window frame, for the admission of a bolt to secure the shutter, a white pudgy finger – first the tip, and then the two first joints – introduced, and turned about this way and that, crooked against the inside, as if in search of a fastening which its owner designed to push aside. When the maid got back into the kitchen we are told 'she fell into "a swounde", and was all the next day very weak'.

Mr Prosser being, I've heard, a hard-headed and conceited sort of fellow, scouted the ghost, and sneered at the fears of his family. He was privately of the opinion that the whole affair was a practical joke or a fraud, and waited an opportunity of catching the rogue in *flagrante delicto*. He did not long keep this theory to himself, but let it out by degrees with no stint of oaths and threats, believing that some domestic traitor held the thread of the conspiracy.

Indeed it was time something were done, for not only his servants, but good Mrs Prosser herself, had grown to look unhappy and anxious. They kept at home from the hour of sunset, and would not venture about the house after nightfall, except in couples.

The knocking had ceased for about a week, when one night, Mrs Prosser being in the nursery, her husband, who was in the parlour, heard it begin very softly at the hall-door. The air was quite still, which favoured his hearing distinctly. This was the first time there had been any disturbance at that side of the house, and the character of the summons was changed.

Mr Prosser, leaving the parlour-door open, it seems, went quietly into the hall. The sound was that of beating on the outside of the stout door, softly and regularly, 'with the flat of the hand'. He was going to open it suddenly, but changed his mind; and went back very quietly, and on to the head of the kitchen stair, where was a 'strong closet' over the pantry, in which he kept his firearms, swords, and canes.

Here he called his manservant, whom he believed to be honest, and, with a pair of loaded pistols in his own coat-pockets, and giving another pair to him, he went as lightly as he could, followed by the man and with a stout walking-cane in his hand, forward to the door.

Everything went as Mr Prosser wished. The besieger of his house, so far from taking fright at their approach, grew more impatient; and the sort of patting which had aroused his attention at first assumed the rhythm and emphasis of a series of double-knocks.

Mr Prosser, angry, opened the door with his right arm across, cane in hand. Looking, he saw nothing; but his arm was jerked up oddly, as it might be with the hollow of a hand, and something passed under it, with a kind of gentle squeeze. The servant neither saw nor felt anything, and did not know why his master looked back so hastily, cutting with his cane, and shutting the door with so sudden a slam.

From that time Mr Prosser discontinued his angry talk and swearing about it, and seemed nearly as averse from the subject as the rest of his family. He grew, in fact, very uncomfortable, feeling an inward persuasion that when, in answer to the summons, he had opened the hall-door, he had actually given admission to the besieger.

He said nothing to Mrs Prosser, but went up earlier to his bed-room, 'where he read a while in his Bible, and said his prayers'. I hope the particular relation of this circumstance does not indicate its singularity. He lay awake a good while, it appears, and, as he supposed about a quarter past twelve, he heard the soft palm of a hand patting on the outside of the bedroom door, and then brushing slowly along it.

Up bounced Mr Prosser, very much frightened, and locked the door, crying, 'Who's there?' but received no answer but the same brushing sound of a soft hand drawn over the panels, which he knew only too well.

In the morning the housemaid was terrified by the impression of a hand in the dust of the 'little parlour' table, where they had been unpacking delft and other things the day before. The print of the naked foot in the sea-sand did not frighten Robinson Crusoe half so much. They were by this time all nervous, and some of them half-crazed, about the hand.

Mr Prosser went to examine the mark and made light of it, but as he swore afterwards, rather to quiet his servants than from any comfortable feeling about it in his own mind; however, he had them all, one by one, into the room, and made each place his or her hand, palm downward, on the same table, thus taking a similar impression from every person in the house, including himself and his wife; and his 'affidavit' deposed that the formation of the hand so impressed differed altogether from those of the living inhabitants of the house, and corresponded with that of the hand seen by Mrs Prosser and by the cook.

Whoever or whatever the owner of that hand might be, they all felt this subtle demonstration to mean that it was declared he was no longer out of doors, but had established himself in the house.

And now Mrs Prosser began to be troubled with strange and horrible dreams, some of which, as set out in detail in Aunt Rebecca's long letter, are really very appalling nightmares. But one night, as Mr Prosser closed his bedchamber-door, he was struck somewhat by the utter silence of the room, there being no sound of breathing, which seemed unaccountable to him, as he knew his wife was in bed, and his ears were particularly sharp.

There was a candle burning on a small table at the foot of the bed, besides the one he held in one hand, a heavy ledger, connected with his father-in-law's business, being under his arm. He drew the curtain at the side of the bed, and saw Mrs Prosser lying, as for a few seconds he mortally feared, dead, her face being motionless, white and covered with a cold dew; and on the pillow, close beside her head, and just within the curtains, was, as he first thought, a toad – but really the same fattish hand, the wrist resting on the pillow, and the fingers extended towards her temple.

Mr Prosser, with a horrified jerk, pitched the ledger right at the curtains, behind which the owner of the hand might be supposed to stand. The hand was instantaneously and smoothly snatched away, the curtains made a great wave, and Mr Prosser got round the bed in time to see the closet-door, which was at the other side, pulled to by the same white, puffy hand, as he believed.

He drew the door open with a fling, and stared in: but the closet was empty, except for the clothes hanging from the pegs on the wall, and the dressing-table and looking-glass facing the windows. He shut it sharply, and locked it, and felt for a minute, he says, 'as if he were like to lose his wits'; then, ringing at the bell, he brought the servants, and with much ado they recovered Mrs Prosser from a sort of 'trance', in which, he says, from her looks, she seemed to have suffered 'the pains of death': and Aunt Rebecca adds, 'from what she told me of her visions, with her own lips, he might have added, "and of hell also".'

But the occurrence which seems to have determined the crisis was the strange sickness of their eldest child, a little boy aged between two and three years. He lay awake, seemingly in paroxysms of terror, and the doctors who were called in set down the symptoms to incipient water on the brain. Mrs Prosser used to sit up with the nurse by the nursery fire, much troubled in mind about the condition of her child.

His bed was placed sideways along the wall, with its head against the door of a press or cupboard, which, however, did not shut quite close. There was a little valance, about a foot deep, round the top of the child's bed, and this descended within some ten or twelve inches of the pillow on which he lay.

They observed that the little creature was quieter whenever they took him up and held him on their laps. They had just replaced him, as he seemed to have grown quite sleepy and tranquil, but he was not five minutes in his bed when he began to scream in one of his frenzies of terror; at the same moment the nurse, for the first time, detected, and Mrs Prosser equally plainly saw, following the direction of her eyes, the real cause of the child's sufferings.

Protruding through the aperture of the press, and shrouded in the shade of the valance, they plainly saw the white fat hand, palm downwards, presented towards the head of the child. The mother uttered a scream, and snatched the child from its little bed, and she and the nurse ran down to the lady's sleeping-room, where Mr Prosser was in bed, shutting the door as they entered; and they had hardly done so, when a gentle tap came to it from the outside.

There is a great deal more, but this will suffice. The singularity of the narrative seems to me to be this, that it describes the ghost of a hand, and no more. The person to whom that hand belonged never once appeared; nor was it a hand separated from a body, but only a hand so manifested and introduced that its owner was always, by some crafty accident, hidden from view.

In the year 1819, at a college breakfast, I met a MrProsser – a thin, grave, but rather chatty old gentleman, with very white hair drawn back into a pigtail – and he told us all, with a concise particularity, a story of his cousin, James Prosser, who, when an infant, had slept for some time in what his mother said was a haunted nursery in an old house near Chapelizod, and who, whenever he was ill, over-fatigued or in anywise feverish, suffered all through his life, as he had done from a time he could scarce remember, from a vision of a certain gentleman, fat and pale, every curl of whose wig, every button and fold of whose laced clothes, and every feature and line of whose sensual, benignant and unwholesome face, was as minutely engraven upon his memory as the dress and lineaments of his own grand-father's portrait, which hung before him every day at breakfast, dinner and supper.

Mr Prosser mentioned this as an instance of a curiously mono-tonous, individualised and persistent nightmare, and hinted at the extreme horror and anxiety with which his cousin, of whom he spoke in the past tense as 'poor Jemmie', was at any time induced to mention it.

I hope the reader will pardon me for loitering so long in the Tiled House, but this sort of lore has always had a charm for me; and people, you know, especially old people, will talk of what most interests themselves, too often forgetting that others may have had more than enough of it.

The Sexton of Cashel

D. R. McANALLY, JR

All over Ireland, from Cork to Belfast, from Dublin to Galway, are scattered the ruins of churches, abbeys, and ecclesiastical buildings, the relics of a country once rich, prosperous and populous. These ruins raise their castellated walls and towers, noble even in decay, sometimes in the midst of a village, crowded with the miserably poor; sometimes on a mountain, in every direction commanding magnificent prospects; sometimes on an island in one of the lakes, which, like emeralds in a setting of deeper green, gem the surface of the rural landscape and contribute to increase the beauty of scenery not surpassed in the world.

Ages ago the voice of prayer and the song of praise ceased to ascend from these sacred edifices, and they are now visited only by strangers, guides, and parties of humble peasants, the foremost bearing on their shoulders the remains of a companion to be laid within the hallowed enclosure, for although the church is in ruins, the ground in and about it is still holy and in service when pious hands lay away in the bosom of earth the bodies of those who have borne the last burden, shed the last tear, and succumbed to the last enemy. But among all the pitiable spectacles presented in this unhappy country, none is better calculated to inspire sad reflections than a rural graveyard. The walls of the ruined church tower on high, with massive cornice and pointed window; within stand monuments and tombs of the Irish great; kings, princes, and arch-bishops lie together, while about the hallowed edifice are huddled the graves of the poor; here, sinking so as to be indistinguishable from the sod; there, rising in new-made proportions; yonder marked with a wooden cross, or a round stick, the branch of a tree rudely trimmed, but significant as the only token bitter poverty could furnish of undying love; while over all the graves, alike of the high born and of the lowly, the weeds and nettles grow.

'Sure there's no saxton, Sorr,' said car-man Jerry Magwire, in answer to a question, 'We dig the graves ourselves whin we put them away, an' sometimes there's a fight in the place whin two berryin's meet. Why is that? Faith, it's not for us to be talkin' o' them deep subjects widout respict, but it's the belafe that the last wan berrid must be carryin' wather all the time to the sowls in Purgathory till the next wan comes to take the place av him. So, ye mind, when two berryin's happen to meet, aitch party is shtrivin' to be done foorst, an' wan thries to make the other lave aff, an' thin they have it. Troth, Irishmen are too handy wid their fishts entirely, it's a weak pint wid 'em. But it's a sad sight, so it is, to see the graves wid the nettles on thim an' the walls all tumblin'. It isn't every owld church that has a caretaker like him of Cashel. Bedad, he was betther nor a flock av goats to banish the weeds.

'Who was he? Faith, I niver saw him but the wan time, an' thin I had only a shot at him as he was turnin' a corner, for it was as I was lavin' Cormac's chapel the time I wint to Cashel on a pinance, bekase av a little throuble on me mind along av a pig that wasn't mine, but got mixed wid mine whin I was afther killin' it. But, as I obsarved, it was only a shot at him I had, for it wasn't aften that he was seen in the daytime, but done all his work in the night, an' it isn't me that'ud be climbin' the Rock av Cashel afther the sun'ud go to slape. Not that there's avil sper'ts there, for none that's bad can set fut on that holy ground day or night, but I'm not afther wantin' to meet a sper't av any kind, even if it's good, for how can ye tell about thim. Sure aven the blessed saints have been desaved, an' it's not for a sinner like me to be settin' up for to know more than thimselves. But it was the long, bent body that he had, like he'd a burdhen on his back, as they say, God be good to him, he had on his sowl, an' the great, blue eyes lookin' out as if he was gazin' on the other worruld. No, I didn't run down the rock, but I didn't walk aither, but jist bechuxt the two, wid a sharp eye round the corners that I passed. No more do I belave there was harrum in him, but, God's prisence be about us, ye can't tell.

'He was a man o' Clare be the name av Paddy O'Sullivan, an' lived on the highway betune Crusheen an' Ennis, an' they do say that whin he was a lad, there wasn't a finer to be seen in the County; a tall, shtrappin' young felly wid an eye like a bay'net, an' a fisht like a shmith, an' the fut an' leg av him'ud turn the hearts o' half the wimmin in the parish. An' they was all afther him, like they always do be whin a man is good lookin', sure I've had a little o' that same experience mesilf. Ye needn't shmile. I know me head has no more hair on it than an egg, an' I think me last tooth'ull come out tomorrer, bad cess to the day, but they do say that forty years ago, I cud have me pick av the gurruls, an' mebbe they're mishtaken an' mebbe not. But I was sayin', the gurruls were afther Paddy like rats afther chaze, an' sorra wan o' thim but whin she spied him on the road, 'ud shlip behind the hedge to shmooth her locks a bit an' set the shawl shtraight on her head. An' whin there was a bit av a dance, niver a boy'ud get a chance till Paddy made his chice to dance wid, an' sorra a good word the rest o' the gurruls'ud give that same. Och, the tongues that wimmin have! Sure they're sharper nor a draggin's tooth. Faith, I know that well too, for I married two o' them an' larned a deal too afther doin' it, an' axin' yer pardon, it's my belafe that if min knewn as much before marryin' as afther, bedad, the owld maid population'ud be greatly incrased.

'Howandiver, afther a bit, Paddy left carin' for thim all, that, in my consate, is a moighty safe way, and begun to look afther wan. Her name was Nora O'Moore, an' she was as clever a gurrul as'ud be found bechuxt Limerick an' Galway. She was kind o' resarved like, wid a face as pale as a shroud, an' hair as black as a crow, an' eyes that looked at ye an' never seen ye. No more did she talk much, an' whin Paddy'ud be sayin' his fine spaches, she'd listen wid her eyes cast down, an' whin she'd had enough av his palaver, she'd jist look at him an' somehow Paddy felt that his p'liteness wasn't the thing to work wid. He cudn't undhershtand her, an' bedad, many's the man that's caught be not undhershtandin' thim. There's rivers that's quiet on top bekase they're deep, an' more that's quiet bekase they're not deep enough to make a ripple, but phat's the differ if ye can't sound thim, an' whin a woman's quiet, begorra, it's not aisy to say if she's deep or shallow. But Nora was a deep wan, an' as good as iver drew a breath. She thought a dale av Paddy, only she'd be torn limb from limb afore she'd let him know it till he confist first. Well, my dear, paddy wint on, at firsht it was only purtindin' he was, an' whin he found she cudn't be tuk wid his chaff, he got in airnest, an' afore he knewn it, he was dead in love wid Nora, an' had as much show for gettin' out agin as a shape in a bog, an' sorra a bit did he know at all at all, whether she cared a traneen for him. It's funny entirely that whin a man thinks a woman is afther him, he's aff like a hare, but if she doesn't car a rap, begob, he'll give the nose aff his face to get her. So it was wid paddy an'

Nora, axceptin' that Paddy didn't know that Nora wanted him as much as he wanted her.

'So, wan night, whin he was bringin' her from a dance that they'd been at, he said to her that he loved her bedther than life an' towld her would she marry him, an' she axed was it jokin' or in airnest he was, an' he said cud she doubt it whin he loved her wid all the veins av his heart, an' she trimbled, turnin' paler than iver, an' thin blushin' rosy red for joy an' towld him yes, an' he kissed her, an' they both thought the throuble was all over foreiver. It's a way thim lovers has,, an' they must be axcused, bekase it's the same wid thim all.

'But it wann't at all, fur Nora had an owld squireen av a father, that was as full av maneness as eggs is av mate. Sure he was the divil entirely at home, an' niver left off wid the crassness that was in im. The timper av him was spiled be rason o' losing his bit o' money wid cards an' racin', an' like some min, he tuk it out wid his wife an' dawther. There was only the three o' thim in it, an' they do say that whin he was crazy wid dhrink, he'd bate thim right an' lift, an' turn thim out o' the cabin into the night, niver heeding, the baste, phat'ud come to thim. But they niver said a word thimselves, an' the nabers only larned av it be seein' thim.

'Well. Whin O'Moore was towld that Paddy was kapin' comp'ny wid Nora, an' the latther an' her mother towld him she wanted fur to marry Paddy, thw owld felly got tarin' mad, fur he was as proud as a paycock, an' though he'd nothin' himself, he riz agin the match, an' all the poor mother an' Nora cud say 'udn't sthir him.

' "Sure I've nothin' agin him," he'd say, "barrin' he's as poor as a fiddler, an' I want Nora to make a good match."

'Now the owld felly had a match in his mind fur Nora, a lad from Tipperary, whose father was a farmer there, an' had a shmart bit av land wid no end av shape grazin' on it, an' the Tipperary boy wasn't bad at all, only as shtupid as a donkey, an' whin he'd come to see Nora, bad cess to the word he'd to say, only look at her a bit an' thin fall aslape an' knock his head agin the wall. But he wanted her, an' his father an' O'Moore put their heads together over a glass an' aggrade that the young wans'ud be married.

' "Sure I don't love him a bit, father," Nora'ud say.

' "Be aff wid yer nonsinse," he'd say to her. "Phat does it matther about love, whin he's got more nor a hundred shape. Sure I wudn't give the wool av thim fur all the love in Clare," says he, an' wid that the argymint'ud end.

'So Nora towld paddy an' Paddy said he'd not give her up for all the men in Tipperary or all the shape in Ireland, an' it was aggrade that in wan way or another, they'd be married in spite av owld O'Moore, though Nora hated to do it, bekase, as I was afther tellin' ye, she was a good gurrul, an' wint to mass an' to her duty reg'lar. But like the angel that she was, she towld her mother an' the owld lady was agrayble, an' so Nora consinted.

'But O'Moore was shrewder than a fox whin he was sober, an' that was whin he'd no money to shpend in dhrink, an' this being' wan o' thim times, he watched Nora an' begun to suspicion somethin'. So he made belave that everything was right an' the next time that Murphy, that bein' the name o' the Tipperary farmer, came, the two owld fellys settled it that O'Moore an' Nora'ud come to Tipperary av the Winsday afther, that bein' the day o' the fair in Ennis that they knew Paddy'ud be at, an' whin they got to Tipperary, they'd marry Nora an' young Murphy at wanst. So owld Murphy was to sind the car afther thim an' everything was made sure. So, av the Winsday, towards noon, says owld O'Moore to Nora: ' "Be in a hurry now, me child, an' make yersel' as fine as ye can, an' Murphy's car'ull be here to take us to the fair."

'Nora didn't want to go, for Paddy was comin' out in the afthernoon, misthrustin' that owld O'Moore'ud be at the fair. But O'Moore only towld her to make hast wid hersilf or they'd be late, an' she did. So the car came, wid a boy dhriving, an' owld O'Moore axed the boy if he wanted to go to the fair, so that Nora cudn't hear him, an' the boy said yes, an' O'Moore towld him to go an' he'd dhrive an' bring him back tomorrer. So the boy wint away, an' O'Moore an' Nora got up an' shtrated. Whin they came to the crass-road, O'Moore tuk the road to Tipperary.

' "Sure father, ye're wrong," says Nora, "that's not the way."

' "No more is it," said the owld desayver, "but I'm afther wantin' to see a frind o' mine over here a bit an' we'll come round to the Ennis road on the other side," says he.

'So Nora thought no more av it, but whin they wint on an' on, widout shtoppin' at all, she begun to be disquisitive agin.

' "Father, is it to Ennis or not ye're takin' me," says she.

'Now, be this time, they'd got on a good bit, an' the owld villin seen it was no use thryin' to desave her any longer.

' "I'm not," says he, "but it's to Tipperary ye're goin', where ye're to be married to Misther Murphy this blessed day, so ye are, an' make no throuble about it aither, or it'll be the worse for ye," says he, lookin' moighty black.

'Well, at first Nora thought her heart'ud shtand still. 'Sure, Father dear, ye don't mane it, ye cudn't be so cruel. It's like a blighted tree I'd be, wid that man,' an' she thried to jump aff the car, but her father held her wid a grip av stale.

' "Kape still," says he wid his teeth closed like a vise. "If ye crass me, I'm like to murdher ye. It's me only escape from prison, for I'm in debt an' Murphy'ull help me," says he. "Sure," says he, saftenin' a bit as he seen the white face an' great pleadin' eyes, "Sure ye'll be happy enough wid Murphy. He loves ye, an' ye can love him, an' besides, think o' the shape."

'But Nora sat there, a poor dumb thing, wid her eyes lookin' deeper than iver wid the misery that was in thim. An' from that minit, she didn't spake a word, but all her sowl was determined that she'd die afore she'd marry Murphy, but how she'd get out av it she didn't know at all, but watched her chance to run.

'Now it happened that owld O'Moore, bein' disturbed in his mind, mistuk the way, an' whin he come to the crass-roads, wan to Tipperary an' wan to Cashel, he tuk the wan for the other, an' whin the horse thried to go home to Tipperary, he wudn't let him, but pulled him into the Cashel road. Faix, he might have knewn that if he'd let the baste alone, he'd take him right, fur horses knows a deal more than ye'd think. That horse o' mine is only a common garron av a baste, but he tuk me from Ballyvaughn to Lisdoon Varna wan night whin it was so dark that ye cudn't find yer nose, an' wint be the rath in a gallop, like he'd seen the good people. But niver mind, I'll tell ye the shtory sometime, only I was thinkin' O'Moore might have knewn betther.

'But they tuk the Cashel road an' wint on as fast as they cud, for it was afthernoon an' gettin' late. An' O'Moore kept lookin' about an' wonderin' that he didn't know the counthry, though he'd niver been to Tipperary but wanst, an' afther a while, he gev up that he was lost entirely. No more wud he ax the people on the road, but gev thim "God save ye" very short, for he was afeared Nora might make throuble. An' by an' by, it come on to rain, an' whin they turned the corner av a hill, he seen the Rock o' Cashel wid the churches onit, an' thin he stopped.

' "Phat's this at all," says he. "Faix, if that isn't Cashel I'll ate it, an' we've come out o' the way altogether."

'Nora answered him niver a word, an' he shtarted to turn round, but whin he looked at the horse, the poor baste was knocked up entirely.

' "We'll go on to Cashel," says he, "an' find a shebeen, an' go back in the mornin'. It's hard luck we're afther havin'," says he.

'So they wint on, an' jist afore they got to the Rock, they seen a nate lodgin' house be the road an' wint in. He left Nora to sit be the fire, while he wint to feed the horse, an' whin he come back in a minit, he looked for her, but faith, she'd given him the shlip an' was gone complately.

' "Where is me dawther?" says he.

' "Faith, I dunno," says the maid. "She walked out av the dure on the minit," says she.

'Owld O'Moore run, an' Satan an' none but himself turned him in the way she was afther takin.' God be good to thim, no wan iver knewn phat tuk place, but whin they wint wid a lanthern to sarch fur thim whin they didn't raturn, they found the marks o' their feet on the road to the strame. Halfway down the path they picked up Nora's shawl that was torn an' flung on the ground an' fut marks in plenty they found, as if he had caught her an' thried to howld her an' cudn't, an' on the marks wint to the high bank av the strame, that was a torrent be razon av the rain. An' there they ended wid a big slice o' the bank fallen in, an' the sarchers crassed thimselves wid fright an wint back an' prayed for the repose av their sowls.

'The next day they found thim, a good Irish mile down the strame, owld O'Moore wid wan hand howlding her gown an' the other wan grippin' her collar an' the clothes half torn aff her poor cowld corpse, her hands stratched out afore her, wid the desperation in her heart to get away, an' her white face wid the great eyes an' the light gone out av thim, the poor craythur, God give her rest, an' so to us all.

'They laid thim dacintly, wid candles an' all, an' the wake that they had was shuparb, fur the shtory was towld in all the counthry, wid the vartues av Nora; an' the O'Brian's come from Ennis, an' the O'Moore's from Crusheen, an' the Murphy's an' their frinds from Tipperary, an' more from Clonmel. There was a power av atin' an' slathers av dhrink fur thim that wanted it, fur, d' ye mind, thim of Cashel thried fur to show the rale Irish hoshpitality bekase O'Moore an' Nora were sint there to die an' they thought it was their juty to thrate thim well. An' all the County Clare an' Tipperary was at the berryin', an' they had three keeners, the best that iver was, wan from

Ennis, wan from Tipperary, an' wan from Limerick, so that the praises av Nora wint on day an' night till the berryin' was done. An' they made Nora's grave in Cormac's Chapel just front o' the Archbishop's tomb in the wall an' berried her first, an' tuk O'Moore as far from her as they cud get him, an' put his grave as clost be the wall as they cud go fur the shtones an' jist ferninst the big gate on the left hand side, an' berried him last, an' sorra the good word they had fur him aither.

'Poor Paddy wint nayther to the wake nor to the berryin', fur afther they towld him the news, he sat as wan in a dhrame, no more cud they rouse him. He'd go to his work very quite, an' niver shpake a word. An' so it was, about a fortnight afther, he says to his mother, says he, "Mother I seen Nora last night an' she stood be me side an' laid her hand on me brow, an' says 'Come to Cashel, Paddy dear, an' be wid me.'" An' his mother was frighted entirely, for she parsaved he was wrong in his head. She thried to aise his mind, but the next night he disappeared. They folly'd him to Cashel, but he dodged an' kept from thim complately whin they come an' so they left him. In the day he'd hide an' slape, an' afther night, Nora's sper't'ud mate him an' walk wid him up an' down the shtones av the Chapel an' undher the arches av the Cathaydral, an' he cared fur her grave, an' bekase she was berried there, fur the gravs av all thim that shlept on the Rock. No more had he any frinds, but thim o' Cashel'ud lave pitaties an' bread where he'd see it an' so he lived. Fur sixty wan years was he on the Rock an' never left it, but he'd sometimes show himself in the day whin there was a berryin', an' say, "Ye've brought me another frind," an' help in the work, an' never was there a graveyard kept like that o' Cashel.

'When he got owld, an' where he cud look into the other worruld, Nora came ivery night an' brought more wid her, sper'ts av kings an' bishops that rest on Cashel, an' there's thim that's seen the owld man walkin' in Cormac's Chapel, Nora holdin' him up an' him discoorsin' wid the mighty dead. They found him wan day, cowld an' shtill, on Nora's grave, an' laid him be her side, God rest his sowl, an' there he slapes today, God be good to him.

'They said he was only a poor owld innocent, but all is aqualised, an' thim that's despised sometimes have betther comp'ny among the angels than that of mortals.'

The Defeat of the Widows

D. R. McANALLY, JR

When superstitions have not yet been banished from any other part of the world it is not wonderful that they should still be found in the country districts of Ireland, rural life being especially favourable to the perpetuation of old ways of living and modes of thought, since in an agricultural district less change takes place in a century than may, in a city, be observed in a single decade. Country people preserve their old legends with their antique styles of apparel, and thus the relics of the pagan ages of Ireland have come down from father to son, altered and adapted to the changes in the country and its population. Thus, for instance, the old-fashioned witch is no longer found in any part of Ireland, her memory lingering only as a tradition, but her modern successor is frequently met with, and in many parishes a retired hovel in a secluded lane is a favourite resort of the neighbouring peasants, for it is the home of the Pishogue, or wise woman, who collects herbs, and, in her way, doctors her patients sometimes with simple medicinal remedies, sometimes with charms, according to their gullibility and the nature of their ailments.

Not far from Ballinahinch, a fishing village on Birterbuy Bay, in the County Galway, and in the most lonely valley of the neighbourhood, there dwells one of these wise women who supplant the ancient witches. The hovel which shelters her bears every indication of wretched poverty; the floor is mud, the smoke escapes through a hole in the thatch in default of a chimney; the bed is a scanty heap of straw in the corner, and two rude shelves, bearing a small assortment of cracked jars and broken bottles, constitute Moll's stock in trade.

The misery of her household surroundings, however, furnished to the minds of her patients no argument against the efficiency of her remedies, Moll being commonly believed to have 'a power av goold,' though no one had ever see any portion thereof. But with all her reputed riches she had no fear of robbers, for 'she could aisily do for thim did they but come as many as the shtraws in the thatch,' and would-be robbers, no doubt understanding that fact, prudently consulted their own safety by staying away from the vicinity of her cabin.

'Owld Moll,' as she was known, was a power in the parish, and her help was sought in many emergencies. Did a cow go dry, Moll knew the reason and might possibly remove the spell; if a baby fell ill, Moll had an explanation of its ailment, and could tell at a glance whether the little one was or was not affected by the evil of a secret enemy. If a pig was stolen, she was shrewd in her conjectures as to the direction its wrathful owner must take in the search. But her forte lay in bringing about love-matches. Many were the charms at her command for this purpose, and equally numerous the successes with which she was accredited. Some particulars of her doings in this direction were furnished by Jerry Magwire, a jolly car-man of Galway, who had himself been benefited by her services.

'Sure I was married meself be her manes,' stated Jerry, 'an' this is the way it was. Forty-nine years ago come next Mickelmas, I was a good-lookin' young felly, wid a nate cabin on the road from Ballinasloe to Ballinamore, havin' a fine car an' a mare an' her colt, that was as good as two horses whin the colt grew up. I was afther payin' coort to Dora O'Callighan, that was the dawther av Misther O'Callighan that lived in the County Galway, an', be the same token, was a fine man. In thim times I used be comin' over here twict or three times a year wid a bagman, commercial thraveller, you'd call him, an' I heard say av Owld Moll, an' she wasn't owld thin, an' the next time I come, I wint to her an' got an inchàntmint. Faix, some av it is gone from me, but I mind that I was to change me garthers, an' tie on me thumb a bit o' bark she gev me, an' go to the churchyard on Halloween, an' take the first chilla-ca-pooka (snail) I found on a tombshtone, an' begob, it was that same job that was like to be the death o' me, it bein' dark an' I bendin' to look clost, a hare jumped in me face from undher the shtone. "Jagers," says I, an' me fallin' on me back on the airth an' the life lavin' me. "Presince o' God be about me," says I, for I knewn the inchantmint wasn't right, no more I oughtn't to be at it, but the hare was skairt like meself an' run, an' I found the shnail an' run too wid the shweat pourin' aff me face in shtrames.

'So I put the shnail in a plate that I covered wid another, an' av the Sunday, I opened it fur to see phat letters it writ, an' bad luck to the wan o' thim cud I rade at all, fur in thim days I cudn't tell A from any other letther. I tuk the plate to Misther O'Callighan, fur he was a fine scholar an' cud rade both books an' writin', an' axed him phat the letters was.

' "A–a–ah, ye ignerant gommoch," says he to me, "yer head's as empty as a drum. Sure here's no writin' at all, only marks that the shnail's afther makin' an' it crawlin' on the plate."

'So I explained the inchantmint to him, an' he looked a little closter, an' thin jumped wid shurprise.

' "Oh," says he. "Is that thrue?" says he. "Ye must axqueeze me, Misther Magwire. Sure the shnails doesn't write a good hand, an' I'm an owld man an' me eyes dim, but I see it betther now. Faith, the first letter's a D," says he, an' thin he shtudied awhile. "An' the next is a O, an' thin there's a C," says he, "only the D an' the C is bigger than the O, an' that's all the letters there is," says he.

' "An' phat does thim letters shpell?" says I, bekase I didn't know.

' "Ah, bad scran to 'em," says he; "there's thim cows in me field agin," says he. "Ax Dora, here she comes," an' away he wint as she come in, an' I axed her phat D.O.C. shpelt; an' she towld me her name, an' I go bail she was surprised to find the shnail had writ thim letters on the plate, so we marr'd the next Sunday.

'But Owld Moll is a knowledgeable woman an' has a power av shpells an' charms. There's Tim Gallagher, him as dhrives the public car out o' Galway, he's bought his luck av her be the month, fur nigh on twinty year, barin' wan month, that he forgot, an' that time he shpilt his load in the ditch an' kilt a horse, bein' too dhrunk to dhrive.

'Whin me dawther Dora, that was named afther her mother, was ill afther she'd been to the dance, whin O'Hoolighan's Peggy was married to Paddy Noonan (she danced too hard in the cabin an' come home in the rain), me owld woman wint to Moll an' found that Dora had been cast wid an avil eye. So she gev her a tay to dhrink an' a charm to wear agin it, an' afther she'd dhrunk the tay an' put on the charm the faver lift her, an' she was well entirely.

'Sure Moll towld me wan magpie manes sorrow, two manes luck, three manes a weddin', an' four manes death; an' didn't I see four o' thim the day o' the fair in Ennis whin O'Dougherty was laid out? An' whin O'Riley cut his arrum wid a billhook, an' the blood was runnin', didn't she tie a shtring on the arrum an' dip a raven's feather into the blood av a black cat's tail, an' shtop the bleedin'? An' didn't she bid me take care o' meself the day I met a red-headed

woman afore dinner, an' it wasn't six months till I met the woman in
the mornin', it a-rainin' an' ivery dhrop the full o' yer hat, an' me
topcoat at home, an' that same night was I tuk wid the roomytics an'
didn't shtir a toe fur a fortnight. Faix, she's an owld wan is Moll;
phat she can't do it n't worth thryin'. If she goes fur to make a
match, all the fathers in Ireland cudn't purvint it, an' it's no use o'
their settin' theirselves agin her, fur her head's as long as a summer
day an' as hard as a shillalee.

'Did iver ye hear how she got a husband for owld Miss Rooney,
the same that married Misther Dooley that kapes the Aygle Inn in
Lisdoon Varna, an' tuk him clane away from the Widdy Mulligan
an' two more widdy's that were comin' down upon him like kites on
a young rabbit?

'Well, it's a mighty improvin' shtory, fur it shows that widdys can
be baten whin they're afther a husband, that some doesn't belave,
but they do say it takes a witch, the divil, an' an owld maid to do it,
an' some think that all o' thim isn't aiquel to a widdy, aven if there's
three o' thim an' but wan av her.

'The razon av it is this. Widdy wimmin are like lobsthers, whin
they wanst ketch holt, begob, they've no consate av lettin' go at all,
but will shtick to ye tighter than a toenail, till ye've aither to marry
thim or murther thim, that's the wan thing in the end; fur if ye
marry thim ye're talked to death, an' if ye murther thim ye're only
dacintly hanged out o' the front dure o' the jail. Whin they're afther
a husband, they're as busy as owld Nick, an' as much in airnest as a
dog in purshoot av a flea. More-be-token, they're always lookin' fur
the proper man, an' if they see wan that they think will shuit, bedad,
they go afther him as strait as an arrer, an' if he doesn't take the
alarum an' run like a shape-thief, the widdy'ull have him afore the
althar an' married fast an' tight while he'd be sayin'a craydo.

'They know so much be wan axpayrience av marryin', that, barrin'
it's a widdy man that's in it, an' he nows as much as thimselves,
they'll do for him at wanst, bekase it's well undhershtood that a
bach'ler, aither young or owld, has as much show av outshtrappin' a
widdy as a mouse agin a weasel.

'Now, this Misther Dooley was an owld bach'ler, nigh on five an'
thirty, an' about fifteen years ago, come next Advint, he come from
Cork wid a bit o' money, an' tuk the farm beyant Misther McCoole's
on the lift as ye come out o' Galway. He wasn't a bad lookin' felly,
an' liked the ladies, an' the first time he was in chapel afther takin'

the farm, aitch widdy an' owld maid set the two eyes av her on him, an' the Widdy Mulligan says to herself, says she, "Faix, that's just the man to take the place av me dear Dinnis," fur, ye see the widdy's always do spake that-a-way av their husbands, a-givin' them the good word after they're dead, so as to make up fur the tonge lashin's they give 'em whin they're alive. It's quare, so it is, phat widdys are like. Whin ye see a widdy at the wake schraimin' fit to shplit yer head wid the noise, an' flingin' herself acrass the grave at the berryin' like it was a bag o'male she was, an' thin spakin' all the time av "me poor dear hushband", I go bail they lived together as paceful as a barrel full o' cats an' dogs; no more is it sorrow that's in it, but raimorse that's tarin' at her, an' the shquailin' an' kickin' is beways av a pinnance fur the gostherin' she done him whin he was livin', fur the more there's in a jug, the less noise it makes runnin' out, an' whin ye've a heavy load to carry, ye nade all yer breath, an' so have none to waste tellin' how it's breakin' yer back.

'So it was wid the Widdy Mulligan, that kept the Shamrock Inn, for her Dinnis was a little ottomy av a gossoon, an' her the full av a dure, an' the arrum on her like a smith an' the fut like a leg o' mutton. Och, she was big enough thin, but she's a horse entirely now, wid the walk av a duck, an' the cheeks av her shakin' like a bowl av shtirabout whin she goes. Her poor Dinnis darn't say his sowl belonged to him, but was conthrolled be her, an' they do say his last words were, "I'll have pace", that was phat he niver had afther he married her, fur she was wan that'ud be shmilin' an' shmilin' an' the tongue av her like a razer. She'd a good bit o' property in the inn, siven beds in the house fur thravellers, an' six childher, the oldest nigh on to twelve, an' from him on down in reg'lar steps like thim in front o' the coorthouse.

'Now, a bit up the shtrate from the Shamrock there was a little shop kept be Missis O'Donnell, the widdy av Tim O'Donnell, that died o' bein' mortified in his legs that broke be his fallin' aff his horse wan night whin he was comin' back from Athlone, where he'd been to a fair. Missis O'Donnell was a wapin' widdy, that's got eyes like a hydrant, where ye can turn on the wather whin ye plaze. Begorra, thim's the widdys that'ull do fur anny man, fur no more can ye tell phat's in their minds be lookin' at their faces than phat kind av close they've got on be lookin' at their shadders, an' whin they corner a man that's tinder-hearted, an' give a shy look at him up out o' their eyes, an' thin look down an' sind two or three dhrops o' wather from undher their eye-lashers, the only salvation fur him is to get up an' run like it was a bag o' gun-powdher she was. So Missis O'Donnell, whin she seen Misther Dooley, tuk the same notion into her head that the Widdy Mulligan did, fur she'd two childher, a boy an' a gurrul, that were growin' up, an' the shop wasn't payin' well.

'There was another widdy in it, the Widdy McMurthry, that aftherwards married a sargeant av the polis, an' lives in Limerick. She was wan o' thim frishky widdy's that shtruts an' wears fine close an' puts on more airs than a paycock. She was a fine-lookin' woman thim times, an' had money in plinty that she got be marryin' McMurthry, that was owld enough to be a father to her an' died o' dhrinkin' too much whishkey at first, an' thin too much sulphur-wather at Lisdoon Varna to set him right agin. She was always ready wid an answer to ye, fur it was quick witted she was, wid slathers o' talk that didn't mane annything, an' a giggle that she didn't nade to hunt fur whin she wanted it to make a show wid. An' she'd a dawther that was a fine child, about siventeen, a good dale like her mother.

'Now, Misther Dooley has a kind heart in his body fur wimmin in gineral, an' as he liked a bit o' chaff wid thim on all occashuns, he wasn't long in gettin' acquainted wid all the wimmin o' the parish, an' was well liked be thim, an', be the same token, wasn't be the men, fur men, be nacher, doesn't like a woman's man anny more than wimmin like a man's woman. But, afther a bit, he begun to centhre himself on the three widdys, an' sorra the day' ud go by whin he come to town but phat he'd give wan or another o' thim a pace av his comp'ny that was very plazin' to thim. Bedad, he done that same very well, for he made a round av it for to kape thim in suspince. He'd set in the ale room o' the Shamrock an hour in the afthernoon an' chat wid the Widdy Mulligan as she was sarvin' the dhrink, an' shtop in the Widdy O'Donnell's shop as he was goin' by, to get a thrifle or a bit av shwates an' give to her childher beways av a complimint, an' thin go to Missis McMurthry's to tay, an' so got on well wid thim all. An' it's me belafe he'd be doin' that same to this blessed day only that the widdys begun to be pressin' as not likin' fur to wait any longer. Fur, mind ye, a widdy's not like a young wan that'll wait fur ye to spake an' if ye don't do it, 'ull go on foriver, or till she gets tired av waitin' an' takes some wan else that does spake, widout sayin' a word to ye at all; but the widdy'ull be hintin' an' hintin', an' her hints'ull be as shtrong as a donkey's kick, so that the head o' ye has to be harder than a pavin'-shtone if ye don't undhershtand, an' ye've got to have more impidince than a monkey if ye don't spake up an' say something about marryin'.

'Well, as I was afther sayin', the widdys begun to be pressin' him clost: the Widdy Mulligan tellin' him how good her business was an' phat a savin' there'd be if a farm an' a public were put together; the Widdy O'Donnell a-lookin' at him out av her tears an' sighin' an' tellin' him how lonely he must be out on a farm an' nobody but a man wid him in the house, fur she was lonesome in town, an' it wasn't natheral at all, so it wasn't, fur aither man or woman to be alone; an' the Widdy McMurthry a palatherin' to him that if he'd a fine, good-lookin' woman that loved him, he'd be a betther man an' a changed man entirely. So they wint on, the widdys a-comin' at him, an' he thryin' to kape wid thim all, as he might have knewn he couldn't do (barrin' he married the three o' thim like a Turk), until aitch wan got to undhershtand, be phat he said to her, that he was goin' to marry her, an' the minnit they got this in their heads, aitch begged him that he'd shtay away from the other two, fur aitch knew he wint to see thim all. By jayminy, it bothered him thin, fur he liked to talk to thim all aiquelly, an' didn't want to confine his agrayable comp'ny to anny wan o' thim. So he got out av it thish-a-way. He promised the Widdy McMurthry that he'd not go to the Shamrock more than wanst in the week, nor into the Widdy O'Donnell's barrin' he naded salt fur his cow; an' said to the Widdy Mulligan that he'd not more than spake to Missis O'Donnell whin he wint in, an' that he'd go no more at all to Missis McMurthry's; an' he towld Missis O'Donnell that whin he wint to the Shamrock he'd get his sup an' thin lave at wanst, an' not go to the Widdy McMurthry's axceptin' whin his horse wanted to be shod, the blacksmith's bein' ferninst her dure that it'ud be convaynient fur him to wait at. So he shmiled wid himself thinkin' he'd done thim complately, an' made up his mind that whin his pitaties were dug he'd give up the farm an' get over into Country Clare, away from the widdys.

'But thim that think widdys are fools are desaved entirely, an' so was Misther Dooley, fur instead av his troubles bein' inded, begob, they were just begun. Ivery time he wint into the Shamrock Missis O'Donnell heard av it an' raymonshtrated wid him, an' 'ud cry at him beways it was dhrinkin' himself to death he was; afther lavin' the Shamrock, the Widdy Mulligan'ud set wan av her boys to watch him up the strate an' see if he shtopped in the shop. Av coorse he cudn't go by, an' whin he come agin, the Widdy Mulligan'ud gosther him about it, an' thin he'd promise not to do it agin. No more cud he go in the Widdy O'Donnell's shop widout meetin' Missis McMurthry's dawther that was always shtreelin' on the strate, an' thin her mother'ud say to him it was a power o' salt his cow was atin', an' the Widdy O'Donnell towld him his horse must be an axpensive baste fur to nade so much shooin'.

'Thin he'd tell thim a lot o' lies that they purtinded to belave an' didn't, bekase they're such desavers thimselves that it isn't aisey fur to do thim, but Dooley begun to think if it got anny hotter fur him he'd lave the pitaties to the widdys to divide bechune thim as a raytribution fur the loss av himself, an' go to Clare widout delay.

'While he'd this bother on him he got to know owld Miss Rooney, that lived wid her mother an' father on the farm next but wan to his own, but on the other side o' the way, an' the manes be which he got to know her was this. Wan mornin', whin Dooley's man, Paddy, wint to milk the cow, bad scran to the dhrop she'd to shpare, an' he pullin' an' pullin', like it was ringin' the chapel bell he was, an' she kickin', an' no milk comin', faix not as much as'ud blind the eye av a midge. So he wint an' towld Misther Dooley.

' "I can get no milk," says he. "Begorra the cow's as dhry as a fiddler's troat," says he.

' "Musha, thin," says Misther Dooley, "it's the lazy omadhawn ye are. I don't belave it. Can ye milk at all?" says he.

' "I can," says Paddy, "as well as a calf," says he. "But phat's the use ov pullin'? Ye'd get the same quantity from a rope," says he.

'So Dooley wint out an' thried himself an' didn't get as much as a shmell of milk.

' "Phat's the matther wid the baste?" says he, "an' her on the grass from sun to sun."

' "Be jakers," says Paddy, "it's my consate that she's bewitched."

' "It's thrue fur ye," says Dooley, as the like was aften knewn. "Go you to Misther Rooney's wid the pail an' get milk fur the calf, an' ax if there's a Pishogue hereabouts."

'So Paddy wint an' come back sayin' that the young lady towld him there was.

' "So there's a young lady in it," thinks Dooley. Faix, the love av coortin' was shtrong on him. "Did ye ax her how to raich the woman?"

' "Bedad, I didn't. I forgot," says Paddy.

' "That's yerself entirely," says Dooley to him agin. "I'd betther thrust me arriants to a four-legged jackass as to wan wid two. He'd

go twict as fast an' remimber as much. I'll go meself," says he, only
wantin' an axcuse, an' so he did. He found Miss Rooney thried to be
plazin', an' it bein' convainient, he wint agin, an' so it was ivery day
whin he'd go fur the calf's milk he'd have a chat wid her, an'
sometimes come over in the avenin', bekase it wasn't healthy fur
him in town just thin.

'But he wint to Owld Moll about the cow, an' the charm she gev
him soon made the baste all right agin, but, be that time, he'd got
used to goin' to Rooney's an' liked it betther than the town, bekase
whinever he wint to town he had to make so many axcuses he was
afeared the widdys'ud ketch him in a lie.

'So he shtayed at home most times and wint over to Rooney's the
rest, fur it wasn't a bad job at all, though she was about one an' forty,
an' had give up the fight fur a husband an' so saiced strugglin'. As
long as they've anny hope, owld maids are the most praypostherous
craythers alive, fur they' ll fit thimselves wid the thrappin's av a
young gurrul an' look as onaisey in thim as a boy wid his father's
britches on. But whin they've consinted to the sitiwation an' saiced
to struggle, thin they begin to be happy an' enjoy life a bit, but
there's no aise in the worruld fur thim till thin. Now Miss Rooney
had gev up the contist an' plasthered her hair down on aitch side av
her face so smooth ye'd shwear it was ironed it was, an' begun to
take the worruld aisey.

'But there's thim that says an owld maid niver does give up her
hope, only lets on to be continted so as to lay in amboosh fur anny
onsuspishus man that happens to shtray along, an' faix, it looks that-
a-way from phat I'm goin' to tell ye, bekase as soon as Misther
Dooley begun to come over an' palather his fine talk to her an' say
shwate things, thin she up an' begins shtrugglin' harder nor iver,
bekase it was afther she'd let go, an' comin' onexpected-like she
thought it was a dispinsation av Providence, whin rayly it was only
an accident it was, beways av Dooley's cow goin' dhry an' the calf
too young to lave suckin' an' ate grass.

'Annyhow, wan day, afther Misther Dooley had talked purty nice
the avenin' afore, she put an her cloak, an' wint to Owld Moll an' in
an' shut the dure.

' "Now, Moll," she says to the owld cuillean, "it's a long time since
I've been to ye, barrin' the time the goat was lost, fur, sure, I lost me
confidince in ye. Ye failed me twict, wanst whin John McCune forgot
me whin he wint to Derry an' thin come back an' married that Mary

O'Niel, the impidint young shtrap, wid the air av her as red as a glowin' coal; an' wanst whin Misther McFinnigan walked aff from me an' married the Widdy Bryan. Now ye must do yer besht, fur I'm thinkin' that, wid a little industhry, I cud get Misther Dooley, the same that the town widdys is so flusthrated wid."

' "An' does he come to see ye, at all?" says Moll.

' "Faith he does, an' onless I'm mishtaken is mightily plazed wid his comp'ny whin it's me that's in it," says Miss Rooney.

' "An' phat widdys is in it," says Moll, as she didn't know, bekase sorra a step did the widdys go to her wid their love doin's, as they naded no help, an' cud thransact thim affairs thimselves as long as their tongues held out.

'So Miss Rooney towld her, an' Moll shuk her head. "Jagers," says she, "I'm afeared yer goose is cooked if all thim widdys is after him. I won't thry," says she.

'But Miss Rooney was as much in airnest as the widdys, troth, I'm thinkin', more, bekase she was fairly aitchin' fur a husband now she'd got her mind on it.

' "Sure, Moll," says she, "ye wouldn't desart me now an' it me last show. Thim widdys can marry who they plaze, bad scran to 'em, but if Misther Dooley gets from me, divil fly wid the husband I'll get at all, at all," beginnin' to cry.

'So, afther a dale av palatherin', Moll consinted to thry, bein' it was the third time Miss Rooney had been to her, besides, she wanted to save her charackther for a knowledgeable woman. So she aggrade to do her best, an' gev her a little bag to carry wid 'erbs in it, an' writ some words on two bits av paper an' the same in Latin. It was an awful charm, no more do I remimber it, fur it was niver towld me, nor to anny wan else, fur it was too dreadful to say axceptin' in Latin an' in a whisper fur fear the avil sper'ts'ud hear it, that don't undhershtand thim dape langwidges.

' "Now, darlint," says owld Moll, a-givin' her wan, "take you this charm an' kape it on you an' the bag besides, an' ye must manage so as this other paper'ull be on Misther Dooley, an' if it fails an he don't marry ye I'll give ye back yer money an' charge ye nothing at all," says she.

'So Miss Rooney tuk the charms an' paid Owld Moll one pound five, an' was to give her fifteen shillins more afther she was married to Dooley.

'She wint home, bothered entirely how she'd get the charm on

Dooley, an' the avenin' come, an' he wid it, an' shtill she didn't know. So he set an' talked an' talked, an' by an' he dhrunk up the rest av the whiskey an' wather in his glass an' got up to go.

' "Why, Misther Dooley," says she, bein' all at wanst shtruck be an idee. "Was iver the like seen av yer coat?" says she. "Sure it's tore in the back. Sit you down agin wan minnit an' I'll mend it afore ye can light yer pipe. Take it aff," says she.

' "Axqueeze me," says Dooley. "I may be a bigger fool than I look, or I may look a bigger fool than I am, but I know enough to kape the coat on me back whin I'm wid a lady," says he.

' "Then take a sate an' I'll sow it on ye," says she to him agin, so he set down afore the fire, an' she, wid a pair av shizzors an' a nadle, wint behind him an' at the coat. 'T was a sharp thrick av her, bekase she took the shizzors, an' whin she was lettin' on to cut aff the t'reads that she said were hangin', she ripped the collar an' shlipped in the bit o' paper, an' sowed it up as nate as a samesthress in less than no time.

' "It's much beholden to ye I am," say Dooley, risin' wid his pipe lit. "An' it's a happy man I'd be if I'd a young woman av yer size to do the like to me ivery day."

' "Glory be to God," says Miss Rooney to herself, fur she thought the charm was beginnin' to work. But she says to him, "Oh, it's talkin' ye are. A fine man like you can marry who he plazes."

'So Dooley wint home, an' she, think' the business as good as done, towld her mother that night she was to marry Misther Dooley. The owld lady cudn't contain herself or the saycret aither, so the next mornin' towld it to her sister, an' she to her dawther that wint to school wid Missis McMurthry's gurrul. Av coorse the young wan cudn't howld her jaw anny more than the owld wans, an' up an' towld the widdy's dawther an' she her mother an' the rest o' the town, so be the next day every wan knew that Dooley was goin' to marry Miss Rooney: that shows, if ye want to shpread a bit o' news wid a quickness aiquel to the tellygraph, ye've only to tell it to wan woman as a saycret.

'Well, me dear, the noise the widdys made'ud shtun a dhrummer. Dooley hadn't been in town fur a week, an' widdys bein' nacherly suspishus, they misthrusted that somethin' was wrong, but divil a wan o' thim thought he'd do such an onmannerly thrick as that. But they all belaved it, bekase widdys judge iverybody be themselves, so they were mighty mad.

'The Widdy McMurthry was first to hear the news, as her dawther towld her, an' she riz in a fury. "Oh the owdashus villin," says she; "to think av him comin' her an' me listenin' at him that was lyin' fasther than a horse'ud throt. But I'll have justice, so I will, an' see if there's a law for a lone widdy. I'll go to the judge, fur, I forgot to tell ye, it was jail delivery an' the coort was settin' an' the judge down from Dublin wid a wig on him the size av a bar'l.

'Whin they towld Missis O'Donnell, she bust out cryin' an' says, "Sure it can't be thrue. It isn't in him to desave a poor widdy wid only two childer, an' me thrustin' on him' so she wint into the back room an' laid on the bed.

'But whin the Widdy Mulligan learned it, they thought she'd take a fit, the face av her got so red an' she chokin' wid rage. "Tatther an' agers," says she. "If I only had that vagabone here five minnits, it's a long day it'ud be afore he'd desave another tinder-hearted faymale."

' "Oh, be aisey," says wan to her, "faix, you're not the onliest wan that's in it. Sure there's the Widdy O'Donnell an' Missis McMurthry that he's desaved aiquelly wid yerself."

' "Is that thrue?" says she; "by this an' by that I'll see thim an' we'll go to the judge an' have him in the prision. Sure the Quane's a widdy herself an' knows how it feels, an' her judge'ull take the part av widdys that's misconshtrewed be a nagurly blaggard like owld Dooley. Bad luck to the seed, breed, an' generation av him. I cud mop up the flure wid him, the divil roast him, an' if I lay me hands on him, I'll do it," says she, an' so she would; an' a blessin it was to Misther Dooley he was not in town just thin, but at home, diggin' pitaties as fast as he cud, an' chucklin' to himself how he'd send the pitaties to town be Paddy, an' himself go to Clare an' get away from the whole tribe av widdys an' owld maids.

'So the Widdy Mulligan wint afther the Widdy O'Donnell an' tuk her along, an' they towld thim av the Widdy McMurthry an' how she was done be him, an they got her too, fur they all said, "Sure we wouldn't marry him fur him, but only want to see him punished fur misconshtructing phat we said to him an' lying to us." Be this time half the town was ready an' aiger to go wid thim to the coort, an' so they did, an' in, wid the offishers thryin' to kape thim out, an' the wimmin shovin' in, an' all their frinds wid 'em, an' the shur'f callin' out "Ordher in the coort", an' the judge lookin' over his shpectacles at thim.

' "Phat's this at all?" says the judge, wid a solemnious voice. "Is it a riat it is, or a faymale convulsion?" – whin he seen all the wimmin. "Phat's the matther?" says he, an' wid that all the wimmin begun at wanst, so as the noise av thim was aiquel to a 'viction.

' "Marcy o' God," says the judge, "phat's in the faymales at all? Are they dishtracted entirely, or bewitched, or only dhrunk?" says he.

' "We're crazy wid graif, yer Lordshap," they schraimed at him at wanst. "It's justice we want agin the uppresser."

' "Phat's the uppresser been a-doin'?" axed the judge.

' "Disthroyin' our pace, an' that av our families," they said to him.

' "Who is the oppresser?" he axed.

' "Owld Dooley," they all shouted at him at the wan time, like it was biddin' at an auction they were.

'So at first the judge cudn't undhershtand at all, till some wan whishpered the truth to him an' thin he scrotched his chin wid a pen.

' "Is it a man fur to marry all thim widdys? By me wig, he's a bowld wan. Go an' fetch him," he says to a consthable. "Be sated, ladies, an' ye'll have justice," he says to the widdys, very p'lite. "Turn out thim other blaggards," he says to the shur'f, an' away wint the polisman afther Dooley.

'He found him at home, wid his coat aff, an' him an' Paddy diggin' away at the pitaties for dear life, bekase he wanted to get thim done.

' "Misther Dooley," says the consthable to him, "ye're me prish'ner. Come along, ye must go wid me at wanst."

'At first, Dooley was surprised in that degray he thought the life'ud lave him, as the consthable come up behind him on the quiet, so as to give him no show to run away.

' "Phat for?" says Dooley to him, whin he'd got his wind agin.

' "Faix, I'm not sartain," says the polisman, that wasn't a bad felly; "but I belave it's along o' thim widdys that are so fond o' ye. The three o' thim's in the coort an' all the faymales in town, an' the judge sint me afther ye, an' ye must come at wanst, so make ready to go immejitly."

' "Don't go wid him," says Paddy, wid his sleeves rowled up an' spitting in his hands. "Lave me at him," says he, but Dooley wouldn't, bekase he was a paceable man. But he wasn't anxshus to go to the coort at all; begob, he'd all the coortin' he naded, but bein' there was no help fur it, he got his coat, the same that Miss Rooney sowed the charm in, an' shtarted wid the consthable.

'Now, it was that mornin' that owld Rooney was in town, thryin' to sell a goat he had, that gev him no end o' throuble be losin' itself part of the time an' the rest be jumpin' on the thatch an' stickin' its feet through. But he cudn't sell it, as ivery wan knew the bast as well as himself, an' so he was sober, that wasn't common wid him. Whin he seen the widdys an' the other wimmin wid thim shtravigerin' through the strate on the way to the coort an' heard the phillaloo they were afther makin', he axed phat the matther was. So they towld him, an' says he, "Be the powers, if it's a question av makin' him marry some wan, me dawther has an inthrust in the matther," so he dhropped the goat's shtring an' shtarted home in a lamp-lighter's throt to fetch her, an' got there about the time the polisman nabbed Dooley.

' "There, they're afther goin' now," says he to her. "Make haste, or we'll lose thim," an' aff they run, she wid her charm an' he widout his coat, grippin' a shillalee in his fisht, an' caught up wid Paddy that was follerin' the polisman an' Dooley.

'So they jogged along, comfortable enough, the polisman an' Dooley in the lade, afther thim owld Rooney an' Paddy, blaggardin' the consthable ivery fut o' the way, an' offerin' fur to bate him so as he wouldn't know himself be lookin' in the glass, an' Miss Rooney in the rare, wondherin' if the charm'ud work right. But Dooley didn't let a word out av his jaw, as knowin' he'd nade all his breath afther gettin' into the coort.

'At the rise o' the hill the pursesshun was met be about a hunderd o' the town boys that come out fur to view thim, an' that yelled at Dooley how the widdys were waitin' to tare him in paces, an' that he was as good as a dead man a'ready, so he was; an' whin they got into town, all the men jined the show, roarin' wid laughter an' shoutin' at Dooley that the judge cudn't do anny more than hang him at wanst, an' to shtand it like a hayro, bekase they'd all be at the hangin' an' come to the wake besides an' have a tundherin' big time. But he answered thim niver a word, so they all wint on to the coort, an' in, bringin' the other half o' the town wid 'em, the faymale half bein' there kapin' comp'ny wid the widdys.

'The minnit they come nie the dure, all the widdys an' wimmin begun in wan breath to make raimarks on thim.

' "A–a–a–ah, the hang-dog face he has," says Missis McMurthry. "Sure hasn't he the look av a shape-thief on the road to the gallus?"

' "See the haythen vagabone," says the Widdy Mulligan. "If I had me tin fingers on him for five minnits, it's all the satiswhackshun I'd ax. Bad cess to the hair I'd lave on the head av him or in his whushkers aither."

'But the Widdy O'Donnell only cried, an' all the wimmin turned their noses up whin they seen Miss Rooney comin' in.

' "Look at that owld thing," says they. "Phat a power av impidince! Mind the consate av her to be comin' here wid him. Sure she hasn't the shame av a shtone monkey," says they av her.

' "Silence in the coort," says the shur'f. "Stop that laughin' be the dure. Git along down out o' thim windys," says he to the mob that Dooley an' the consthable brought wid them.

' "Misther Dooley," says the judge, "I'm axed to b'lave ye're thryin' to marry four wimmin at wanst, three av the same aforeshed bein' widdys an' the other wan not. Is it thrue, or do ye plade not guilty?" says he.

' "It's not thrue, yer Lordshap," says Dooley, shpakin' up, bekase he seen he was in for it an' put on a bowld face. "Thim widdys is crazy to get a husband, an' misconsayved the manin' o' me words," says he, an' that minnit you'd think a faymale lunattic ashylum broke loose in the coort.

'They all gabbled at wanst like a field av crows. They said he was a haythen, a Toork, a vulgar shpalpeen, a lyin' blaggard, a uppresser av the widdy, a robber av the orphin, he was worse than a nagur, he was, so he was, an' they niver thought av belavin' him, nor av marryin' him aither till he axed thim, an' so on.

'The judge was a married man himself an' knewn it was no use thryin' to shtop the gostherin', for it was a joke av him to say that the differ bechuxt a woman an' a book was you cud shut up a book, so he let thim go on till they were spint an' out o' breath an' shtopped o' thimselves like an owld clock that's run down.

' "The sintince av this coort, Misther Dooley, is, that ye marry wan av 'em an' make compinsation to the other wans in a paycoonyary way be payin' thim siven poun' aitch."

' "Have marcy, yer Lordshap," says Dooley, bekase he seen himself shtripped av all he had. "Make it five poun', an' that's more than I've got in money."

' "Siven pound, not a haporth less," says the judge. "if ye haven't the money ye can pay it in projuice. An' make yer chice bechune the wimmin who ye'll marry, as it's married ye'll be this blessed day, bekase ye've gone too long a'ready," says the judge, very starn, an' thin the widdys all got quite, an' begun to be sorry they gev him so many hard names.

' "Is it wan o' the widdy's must I marry?" says Dooley, axin' the judge, an' the charm in his coller beginnin' to work hard an' remind him av Miss Rooney, that was settin' on wan side, trimblin'.

' "Tare an' 'ouns," says the judge. "Bad luck to ye, ye onmannerly idjit," as he was gettin' vexed wid Dooley, that was shtandin', acrotchin' the head av him like he was thryin' to encourage his brains. "Wasn't it wan o' the wimmin that I tould ye to take?" says he.

' "If that's phat yer Lordshap syas, axin' yer pardin an' not misdoubtin' ye, if it's plazin' to ye, bedad, I'll take the owld maid, bekase thim widdys have got a sight av young wans, an' childer are like toothpicks, ivery man wants his own an' not another felly's." But he had another razon that he towld to me afther; says he, "If I've got to have a famly, be jakers, I want to have the raisin' av it meself," an' my blessin' on him for that same.

'But whin he was spakin' an' said he'd take Miss Rooney, wid that word she fainted away fur dead, an' was carried out o' the coort be her father an' Paddy.

'So it was settled, an' as Dooley didn't have the money, the widdys aggrade to take their pay some other way. The Widdy Mulligan tuk the pitaties he was diggin' whin the polisman gripped him, as she said they'd kape the inn all winter. The Widdy McMurthry got his hay, which come convaynient, bekase her brother kep post horses an' tuk the hay av her at two shillins undher the market. Missis O'Donnell got the cow that made all the throuble be goin' dhry at the wrong time, an' bein' it was a good cow was vally'd at tin poun' so she geve him three poun', an' was to sind him the calf whin it was weaned. So the widdys were all paid for bein' wounded in their hearts be Misther Dooley, an' a good bargain they made av it, bekase a widdy's affections are like garden weeds, the more ye thrample thim the fasther they grow.

'Misther Dooley got Miss Rooney, an' she a husband, fur they pulled her out av her faint wid a bucket o' wather, an' the last gossoon in town wint from the coort to the chapel wid Miss Rooney an Misther Dooley, the latther crassin' himself ivery minnit an' blessin' God ivery step he tuk that it wasn't the jail he was goin' to, an' they were married there wid a roarin' crowd waitin' in the strate fur to show thim home. But they sarcumvinted thim, bekase they wint out the back way an' through Father O'Donohue's garden, an' so home, lavin' the mob howlin' before the chapel dure like wild Ingines.

'An' that's the way the owld maid defated three widdys, that isn't often done, no more would she have done it but for owld Moll an' the charm in Dooley's coat. But he's very well plazed, an' that I know, for afther me first wife died, her I was tellin' ye av, I got the roomytics in me back like tin t'ousand divils clawin' at me backbone, an' I made me mind up that I'd get another wife, bekase I wanted me back rubbed, sence it'ull be chaper, says I, to marry some wan to rub it than to pay a boy to do that same. So I was lookin' roun' an' met Misther Dooley an' spake av it to him, an' good luk it'ud have been if I'd tuk his advice, but I didn't, bein' surrounded be a widdy afther, that's rubbed me back well fur me only wid a shtick. But says he to me, "Take you my advice Misther Magwire, an' whin ye marry, get you an owld maid, if there's wan to be had in the counthry. Gurruls is flighty an' axpectin' too much av ye, an' widdys is greedy buzzards as ye've seen by my axpayriences, but owld maids is humble, an' thankful for gettin' a husband at all, God bless 'em, so they shtrive to plaze an' do as ye bid thim widout grumblin' or axin' throublesome questions." '

The Henpecked Giant

D. R. McANALLY, JR

No locality of Ireland is fuller of strange bits of fanciful legend than the neighbourhood of the Giant's Causeway. For miles along the coast the geological strata resemble that of the Causeway, and the gradual disintegration of the stone has wrought many peculiar and picturesque effects among the basaltic pillars, while each natural novelty has woven round it a tissue of traditions and legends, some appropriate, others forced, others ridiculous misapplications of commonplace tales. Here, a long straight row of columns known as the 'Giant's Organ', and tradition pictures the scene when the giants of old, with their gigantic families, sat on the Causeway and listened to the music; there, a group of isolated pillars is called the 'Giant's Chimneys', since they once furnished an exit for the smoke of the gigantic kitchen. A solitary pillar, surrounded by the crumbling remains of others, bears a distant resemblance to a seated female figure, the 'Giant's Bride', who slew her husband and attempted to flee, but was overtaken by the power of a magician, who changed her into stone as she was seated by the shore, waiting for the boat that was to carry her away. Further on, a cluster of columns forms the 'Giant's Pulpit', where a presumably outspoken gigantic preacher denounced the sins of a gigantic audience. The Causeway itself, according to legend, formerly extended to Scotland, being originally constructed by Finn Maccool and his friends, this notable giant having invited Benandoner, a Scotch giant of much celebrity, to come over and fight him. The invitation was accepted, and Maccool, out of politeness, built the Causeway the whole distance, the big Scotchman thus walking over dry-shod to receive his beating.

Some distance from the mainland is found the Ladies' Wishing Chair, composed of blocks in the Great Causeway, wishes made while seated here being certain of realisation. To the west of the Wishing Chair a solitary pillar rises from the sea, the 'Grey Man's Love'. Look to the mainland, and the mountain presents a deep, narrow cleft, with perpendicular sides, the 'Grey Man's Path'. Out in the sea, but unfortunately not often in sight, is the 'Grey Man's Isle', at present inhabited only by the Grey Man himself. As the island, however, appears but once in seventeen years, and the Grey Man is never seen save on the eve of some awful calamity, visitors to the Causeway have a very slight chance of seeing either island or man. There can be no doubt though of the existence of both, for everybody knows he was one of the greatest of the giants during his natural lifetime, nor could any better evidence be asked than the facts that his sweetheart, turned into stone, still stands in sight of the Causeway; the precipice, from which she flung herself into the sea, is still known by the name of the 'Lovers' Leap'; and the path he made through the mountain is still used by him when he leaves his island and comes on shore.

It is not surprising that so important a personage as the Grey Man should be the central figure of many legends, and indeed over him the story-makers seem to have had vigorous competition, for thirty or forty narratives are current in the neighbourhood concerning him and the principal events of his life. So great a collection of legendary lore on one topic rendered the choice of a single tradition which should fairly cover the subject a matter of no little difficulty. As sometimes happens in grave undertakings, the issue was determined by accident. A chance boat excursion led to the acquaintance of Mr Barney O'Toole, a fisherman, and conversation developed the fact that this gentleman was thoroughly posted in the local legends, and was also the possessor of a critical faculty which enabled him to differentiate between the probable and the improbable, and thus to settle the historical value of a tradition. In his way, he was also a philosopher, having evidently given much thought to social issues, and expressing his conclusions thereupon with the ease and freedom of a master mind.

Upon being informed of the variety and amount of legendary material collected about the Grey Man and his doings, Barney unhesitatingly pronounced the entire assortment worthless, and condemned all the gathered treasures as the creations of petty intellects, which could not get out of the beaten track, but sought in the supernatural a reason for and explanation of every fact that seemed at variance with the routine of daily experience. In his opinion, the Grey Man is never seen at all in our day and generation, having been gathered to his fathers ages ago; nor is there any enchanted island; to use his own language, 'all thim shtories bein' made be thim blaggard guides that set up av a night shtringin' out laigends for to enthertain the quol'ty.'

'Now, av yer Anner wants to hear it, I can tell ye the thrue shtory av the Grey Man, no more is there anny thing wondherful in it, but it's just as I had it from me grandfather, that towld it to the childher for to entertain thim.

'It's very well beknownst that in thim owld days there were gionts in plinty hereabouts, but they didn't make the Causeway at all, for that's a work o' nacher, axceptin' the Grey Man's Path, that I'm goin' to tell ye av. But ivery wan knows that there were gionts, bekase if there wasn't, how cud we know o' thim at all, but wan thing's sartain, they were just like us, axceptin' in the matther o' size, for wan ov thim'ud make a dozen like the men that live now.

'Among the gionts that lived about the Causeway there was wan, a young giont named Finn O'Goolighan, that was the biggest av his kind, an' none o' them cud hide in a kish. So Finn, for the size av him, was a livin' terror. His little finger was the size av yer Anner's arrum, an' his wrist as big as yer leg, an' so he wint, bigger an' bigger. Whin he walked he carried an oak tree for a shtick, ye cud crawl into wan av his shoes, an' his caubeen'ud cover a boat. But he was a good-humoured young felly wid a laugh that'ud deefen ye, an' a plazin' word for all he met, so as if ye run acrass him in the road, he'd give ye "good morrow kindly", so as ye'd feel the betther av it all day. He'd work an' he'd play an' do aither wid all the might that was in him. Av a week day you'd see him in the field or on the shore from sun to sun as busy as a hen wid a dozen chicks; an' av a fair-day or av a Sunday, there he'd be, palatherin' at the girls, an' dancin' jigs that he done wid extrame nateness, or havin' a bout wid a shtick on some other felly's head, an' indade, at that he was so clever that it was a delight for to see him, for he'd crack a giont's shkull that was as hard as a pot wid wan blow an' all the pleasure in life. So he got to be four or five an' twinty an' not his betther in the County Antrim.

'Wan fine day, his father, Bryan O'Goolighan, that was as big a giont as himself, says to him, says he, "Finn, me Laddybuck, I'm thinkin' ye'll want to be gettin' marr'd."

' "Not me," says Finn.

' "An' why not?" says his father.

' "I've no consate av it," says Finn.

' "Ye'd be the betther av it," says his father.

' "Faix, I'm not sure o' that," says Finn; "gettin' marr'd is like turnin' a corner, ye don't know phat ye're goin' to see," says he.

' "Thrue for ye,' says owld Bryan, for he'd had axpayrience himself, "but if ye'd a purty woman to make the stir-about for ye av a mornin' wid her won white hands, an' to watch out o' the dure for ye in the avenin,' an' put on a sod o' turf whin she sees ye comin', ye'd be a bether man," says he.

' "Bedad, it's not aisey for to conthravene that same,' says Finn, "barrin' I mightn't git wan like that. Wimmin is like angels," says he. "There's two kinds av 'em, an' the wan hat shmiles like a dhrame o' heaven afore she's marr'd, is the wan that gits to be a tarin' divil afther her market's made an' she's got a husband."

'Ye see Finn was a mighty smart young felly, if he was a giont, but his father didn't give up hope av gettin' him marr'd, for owld folks that's been through a dale o' throuble that-a-way always thries to get the young wans into the same thrap, beways, says they, av taichin' them to larn something. But Bryan was a wise owld giont, an' knewn, as the Bible says, there's time enough for all things. So he quit him, an' that night he spake wid the owld woman an' left it wid her, as knowin' that whin it's a matther o' marryin', a woman is more knowledgable an' can do more to bring on that sort o' mis'ry in wan day than a man can in all the years God gives him.

'Now, in ordher that ye see the pint, I'm undher the needcessity av axplainin' to yer Anner that Finn didn't be no manes have the hathred at wimmin that he purtinded, for indade he liked them purty well, but he thought he undhershtood thim well enough to know that the more ye talk swate to thim, the more they don't like it, barrin' the're fools, that sometimes happens. So whin he talked wid 'em or about thim, he spake o' thim shuperskillious, lettin' on to despise the lasht wan o' thim, that was a takin' way he had, for wimmin love thimselves a dale bether than ye'd think, unless yer Anner's marr'd an' knows, an' that Finn knew, so he always said o' thim the manest things he cud get out av his head, an' that made thim think av him, that was phat he wanted. They purtinded to hate him for it, but he didn't mind that, for he knewn it was only talk, an' there wasn't wan o' thim that wouldn't give the lasht tooth out av her jaw to have him for a husband.

'Well, as I was sayin', afther owld Bryan give Finn up, his mother tuk him in hand, throwin' a hint at him wanst in a while, sighin' to him how glad she'd be to have a young lady giont for a dawther, an' dhroppin' a word about phat an iligant girl Burthey O'Ghallaghy was, that was the dawther av wan o' the naburs, that she got Finn, unbeknownst to himself, to be thinkin' about Burthey. She was a fine young lady giont, about tin feet high, as broad as a cassel dure, but she was good size for Finn, as ye know be phat I said av him. So when Finn's mother see him takin' her home from church afther benediction, an' the nabers towld her how they obsarved him lanin' on O'Ghallaghy's wall an' Burthey lightin' his pipe wid a coal, she thought to herself, "fair an' aisey goes far in a day," an' made her mind up that Finn'ud marry Burthey. An' so, belike, he'd a' done, if he hadn't gone over, wan onlucky day, to the village beyant, where the common people like you an' me lived.

'When he got there, in he wint to the inn to get him his dhrink, for it's a mishtake to think that thim gionts were all blood-suckin' blaggards as the Causeway guides say, but, barrin' they were in dhrink, were as paceable as rabbits. So when Finn wint in, he says, "God save ye," to thim settin', an' gev the table a big crack wid his shillaylah as for to say he wanted his glass. But instead o' the owld granny that used for to fetch him his potheen, out shteps a nate little woman wid hair an' eyes as black as a crow an' two lips on her as red as a cherry an' a quick sharp way like a cat in a hurry.

' "An' who are you, me Dear?" says Finn, lookin' up.

' "I'm the new barmaid, Sorr, av it's plazin' to ye," says she, makin' a curchey, an' lookin' shtrait in his face.

' "It is plazin'," says Finn. " 'tis I that's glad to be sarved be wan like you. Only," says he, "I know be the look o' yer eye ye've a timper."

' "Dade I have," says she, talkin' back at him, "an' ye'd betther not wake it."

'Finn had more to say an' so did she, that I won't throuble yer Anner wid, but when he got his fill av dhrink an' said all he'd in his head, an' she kep' aven wid him at ivery pint, he wint away mightily plazed. The next Sunday but wan he was back agin, an' the Sunday afther, an' afther that agin. By an' by, he'd come over in the avenin' afther the work was done, an' lane on the bar or set on the table, talkin' wid the barmaid, for she was as sharp as a thornbush, an' sorra a word Finn'ud say to her in impidince or anny other way, but she'd give him his answer afore he cud get his mouth shut.

'Now, be this time, Finn's mother had made up her mind that Finn'ud marry Burthey, an' so she sent for the matchmaker, an' they talked it all over, an' Finn's father seen Burthey's father, an' they settled phat Burthey'ud get an' phat Finn was to have, an' were come to an agraymint about the match, onbeknownst to Finn, bekase it was in thim days like it is now, the matches bein' made be the owld people, an' all the young wans did was to go an' be marr'd an' make the best av it. Afther all, maybe that's as good a way as anny, for whin ye've got all the throuble on yer back ye can stagger undher, there's not a haporth o' differ whether ye got undher it yerself or whether it was put on ye, an' so it is wid gettin' marr'd, at laste so I'm towld.

'Annyhow, Finn's mother was busy wid preparin' for th weddin' whin she heard how Finn was afther puttin' in his time at the village.

' "Sure that won't do," she says to herself; "he ought to know betther than to be spendin' ivery rap he's got in dhrink an' gostherin' at that black-eyed huzzy, an' he to be marr'd to the best girl in the county." So that night, when Finn come in, she spake fair an' soft to him that he'd give up goin' to the inn, an' get ready for to be marr'd at wanst. An' that did well enough till she got to the marryin', when Finn riz up aff his sate, an' shut his taith so hard he bruk his pipestem to smithereens.

' "Say no more, mother," he says to her. "Burthey's good enough, but I wouldn't marry her if she was made av goold. Begob, she's too big. I want no hogs'ead av a girl like her," says he. "If I'm to be marr'd, I want a little woman. They're betther o' their size, an' it don't take so much to buy gowns for thim, naither do they ate so much," says he.

' "A-a-ah, baithershin," says his mother to him; "phat d'ye mane be talkin' that-a-way, an' me workin' me fingers to the bone clanin' the house for ye, an' relavn' ye av all the coortin' so as ye'd not be bothered in the laste wid it."

' "Shmall thanks to ye," says Finn, 'sure isn't the coortin' the best share o' the job?'

' "Don't ye mane to marry her?" says his mother.

' "Divil a toe will I go wid her," says Finn.

' "Out, ye onmannerly young blaggard, I'd tell ye to go to the divil, but ye're on the way fast enough, an' bad luck to the fut I'll shtir to halt ye. Only I'm sorry for Burthey," says she, "wid her new gown made. When her brother comes back, begob 'tis he that'll be the death av ye immedjitly afther he dhrops his two eyes on ye."

' "Aisey now," says Finn, "if he opens his big mouth at me, I'll make him wondher why he wasn't born deef an' dumb," says he, an' so he would, for all that he was so paceable.

'Afther that, phat was his mother to do but lave aff an' go to bed, that she done, givin' Finn all the talk in her head an' a million curses besides, for she was mightily vexed at bein' bate that way an' was in a divil av a timper along o' the house-clanin', that always puts wimmin into a shtate av mind.

'So the next day the news was towld, an' Finn got to be a holy show for the nabers, bekase av not marryin' Burthey an' wantin' the barmaid. They were afeared to say annything to himself about it, for he'd an arm on him the thick o' yer waist, an' no wan wanted to see how well he cud use it, but they'd whisper afther him, an' whin he wint along the road, they'd pint afther him, an' by an' by a giont like himself, an uncle av him towld him he'd betther lave the counthry, an' so he thought he'd do an' made ready for to shtart.

'But poor Burthey pined wid shame an' grief at the loss av him, for she loved im wid all the heart she had, an' that was purty big. So she fell aff her weight, till from the size av a hogs'ead she got no bigger round than a barrel an' was like to die. But all the time she kept on hopin' that he'd come to her, but whin she heard for sartain he was goin' to lave the counthry she let go an' jumped aff that clift into the say an' committed shooicide an' drownded herself. She wasn't turned into a pillar at all, that's wan o' thim guides' lies; she just drownded like anybody that fell into the wather would, an' was found afther an' berrid be the fishermen, an' a hard job av it they had, for she weighed a ton. But they called the place the Lovers' Lape, bekase she jumped from it, an' lovin' Finn the way she did, the lape she tuk made the place be called afther her an' that's razon enough.

'Finn was showbogher enough afore, but afther that he seen it was no use thryin' for to live in Ireland at all, so he got the barmaid, that was aiquel to goin' wid him, the more that ivery wan was agin him, that's beway o' the conthrariness av wimmin, that are always ready for to do annything ye don't want thim to do, an' wint to Scotland an' wasn't heard av for a long time.

'About twelve years afther, there was a great talk that Finn had got back from Scotland wid his wife an' had taken the farm over be the village, the first on the left as ye go down the mountain. At first there was no end av the fuss that was, for Burthey's frinds hadn't forgotten, but it all come to talk, so Finn settled down quite enough an' wint to work. But he was an althered man. His hair an' beard were grey as a badger, so they called him the Grey Man, an' he'd a look on him like a shapestalin' dog. Everybody wondhered, but they didn't wondher long, for it was aisely persaived he had cause enough, for the tongue o' Missis Finn wint like a stame-ingine, kapin' so far ahead av her branes that she'd have to shtop an' say "an'–uh, an'–uh," to give the latther time for to ketch up. Jagers, but she was the woman for to talk an' schold an' clack away till ye'd want to die to be rid av her. When she was young she was a purty nice girl, but as she got owlder her nose got sharp, her lips were as thin as the aidge av a sickle, an' her chin was as pinted as the bow av a boat. The way she managed Finn was beautiful to see, for he was that afeared av her tongue that he darn't say his sowl belonged to him when she was by.

'When he got up airly in the mornin', she'd ax, 'Now phat are ye raisin' up so soon for, an' me just closin' me eyes in slape?' an' if he'd lay abed, she'd tell him to "get along out o' that now, ye big gossoon; if it wasn't for me ye'd do nothin' at all but slape like a pig." If he'd go out, she'd gosther him about where he was goin' an' phat he meant to do when he got there; if he shtayed at home, she'd raymark that he done nothin' but set in the cabin like a boss o' shtraw. When he thried for to plaze her, she'd grumble at him bekase he did 't thry sooner; when he let her be, she'd fall into a fury an' shtorm till his hair shtud up like it was bewitched it was.

'She'd more thricks than a showman's dog. If scholdin' didn't do for Finn, she'd cry at him, an' had tin childher that she larned to cry at him too, an' when she begun, the tin o' thim'ud set up a yell that'ud deefen a thrumpeter, so Finn'ud give in.

'She cud fall ill on tin minnits notice, an' if Finn was obsthreperous in that degray that she cudn't do him no other way, she'd let on her head ached fit to shplit, so she'd go to bed an' shtay there till she'd got him undher her thumb agin. So she knew just where to find him whin she wanted him; that wimmin undhershtand, for there's more divilmint in wan woman's head about gettin' phat she wants than in tin men's bodies.

'Sure, if iver anybody had raison to remimber the ould song, 'When I was single,' it was Finn.

'So, ye see, Finn, the Grey Man, was afther havin' the divil's own time, an' that was beways av a mishtake he made about marryin'. He thought it was wan o' thim goold bands the quol'ty ladies wear on their arrums, but he found it was a handcuff it was. Sure wimmin are quare craythers. Ye think life wid wan o' thim is like a sunshiny day an' it's nothing but drizzle an' fog from dawn to dark, an' it's my belafe that Misther O'Day wasn't far wrong when he said wimmin are like the owld gun he had in the house an' that wint aff an the shly wan day an' killed the footman. "Sure it looked innycent enough," says he, "but it was loaded all the same an' only waitin' for an axcuse to go aff at some wan, an' that's like a woman, so it is," he'd say, an' ivery wan'ud laugh when he towld that joke, for he was the landlord, "That's like a woman, for she's not to be thrusted avin when she's dead.' "

'But it's me own belafe that the most sarious mishtake av Finn's was in marryin' a little woman. There's thim that says all wimmin is a mishtake be nacher, but there's a big differ bechuxt a little woman an' a big wan, the little wans have sowls too big for their bodies, so are always lookin' out for a big man to marry, an' the bigger he is, the betther they like him, as knowin' they can manage him all the aisier. So it was wid Finn an' his little wife, for be hook an' be crook she rejuiced him in that obejince that if she towld him for to go an' shtand on his head in the corner, he'd do it wid the rish av his life, bekase he'd wanted to die an' go to heaven as he heard the priest say there was no marryin' there, an' though he didn't dare to hint it, he belaved in his sowl that the rayzon was the wimmin didn't get that far.

'Afther they'd been living here about a year, Finn thought he'd fish a bit an' so help along, considherin' he'd a big family an' none o' the childher owld enough for to work. So he got a boat an' did purty well an' his wife used to come acrass the hill to the shore to help him wid the catch. But it was far up an' down agin an' she'd get tired wid climbin' the hill an' jawing at Finn on the way.

'So wan day as they were comin' home, they passed a cabin an' there was the man that lived there, that was only a ditcher, a workin' away on the side av the hill down the path to the shpring wid a crowbar, movin' a big shtone, an' the shweat rollin' in shtrames aff his face.

' "God save ye," says Finn to him.

'God save ye kindly," says he to Finn.

' "It's a bizzy man ye are," says Finn.

' "Thrue for ye," says the ditcher. "It's along o' the owld woman. 'The way to the shpring is too stape an' shtoney,' says she to me, an' sure, I'm afther makin' it aisey for her."

' "Ye're the kind av a man to have," says Missis Finn, shpakin' up.

"Sure all wimmin isn't blessed like your wife," says she, lookin' at Finn, who let on to laugh when he wanted to shwear. They had some more discoorse, thin Finn an' his wife wint on, but it put a big notion into her head. If the bogthrotter, that was only a little ottommy, 'ud go to work like that an' make an aisey path for his owld woman to the shpring, phat's the rayzon Finn cudn't fall to an' dig a path through the mountains, so she cud go to the say an' to the church on the shore widout breakin' her back climbin' up an' then agin climbin' down. 'T was the biggest consate iver in the head av her, an' she wasn't wan o' thim that'ud let it cool aff for the want o' talkin' about it, so she up an' towld it to Finn, an' got afther him to do it. Finn wasn't aiger for to thry, bekase it was Satan's own job, so he held out agin all her scholdin' an' beggin' an' cryin'. Then she got sick on him, wid her headache, an' wint to bed, an' whin Finn was about she'd wondher out loud phat she was iver born for an' why she cudn't die. Then she'd pray, so as Finn'ud hear her, to all the saints to watch over her big gossoon av a husband an' not forget him just bekase he was a baste, an' if Finn'ud thry to quiet her, she'd pray all the louder, an' tell him it didn't matther, she was dyin' an' 'ud soon be rid av him an' his brutal ways, so as Finn got half crazy wid her an' was ready to do annything in the worruld for to get her quiet.

'Afther about a week av this thratemint, Finn give in an' wint to work wid a pick an' shpade on the Grey Man's Path. But thim that says he made it in wan night is ignerant, for I belave it tuk him a month at laste; if not more. So that's the thrue shtory av the Grey Man's Path, as me grandfather towld it, an' shows that a giont's size isn't a taste av help to him in a contist wid a woman's jaw.

'But to be fair wid her, I belave the onliest fault Finn's wife had was, she was possist be the divil, an' there's thim that thinks that's enough. I mind me av a young felly wan time tatt was in love, an' so to be axcused, that wished he'd a hunderd tongues so to do justice to his swateheart. So after that he marr'd her, an' whin they'd been marr'd a while an' she'd got him undher her fisht, says they to him, "An' how about yer hunderd tongues?" "Begorra," says he to thim agin, "wid a hunderd I'd get along betther av coorse than wid wan, but to be ayquel to the waggin' av her jaw I'd nade a hunderd t'ousand."

'So it's a consate I have that Missis Finn was not a haporth worse nor the rest o' thim, an' that's phat me grandfather said too, that had been marr'd twict, an' so knewn phat he was talkin' about. An' whin he towld the shtory av the Grey Man, he'd always end it wid a bit av poethry:

> 'The first rib did bring in ruin
> As the rest have since been doin';
> Some be wan way, some another,
> Woman shtill is mischief's mother.

> 'Be she good or be she avil,
> Be she saint or be she divil,
> Shtill unaisey is his life
> That is marr'd wid a wife.'

The Leprechaun

D. R. McANALLY, JR

Every mythology has its good and evil spirits which are objects of adoration and subjects of terror, and often both classes are worshipped from opposite motives; the good, that the worshipper may receive benefit; the evil, that he may escape harm. Sometimes good deities are so benevolent that they are neglected, superstitious fear directing all devotion towards the evil spirits to propitiate them and avert the calamities they are ever ready to bring upon the human race; sometimes the malevolent deities have so little power that the prayer of the pious is offered up to the good spirits that they may pour out still further favours, for man is a worshipping being, and will prostrate himself with equal fervour before the altar whether the deity be good or bad.

Midway, however, between the good and evil beings of all mythologies there is often one whose qualities are mixed; not wholly good nor entirely evil, but balanced between the two, sometimes doing a generous action, then descending to a petty meanness, but never rising to nobility of character nor sinking to the depths of depravity; good from whim, and mischievous from caprice.

Such a being is the leprechaun of Ireland, a relic of the pagan mythology of that country. By birth the leprechaun is of low descent, his father being an evil spirit and his mother a degenerate fairy; by nature he is a mischief-maker, the Puck of the Emerald Isle. He is of diminutive size, about three feet high, and is dressed in a little red jacket or roundabout, with red breeches buckled at the knee, grey or black stockings, and a hat, cocked in the style of a century ago, over a little, old, withered face. Round his neck is an Elizabethan ruff, and frills of lace are at his wrists. On the wild west coast, where the Atlantic winds bring almost constant rains, he dispenses with ruff and frills and wears a frieze overcoat over his pretty red suit, so that, unless on the lookout for the cocked hat, 'ye might pass a leprechaun on the road and never know it's himself that's in it at all.'

In Clare and Galway, the favourite amusement of the leprechaun is riding a sheep or goat, or even a dog, when the other animals are not available, and if the sheep look weary in the morning or the dog is muddy and worn out with fatigue, the peasant understands that the local leprechaun has been going on some errand that lay at a greater distance than he cared to travel on foot. Aside from riding the sheep and dogs almost to death, the leprechaun is credited with much small mischief about the house. Sometimes he will make the pot boil over and put out the fire, then again he will make it impossible for the pot to boil at all. He will steal the bacon-flitch, or empty the potatokish, or fling the baby down on the floor, or occasionally will throw the few poor articles of furniture about the room with a strength and vigour altogether disproportioned to his diminutive size. But his mischievous pranks seldom go further than to drink up all the milk or despoil the proprietor's bottle of its poteen, sometimes, in sportiveness, filling the bottle with water, or, when very angry, leading the fire up to the thatch, and then startling the inmates of the cabin with his laugh as they rise, frightened, to put out the flames.

To offset these troublesome attributes, the leprechaun is very domestic, and sometimes attaches himself to a family, always of the 'rale owld shtock', accompanying its representatives from the castle to the cabin and never deserting them unless driven away by some act of insolence or negligence, 'for, though he likes good atin', he wants phat he gets to come wid an open hand, an' 'ud laver take the half av a pratee that's freely given than the whole av a quail that's begrudged him.' But what he eats must be specially intended for him, an instance being cited by a Clare peasant of a leprechaun that deserted an Irish family, because, on one occasion, the dog having left a portion of his food, it was set by for the leprechaun. 'Jakers, 't was as mad as a little wasp he was, an' all that night they heard him workin' away in the cellar as busy as a nailer an' a sound like a catheract av wather goin' widout sayein'. In the mornin' they wint to see phat he'd been at, but he was gone, an' whin they come to thry for the wine, bad loock to the dhrop he'd left, but all was gone from ivory cask an' bottle, and they were filled wid say-wather, beways av rayvinge o' phat they done him.'

In different country districts the leprechaun has different names. In the northern counties he is the logheryman; in Tipperary, he is the lurigadawne; in Kerry, the luricawne; in Monaghan, the cluricawne.

The dress also varies. The logheryman wears the uniform of some British infantry regiments, a red coat and white breeches, but instead of a cap, he wears a broad-brimmed, high, pointed hat, and after doing some trick more than usually mischievous, his favourite position is to poise himself on the extreme point of his hat, standing at the top of a wall or on a house, feet in the air, then laugh heartily and disappear. The lurigadawne wears an antique slashed jacket of red, with peaks all round and a jockey cap, also sporting a sword, which he uses as a magic wand. The luricawne is a fat, pursy little fellow whose jolly round face rivals in redness the cutaway jacket he wears, that always has seven rows of seven buttons in each row, though what use they are has never been determined, since his jacket is never buttoned, nor, indeed, can it be, but falls away from a shirt invariably white as the snow. When in full dress he wears a helmet several sizes too large for him, but, in general, prudently discards this article of headgear as having a tendency to render him conspicuous in a country where helmets are obsolete, and wraps his head in a handkerchief that he ties over his ears.

The cluricawne of Monaghan is a little dandy, being gorgeously arrayed in a swallow-tailed evening coat of red with green vest, white breeches, black stockings, and shoes that 'fur the shine av 'em 'ud shame a lookin'-glass'. His hat is a long cone without a brim, and is usually set jauntily on one side of his curly head. When greatly provoked, he will sometimes take vengeance by suddenly ducking and poking the sharp point of his hat into the eye of the offender. Such conduct is, however, exceptional, as he commonly contents himself with soundly abusing those at whom he has taken offence, the objects of his anger hearing his voice but seeing nothing of his person.

One of the most marked peculiarities of the leprechaun family is their intense hatred of schools and schoolmasters, arising, perhaps, from the ridicule of them by teachers, who affect to disbelieve in the existence of the leprechaun and thus insult him, for 'it's very well beknownst, that unless ye belave in him an' thrate him well, he'll lave an' come back no more.' He does not even like to remain in the neighbourhood where a national school has been established, and as such schools are now numerous in Ireland, the leprechauns are becoming scarce. 'Wan gineration of taichers is enough for thim, bekase the families where the little fellys live forgit to set thim out the bit an' sup, an' so they lave.' The few that remain must have a hard time keeping soul and body together for nowhere do they now receive any attention at meal-times, nor is the anxiety to see one by any means so great as in the childhood of men still living. Then, to catch a leprechaun was certain fortune to him who had the wit to hold the mischief-maker a captive until demands for wealth were complied with.

'Mind ye,' said a Kerry peasant, 'the onliest time ye can ketch the little vagabone is whin he's settin' down, an' he niver sets down axceptin' whin his brogues want mendin'. He runs about so much he wears thim out, an' whin he feels his feet on the ground, down he sets undher a hidge or behind a wall, or in the grass, an' takes thim aff an' mends thim. Thin comes you by, as quiet as a cat an' sees him there, that ye can aisily, be his red coat, an' you shlippin' up on him, catches him in yer arrums.

' "Give up yer goold," says you.

' "Begob, I've no goold," says he.

' "Then outs wid yer magic purse," says you.

'But it's like pullin' a hat full av taith to get aither purse or goold av him. He's got goold be the ton, an' can tell ye where ye can put yer finger on it, but he wont, till ye make him, an' that ye must do be no aisey manes. Some cuts aff his wind be chokin' him, an' some bates him, but don't for the life o' ye take yer eyes aff him, fur if ye do, he's aff like a flash an' the same man niver sees him agin, an' that's how it was wid Michael O'Dougherty.

'He was afther lookin' for wan nigh a year, fur he wanted to get married an' hadn't any money, so he thought the aisiest was to ketch a luricawne. So he was lookin' an' watchin' an' the fellys makin' fun av him all the time. Wan night he was comin' back afore day from a wake he'd been at, an' on the way home he laid undher the hidge an' shlept awhile, thin riz an' walked on. So as he was walkin', he seen a luricawne in the grass be the road a-mendin' his brogues. So he shlipped up an' got him fast enough, an' thin made him tell him where was his goold. The luricawne tuk him to nigh the place in the break o' the hills an' was goin' fur to show him, when all at wanst Mike heard the most outprobrious scraich over the head av him that'ud make the hairs av ye shtand up like a mad cat's tail.

' "The saints defind me," says he, "phat's that?" an' he looked up from the luricawne that he was carryin' in his arrums. That minnit the little attomy wint out av his sight, fur he looked away from it an' it was gone, but he heard it laugh when it wint an' he niver got the goold but died poor, as me father knows, an' he a boy when it happened.'

Although the leprechauns are skilful in evading curious eyes, and, when taken, are shrewd in escaping from their captors, their tricks are sometimes all in vain, and after resorting to every device in their power, they are occasionally compelled to yield up their hidden stores, one instance of which was narrated by a Galway peasant.

'It was Paddy Donnelly av Connemara. He was always hard at work as far as anny wan seen, an' bad luck to the day he'd miss, barrin' Sundays. When all'ud go to the fair, sorra a fut he'd shtir to go near it, no more did a dhrop av dhrink crass his lips. When they'd ax him why he didn't take divarshun, he'd laugh an' tell thim his field was divarshun enough fur him, an' by an' by he got rich, so they knewn that when they were at the fair or wakes or shports, it was lookin' fur a leprechaun he was an' not workin', an' he got wan too, fur how else cud he get rich at all.'

And so it must have been, in spite of the denials of Paddy Donnelly, though, to do him justice, he stoutly affirmed that his small property was acquired by industry, economy, and temperance. But according to the opinions of his neighbours, 'bad scran to him 't was as greedy as a pig he was, fur he knewn where the goold was, an' wanted it all fur himself, an' so lied about it like the leprechauns, that's known to be the biggest liars in the world.'

The leprechaun is an old bachelor elf who successfully resists all efforts of scheming fairy mammas to marry him to young and beautiful fairies, persisting in single blessedness even in exile from his kind, being driven off as a punishment for his heterodoxy on matrimonial subjects. This is one explanation of the fact that leprechauns are always seen alone, though other authorities make the leprechaun solitary by preference, he having learned the hollowness of fairy friendship and the deceitfulness of fairy femininity, and left the society of his kind in disgust at its lack of sincerity.

It must be admitted that the latter explanation seems the more reasonable, since whenever the leprechaun has been captured and forced to engage in conversation with his captor he displayed conversational powers that showed an ability to please, and as woman kind, even among fairy circles, are, according to an Irish proverb, 'aisily caught be an oily tongue', the presumption is against the expulsion of the leprechaun and in favour of his voluntary retirement.

However this may be, one thing is certain to the minds of all wise women and fairy-men, that he is the 'thrickiest little divil that iver wore a brogue', whereof abundant proof is given. There was Tim O'Donovan, of Kerry, who captured a leprechaun and forced him to disclose the spot where the 'pot o' goold' was concealed. Tim was going to make the little rogue dig up the money for him, but, on the leprechaun advancing the plea that he had no spade, released him, marking the spot by driving a stick into the ground and placing his hat on it. Returning the next morning with a spade, the spot pointed out by the 'little ottomy av a desaver' being in the centre of a large bog, he found, to his unutterable disgust, that the leprechaun was too smart for him, for in every direction innumerable sticks rose out of the bog, each bearing aloft an old 'caubeen' so closely resembling his own that poor Tim, after long search, was forced to admit himself baffled and give up the gold that, on the evening before, had been fairly within his grasp, if 'he'd only had the brains in his shkull to make the leprechaun dig it for him, shpade or no shpade.'

Even when caught, therefore, the captor must outwit the captive, and the wily little rascal, having a thousand devices, generally gets away without giving up a penny, and sometimes succeeds in bringing the eager fortune hunter to grief, a notable instance of which was the case of Dennis O'Bryan, of Tipperary, as narrated by an old woman of Crusheen.

'It's well beknownst that the leprechaun has a purse that's got the charmed shillin'. Only wan shillin', but the wondher av the purse is this: No matther how often ye take out a shillin' from it, the purse is niver empty at all, but whin ye put yer finger in agin, ye always find wan there, fur the purse fills up when ye take wan from it, so ye may shtand all day countin' out the shillin's an' they comin', that's a thrick av the good peoples an' be magic.

'Now Dinnis was a young blaggard that was always afther peepin' about undher the hidge fur to ketch a leprechaun, though they do say that thim that doesn't sarch afther thim see thim oftener that thim that does, but Dinnis made his mind up that if there was wan in the counthry, he'd have him, fur he hated work worse than sin, an' did be settin' in a shebeen day in an' out till you'd think he'd grow on the sate. So wan day he was comin' home, an' he seen something red over in the corner o' the field, an' in he goes, as quiet as a mouse, an' up on the leprechaun an' grips him be the collar an' down's him on the ground.

' "Arrah, now, ye ugly little vagbone," says he, "I've got ye at last. Now give up yer goold, or by jakers I'll choke the life out av yer pin-squazin' carkidge, ye owld cobbler, ye," says he, shakin' him fit to make his head dhrop aff.

'The leprechaun begged, and scritched, an' cried, an' said he wasn't a rale leprechaun that was in it, but a young wan that hadn't anny goold, but Dinnis wouldn't let go av him, an' at last the leprechaun said he'd take him to the pot ov goold that was hid be the say, in a glen in Clare. Dinnis didn't want to go so far, bein' afeared the leprechawn'ud get away, an' he thought the divilish baste was afther lyin' to him, bekase he knewn there was goold closter than that, an' so he was chokin' him that his eyes stood out till ye cud knock 'em aff wid a shtick, an' the leprechaun axed him would he lave go if he'd give him the magic purse. Dinnis thought he'd bhether do it, fur he was mortially afeared the oudacious little villin'ud do him so thrick an' get away, so he tuk the purse, afther lookin' at it to make sure it was red shilk, an' had the shillin' in it, but the minnit he tuk his two eyes aff the leprechaun, away wint the rogue wid a laugh that Dinnis didn't like at all.

'But he was feelin' very comfortable be razon av gettin' the purse, an' says to himself, "Begorra, 'tis mesilf that'll ate the full av me waistband fur wan time, an' dhrink till a stame-ingine can't squaze wan dhrop more down me neck," says he, and aff he goes like a quarther-horse fur Miss Clooney's sheebeen, that's where he used fur to go. In he goes, an' there was Paddy Grogan, an' Tim O'Donovan, an' Mike Conathey, an' Bryan Flaherty, an' a shtring more av 'om settin' on the table, an' he pulls up a sate an' down he sets, a-callin' to Miss Clooney to bring her best.

' "Where's yer money?" says she to him, fur he didn't use to have none barrin' a tuppence or so.

' "Do you have no fear," says he, "fur the money," says he, "ye pinny-schrapin' owld shkeleton," this was beways av a shot at her, fur it was the size av a load o' hay she was, an' weighed a ton. "Do you bring yer best," says he. "I'm a gintleman av forchune, bad loock to the job o' work I'll do till the life laves me. Come, jintlemin, dhrink at my axpinse." An' so they did an' more than wanst, an' afther four or five guns apace, Dinnis ordhered dinner fur thim all, but Miss Clooney towld him sorra the bit or sup more'ud crass the lips av him till he paid fur that he had. So out he pulls the magic purse fur to pay, an' to show it thim an' towld thim phat it was an' where he got it.

' "And was it the leprechaun gev it ye?" says they.

' "It was," says Dinnis, "an' the varchew av this purse is sich, that if ye take shillin's out av it be the handful all day long, they'll be comin' in a shtrame like whishkey out av a jug," says he, pullin' out wan.

'And thin, me jewel, he put in his fingers afther another, but it wasn't there, for the leprechaun made a ijit av him, an' instid o' givin' him the right purse, gev him wan just like it, so as onless ye looked clost, ye cudn't make out the differ betune thim. But the face on Dinnis was a holy show when he seen the leprechaun had done him, an' he wid only a shillin', an' half a crown av dhrink down the troats av thim.

' "To the divil wid you an' yer leprechauns, an' purses, an' magic shillin's," schreamed Miss Clooney, belavin', an' small blame to her that's, that it was lyin' to her he was. "Ye're a thafe, so ye are, dhrinkin' up me dhrink, wid a lie on yer lips about the purse, an' insultin' me into the bargain," says she, thinkin' how he called her a shkeleton, an' her a load fur a waggin. "Yer impidince bates owld Nick, so it does," says she; so she up an' hits him a power av a crack on the head wid a bottle; an' the other felly's, a thinkin' sure that it was a lie he was afther tellin' them, an' he laving thim to pay fur the dhrink he'd had, got on him an' belted him out av the face it was nigh on to dead he was. Then a consthable comes along an' hears the phillaloo they did be makin' an' comes in.

' "Tatther an' agers," says he, "lave aff. I command the pace. Phat's the matther here?"

'So they towld him an' he consayved that Dinnis shtole the purse an' tuk him be the collar.

' "Lave go," says Dinnis. "Sure phat's the harrum o' getting the purse av a leprechaun?"

' "None at all," says the polisman, "av ye projuice the leprechaun an' make him teshtify he gev it ye an' that ye haven't been burglarious an' sacrumvinted another man's money," says he.

'But Dinnis cudn't do it, so the cunsthable tumbled him into the jail. From that he wint to corrt an' got thirty days at hard labour, that he niver done in this life afore, an' afther he got out, he said he'd left lookin' for leprechauns, fur they were too shmart fur him entirely, an' it's thrue fur him, bekase I belave they were.'

The Prisoner

DOROTHY MACARDLE

It was on an evening late in May that Liam Daly startled us by strolling into Una's room, a thin, laughing shadow of the boy we had known at home. We had imagined him a helpless convalescent still in Ireland and welcomed him as if he had risen from the dead. For a while there was nothing but clamourous question and answer, raillery, revelry and the telling of news; his thirty-eight days' hunger-strike had already become a theme of whimsical wit; but once or twice as he talked his face sobered and he hesitated, gazing at me with a pondering burdened look.

'He holds me with his glittering eye!' I complained at last. He laughed.

'Actually,' he said, 'you're right. There *is* a story I have to tell – sometime, somewhere, and if you'll listen, I couldn't do better than to tell it here and now.'

He had found an eager audience, but his grace face quieted us and it was in an intent silence that he told his inexplicable tale.

'You'll say it was a dream,' he began, 'and I hope you'll be right; I could never make up my mind; it happened in the gaol. You know Kilmainham?' He smiled at Larry who nodded. 'The gloomiest prison in Ireland, I suppose – goodness knows how old. When the strike started I was in a punishment cell, a "noisome dungeon", right enough, complete with rats and all, dark always, and dead quiet; none of the others were in that wing. It amounted to solitary con-finement, of course, and on hunger-strike that's bad, the trouble is to keep a hold of your mind.

'I think it was about the thirtieth day I began to be afraid – afraid of going queer. It's not a pretty story, all this,' he broke off, looking remorsefully at Una, 'but I'd like you to understand – I want to know what you think.

'They'd given up bringing in food and the doctor didn't trouble himself overmuch with me; sometimes a warder would look through the peep-hole and shout a remark; but most of the day and all night I was alone.

'The worst was losing the sense of time; you've no idea how that torments you. I'd doze and wake up and not know whether a day or only an hour had gone; I'd think sometimes it was the fiftieth day, maybe, and we'd surely be out soon; then I'd think it was the thirtieth still; then a crazy notion would come that there was no such thing as time in prison at all; I don't know how to explain – I used to think that time went past outside like a stream, moving on, but in prison you were in a kind of whirlpool – time going round and round with you, so that you'd never come to anything, even death, only back again to yesterday and round to today and back to yesterday again. I got terrified, then, of going mad; I began talking and chattering to myself, trying to keep myself company, and that only made me worse because I found I couldn't stop – something seemed to have got into my brain and to be talking – talking hideous, blasphemous things, and I couldn't stop it. I thought I was turning into that – Ah, there's no describing it!

'At times I'd fight my way out of it and pray. I knew, at those times, that the blaspheming thing wasn't myself; I thought 'twas a foul spirit, some old criminal maybe, that had died in that cell. Then the fear would come on me that if I died insane he'd take possession of me and I'd get lost in Hell. I gave up praying for everything except the one thing, then – that I'd die before I went mad. One living soul to take to would have saved me; when the doctor came I'd all I could do to keep from crying out to him not to leave me alone; but I'd just sense enough left to hold on while he was there.

'The solitude and the darkness were like one – the one enemy – you couldn't hear and you couldn't see. At times it was pitch black; I'd think I was in my coffin then and the silence trying to smother me. Then I'd seem to float up and away – to lose my body, and then wake up suddenly in a cold sweat, my heart drumming with the shock. The darkness and I were two things hating one another, striving to destroy one another – it closing on me, crushing me, stifling the life out of my brain – I trying to pierce it, trying to see – My God, it was awful!

'One black night the climax came. I thought I was dying and that 'twas a race between madness and death. I was striving to keep my mind clear till my heart would stop, prying to go sane to God. And the darkness was against me – the darkness, thick and powerful and black. I said to myself that if I could pierce that, if I could make myself see – see anything, I'd not go mad. I put out all the strength I had, striving to see the window or the peep-hole or the crucifix on the wall, and failed. I knew there was a little iron seat clamped into the wall in the corner opposite the bed. I willed, with a desperate, frenzied intensity, to see that; and I did see it at last. And when I saw it all the fear and strain died away in me, because I saw that I was not alone.

'He was sitting there quite still, a limp, despairing figure, his head bowed, his hands hanging between his knees; for a long time I waited, then I was able to see better and I saw that he was a boy – fair-haired, white-faced, quite young, and there were fetters on his feet. I can tell you, my heart went out to him, in pity and thankfulness and love.

'After a while he moved, lifted up his head and stared at me – the most piteous look I have ever seen.

'He was a young lad with thin, starved features and deep eye-sockets like a skull's; he looked, then bowed his head down hopelessly again, not saying a word. But I knew that his whole torment was the need to speak, to tell something; I got quite strong and calm, watching him, waiting for him to speak.

'I waited a long while, and that dizzy sense of time working in a circle took me, the circles getting larger and larger, like eddies in a pool, again. At last he looked up and rested his eyes beseechingly on me as if imploring me to be patient; I understood; I had conquered the dark – he had to break through the silence – I knew it was very hard.

'I saw his lips move and at last I heard him – a thin, weak whisper came to me: "Listen – listen – for the love of God!"

'I looked at him, waiting; I didn't speak; it would have scared him. He leaned forward, swaying, his eyes fixed, not on mine, but on some awful vision of their own; the eyes of a soul in purgatory, glazed with pain.

' "Listen, listen!" I heard, "the truth! You must tell it – it must be remembered; it must be written down!"

' "I will tell it," I said, very gently, "I will tell it if I live."

' "Live, live, and tell it!" he said, moaningly and then, then he began. I can't repeat his words, all broken, shuddering phrases; he talked as if to himself only – I'll remember as best I can.

' "My mother, my mother!" he kept moaning, and "the name of shame!" "They'll put the name of shame on us," he said, "and my mother that is so proud – so proud she never let a tear fall, though they murdered my father before her eyes! Listen to me!" He seemed in an anguish of haste and fear, striving to tell me before we'd be lost again. "Listen! Would I do it to save my life? God knows I wouldn't, and I won't! But they'll say I did it! They'll say it to her. They'll be pouring out their lies through Ireland and I cold in my grave!"

'His thin body was shaken with anguish; I didn't know what to do for him. At last I said, "Sure, no one'll believe their lies."

' "My Lord won't believe it!" he said vehemently. "Didn't he send me up and down with messages to his lady? Would he do that if he didn't know I loved him – know I could go to any death?"

' " 'Twas in the Duke's Lawn they caught me," he went on. " 'Twas on Sunday last and they're starving me ever since; trying night and day they are to make me tell them what house he's in – and God knows I could tell them! I could tell!"

'I knew well the dread that was on him. I said, "There's no fear," and he looked at me a little quieter then.

' "They beat me," he went on. "They half strangled me in the Castle Yard and then they threw me in here. Listen to me! Are you listening?" he kept imploring. "I'll not have time to tell you all!"

' "Yesterday one of the redcoats came to me – an officer, I suppose, and he told me my Lord will be caught. Some lad that took his last message sold him . . . He's going to Moira House in the morning, disguised; they'll waylay him – attack him in the street. They say there'll be a fight – and sure I know there will – and he'll be alone; they'll kill him. He laughed, the devil – telling me that! He laughed, I tell you, because I cried.

' "A priest came in to me then – a priest! My God, he was a fiend! He came in to me in the dead of night, when I was lying shivering and sobbing for my Lord. He sat and talked to me in a soft voice – I thought at first he was kind. Listen till I tell you! Listen till you hear all! He told me I could save my Lord's Life. They'd go quietly to his house and take him; there'd be no fighting and he'd not be hurt. I'd only have to say where his lodging was. My God, I stood up and cursed him! He, a priest! God forgive me if he was."

' "He was no priest," I said, trying to quiet him. "That's an old tale."

' "He went out then," the poor boy went on, talking feverishly, against time. "And a man I'd seen at the Castle came in, a man with a narrow face and a black cloak. The priest was with him and he began talking to me again, the other listening, but I didn't mind him or answer him at all. He asked me wasn't my mother a poor widow, and wasn't I her only son. Wouldn't I do well to take her to America, he said, out of the hurt and harm, and make a warm home for her, where she could end her days in peace. I could earn the right to it, he said – good money, and the passage out, and wasn't it my duty as a son. The face of my mother came before me – the proud, sweet look she has, like a queen; I minded the loving voice of her and she saying, 'I gave your father for Ireland and I'd give you.' My God, my God, what were they but fiends? What will I do, what will I do at all?"

'He was in an agony, twisting his thin hands.

' "You'll die and leave her her pride in you," I said.

'Then, in broken gasps he told me the rest.

' "The Castle man – he was tall, he stood over me – he said, 'You'll tell us what we want to know.' "

' "I'll die first," I said to him and he smiled. He had thin, twisted lips – and he said, "You'll hang in the morning like a dog."

' "Like an Irishman, please God," I said.

' "He went mad at that and shook his first in my face and talked sharp and wicked through his teeth. O my God! I went down on my knees to him, I asked him in God's holy name! How will I bear it? How will I bear it at all?"

'He was overwhelmed with woe and terror; he bowed his head and trembled from head to foot.

' "They'll hang me in the morning," he gasped, looking at me haggardly. "And they'll take him and they'll tell him I informed. The black priest'll go to my mother – he said it! Himself said it! He'll tell her I informed! It will be the death blow on her heart – worse than death! 'Twill be written in the books of Ireland to the end of time. They'll cast the word of shame on my grave."

'I never saw a creature in such pain – it would break your heart. I put out all the strength I had and swore an oath to him. I swore that if I lived I'd give out the truth, get it told and written through Ireland. I don't know if he heard; he looked at me wearily, exhausted, and sighed and leaned his head back against the wall.

'I was tired out and half conscious only, but there was a thing I was wanting to ask. For a while I couldn't remember what it was, then I remembered again and asked it: "Tell me, what is your name?"

'I could hardly see him. The darkness had taken him again, and the silence; his voice was very far off and faint.

' "I forget," it said. "I have forgotten. I can't remember my name."

'It was quite dark then. I believe I fainted. I was unconscious when I was released.'

*   *   *

Max Barry broke the puzzled silence with a wondering exclamation: 'Lord Edward! More than a hundred years!'

'Poor wretch!' laughed the irrepressible Frank. 'In Kilmainham since ninety-eight!'

'Ninety-eight?' Larry looked up quickly. 'You weren't in the hospital were you, Liam? I was. You know it used to be the condemned cell. There's a name carved on the window-sill, and a date in ninety-eight – I can't – I can't remember the name.'

'Was there anyone accused, Max?' Una asked. 'Any record of a boy?'

Max frowned: 'Not that I remember – but so many were suspect – it's likely enough – poor boy!'

'I never could find out,' said Liam. 'Of course I wasn't far off delirium. It may have been hallucination or a dream.'

I did not believe he believed that and looked at him. He smiled.

'I want you to write it for me,' he pleaded quietly. 'I promised, you see.'

Far Darrig in Donegal

LETITIA MACLINTOCK

Pat Diver, the tinker, was a man well accustomed to a wandering life, and to strange shelters; he had shared the beggar's blanket in smoky cabins; he had crouched beside the still in many a nook and corner where poteen was made on the wild Innishowen mountains; he had even slept on the bare heather, or on the ditch, with no roof over him but the vault of heaven; yet were all his nights of adventure tame and commonplace when compared with one especial night.

During the day preceding that night, he had mended all the kettles and saucepans in Moville and Greencastle, and was on his way to Culdaff, when night overtook him on a lonely mountain road.

He knocked at one door after another asking for a night's lodging, while he jingled the halfpence in his pocket, but was everywhere refused.

Where was the boasted hospitality of Innishowen, which he had never before known to fail? It was of no use to be able to pay when the people seemed so churlish. Thus thinking, he made his way toward a light a little further on, and knocked at another cabin door.

An old man and woman were seated one at each side of the fire.

'Will you be pleased to give me a night's lodging, sir?' asked Pat respectfully.

'Can you tell a story?' returned the old man.

'No, then, sir, I canna say I'm good at storytelling' replied the puzzled tinker.

'Then you maun just gang further, for none but them that can tell a story will get in here.'

This reply was made in so decided a tone that Pat did not attempt to repeat his appeal, but turned away reluctantly to resume his weary journey.

'A story, indeed,' muttered he. 'Auld wives fables to please the weans!'

As he took up his bundle of tinkering implements, he observed a barn standing rather behind the dwelling house, and, aided by the rising moon, he made his way toward it.

It was a clean, roomy barn, with a piled-up heap of straw in one corner, Here was a shelter not to be despised; so Pat crept under the straw, and was soon asleep.

He could not have slept very long when he was awakened by the tramp of feet, and, peeping cautiously through a crevice in his straw covering, he saw four immensely tall men enter the barn, dragging a body, which they threw roughly upon the floor.

They next lighted a fire in the middle of the barn, and fastened the corpse by the feet with a great rope to a beam in the roof. One of them then began to turn it slowly before the fire. 'Come on,' said he, addressing a gigantic fellow, the tallest of the four – 'I'm tired; you be to tak' your turn.'

'Faix an' troth, I'll no turn him,' replied the big man. 'There's Pat Diver in under the straw, why wouldn't he tak' his turn?'

With hideous clamour the four men called the wretched Pat, who, seeing there was no escape, thought it was his wisest plan to come forth as he was bidden.

'Now, Pat,' said they, 'you'll turn the corpse, but if you let him burn you'll be tied up there and roasted in his place.'

Pat's hair stood on end, and the cold perspiration poured from his forehead, but there was nothing for it but to perform his dreadful task.

Seeing him fairly embarked in it, the tall men went away.

Soon, however, the flames rose so high as to singe the rope, and the corpse fell with a great thud upon the fire, scattering the ashes and embers, and extracting a howl of anguish from the miserable cook, who rushed to the door, and ran for his life.

He ran on until he was ready to drop with fatigue, when, seeing a drain overgrown with tall, rank grass, he thought he would creep in there and lie hidden till morning.

But he was not many minutes in the drain before he heard the heavy tramping again, and the four men came up with their burthen, which they laid down on the edge of the drain.

'I'm tired,' said one, to the giant; 'it's your turn to carry him a piece now.'

'Faix and troth, I'll no carry him,' replied he, 'but there's Pat Diver in the drain, why wouldn't he come out and tak' his turn?'

'Come out, Pat, come out,' roared all the men, and Pat, almost dead with fright, crept out.

He staggered on under the weight of the corpse until he reached Kiltown Abbey, a ruin festooned with ivy, where the brown owl hooted all night long, and the forgotten dead slept around the walls under dense, matted tangles of brambles and ben-weed.

No one ever buried there now, but Pat's tall companions turned into the wild graveyard, and began digging a grave.

Pat, seeing them thus engaged, thought he might once more try to escape, and climbed up into a hawthorn tree in the fence, hoping to be hidden in the boughs.

'I'm tired,' said the man who was digging the grave; 'here, take the spade,' addressing the big man, 'it's your turn.'

'Faix an' troth, it's no my turn,' replied he, as before. 'There's Pat Diver in the tree, why wouldn't he come down and tak' his turn?'

Pat came down to take the spade, but just then the cocks in the little farmyards and cabins round the abbey began to crow, and the men looked at one another.

'We must go,' said they, 'and well is it for you, Pat Diver, that the cocks crowed, for if they had not, you'd just ha' been bundled into that grave with the corpse.'

Two months passed, and Pat had wandered far and wide over the county Donegal, when he chanced to arrive at Raphoe during a fair.

Among the crowd that filled the Diamond he came suddenly on the big man.

'How are you, Pat Diver?' said he, bending down to look into the tinker's face.

'You've the advantage of me, sir, for I havna' the pleasure of knowing you,' faltered Pat.

'Do you not know me, Pat?' Whisper – 'When you go back to Innishowen, you'll have a story to tell!'

Jamie Freel and the Young Lady

LETITIA MACLINTOCK

Down in Fannet, in time gone by, lived Jamie Freel and his mother. Jamie was the widow's sole support; his strong arm worked for her untiringly, and as each Saturday night came round he poured his wages into her lap, thanking her dutifully for the halfpence which she returned him for tobacco.

He was extolled by his neighbours as the best son ever known or heard of. But he had neighbours of whose opinion he was ignorant – neighbours who lived pretty close to him, whom he had never seen, who are, indeed, rarely seen by mortals, except on May Eves and Halloweens.

An old ruined castle, about a quarter of a mile from his cabin, was said to be the abode of the 'wee folk'. Every Halloween were the ancient windows lighted up, and passers-by saw little figures flitting to and fro inside the building, while they heard the music of flutes and pipes.

It was well known that fairy revels took place; but nobody had the courage to intrude on them.

Jamie had often watched the little figures from a distance, and listened to the charming music, wondering what the inside of the castle was like; but one Halloween he got up, and took his cap, saying to his mother, 'I'm awa to the castle to seek my fortune.'

'What!' cried she. 'Would you venture there – you that's the widow's one son? Dinna be sae venturesome and foolitch, Jamie! They'll kill you, an' then what'll come o' me?'

'Never fear, mother; nae harm'll happen me, but I maun gae.'

He set out, and, as he crossed the potato field, came in sight of the castle, whose windows were ablaze with light that seemed to turn the russet leaves, still clinging to the crab tree branches, into gold.

Halting in the grove at one side of the ruin, he listened to the elfin revelry, and the laughter and singing made him all the more determined to proceed.

Numbers of little people, the largest about the size of a child of five years old, were dancing to the music of flutes and fiddles, while others drank and feasted.

'Welcome, Jamie Freel! welcome, welcome, Jamie!' cried the company, perceiving their visitor. The word 'Welcome' was caught up and repeated by every voice in the castle.

Time flew, and Jamie was enjoying himself very much, when his hosts said, 'We're going to ride to Dublin tonight to steal a young lady. Will you come too, Jamie Freel?'

'Ay, that I will,' cried the rash youth, thirsting for adventure.

A troop of horses stood at the door. Jamie mounted, and his steed rose with him into the air. He was presently flying over his mother's cottage, surrounded by the elfin troop, and on and on they went, over bold mountains, over little hills, over the deep Lough Swilley, over towns and cottages, where people were burning nuts and eating apples and keeping merry Halloween. It seemed to Jamie that they flew all round Ireland before they got to Dublin.

'This is Derry,' said the fairies, flying over the cathedral spire; and what was said by one voice was repeated by all the rest, till fifty little voices were crying out, 'Derry! Derry! Derry!'

In like manner was Jamie informed as they passed over each town on the route, and at length he heard the silvery voices cry, 'Dublin! Dublin!'

It was no mean dwelling that was to be honoured by the fairy visit, but one of the finest houses in Stephen's Green.

The troop dismounted near a window, and Jamie saw a beautiful face on a pillow in a splendid bed. He saw the young lady lifted and carried away, while the stick which was dropped in her place on the bed took her exact form.

The lady was placed before one rider and carried a short way, then given to another, and the names of the towns were cried out as before.

They were approaching home. Jamie heard 'Rathmullan', 'Milford', 'Tamney', and then he knew they were near his own house.

'You've all had your turn at carrying the young lady,' said he. 'Why wouldn't I get her for a wee piece?'

'Ay, Jamie,' replied they pleasantly, 'you may take your turn at carrying her, to be sure.'

Holding his prize very tightly he dropped down near his mother's door.

'Jamie Freel! Jamie Freel! is that the way you treat us?' cried they, and they, too, dropped down near the door.

Jamie held fast, though he knew not what he was holding, for the little folk turned the lady into all sorts of strange shapes. At one moment she was a black dog, barking and trying to bite; at another a glowing bar of iron, which yet had no heat; then again a sack of wool.

But still Jamie held her, and the baffled elves were turning away when a tiny woman, the smallest of the party, exclaimed, 'Jamie Freel has her awa frae us, but he sall nae hae gude of her, for I'll mak' her deaf and dumb,' and she threw something over the young girl.

While they rode off, disappointed, Jamie Freel lifted the latch and went in.

'Jamie, man!' cried his mother, 'you've been awa all night. What have they done to you?'

'Naething bad, mother; I hae the very best o' gude luck. Here's a beautiful young lady I hae brought you for company.'

'Bless us and save us!' exclaimed the mother; and for some minutes she was so astonished she could not think of anything else to say.

Jamie told the story of the night's adventure, ending by saying, 'Surely you wouldna have allowed me to let her gang with them to be lost for ever?'

'But a *lady*, Jamie! How can a lady eat we'er [our] poor diet and live in we're poor way? I ax you that, you foolitch fellow!'

'Well, mother, sure it's better for her to be here nor yonder,' said he pointed in the direction of the castle.

Meanwhile, the deaf and dumb girl shivered in her light clothing, stepping close to the humble turf fire.

'Poor crathur, she's quare and handsome! Nae wonder they set their hearts on her,' said the old woman, gazing at their guest with pity and admiration. 'We maun dress her first; but what in the name o' fortune, has I fit for the likes o' her to wear?'

She went to her press in 'the room' and took out her Sunday gown of brown drugget. She then opened a drawer and drew forth a pair of white stockings, a long snowy garment of fine linen, and a cap, her 'dead dress,' as she called it.

These articles of attire had long been ready for a certain triste ceremony, in which she would someday fill the chief part, and only saw the light occasionally when they were hung out to air; but she was willing to give even these to the fair trembling visitor, who was turning in dumb sorrow and wonder from her to Jamie, and from Jamie back to her.

The poor girl suffered herself to be dressed, and then sat down on a 'creepie' in the chimney corner and buried her face in her hands.

'What'll we do to keep us a lady like thou?' cried the old woman.

'I'll work for you both, mother,' replied the son.

'An' how could a lady live on we're poor diet?' she repeated.

'I'll work for her,' was all Jamie's answer.

He kept his word. The young lady was very sad for a long time, and tears stole down her cheeks many an evening, while the old woman spun by the fire and Jamie made salmon nets, an accomplishment acquired by him in hopes of adding to the comfort of his guest.

But she was always gentle, and tried to smile when she perceived them looking at her; and by degrees she adapted herself to their ways and mode of life. It was not very long before she began to feed the pig, mash potatoes and meal for the fowls, and knit blue worsted socks.

So a year passed and Halloween came round again. 'Mother,' said Jamie, taking down his cap, 'I'm off to the ould castle to seek my fortune.'

'Are you mad, Jamie?' cried his mother in terror; 'sure they'll kill you this time for what you done on them last year.'

Jamie made light of her fears and went his way.

As he reached the crab tree he saw bright lights in the castle windows as before, and heard loud talking. Creeping under the window he heard the wee folk say, 'That was a poor trick Jamie Freel played us this night last year, when he stole the nice young lady from us.'

'Ay,' said the tiny woman, 'an' I punished him for it, for there she sits a dumb image by the hearth, but he does na' know that three drops out o' this glass that I hold in my hand wad gie her her hearing and her speech back again.'

Jamie's heart beat fast as he entered the hall. Again he was greeted by a chorus of welcomes from the company – 'Here comes Jamie Freel! Welcome, welcome, Jamie!'

As soon as the tumult subsided the little woman said, 'You be to drink our health, Jamie, out o' this glass in my hand.'

Jamie snatched the glass from her and darted to the door. He never knew how he reached his cabin, but he arrived there breathless and sank on a stove by the fire.

'You're kilt, surely, this time, my poor boy,' said his mother.

'No, indeed, better luck than ever this time!' and he gave the lady three drops of the liquid that still remained at the bottom of the glass, notwithstanding his mad race over the potato field.

The lady began to speak, and her first words were words of thanks to Jamie.

The three inmates of the cabin had so much to say to one another that, long after cockcrow, when the fairy music had quite ceased, they were talking round the fire.

'Jamie,' said the lady, 'be pleased to get me paper and pen and ink that I may write to my father and tell him what has become of me.'

She wrote, but weeks passed and she received no answer. Again and again she wrote, and still no answer.

At length she said, 'You must come with me to Dublin, Jamie, to find my father.'

'I hae no money to hire a car for you,' he answered; 'an' how can you travel to Dublin on your foot?'

But she implored him so much that he consented to set out with her and walk all the way from Fannet to Dublin. It was not as easy as the fairy journey; but at last they rang the bell at the door of the house in Stephen's Green.

'Tell my father that his daughter is here,' said she to the servant who opened the door.

'The gentleman that lives here has no daughter, my girl. He had one, but she died better nor a year ago.'

'Do you not know me, Sullivan?'

'No, poor girl, I do not.'

'Let me see the gentleman. I only ask to see him.'

'Well, that's not much to ax. We'll see what can be done.'

In a few moments the lady's father came to the door.

'How care you call me your father?' cried the old gentleman angrily. 'You are an impostor. I have no daughter.'

'Look in my face, father, and surely you'll remember me.'

'My daughter is dead and buried. She died a long, long time ago.' The old gentleman's voice changed from anger to sorrow. 'You can go,' he concluded.

'Stop, dear father, till you look at this ring on my finger. Look at your name and mine engraved on it.'

'It certainly is my daughter's ring, but I do not know how you came by it. I fear in no honest way.'

'Call my mother – she will be sure to know me,' said the poor girl, who by this time was weeping bitterly.

'My poor wife is beginning to forget her sorrow. She seldom speaks of her daughter now. Why should I renew her grief by reminding her of her loss?'

But the young lady persevered till at last the mother was sent for.

'Mother,' she began, when the old lady came to the door, 'don't you know your daughter?'

'I have no daughter. My daughter died, and was buried a long, long time ago.'

'Only look in my face and surely you'll know me.'

The old lady shook her head.

'You have all forgotten me; but look at this mole on my neck. Surely, mother, you know me now?'

'Yes, yes,' said the mother, 'my Gracie had a mole on her neck like that; but then I saw her in her coffin, and saw the lid shut down upon her.'

It became Jamie's turn to speak, and he gave the history of the fairy journey, of the theft of the young lady, of the figure he had seen laid in its place, of her life with his mother in Fannet, of last Halloween, and of the three drops that had released her from her enchantments.

She took up the story when he paused and told how kind the mother and son had been to her.

The parents could not make enough of Jamie. They treated him with every distinction, and when he expressed his wish to return to Fannet, said they did not know what to do to express their gratitude.

But an awkward complication arose. The daughter would not let him go without her. 'If Jamie goes, I'll go, too,' she said. 'He saved me from the fairies, and has worked for me ever since. If it had not been for him, dear father and mother, you would never have seen me again. If he goes, I'll go, too.'

This being her resolution, the old gentleman said that Jamie should become his son-in-law. The mother was brought from Fannet in a coach-and-four, and there was a splendid wedding.

They all lived together in the grand Dublin house, and Jamie was heir to untold wealth at his father-in-law's death.

A Vision of Purgatory

WILLIAM MAGINN

The churchyard of Inistubber is as lonely a one as you would wish to see on a summer's day or avoid on a winter's night. It is situated in a narrow valley, at the bottom of three low, barren, miserable hills, on which there is nothing green to meet the eye – tree or shrub, grass or weed. The country beyond these hills is pleasant and smiling: rich fields of corn, fair clumps of oaks, sparkling streams of water, houses beautifully dotting the scenery, which gently undulates round and round as far as the eye can reach; but once across the north side of Inistubber Hill, and you look down upon desolation. There is nothing to see but, down in the hollow, the solitary churchyard with its broken wall, and the long lank grass growing over the gravestones, mocking with its melancholy verdure the barrenness of the rest of the landscape. It is a sad thing to reflect that the only green spot in the prospect springs from the grave!

Under the east window is a mouldering vault of the de Lacys, a branch of a family descended from one of the conquerors of Ireland; and there they are buried when the allotted time calls them to the tomb. On these occasions a numerous cavalcade, formed from the adjoining districts in all the pomp and circumstance of woe, is wont to fill the deserted churchyard, and the slumbering echoes are awakened to the voice of prayer and wailing, and charged with the sigh that marks the heart bursting with grief, or the laugh escaping from the bosom mirth-making under the cloak of mourning. Which of these feelings was predominant when Sir Theodore de Lacy died is not written in history; nor is it necessary to enquire. He had lived a jolly, thoughtless life, rising early for the hunt, and retiring late from the bottle; a good-humoured bachelor who took no care about the management of his household, provided that the hounds were in order for his going out, and the table ready on his coming in; as for the rest, an easy landlord, a quiet master, a lenient magistrate (except to poachers), and a very excellent foreman of a grand jury. He died one evening while laughing at a story which he had heard regularly thrice a week for the last fifteen years of his life; and his spirit mingled with the claret.

In former times, when the De Lacys were buried, there was a grand breakfast, and all the party rode over to the church to see the last rites paid. The keeners lamented; the country people had a wake before the funeral and a dinner after it – and there was an end. But with the march of mind came trouble and vexation. A man has nowadays no certainty of quietness in his coffin – unless it be a patent one. He is laid down in the grave and, the next morning, finds himself called up to demonstrate and interesting fact! No one, I believe, admires this ceremony; and it is not to be wondered at that Sir Theodore de Lacy held it in especial horror. 'I'd like,' he said one evening, 'to catch one of the thieves coming after me when I'm dead. By the God of War, I'd break every bone in his body! But,' he added with a sigh, 'as I suppose I'll not be able to take my own part then, upon you I leave it, Larry Sweeney, to watch me three days and three nights after they plant me under the sod. There's Doctor Dickenson there – I see the fellow looking at me. Fill your glass, doctor: here's your health! And shoot him, Larry (do you hear?), shoot the doctor like a cock if he ever comes stirring up my poor old bones from their roost of Inistubber.'

'Why, then,' Larry answered, accepting the glass which followed this command, 'long life to both your honours; and it's that I would like to be putting a bullet into Dr Dickenson – Heaven between him and harm! – for wanting your honour away, as if you was a horse's head, to a bonfire. There's nothing, I 'shure you, gintlemin, poor as I am, that would give me greater pleasure.'

'We feel obliged, Larry,' said Sir Theodore, 'for your good wishes.'

'Is it I pull you out of the grave, indeed?' continued the whipper-in (for such he was); 'I'd let nobody pull your honour out of any place, saving 'twas Purgatory; and out of that I'd pull you myself, if I saw you going *there*.'

'I am of opinion, Larry,' said Dr Dickenson, 'you'd turn tail if you saw Sir Theodore on that road. You might go farther and fare worse, you know.'

'Turn tail!' replied Larry. 'It's I that wouldn't – I appale to St Patrick himself over beyond' – pointing to a picture of the Prime Saint of Ireland which hung in gilt daubery behind his master's chair, right opposite to him.

To Larry's horror and astonishment the picture, fixing its eyes upon him, winked with the most knowing air, as if acknowledging the appeal.

'What makes you turn so white, then, at the very thought?' said the doctor, interpreting the visible consternation on our hero in his own way.

'Noting particular,' answered Larry; 'but a wakeness has come strong over me, gintlemin; and, if you have no objection, I'd like to go into the air for a bit.'

Leave was of course granted, and Larry retired amid the laughter of the guests; but, as he retreated, he could not avoid casting a glance on the awful picture; and again the saint winked, with a most malicious smile. It was impossible to endure the repeated infliction, and Larry rushed down the stairs in an agony of fright and amazement.

'Maybe,' thought he, 'it might be my own eyes that wasn't quite steady – or the flame of the candle. But no! He winked at me as plain as ever I winked at Judy Donaghue of a May morning. What he manes by it I can't say; but there's no use of thinking about it; no, nor of talking neither, for who'd believe me if I tould them of it?'

The next evening Sir Theodore died, as has been mentioned, and in due time thereafter was buried, according to the custom of the family, by torchlight in the churchyard of Inistubber. All was fitly performed; and although Dickenson had no design upon the jovial knight – and, if he had not, there was nobody within fifteen miles that could be suspected of such an outrage – yet Larry Sweeney was determined to make good his promise of watching his master. 'I'd think little of telling a lie to him, by the way of no harm, when he was alive,' said he, wiping his eyes as soon as the last of the train had departed, leaving him with a single companion in the lonely cemetery; 'but now that he's dead – God rest his soul! – I'd scorn it. So Jack Kinaley, as behoves my first cousin's son, stay you with me here this blessed night, for betune you and I it ain't lucky to stay by one's self in this ruinated old rookery, where ghosts (God help us!) is as thick as bottles in Sir Theodore's cellar.'

'Never you mind that, Larry,' said Kinaley, a discharged soldier who had been through all the campaigns of the Peninsula: 'never mind, I say, such botherations. Hain't I lain in bivouack on the field at Salamanca, and Tallawora, and the Pyrumnees, and many another place beside, when there was dead corpses lying about in piles, and there was no more ghosts than knee buckles in a ridgemint of High-landers. Here! Let me prime them pieces, and hand us over the bottle. We'll stay snug under this east window, for the wind's coming down the hill and I defy – '

'None of that bould talk, Jack,' said his cousin. 'As for what ye saw in foreign parts, of dead men killed a-fighting, sure that's nothing to the dead – God rest 'em! – that's here. There, you see, they had company, one with the other, and, being killed fresh-like that morning, had no heart to stir; but here, faith! 'tis a horse of another colour.'

'Maybe it is,' said Jack; 'but the night's coming on; so I'll turn in. Wake me if you see anything; and, after I've got my two hours' rest, I'll relieve you.'

With these words the soldier turned on his side under shelter of a grave, and, as his libations had been rather copious during the day, it was not long before he gave audible testimony that the dread of supernatural visitants had had no effect in disturbing the event current of his fancy.

Although Larry had not opposed the proposition of his kinsman, yet he felt by no means at ease. He put in practice all the usually recommended nostrums for keeping away unpleasant thoughts. He whistled; but the echo sounded so sad and dismal that he did not venture to repeat the experiment. He sang; but, when no more than five notes had passed his lips, he found it impossible to get out a sixth, for the chorus reverberated from the ruinous walls was destruction to all earthly harmony. He cleared his throat; he hummed, he stamped; he endeavoured to walk. All would not do. He wished sincerely that Sir Theodore had gone to Heaven – he dared not suggest even to himself, just then, the existence of any other region – without leaving on him the perilous task of guarding his mortal remains in so desperate a place. Flesh and blood could hardly resist it! Even the preternatural snoring of Jack Kinaley added to the horrors of his position; and, if his application to the spirituous soother of grief beside him was frequent, it is more to be deplored on the score of morality than wondered at on the score of meta-physics. He who censures our hero too severely has never watched the body of a dead baronet in the churchyard of Inistubber at mid-night. 'If it was a common, decent, quite, well-behaved churchyard a'self,' thought Larry half aloud, 'but when 'tis a place like this forsaken ould berrin' ground, which is noted for villainy – '

'For what, Larry?' enquired a gentleman stepping out of a niche which contained the only statue time had spared. It was the figure of St Colman, to whom the church was dedicated. Larry had been looking at the figure as it shone forth in ebon and ivory in the light and shadow of the now high-careering moon.

'For what, Larry?' said the gentleman; 'for what do you say the church is noted?'

'For nothing at all, please your honour,' replied Larry, 'except the height of gentility.'

The stranger was about four feet high, dressed in what might be called glowing garments if, in spite of their form, their rigidity did not deprive them of all claim to such an appellation. He wore an antique mitre upon his head; his hands were folded upon his breast; and over his right shoulder rested a pastoral crook. There was a solemn expression in his countenance, and his eye might truly be called stony. His beard could not well be said to wave upon his bosom; but it lay upon it in ample profusion, stiffer than that of a Jew on a frosty morning after mist. In short, as Larry soon discovered to his horror on looking up at the niche, it was no other than St Colman himself, who had stepped forth indignant, in all probability, at the stigma cast by the watcher of the dead on the churchyard of which his saintship was patron.

He smiled with a grisly solemnity – just such a smile as you might imagine would play round the lips of a milestone (if it had any) – at the recantation so quickly volunteered by Larry. 'Well,' said he, 'Lawrence Sweeney – '

'How well the old rogue,' thought Larry, 'knows my name!'

'Since you profess yourself such an admirer of the merits of the churchyard of Inistubber, get up and follow me, till I show you the civilities of the place, for I'm master here, and must do the honours.'

'Willingly would I go with your worship,' replied our friend; 'but you see here I am engaged to Sir Theodore, who, though a good master, was a mighty passionate man when everything was not done as he ordered it, and I am feared to stir.'

'Sir Theodore,' said the saint, 'will not blame you for following me. I assure you he will not.'

'But then – ' said Larry.

'Follow me!' cried the saint in a hollow voice; and, casting upon him his stony eye, drew poor Larry after him, as the bridal guest was drawn by the lapidary glance of the Ancient Mariner, or, as Larry himself afterwards expressed it, 'as a jaw-tooth is wrinched out of an ould woman with a pair of pincers.'

The saint strode before him in silence, not in the least incommoded by the stones and rubbish which at every step sadly contributed to the discomfiture of Larry's shins, who followed his marble conductor into a low vault situated at the west end of the church. In accomplishing this, poor Larry contrived to bestow upon his head an additional organ, the utility of which he was not craniologist enough to discover.

The path lay through coffins piled up on each side of the way in various degrees of decomposition; and excepting that the solid footsteps of the saintly guide, as they smote heavily on the floor of stone, broke the deadly silence, all was still. Stumbling and staggering along, directed only by the casual glimpse of light afforded by the moon where it broke through the dilapidated roof of the vault and served to discover only sights of woe, Larry followed. He soon felt that he was descending, and could not help wondering at the length of the journey. He began to entertain the most unpleasant suspicions as to the character of his conductor; but what could he do? Flight was out of the question, and to think of resistance was absurd. 'Needs must, they say,' thought he to himself, 'when the Devil drives. I see it's much the same when a saint leads.'

At last the dolorous march had an end; and, not a little to Larry's amazement, he found that his guide had brought him to the gate of a lofty hall before which a silver lamp, filled with naphtha, 'yielded light as from a sky.' From within loud sounds of merriment were ringing; and it was evident, from the jocular harmony and the tinkling of glasses, that some subterranean catch-club was not idly employed over the bottle.

'Who's there?' said a porter, roughly responding to the knock of St Colman.

'Be so good,' said the saint mildly, 'my very good fellow, as to open the door without further questions, or I'll break your head. I'm bringing a gentleman here on a visit, whose business is pressing.'

'Maybe so,' thought Larry; 'but what that business may be is more than I can tell.'

The porter sulkily complied with the order, after having apparently communicated the intelligence that a stranger was at hand; for a deep silence immediately followed the tipsy clamour, and Larry, sticking close to his guide, whom he now looked upon almost as a

friend when compared with these underground revellers to whom
he was about to be introduced, followed him through a spacious
vestibule, which gradually sloped into a low-arched room where the
company was assembled.

And a strange-looking company it was. Seated round a long table
were three and twenty grave and venerable personages, bearded,
mitred, stoled and croziered – all living statues of stone, like the
saint who had walked out of his niche. On the drapery before them
were figured the images of the sun, moon and stars – the inexplicable
bear – the mystic temple built by the hand of Hiram – and other
symbols of which the uninitiated know nothing. The square, the
line, the trowel were not wanting, and the hammer was lying in
front of the chair. Labour, however, was over, and, the time for
refreshment having arrived, each of the stony brotherhood had a
flagon before him; and when we mention that the saints were Irish,
and that St Patrick in person was in the chair, it is not to be
wondered at that the mitres, in some instances, hung rather loosely
on the side of the heads of some of the canonised compotators.
Among the company were found St Senanus of Limerick, St Declan
of Ardmore, St Canice of Kilkenny, St Finbar of Cork, St Michan of
Dublin, St Brandon of Kerry, St Fachnan of Ross, and others of that
holy brotherhood. A vacant place, which completed the four-and-
twentieth, was kept for St Colman, who, as everybody knows, is of
Cloyne; and he, having taken his seat, addressed the President to
inform him that he had brought the man.

The man (Larry himself) was awestruck with the company in
which he so unexpectedly found himself, and trembled all over when,
on the notice of his guide, the eight-and-forty eyes of stone were
turned directly upon himself.

'You have just nicked the night to a shaving, Larry,' said St Patrick.
'This is our chapter night, and myself and brethren are here
assembled on merry occasion! – You know who I am?'

'God bless you riverince!' said Larry, it's I that do well. Often did
I see your picture hanging over the door of places where it is' –
lowering his voice – 'pleasanter to be than here, buried under an
ould church.'

'You may as well say it out, Larry,' said St Patrick. 'And don't
think I'm going to be angry with you about it, for I was once flesh
and blood myself. But you remember the other night saying that
you would think nothing of pulling your master out of Purgatory if

you could get at him there, and appealing to me to stand by your words.'

'Y–e–e–s,' said Larry most mournfully, for he recollected the significant look he had received from the picture.

'And,' continued St Patrick, 'you remember also that I gave you a wink, which, you know, is as good any day as a nod – at least, to a blink horse.'

'I'm sure your Riverince,' said Larry with a beating heart, 'is too much of a gintleman to hold a poor man hard to every word he may say of an evening; and therefore – '

'I was thinking so,' said the saint. 'I guessed you'd prove a poltroon when put to the push. What do you think, my brethren, I should do to this fellow?'

A hollow sound burst from the bosoms of the unanimous assembly. The verdict was short but decisive: 'Knock out his brains!'

And, in order to suit the action to the word, the whole four-and-twenty rose at once, and, with their immovable eyes fixed firmly on the face of our hero – who, horror-struck with the sight as he was, could not close his – they began to glide slowly but regularly towards him, bending their line into the form of a crescent so as to environ him on all sides. In vain he fled to the door; its massive folds resisted mortal might. In vain he cast his eyes around in quest of a loophole of retreat – there was none. Closer and closer pressed on the slowly-moving phalanx, and the uplifted croziers threatened soon to put their sentence into execution. Supplication was all that remained – and Larry sank upon his knees.

'Ah then!' said he, 'gintlemin and ancient ould saints as you are, don't kill the father of a large small family who never did hurt to you or yours. Sure, if 'tis your will that I should go to – no matter who, for there's no use in naming his name – might I not as well make up my mind to go there alive and well, stout and hearty, and able to face him, as with my head knocked into bits, as if I had been after a fair or a patthren?'

'You say right,' said St Patrick, checking with a motion of his crozier the advancing assailants, who thereupon returned to their seats. 'I'm glad to see you coming to reason. Prepare for your journey.'

'And how, please your saintship, am I to go?' asked Larry.

'Why,' said St Patrick, 'as Colman here has guided you so far, he may guide you further. But as the journey is into foreign parts, where you aren't likely to be known, you had better take this letter of introduction, which may be of use to you.'

'And here, also Lawrence,' said a Dublin saint (perhaps Michan), 'take you this box also, and make use of it as he to whom you speak shall suggest.'

'Take a hold, and a firm one,' said St Colma, 'Lawrence, of my cassock, and we'll start.'

'All right behind?' cried St Patrick.

'All right!' was the reply.

In an instant vault, table, saints, bell, church faded into air; a rustling hiss of wings was all that was heard, and Larry felt his cheek swept by a current, as if a covey of birds of enormous size were passing him. [It was in all probability the flight of the saints returning to Heaven; but on that point nothing certain has reached us up to the present time of writing.] He had not a long time to wonder at the phenomenon, for he himself soon began to soar, dangling in mid-sky to the skirt of the cassock of his sainted guide. Earth, and all that appertains thereto, speedily passed from his eyes, and they were alone in the midst of circumfused ether, glowing with a sunless light. Above, in immense distance, was fixed the firmament, fastened up with bright stars, fencing around the world with its azure wall. They fled far before any distinguishable object met their eyes. At length a long white streak, shining like silver in the moonbeam, was visible to their sight.

'That,' said St Colman, 'is the Limbo which adjoins the earth, and is the highway for ghosts departing the world. It is called in Milton, a book which I suppose, Larry, you never have read – '

'And how could I, please your worship,' said Larry, 'seein' I don't know a B from a bull's foot?'

'Well, it is called in Milton the 'Paradise of Fools'; and, if it were indeed peopled by all of that tribe who leave the world, it would contain the best company that ever figured on the earth. To the north you see a bright speck?'

'I do.'

'That marks the upward path – narrow and hard to find. To the south you may see a darksome road – broad, smooth, and easy of descent. That is the lower way. It is thronged with the great ones of the world; you may see their figures in the gloom. Those who are soaring upwards are wrapped in the flood of light flowing perpetually from that single spot, and you cannot see them. The silver path on which we enter is the Limbo. Here I part with you. You are to give your letter to the first person you meet. Do your best; be courageous, but observe particularly that you profane no holy name, or I will not answer for the consequences.'

His guide had scarcely vanished when Larry heard the tinkling of a bell in the distance; and, turning his eyes in the quarter whence it proceeded, he saw a grave-looking man in black, with eyes of fire, driving before him a host of ghosts with a switch, as you see turkeys driven on the western road at the approach of Christmas. They were on the highway to Purgatory.

The ghosts were shivering in the thin air, which pinched them severely now that they had lost the covering of their bodies. Among the group Larry recognised his old mastser, by the same means that Ulysses, Aeneas, and others recognised the bodiless forms of their friends in the regions of Acheron.

'What brings a living person,' said the man in black, 'on this pathway? I shall make legal capture of you, Larry Sweeney, for trespassing. You have no business here.'

'I have come,' said Larry, plucking up courage, 'to bring your honour's glory a letter from a company of gintlemin with whom I had the pleasure of spending the evening underneath the ould church of Inistubber.'

'A letter?' said the man in black. 'Where is it?'

'Here, my lord,' said Larry.

'Ho!' cried the black gentleman on opening it; 'I know the hand-writing. It won't do, however, my lad; – I see they want to throw dust in my eyes.'

'Whew!' thought Larry. 'That's the very thing. 'Tis for that the ould Dublin boy gave me the box. I'd lay a tenpenny to a brass farthing that it's filled with Lundyfoot.'

Opening the box, therefore, he flung its contents right into the fiery eyes of the man in black, while he was still occupied in reading the letter; – and the experiment was successful.

'Curses! Tche – tche – tche – Curses on it!' exclaimed he, clapping his hands before he eyes, and sneezing most lustily.

'Run, you villains, run,' cried Larry to the ghosts; 'run, you villains, now that his eyes are off you. O master, master! Sir Theodore, jewel! Run to the right-hand side, make for the bright speck, and God give you luck!'

He had forgotten his injunction. The moment the word was

uttered he felt the silvery ground sliding from under him; and with the swiftness of thought he found himself on the flat of his back, under the very niche of the old church wall whence he had started, dizzy and confused with the measureless tumble. The emancipated ghosts floated in all directions, emitting their shrill and stridulous cries in the gleaming expanse. Some were again gathered by their old conductor; some, scudding about at random, took the right-hand path, others the left. Into which of them Sir Theodore struck is not recorded; but, as he had heard the direction, let us hope he made the proper choice.

Larry had not much time given him to recover from his fall, for almost in an instant he heard an angry snorting rapidly approaching; and, looking up, whom should he see but the gentleman in black, with eyes gleaming more furiously than ever, and his horns (for in his haste he had let his hat fall) relieved in strong shadow against the moon? Up started Larry; – away ran his pursuer after him. The safest refuge was, of course, the church. Thither ran our hero,

> As darts the dolphin from the shark,
>
> Or the deer before the hounds;

and after him – fiercer than the shark, swifter than the hounds – fled the black gentleman. The church is cleared, the chancel entered; and the hot breath of his pursuer glows upon the outstretched neck of Larry. Escape is impossible, the extended talons of the fiend have clutched him by the hair.

'You are mine!' cried the demon. 'If I have lost any of my flock, I have at least got you!'

'O St Patrick!' exclaimed our hero in horror. 'O St Patrick, have mercy upon me, and save me!'

'I tell you what, Cousin Larry,' said Kinaley, chucking him up from behind a gravestone where he had fallen; 'all the St Patricks that ever were born would not have saved you from ould Tom Picton if he caught you sleeping on your post as I've caught you now. By the world of an ould soldier he'd have had the provost-marshal upon you, and I'd not give twopence for the loan of your life. And then, too, I see you have drunk every drop in the bottle. What can you say for yourself?'

'Nothing at all,' said Larry, scratching his head, 'but it was an unlucky dream, and I'm glad it's over.'

A Play-House in the Waste

GEORGE MOORE

'It's a closed mouth that can hold a good story,' as the saying goes, and very soon it got about that Father MacTurnan had written to Rome saying he was willing to take a wife to his bosom for patriotic reasons, if the Pope would relieve him of his vow of celibacy. And many phrases and words from his letter (translated by whom – by the Bishop or Father Meehan? – nobody ever knew) were related over the Dublin firesides, till at last out of the talk a tall gaunt man emerged, in an old overcoat, green from weather and wear, the tails of it flapping as he rode his bicycle through the great waste bog that lies between Belmullet and Crossmolina. His name! We liked it. It appealed to our imagination. MacTurnan! It conveyed something from afar like Hamlet or Don Quixote. He seemed as near and as far from us as they, till Pat Comer, one of the organisers of the IAOS, came in and said, after listening to the talk that was going round: 'Is it of the priest that rides in the great Mayo bog you are speaking? If it is, you haven't got the story rightly.'

As he told us the story, so it is printed in this book. And we sat wondering greatly, for we seemed to see a soul on its way to heaven. But round a fire there is always one who cannot get off the subject of women and blasphemy – a papist generally he is; and it was Quinn that evening who kept plaguing us with jokes, whether it would be a fat girl or a thin that the priest would choose if the Pope gave him leave to marry, until at last, losing all patience with him, I bade him be silent, and asked Pat Comer to tell us if the Priest was meditating a new plan for Ireland's salvation.

'For a mind like his,' I said, 'would not stand still and problems such as ours waiting to be solved.'

'You're wrong there! He thinks no more of Ireland, and neither reads nor plans, but knits stockings ever since the wind took his playhouse away.'

'Took his playhouse away!' said several.

'And why would he be building a playhouse,' somebody asked, 'and he living in a waste?'

'A queer idea, surely!' said another. 'A playhouse in the waste!'

'Yes, a queer idea,' said Pat, 'but a true one all the same, for I have seen it with my own eyes – or the ruins of it – and not later back than three weeks ago, when I was staying with the priest himself. You know the road, all of you – how it straggles from Foxford through the bog alongside of bog holes deep enough to drown one, and into which the jarvey and myself seemed in great likelihood of pitching, for the car went down into great ruts, and the horse was shying from one side of the road to the other, and at nothing so far as we could see.'

'There's nothing to be afeared of, yer honour; only once was he near leaving the road, the day before Christmas, and I driving the doctor. It was here he saw it – a white thing gliding – and the wheel of the car must have gone within an inch of the bog hole.'

'And the doctor. Did he see it?' I said.

'He saw it too, and so scared was he that the hair rose up and went through his cap.'

'Did the jarvey laugh when he said that?' we asked Pat Comer; and Pat answered: 'Not he! Them fellows just speak as the words come to them without thinking. Let me get on with my story. We drove on for about a mile, and it was to stop him from clicking his tongue at the horse that I asked him if the bog was Father MacTurnan's parish.' 'Every mile of it, sir,' he said, 'every mile of it, and we do be seeing him buttoned up in his old coat riding along the roads on his bicycle going to sick calls.'

'Do you often be coming this road?' says I.

'Not very often, sir. No one lives here except the poor people, and the priest and the doctor. Faith! there isn't a poorer parish in Ireland, and everyone of them would have been dead long ago if it had not been for Father James.'

'And how does he help them?'

'Isn't he always writing letters to the Government asking for relief works? Do you see those bits of roads?'

'Where do those roads lead to?'

'Nowhere. Them roads stops in the middle of the bog when the money is out.'

'But,' I said, 'surely it would be better if the money were spent upon permanent improvements – on drainage, for instance.'

The jarvey didn't answer; he called to his horse, and not being able to stand the clicking of his tongue, I kept on about the drainage.

'There's no fall, sir.'

'And the bog is too big,' I added, in hope of encouraging conversation.

'Faith it is, sir.'

'But we aren't very far from the sea, are we?'

'About a couple of miles.'

'Well then,' I said, 'couldn't a harbour be made?'

'They were thinking about that, but there's no depth of water, and everyone's against emigration now.'

'Ah! the harbour would encourage emigration.'

'So it would, your honour.'

'But is there no talk about home industries, weaving, lacemaking?'

'I won't say that.'

'But has it been tried?'

'The candle do be burning in the priest's window till one in the morning, and he sitting up thinking of plans to keep the people at home. Now, do ye see that house, sir, fornint my whip at the top of the hill? Well, that's the playhouse he built.'

'A playhouse?'

'Yes, yer honour. Father James hoped the people might come from Dublin to see it, for no play like it had ever been acted in Ireland before, sir!'

'And was the play performed?'

'No, yer honour. The priest had been learning them all the summer, but the autumn was on them before they had got it by rote, and a wind came and blew down one of the walls.'

'And couldn't Father MacTurnan get the money to build it up?'

'Sure, he might have got the money, but where'd be the use when there was no luck in it?'

'And who were to act the play?'

'The girls and the boys in the parish, and the prettiest girl in all the parish was to play Good Deeds.'

'So it was a miracle play,' I said.

'Do you see that man? It's the priest coming out of Tom Burke's cabin, and I warrant he do be bringing him the Sacrament, and he having the holy oils with him, for Tom won't pass the day; we had the worst news of him last night.'

'And I can tell you,' said Pat Comer, dropping his story for a moment and looking round the circle, 'it was a sad story the jarvey told me. He told it well, for I can see the one-roomed hovel full or peat smoke, the black iron pot with traces of the yellow stirabout in it on the hearth, and the sick man on the pallet bed, and the priest by his side mumbling prayers together. Faith! these jarveys can tell a story—none better.'

'As well as yourself, Pat,' one of us said. And Pat began to tell of the miles of bog on either side of the straggling road, of the hilltop to the left, with the playhouse showing against the dark and changing clouds; of a woman in a red petticoat, a handkerchief tied round her head, who had flung down her spade the moment she caught sight of the car, of the man who appeared on the brow and blew a horn. 'For she mistook us for bailiffs,' said Pat, 'and two little sheep hardly bigger than geese were driven away.'

'A playhouse in the waste for these people,' I was saying to myself all the time, till my meditations were interrupted by the jarvey telling that the rocky river we crossed was called the Greyhound – a not inappropriate name, for it ran swiftly . . . Away down the long road a white cottage appeared, and the jarvey said to me, 'That is the priest's house.' It stood on the hillside some little way from the road, and all the way to the door I wondered how his days passed in the great loneliness of the bog.

'His reverence isn't at home, yer honour – he's gone to attend a sick call.'

'Yes, I know – Tom Burke.'

'And is Tom better, Mike?'

'The devil a bether he'll be this side of Jordan,' the jarvey answered, and the housekeeper showed me into the priest's parlour. It was lined with books, and I looked forward to a pleasant chat when we had finished our business. At that time I was on a relief committee, and the people were starving in the poor parts of the country.

'I think he'll be back in about an hour's time, yer honour.' But the priest seemed to be detained longer than his housekeeper expected, and the moaning of the wind round the cottage reminded me of the small white thing the horse and the doctor had seen gliding along the road. 'The priest knows the story – he will tell me,' I said, and piled more turf on the fire – fine sods of hard black turf they were, and well do I remember seeing them melting away. But all of a sudden my eyes closed. I couldn't have been asleep more than a few minutes when it seemed to me a great crowd of men and women had gathered about the house, and a moment after the door was flung open, and a tall, gaunt man faced me.

'I've just come,' he said, 'from a deathbed, and they that have followed me aren't far from death if we don't succeed in getting help.' I don't know how I can tell you of the crowd I saw round the house that day. We are accustomed to see poor people in towns cowering under arches, but it is more pitiful to see people starving in the fields on the mountain side. I don't know why it should be so, but it is. But I call to mind two men in ragged trousers and shirts as ragged, with brown beards on faces yellow with famine; and the words of one of them are not easily forgotten: 'The white sun of Heaven doesn't shine upon two poorer men than upon this man and myself.' I can tell you I didn't envy the priest his job, living all his life in the waste listening to tales of starvation, looking into famished faces. There were some women among them, kept back by the men, who wanted to get their word in first. They seemed to like to talk about their misery . . . and I said: 'They are tired of seeing each other. I am a spectacle, a show, an amusement for them. I don't know if you can catch my meaning?'

'I think I do,' Father James answered. And I asked him to come for a walk up the hill and show me the playhouse.

Again he hesitated, and I said: 'You must come, Father MacTurnan, for a walk. You must forget the misfortunes of those people for a while.' He yielded, and we spoke of the excellence of the road under our feet, and he told me that when he conceived the idea of a playhouse, he had already succeeded in persuading the inspector to agree that the road they were making should go to the top of the hill. 'The policy of the Government,' he said, 'from the first was that relief works should benefit nobody except the workers, and it is sometimes very difficult to think out a project for work that will be perfectly useless. Arches have been built on the top of hills, and roads that lead nowhere. A strange sight to the stranger a road must be that stops suddenly in the middle of a bog. One wonders at first how a Government could be so foolish, but when one thinks of it, it is easy to understand that the Government doesn't wish to spend money on works that will benefit a class. But the road that leads nowhere is difficult to make, even though starving men are employed upon it; for a man to work well there must be an end in view, and I can tell you it is difficult to bring even starving men to engage on a road that leads nowhere. If I'd told everything I am telling you to the inspector, he wouldn't have agreed to let the road run to the top of the hill; but I said to him: 'The road leads nowhere; as well let it end at the top of the hill as down in the valley.' So I got the money for my road and some money for my playhouse, for of course the playhouse was as useless as the road; a playhouse in the waste can neither interest of benefit anybody! But there was an idea at the back of my mind all the time that when the road and the playhouse were finished, I might be able to induce the Government to build a harbour?'

'But the harbour would be of use.'

'Of very little,' he answered. 'For the harbour to be of use a great deal for dredging would have to be done.'

'And the Government needn't undertake the dredging. How very ingenious! I suppose you often come here to read your breviary?'

'During the building of the playhouse I often used to be up here, and during the rehearsals I was here every day.'

'If there was a rehearsal,' I said to myself, 'there must have been a play.' And I affected interest in the grey shallow sea and the erosion of the low-lying land – a salt marsh filled with pools.

'I thought once,' said the priest, 'that if the play were a great success, a line of flat-bottomed steamers might be built.'

'Sitting here in the quiet evenings,' I said to myself, 'reading his breviary, dreaming of a line of steamships crowded with visitors! He has been reading about the Oberammergau performances.' So that was his game – the road, the playhouse, the harbour – and I agreed with him that no one would have dared to predict that visitors would have come from all sides of Europe to see a few peasants performing a miracle play in the Tyrol.

'Come,' I said, 'into the playhouse and let me see how you built it.'

Half a wall and some of the roof had fallen, and the rubble had not been cleared away, and I said: 'It will cost many pounds to repair the damage, but having gone so far you should give the play a chance.'

'I don't think it would be advisable,' he muttered, half to himself, half to me.

As you may well imagine, I was anxious to hear if he had discovered any aptitude for acting among the girls and the boys who lived in the cabins.

'I think' he answered me, 'that the play would have been fairly acted; I think that, with a little practice, we might have done as well as they did at Oberammergau.'

An odd man, more willing to discuss the play that he had chosen than the talents of those who were going to perform it, and he told me that it had been written in the fourteenth century in Latin, and that he had translated it into Irish.

I asked him if it would have been possible to organise an excursion from Dublin – 'Oberammergau in the West.'

'I used to think so. But it is eight miles from Rathowen, and the road is a bad one, and when they got here there would be no place for them to stay; they would have to go all the way back again, and that would be sixteen miles.'

'Yet you did well, Father James, to build the playhouse, for the people could work better while they thought they were accomplishing something. Let me start a subscription for you in Dublin.'

'I don't think that it would be possible – '

'Not for me to get fifty pounds?'

'You might get the money, but I don't think we could ever get a performance of the play.'

'And why not?' I said.

'You see, the wind came and blew down the wall. The people are very pious; I think they felt that the time they spent rehearsing might have been better spent. The playhouse disturbed them in their ideas. They hear Mass on Sundays, and there are the Sacraments, and they remember they have to die. It used to seem to me a very sad thing to see all the people going to America; the poor Celt disappearing in America, leaving his own country, leaving his language, and very often his religion.'

'And does it no longer seem to you sad that such a thing should happen?'

'No, not if it is the will of God. God has specially chosen the Irish race to convert the world. No race has provided so many missionaries, no race has preached the Gospel more frequently to the heathen; and once we realise that we have to die, and very soon, and that the Catholic Church is the only true Church, our ideas about race and nationality fade from us. We are here, not to make life successful and triumphant, but to gain heaven. That is the truth, and it is to the honour of the Irish people that they have been selected by God to preach the truth, even though they lose their nationality in preaching it. I do not except you to accept these opinions. I know that you think very differently, but living here I have learned to acquiesce in the will of God.'

He stopped speaking suddenly, like one ashamed of having expressed himself too openly, and soon after we were met by a number of peasants, and the priest's attention was engaged; the inspector of the relief works had to speak to him; and I didn't see him again until dinner-time.

'You have given them hope,' he said.

This was gratifying to hear, and the priest sat listening while I told him of the looms already established in different parts of the country. We talked about half an hour, and then, like one who suddenly remembers, the priest got up and fetched his knitting.

'Do you knit every evening?'

'I have got into the way of knitting lately – it passes the time.'

'But do you never read?' I asked, and my eyes went towards the bookshelves.

'I used to read a great deal. But there wasn't a woman in the parish that could turn a heel properly, so I had to learn to knit.'

'Do you like knitting better than reading?' I asked, feeling ashamed of my curiosity.

'I have constantly to attend sick calls, and if one is absorbed in a book one doesn't like to put it aside.'

'I see you have two volumes of miracle plays!'

'Yes, and that's another danger: a book begets all kinds of ideas and notions into one's head. The idea of that playhouse came out of those books.'

'But,' I said, 'you don't think that God sent the storm because He didn't wish a play to be performed?'

'One cannot judge God's designs. Whether God sent the storm or whether it was accident must remain a matter for conjecture; but it is not a matter of conjecture that one is doing certain good by devoting oneself to one's daily task, getting the Government to start new relief works, establishing schools for weaving. The people are entirely dependent upon me, and when I'm attending to their wants I know I'm doing right'.

The playhouse interested me more than the priest's ideas of right and wrong, and I tried to get him back to get him back to it; but the subject seemed a painful one, and I said to myself: 'The jarvey will tell me all about it tomorrow. I can rely on him to fin out the whole story from the housekeeper in the kitchen.' And sure enough, we hadn't got to the Greyhound River before he was leaning across the well of the car talking to me and asking if the priest was thinking of putting up the wall of the playhouse.

'The wall of the playhouse?' I said.

'Yes, yer honour. Didn't I see both of you going up the hill in the evening time?'

'I don't think we shall ever see a play in the playhouse.'

'Why would we, since it was God that sent the wind that blew it down?'

'How do you know it was God that sent the wind? It might have been the devil himself, or somebody's curse.'

'Sure it is of Mrs Sheridan you do be thinking, yer honour, and of her daughter – she that was to be playing Good Deeds in the play, yer honour; and wasn't she wake coming home from the learning of the play? And when the signs of her wakeness began to show, the widow Sheridan took a halter off the cow and tied Margaret to the wall, and she was in the stable till the child was born. Then didn't her mother take a bit of string and tie it round the child's throat, and bury it near the playhouse; and it was three nights after that the storm rose, and the child pulled the thatch out of the roof.'

'But did she murder the child?'

'Sorra wan of me knows. She sent for the priest when she was dying, and told him what she had done.'

'But the priest wouldn't tell what he heard in the confessional,' I said.

'Mrs Sheridan didn't die that night; not till the end of the week, and the neighbours heard her talking of the child she had buried, and then they all knew what the white thing was they had seen by the roadside. The night the priest left her he saw the white thing standing in front of him, and if he hadn't been a priest he'd have dropped down dead; so he took some water from the bog hole and dashed it over it, saying, "I baptise thee in the name of the Father, and of the Son, and of the Holy Ghost!" '

The driver told his story like one saying his prayers, and he seemed to have forgotten that he had a listener.

'It must have been a great shock to the priest.'

'Faith it was, sir, to meet an unbaptised child on the roadside, and that child the only bastard that was ever born in the parish – so Tom Mulhare says, and he's the oldest man in the county.'

'I was altogether a very queer idea – this playhouse.'

'It was indeed, sir, a quare idea, but you see he's quare man. He has been always thinking of something to do good, and it is said that he thinks too much. Father James is a very quare man, your honour'

The Ghost at the Rath

ROSA MULHOLLAND

Many may disbelieve this story, yet there are some still living who can remember hearing, when children, of the events which it details, and of the strange sensation which their publicity excited. The tale, in its present form, is copied, by permission, from a memoir written by the chief actor in the romance, and preserved as a sort of heirloom in the family whom it concerns.

In the year —, I, John Thunder, Captain in the — Regiment, having passed many years abroad following my profession, received notice that I had become owner of certain properties which I had never thought to inherit. I set off for my native land, arrived in Dublin, found that my good fortune was real, and at once began to look about me for old friends. The first I met with, quite by accident, was curly-headed Frank O'Brien, who had been at school with me, though I was ten years his senior. He was curly-headed still, and handsome, as he had promised to be, but careworn and poor. During an evening spent at his chambers I drew all his history from him. He was a briefless barrister. As a man he was not more talented than he had been as a boy. Hard work and anxiety had not brought him success, only broken his health and soured his mind. He was in love, and he could not marry. I soon knew all about Mary Leonard, his fiancée, whom he had met at a house in the country somewhere, in which she was governess. They had now been engaged for two years – she active and hopeful, he sick and despondent. From the letters of hers which he showed me, I thought she was worth all the devotion he felt for her. I considered a good deal about what could be done for Frank, but I could not easily hit upon a plan to assist him. For ten chances you have of helping a sharp man, you have not two for a dull one.

In the meantime my friend must regain his health, and a change of air and scene was necessary. I urged him to make a voyage of discovery to the Rath, an old house and park which had come into my possession as portion of my recently acquired estates. I had never been to the place myself but it had once been the residence of Sir Luke Thunder, of generous memory, and I knew that it was furnished, and provided with a caretaker. I pressed him to leave Dublin at once, and promised to follow him as soon as I found it possible to do so.

So Frank went down to the Rath. The place was two hundred miles away; he was a stranger there, and far from well. When the first week came to an end, and I had heard nothing from him, I did not like the silence; when a fortnight had passed, and still not a word to say he was alive, I felt decidedly uncomfortable; and when the third week of his absence arrived at Saturday without bringing me news, I found myself whizzing through a part of the country I had never travelled before, in the same train in which I had seen Frank seated at our parting.

I reached D—, and, shouldering my knapsack, walked right into the heart of a lovely woody country. Following the directions I had received, I made my way to a lonely road, on which I met not a soul, and which seemed cut out of the heart of a forest, so closely were the trees ranked on either side, and so dense was the twilight made by the meeting and intertwining of the thick branches overhead. In these shades I came upon a gate, like a gate run to seed, with tall, thin, brick pillars, brandishing long grasses from their heads, and spotted with a melancholy crust of creeping moss. I jangled a cracked bell, and an old man appeared from the thickets within, stared at me, then admitted me with a rusty key. I breathed freely on hearing that my friend was well and to be seen. I presented a letter to the old man, having a fancy not to avow myself.

I found my friend walking up and down the alleys of a neglected orchard, with the lichened branches tangled above his head, and ripe apples rotting about his feel. His hands were locked behind his back, and his heard was set on one side, listening to the singing of a bird. I never had seen him look so well; yet there was a vacancy about his whole air which I did not like. He did not seem at all surprised to see me, asked had he really not written to me; thought he had; was so comfortable that he had forgotten everything else. He fancied he had only been there about three days; could not imagine how the time had passed. He seemed to talk wildly, and this, coupled with the unusual happy placidity of his manner, confounded me. The place knew him, he told me confidentially; the place belonged to him, or should; the birds sang him this, the very trees bent before him as he passed, the air whispered him that he had been long expected, and should be poor no more. Wrestling with my judgement ere it might pronounce him mad, I followed him indoors. The Rath was no ordinary old country-house. The acres around it were so wildly overgrown that it was hard to decide which had been pleasure-ground and where the thickets had begun. The plan of the house was fine, with mullioned windows, and here and there a fleck of stained glass flinging back the challenge of an angry sunset. The vast rooms were full of a dusky glare from the sky as I strolled through them in the twilight. The antique furniture had many a blood-red stain on the abrupt notches of its dark carvings; the dusty mirrors flared back at the windows, while the faded curtains produced streaks of uncertain colour from the depths of their sullen foldings.

Dinner was laid for us in the library, a long wainscoted room, with an enormous fire roaring up the chimney, sending a dancing light over the dingy titles of long unopened books. The old man who had unlocked the fate for me served us at table, and, after drawing the dusty curtains, and furnishing us with a plentiful supply of fuel and wine, left us. His clanking hobnailed shoes went echoing away in the distance over the unmatted tiles of the vacant hall till a door closed with a resounding clang very far away, letting us know that we were shut up together for the night in this vast, mouldy, oppressive old house.

I felt as if I could scarcely breathe in it. I could not eat with my usual appetite. The air of the place seemed heavy and tainted. I grew sick and restless. The very wine tasted badly, as if it had been drugged. I had a strange feeling that I had been in the house before, and that something evil had happened to me in it. Yet such could not be the case. What puzzled me most was, that I should feel dissatisfied at seeing Frank looking so well, and eating so heartily. A little time before I should have been glad to suffer something to see him as he looked now; and yet not quite as he looked now. There was a drowsy contentment about him which I could not understand. He did not talk of his work, or of any wish to return to it. He seemed to have no thought of anything but the delight of hanging about that old house, which had certainly cast a spell over him.

About midnight he seized a light, and proposed retiring to our rooms. 'I have such delightful dreams in this place,' he said. He volunteered, as we issued into the hall, to take me upstairs and show me the upper regions of his paradise. I said, 'Not tonight.' I felt a strange creeping sensation as I looked up the vast black staircase, wide enough for a coach to drive down, and at the heavy darkness bending over it like a curse, while our lamps made drips of light down the first two or three gloomy steps. Our bedrooms were on the ground floor, and stood opposite on another off a passage which led to a garden. Into mine Frank conducted me, and left me for his own.

The uneasy feeling which I have described did not go from me with him, and I felt a restlessness amounting to pain when left alone in my chamber. Efforts had evidently been made to render the room habitable, but there was a something antagonistic to sleep in every angle of its many crooked corners. I kicked chairs out of their prim order along the wall, and banged things about here and there; finally, thinking that a good night's rest was the best cure for an inexplicably disturbed frame of mind, I undressed as quickly as possible, and laid my head on my pillow under a canopy, like the wings of a gigantic bird of prey wheeling above me ready to pounce.

But I could not sleep. The wind grumbled in the chimney, and the boughs swished in the garden outside; and between these noises I thought I heard sounds coming from the interior of the old house, where all should have been still as the dead down in their vaults. I could not make out what these sounds were. Sometimes I thought I heard feet running about, sometimes I could have sworn there were double knocks, tremendous tantarararas at the great hall door. Sometimes I heard the clashing of dishes, the echo of voices calling, and the dragging about of furniture. While I sat up in bed trying to account for these noises, my door suddenly flew open, a bright light streamed in from the passage without, and a powdered servant in an elaborate livery of antique pattern stood holding the handle of the door in his hand, and bowing low to me in the bed.

'Her ladyship, my mistress, desires your presence in the drawing-room, sir.'

This was announced in the measured tone of a well-trained domestic. Then with another bow he retired, the door closed, and I was left in the dark to determine whether I had not suddenly awakened from a tantalising dream. In spite of my very wakeful sensations, I believe I should have endeavoured to convince myself that I had been sleeping, but that I perceived light shining under my door, and through the keyhole, from the passage. I got up, lit my lamp, and dressed myself as hastily as I was able.

I opened my door, and the passage down which a short time before I had almost groped my way, with my lamp blinking in the dense foggy darkness, was now illuminated with a light as bright as gas. I walked along it quickly, looking right and left to see whence the glare proceeded. Arriving at the hall, I found it also blazing with light, and filled with perfume. Groups of choice plants, heavy with blossoms, made it look like a garden. The mosaic floor was strewn with costly mats. Soft colours and gilding shone from the walls, and canvases that had been black gave forth faces of men and women looking brightly from their burnished frames. Servants were running about, the dining-room and drawing-room doors were opening and shutting, and as I looked through each I saw vistas of light and colour, the moving of brilliant crowds, the waving of feathers, and glancing of brilliant dresses and uniforms. A festive hum reached me with a drowsy subdued sound, as if I were listening with stuffed ears. Standing aside by an orange tree, I gave up speculating on what this might be, and concentrated all my powers on observation.

Wheels were heard suddenly, and a resounding knock banged at the door till it seemed that the very rooks in the chimneys must be startled out of their nests. The door flew open, a flaming of lanterns was seen outside, and a dazzling lady came up the steps and swept into the hall. When she held up her cloth of silver train, I could see the diamonds that twinkled on her feet. Her bosom was covered with roses, and there was a red light in her eyes like the reflection from a hundred glowing fires. Her black hair went coiling about her head, and couched among the braids lay a jewel not unlike the head of a snake. She was flashing and glowing the gems and flowers. Her beauty and brilliance made me dizzy. Then came faintness in the air, as if her breath had poisoned it. A whirl of storm came in with her, and rushed up the staircase like a moan. The plants shuddered and shed their blossoms, and all the lights is grew dim a moment, then flared up again.

Now the drawing-room door opened, and a gentleman came out with a young girl learning on his arm. He was a fine-looking, middle-aged gentleman, with a mild countenance.

The girl was a slender creature, with golden hair and a pale face. She was dressed in pure white, with a large ruby like a drop of blood at her throat. They advanced together to receive the lady who had arrived. The gentleman offered his arm to the stranger, and the girl who was displaced for her fell back, and walked behind them with a downcast air. I felt irresistibly impelled to follow them, and passed with them into the drawing-room. Never had I mixed in a finer, gayer crowd. The costumes were rich and of an old-fashioned pattern. Dancing was going forward with spirit – minuets and country dances. The stately gentleman was evidently the host, and moved among the company, introducing the magnificent lady right and left. He led her to the head of the room presently, and they mixed in the dance. The arrogance of her manner and the fascination of her beauty were wonderful.

I cannot attempt to describe the strange manner in which I was in this company, and yet not of it. I seemed to view all I beheld through some fine and subtle medium. I saw clearly, yet I felt that it was not with my ordinary naked eyesight. I can compare it to nothing but looking at a scene through a piece of smoked or coloured glass. And just in the same way (as I have said before) all sounds seemed to reach me as if I were listening with ears imperfectly stuffed. No one present took any notice of me. I spoke to several, and they made no reply – did not even turn their eyes upon me, nor show in any way that they heard me. I planted myself straight in the way of a fine fellow in a general's uniform, but he, swerving neither to right nor left by an inch, kept on his way, as though I were a streak of mist, and left me behind him. Everyone I touched eluded me somehow. Substantial as they all looked, I could not contrive to lay my hand on anything that felt like solid flesh. Two or three times I felt a momentary relief from the oppressive sensations which distracted me, when I firmly believed I saw Frank's head at some distance among the crowd, now in one room and now in another, and again in the conservatory, which was hung with lamps, and filled with people walking about among the flowers. But, whenever I approached, he had vanished. At last I came upon him, sitting by himself on a couch behind a curtain watching the dancers. I laid my hand upon his shoulder. Here was something substantial at last. He did not look up; he seemed aware neither of my touch not my speech. I looked in his staring eyes, and found that he was sound asleep. I could not wake him.

Curiosity would not let me remain by his side. I again mixed with the crowd, and found the stately host still leading about the magnificent lady. No one seemed to notice that the golden-haired girl was sitting weeping in a corner; no one but the beauty in the silver train, who sometimes glanced at her contemptuously. While I watched her distress a group came between me and her, and I wandered into another room, where, as though I had turned from one picture of her to look at another, I beheld her dancing gaily, in the full glee of Sir Roger de Coverley, with a fine-looking youth, who was more plainly dressed than any other person in the room. Never was a better-matched pair to look at. Down the middle they danced, hand in hand, his face full of tenderness, hers beaming with joy, right and left bowing and curtseying, parted and meeting again, smiling and whispering; but over the heads of smaller women there were the fierce eyes of the magnificent beauty scowling at them. Then again the crowd shifted around me, and this scene was lost.

For some time I could see no trace of the golden-haired girl in any of the rooms. I looked for her in vain, till at last I caught a glimpse of her standing smiling in a doorway with her finger lifted, beckoning. At whom? Could it be at me? Her eyes were fixed on mine. I hastened into the hall, and caught sight of her white dress passing up the wide black staircase from which I had shrunk some hours earlier. I followed her, she keeping some steps in advance. It was intensely dark, but by the gleaming of her gown I was able to trace her flying figure. Where we went I knew not, up how many stairs, down how many passages, till we arrived at a low-roofed large room with sloping roof and queer windows where there was a dim light, like the sanctuary light in a deserted church. Here, when I entered, the golden head was glimmering over something which I presently discerned to be a cradle wrapped round with white curtains, and with a few fresh flowers fastened up on the hood of it, as if to catch a baby's eye. The fair sweet face looked up at me with a glow of pride on it, smiling with happy dimples. The white hands unfolded the curtains, and stripped back the coverlet. Then, suddenly there went a rushing moan all round the weird room, that seemed like a gust of wind forcing in through the crannies, and shaking the jingling old windows in their sockets. The cradle was an empty one. The girl fell back with a look of horror on her pale face that I shall never forget, then, flinging her arms above her head, she dashed from the room.

I followed her as fast as I was able, but the wild white figure was too swift for me. I had lost her before I reached the bottom of the staircase. I searched for her, first in one room, then in another, neither could I see her foe (as I already believed to be), the lady of the silver train. At length I found myself in a small anteroom, where a lamp was expiring on the table. A window was open, close by it the golden-haired girl was lying sobbing in a chair, while the magnificent lady was bending over her as if soothingly, and offering her something to drink in a goblet. The moon was rising behind the two figures. The shuddering light of the lamp was flickering over the girl's bright head, the rich embossing of the golden cup, the lady's silver robes, and, I thought, the jewelled eyes of the serpent looked out from her bending head. As I watched, the girl raised her face and drank, then suddenly dashed the goblet away; while a cry such as I never heard but once, and shiver to remember, rose to the very roof of the old house, and the clear sharp word '*Poisoned!*' rang and reverberated from hall and chamber in a thousand echoes, like the clash of a peal of bells. The girl dashed herself from the open window, leaving the cry clamouring behind her. I heard the violent opening of doors and running of feet, but I waited for nothing more. Maddened by what I had witnessed, I would have felled the murderess, but she glided unhurt from under my vain blow. I sprang from the window after the wretched white figure. I saw it flying on before me with a speed I could not overtake. I ran till I was dizzy. I called like a madman, and heard the owls croaking back to me. The moon grew huge and bright, the trees grew out before it like the bushy heads of giants, the river lay keen and shining like a long unsheathed sword, couching for deadly work among the rushes. The white figure shimmered and vanished, glittered brightly on before me, shimmered and vanished again, shimmered, staggered, fell, and disappeared in the river. Of what she was, phantom or reality, I thought not at the moment; she had the semblance of a human being going to destruction, and I had the frenzied impulse to save her. I rushed forward with one last effort, struck my foot against the root of a tree, and was dashed to the ground. I remember a crash, momentary pain and confusion; then nothing more.

When my senses returned, the red clouds of the dawn were shining in the river beside me. I arose to my feet, and found that, though much bruised, I was otherwise unhurt. I busied my mind in recalling the strange circumstances which had brought me to that place in the dead of the night. The recollection of all I had witnessed was vividly present to my mind. I took my way slowly to the house, almost expecting to see the marks of wheels and other indications of last night's revel, but the rank grass that covered the gravel was uncrushed, not a blade disturbed, not a stone displaced. I shook one of the drawing-room windows till I shook off the old rusty hasp inside, flung up the creaking sash, and entered. Where were the brilliant draperies and carpets, the soft gilding, the vases teeming with flowers, the thousand sweet odours of the night before? Not a trace of them; no, nor even a ragged cobweb swept away, nor a stiff chair moved an inch from its melancholy place, nor the face of a mirror relieved from one speck of its obscuring dust!

Coming back into the open air, I met the old man from the gate walking up one of the weedy paths. He eyed me meaningly from head to foot, but I gave him good-morrow cheerfully.

'You see I am poking about early,' I said.

'I' faith, sir,' said he, 'an' ye look like a man that had been pokin' about *all night*.'

'How so?' said I.

'Why, ye see, sir,' said he, 'I'm used to 't, an' I can read it in yer face like prent. Some sees one thing an' some another, an' some only feels an' hears. The poor jintleman inside, *he* says nothin', but he has beautyful dhrames. An' for the Lord's sake, sir, take him out o' this, for I've seen him wandherin' about like a ghost himself in the heart of the night, an' him that sound sleepin' that I couldn't wake him!'

*　　*　　*

At breakfast I said nothing to Frank of my strange adventures. He had rested well, he said, and boasted of his enchanting dreams. I asked him to describe them, when he grew perplexed and annoyed. He remembered nothing, but that his spirit had been delightfully entertained while his body reposed. I now felt a curiosity to go through the old house, and was not surprised, on pushing open a door at the end of a remote mouldy passage, to enter the identical chamber into which I had followed the pale-faced girl when she beckoned me out of the drawing-room. There were the low brooding roof and slanting walls, the short wide latticed windows to which the noonday sun was trying to pierce through a forest of leaves. The hangings rotting with age shook like dreary banners at the opening of the door, and there in the middle of the room was the cradle; only the curtains that had been white were blackened with dirt, and laced and overlaced with cobwebs. I parted the curtains, bringing down a shower of dust upon the floor, and saw lying upon the pillow, within, a child's tiny shoe, and a toy. I need not describe the rest of the house. It was vast and rambling, and, as far as furniture and decorations were concerned, the wreck of grandeur.

Having strange subject for meditation, I walked alone in the orchard that evening. This orchard sloped towards the river I have mentioned before. The trees were old and stunted, and the branches tangled overhead. The ripe apples were rolling in the long bleached grass. A row of taller trees, sycamores and chestnuts, straggled along by the river's edge, ferns and tall weeds grew round and among them, and between their trunks, and behind the rifts in the foliage, the water was seen to flow. Walking up and down one of the paths I alternately faced these trees and turned my back upon them. Once when coming towards them I chanced to lift my glance, started, drew my hands across my eyes, looked again, and finally stood still gazing in much astonishment. I saw distinctly the figure of a lady standing by one of the trees, bending low towards the grass. Her face was a little turned away, her dress a bluish-white, her mantle a dun-brown colour. She held a spade in her hand, and her foot was upon it, as if she were in the act of digging. I gazed at her for some time, vainly trying to guess at whom she might be, then I advanced towards her. As I approached, the outlines of her figure broke up and disappeared, and I found that she was only an illusion presented to me by the curious accidental grouping of the lines of two trees which had shaped the space between them into the semblance of the form I have described. A patch of the flowing water had been her robe, a piece of russet moorland her cloak. The spade was an awkward young shoot slanting up from the root of one of the trees. I stepped back and tried to piece her out again bit by bit, but could not succeed. That night I did not feel at all inclined to return to my dismal chamber, and lie awaiting such another summons as I had once received. When Frank bade me good-night, I heaped fresh coals on the fire, took down from the shelves a book, from which I lifted the dust in layers with my penknife, and, dragging an armchair close to the hearth, tried to make myself as comfortable as might be. I am a strong, robust man, very unimaginative, and little troubled with affections of the nerves, but I confess that my feelings were not enviable, sitting thus alone in that queer old house, with last night's strange pantomime still vividly present to my memory. In spite of my efforts at coolness, I was excited by the prospect of what yet might be in store for me before morning. But these feelings passed away as the night wore on, and I nodded asleep over my book.

I was startled by the sound of a brisk light step walking overhead. Wide awake at once, I sat up and listened. The ceiling was low, but I could not call to mind what room it was that lay above the library in which I sat. Presently I heard the same step upon the stairs, and the loud sharp rustling of a silk dress sweeping against the banisters. The step paused at the library door, and then there was silence. I got up, and with all the courage I could summon seized a light, and opened the door; but there was nothing in the hall but the usual heavy darkness and damp mouldy air. I confess I felt more uncomfortable at that moment than I had done at any time during the preceding night. All the visions that had then appeared to me had produced nothing like the horror of thus feeling a supernatural presence which my eyes were not permitted to behold.

I returned to the library, and passed the night there. Next day I sought for the room above it in which I had heard the footsteps, but could discover no entrance to any such room. Its windows, indeed, I counted from the outside, though they were so overgrown with ivy I could hardly discern them, but in the interior of the house I could find no door to the chamber. I asked Frank about it, but he knew and cared nothing on the subject; I asked the old man at the lodge, and he shook his head.

'Och!' he said, 'don't ask about that room. The door's built up, and flesh and blood have no consarn wid it. It was *her own* room.'

'Whose own?' I asked.

'Ould Lady Thunder's. An' whist, sir! *that's her grave!*'

'What do you mean?' I said. 'Are you out of your mind?'

He laughed queerly, drew nearer, and lowered his voice. 'Nobody has asked about the room these years but yourself,' he said. 'Nobody misses it goin' over the house. My grandfather was an old retainer o' the Thunder family, my father was in the service too, an' I was born myself before the ould lady died. Yon was her room, an' she left her eternal curse on her family if so be they didn't lave her coffin there. *She* wasn't goin' undher the ground to the worms. So there it was left, an' they built up the door. God love ye, sir, an' don't go near it. I wouldn't have told you, only I know ye've seen plenty about already, an' ye have the look o' one that'd be ferretin' things out, savin' yer presence.'

He looked at me knowingly, but I gave him no information, only thanked him for putting me on my guard. I could scarcely credit what he told me about the room; but my curiosity was excited regarding it. I made up my mind that day to try and induce Frank to quit the place on the morrow. I felt more and more convinced that the atmosphere was not healthful for his mind, whatever it might be for his body. The sooner we left the spot the better for us both; but the remaining night which I had to pass there I resolved on devoting to the exploring of the walled-up chamber. What impelled me to this resolve I do not know. The undertaking was not a pleasant one, and I should hardly have ventured on it had I been forced to remain much longer at the Rath. But I knew there was little chance of sleep for me in that house, and I thought I might as well go and seek for my adventures as sit waiting for them to come for me, as I had done the night before. I felt a relish for my enterprise, and expected the night with satisfaction. I did not say anything of my intention either to Frank or the old man at the lodge. I did not want to make a fuss, and have my doings talked of all over the country. I may as well mention here that again, on this evening, when walking in the orchard, I saw the figure of the lady digging between the trees. And again I saw that this figure was an illusive appearance; that the water was her gown, and the moorland her cloak, and a willow in the distance her tresses.

As soon as the night was pretty far advanced, I placed a ladder against the window which was least covered over with the ivy, and mounted it, having provided myself with a dark lantern. The moon rose full behind some trees that stood like a black bank against the horizon, and glimmered on the panes as I ripped away branches and leaves with a knife, and shook the old crazy casement open. The sashes were rotten, and the fastenings easily gave way. I placed my lantern on a bench within, and was soon standing beside it in the chamber. The air was insufferably close and mouldy, and I flung the window open to the widest, and beat the bowering ivy still further back from about it, so as to let the fresh air of heaven blow into the place. I then took my lantern in hand, and began to look about me.

The room was vast and double; a velvet curtain hung between me and an inner chamber. The darkness was thick and irksome, and the scanty light of my lantern only tantalised me. My eyes fell on some tall spectral-looking candelabra furnished with wax candles, which, though black with age, still bore the marks of having been guttered by a draught that had blown on them fifty years ago. I lighted these; they burned up with a ghastly flickering, and the apartment, with its fittings, was revealed to me. These latter had been splendid in the days of their freshness: the appointments the rest of the house were mean in comparison. The ceiling was painted with fine allegorical figures, also spaces of the walls between the dim mirrors and the sumptuous hangings of crimson velvet, with their tarnished golden tassels and fringes. The carpet still felt luxurious to the tread, and the dust could not altogether obliterate the elaborate fancy of its flowery design. There were gorgeous cabinets laden with curiosities, wonderfully carved chairs, rare vases, and antique glasses of every description, under some of which lay little heaps of dust which had once no doubt been blooming flowers. There was a table laden with books of poetry and science, drawings and drawing materials, which showed that the occupant of the room had been a person of mind. There was also a writing-table scattered over with yellow papers, and a work-table at a window, on which lay reels, a thimble, and a piece of what had once been white muslin, but was now saffron colour, sewn with gold thread, a rusty needle sticking in it. This and the pen lying on the inkstand, the paperknife between the leaves of a book, the loose sketches shaken out by the side of a portfolio, and the ashes of a fire on the wide mildewed hearth-place, all suggested that the owner of this retreat had been snatched from it without warning, and that whoever had thought proper to build up the doors, had also thought proper to touch nothing that had belonged to her.

Having surveyed all these things, I entered the inner room, which was a bedroom. The furniture of this was in keeping with that of the other chamber. I saw dimly a bed enveloped in lace, and a dressing-table fancifully garnished and draped. Here I espied more candelabra, and going forward to set the lights burning, I stumbled against something. I turned the blaze of my lantern on this something, and started with a sudden thrill of horror. It was a large stone coffin.

I own that I felt very strangely for the next few minutes. When I had recovered the shock, I set the wax candles burning, and took a better survey of this odd burial-place. A wardrobe stood open, and I saw dresses hanging within. A gown lay upon a chair, as if just thrown off, and a pair of dainty slippers were beside it. The toilet-table looked as if only used yesterday, judging by the litter that covered it; hairbrushes lying this way and that way, essence-bottles with the stoppers out, paint pots uncovered, a ring here, a wreath of artificial flowers there, and in front of tall that the coffin, the tarnished Cupids that bore the mirror between their hands smirking down at it with a grim complacency.

On the corner of this table was a small golden salver, holding a plate of some black mouldered food, an antique decanter filled with wine, a glass, and a phial with some thick black liquid, uncorked. I felt weak and sick with the atmosphere of the place, and I seized the decanter, wiped the dust from it with my handkerchief, tasted, found that the wine was good, and drank a moderate draught. Immediately it was swallowed I felt a horrid giddiness, and sank upon the coffin. A raging pain was in my head and a sense of suffocation in my chest. After a few intolerable moments I felt better, but the heavy air pressed on me stiflingly, and I rushed from this inner room into the larger and outer chamber. Here a blast of cool air revived me, and I saw that the place was changed.

A dozen other candelabra besides those I had lighted were flaming round the walls, the hearth was all ruddy with a blazing fire, everything that had been dim was bright, the lustre had returned to the gilding, the flowers bloomed in the vases. A lady was sitting before the hearth in a low armchair. Her light loose gown swept about her on the carpet, her black hair fell round her to her knees, and into it her hands were thrust as she leaned her forehead upon them, and stared between them into the fire. I had scarcely time to observe her attitude when she turned her head quickly towards me, and I recognised the handsome face of the magnificent lady who had played such a sinister part in the strange scenes that had been enacted before me two nights ago. I saw something dark looming behind her chair, but I thought it was only her shadow thrown backward by the firelight.

She arose and came to meet me, and I recoiled from her. There was something horridly fixed and hollow in her gaze, and filmy in the stirring of her garments. The shadow, as she moved, grew more firm and distinct in outline, and followed her like a servant where she went.

She crossed half of the room, then beckoned me, and sat down at the writing-table. The shadow waited beside her, adjusted her paper, placed the ink-bottle near her and the pen between her fingers. I felt impelled to approach her, and to take my place at her left shoulder, so as to be able to see what she might write. The shadow stood motionless at her other hand. As I became accustomed to the shadow's presence he grew more visibly loathsome and hideous. He was quite distinct from the lady, and moved independently of her with long ugly limbs. She hesitated about beginning to write, and he made a wild gesture with his arm, which brought her hand quickly to the paper, and her pen began to move at once. I needed not to bend and scrutinise in order to read. Every words as it was forming flashed before me like a meteor.

'I am the spirit of Madeline, Lady Thunder, who lived and died in this house, and whose coffin stands in yonder room among the vanities in which I delighted. I am constrained to make my confession to you, John Thunder, who are the present owner of the estates of your family.'

Here the hand trembled and stopped writing. But the shadow made a threatening gesture, and the hand fluttered on.

'I was beautiful, poor, and ambitious, and when I entered this house first on the night of a ball given by Sir Luke Thunder, I determined to become its mistress. His daughter, Mary Thunder, was the only obstacle in my way. She divined my intention, and stood between me and her father. She was a gentle, delicate girl, and no match for me. I pushed her aside, and became Lady Thunder. After that I hated her, and made her dread me. I had gained the object of my ambition, but I was jealous of the influence possessed by her over her father, and I revenged myself by crushing the joy out her young life. In this I defeated my own purpose. She eloped with a young man who was devoted to her, though poor, and beneath her in station. Her father was indignant at first, and my malice was satisfied; but as time passed on I had no children, and she had a son, soon after whose birth her husband died. Then her father took her back to his heart, and the boy was his idol and heir.'

Again the hand stopped writing, the ghostly head drooped, and the whole figure was convulsed. But the shadow gesticulated fiercely, and, cowering under its menace, the wretched spirit went on: 'I caused the child to be stolen away. I thought I had done it cunningly, but she tracked the crime home to me. She came and accused me of it, and in the desperation of my terror at discovery, I gave her poison to drink. She rushed from me and from the house in frenzy, and in her mortal anguish fell in the river. People thought she had gone mad from grief for her child, and committed suicide. I only knew the horrible truth. Sorrow brought an illness upon her father, of which he died. Up to the day of his death he dad search made for the child. Believing that it was alive, and must be found, he willed all his property to it, his rightful heir, and to its heirs for ever. I buried the deeds under a tree in the orchard, and forged a will, in which all was bequeathed to me during my lifetime. I enjoyed my state and grandeur till the day of my death, which came upon me miserably, and, after that, my husband's possessions went to a distant relation of his family. Nothing more was heard of the fate of the child two was stolen; but he lived and married, and his daughter now toils for her bread – his daughter, who is the rightful owner of all that is said to belong to you, John Thunder. I tell you this that you may devote yourself to the task of discovering this wronged girl, and giving up to her that which you are unlawfully possessed of. Under the thirteenth tree standing on the brink of the river at the foot of the orchard you will find buried the genuine will of Sir Luke Thunder. When you have found and read it, do justice, as you value your soul. In order that you may know the grandchild of Mary Thunder when you find her, you shall behold her in a vision – '

The last words grew dim before me; the light faded away, and all the place was in darkness, except one spot on the opposite wall. On this spot the light glimmered softly, and against the brightness the outlines of a figure appeared, faintly at first, but, growing firm and distinct, became filled in and rounded at last to the perfect semblance of life. The figure was that of a young girl in a plain black dress, with a bright, happy face, and pale gold hair softly banded on her fair forehead. She might have been the twin-sister of the pale-faced girl whom I had seen bending over the cradle two nights ago; but her healthier, gladder, and prettier sister. When I had gazed on her some moments, the vision faded away as it had come; the last vestige of the brightness died out upon the wall, and I found myself once more in total darkness. Stunned for a time by the sudden changes, I stood watching for the return of the lights and figures; but in vain. By and by my eyes grew accustomed to the obscurity, and I saw the sky glimmering behind the little window which I had left open. I could soon discern the writing-table beside me, and possessed myself of the slips of loose paper which lay upon it. I then made my way to the window. The first streaks of dawn were in the sky as I descended my ladder, and I thanked God that I breathed the fresh morning air once more, and heard the cheering sound of the cocks crowing.

* * *

All thought of acting immediately upon last night's strange revelations, almost all memory of them, was for the time banished from my mind by the unexpected trouble of the next few days. That morning I found an alarming change in Frank. Feeling sure that he was going to be ill, I engaged a lodging in a cottage in the neighbourhood, whither we removed before nightfall, leaving the accursed Rath behind us. Before midnight he was in the delirium of a raging fever.

I thought it right to let his poor little fiancée know his state, and wrote to her, trying to alarm her no more than was necessary. On the evening of the third day after my latter went I was sitting by Frank's bedside, when an unusual bustle outside aroused my curiosity, and going into the cottage kitchen I saw a figure standing in the firelight which seemed a third appearance of that vision of the pale-faced golden-haired girl which was now thoroughly imprinted on my memory – a third, with all the woe of the first and all the beauty of the second. But this was a living, breathing apparition. She was throwing off her bonnet and shawl, and stood there at home in a moment in her plain black dress. I drew my hand across my eyes to make sure that they did not deceive me. I had beheld so many supernatural visions lately that it seemed as thought I could scarcely believe in the reality of anything till I had touched it.

'Oh, sir,' said the visitor, 'I am Mary Leonard, and are you poor Frank's friend? Oh, sir, we are all the world to one another, and I could not let him die without coming to see him!'

And here the poor little traveller burst into tears. I cheered her as well as I could, telling her that Frank would soon, I trusted, be out of all danger. She told me that she had thrown up her situation in order to come and nurse him. I said we had got a more experienced nurse than she could be, and then I gave her to the care of our landlady, a motherly countrywoman. After that I went back to Frank's bedside, nor left it for long till he was convalescent. The fever had swept away all that strangeness in this manner which had afflicted me, and he was quite himself again.

There was a joyful meeting of the lovers. The more I saw of Mary Leonard's bright face the more thoroughly was I convinced that she was the living counterpart of the vision I had seen in the burial chamber. I made enquiries as to her birth, and her father's history, and found that she was indeed the grandchild of that Mary Thunder whose history had been so strangely related to me, and the rightful heiress of all those properties which for a few months only had been mine. Under the tree in the orchard, the thirteenth, and that by which I had seen the lady digging, were found the buried deeds which had been described to me. I made an immediate transfer of property, whereupon some others who thought they had a chance of being my heirs disputed the matter with me, and went to law. Thus the affair has gained publicity, and become a nine days' wonder. Many things have been in my favour, however: the proving of Mary's birth and of Sir Luke's will, the identification of Lady Thunder's handwriting on the slips of paper which I had brought from the burial chamber; also other matters which a search in that chamber brought to light. I triumphed, and I now go abroad, leaving Frank and his Many made happy by the possession of what could only have been a burden to me.

So the manuscript ends. Major Thunder fell in battle a few years after the adventure it relates. Frank O'Brien's grandchildren hear of him with gratitude and awe. The Rath has been long since totally dismantled and left to go to ruin.

The Living Ghost

ROSA MULHOLLAND

I

A dear old lady tells us this story in the late autumn evenings. Now the harvest is in, huge haycocks shelter the gable, the honey is strained and put by in jars, the apples are ripened and stored; the logs begin to sputter and sing in the big parlour at evening, hot cakes to steam on the tea-table, and the pleasant lamplit hours to spread themselves. Indoor things begin to have meaning looks of their own, our limbs grow quiet, and our brains begin to work. The moors beyond the window take strange expressions in the twilight, and fold mysteries into their hollows with the shadows of the night. The maids in the kitchen sing wild ballads to one another round the ingle; and when one of us young folks threads the rambling passages above to fetch a stray thimble from one of the lavender-scented bedrooms, she comes back flying down the great hollow staircase as if a troop of ghosts were at her heels. It is the time to enjoy a story, a true story, the story of a real life; and here it is, as our dear old lady is telling it to us.

*   *   *

When I first learned, my children, that I was the ward of my mother's early friend, Mrs Hollingford, and was to live under her roof after my departure from school, I little thought that a place like Hillsbro' Farm was ever likely to be my home. I was a conceited young person, and fond of giving myself airs. My father was colonel of his regiment, and I thought I had a right to look down on Lydia Brown, whose father was in business, though she wore velvet three inches deep upon her frocks, while mine had no better trimming than worsted braid. I had spent all my life at school, from the day when my father and mother kissed me for the last time in Miss Sweetman's parlour. I remember yet my pretty mother's pale tearful face as she looked back at me through the carriage window, and my own paroxysm of despairing tears on the mat when the door was shut. After that I had a pleasant enough life of it. I was a favourite at school, having a disposition to make myself and others as happy as I could. I required a good deal of snubbing, but when properly kept down I believe I was not a disagreeable girl.

My Indian letters generally contained some bit of news to amuse or interest my companions, and now and again captain or ensign somebody, home upon sick leave, called and presented himself in Miss Sweetman's parlour, with curious presents for me, my mistresses or my favourite companions. I remember well the day when Major Guthrie arrived with the box of stuffed birds. Miss Kitty Sweetman, our youngest and best-loved mistress, was sent on before me to speak civilly to the gentleman in the parlour, and announce my coming. Miss Kitty was the drudge of the school, the sweetest-tempered drudge in the world. She was not so well informed as her elder sisters, and had to make up in the quantity of her teaching what it lacked in the quality. She was fagged, and hunted, and worried from morning till night by all the small girls in the school. She would have been merry if she had had time, and she was witty whenever she could get the chance of being anything but a machine; but she was not always happy, for I slept in her room, and I sometimes heard her crying in the night. As I remember her first she was young and pretty, but as time went on she grew a little faded, and a little harassed-looking; though I still thought her sweet enough for anything.

Well, Miss Kitty went down to the major, and I, following close upon her heels, heard a little scream as I paused at the parlour door, and there when I went in was a bronzed-looking gentleman holding Miss Kitty's two hands in his, and looking in her face. And I could not care about the birds for thinking of it, and when we went up to bed Miss Kitty told me that Major Guthrie was an old friend of her family, and that he had said he would call again. And surely enough he did call again; and then it happened that the three Miss Sweetmans were invited out to an evening party – a great event for them. I thought there was something very particular about it, and so I took care to dress Miss Kitty with my own hands. She had a plain white dress, and I insisted on lending her my blue sash and coral necklace; and when she was dressed she put her finger in her mouth, and asked, between laughing and crying, whether I could further accommodate her with a coral and bells. She looked as young as anybody, though she would make fun of herself. And when she came in that night, and saw my open eyes waiting for her, she sat down on my bed and began to cry, and told me that Major Guthrie had asked her to marry him, and she was going to India as his wife. Then I heard the whole story; how he had loved her dearly long ago; how her family had refused him because he was too poor, and she was too young; how after he had gone off in a passion reverses had come upon them, and she and her sisters had been obliged to open a school. And so Miss Kitty went out to India, and the only thing that comforted me for her loss was the fact that she took with her the embroidered handkerchief for my mother and the wrought cigar-case for my father which it had taken my idleness a whole year to produce. Ah, me! and my eyes never beheld either of these three again: friend, father or mother.

My first recollections of Mrs Hollingford are associated with plum-cake, birthdays and bon-bons. I remember her as an erect, dignified-looking lady in a long velvet cloak, and with a peculiarly venerable face, half severe, half benevolent. I used to feel a little nervous about speaking to her, but I liked to sit at a distance and look at her. I had a superstition that she was the most powerful universal agent in existence; that she had only to say, 'Let there be plum-cake,' and immediately it would appear on the table; or, 'This little girl requires a new doll,' and at once a waxen cherub would repose in my arms. The Miss Sweetmans paid her the greatest deference, and the girls used to peep over the blinds in the school-room at her handsome carriage and powdered servants. I remember, when a very little girl, presenting myself before Miss Sweetman one day and popping up my hand as a sign that I wanted to ask a question. 'What is the reason, Miss Sweetman,' I asked, 'that Mrs Hollingford makes me think of the valiant woman of whom we were reading in the Bible yesterday?' But Miss Sweetman was busy, and only puckered up her mouth and ordered me back to my seat. Mrs Hollingford used to take me on her knee and tell me of a little girl of hers who was at school in France, and with whom I was one day to be acquainted; and a tall lad, who was her son, used to call sometimes with bouquets for Miss Sweetman or sugar-plums for me; but I was never in her house, which I believed to be a palace, nor did I ever see Mr Hollingford, who was a banker in the city. After my twelfth birthday I saw them no more. I missed the periodical appearance of the noble countenance in the parlour. Miss Sweetman, with a very long face, told me something of the breaking of a bank, ruin and poverty. I was very sorry, but I was too young to realise it much; and I went on thinking of Mrs Hollingford, in trouble, no doubt, and unfortunately removed from me, but still going about the world in her long velvet cloak and with her hands full of plum-cake.

So my youth went on till I was sixteen, pretty well grown for my years, a little pert, a little proud, a little fond of tinsels and butterflies, a little too apt to make fun of my neighbours and to believe that the sun had got a special commission to shine upon me, but withal sympathetic and soft-hearted enough when in my right senses, and, as I said before, not a bad sort of girl when properly kept down by a judicious system of snubbing. I had already begun to count the months to the happy time, two years hence, when, my education being finished, I should at last rejoin my parents in India; and I was fond of describing all the beautiful things I would send as presents to the friends who had been kind to me in England. And then one fearful day came the black letter bearing the terrible news which bowed my head in the dust, scattered my girlish vanities, and altered my fate for life. Everyone in the house learned the news before me. I saw blank faces all around, and could only guess the cause, so careful were they to break it to me gradually. For two dreadful days they kept me on the rack of suspense, while I did not know whether it was my father or mother who was dead, or whether both were ill, or only one. But I learned all soon enough. There had been a fever, and both were dead. I was an orphan, quite alone in the world.

For three years after this I remained with the Miss Sweetmans, during which time I regained much of my old cheerfulness, and also some degree of my natural pride and impertinence. My father and mother had been to me a memory and a hope; now they were a memory only. After my first grief and sense of desolation had passed, I went on with the routine of my days much as before. I did not miss my father and mother every hour as though I had lived under their roof and been familiar with their faces and caresses. But the bright expectation of my youth was extinguished, and I suffered secretly a great yearning for the love which I had now no right to claim from anyone. The time was fast approaching when I must take my school-books down from the Miss Sweetmans' shelves, pack up my trunks, and go forth among strangers. I had some property, more than enough for my needs, and I was to dwell under the roof of my guardian, Mrs Hollingford. In the meantime, I paid several visits to the home of a wealthy schoolfellow, who had entered upon fashionable life, and who was eager to give me a taste of its delights before I yielded myself to the fate that was in store for me. I learned to dress with taste, to wear my hair in the newest style, and to waltz to perfection. But I could not go on paying visits for ever, and the time arrived when I found it necessary to turn my back on lively scenes and prepare for the obscurity of Hillsbro'. This was a remote place in the north country, from whence were dated all the letters addressed by Mrs Hollingford to me since the time when she had become my guardian.

I did not go to Hillsbro' Farm in any unfair state of ignorance as to the present worldly position of its owners. Grace Tyrrell (my schoolfellow) was careful to let me know the depth of the degradation to which these friends of an old time had fallen from their once high estate; also to make me aware of the estimation in which they were held by the people of her world. The idea of my going to Hillsbro' was ridiculed till I got angry, but not ashamed.

'Those poor Hollingfords!' said one lady. 'I am sure it is very kind of you, Miss Dacre, to pay them a visit; but *live* with them, my dear! – you could not think of identifying yourself with such people. Are you aware that the father ruined numbers of people, absconded with his pockets full of money, and never was heard of since?'

'Yes,' said I; 'but I have nothing to do with Mr Hollingford. And I dare say if his wife had taken ill-gotten riches down to Hillsbro' with her, the police would have followed her before this; for she gives her address quite openly.'

I afterwards heard this lady telling Grace that her friend was a very pert young woman. I did not mind, for, through fighting Mrs Hollingford's battles, I had come to think that I loved her memory; and I tried to do so for my mother's sake.

'It is not at all necessary to live with a guardian,' said Grace. 'They say Mrs Hollingford makes butter and sells it; and Frederick says the son is a mere ploughman. He is Mr Hill's agent; Frederick met him by chance, quite lately, when he was shooting at Hillsbro'.'

'Agent, is he?' said I, mischievously. 'Then I should think he must at least know how to read and write. Come, that is not so bad!'

'You will get the worst of it, Grace,' said Frederick Tyrrell, who was listening. 'Lucky fellow, Hollingford, to have such a champion!'

So here I had better explain to you, my dears, that Captain Tyrrell

was, even at this time, what old-fashioned people used to call a great
beau of mine; that he was fond of dangling about my skirts and
picking up my fan. Nothing more on this subject is necessary here.
If you desire to know what he is like, I refer you to an old water-
colour sketch of a weak-faced, washed-out-looking young man, with
handsome features, and a high-collared coat, which you will find in
an old portfolio upstairs, on the top shelf of the wardrobe, in the
lumber-room. It was done by Grace's own hand, a portrait of her
brother, and presented to me in those days. It has lain in that
portfolio ever since.

Though I fought for the Hollingfords, and would hear no word
against them, I do confess that I suffered much fear as to how I
should manage to accommodate myself to the life which I might
find awaiting me at Hillsbro' Farm. That idea of the butter-making,
for instance, suggested a new train of reflections. The image of Mrs
Hollingford began to divest itself gradually of the long velvet cloak
and majestic mien which it had always worn in my mind, and I
speculated as to whether I might not be expected to dine in a kitchen
with the farm-servants, and to assist with the milking of the cows.
But I contrived to keep my doubts to myself, and went on packing
my trunks with a grudging conviction that at least I was doing my
duty.

And it is here, just when my packing was half done, that the
strange, beautiful face of Rachel Leonard rises up to take its place in
my history. I was introduced to her by chance; I did not know her
story, nor that she had a story, nor yet that she was connected with
any people whose intimate acquaintance I was likely to make in the
future.

We met at a small musical party, where we had opportunities for
conversation. She wore a white Indian muslin, with a bunch of scarlet
flowers in the bosom. We were sitting in a softly lighted corner, and
her figure was in relief against a dark curtain. Her face was oval and
olive, with an exquisite mingling of warmth and purity, depth and
delicacy, in its tone. Her dark hair was swept up to the top of her
head in a crown of braids, as it was then worn. Her eyes were dark
grey, and very sweet, with a mysterious shadow of sadness about
them when her face was in repose; yet, when they smiled they shone
more than any eyes I have ever seen.

'Miss Dacre and Miss Leonard, I must make you acquainted,' said
our hostess (the meddling lady whom I have already quoted on the

subject of the Hollingford misdemeanours). 'You intend passing the winter at Hillsbro', Miss Leonard.'

'Yes,' replied Rachel; 'I believe we shall be at the hall about Christmas.'

'Ah! and you have never been there before? I can assure you it is the most dreary place; you will be glad of a young friend in the neighbourhood. Miss Dacre's whim is one of our amusements at present. She is going to Hillsbro' to stay with a lady who is the mother of Mr Hill's agent.'

'Mrs Cowan?' said Miss Leonard, with a ladylike assumption of interest in the subject.

'Not at all, my dear; the Cowans were worthy people, but Mr Hill has changed his agent. Have you not heard? No, of course. Hollingford is the name of these people. The father was a banker, the bank smashed, and he ran away with large sums of money.'

I thought – nay, I was quite sure – that Miss Leonard started at the mention of the word Hollingford; and I also thought that she turned deathly pale; but she bent over her flowers at the moment, and the light was very subdued. No one else seemed to notice it, so it is just possible I may have been mistaken.

'Mr Hill's new agent is, then, the son of Mr Hollingford, the banker?' said Miss Leonard, after a pause. 'I did not know that they belonged to that part of the country.'

'Oh! I do not know about that; but the mother and son have taken a farm there lately, trying to make shift for themselves, poor things! They say young Hollingford has some Quixotic ideas about paying some of his father's liabilities; and if he has, I am sure it is very creditable to him. But I for one am inclined to doubt it. Bad conduct generally runs in families.'

'Madam,' said I, with my cheeks getting very hot, 'Mrs Hollingford was my mother's dear friend.'

'Highty tighty, Miss Dacre,' said the lady, 'we never know how our friends are going to turn out. I say nothing but what is true. And allow me to warn you, my dear, that if you will persist in identifying yourself with such people you must make up your mind to hear them spoken of as they deserve.'

'Madam,' said I again, flashes of lightning now dancing before my eyes, 'I am very sorry I ever entered your house; and I shall certainly never enter it again.'

Not waiting for more I made her a curtsy, and walked out of the room. I found the dressing-room where I had left my cloak, fully determined to go home at once, if I could only get the carriage. I had to wait some time, however, and while I sat alone the door opened and Rachel Leonard came hurriedly up to my side.

'I could not go away without bidding you good-night,' she said, holding both my hands in both of hers. 'Perhaps we may meet again. God bless you!'

Her voice was unsteady, her face pale, her eyes wet. A lady came to the door and said, 'Now, Rachel, we are waiting!' She dropped my hand and was gone.

'Who is she?' I asked of Grace, as soon as we were together, 'What relation is she to the Hills?'

'None whatever,' said Grace; 'only an adopted daughter. There is some romantic story about her, I believe. She went to Mrs Hill as a companion first. The Hills, who are the most eccentric old couple in the world, took a violent fancy to her, and adopted her for their own. I believe she is an orphan of a very good family. They keep up a wonderful fuss about her; and people say they have made her their heiress.'

'I wonder why she looked so strangely at the mention of the Hollingfords?' I said musingly.

'My dear Margery,' said Grace, shaking her head, 'I give you up. You are perfectly insane on the subject of the Hollingfords. What will you imagine next?'

'I do not think I imagined it,' said I. 'I am sure that she turned as white as your cloak.'

'Well, well,' said Grace, 'there may be some deep mystery for all I know. Miss Leonard may, like yourself, have a taste for agriculture; or may have known young Mr Hollingford before he turned plough-man. I advise you to think about it. You have materials for a pretty romance to take into exile with you.'

And I did think about it long afterwards.

2

My children, you must remember that I am speaking of an old-fashioned time, and I travelled down to Hillsbro' by coach. The promenade of a fashionable watering-place had hitherto been my idea of the country. Imagine, then, how my hungry eyes devoured the new beauties presented to them. I had provided myself with a book, and I had hoped to fall asleep over it, yet here I was with my eyes riveted to a pane of glass, afraid to wink lest I should miss something. Grace's warning, 'You will fret yourself to death and you will be back before a month,' grew faint in my ears. When night shut out my new world and I fell asleep, I dreamed of extraordinary phenomena – trees stalking about the plains, fairies leaping out of the foam of the rivers.

I opened my eyes to a rose-coloured dawn. We had stopped before a little village inn. A row of pigeons with burnished necks looked down on me from their perch on the signboard above the door; a half-dressed, curly-headed child peeped out of a window from under the eaves, and clapped his hands at the steaming horses; and a young man walked out of the inn with a whip in his hand, and asked if there might be a lady inside the coach whose destination was Hillsbro' Farm.

I was soon seated by his side in a gig. By a few careful glances I had easily assured myself that there was nothing of the ploughman in the appearance of Mrs Hollingford's son. You will want to know what I thought of him that morning, and I will tell you. He seemed to me the beau ideal of a country gentleman: nothing less than this, and something more. You have known him, my dears, stooped and white-haired, and have loved him in his age for the sake of the heart that never grew old. But on that brilliant autumn morning when he and I first sat side by side, the same lovable spirit was clothed with the strength and beauty of mortal youth.

The vivid life of the country was sweet to me that early morning. Carts of hay lumbered past us, almost crushing us into the hedges as they swept along heavily, leaving a trail of fragrance in the air. Red and brown leaves lay thick on the ground, making beautiful the undulations of the roads. Mists of dew hung among the purple folds of the hills, and the sun dashed the woods and streams with kindling gold. By and by the whole countryside was laughing in the full face of the day.

Hillsbro' Farmhouse was, and is, a low long dwelling built of dark bricks, and standing among orchards and meadows, green pasture lands and running streams. Its ivied chimneys had for background the sombre lines of a swelling moor, belted by a wood of pines which skirted the hollow wherein the earth nourished the fatness and sweetness of the thrifty farm acres. Along the edge of the moor the road ran that led to Hillsbro' Hall, and a short cut through the wood brought one down upon a back entrance to the squire's own grounds.

The dear old farm! Roses were blowing in that morning at the open sashes of the big, heavy, roughly hung windows. Two young girls, who were afterwards dear to me as fibres of my heart, lingered beside the open door; stately handsome Jane, with her solemn observant black eyes and trim dark dress, and frolicsome Mopsie, with her laughing face, and her hat tied down, gypsy fashion, with a red ribbon. They lingered to see me, to take their share in giving me a welcome, and then set out on their long walk, discussing me by the way. They told me of it afterwards. Jane said I was only fit for a glass case, and Mopsie declared I alighted from the old gig as if I had a mind to dance. They were awed by the high heels on my boots, the feather in my hat, and the quilted satin of my pelisse. They wondered I could deign to speak anything but French, and concluded I did so only out of compliment to their homeliness.

And I, meanwhile, decked in all the fanciful elegancies of a London toilette, sat down to breakfast in the long parlour at Hillsbro' Farm, with something in my heart that would not let me eat though I was hungry, and something in my eyes that would not let me see very well, though the sun came rich and yellow through each of the wide windows, forming one broad golden path down the middle of the room. I saw but dimly the dark brown walls and ceiling, the stiff-backed chairs with their worn covers, the jar full of late roses that stood in either window, the heap of trailing ivy that overran the huge grate. It was Mrs Hollingford's face that did it as she sat, kind, careful, hospitable, pressing on me sweet home-made cakes, fresh butter, fragrant tea, delicious cream and delicate pink eggs. Ah me! it was her face that did it. There was my great lady, my beneficent friend, my valiant woman. Her eyes were somewhat sunken, the fire of their energy a trifle slackened, her brow a little seamed; the strain of fortitude had drawn a tight cord about her mouth. Whence, then, that new touching beauty that made one see the stamp of heaven's nobility shining on her face? Had I quite forgotten her, or was she indeed something new? It was as if grief had chiselled her features afresh out of the superfluous roundings of prosperity, wasted them into perfect sweetness, hacked them into purer refinement. She wore a strait black gown of the coarsest material, only the fair folds of muslin about her throat giving daintiness to her attire. Her son breakfasted with us, and I fancied he often looked at me curiously as if to say, 'What concern can she have with us? why did she come? how long will she remain?' I had talked to him without embarrassment as we drove along, but now I could hardly speak. Never had I felt so shy in any company as I did in the presence of my mother's friend.

After breakfast she led me to my room, bright and airy, but scantily furnished. It had a window looking out on an orchard threaded by long alleys, over which hung a glowing roof of fruit-laden branches. And here I unpacked my trunks and stowed away my elegant dresses in a huge painted wardrobe smelling of apples. I laid aside with a kind of shame all the little ornaments I was accustomed to wear, and dressed myself in the plainest gown I possessed. Descending the quaint old staircase again, I found Mrs Hollingford walking up and down the hall waiting patiently for my appearance.

'What a great woman you have grown, my love!' she said, drawing my hand within her arm, and leading me through the open hall door. 'But you have still your mother's fair hair and sunny eyes. Will you walk with me for an hour? I have much to say to you, and the sooner it is said the better.'

Then she told me the story of her life, and misfortunes, sternly, sweetly, with strange humility and fortitude. I knew much of it before, but she would tell it all.

'And now, my love,' she said, 'you know us as we are. Your mother, when she made me your guardian, did not foresee the changes that were to take place. You have other friends who are willing to give you a home. You have come here of your own will. When you wish to leave us we shall not wonder.'

I threw my arms round her neck and told her I would not leave her. Never, since Miss Kitty Sweetman went to India, had my heart gone forth so completely to anyone.

She bade me not be too hasty. 'You will find our life so different from anything you have ever known,' she said. 'We all fear it for you. We are so busy here. We have always a purpose before our eyes to make us work.'

'Then I shall work too,' I said. 'I will not be the only drone in such a thrifty hive.'

She smiled at this, and shook her head. But I immediately began to cast about for the means by which I might find it possible to keep my word.

I soon learned to love the farm. I began to know the meaning of the word 'home.' The beauty and lovableness of some persons and places takes you by surprise; with others they steal upon you by degrees; but there was that about Hillsbro' Farm which I loved much at once and more afterwards. Looking at it in the most commonplace way, it had all the peace and plenty of an English farmhouse, while for eyes that sought more they would find enough that was picturesque in the orchard's ruddy thickets, where the sun struck fire on frosty mornings; in the wide pasture lands sloping to the sedgy river, where the cows cooled their feet on sultry evenings. You know as well as I the curious bowery garden beyond the lower window of the parlour, stocked with riches and sweets of all kinds, rows of beehives standing in the sun, roses and raspberries growing side by side. The breaths of thyme and balm, lavender and myrtle, were always in that parlour. You know the sheepfold and the paddock, the old tree over the west gable where the owl made his nest – the owl that used to come and sit on our schoolroom windowsill and hoot at night. You know the sundial where the screaming peacock used to perch and spread his tail; the dovecote, where the silver-necks and fantails used to coo and ruffle their feathers. You know, too, all the quaint plannings and accidents of the old house; how the fiery creeper ran riot through the ivy on the dark walls, dangling its burning wreaths over the windows; how the hall door lay open all day with the dogs sleeping on the broad doorstep. Also, within, that there were long dark passages, rooms with low ceilings; a step up here, and a step down there; fireplaces twisted into odd corners, narrow pointed windows, and wide latticed ones. You know all the household recesses, the dairies and pantries and storerooms; but you cannot know how Mrs Hollingford toiled among them, filling them with her industry one day that they might be emptied the next; hardening her delicate hands with labour to the end that justice might be done, that some who had lost might gain, that a portion of her husband's heavy debts might be paid, and a portion of the curse of the impoverished lifted from his guilty shoulders.

No luxury was ever permitted in that household. Old gowns were worn and mended till they could be worn and mended no longer.

The girls were of an age to go abroad to school, but they must be contented with such education as they could pick up at home, so long as one poor creature suffered straits through their father's fault. The only indulgence allowed was almsgiving. Mopsie might divide her dinner with a hungry child, or Jane bestow her new petticoat on an aged woman; but they must, in consequence, deny themselves and suffer inconvenience till such time as it came to be again their turn to have their absolute wants relieved.

I did, indeed, feel like a drone in a hive when, on leaving my room in the mornings, I met Mrs Hollingford coming from her work in the dairy, John Hollingford arriving from his early visit to a distant part of the farm, Jane from her sewing closet where she made and mended the linen of the household, and Mopsie from the kitchen with a piled dish of breakfast-cakes, showing what her morning task had been. I could not eat for envy. Why could I not be of use to somebody? I gave Mopsie some gay ribbons, which were returned to me by her mother. Nothing might she wear but her plain black frock and white frill. I gave Jane a book of poems with woodcuts, and that was accepted with rapture. This encouraged me. I picked up two little children on the road, and to one I gave a bright silk girdle for a skipping-rope, and to the other a doll dressed from the materials of a fine gauze hat, which I picked to pieces for the purpose. I was not going to be a peony flaunting among thrifty modest vetches. At first I was sorry for the destruction of my pretty things, but soon I grew to admire the demureness of my grey gown and little black apron. I learned to make pies and cakes, to sweep a room and set it to rights, to wash and get up linen and laces, to churn to make butter. But as many hands were engaged in these matters, I was often thrown out of employment. I made music for my friends in the evenings, and, as they liked it, this was something; but it was not enough. A new spirit had entered into me. I felt my old self lost in the admiration which I had conceived for the new friends who had accepted me among them.

By and by I found out a little niche of usefulness for myself. Jane and Mopsie attended the village school. One day I went to the town to buy some trifle and call for the girls. It was past the hour for breaking up, and I found Mopsie romping with some rude-looking girls on the green, while Jane, detained for some fault, sat alone in the schoolroom, perched on a bench, her arms folded and her eyes gloomily fixed on the wall. When I entered she blushed crimson.

She was a proud girl, and I knew she was hurt at my seeing her disgrace. I coaxed her to speak out her trouble.

'I could teach the whole school,' she said, fiercely – 'master, mistress, and all – and yet I am kept sitting over a, b, c, like a baby. I get so sick of it that sometimes I answer wrong by way of novelty. Then I have to hold out my hand for the rod. Today I drew Portia and Shylock on my slate, and forgot to finish my sum; therefore I am disgraced!'

I seized the happy moment and offered myself to the girls as a governess. Mopsie stopped on the road and hugged me in delight. Jane squeezed my hand and was silent during the rest of the walk, except when she said, 'Mother will never consent. I am too proud, and she wants me to be humbled. She thinks it is good for me to go to the village school.'

That night, however, I laid my plan before Mrs Hollingford, and, after some trouble, I attained my point.

We chose for our schoolroom an unoccupied chamber at the end of a long passage upstairs. It was furnished with a deal table and chairs, and a small square of green carpet laid upon the sanded floor. It had three latticed windows looking westward, and one of those odd grates I have mentioned, large enough to cook a dinner. We kept it filled with logs, and in the evenings, after we had drawn the curtains in the parlour, set the tea-table, and made Mrs Hollingford comfortable on the sofa for an hour's rest, we three retreated to our schoolroom for a chat in the firelight. Here John joined us when he happened to come home early, and many a happy hour we passed, four of us sitting round the blazing logs, talking and roasting apples. We told stories, tales of the outer world, and legends of the country around us. We described places and people we had seen, and our fancies about others we had not seen. John, who had travelled, was the most frequent speaker, and as I was a wonder of experience to his sisters, just so was he a wonder to me. We laughed, cried, or listened in breathless silence, all as he willed, while the purple and yellow lingered in the sky behind the lattice, and the moaning of the wind through the forlorn fields, the hissing of the roasting apples and the crackling of the burning wood kept up an accompaniment to his voice.

There were other evenings, too, when John was late, and Mopsie, having grown tired of serious talk, tripped off to hear the lasses singing Bold Robin Hood in the kitchen. Then Jane used to open her heart to me, and talk about the troubles of the family. Her heart was stern and bitter against her father. Well had she said she was proud; well had her mother wished to humble her, if that could be done. She had, I believe, a great intellect, and she had much personal beauty of a grand character. I do not think she thought much about the latter, but she felt her mental powers. She knew she was fitted to move in a high sphere, and chafed against her fate; still more against the fate of her brother.

I can see her now, on her low seat before the fire, her hands clasping one knee, her dark head thrown back, and her eyes fixed on the dancing shadows above the chimney.

'To think of John settling down as a farmer!' she said. 'John, who for cleverness might be prime minister. And there is no hope of his getting away from it; none whatever.'

I could not but agree to this, though the thought occurred to me that the farm might not be so pleasant a home if John had to go away and be prime minister. All I could say I said to combat her rebellious despondency as to her own future.

'If you knew the emptiness and foolishness of the gay world,' I said in a sage manner, 'you would be thankful for our quiet life at Hillsbro'.'

'It is not the gay world I think of,' she said. 'It is the world of thought, of genius.'

'Well, Jane,' said I, cheerfully, 'you may pierce your way to that yet.'

'No!' she said. 'If I had a clean name I would try to do it. As it is, I will not hold up my head only to be pointed at. But I will not spend my life at Hillsbro', moping. I will go away and work – teach, or write, if I can.'

I saw her eyes beginning to flash, and I did not like these fierce moods in Jane. I was turning over a book at the time, and, to divert her attention, I read aloud the name written on the title-page.

'Mary Hollingford,' I said. 'Was not she your elder sister?'

Jane started. 'Yes,' she said. 'Who mentioned her to you?'

'Your mother,' I said, 'used to tell me of her little Mary, who was at school in France. I cannot recollect who told me of her death. Do you remember her?'

'Oh yes,' said Jane, 'perfectly. We did not lose her till after – my father went away.'

'I suppose she took the trouble to heart,' I said, reflectively; and then was sorry I had said it. But Jane answered,

'Yes,' readily; then dropped her face between her hands, and remained plunged in one of her motionless fits of abstraction for half an hour.

I never alluded to this subject again to Jane, but one evening when Mopsie and I were alone together, the child spoke of it herself.

'Margery,' she said, 'you are holding me now just as sister Mary used to hold me with both her arms round my waist, when I was a tiny little thing and she used to play with me in our nursery in London.'

'You remember her, then?' I said.

'Yes,' said Mopsie. 'I remember her like a dream. She used to come home for the holidays, and a handsome French lady with her, who used to throw up her hands if we had not ribbons in our sleeves and smart rosettes on our shoes. I remember sister Mary in a pretty white frock trimmed with lace, and her hair curled down to her waist. I used to think her like one of the angels. But we never speak of her now, nor of papa, because it pains mother and John. I used to speak of her to Jane sometimes in the night, just to ask her did she think sister Mary was thinking of us in heaven; but Jane used to get into such dreadful fits of crying that I grew afraid. I wish someone would talk of her. I think it is cruel of us all to forget her because she is dead.'

And tears stood in Mopsie's blue eyes. But the next half hour she was singing like a skylark over some household task.

4.

The winter deepened. Christmas was drawing near, and workmen were busy setting the old Hall to rights for the reception of Mr Hill and his family. John had been requested to oversee the arrangements, for the place had been unoccupied for years, and there were many alterations to be made, and much new furnishing to be done. The housekeeper, who had quietly dozed away half her life in two rooms in a corner of the house, now bestirred herself joyfully to open shutters, kindle fires, see to the sweeping and scrubbing, keep her eye upon painters and charwomen, and make ready store of pickles and preserves for the adornment of her pantry shelves.

This good woman was an old acquaintance of our two girls, their long walks often leading them across the moor and through the grounds to the Hall. Mrs Beatty, from her lonely window, had always espied their approach, and many a winter day had she fed them with sweets by her fireside, while she dried their wet wrappings, and told them stories of the pictures in the dining-room. Later, they had discovered the library, a sunny room at the south side of the house, stored with an excellent collection of books, and had gone there to read when it pleased them. I, in my capacity of governess, encouraged them in this habit, and at least once a week we had a 'reading day', as we called it. Mrs Beatty knew our day, and had coffee and a blazing fire awaiting us. And here we had delicious times of study, with our books in our laps, perched on the steps of the little ladder, or buried in the recesses of the deep leathern chairs.

Now, however, the luxury of our quiet days was interfered with. Workmen hammered about our ears, and an impertinent odour of paint annoyed us. We turned our reading days into days of general inspection, and amused ourselves with watching how the dingy corners threw off their cobwebs one after another, and came forth into the light with clean and brilliant faces. It was pleasant to know that I was useful to John in those days, for his mother did not interfere in this affair, and he needed a woman's taste to help him. It was I who selected the colours for Mrs Hill's drawing-room carpet, I who chose the silk hangings for Miss Leonard's boudoir, I who rearranged in the cabinets the curiosities about which no one but a stray mouse or two had been curious for many years. I knew well that I did nothing but what any other person could do, yet it pleased me to see how John overrated my services. It delighted me to hear him praise to his mother my 'exquisite taste and skill'; but it pained me to see her anxious look from him to me. I knew she feared that he was getting to love me well; sometimes with a mixture of fear and joy I thought it myself. I guessed that his mother would rather keep her son by her side unwed – perhaps that he could not afford to marry. I often longed to slip my hand in hers, and say, 'Be not afraid, I am true;' but I could only look straight in her eyes and be silent. And this thought, perhaps because I might not speak it out and have done with it, remained with me, and preyed upon my mind. About this time I began to lie awake at nights, planning how I might show Mrs Hollingford that I had no wish to thrust myself between her and her son.

And so it came that there arose a strangeness between John and me. I did not wish it to be so, but it happened naturally as a consequence of all my thinking and planning. It grew up in the midst of our pleasant work at the Hall, and it was burthensome, for it took the joyous adornment off everything, made handsome things ugly, and comfortable things dreary. It made the snowy landscape lonely, and the red sun angry. It made me cold and disobliging, the girls dull and John proud and reserved. Jane spoke of it to me; she said: 'What is the matter between you and John? You used to be such good friends. Now you hurry downstairs in the evenings, though you know he likes our chat round the schoolroom fire. And when we go to the Hall you start early for the purpose of walking home without him.'

'Don't be foolish, Jane,' I said; 'John and I are just as good friends as ever. But you must not suppose he always cares for our women's chatter. We must give him a little rest sometimes.'

Jane was silenced, but not satisfied. She thought I was beginning to look down on her brother. The proud, loving heart would not brook this, and she, too, estranged herself from me. The girl was very dear to me, and it was a trial.

Thus a division grew up among us. It was in the bright frosty days before Christmas, when the fields and dales were wrapped in snow, when the logs burned merrily and the crickets sang, when fairyland was painted on every window-pane, when our superintendence at the Hall was over, when all things there had been placed in readiness, even to the lighting of the fires in the bedchambers. We had left Mrs Beatty in possession of her domain, and in daily expectation of an announcement of the intended arrival of her master and mistress. Things were in this way when one day a carriage dashed up to our farmhouse door, and out stepped Grace Tyrrell and her brother Frederick.

Jane shrank into a corner when I asked her to accompany me downstairs, murmuring something I would not hear about my 'fine friends'. But Mopsie smoothed her curly locks, put on her best apron, and slipped her hand in mine as I went down to the parlour.

Grace was impatiently tripping about the room, making faces at the bare walls and laughing at the old-fashioned furniture. She was clothed in velvet and fur with feathers nodding from her hat. She put her hands on my shoulders and eyed me all over critically.

'Pray, little Quakeress,' said she, 'can you tell me what has become of my friend Margery?'

'Yes,' said I laughing, 'I actually happen to have her about me. What do you want with her?'

'Only to ask her what sin she has committed that she shuts herself up from the world, starves herself to skin and bone, and dresses herself in sackcloth?' she replied, touching my dress, and trying its texture between her finger and thumb.

'We do not starve her,' put in Mopsie stoutly.

'And who are you, little miss?' said Grace, using a gold-rimmed eyeglass, which nearly annihilated poor Mopsie.

'No matter,' said the little one, scarlet and trembling. 'We are all Margery's friends, and we love her dearly.'

Grace laughed at the child's ardour, as if it were something very funny and original; but Mopsie, never flinching, held my hand all the time.

'And what about the ploughman, dear?' Grace went on; 'would it be possible to get a sight of him? Yes, do go' (to Mopsie), 'like a useful little girl, and see about getting us some lunch. We are staying in this country at present, Margery, and when we return to London we intend to take you with us.'

Mopsie's eyes dilated dangerously, but she retreated to the door at a whisper from me.

'Frederick,' said Grace, 'come and help me to persuade Margery;' and Mopsie vanished.

I said something about Frederick Tyrrell before, but I can hardly describe how excessively slim, and elegant, and effeminate he looked to me that day in particular. His dress and his manners amused me very much. While staying with the Tyrrells one of my chief occupations had been making fun of this young man, a fact of which I believe he was blissfully unconscious. Perhaps experience had made him incredulous as to the indifference any young lady might feel to his special favour; or it might have been conceit; I will not pretend to decide which. But when he drew near me, murmuring (shall I say lisping?), 'Oh, do come; pray, take pity on us – we have missed you so dreadfully,' I am sure he thought he did enough to make any reasonable young woman desire to leave Hillsbro' on the instant.

But I did not want to leave Hillsbro', I felt a pang of keen pain at the very suggestion; yet at the same moment an idea came into my mind that it might be a good thing that I should leave it for a time. I hesitated, asked Grace when she intended returning to London, and, while we were parleying about the matter, Mopsie returned. During the remainder of the visit the little girl listened earnestly to everything we said on the subject, and when I parted from my friends at the gate, leaving it undecided whether I should go with them to London or not, Mopsie burst into tears and clung to my neck.

'Do not go with them,' she said; 'they cannot love you as we do.'

'Mopsie, my pet,' I said, 'don't be a little goose. Neither do I love them as I love you. If I go away for a time I will be sure to come back.'

Mopsie whispered her fears to Jane, and all that evening Jane kept aloof from me. My head ached with trying to think of what I ought to do, and I sat alone by the schoolroom hearth in the firelight considering my difficulties, fighting against my wishes, and endeavouring in vain to convince myself that I had no wishes at all. Mopsie came in and lay down at my feet, with her face rolled up in my gown; and so busy was I that I did not know she was crying. John came in and found her out. He took her on his knee and stroked her as if she had been a kitten. Mopsie would not be comforted. I felt guilty and said nothing. John looked from her to me, wondering. At last Mopsie's news came out.

'Margery's grand London friends have been here, and they want to take her away.'

'What grand London friends?' asked John, looking at me, but talking to her.

'Oh, Mr and Miss Tyrrell, a pretty lady with long feathers and ringlets, and flounces on her dress, and a handsome gentleman who said they had missed Margery dreadfully. And Margery is thinking of going back to them.'

John suddenly stopped stroking her, and sat quite still. I felt him looking at me earnestly, and at last I had to look up, which I did smiling, and saying, 'I did not know Mopsie cared so much about me.'

Then John kissed the little girl, and said, 'Go downstairs to Jane, dear. I have something particular to say to Margery.'

I was completely taken by surprise. He closed the door upon Mopsie, and came back and reseated himself at the fire. He sat on one side of the fireplace, and I at the other, and the flames danced between us. He shaded his face with his hand, and looked across at me; and I watched intently a great tree falling in the depths of a burning forest among the embers.

'Is this true, Margery,' said John, 'that you are going to leave us, and return to London?'

'I am thinking of it,' I said pleasantly.

'I thought – I had hoped you were happy with us,' he said.

'Yes,' I said, 'I have been very happy, but I think I want a little change.'

How my heart ached with the effort of uttering that untruth! I knew that I wanted no change.

'I do not wonder at it,' he said after a pause. 'We have made a slave of you. You are tired of it, and you are going away.'

He said this bitterly and sorrowfully, shading his eyes still more with his hand.

'No, no,' I said, 'you must not say that. I never was so happy in my life as I have been here.'

I spoke more eagerly than I meant to do, and my voice broke a little in spite of me. John left his seat and bent down beside me, so that he could see my face, which could not escape him.

'Margery,' said he, 'I have seen that you have made yourself happy, and I have been sometimes wild enough to hope that you would be content to spend your life among us. When you came first I feared to love you too well, but your sweet face and your sweet ways have been too much for me. It may be ungenerous in me to speak, seeing that I only have to offer you a true love, truer maybe than you will meet with in the gay world, a tarnished name, and a very humble home. I have debts to pay, and a soil to wash off my name; but still, Margery, will you be my wife? With your love nothing will be dark or difficult to me.'

It was very hard. My heart was brimming over with a joyous reply to this appeal; but Mrs Hollingford's uneasy face was vividly before my eyes all the time, and I could only say distressedly, 'It cannot be, John. It cannot, cannot be.'

'Why?' he asked, almost sternly, and he rose up and stood above me. 'Tell me that you cannot love me – tell me you would rather save yourself for more honour, more prosperity, and I will never trouble you again. Were I differently circumstanced I might plead, but I could not live to see you discontented, ashamed. Why can it not be, Margery?'

I clasped my hands in my lap, and tried to speak firmly. 'For a reason that I cannot give to you, John. Let us be good friends.'

'Friends!' he echoed bitterly. 'Well! I was wrong to think of my own happiness before your worldly advantage. Goodbye, Margery. I am going to London in the morning. Perhaps you may be gone before I come back.'

And with this he abruptly walked out of the room. But afterwards

I sat there an hour, wondering if what had passed so quickly were true, and I had really refused to be John Hollingford's wife.

After tea he left us early, saying he must start from Hillsbro' at four in the morning. Mopsie fell asleep, and Jane absorbed herself in her books. Mrs Hollingford and I held some embroidery in our hands, but my fingers trembled so that the stitches went all wrong. Now and again, glancing up, I encountered long troubled looks from Mrs Hollingford. She had seen that something was amiss between me and John, and I guessed that her mind was at work with fears. I could not bear it; I thought it was not fair after what I had done. For the first and last time I felt angry and impatient with the dear old lady. Would she herself, in her own young days, have sacrificed as much? Jane shut up her books at last, and carried Mopsie off with her to bed, and Mrs Hollingford and I were left sitting facing one another.

'Mrs Hollingford,' I said, dropping my work with almost a sob, 'don't look at me like that. I cannot bear it, and I do not deserve it.'

What made me say it I cannot think. The moment before I spoke I had no intention of speaking. Mrs Hollingford dropped her work in dismay.

'My love,' she said, 'what do you mean? I do not understand. What do my looks say that you cannot bear?'

'Oh, Mrs Hollingford,' I said, covering my burning cheeks with my hands, 'you must know what I mean. You look at me, and look at me, and I see what is in your mind. How can I help it?'

'My dear,' said she, 'is it anything about John?'

'Yes,' said I desperately, 'it is about John. You think I want to take him from you, and I do not, and I never will, and I have told him so. I am going away to London with my friends the Tyrrells, and I will never trouble you any more.'

I was rather blind by this time, and I was not sure of what part of the room I was in; but Mrs Hollingford had come to my side, and she put her arms round about me and fondled my head on her breast.

'My dear,' she said, 'and is this the secret that has made the trouble between us? I never thought that you wanted to take him from me; on the contrary, I feared that you might be too young to understand his worth. I dreaded sorrow and suffering for my son, nothing else.'

My face was hidden in her motherly embrace. I could not speak for some moments, and I thought my heart had stopped beating. At last I whispered: 'Oh, Mrs Hollingford, I have made a great mistake. Can it be that you really – '

'Will have you for a daughter?' she asked, smiling. 'Gladly, thankfully, my darling, if it be for your happiness. But you must not decide hastily; there are great disadvantages which you must consider, and I, as your guardian and friend, must point them out to you. I must forget my son's interests in the faithful discharge of my trust. John has a cloud upon his name.'

'Don't, don't!' I said, 'if he had a hundred clouds upon his name it would be all the same to me.'

'Then you love him well?' she said tenderly, sighing and smiling at the same time.

'I think I do,' I said; 'but that is only a misfortune, for you know I have refused him.'

'Well,' she said cheerfully, 'perhaps it is for the best. You must go to London with your friends, and test your feeling by absence and the society of others. If you remain unattracted by those who are better placed in the world, I think John will try again, in spite of his pride. I know I should in his place,' she said, lifting up my disturbed face, and looking in it with a half quizzical fondness.

I answered by throwing my arms round her neck in a long tearful embrace, and after that we sat long by the fireside talking the matter over. The consequence was, oddly enough, that I went upstairs to bed feeling so extremely sober that, before I laid my head upon my pillow, I had begun to doubt whether I cared for John Hollingford at all. It was not that I shrank from what his mother had called the 'sacrifices' I should make in becoming his wife. I never even thought of them. I had found too much happiness at Hillsbro' Farm to be able to realise their existence. But I had a superstition that I ought to feel very joyfully excited about all I had learned that evening; first, that John really loved me, and, secondly, that his mother was ready to take me to her heart. Yet I only felt sobered to the last degree, and exceedingly afraid of seeing John again. I heard him driving away from the door before daybreak, and I found myself hoping that he might not come back for a week.

The next day I was in the same mood. I felt so grave and quiet that I made up my mind I could not have that wonderful love for John which I believed to be the duty of a wife. I thought I had better write to Grace, and arrange about going with her to London. Then I grew miserable at the thought of leaving the farm, and wished I had never seen it. For three days I tormented myself thus, and then there came a shock which brought me cruelly to my senses.

On the fourth day after John had left us, I was walking up and down the frosty avenue just as the evening was coming on. The sun was setting redly behind the brown wood, and blushing over the whitened fields and hedgerows. A man came up the avenue and pulled off his hat as he approached me. I recognised in him an Irish labourer whom I had seen working in the gardens at the Hall.

'Beg pardon, miss!' said he, 'but be you Miss Margery Dacre?'

'Yes, Pat,' said I. 'This is a fine evening, is it not? What do you want with me?'

'Oh then, a fine evenin' it is; glory be to God!' said Pat; 'but all the same, Mrs Beatty is mortial anxious for you to step over to the Hall the soonest minute ye can, as she has somethin' very sarious to say to ye.'

'Step over to the Hall?' I exclaimed. 'Do you know what o'clock it is, Pat?'

'Oh yis, miss!' said Pat; 'it's three o'clock, an' the sun low, but niver fear; I'll walk behind ye ivery step o' the way, an' if as much as a hare winks at ye, he'll rue the day. Mrs Beatty would ha' come over here to spake to ye, only for fear o' hersel' at the farm,' said Pat, jerking his thumb in the direction of the house. 'God keep sorrow from her door; but I'm feared there's throuble in the wind!'

I did not quite understand whether the threatened trouble was for Mrs Beatty or Mrs Hollingford. I guessed the latter, and thought immediately of the absent husband and father. I felt that I could not do better than obey the summons. Pat promised to wait for me at the gate, and I hastened into the house to prepare for my journey.

'I am going for a walk, Jane,' I said, looking in at the schoolroom door. 'Don't be surprised if I am not in before dark.'

'But, Margery!' I heard her beginning, and did not wait to hear any more.

How I racked my brains during that walk to try and guess the cause of my sudden summons. The only thing I could think of was that Mr Hollingford was in prison. I never fancied anything approaching to the truth.

Mrs Beatty was anxiously watching at the door for my arrival. She had tea waiting for me, and began pulling off my bonnet and boots at her fireside. But her hands were shaking, and her eyes red and watering.

'Never mind me, Mrs Beatty,' I said, imploringly; 'tell me what is the matter.'

'Take a sup of tea first, my dear young lady,' said she; 'ill news is heard soon enough.'

'I won't taste it,' I said, pushing it away. 'Tell me this instant!' I said, as a dim fear of the truth came across my brain.

'Well, my dear,' she said, beginning to cry outright, 'you see there has been a terrible smash of the coach from London. The horses fell crossing a bridge, and the coach was overturned into the river; and they do say everybody was killed or drowned. And poor young Mr Hollingford was in the coach; and, oh! that I should have to say it, he's met a cruel death. I sent for you, dear young lady, that you might break the news gently to his mother; for there's not a soul in the countryside dare carry the story to her door, and they'll maybe be bringing home the bodies.'

'Stop!' said I. 'Mrs Beatty – are you sure – '

And the next thing I knew was a sensation of coldness and wetness upon my face, and a smell of vinegar and wine, and a sound of murmuring and crying.

'Dear heart, dear heart! to think of her taking on so!' I heard the good woman saying, and I crept to my feet, and began tying on my bonnet in spite of her entreaties that I would lie still.

'No, no, I must get home!' I said, shuddering. 'Someone else will come and tell her, and it will kill her. Let me go at once! Let me go!'

At the door in the frosty dusk Pat was waiting with a horse and gig.

'I was thinkin' ye'd be a bit staggered by the news, miss,' he said, 'an' I put the mare to this ould shandheradan. It's not very fit for a lady, bad manners to it! but it'll be betther nor the slippery roads undher yer feet.'

I do not know how the drive passed. I remember saying once to Pat, 'Are they quite, quite sure that Mr Hollingford was – was – '

'No indeed, miss,' was the answer, 'sorra sure at all. They do say he was in the coach, but no wan seen him dead, as far as I can hear tell.'

I made the man set me down at the farm gate, and walked up the avenue just as the early moonlight was beginning to light up the frosty world. As I came near the door, I fancied I heard crying and wailing; but it was only Mopsie singing in the hall. Behind the parlour window I saw Jane stepping about briskly in the firelight, arranging the table for tea. All was quiet and peaceful as when I had left the place two hours before.

The children followed me to my room, wondering where I could have been so late. I said I was tired, and begged them to leave me alone. Then I locked my door, and a solitary hour of anguish passed. The fever of uncertainty would not let me weep; I suffered without much sign, but in such a degree as I had never dreamed of before.

There was something horrible that I had to realise and could not. John hurt and dying away from his home, without one by to comfort him, without his mother's blessing, without a whisper to tell him that I had loved him and would mourn for him all my life! John vanished from the earth – lost to us for ever! The sickly moonlight fell about me with a ghastly peace, and the horror of death froze my heart.

Tea-hour arrived, and the girls knocked at the door. Mrs Hollingford came to me, questioning me anxiously, and pressing my burning temples between her cool palms; and there I lay under her hands, crushed with my cruel secret. I could not tell it. Not that night. When the worst must be known it would be my place to help them all in their agony; and was I fit for such a task now? Besides, there was still a hope, and I clung to it with wild energy.

They left me for the night, thinking I slept, but when the clock struck five I wrapped myself in a cloak, and went out and down the avenue. I was half afraid of the ghostly trees, so black against the snow, but I was more in terror of the melancholy corners of my own room, the solitary light, the dreary ashes in the grate. I walked as far as the gate, and even ventured out on the road, hoping to see some wayfarer coming past who might be able to tell me something of the accident. I tried to consider how far it might be to the nearest wayside cottage, where I might possibly learn some news that might break the awful suspense. But my head was confused, and I suppose I did not calculate the distance rightly, for after I had walked a mile I could see no dwelling. The morning was breaking now, and the world looked pallid and dreary. Suddenly my strength failed, I felt faint and dizzy, and sat down upon a heap of stones, drawing my cloak over my face. My thoughts became broken and confused, and my senses numb. I remained, lost in a sort of stupid dream of trouble, I do not know how long, when the touch of a hand on my shoulder made me start, and a voice said, 'What is the matter with you, my poor woman?'

It was a man's voice – a familiar voice; my children, it was the voice of John Hollingford. With a cry I flung back the cloak from my face. 'John! – John!' I cried, and grasped him by both hands. There he stood unhurt. I burst into a fit of weeping, though not a tear had I shed all the while I had pictured him lying dead or dying. 'I thought I never should have seen your face again except in the coffin!'

I sobbed in my joy, hardly knowing what I said.

'Margery!' he said. 'Is this all for me?'

'I cannot help it,' I said. 'I ought, but I cannot. No one knows but me. I heard it last night – '

'You are killing yourself sitting here in the cold,' said John. 'You are nearly frozen to death.' He wrapped my cloak round me, and drew my arm through his.

'Who told you of the accident?' he said.

'Mrs Beatty.'

'She might have kept her own counsel till today. Several poor fellows have been killed, but many escaped, like myself, unhurt. And so you kept it from my mother, and you grieved for me. Margery, may I ask again that question I asked you the night before I went away? If it pains you, say nothing.'

'You may ask it.'

'And what will you answer?'

'Anything you like.'

'And you do not want to go to London?'

'Not unless you turn me out of doors.'

'My darling!' he said. And so we became engaged there upon the snow.

How wonderful the sun rose that morning. How I walked home through Paradise, forgetting that there was such a thing as suffering in the world. How the girls hugged me when they knew all. How Mrs Hollingford smiled upon us. And how sweet the honey and rice-cakes tasted at breakfast. It was arranged that, all things considered, we had better not be married for a year.

I remember our gathering round the fire that evening, the curtains unclosed, the mild moonshine behind the window, the room half black shade and half red light, the dear faces beaming round. That evening I wrote my letter to Grace Tyrrell to say that I should not go to London. That evening, also, there came a letter from Mr Hill to John, saying that he hoped to arrive at the Hall on the morrow or next day. At tea we talked about Rachel Leonard. Thinking of her, the scene at the party came vividly back – the occasion on which I had defended Mr Hollingford so hotly; and also my conversation with Grace Tyrrell on the subject in the carriage coming home. After musing a little while, I said: 'John, are you quite sure that you never met Miss Leonard when you were abroad?'

'Quite,' said John, looking at me curiously. 'Why do you ask me that question so often, Margery?'

'Have I asked it often?' I said, 'I don't remember; but I fancied from her manner that she knew something about you.'

'It is not likely,' said John, 'for I know nothing about her.' And so this matter dropped.

6

John made me promise to go out to meet him next morning on his return from his early walk across the farm. I remember so well how gladly I sprang from my bed that morning, how tedious my dressing seemed, and yet how I lingered over it at the last, anxious to make myself more pleasing in the eyes which I knew would be watching for me from the hill. I remember how, in the tenderness of my joy, I opened my sash to feed the robins, and how gay and fair the world looked in its robe of white. I remember how I ran after a little beggar boy to give him sixpence, and how afterwards I went along the path through the fields singing aloud for mere happiness. And yet a little cloud had already risen out of the glories of the shining east, and was spreading and moving towards me.

John and I walked home together, side by side, and we talked the happiest talk that ever was written or spoken. The world was all radiant over our heads and under our feet, and we could not see even the shadow of the cloud that was coming, fast as the wheels that were rolling towards us from the distance.

'Look, Margery!' said John, 'do you see a carriage on the road?'

I shaded my eyes with my hand, and I saw the carriage.

'I dare say it is the Hills',' I said, and then we walked on through the white fields and between the bare hedges till we came out upon the road which leads away across the moor between Hillsbro' Farm and Hillsbro' Hall. There is a spot on this road which you know well, where the ground sinks into a hollow, and then rises in a steep abrupt hill, on the top of which any object suddenly appearing stands out in sharp relief against the sky, in the eyes of the traveller below. We reached the foot of this hill, John and I; we began to ascend; I raised my eyes, and saw a figure appear on the brink of the hill, a woman's figure with draperies fluttering a little as the petticoats of the market women flutter when they tramp the road to Hillsbro'. I raised my eyes again, and came face to face with Rachel Leonard.

She was walking quickly, pressing forward, wrapped in a fur mantle, with a Shetland snood drawn round her face. I remember the momentary expression of that face before it changed at sight of us; the delicate brows knitted as if in pain or anxiety; the wide dark eyes intent upon the scenes opening before them; the scarlet lips parted in fatigue; the glow of exercise wandering over the cheeks.

She did not see us at first; the sun was in her eyes; but I spoke her name aloud, and held out my hand. She started violently, and all the colour flew out of her cheeks. She took my hand, and held it mechanically, but her eyes were fixed on John. I looked at him in amazement, seeking for some explanation of the strange long look in her eyes, and the trembling of her white lips, only to see both repeated in his face, which had been ruddy and smiling the minute before. They stood gazing in one another's eyes as if both were magnetised, without either advancing a hand or attempting a word. An indescribable chill crept over my heart as I looked at them, and I drew my hand from John's arm, and turned impatiently away.

He did not seem conscious of the action, but it roused Rachel. She smiled, and extending her hand, said, with quivering lips, which she made vain efforts to compose: 'Mr Hollingford, do you not remember me? My name is Rachel Leonard.'

John's gaze had never left her face, and he could not but note the imploring look that came into her eyes as she said these words.

'Yes,' he answered, and his voice shook, though his face kept a fixed, stern gravity. 'Yes, surely I remember you – Miss Leonard.'

At this the sound of wheels was heard coming up the hill, and with a sudden effort Rachel changed her manner.

'Here is the carriage,' she said. 'I hope, Mr Hollingford, you will not greet Mr and Mrs Hill with that panic-stricken look. You are a great favourite with them, and they will be glad to see you. Pray do not look so shocked. They will think you have seen a ghost.'

'Would to God I had – rather than have seen you,' he murmured to himself, and I heard him.

The carriage drew up beside us, and Mr Hill jumped out. He was an odd-looking man, with a bald, benevolent forehead, a pair of honest brown eyes, which glared about with a sort of fierce good-humour, white hair and white thickset whiskers. Mrs Hill sat within the carriage, a mild-looking fat little lady, with rosy cheeks and a piping voice, holding hugged in her arms something which looked like a bundle of fleecy wool, but which I afterwards knew to be a favourite dog.

'Eh, Hollingford, my lad, I am glad to see you. How are you? and your good mother?' said the old gentleman, grasping John's hand, and glaring kindly in his face.

'Well, Mr Hill; well, thank you,' answered John, but he kept his stern, absent demeanour, as if he could not, or would not, shake off the spell that had come over him, which made him look like a cold, unfaithful, unlifelike copy of himself.

The sharp trebles of the ladies' voices rang about my ears, but it was only by an effort that I could take in the meaning of what they said, so observant was I of John's severe glance, which followed every movement of Rachel as she stood chatting to me with a merriment which I could not but think was nervous and assumed.

Mr Hill was rallying John upon his gravity, kindly and delicately, even in the midst of the natural noisy bluster of his manner. And somehow I divined readily, even out of the distraction of wonder that had come upon me, that the fine old gentleman, remembering certain thorns in John's way, was touched at seeing him proud and reserved in the presence of his natural equals, who had not sunk in the world's favour, and who had got no stain upon their name.

'Will you come and dine with us this evening at seven?' said Mr Hill. 'You and I must have much to talk about. I have been too long absent from this place, but even already I see new things around which delight me. I shall be blind and helpless here till you open my eyes and set me on my feet.'

I noticed, or I fancied I noticed, that Rachel faltered on the words she was speaking at this moment, and that she held her breath to hear John's reply to the invitation.

'I will come with pleasure, sir,' said John.

'And Miss Dacre?' piped Mrs Hill. 'Will she not also come and dine with us?'

'I fear we should be bad company tonight,' put in Rachel quickly. 'We shall be so tired; it would be a poor compliment to ask her to come and look at us nodding in our chairs. Say tomorrow, instead. Margery Dacre, will you come and spend a long day with us tomorrow?'

But Margery Dacre had at that moment no wish to spend such a day. I said, 'No, thank you, Miss Leonard; I shall be otherwise engaged both today and tomorrow.' And then, feeling that I had spoken very coldly, and seeing that she looked troubled, I added, forcing a smile, 'The winter will be long enough for our civilities.'

'But not for our friendship, I trust,' she replied quickly, seizing my hands, while her face cleared, and sincerity seemed to beam out of it, like the sun out of a May sky. I felt her fascination; but it sickened me somehow, and I dropped her hands, and thought of saying good-morning to the group, and returning to the farm alone, so that John might not feel himself hindered from going to breakfast as well as to dine with these new old friends of his who were so eager for his company. But before I had time to act upon the thought, Mr Hill handed Rachel into the carriage, followed her himself, and the carriage rolled away. John and I were left standing there together; I stupid, like one awakened from a dream, staring at the wheel-marks on the snow and at other signs which these people, in passing, had left behind them.

I turned and walked on silently towards the farm, and John walked beside me. A weight of doubt and wonder pressed on my heart like a load of ice. Why had John wanted to conceal from me his acquaintance with Rachel Leonard? Why had they both been so strangely moved at meeting? I longed to ask a question; but I could not find my voice. I longed for John to speak, and tell me something – anything at all that he liked; and were it the strangest puzzle that ever failed to be unriddled, I swore to my own heart that I would believe him.

'Margery,' said John, speaking as if in answer to my thought – and he came nearer to me, for we had walked a little apart, and drew my hand through his arm, and looked down in my face – 'Margery,' he said, 'look me straight in the eyes,' and I looked, and saw them full of grievous trouble.

'You are blaming me in your heart,' he said, 'and saying to yourself that I have deceived you. Will you trust me that I did not mean to do so? I have got a cruel shock, dearest, and I beg of you to be kind and forbearing with me. I owe you an explanation, and I will give it the earliest moment I can. I cannot till I see further. In the meantime, I swear to you that there is nothing in this that should shake your faith in me. Do you trust me, Margery?'

'I would trust you against the whole world, John!' I cried, in a sudden remorse for having ever doubted him. And, smiling and happy, I walked by the side of his horse that evening down the avenue, and kissed my hand to him over the gate as he rode away to dine at the Hall.

'Do not say anything to my mother about my knowing Miss Leonard,' he said, the last thing at parting; and I nodded and said no, not unless he bade me; and I tried not to wonder, and went back to the house satisfied. And I was very merry all the evening; but at night, in my bed, I listened for his return. An evil spirit reminded me of Rachel's face when John said, 'I will come,' and her quickness in arranging that I should not accompany him. I said, 'Margery, I am ashamed of you; curiosity and jealousy are hateful; have nothing to do with them.' And I turned on my pillow and prayed for John; and then I heard him coming into the house. So utterly still was everything by reason of the snow, that I heard his every movement. Even after he had closed his door, I thought I heard him walking about his room. And the wonder leaped up in me again – why was he troubled? why could he not rest? I got up, and laid my heart and ear against his door in a passion of dismay and sympathy. Up and down, up and down; no thought of sleep after his fatigue. Oh, what was this that had come between us? I went back to my bed and wept.

That was the first beginning of the trouble about Rachel Leonard. From that day a shadow hung upon John. He went often to the Hall, for Mr Hill fastened upon him, and delighted in him, and would not live without him. But the more he went to the Hall, the more the trouble grew upon him; and I could not but date its beginning from the arrival of Rachel Leonard, seeing that, before he met her that morning upon the road, he had seemed as radiantly happy as it is possible for any man to be. And the more the trouble grew upon him, the more reserved he became on the subject of the people at the Hall. His mother began to guess that he must be annoyed with business, and the girls to fancy that he and I had quarrelled. And I silently let them think that it was so, the better to keep his secret.

My own heart was aching, but I would not speak. I had promised not to doubt him, and I feared lest he should think, even by my face or manner, that I was weak enough to break my word.

Several weeks passed before I saw anything more of Rachel Leonard following my passing glimpse of her in the snow at sunrise. Mrs Hollingford, who never had been in any but the poorest houses on the estate, walked over with me, at Mrs Hill's request, to pay a morning visit at the Hall. On that occasion no Miss Leonard was to be seen. She must have gone out walking – so said the maid who went to seek her in her room; and we came back to the farm without having seen her. Then arrived Mrs Hill to return the visit, but no Miss Leonard accompanied her. Rachel was confined to bed with a cold. The girls, who had hoped for a sight of her, were disappointed.

And so the days went on, till it happened that I went to stay at the Hall. I had received two or three invitations, and had always found an excuse to stay away. At last it seemed ungracious to stay away any longer, and I went.

How the house was changed since the quiet time of our 'reading days', when the solitary wreath of smoke went up from Mrs Beatty's chimney, and the echo of one's step on the stone stair rang round the gallery above! Now the hall, that had used to look so wide and chilly with its grim ornaments of busts of authors, was decorated with flowers from the hothouse, and cheered by a blazing fire. A soft murmur of prosperity was heard throughout the house, as if Luxury were gliding about in her velvet slippers, giving orders in her modulated voice, and breathing her perfumed breath into all the corners. The presence of life had wrought upon the handsome sticks and stones that furnished the rooms, and transformed them into household gods. Firelight twinkled in all the chambers, bringing out the lustre of coloured glass and costly hangings into the sallow daylight of the winter noon. I do not know how it was that on the day of my arrival at the Hall I made my appearance at an earlier hour than they expected me. I learned afterwards, by chance, that they had not looked for me till the dinner hour, while I understood that it was desired of me to present myself early in the day, so that Rachel and I might have some quiet hours during which to renew our acquaintance before we should be called upon to mix among the company now staying at the Hall. Good Mrs Hill was one of those people whose manner would make you believe that if you deny them the thing they desire at your hands, you will undoubtedly destroy their peace, but who will probably have forgotten their request and its motive while you are yet pondering it, and forcing your own will that it may be complied with. The mistake about the hour of my arrival was one of those pieces of confusion which seem too trifling ever to be worth clearing up. But it was a mistake which caused me months of unutterable misery.

The idea of the visit had always been distasteful to me; but, having made up my mind to go, I thought it was better to be amiable for John's sake. About midday I said goodbye to the three who were already my mother and sisters, and set out to walk across the moor to the Hall. John was to dine with the Hills that day, so I knew I should see him in the evening. My baggage had been sent on before me early in the morning. It seemed very absurd to feel so sorry at leaving home to stay at a fine house, where the hours were to be filled with feasting and merry-making. In earlier days it would have been otherwise. But the farm, with its busy inmates, its old-fashioned nooks and corners, its homely sights and sounds, had grown strangely sufficient for the desires of my life.

I arrived at the Hall, gaining the grounds by a descent from the hill at their back, and coming, so, round by the gardens to the house. Mrs Hill was driving with some of her guests. Mr Hill was out walking with some of his guests. A maid would go and seek for Miss Leonard, and in the meantime I was conducted to my room.

Such a room as it was. I smiled at myself for thinking it so grand, for I had certainly slept in as fine a chamber before. But of late I had forgotten how long is wealth's list of necessities, and had learned to live without a velvet couch at the fireside of my sleeping apartment, branches of wax-candles on the mantel, and long mirrors on every side to make me feel as if half a dozen impertinent young women were for ever prying into, and making a mockery of, my movements. I had lately been accustomed to hear the heels of my shoes go clinking over the well-waxed boards of my simple room, and to look out at the woods and fields through a narrow framework of white dimity. Here were voluptuous curtains and carpets that forbade sound, and denied the daylight. The farm was my beau ideal of a home; therefore my room at the farm was my beau ideal of a room; therefore all this comfort was oppressive and ridiculous.

Miss Leonard did not come to seek me. Perhaps she was out. I guessed there was a mistake, and made myself content. I declined the services of a maid, unpacked my trunk, and laid out my dinner dress upon the bed. After this I knew not what to do, and sat down to rest. I looked at the swelling couch over whose cushions the firelight wavered drowsily. 'We are not likely to have velvet couches at the farm,' I thought, 'and it is better to despise such foolish luxuries.' So I drew out a stiff-backed chair, and sat down to muse before the fire.

I soon got tired of this, for I could not think without conjuring up my familiar wonders and forebodings, and these must be kept in the background in order that I might conduct myself properly in this house. I opened my door and looked around me. I knew the place well, but I did not care to be seen roaming about before I had received a welcome from my host or hostess. Weariness enabled me to overcome this difficulty, and I presently found myself in the gallery where the pictures hung and the curiosities were displayed in their cabinets; where chairs were placed for people to sit upon, and screens erected to keep away the draughts; and where the light from the dome in the roof fell mellowly over the knight made of armour, who stood quite at the end of the gallery, near a narrow staircase which led down to the back premises of the house. This knight was an old friend. Mopsie had been very fond of a nook formed by the angle of the wall at his back, and in the days of our 'readings' had dragged a deep-seated armchair from a near room, and arranged a tall light screen behind his shoulders, forming a tiny triangular chamber. When I came upon this retreat now I took possession of it, for it was a pleasant place to sit in. The massive helmet of the knight on his pedestal soared above the top of the screen, and stood out in bold relief against the soft brilliance of the painted dome. I seated myself in Mopsie's chair, and drew a little book from my pocket. In this little book John had copied out for me some sweet quaint rhymes which were favourites of his and mine, and because I had thought the writing and the writer could never be glorified enough, I had wrought round the margin of the pages a border of fanciful arabesque, which I had filled in with colours and gold.

I turned over the pages absently. By and by I heard footsteps coming down the gallery, and voices drawing near me. I hoped that, whoever the people were, they might pass on without perceiving me. I did not like the idea of strangers peeping in behind the screen and wondering who I could be. But the people came nearer, still conversing in low earnest tones, the sound of which made me start and wonder. They came up to the screen, which was just at the end of the gallery, and stopped there as people will pause at the extremity of a walk before they turn to retrace their steps. And it seemed as if my heart paused with them, for the speakers were Rachel Leonard and John Hollingford, and this was the conversation I heard: 'I think you are very unkind, John,' said Rachel; and she spoke sullenly, and as if she had been crying. 'I only ask you not to hurry me, to give me time, and you complain as if I had refused altogether.'

'I do not understand why you should want time,' replied John; 'if what you have told me is true, if what you have promised is in good faith, I do not see why you should delay making everything known.'

'Nor do I see why you should wish for haste,' said Rachel. 'The announcement will be painful enough when it must be made. Have you ever thought of what Margery will say?'

'Margery! God bless her!' said John earnestly, 'Sweet, unselfish soul! It will be a shock, but she will get over it. While this is going on, her eyes are a continual reproach to me. The position is intolerable. If you will not speak soon I must break my promise to you, and enlighten her.'

'No, no, no!' said Rachel passionately. 'She suspects nothing, and let her rest awhile. She will not take it so quietly as you think. Every one will cry out at me, and I know that I deserve it. Pity me, John' – here her voice broke down – 'but, for God's sake, leave me to myself for a time.'

'Let it be a short time, then,' said John, sadly. 'I must say I am grieved to see that this is such a hard trial to you. After all that has been, all you have told me, I did not expect to find you so weak and selfish.'

'I am weak and I am selfish,' sobbed Rachel; 'do not expect to find me anything else. I am struggling to be something better; but whatever I am, John, be sure that I love you, and have loved you all these years. Leave me a little time, and I will do everything you wish.'

'Let it be so, then,' said John – 'a short time, remember. My poor, dear girl! My lost darling, so unexpectedly found.'

And they walked away together down the gallery talking till their voices and their steps died away. The thick yellow daylight was almost extinct in the gallery by this time, and it was nearly dark behind the screen. It was night at four o'clock in those days, and it was not till the dressing-bell for dinner rang at near seven that I went, feeling my way along the gallery, back to my own chamber. I do not know what I had been doing in the meantime. A chorus of soft voices warbled in conversation on the stairs as a band of graceful ladies tripped up to their several apartments. Miss Leonard came to me in my rich, hot, heavy room and helped me to dress. I told her I had come too soon, and had been rambling about. I believe that was what I said. She fastened my sash, and even tied my sandals, for my fingers were shaking. She bent over my feet with her glorious face and her firm white hands. I think she had a black velvet frock and a diamond waist buckle; but I am not sure. The charm of her beauty overshone these things. As she busied herself among my hooks and eyes, I saw our two reflections, in a glass – she who had loved John for years, and I who had only known him for a few short months.

As I went down the stairs with Rachel, I told myself it was true what John said, that I should get over it. The drawing-room was full of gay people, and my first thought was, looking round it, that there was no man there equal to John – no woman there equal to Rachel. Why had I thrust myself between them?

When John took my hand with just his old loving pressure, the first wave of despair broke over me. 'Get over it?' I asked myself; but that was all. I believed that John was sitting by Rachel, but I did not see the dinner-table, nor the people sitting at it. They thought I was shy or proud, and did not trouble me with conversation. A sound was in my ears, which I thought was like the rushing of a storm in an Indian forest. All my life lay before me like a blot of ink on a bright page. Why must I give trouble, and carry a sore heart? Why was I left behind to come to Hillsbro'? Why did not my father and mother take me with them that I might have died of their fever and been buried in their Indian grave? But how Rachel laughed. All the evening she was the most brilliant, beautiful, witty creature that ever enlivened a company.

8

My children, when I sat that night over the embers of my dying fire in my chamber at Hillsbro' Hall, while everyone else was asleep, there has never been a more desolate creature in the world than I felt myself to be. I had behaved all the evening very meekly and quietly, keeping out of John's way, accepting Rachel's attentions, watching and admiring her with a dull kind of fascination. I remember observing absently, in a mirror at the other end of the room, the white pensive face of a young girl sitting very still in a corner, rapt in thought or pain. I wondered whether she was sick or in trouble; but afterwards I found by accident that I had been speculating about myself. A little chill smile came to my lips at this discovery; but I felt hardly any surprise at seeing myself thus so different from what I had ever been before. The world had changed, and I with it, since the fall of twilight in the gallery.

Rachel sang and the room applauded; people danced and Rachel among them; young gentlemen were introduced to me, and I told them, 'I don't dance,' with my cold lips. There was an agonising pressure on my senses, of sound, light, perfume. I thought it was these things that gave the pain, while from my heart, which seemed perfectly still, came forth at intervals the repetition, 'I will get over it, I will get over it.' John found me out, and said, quite startled, 'What is the matter with you, Margery?' I complained of 'my head', and drew back within the shelter of a curtain. 'Margery, my dearest, you are ill,' he said, and then the flood-gates of bitterness opened in my heart. How long was he going to act a cruel lie to me? I said, 'I am ill; I must go to bed.' He followed me out of the room, questioned me anxiously, wrapped me in a shawl, stood at the foot of the stairs watching till I passed out of sight; all as if he had still loved me.

When I reached my room I blew out my candles, and the fireplace was the only spot of light in the large shadowy room. I walked up and down in the dark, thinking about it all. I could imagine how Rachel and John had met while I was still in Miss Sweetman's schoolroom. There had been a quarrel, and then had come John's misfortunes, and they had never met again till that morning in the sunrise on the snow. I knew the story as perfectly as if the firelight were printing it all over the walls for me to read. And then I had risen up between them, and here I stood between them now, when all their mistakes had been cleared up, and all their old feelings revived. Well, I would not be in their way. I would go away from Hillsboro'.

I crept over to the fire, drew the embers together, and watched them waning and dying in the grate. I no longer told myself that I should get over it. I knew that I should not die, or go mad, nor do anything that people could talk about; but deep in my heart I knew that here was a sorrow that would go with me to my grave. I felt that

I was not a girl to put my foot on the memory of it, and go out into the world again to be wooed and won afresh. I knew that the spring of my days was going to end in winter. Then I thought of how I had turned my back upon the whole world, all the world that I knew, to follow my mother's friends to Hillsbro'; how I had loved them, how I had given my whole heart and faith to John; how trusting, how satisfied, how happy I had been. At last my heart swelled up in softer grief, and I wept with my face buried in my arms where I lay upon the hearthrug. And so after long grieving I sobbed myself to sleep, and wakened in the dark, towards morning, shuddering with cold in my thin dress.

The next day I was ill with a feverish cold, and Rachel tended me. Never was there a nurse more tender, more patient, more attentive. I was not at all so ill as to require constant watching, but she hovered about my bed, applying remedies, tempting me with dainties, changing my pillows, shifting the blinds so as to keep the room cheerful, yet save my burning eyes from the light. She would not be coaxed away from me even for an hour. Mrs Hill, though kind and sympathetic herself, in a different way, was dissatisfied, I think. There were other guests, and she was a lady who took the duties of hospitality seriously to heart. But Rachel, charming, even when provoking, knew how to manage her adopted mother. There were whispered discussions between them, of which I, lying with closed eyes, was supposed to know nothing, and then Rachel would steal her graceful arm round Mrs Hill's portly waist, and kiss her, and put her out of the room. Mrs Hill was very good to me, and scrupulously left her poodle dog on the mat outside the door when she came to visit me; but her vocation was not for waiting in sick-rooms.

Rachel, soft-voiced, light-footed as a sister of mercy, moved about in her pale grey woollen gown, with a few snowdrops in her breast, her face more thoughtful and sad, yet sweeter than I had ever seen it. She had a work-basket beside her, and a book, while she sat by the head of my bed, but I saw that she occupied herself only with her thoughts, sitting with her hands laced loosely together in her lap, gazing across the room through a distant window at the ragged scratchy outlines of the bare brown wood that hid the chimneys of the farm from the view of the inmates of the Hall.

It needed no witchcraft to divine her thoughts. She was thinking of John at the farm, and possibly of all that had passed there between him and me. It saddened her, but I thought she must be very secure in her faith, for there was no angry disturbance in her anxious eyes, no bitterness of jealousy about her soft sweet lips. I read her behaviour all through like a printed legend; her faithful kindness, her tender care, her thoughtful regret. She was feeling in her woman's heart the inevitable wrong she was about to do me, measuring my love by the strength and endurance of her own, and pitying me with a pity which was great in proportion to the happiness which was to be her own lot for life.

Everywhere she moved I followed her with John's eyes, it seemed, seeing new beauties in her, feeling how he must love her. In my weak desolation I wished to die, that I might slip quietly out of the hold of my kind enemy, leaving vacant for her the place from which she was going to thrust me with her strong gentle hands. But under her care I recovered quickly.

Never had there been such a nurse, such a petting, fondling, bewitching guardian of an ill-humoured, nervous, thankless patient. How lovingly she tucked me up on the couch by the fireside; how unweariedly she sought to amuse me with her sprightly wit; how nimbly her feet went and came; how deftly and readily her hands ministered; I could never tell you half of it, my dears! If her face fell into anxious lines while my eyes were closed, no sooner did I seem to wake to consciousness again than the sunshine and the archness beamed out. Once or twice it smote me that she wondered at my petulance and gloom – wondered, not knowing that my time had already come, that the burden of the sorrow she had brought me was already upon my shoulders. 'Are you in pain, dear?' she would ask, perplexed. 'I am afraid you are worse than we think;' and I would answer coldly, 'Thank you; I suffer a little, but it will pass away. It is only weakness. Pray, do not trouble yourself so much about me.'

My only excuse was that my heart was breaking; but this I could not explain. And still she was faithful and winning, would not take offence, and would not be repelled. It was hard work trying to hate her, and I gave it up at last. One time when her hand hovered by me I caught it going past, kissed it, and burst into tears. 'Forgive me,' I said; 'you are an angel, and I – ' I felt that I had been something very evil in the past few days. 'My poor little nervous darling!' she said, down on her knees, with her arms about me, 'what shall we do to make you strong?' 'Little' she called me, though I was as tall as she. I acknowledged her superior greatness for compelling love, and letting the bitterness roll out of my heart for the time, like a huge load, I laid my head upon her shoulder for a long miserable cry. Desperately I invented excuses for my tears, but I shed them, and they did me good. After that I no longer struggled against the spell of her attraction. I loved her even out of the depths of the misery she had caused.

She saw that I was growing to love her, and she was glad, and I winced at her delight. She was thinking that by and by, when I should have 'got over it', she and I would be friends. I smarted silently, and smiled. I would not be a weeping, deserted damsel. I would try to be strong and generous, and keep my sorrow to myself.

During this illness of mine, which lasted about a week, John came often to the Hall to enquire for me. Good little Mrs Hill would come into the room smiling, and say, 'Rachel, you must go down to Mr Hollingford. He wants to hear from your own lips about your patient.' And she would sit with me, talking about her dogs and the county families, till Rachel's return, who always brought me kind messages, and seemed anxious to deliver them faithfully. I thought she always came back with signs of disturbance in her face, either very pale or with a heightened colour. Once I thought she looked as if she had been crying; she pulled down the blinds immediately on entering the room, and sat with her back to the light.

'Margery,' said she by and by, 'Mrs Hollingford is coming to see you tomorrow.'

'Is she?' said I, with a great pang at my heart.

I could not say, 'I am glad,' for the dear old lady's true face rose up before me, a treasure I had lost, and I lay back among my cushions, and thought it would be well if I could die.

The next morning Rachel was restless and absent. Early in the day she left me suddenly, and came back dressed in her riding-habit.

'I am going for a ride, dear,' she said hurriedly. 'I am not very well; I need fresh air. You can do without me for a few hours, I dare say.'

Something in her manner made me wonder. I heard the mustering of horses on the gravel, and dragged myself to the window to see if John Hollingford were of the party. But he was not there. Lying on my sofa afterwards I remembered Mrs Hollingford's expected visit, and felt sure that Rachel had gone away to avoid her. I remembered that they had never yet met, and I easily saw a reason for Rachel's fearing her eyes at present. In the midst of these reflections came my dear second mother.

Mrs Hill brought her to me. The contrast between the two was striking. Mrs Hill was short, fat and plain, and had narrowly escaped from nature's hands without the stamp of a vulgar little woman. Mrs Hollingford was tall and slender, with a worn noble face, and, in spite of all circumstances, looked the ideal of an ancient 'high-born ladye'.

When I looked at her, I felt that it would be impossible for me to go back to the farm. I thought that when we found ourselves alone I would tell her what I had learned, and beg of her to permit me to go straight from the Hall to London, whence I could write a letter of release to John. But Mrs Hill stayed with us some time, and in the meantime my courage oozed away. When I found myself face to face with her, and no one else there, I could not say a word of my confession. I realised what would be her dismay, her indignation, and worst of all, I feared, her incredulity. She would assuredly speak to John when she went home, and all my pride revolted at the thought. So I let the opportunity go by.

I told her of Miss Leonard's kindness. She had been a little hurt, I think, at the young lady's absence, but she was never used to look for slights, and my testimony cleared away all shadow of offence. Afterwards I found that the girls at home were indignant at Miss Leonard's hauteur. They had expected something different. She had disappointed them. Mrs Hill was courteous, Mr Hill was kind, but Miss Leonard ignored the dear old mother altogether.

' 'Tis always the way with upstarts,' said Jane; and the foolish little hearts were up in arms.

'Tell me, my darling,' said Mrs Hollingford, with her arm round my neck, 'is there anything amiss between you and John?'

'What could there be amiss?' I said, kissing her hand, and avoiding her eyes. 'I have not seen him since the day I came here. He has called to enquire for me constantly.'

'I thought of it before you left us,' she said sadly, 'and I fear it more every day. He is – you are both strangely altered. Margery, don't jilt my son. He is not as fine a gentleman as others you may see, but you will never meet his like.'

I turned my head away, and said nothing. What was there that I could say? My heart was big with much that I could not tell, and I was silent. And so the occasion passed away. Mrs Hollingford went home with a bitter doubt in her heart; and the doubt was all of me.

After she had gone, Mrs Hill came and sat with me, and tried to amuse me. She was a good little woman, but her gossip was tiresome and her anecdotes worldly. I was glad when her duty to her other

guests carried her away. You will find it hard, my dears, to understand from my account of this time that I was staying at a pleasant
country-house full of merry-making people. But the people were
only shadows to me, and the time a puzzle. What was not real to me
then, I cannot make real to you now.

The afternoon was wet and windy, and the riding-party returned
early, all but Rachel and another lady and gentleman. These came
home later. I was sitting in my room, in the firelight, alone, when
Rachel came to me, laughing, in her wet riding-habit, saying she had
had enough of the weather.

I said, 'Yes, it is a pity you went.'

'No, not a pity,' she said. Then, 'Has not Mrs Hollingford been
here?'

'Yes,' I said.

'Here, in this room, with you?'

'There, in that chair, by your side.'

She turned and looked at the chair with a strange look, which was
wonderful to see, but quite indescribable. She drew it to the hearth,
and sat down in it, throwing back her wet skirts and leaning towards
the fire. Then I saw that she looked pale and worn, as if her riding
had not done her much good.

'Do you not love her, this Mrs Hollingford?' she said, presently.

'Dearly,' I said.

'Will you describe her to me?' said Rachel.

'She is tall and handsome,' I began.

'Yes,' put in Rachel, 'I have heard so.'

'There is something grand about her, though she dresses as gravely
and poorly as a nun. Her face is sweet and sad, and can be stern. Her
hair is silver grey – '

'No,' said Rachel hurriedly, 'brown. I heard that it was a beautiful
chestnut-brown.'

'It is nearly white now,' said I.

Rachel did not speak again for some minutes. Looking at her
presently, I was surprised to see her face quivering, and great shining
tears following one another swiftly and silently into her lap.

'Do not mind me,' she said. 'I went to see a poor girl on the estate,
who is dying. Her mother was sitting at the head of her bed. She
told me the girl had never vexed her in her life.'

'And has that made you sad?' asked I, thinking the girl was to be
envied.

'Very sad,' said Rachel; 'sadder than I could tell.'

We were silent awhile, and then said Rachel: 'It must have made her grow old before her time, that trouble.'

'Do you mean Mrs Hollingford?' said I.

'Yes,' said Rachel. 'The grief, and the shame, and the blight.'

'There should be no shame, no blight for the innocent,' I said.

'The world does not think so,' said Rachel, with a stern cloud on her face.

'The world!' I said contemptuously.

She lifted her eyes from the fire to my face. 'Yes, I know you are a brave independent little soul,' she said. 'Will you answer me one thing truly? Did you not feel even a shadow of shrinking or regret when you promised to marry John Hollingford?'

'Not a shadow,' I said bitterly. 'I accepted him for what I believed him to be, not for what the world might think of him.'

'I wish God had made me like you,' she said solemnly; and then got up, with a wild sad look in her face, and left me without another word, forgetting to lift up her wet trailing habit, which she dragged along the ground as she went.

After she had gone I sat there, angry, amazed and sick at heart. I thought she had well said to John, 'I am weak and selfish.' I had never told her of my engagement, and she had talked to me of it unblushingly. Thinking of her own sacrifice, she had forgotten my wrong and pain. I had seen into the working of her thoughts. She could love John and injure me, but she could not be content without the approval of the world. The young farmer was worthy of love, but he was not rich enough, nor grand enough, nor was his soiled name fitted for the spoilt child of wealth. She could steal away my treasure without enriching herself – could destroy the peace of two minds, without creating any contentment for herself out of the wreck. 'Poor John!' I thought, 'your chances of happiness are no better than my own, even though you have paid a dishonourable price for them.' And I hated her after that.

9

The winter was passing away at this time, and spring days were beginning to shine. I walked out of my bedroom into the bright March world and saw the primroses laughing in the hollows. I thought my heart broke outright when I heard the first lark begin to sing. After that things went still further wrong. John came to take me out for a drive one day, and I would not go. And the Tyrrells were staying at the Hall.

Whether it was that Rachel shunned me of her own wish, or because she saw that I had learned to despise her, I do not know; but we kept apart. My poor soul was quite adrift. Anguish for the past, disgust at the present, terror of the future, all weighed on it. If I had known of any convent of saintly nuns, such as I had read of in poems and legends, who took the weary in at their door and healed the sick, who would have preached to me, prayed with me, let me sit at their feet and weep at their knees till I had struggled through this dark phase of my life, I would have got up and fled to them in the night, and left no trace behind me.

I hated to stay at the Hall, and yet I stayed. Mr Hill – kind heart! – said he would bar the gates, and set on the dogs if I attempted to move. He and his wife both fancied at this time to make a pet of me. I had been ill in their house, and I must get well in their house. They would warrant to make the time pleasant. So the Tyrrells were bidden to come and stay a month. Grace Tyrrell arrived with her high spirits, her frivolity, her odour of the world, took me in her hands, and placed herself at once between me and Rachel. She found me weak, irritable, woebegone. She questioned, petted, coaxed. Partly through curiosity, and partly through good-nature, she tried to win my confidence, and in an evil hour I told her all my trouble. I listened to her censure, scoffs, counsels, and my heart turned to steel against John.

She was older than me by five or six years. I was a good little simple babe, she said, but she, she knew the world. It was only in story books or by younglings like me that lovers were expected to be true. Miss Leonard was an 'old flame', and, if all that was said might be true, would be heiress of Hillsbro'. Yes, yes, she knew; I need not blaze out. I had made myself a hero, as simple hearts do, but my idol was clay all the same. Wealth and power would do for John Hollingford what his father's misconduct had undone. It was utter silliness my abasing myself, saying that Rachel Leonard was more lovable than I. Her rich expectations were her superior charm. Oh me! how people will talk, just to be thought knowing, just to be thought wise, just to dazzle and to create an excitement for the hour.

I do think that Grace Tyrrell loved me after her own fashion, and that she thought I had been hardly used; but the sympathy she gave me was a weak sympathy, that loved to spend itself in words, that was curious to sift out the matter of my grief, that laid little wiles to prove the judgement she had given me true. She had watched them (Rachel and John), she said, and John's manner was not the manner of a lover, though he affected it as much as he could. He was trying to bind her with promises, but she would not be bound. Yes, she, Grace, had watched them, and would watch them. Every night she brought me into her room, and detailed her observations of the day, and pitied and petted and caressed her poor darling. I was weak in health, and unutterably lonely and sad, and I clung to her protection and kindness. But instinctively I distrusted her judgement. I disliked her coarse views of things, and followed her counsels doubtingly.

I have not described her to you yet, my children. Imagine, then, a showy, frivolous-looking, blonde young woman, fond of pretty feathers, and flowers, and gay colours; pretty enough in her way, good-humoured and talkative.

I thought, then, that I had every reason to be grateful to her, and I blamed myself for not loving her spontaneously, as I had loved, as I still fought against loving Rachel. I think now that I had no reason to be grateful to her. If she had not been always by my side, so faithful, so watchful, so never-failing with her worldly lesson, I think I should have found a way out of the darkness of my trouble. I think I should have softened a little when Rachel met me in the gallery, twined her soft arm round my neck, and asked me why we two should be so estranged. I think I should have wept when John took my hand between his two and asked me, in God's name, to tell him why I had grown so altered. But I was blind, deaf and dumb to their advances. Their reproaches were meaningless, their caresses treacherous, and I would have none of them. I would stand where they themselves had placed me, but I would draw no nearer to set their consciences at rest. And then there was Captain Tyrrell at the Hall.

Why did Grace Tyrrell want me to marry her brother? I do not know; unless because she liked me, for she was fond of him; unless because my substantial dowry would be of use to the needy man of fashion. I had heard before that he had made two unsuccessful attempts to marry an heiress. I was not an heiress, but the hand that I should give to a husband would be pretty well filled. At all events he was ever by my side, and Grace (I am now sure) helped him to contrive that it should be so. I did not like him, I never had liked him. Before I had come to Hillsbro' he had wearied me with compliments and attentions. When he had visited me at the farm, elegant as he was, I had contrasted him unfavourably with the absent 'ploughman', wondering that language had only provided one word, 'man', by which to designate two creatures so different. He was the same now that he had been then; but I, who had soared to things higher, had fallen. Anyone was useful to talk to, to walk with, to drive with, so that time might pass; any noise, any bustle, that would keep me from thinking, was grateful. So I tolerated the attention of Captain Tyrrell, and he and Grace hemmed me in between them. Rachel looked on in silence, sometimes with contempt, sometimes with wondering pity. John kept further and further aloof, and his face got darker, and sadder, and sterner to me. And this it was that bewildered and chafed me more than anything I had suffered yet. Why, since he had turned his back upon me, would he keep constantly looking over his shoulder? And, oh me! how Grace did whisper; and how her whispers fired me with pride, while the confidence I had foolishly given her daily wore away my womanly self-respect.

My children, you will wonder why I did not behave heroically under this trial. You despise a heroine who is subject to the most common faults and failings. The old woman now can look back and mark out a better course of conduct for the girl. But the girl is gone – the past is past, the life is lived. I was full of the humours and delusions of nineteen years, and I saw the glory and delight of my youth wrecked. Existence was merely inextricable confusion in the dark. I never dreamt of a path appearing, of a return of sunshine, of a story like this to be afterwards told.

Rachel's conduct was variable and strange to me at this time. She kept aloof from me, as I have told you, looking on at my poor little frantic efforts to be careless with a grand contempt. She watched me as closely as Grace watched her; but one day, I know not how it happened, some word of jealous misery escaped me, and Rachel grew very white and silent, and there was a long pause of days before either of us addressed the other again; but Rachel's look and manner were altered to me from that moment. A long, tender, wistful gaze followed me about. She did not venture to dispute Grace Tyrrell's possession of me, but it made her uneasy. She was observant and sad, patient and kind, while my manner to her was often irritable and repellent. One night she stole into my room when I was sinking to sleep, and bent over me in my bed. 'My darling, my sister!' she said, 'let me kiss you, let me put my arms round you. Oh! why will you always turn away from me?'

I did not answer, except by moving my face shudderingly aside.

'Margery,' she whispered again, 'tell me why you have turned against me and John Hollingford.'

'You and John!' said I, opening my eyes and looking at her. 'Yes, that is it. You and John. Dear me; am I not grateful to you both? How odd!'

'Margery, shall I swear that you have no reason to be jealous of me?'

'Oh, no, Rachel,' I said; 'don't swear. Go away and be happy, as I am, and sleep soundly.'

She moved away a step or two, but came back hesitatingly.

'Margery,' said she, 'I want to tell you – if you will listen to me – I have a great trouble.'

'Have you?' said I. 'To think of anyone having a trouble in this world! I can't believe it.'

'But, Margery,' she said, putting her hands on my shoulders, and looking down at me, 'I have a secret, and I came here to tell it to you, and you must listen, for it concerns you.'

'Does it?' said I; 'then you had better not trust me with your secret, Rachel. I think I have a wild creature chained up in me somewhere, and it might do you harm. I advise you not to have anything to do with me. Good-night.'

'Ah!' said she bitterly, turning away, 'was ever anyone so changed in so short a time. This is Miss Tyrrell's doing. She is a spy upon me, and yet I defy her to know anything about me. She has filled you with her own cruel prejudice.'

'Do not say anything against the Tyrrells in my hearing,' I said. 'They are the dearest friends I have.'

'If that be true,' answered Rachel thoughtfully, 'I have nothing more to say. The thing that I was going to tell you does not concern you, and I have been spared a humiliation for the present. When you know all, you can cry out against me with the rest. Remember,' she added distinctly with proud bitterness, 'I give you full permission.'

She turned away and moved across the room; she stopped before the dying fire, standing above it, and looking down into it. I saw her dark figure between me and the fading glare, her head lowered on her breast, her arms hanging dejectedly by her side. She mused there a few minutes, and then went noiselessly out of the room.

10

Early summer was already upon the land, flowers were blooming, and the reign of sunshine had begun. The cuckoo haunted the Hall gardens, rabbits basked in the glades, and the woods were alive with singing birds.

A little thing happened which surprised me. A troop of us were riding one day along the moor, and by the outskirts of the road, I, being foremost, espied two figures at a distance among the trees, and recognising the girls from the farm, I pressed on and came on them unawares, where they were down on their knees, gathering mosses out of the grass. Mopsie was on my neck in a moment, but Jane was a little shy. I had to coax her to be frank.

She thought I must be changed, she said, I had stayed away so long. If I cared for them any more, I would have come to see them. Mother was not very well, and John, when at home, was dull. He fretted about something. Did I not know what it was about?

'Whether I come or stay, you must believe in me, Jane,' said I; 'I am not one of those that change. I will go back with you now and see your mother. Here are the rest of our party coming; we will meet them and tell them what I am going to do.

'That is Miss Leonard,' I added, seeing Rachel riding foremost. 'Are you not curious to see her?'

Jane said, 'Yes,' and walked on beside me, holding my whip.

The sun was in Rachel's face till she passed into the shade right before us. She raised her eyes then and looked at us, started violently and gave her reins a sudden wild pluck; the horse reared, plunged, and flung her. I screamed and sprang to the ground, but Jane stood immovable, looking at Rachel where she lay, staring at her with a face which had changed from glowing red to white. I pushed her aside to reach Rachel. She turned quickly round, and, without a word, began walking rapidly towards home. She passed out of sight without once looking back. It all occurred in a minute.

The other riders came up; Rachel was not injured, only a little bruised and faint. She was too nervous to remount. Our party rode home, and I sat with Rachel on the grass till a servant came with a pony carriage. The man took our horses, and I drove Rachel home. She cried hysterically all the time while we waited in the wood. I did not see any more of Jane, and, of course, I did not pay my proposed visit to her mother. Rachel did not attempt to explain the cause of her accident, and I did not ask her anything about it. I remembered Jane's face, and I puzzled over her strange conduct in silence. It was impossible not to think that she had beheld in Rachel someone whom she had not expected, and was not well pleased to see. Yet this young girl had been a child when she had come to Hillsbro', and she had not known Rachel by name. My head ached distressfully over the puzzle, but I could make nothing of it. Jane was an odd girl; she had conceived a prejudice against Miss Leonard, and had taken a whimsically rude way of showing it. This was all the conclusion I could come to on the subject.

One evening we had a dinner party, and a good many young people being present, we danced a little. I danced more gaily than the rest, for my heart was unusually sore. Grace Tyrrell had told me that day that she purposed leaving the Hall next week, and had pressed me to go with her to London. I thought I had better go, yet I had refused her. I knew I must leave Hillsbro', yet I shrank from the great effort of tearing myself away. Here I had been loved and happy; the trees and the moors knew it; even the strange faces of the country people passing on the roads had seemed to be in my secret, and had played their simple part in my dream. I felt that, once gone, I could never return, and I must first have an explanation with John, and put an end to our engagement. Yet how to seek him for such a purpose? I had kept at so great a distance from him lately that it seemed impossible. I felt that he would be relieved by my absence, and glad of his release, but my own woe pressed upon me. I feared to make a fool of myself, if he was kind as of old when we said goodbye.

So I was dancing with the rest, and Captain Tyrrell was my partner. We were very merry. Grace was playing for us, and looked approvingly over her shoulders. John had been with us at dinner, but I had lost sight of him, and as I did not see Rachel either, my fancy saw them walking in the moonlight without. For it was a warm evening, the windows were open, the stars bright, and people went in and out at their pleasure. The flowers smelt sweetly in the dew, and the nightingales were singing. There was a game of hide-and-seek on the lawn, and when the shrieks and laughter were subsiding, someone began to sing within. Rachel was entertaining the old ladies and gentlemen, and the rovers flocked round the windows to listen. I had sauntered with Captain Tyrrell into a grove to hear a nightingale, and I was weary to death of his company. He was trying to make me promise to go to London. 'Oh, let it rest,' I said, 'we will talk about it tomorrow. Let us be merry tonight. We will play hide-and-seek again!' and I darted suddenly among the trees, and lay close behind a great oak. My squire lost me; I heard him go past plunging through the underwood, and swearing a little. I lay still till he had given up the search and gone towards the house, and then, like the silly lamb in the spelling-book story, I came forth in the moonlight, and if I did not skip and frisk about with delight, I at least enjoyed myself after the only dismal fashion I could command. Captain Tyrrell was to me, in these days, a veritable old man of the sea, I could not get rid of him, and sometimes I thought in my most despairing moods that it was going to be my lot to carry him on my shoulders for the remainder of my life.

I was walking slowly, musing ruefully, when I saw a figure advancing to meet me on the path. I saw at a glance that it was John Hollingford. The time had been when I would have flown gladly to meet him, linked my arm in his, and seized the opportunity for one of our old talks about pleasant fancies. But this was not the friend I had known, nor was I any longer the simple girl who could open her heart to trust, and delight in shining dreams. The pleasant fancies had been proved cheats, the stars had fallen. I no longer looked up at the sky, but down to the ground. For a moment I shrank back, and would have hidden, but then I thought bitterly, what did it matter? Unpleasant words must be said between us, sooner or later. A very few would suffice. Better they were said at once.

'Margery,' said John, 'people are looking for you, and talking about you. I have come to fetch you to the house. To tell the truth I am glad of the opportunity of saying something which has been long upon my mind. Will you bear with me a few minutes?'

'Yes,' I said, 'certainly. As long as you please,' and I tossed little pieces of twig over my shoulder, and prepared myself to listen. Oh, my dears, how defiant women will be, just for the fear of being pitied.

'You must know very well,' he continued, 'what I am going to say. I have a right to ask you for an explanation of your conduct for the past few weeks. People are coupling your name with that of Captain Tyrrell, and with good reason. You are so changed that I scarcely see a trace of the Margery I once knew. Child! if you repent of the promise you have given me, tell me now and I will set you free. I remember the circumstances under which that promise was given. You, perhaps, exaggerated your own feelings; you have since renewed your acquaintance with people and ways of life that suit you best. I will try not to blame you. Speak out at once, and do not think of me.'

The truthful ring of feeling and reproach in his voice startled my ears, and set my heart struggling for liberty to give an honest response to this appeal. A few simple words would have been enough, but the recollection of all that I knew came back too quickly. The conviction of his insincerity and injustice suddenly bewildered me with anger, keen in proportion to the desolation I had suffered.

'Sir,' said I (we said 'sir' for politeness in those days, my dears), loftily, coldly, and in utter despair, 'I will take you at your word. Let the promise between us be broken from this moment!'

He heaved a great sigh, of relief, I thought, and being near the house we parted with much politeness. Thus we put an end to our engagement. Holy and indestructible I had believed it to be; but then I was an ignorant little fool. People shake hands and say good-bye every day, and never dream of being so mad as to spoil tomorrow with tears. As for me I did not wait for tomorrow. That night was piteous with the rain of my grief. But Grace was at hand to comfort, to counsel, to instruct, which she did with her own peculiar figures of speech.

'You are a brave little thing!' she said. 'I am glad you had spirit to act on the first notice to quit. It would have been so much more humiliating to have waited for a forcible ejectment.'

And I promised to accompany her to London.

I I

Mrs Hill had a pretty little bedizened boudoir, blue silk hangings elegantly festooned with bird cages; couches and divans for its mistress's dogs and cats; with a spare seat for a friend who might venture in at any time for a dish of private chit-chat with the lady of the Hall. Into this apartment I was confidentially drawn by Mrs Hill on the morning after my moonlight conversation with John, as with heavy eyes and hectic cheeks, but with a saucy tongue in reserve, specially sharpened, and a chin held at the extreme angle of self-complacency and no toleration of interference from others, I was sailing majestically downstairs to put my melancholy finger as usual into the pie of the pleasures and pastimes of the day.

'Come in, my dear,' she said mysteriously, with her finger to her lip, nodding her little fat face good-humouredly at me, and making all her little curls shake. 'I think you are a very safe person, my love, and, besides, so fond of Rachel. I would not trouble you with my news, only that it is a secret, and a secret is a thing that I never could endure for any length of time without bringing on hysterics. You are not fond of my darlings, I know. There, we will send away the noisiest.'

And Mrs Hill hereupon tumbled some half-dozen fluffy bodies out of the window on to the verandah below, and stood for the next few moments wagging her head and coquetting down at the ill-tempered little brutes, who whined and scowled their resentment of the disrespectful treatment they had received.

'Ho, my beauties! run, skip, jump!' cried the lady, throwing up her little fat arms. And the dogs, rolling their bodies away into the sun at last, her attention returned to me.

'I must first tell you, my love,' said she, drawing a letter from her pocket, and smoothing it open on her knee, 'I must first confide to you in strict secrecy that our dear Rachel is engaged to be married.'

Here the ecstatic fury of the singing-birds reached such a deafening climax that their mistress was obliged to pause in her communication, and to go round the room dropping extinguishers of silk and muslin over the cages. 'When the pie was opened the birds began to sing,' thought I, the pie being Mrs Hill's budget, and I had also time to consider that John must have sat up very late last night, or risen very early this morning, to have matters already so very happily matured. 'I wonder if Grace would mind travelling a day sooner than she named,' was the third thought that went whizzing through my head before Mrs Hill could proceed any further with the news that she had in store for me.

'Yes,' said Mrs Hill, 'it is true that we are destined to lose her, and it is very kind and sympathising of you, my dear, to look so miserable. You can readily imagine how I shall suffer – I, who have loved that girl far more than if I had been ten times over her mother.' And the little lady wiped her eyes. 'I told you, my dear, that the matter is a secret. Old Sir Arthur wants his son to marry another lady, and Arthur Noble cannot marry without his father's consent. But, in the meantime, the children are engaged, hoping for better days. And now there is a letter from the dear fellow saying he will be here this evening. Only I am not to tell Rachel, as he wants to surprise her. You will keep my counsel, Miss Dacre?'

I murmured, 'Oh, certainly;' but the things in the room were swimming about strangely, and my wits were astray.

'And do you know, my dear (I feel I can trust you thoroughly), do you know I am exceedingly glad of this for many reasons. I have noticed poor young Hollingford! Rachel is an attractive creature, and I fear a little inconsiderate. But the queen of beauty must be excused, my dear, and she is a queen, our Rachel. We cannot help the moths getting round the candle, can we?'

After this I curtsied, and made my escape as quickly as possible. 'Poor young Hollingford! Oh, John, John! why have you brought yourself so low as this?' I cried across the wood to the farm chimneys.

My children, there is a rambling old garden at the back of the hall, a spot which the sun never leaves. Wild tangles of shadow fall now as then on the paths from the gnarled branches of moss-eaten apple-trees. In the season of fruit, blushing peaches and plums, yellow and transparent as honey, hung from its ancient lichen-covered walls. Raspberry brambles, borne out of their ranks by the weight of their crimson berries, strayed across the path. There were beehives ranged against the fiery creeper on the far-end wall, and the booming of the bees made a drowsy atmosphere in the place. This, together with the odour of stocks and wallflowers, was deliciously perceived as soon as your hand lifted the latch of the little green door, and regretfully missed when you closed it behind you.

You know it, my children. I need not tell you that it is a homely retreat compared with the other gardens near, costly, curious and prim, where the beds are like enormous bouquets dropped on the grass, and the complexion of every flower is suited with that of its neighbour. But this old garden was always a favourite, for its unfailing sunshine, its murmurous repose, and the refreshing fragrance of its old-fashioned odours.

Well, my dears, all day long I stayed in my room, fighting a battle of sorrow and passion, and when evening came I stood at the window and saw the sun go down behind the trees of the old garden. I bethought me of its soothing sights and sounds, and fled away to it, as to a sanctuary. There is an arbour under the wall, in the midst of a bed of lilies. I hid myself there, and looked out on the lily-cups brimming with sunset light, on the diving up and down of the birds, on the little golden clouds transfixed in the glory of the heavens. Not a soul breathed within the four high walls but myself, till the latch of the little green door clicked, and who should come hieing along the path but Rachel, her white evening dress tucked to one side, and a watering-pot in her hand. She had a favourite corner in this garden, which it was her pleasure to tend with her own hands. The sun was down, and the plants were thirsting. Rachel was kind to all: kind to the daisies and me, kind to John, kind to her betrothed, Arthur Noble (I had not failed to pick up the name), who was coming this evening to surprise her. When and in what corner would the kindness end and cruelty begin? Watching, through a rent screen of tangled flowers, the fair shapely figure flitting and swaying in the after glory of the sunset, I wondered about it all. How would she act when her other lover arrived? Would she turn her face, in which lived such pathetic truth, first on one and then on the other? Would she for a time give a hand in the dark to each, lacking courage to fling love for ever over her shoulder, and declare at once for the world? Would she honestly dismiss John, confessing that she had chosen her path? or would she bravely destroy that which was unholy, and give her hand to him before the world? Contemplating this possibility, I felt my heart swell with something that was not selfishness; and I built a palace in the air for John.

Having done so, I heard the garden door click again, and starting, looked, expecting to see John coming in to take possession of his palace on the instant. A man came in, but he was a stranger. He took first one path, and then another, and glanced about him with eyes unused to the place. Here, then, was Arthur Noble, arrived. He passed along the path below the lily-bed, and I saw him well. He was a fine-looking fellow, sunburnt, like one who had seen foreign service, and handsome: physically handsomer than John, I could see, with more of the dash of gallantry and air of the grand gentleman, but with less of that something I have hinted at before, soul, spirituality – what shall I call it, my dears, to escape being smiled at? You have known John Hollingford, and you will recognise the charm that I mean, something that – sick, or afflicted, or disfigured, or aged – must always make him lovable, and attract the pure of heart to his side.

Well, Arthur Noble was of a different stamp. How he would have looked out of the sunshine of prosperity, I do not know; but he seemed made to be gilt by it from head to foot. He had a pleasant face, sunny and frank, a high-bred, masterful air, and an amiable courtly manner. Physically he had all the fine points of a Saxon hero, fair hair, blue eyes, powerful frame. Yet, gay and debonair and happy as he looked, I pitied him a little, going past to find Rachel. A little, not a great deal, for I judged him (wrongly, as it afterwards proved) to be one who would love lightly, and be easily consoled by a world whose darling he must be.

I saw their meeting, and John's aerial palace crumbled away into dust. There was no mistaking Rachel's face, the glow that transfigured it when she turned by chance and saw the figure advancing towards her. She sprang to meet him with hands extended, gown tucked aside as it was, and visibly flying feet; and he, striding on, opened his arms to receive her, and folded them reverently about her, like a true knight embracing his bride.

'And what about John?' I said angrily, as I watched the two walking up and down between the roses, talking as eagerly and joyously as if they had just received a charter for perpetual happiness.

That was a dull evening for some of us at the Hall. Rachel and her betrothed sat apart and talked. Grace played chess with Mr Hill, and, to escape from Captain Tyrrell, I kept close to Mrs Hill.

'I am quite in a dilemma, my dear,' she whispered to me. 'There is young Hollingford, who has been coming about the Hall so much, and will be coming about; and then here is Arthur Noble; and you know, my dear, or perhaps you do not know that there has been a deadly feud between their fathers. They were once friends; but poor Mr Hollingford – you know all about him, and Sir Arthur Noble was a heavy loser. Sir Arthur is very vindictive, I must say. I do not think his son is of the same temper, but it might be unpleasant, their meeting. Mr Hill, who is quite bewitched about young Hollingford, will say, "Pooh pooh! let the lads meet and be friends;" but I am not at all so sure that there will not be an awkwardness. I declare I am quite at my wits' end.'

I professed myself unable to give advice on this subject; and, indeed, I felt that I ought now to regard myself as a dying person, who has no further concern with the interests and people around me. I saw a reason why John Hollingford and Mr Noble were not likely to be friends, even if their fathers had been brothers. And the little lady's petty grievance worried me. And all things troubled me, for in three days I was to leave Hillsbro' for London with the Tyrrells.

12

The next morning I set off for a solitary walk to the farm. I was going to ask of Mrs Hollingford formal permission for my visit to London, and to say goodbye to her and the girls. I cried sadly to myself walking over the happy moor and through the wood. I felt unutterably lonely and woebegone. I was going to part from my only friends, and the separation was at hand. I knew that Mrs Hollingford would blame me, and I felt it hardly worth my while to defend myself. I had quarrelled with John, and broken our engagement. I was going to London with gayer friends. Everything was against me; all the wrong seemed mine. I knew that the dear old lady would say little, only look sad and disappointed, thinking in her heart that things were turning out as she had prophesied; would give me full permission to go where I pleased, and do what I pleased; would kiss and bless me; and then I should have the wide world before me.

It was a radiant May day. A saint has said that 'peace is the tranquillity of order'; and such a peace brooded over the happy farm as I crossed its sunny meadows, heard the bleating of its lambs, the lowing of its kine, met its labourers coming and going. An idler was piping somewhere in the fields, the rooks were cawing, the leaves on the boughs just winked in the breeze, the Hall door lay open as usual. I did not see a soul about, and I walked in without summoning anyone. I opened the parlour door; the place smelt of May and myrtle, and there were fresh roses in the jars, but there was no one there. No one in the kitchen, dairy, still-room; the maids were abroad this glorious noon. I went upstairs, looking for a face in vain till I came to our schoolroom. There was Jane alone, sitting at the table over some books, her head between her hands, her hair thrust back from her face, looking older and paler and thinner since I had seen her; a stern, sad-looking young student, with her back to the sun that burned upon the lattice.

Her face turned scarlet when she saw me, and then became paler than before. She gave me her hand coldly, as if she would rather have held it by her side. Her mother was out, she said; had gone to visit at a poor house where there was death and trouble, and would not be home till evening. Mopsie had taken the dogs for a ramble. Then we both sat down and were silent, and Jane's eyes wandered over everything in the room, but would not meet mine.

'I am going to London, Jane,' I said, 'and I came to bid you goodbye.'

'I know,' she said. 'John told me.' And she blushed again fiercely. 'I am very glad. I have thought for a long time that London was the place that would suit you best. I knew you would soon tire of the farm.'

'I have not tired of the farm,' I said, 'but the farm has tired of me.'

She glanced up amazed, then smiled bitterly, and turned aside her head without speaking, as if such utter nonsense could not be thought worthy of an answer.

'However,' I added, 'I did not come here to talk about that – '

'No,' she interrupted hastily, 'it is not worth your while to make any pretence to us. We do not expect to have friends; we never thought of it till you came. In time we shall get used to the curse our father left upon us.'

'Jane, Jane,' I said angrily, 'how can you be so wicked?'

'How can I help being wicked?' she asked. 'I heard that it was prophesied of us that we should all turn out badly, because ill conduct runs in the blood.'

'You do not deserve to have such a mother,' I said.

'Oh! my mother!' she said in an altered tone. 'But she has given all her sweetness to Mopsie, and – to John,' she added, with an effort, a tear starting in her eye. 'But I am my father's daughter. She would cure me too, if she knew of my badness; but she is a saint, and thinks no evil. I work hard at my books, and she calls me a good industrious girl. I will never pour out my bitterness on her. But if my father were here I would let him know what he has done.'

The hopeless hardness of her young voice smote me with pain, but I could think of nothing to say to her. I felt that she thought I had been false to John, and that her sympathy for him had stirred all the latent bitterness of her nature.

'And how is the young lady at the Hall?' she asked suddenly.

'Do you mean Miss Leonard?' I said.

'Oh, yes – Miss Leonard,' said Jane, dropping her eyes on the floor with a strange look.

'Very well,' I answered, thinking of the jubilee that was going on at the Hall.

'There is more wickedness in the world than mine,' said Jane still frowning at the carpet. 'She is false, and you are false – everyone is false. I only know of two grand souls in the world – my mother and

John. But the wicked ones will prosper, see if they don't – those who are gay and charming, at least. Bad ones like me go down like a stone, and lie at the bottom.'

At this moment an eager treble voice was heard on the stairs, and the next Mopsie and I were crying, with our heads together, on the lobby.

'Oh, Margery, Margery!' sobbed the little one – 'dear, darling, *sweet* Margery! why are you going away? You promised you would always stay. Oh, oh, Margery!'

An hour passed before I could tear myself away from the child. Jane prepared luncheon, which was not eaten; but she did not attempt to share in our sorrow and caresses. When I turned from the door Mopsie was prostrate, weeping on the mat; and Jane was standing upright in the doorway, straight, stern and pale. So I went sorrowing back to the Hall. And I had not seen Mrs Hollingford.

Had I seen her that day, had her errand of mercy not taken her away from her home and kept her away while I stayed, the whole current of my life and of the lives of others might have been changed. She would then have had no reason to come and visit me the next morning at the Hall, as she did.

I was busy packing in my own room, enlivening my work by humming gay airs, just to make-believe to myself that I was very merry at the prospect of my visit to London. The door opened quickly, and Rachel came in, walking on tiptoe, with her hand to her lips in trepidation. Her face was as pale as snow, and large tears stood in her eyes.

'My mother, my mother!' she said like one talking in her sleep. 'I have seen my mother.'

'What do you mean, Rachel?' I cried quite panic-stricken; for I thought that her mother was dead, and she must have seen a ghost.

'My mother – Mrs Hollingford; you know her; you are her true daughter; I am nobody – a liar, an outcast. Oh, Margery! she did not know me. Am I changed? I was a child then. And she! – how sunken her eyes are, and dim! – she did not know me. "And this is Miss Leonard!" she said; and I hung my false face, and curtsied from the distance, and ran away. Oh, my mother! Margery, Margery!'

The strange confused words passed like light into my brain. First the room grew dark, and then so bewilderingly bright, that I could see nothing. But presently Rachel's white face, with its piteous look came glimmering towards me. I stretched out both my hands to her, but she melted from my touch; what colour of life remained in her face faded away from it, and she fell in a swoon at my feet.

13

A messenger came to my door to tell me that Mrs Hollingford was waiting to see me. Rachel, restored to her senses, was lying upon my bed with her face hidden on my hands.

'Rachel,' I said, 'I must go to her; but before I go tell me, assure me, that what you have said is true, that you are truly the daughter of Mrs Hollingford.'

'I am truly her daughter, Mary Hollingford,' said Rachel (for I cannot but still call her Rachel); 'I am John's sister. That is the secret I wanted to tell you one night, when you were jealous. But you would not listen. I have more, much more, to tell you; but go now. One thing I beg you to promise me – that you will tell her you have changed your mind about going to London. Let the Tyrrells go, and stay with me – oh, stay with me! I want you so badly; and, now that I have once spoken, I will trust you with everything – all my wickedness and weakness, all my troubles and difficulties.'

She spoke entreatingly, and her tears fell over my hands as she kissed them.

'I will stay,' I said; and the sun began to dance on the walls, it seemed. 'I will help you all I can; and, oh, how glad I shall be to let the Tyrrells go without me!'

And then I went downstairs.

I found my dear old lady looking very sad and worn and anxious. I threw myself into her arms and sobbed on her neck.

'What is this, my love?' she said. 'Is it a mistake, after all? And whose is the fault? Is it yours, or is it John's?'

'Mine – mine,' I cried. 'And I am not going to London. But you must not tell John this, because he might think – '

'Think what?' she said smiling.

'Oh, I don't know; but you must only tell him that I have deferred my visit because Miss Leonard,' I choked a little over the word, 'has pressed me to remain here longer.'

She went away smiling and satisfied, and I went wondering back to my room to hear Rachel's story.

I found her standing, as pale as a ghost, at my window, which commanded a view of the approach to the house. Looking over her shoulder, I saw Mrs Hollingford's black robe disappearing among the trees.

'Now, Rachel,' I said – 'now for your story. I have done what you bid me. I am going to stay with you. Trust me with everything; I am full of anxiety and wonder.'

But at that moment a messenger came to the door seeking Miss Leonard. Mr Noble was waiting for her to walk with him.

Rachel flushed at the summons.

'Do not go; send him word that you are engaged – what can it matter?' I said eagerly.

'No, no,' said Rachel confusedly. 'You must excuse me now, Margery. I must go. Have patience with me, dear,' she added wistfully. 'I will come to your room tonight.'

And she went away sadly.

She came to me that night surely. She asked me to put out the lights, and crouching on a low seat by the fire, she told me her story.

'Do not ask me to look in your face till I have done,' she said, 'but let me hold your hand, and whenever you are too much disgusted and sickened with me to hear me any longer draw away your hand, that I may know.'

Poor Rachel! that was what she said in beginning. I will tell you her history as nearly as possible in the way that she related it, but I cannot now recollect, and it were useless to repeat, one half the bitter words of self-condemnation which she used.

*   *   *

When quite a little girl (she said) I was sent to a school in Paris. Oh, why did my mother send me so early from her side? It was a worldly school – worldly to the last degree. I learned chiefly to think that in proportion as my father was honoured and wealthy, my friends gay and extravagant, just so were my chances of happiness in life. I had handsome clothes and rich presents, and I was a great favourite.

There was a lady, a friend of my father's, who lived in Paris, and who had liberty to take me for holidays to her house as often as she pleased. She made a pet of me, and I spent at least half my time in her carriage or her salon. She had charming toilettes prepared for me, which I was enchanted to wear. Thus I was early introduced to the gay world of Paris, and learned its lessons of folly and vanity by heart. I can remember myself, dressed like a fantastic doll, flitting from one room to another, listening to the conversation of the ladies and admiring their costumes. Every summer I came home for a time, but I found home dull after Paris, and I was rather in awe of my mother's grave face and quiet ways. She always parted with me against her will – I knew that – but it was my father's wish that I should have a Parisian education.

I was just seventeen, on the point of leaving school, bewitched by vanity and arrogance and the delights of the world, when the dreadful news came – you know – about my father, his ruin and disgrace. The effect on me was like nothing you could enter into or conceive. I think it deprived me even of reason, such reason as I had. I had nothing in me – nothing had ever been put in me – to enable me to endure such a horrible reverse.

My mother had written to that friend, the lady I have mentioned, begging her to break the news to me. She, however, was on the point of leaving Paris for her country château, and simply wrote to madame, the mistress of my school, transferring the unpleasant task to her. She sent her love to me, and assured me she was very sorry, *desolée*, that she could not delay, to pay me a visit. I have never seen her since.

And so the whole school knew of my fall and disgrace as soon as I learned it myself. The first thing I did when I understood the full extent of my humiliation was to seize my hat and cloak, and rush out of the house with the intention of never coming back, never being seen again by anyone who had known me. But after walking Paris for several hours, and getting two or three rough frights through being alone and unprotected, I was overcome with fear and fatigue, and was obliged to return by evening, hungry, weary and sullen, to the school.

I took it for granted that all the world would now be my enemy, and, determined not to wait to be shuffled off by my friends, I assumed at once an air of hauteur and defiance which estranged me from everyone. My mother, my poor mother, wrote to me, begging me to be patient until she should find it convenient to bring me home. Patient! Oh dear, I did not know the meaning of the word! No, I would not go home; I would change my name and never willingly see again the face of one who knew me.

Every day I searched the papers, and soon saw an advertisement which I thought might suit me. An English lady in Paris required an English companion, 'young, cheerful and well-educated'. Without losing a moment I went straight to the hotel where the lady lived, saw her, pleased her; she was good, kind Mrs Hill.

I gave her an assumed name, the first that entered my head, and referred her to madame, at my school. When I returned home I said: 'Madame, I have two hundred francs here in my desk; they shall be yours if you will not undeceive a lady who is coming here to assure herself that I am respectable and well-educated, and that I am Miss Leonard, an orphan, and of an honourable family.'

Madame coloured and hesitated; she was surprised at my audacity; but I knew that she had bills coming due just then, and that she was extravagant. We, her pupils, had talked over these things. She hesitated, but in the end agreed to oblige her dear child, who had been to her so good and so profitable a pupil. Perhaps she thought I acted with the consent of my mother, that it was not her affair, and that Providence had sent her my little offering to help her to pay her just debts.

Mrs Hill came the next day; a word satisfied her, and she only stayed about three minutes. She was preparing to leave Paris for Rome, and had many affairs to attend to in the meantime. She urged me to come to her without delay, and in a few hours I was established under her roof.

I was then quite unaware that I had omitted to mention Mrs Hill's name or address to madame, and that madame had forgotten, or had not been sufficiently interested in the matter to ask it. As I said before, I think it is likely that madame believed I acted with the consent of my friends, and that she had no further concern in the matter. Indeed, indeed, I had then no idea of deserting my mother altogether. I was hurried along by impulse, and I intended, when the hurry of action should be over, to write and tell her of all I had done. I little thought that when I quitted my school that day, without leaving behind me the name and address of my new protector, I cut away the only clue by which it might be possible my mother should find me in the future. I did not know that I should afterwards deliberately turn my back upon her, and hide myself from her.

Arthur Noble dined with us on that very first evening of my acquaintance with the Hills. You know that I have been long engaged to Arthur, and I will speak to you freely about him. He has often told me since that he liked me from the first moment he saw me. I felt it even that evening; though I could not believe in it. But the possibility of it dazzled and bewildered me, so powerful was the fascination he possessed for me.

When I went to bed that night I felt my heart strangely softened and opened. I thought a great deal about my mother and my home, of which I knew so little, and for the first time feared that I had done very wrong, and resolved to write to my mother surely on the morrow. I felt myself to be an impostor and a liar, and I trembled, thinking of her just anger at my falsehood and cowardice. I felt that when writing to her I must make up my mind to confess to Mrs Hill that I had deceived her respecting my name and condition, and bribed my schoolmistress to deceive her also. I knew that my mother would not tolerate the deceit; but the thought of the confession was insufferable to me.

The next day, while we sat together, Mrs Hill talked to me about Arthur Noble. He was a great pet of hers, and at present she was particularly interested in his circumstances. He had a cousin in England who was a great heiress, and whom his father wanted him to marry. Arthur disliked the idea extremely; and as the lady was supposed to be very well inclined towards him, he was anxious to avoid danger by prolonging his tour abroad. He had arranged to go on to Rome with them, the Hills; but only yesterday, his father, Sir Arthur Noble, had met him in Paris, urging him to give up the project, and return at once to England. He, Sir Arthur, had lost heavily by the failure and bad conduct of a London banker – a gentleman who had been his personal friend. My heart beat thickly as I heard her say this; but I did not dare to ask the name of that banker. In the midst of my dismay, Arthur Noble came in to assure Mrs Hill that he still intended to be of the party to Rome. His father's ill-humour would subside by and by. He was only a little upset by the shocking conduct of his friend Mr Hollingford. Then Mrs Hill asked questions on the subject, and I sat by stitching at my embroidery while Arthur described my father's disgrace.

My letter to my mother was not written that day. In the afternoon we went out, and in the excitement of shopping I tried to forget everything – who I was, what I was, what I had done, and what I ought to do. In the evening Arthur Noble appeared again, and with him came his father. Sir Arthur and Mr Hill conversed apart, but I could hear the fiery old baronet giving vent to his anger against my father. Arthur devoted himself to Mrs Hill and me. I was bewildered and distracted at the position in which my rash conduct had placed me, and I was very silent. Arthur exerted himself to amuse me, and under the spell of his attractions my remorse was smothered.

I have not spoken to you yet of the wonderful affection which Mrs Hill lavished on me. You have seen it lately, but it was the same from the first. She made me her daughter at once, as far as her conduct to me could do so, though I had been some months her companion before she declared her intention of formally adopting me.

Day followed day, and Arthur was always by my side. A new feverish dream of happiness encompassed me, and it was only in the quiet of wakeful nights that I thought of my mother and sisters and brother, and longed to hear some news of my sorrowful home. Every night my wrestlings with my selfish nature grew weaker and weaker. I could not risk exposure and banishment from Arthur's presence. I left Paris for Rome without writing to my mother.

You will hate me, Margery. I hate myself. I gave myself up to the delight of the hour, and in selfish happiness drowned the reproaches of my conscience, till I told myself at last that it was too late to undo what I had done. Time flew, and I became engaged to Arthur, secretly at first, for he dreaded his father's displeasure. We went from place to place, staying a few months here and a few months there. We spent a year at Rome, and Arthur was with us nearly all the time. When we had been some time engaged, Arthur confided in his father, and asked his consent to our marriage. Sir Arthur was hopelessly enraged at the idea, and, as we could not marry without his consent, we have been obliged to be patient ever since. Arthur has always kept telling me that he knew his father would relent in time. And he was right. The time has come. Sir Arthur has at last reluctantly withdrawn his opposition, and we may be married on any day in the future which I may choose to name.

Stay, stay! do not ask me any questions, or I shall not be able to go on. Let me tell you everything before I stop. I used to dream that when I was married to Arthur, when no power on earth could separate us, I would confess who I was, seek out my mother, and ask her forgiveness. Remorse never left me, and I had bitterness in the midst of my happiness. Arthur suspected that I had trouble which I would not share with him, yet I could not bring myself to confess, so great was my fear of being parted from him.

Some time before that evening when I first met you in London, I went to see some friends of Arthur's. During that time, for several months, I had not seen Mr or Mrs Hill; but in the meanwhile Mrs

Hill had written to me of their intention of coming here to Hillsbro', saying that Mr Hill's new agent had written such cheerful accounts of the estate, that he felt a longing to be on the spot, giving encouragement to the improvements which were going forward. She did not mention the name of the new agent, and it was only on that evening when I first met you, when with shame and bitter self-reproach I heard you defend my poor mother so valiantly, it was only then I knew that the agent was my brother, and that I was actually coming to live within a few miles of my deserted home.

My first thought was that now, indeed, the time for making all the crooked things straight had come; but, oh Margery, you cannot imagine – one like you never could imagine anything so wickedly weak as I am. The old bugbear of our family disgrace, the old terror of Arthur's throwing me off in disgust, rose up again with all their former strength, and I came here torn by conflicting feelings. You saw my meeting with John. The next day, when he came here to dine, I found an opportunity of telling him my story. He was very severe with me at first, though not so much so as I deserved; but he forgave me at last, on condition that I would make up my mind to be honest with everyone, let the consequences be what they might. I promised this; but again and again my courage has failed. He has been so good, so kind, so patient with me. He told me of my mother, of the children, of you, and, oh, how he chafed at the thought of what you would feel about the affair. Every time we met he reproached me with my cowardice and delay, and I made fresh promises; but Arthur's letters invariably broke down my courage and destroyed my resolutions. Again and again John has asked me to allow him to tell you who I was, but I would not suffer it. I could see no reason for humbling myself sooner to you than to anyone else, until one day it flashed on me that you were jealous of me. Then, after a hard struggle, I came to you to tell my story. You repulsed me, you even assured me that the Tyrrells were your best friends. I was glad of the excuse to spare myself and my secret. And so it has gone on. Latterly John has scarcely spoken to, hardly looked at me. I think he has given me up. I know not what he means to do, but I think he means to let me have my own way. I think I should have been silent to the last, but that I saw my mother today. I saw her! I saw her!

*　　*　　*

'And now you will tell her all – everything,' I said, squeezing her hands, while the tears were raining down my face.

'Margery, Margery!' cried Rachel, 'how can I give up Arthur? Here he has come to me after these years of waiting, and presses me to name a day for our marriage, and I am to meet him with a story like this! He would despise me.'

'I think,' said I, 'that if he be a generous man he will forgive you. After loving you so long, he will not give you up so easily. And your mother,' I added. 'Think of all she has suffered. Is she worth no sacrifice?'

'She never knew me,' said Rachel gloomily, 'and she will be happier never to know me. She could not have smiled as she did today if she had not forgotten that I ever existed.'

'That is a selfish delusion,' I said. 'If your mother never knew you, it is plain, at least, that you have never known her. Such a woman could not forget her child. You cannot think that she has not sought for you, and mourned for you, all these years?'

'Oh no,' said Rachel, with another burst of sorrow, 'John has told me. They searched, they advertised, they suffered agony, and feared every terrible thing, till at last they were obliged to soothe one another by trying to think and speak of me as dead. Little Mopsie thinks I am dead. So it has been, and so it must be.'

'So it must not be,' I persisted, and I fought with her all night. The dawn was in the room before she got up to leave me, pale, and worn, and weary, but promising that she would make yet one more great struggle with herself to break the chain of deceit with which one rash falsehood had so strongly bound her.

14

I had the happiness of seeing my friends the Tyrrells depart for London without me. I think they were both, brother and sister, somewhat tired of my inconsistencies and vagaries, and I dare say they felt as little sorrow at parting as I did.

The long hot days of summer followed one another in a slow wandering fashion. No news reached us from the farm. I had vaguely hoped that John would come and speak to me again; but we neither saw him nor heard from him. Mr Hill was from home during these days, and there was no necessity for John to present himself among us, though there might have been many an opportunity if he had cared to seek one. All the light short nights I lay awake, wondering what was going to become of my life.

And Rachel? Was she mindful of the promise she had given me on that night? Alas! no, my dears. She was absorbed in her Arthur. They went here and there together; they were ever side by side, dreaming away the time; seeming lost to everyone else in their happiness. I should have thought that Rachel had forgotten all her confession to me, all that had passed between us on the subject, but for a piteous look which she gave me now and again when no one was by.

At last an early day was fixed for the marriage, and a wonderful trousseau came down from London for Rachel. The pretty things were hardly looked at by her, and were packed away out of sight. Then I saw that two warring spirits were striving within Rachel. The colour left her face, she grew thin, she started and trembled at a sudden word or noise. Sometimes in the middle of the summer nights, just as the earliest birds were beginning to stir, she would come into my room and throw herself weeping across my bed. But I dared not speak to her then. She would not tolerate a word. And so she took her way.

One morning Arthur went off to explore some place alone – a most unusual event. I was in my own room when Rachel came in to me, suddenly and quickly, and very pale.

'Come,' she said, 'come now, I have got courage to go this moment, but I must not delay. Come, come!'

'Where are you going,' I asked.

'You know well,' she said impatiently; 'to my mother. See, I am taking nothing valuable with me.'

She had on a calico morning dress, and plain straw hat. She had taken the earrings out of her ears, the rings off her fingers.

I was ready in an instant, and we went off through the wood together. I did not attempt to ask her what she meant to do; she was not in a mood for answering questions. She took my hand as we walked, and held it tightly, and we went along as children do when they are going through the green wood in quest of May flowers, only our steps were more fearful and our faces paler than children's are wont to be. We went on very silently and bravely, till we were about halfway, deep in the wood, when a cheerful shout came across our ears, and there was a swaying and crackling of bushes; and Arthur

Noble's handsome genial face and stalwart figure confronted us on the path.

'Maids a-Maying!' he said. 'A pretty picture, on my word. Whither be you bound, fair ladies, and will you accept the services of a true knight-errant?'

Rachel's hand had turned cold in mine. 'We are going to the farm to visit Mrs Hollingford,' I said stoutly, 'and as you are not acquainted with the lady you had better go home alone, and amuse Mrs Hill till we come back.'

'Ah! but I do not like that arrangement at all,' said Arthur. 'Why should the lady at the farm not receive me? Has anyone been giving me a bad character? Speak, Rachel, may I not go with you?'

'I cannot go any further,' said Rachel; 'I am not well.' And indeed she looked ill.

'Rest a little,' I said pitylessly, 'and by and by you will be able to go on.'

But Arthur, all alarmed, looked at me with surprise and reproach, drew Rachel's hand within his own, and began walking slowly towards the Hall. I followed, with no company but my reflections, which were odd enough; and so ended this adventure.

And now what I think the most startling occurrence of my story has got to be related, and, when it is told, all will be pretty nearly finished.

It was arranged that the wedding should be very private. Sir Arthur, although he had reluctantly withdrawn his opposition, had refused to be present at the marriage, therefore, no other guests were invited. The eve of the day arrived, and I had spent the forenoon in decorating the little church with white flowers. Early in the morning Rachel and Arthur, with Mr and Mrs Hill and myself, were to proceed thither, and an hour later the husband and wife were to depart on their life's adventure together.

I remember the kind of evening it was. There was a great flush in the sky, and a great glow on the earth, that made the garden paths hot to the tread, and crisped up the leaves of the full-blown roses. There was a rare blending of heaven and earth in lovely alluring distances, and a luscious odour of sweet ripe things athirst for rain. The drawing-room windows were thrown up as high as they would go, and it was cooler within than without. Upstairs the bride's trunks were packed, and the white robe was spread out in state, waiting its moment. We were all in the drawing-room, Mr and Mrs Hill variously unoccupied, Rachel and Arthur sitting together before a window. In another window I was down on my knees leaning my elbows on the open sash, and gazing out on the idealised world of the hour in a kind of restful reverie, which held the fears and pains and unsatisfied hopes of my heart in a sweet thrall, even as the deep-coloured glory that was abroad fused into common beauty all the rough seams and barren places of the unequal land. Suddenly out of the drowsy luxury of stillness there came a quick crushing sound, flying feet on the gravel, and a dark slim figure dashed through the light. Whose was the figure? I could not be sure till I sprang with a shock to my feet, and went to the window where Rachel and Arthur were sitting. Then there was no mistake about it. Here was Jane Hollingford, suddenly arrived.

She stood strangely at the window, with one foot on the low sash, so that she could look searchingly into the room. She had on no bonnet or hat, and the dust of the road was in her hair; it was also white, up to the knees, on her black dress. She was quite breathless, and looked sick and faint with over-running. But there was Jane's wild spirit shining as strong as ever out of her black eyes. She drew breath a moment and looked eagerly into the room with a half-blinded searching look out of the dazzling light into the shade. Then her eyes fell on Rachel, and she spoke, and said a few words which electrified us all.

'Mary Hollingford,' she said; 'come home. Your father is dying, and he wants to see you.'

Mr and Mrs Hill came to the window to see what it was. We were all silent from surprise for about a minute. Then Rachel rose trembling.

'Sit still, my love,' said Arthur; 'it is only a mad gypsy girl.' And Jane was not unlike a gypsy.

'Come, come!' cried Jane, stamping her foot with impatience, not vouchsafing even a look at Arthur. 'Come, or you will be too late; there is not a moment to lose.'

I think Mrs Hill's voice piped shrill exclamations at my ear, but I remember nothing that she said. Mr Hill, who knew Jane by appearance, was speechless. Arthur had risen, and stood by Rachel, looking amazedly from her to Jane, and from Jane to her. Rachel turned on him a grievous look which I have never forgotten, and pushed him from her with both her hands back into the room. Then she glanced at me with a mute entreaty, and I stepped with her out of the window, and we went across the lawn and through the trees, and away along all the old tracks to the farm, following Jane, who, knowing we were behind her, flew like the wind, without once looking back. We soon lost her, for we often paused to pant and lean against one another for a moment's respite in this strange memorable race. We did not speak, but I looked at Rachel, and she was like a poor lily soiled and crushed by the storm, with her white dress trailing through the dust, and her satin shoes torn on her feet. But that was nothing. We reached the farmhouse. There was someone moving to meet white dishevelled, quivering Rachel. There was a cry, smothered at once in the awful hush of the place, and Rachel fell, clasping her mother's knees. I left them alone. What sobbings and whisperings, what confession and forgiveness followed, God and his angels heard.

I went blindly into the hall, knowing nothing of what I did. I met John coming to me. I had no words. I stretched out my hands to him. He took them, took me in his arms, and that was our reconciliation.

That night we were all present at a deathbed. It was only bit by bit that I learned the story of how the dying man came to be there. The poor erring father, reduced by want and smitten by disease, had crept back in the disguise of a beggar to ask the charity of his deserted wife and children, and to breathe his last sigh among loving forgiving hearts. It was Jane, stern Jane, who had denounced him so cruelly, cherished such bitter resentment against him; it was Jane, who had happened, of a summer evening in her mother's absence, to open the door to his knock, had taken him into her arms and into her heart, had nursed him, caressed him, watched and prayed with him. So that was the end of poor Jane's hardness of heart. It was all washed away in tears at her father's deathbed. The last trace of it vanished at sight of Rachel's remorse.

My dear Mrs Hollingford, my sweet old mother! These two shocks well nigh caused her death; but when she had nobly weathered the storm she found a daughter whom she had mourned as lost, living and breathing and loving in her arms, and her brave heart accepted much comfort.

And what about those three kind souls whom we left in such sudden consternation by the open window in the drawing-room at the Hall? Why, of course, they came to enquire into the mystery. I was the one who had to tell them Rachel's story, as kindly and delicately as I might. You will be glad, my children, to know that they made very little of their darling's fault. Mr Hill was somewhat grave over the matter, but Mrs Hill would not allow a word of blame to be uttered against her pet. She urged, she invented a hundred excuses; good, kind soul. As for Arthur Noble, he readily discerned love for himself as the cause of her unwilling desertion of others. His nature was large enough to appreciate the worth of my John and his mother. As he had been willing, he said, to wed Rachel friendless, so was he now more willing to wed Rachel with friends whom he could love. So the beloved culprit was tried and acquitted, and after many days had passed, and the poor father had been laid in the earth, a chastened Rachel was coaxed back to her lover's side, and, I have no doubt, told him her own story in her own way.

But old Mr Hill was, to my mind, the most sensible of them all, who said to his wife: 'They may say what they please, sweetheart, but, to my thinking, the lad, John, is by far the flower of the Hollingford flock!' And the fine old gentleman proved his goodwill after years had passed that were then to come. When called upon to follow his wife, who died before him, he bequeathed the Hillsbro' estate to my husband.

Rachel (he always called her Rachel) and Arthur went to live in Paris; Jane married a great doctor of learning, and found her home in London; and Mopsie made a sweet little wife for a country squire, and stayed among the roses and milk-pans.

For John and me, our home was the farm, till fortune promoted us to the Hall. Thither the dear mother accompanied us, and there she died in my arms. There, also, at last, my husband. And now, my darlings, your father, my son, is the owner of Hillsbro' and the Hall is your own happy home.

And the old woman has returned to the farm.

Courage

FORREST REID

When the children came to stay with their grandfather, young Michael Aherne, walking with the others from the station to the rectory, noticed the high grey wall that lined one side of the long, sleepy lane, and wondered what lay beyond it. For above his head, over the tops of the mossy stones, trees stretched green arms that beckoned to him, and threw black shadows on the white, dusty road. His four brothers and sisters, stepping demurely beside tall, rustling Aunt Caroline, left him lagging behind, and, when a white bird fluttered out for a moment into the sunlight, they did not even see it. Michael called to them, and eight eyes turned straightaway to the trees, but were too late. So he trotted on and took fat, tried Barbara's place by Aunt Caroline.

'Does anybody live there?' he asked; but Aunt Caroline shook her head. The house, whose chimneys he presently caught a glimpse of through the trees, had been empty for years and years; the people to whom it belonged lived somewhere else.

Michael learned more than this from Rebecca, the cook, who told him that the house was empty because it was haunted. Long ago a lady lived there, but she had been very wicked and very unhappy, poor thing, and even now could find no rest in her grave . . .

*   *   *

It was on an afternoon when he was all alone that Michael set out to explore the stream running past the foot of the rectory garden. He would follow it, he thought, wherever it led him; follow it just as his father, far away in wild places, had followed mighty rivers into the heart of the forest. The long, sweet, green grass brushed against his legs, and a white cow, with a buttercup hanging from the corner of her mouth, gazed at him in mild amazement as he flew past. He kept to the meadow side, and on the opposite bank the leaning trees made little magic caves tapestried with green. Black flies darted restlessly about, and every now and again he heard strange splashes – splashes of birds, of fish; the splash of a rat; and once the heavy, floundering splash of the cow herself, plunging into the water up to her knees. He watched her tramp through the sword-shaped leaves of a bed of irises, while the rich black mud oozed up between patches of bright green weed. A score of birds made a quaint chorus of trills and peeps, chuckles and whistles; a wren, like a tiny winged mouse, flitted about the ivy-covered bole of a hollow elm. Then Michael came unexpectedly to the end of his journey, for an iron gate was swung here right across the stream, and on either side of it, as far as he could see, stretched a high grey wall.

He paused. The gate was padlocked, and its spiked bars were so narrow that to climb it would not be easy. Suddenly a white bird rose out of the burning green and gold of the trees, and for a moment, in the sunlight, it was the whitest thing in the world. The it flew back again into the mysterious shadow, and Michael stood breathless.

He knew now where he was, knew that this wall must be a continuation of the wall in the lane. The stooping trees leaned down as if to catch him in their arms. He looked at the padlock on the gate and saw that it was half eaten by rust. He took off his shoes and stockings. Stringing them about his neck, he waded through the water and with a stone struck the padlock once, twice – twice only, for at the second blow the lock dropped into the stream, with a dull splash. Michael tugged at the rusty bolt, and in a moment or two the gate was open. On the other side he clambered up the bank to put on his shoes, and it was then that, as he glanced behind him, he saw the gate swing slowly back in silence.

That was all, yet it somehow startled him, and he had a fantastic impression that he had not been meant to see it. 'Of course it must have moved of its own weight,' he told himself, but it gave him an uneasy feeling as of someone following stealthily on his footsteps, and he remembered Rebecca's story.

Before him was a dark, moss-grown path, like the narrow aisle of a huge cathedral whose pillars were the over-arching trees. It seemed to lead on through an endless green stillness, and he stood dreaming on the outermost fringe, wondering, doubting, not very eager to explore further.

He walked on, and the noise of the stream died away behind him, like the last warning murmur of the friendly world outside. Suddenly, turning at an abrupt angle, he came upon the house. It lay beyond what had once been a lawn, and the grass, coarse and matted, grew right up to the doorsteps, which were green, with gaping apertures between the stones. Ugly, lived stains, lines of dark moss and lichen, crept over the red bricks; and the shutters and blinds looked as if they had been closed for ever. Then Michael's heart gave a jump, for at that moment an uneasy puff of wind stirred one of the lower shutters, which flapped back with a dismal rattle.

He stood there while he might have counted a hundred, on the verge of flight, poised between curiosity and fear. At length curiosity, the spirit of adventure, triumphed, and he advanced to a closer inspection. With his nose pressed to the pane, he gazed into a large dark room, across which lay a band of sunlight, thin as a stretched ribbon. He gave the window a tentative push, and, to his surprise, it yielded. Had there been another visitor here? he wondered. For he saw that the latch was not broken, must have been drawn back from within, or forced, very skilfully, in some way that had left no mark upon the woodwork. He made these reflections and then, screwing up his courage, stepped across the sill.

Once inside, he had a curious sense of relief. He could somehow *feel* that the house was empty, that not even the ghost of a ghost lingered there. With this certainty, everything dropped consolingly, yet half disappointingly, back into the commonplace, and he became conscious that outside it was broad daylight, and that ghost stories were nothing more than a kind of fairytale. He opened the other shutters, letting the rich afternoon light pour in. Though the house had been empty for so long, it smelt sweet and fresh, and not a speck of dust was visible anywhere. He drew his fingers over the top of one of the little tables, but so clean was it that might have been polished that morning. He touched the faded silks and curtains, and sniffed at faintly smelling china jars. Over the wide carved chimney-piece hung a picture of a lady, very young and beautiful. She was sitting in a chair, and beside her stood a tall, delicate boy of Michael's own age. One of the boy's hands rested on the lady's shoulder, and the other held a gilt-clasped book. Michael, gazing at them, easily saw that they were mother and son. The lady seemed to him infinitely lovely, and presently she made him think of his own mother, and with that he began to feel homesick, and all kinds of memories returned to him. They were dim and shadowy, and, as he stood there dreaming, it seemed to him that somehow his mother was bound up with this other lady – he could not tell how – and at last he turned away, wishing that he had not looked at the picture. He drew from his pocket the letter he had received that morning. His mother was better; she would soon be quite well again. Yesterday she had been out driving for more than an hour, she told him, and today she felt a little tired, which was why her letter must be rather short . . . And he remembered, remembered through a sense of menacing trouble only half realised during those days of uneasy waiting in the silent rooms at home; only half realised even at the actual moment of goodbye – remembered that last glimpse of her face, smiling, smiling so beautifully and bravely . . .

He went out into the hall and unbarred and flung wide the front door, before ascending to the upper storeys. He found many curious things, but, above all, in one large room, he discovered a whole store of toys – soldiers, puzzles, books, a bow and arrows, a musical box with a little silver key lying beside it. He wound it up, and a gay, sweet melody tinkled out into the silence, thin and fragile, losing itself in the empty vastness of that still house, like the flicker of a taper in a cave.

He opened a door leading into a second room, a bedroom, and, sitting down in the window-seat, began to turn the pages of an old illuminated volume he found there, full of strange pictures of saints and martyrs, all glowing in gold and bright colours, yet somehow sinister, disquieting. It was with a start that, as he looked up, he noticed how dark it had become indoors. The pattern had faded out of the chintz bed curtains, and he could no longer see clearly into the further corners of the room. It was from these corners that the darkness seemed to be stealing out, like a thin smoke, spreading slowly over everything. Then a strange fancy came to him, and it seemed to him that he had lived in this house for years and years, and that all his other life was but a dream. It was so dark now that the bed curtains were like pale shadows, and outside, over the trees, the moon was growing brighter. He must go home . . .

He sat motionless, trying to realise what had happened, listening, listening, for it was as if the secret, hidden heart of the house had begun very faintly to beat. Faintly at first, a mere stirring of the vacant atmosphere, yet, as the minutes passed, it gathered strength, and with this consciousness of awakening life a fear came also. He listened in the darkness, and though he could hear nothing, he had a vivid sense that he was no longer alone. Whatever had dwelt here before had come back, was perhaps even now creeping up the stairs. A sickening, stupefying dread paralysed him. It had not come for him, he told himself – whatever it was. It wanted to avoid him, and perhaps he could get downstairs without meeting it. Then it flashed across his mind, radiantly, savingly, that if he had not seen it by now it was only because it *was* avoiding him. He sprang to his feet and opened the door – not the door leading to the other room, but one giving on the landing.

Outside, the great well of the staircase was like a yawning pit of blackness. His heart thumped as he stood clutching at the wall. With shut eyes, lest he should see something he had no desire to see, he took two steps forward and gripped the balusters. Then, with eyes still tightly shut, he ran quickly down – quickly, recklessly, as if a fire were at his heels.

Down in the hall, the open door showed as a dim silver-grey square, and he ran to it, but the instant he passed the threshold his panic left him. A fear remained, but it was no longer blind and brutal. It was as if a voice had spoken to him, and, as he stood there, a sense that everything swayed in a balance, that everything depended upon what he did next, swept over him. He looked up at the dark, dreadful staircase. Nothing had pursued him, and he knew now that nothing *would* pursue him. Whatever was there was not there for that purpose, and if he were to see it he must go in search of it. But if he left it? If he left it now, he knew that he should leave something else as well. In forsaking one he should forsake both; in losing one he should lose both. Another spirit at this moment was close to him, and it was the spirit of his mother, who, invisible, seemed to hold his hand keep him there upon the step. But why – why? He could only tell that she *wanted* him to stay: but of that he was certain. If he were a coward she would know. It would be impossible to hide it from her. She might forgive him – she would forgive him – but it could never be the same again. He steadied himself against the side of the porch. The cold moonlight washed through the dim hall, and turned to a glimmering greyness the lowest flight of stairs. With sobbing breath and wide eyes he retraced his steps, but at the foot of the stairs he stopped once more. The greyness ended at the first landing; beyond that, an impenetrable blackness led to those awful upper storeys. He put his foot on the lowest stair, and slowly, step by step, he mounted, clutching the balusters. He did not pause on the landing, but walked on into the darkness, which seemed to close about his slight figure like the heavy wings of a monstrous tomb.

On the uppermost landing of all, the open doors allowed a faint light to penetrate. He entered the room of the toys and stood beside the table. The beating of the blood in his ears almost deafened him. 'If only it would come now!' he prayed, for he felt that he could not tolerate the strain of waiting. But nothing came; there was neither sight nor sound. At length he made his final effort, and crossing to the door, which was now closed, turned the handle. For a moment the room seemed empty, and he was conscious of a sudden, an immense relief. Then, close by the window-seat, in the dim twilight, he perceived something. He stood still, while a deathly coldness descended upon him. At first hardly more than a shadow, a thickening of the darkness, what he gazed upon made no movement, and so long as it remained thus, with head mercifully lowered, he felt that he could bear it. But the suspense tortured him, and presently a faint moan of anguish rose from his dry lips. With that, the grey, marred face, the face he dreaded to see, was slowly lifted. He tried to close his eyes, but could not. He felt himself sinking to the ground, and clutched at the doorpost for support. Then suddenly he seemed to know that it, too, this – this thing – was afraid, and that what it feared was his fear. He saw the torment, the doubt and despair, that glowed in the smoky dimness of those hollowed, dreadful eyes. How changed was this lady from the bright, beautiful lady of the picture! He felt a pity for her, and as his compassion grew his fear diminished. He watched her move slowly towards him – nearer, nearer – only now there was something else that mingled with his dread, battling with it, overcoming it; and when at last she held out her arms to him, held them wide in a supreme, soundless appeal, he knew that it had conquered. He came forward and lifted his face to hers. At the same instant she bent down over him and seemed to draw him to her. An icy coldness, as of a dense mist, enfolded him, and he felt and saw no more . . .

*   *   *

When he opened his eyes the moon was shining upon him, and he knew at once that he was alone. He knew, moreover, that he was now free to go. But the house no longer held any terror for him, and, as he scrambled to his feet, he felt a strange happiness that was very quiet, and a little like that he used to feel when, after he had gone up to bed, he lay growing sleepier and sleepier, while he listened to his mother singing. He must go home, but he would not go for a minute or two yet. He moved his hand, and it struck against a box of matches lying on a table. He had not known they were there, but now he lighted the tall candles on the chimney-piece, and as he did so he became more vividly aware of what he had felt dimly ever since he had opened his eyes. Some subtle atmospheric change had come about, though in what it consisted he could not at once tell. It was like a hush in the air, the strange hush which comes with the falling of snow. But how could there be snow in August? and, moreover, this was within the house, not outside. He lifted one of the candlesticks and saw that a delicate powder of dust had gathered upon it. He looked down at his own clothes – they, too, were covered with that same thin powder. Then he knew what was happening. The dust of years had begun to fall again; silently, slowly, like a soft and continuous caress, laying everything in the house to sleep.

Dawn was breaking when, with a candle in either hand, he descended the broad, whitening staircase. As he passed out into the garden he saw lanterns approaching, and knew they had come to look for him. They were very kind, very gentle with him, and it was not till the next day that he learned of the telegram which had come in his absence.

Hertford O'Donnell's Warning

CHARLOTTE RIDDELL

Many a year, before chloroform was thought of, there lived in an old rambling house, in Gerrard Street, Soho, a clever Irishman called Hertford O'Donnell.

After Hertford O'Donnell he was entitled to write, MRCS for he had studied hard to gain this distinction, and the older surgeons at Guy's (his hospital) considered him one of the most rising operators of the day.

Having said chloroform was unknown at the time this story opens, it will strike my readers that, if Hertford O'Donnell were a rising and successful operator in those days, of necessity he combined within himself a larger number of striking qualities than are by any means necessary to form a successful operator in these.

There was more than mere hand skill, more than even thorough knowledge of his profession, then needful for the man, who, dealing with conscious subjects, essayed to rid them of some of the diseases to which flesh is heir. There was greater courage required in the manipulator of old than is altogether essential at present. Then, as now, a thorough mastery of his instruments, a steady hand, a keen eye, a quick dexterity were indispensable to a good operator; but, added to all these things, there formerly required a pulse which knew no quickening, mental strength which never faltered, a ready power of adaptation in unexpected circumstances, fertility of resource in difficult cases, and a brave front under all emergencies.

If I refrain from adding that a hard as well as a courageous heart was an important item in the program, it is only out of deference to general opinion, which, among other strange delusions, clings to the belief that courage and hardness are antagonistic qualities.

Hertford O'Donnell, however, was hard as steel. He understood his work, and he did it thoroughly; but he cared no more for quivering nerves and shrinking muscles, for screams of agony, for faces white with pain, and teeth clenched in the extremity of anguish, than he did for the stony countenances of the dead, which so often in the dissecting room appalled younger and less experienced men.

He had no sentiment, and he had no sympathy. The human body was to him merely an ingenious piece of mechanism, which it was at once a pleasure and a profit to understand. Precisely as Brunel loved the Thames Tunnel, or any other singular engineering feat, so O'Donnell loved a patient on whom he had operated successfully, more especially if the ailment possessed by the patient were of a rare and difficult character.

And for this reason he was much liked by all who came under his hands, since patients are apt to mistake a surgeon's interest in their cases for interest in themselves; and it was gratifying to John Dicks, plasterer, and Timothy Regan, labourer, to be the happy possessors of remarkable diseases, which produced a cordial understanding between them and the handsome Irishman.

If he had been hard and cool at the moment of hacking them to pieces, that was all forgotten or remembered only as a virtue, when, after being discharged from hospital like soldiers who have served in a severe campaign, they met Mr O'Donnell in the street, and were accosted by that rising individual just as though he considered himself nobody.

He had a royal memory, this stranger in a strange land, both for faces and cases; and like the rest of his countrymen, he never felt it beneath his dignity to talk cordially to corduroy and fustian.

In London, as at Calgillan, he never held back his tongue from speaking a cheery or a kindly word. His manners were pliable enough, if his heart were not; and the porters, and the patients, and the nurses, and the students at Guy's were all pleased to see Hertford O'Donnell.

Rain, hail, sunshine, it was all the same; there was a life and a brightness about the man which communicated itself to those with whom he came in contact. Let the mud in the Borough be a foot deep or the London fog as thick as pea soup, Mr O'Donnell never lost his temper, never muttered a surly reply to the gatekeeper's salutation, but spoke out blithely and cheerfully to his pupils and his patients, to the sick and to the well, to those below and to those above him.

And yet, spite of all these good qualities, spite of his handsome face, his fine figure, his easy address, and his unquestionable skill as an operator, the dons, who acknowledged his talent, shook their heads gravely when two or three of them in private and solemn conclave talked confidentially of their younger brother.

If there were many things in his favour, there were more in his disfavour. He was Irish – not merely by the accident of birth, which might have been forgiven, since a man cannot be held accountable for such caprices of Nature, but by every other accident and design which is objectionable to the orthodox and respectable and representative English mind.

In speech, appearance, manner, taste, modes of expression, habits of life, Hertford O'Donnell was Irish. To the core of his heart he loved the island which he declared he never meant to re-visit; and among the English he moved to all intents and purposes a foreigner, who was resolved, so said the great prophets at Guy's, to rush to destruction as fast as he could, and let no man hinder him.

'He means to go the whole length of his tether,' observed one of the ancient wiseacres to another; which speech implied a conviction that Hertford O'Donnell, having sold himself to the Evil One, had determined to dive the full length of his rope into wickedness before being pulled to that shore where even wickedness is negative – where there are no mad carouses, no wild, sinful excitements, nothing but impotent wailing and gnashing of teeth.

A reckless, graceless, clever, wicked devil – going to his natural home as fast as in London anyone possibly speeds thither; this was the opinion his superiors held of the man who lived all alone with a housekeeper and her husband (who acted as butler) in his big house near Soho.

Gerrard Street – made famous by De Quincey – was not then an utterly shady and forgotten locality; carriage-patients found their way to the rising young surgeon – some great personages thought it not beneath them to fee an individual whose consulting rooms were situated on what was even then considered the wrong side of Regent Street. He was making money, and he was spending it; he was over head and ears in debt – useless, vulgar debt – senselessly contracted, never bravely faced. He had lived at an awful pace ever since he came to London, a pace which only a man who hopes and expects to die young can ever travel.

Life was good, was it? Death, was he a child, or a woman, or a coward, to be afraid of that hereafter? God knew all about the trifle which had upset his coach, better than the dons at Guy's.

Hertford O'Donnell understood the world pretty thoroughly, and the ways thereof were to him as roads often traversed; therefore, when he said that at the Day of Judgment he felt certain he should come off as well as many of those who censured him, it may be assumed, that, although his views of post-mortem punishment were vague, unsatisfactory and infidel, still his information as to the peccadilloes of his neighbours was such as consoled himself.

And yet, living all alone in the old house near Soho Square, grave thoughts would intrude into the surgeon's mind – thoughts which were, so to say, italicised by peremptory letters, and still more peremptory visits from people who wanted money.

Although he had many acquaintances he had no single friend, and accordingly these thoughts were received and brooded over in solitude – in those hours when, after returning from dinner, or supper, or congenial carouse, he sat in his dreary rooms, smoking his pipe and considering means and ways, chances and certainties.

In good truth he had started in London with some vague idea that as his life in it would not be of long continuance, the pace at which he elected to travel could be little consequence; but the years since his first entry into the Metropolis were now piled one on the top of another, his youth was behind him, his chances of longevity, spite of the way he had striven to injure his constitution, quite as good as ever. He had come to that period in existence, to that narrow strip to tableland, whence the ascent of youth and the descent of age are equally discernible – when, simply because he has lived for so many years, it strikes a man as possible he may have to live for just as many more, with the ability for hard work gone, with the boon companions scattered, with the capacity for enjoying convivial meetings a mere memory, with small means perhaps, with no bright hopes, with the pomp and the circumstance and the fairy carriages, and the glamour which youth flings over earthly objects, faded away like the pageant of yesterday, while the dreary ceremony of living has to be gone through today and tomorrow and the morrow after, as though the gay cavalcade and the martial music, and the glittering helmets and the prancing steeds were still accompanying the wayfarer to his journey's end.

Ah! my friends, there comes a moment when we must all leave the coach, with its four bright bays, its pleasant outside freight, its cheery company, its guard who blows the horn so merrily through villages and along lonely country roads.

Long before we reach that final stage, where the black business claims us for its own special property, we have to bid goodbye to all easy, thoughtless journeying, and betake ourselves, with what zest we may, to traversing the common of reality. There is no royal road across it that ever I heard of. From the king on his throne to the labourer who vaguely imagines what manner of being a king is, we have all to tramp across that desert at one period of our lives, at all events; and that period usually is when, as I have said, a man starts to find the hopes, and the strength, and the buoyancy of youth left behind, while years and years of life lie stretching out before him.

The coach he has travelled by drops him here. There is no appeal, there is no help; therefore, let him take off his hat and wish the new passengers good speed, without either envy or repining.

Behold, he has had his turn, and let whosoever will mount on the box-seat of life again, and tip the coachman and handle the ribbons – he shall take that pleasant journey no more, no more forever.

Even supposing a man's springtime to have been a cold and ungenial one, with bitter easterly winds and nipping frosts biting the buds and retarding the blossoms, still it was spring for all that – spring with the young green leaves sprouting forth, with the flowers unfolding tenderly, with the songs of the birds and the rush of waters, with the summer before and the autumn afar off, and winter remote as death and eternity, but when once the trees have donned their summer foliage, when the pure white blossoms have disappeared, and the gorgeous red and orange and purple blaze of many-coloured flowers fills the gardens, then if there come a wet, dreary day, the idea of autumn and winter is not so difficult to realise. When once twelve o'clock is reached, the evening and night become facts, not possibilities; and it was of the afternoon, and the evening, and the night, Hertford O'Donnell sat thinking on the Christmas Eve, when I crave permission to introduce him to my readers.

A good-looking man ladies considered him. A tall, dark-complectioned, black-haired, straight-limbed, deeply divinely blue-eyed fellow, with a soft voice, with a pleasant brogue, who had ridden like a centaur over the loose stone walls in Connemara, who had danced all night at the Dublin balls, who had walked across the Bennebeola Mountains, gun in hand, day after day, without weariness, who had fished in every one of the hundred lakes you can behold from the top of that mountain near the Recess Hotel, who had led a mad, wild life in Trinity College, and a wilder, perhaps, while 'studying for a doctor' – as the Irish phrase goes – in Edinburgh, and who, after the death of his eldest brother left him free to return to Calgillan, and pursue the usual utterly useless, utterly purposeless, utterly pleasant life of an Irish gentleman possessed of health, birth, and expectations, suddenly kicked over the paternal traces, bade adieu to Calgillan Castle and the blandishments of a certain beautiful Miss Clifden, beloved of his mother, and laid out to be his wife, walked down the avenue without even so much company as a gossoon to carry his carpetbag, shook the dust from his feet at the lodge gates, and took his seat on the coach, never once looking back at Calgillan, where his favourite mare was standing in the stable, his greyhounds chasing one another round the home paddock, his gun at half-cock in his dressing-room and his fishing-tackle all in order and ready for use.

He had not kissed his mother, or asked for his father's blessing; he left Miss Clifden, arrayed in her brand-new riding-habit, without a word of affection or regret; he had spoken no syllable of farewell to any servant about the place; only when the old woman at the lodge bade him good-morning and God-blessed his handsome face, he recommended her bitterly to look at it well for she would never see it more.

Twelve years and a half had passed since then, without either Miss Clifden or any other one of the Calgillan people having set eyes on Master Hertford's handsome face.

He had kept his vow to himself; he had not written home; he had not been indebted to mother or father for even a tenpenny-piece during the whole of that time; he had lived without friends; and he had lived without God – so far as God ever lets a man live without him.

One thing only he felt to be needful – money; money to keep him when the evil days of sickness, or age, or loss of practice came upon him. Though a spendthrift, he was not a simpleton; around him he saw men, who, having started with fairer prospects than his own, were, nevertheless, reduced to indigence; and he knew that what had happened to others might happen to himself.

An unlucky cut, slipping on a piece of orange-peel in the street, the merest accident imaginable, is sufficient to change opulence to beggary in the life's program of an individual, whose income depends on eye, on nerve, on hand; and, besides the consciousness of this fact, Hertford O'Donnell knew that beyond a certain point in his profession, progress was not easy.

It did not depend quite on the strength of his own bow and shield whether he counted his earnings by hundreds or thousands. Work may achieve competence; but mere work cannot, in a profession, at all events, compass fortune.

He looked around him, and he perceived that the majority of great men – great and wealthy – had been indebted for their elevation, more to the accident of birth, patronage, connection, or marriage, than to personal ability.

Personal ability, no doubt, they possessed; but then, little Jones, who lived in Frith Street, and who could barely keep himself and his wife and family, had ability, too, only he lacked the concomitants of success.

He wanted something or someone to puff him into notoriety – a brother at Court – a lord's leg to mend – a rich wife to give him prestige in Society; and in his absence of this something or someone, he had grown grey-haired and fainthearted while labouring for a world which utterly despises its most obsequious servants.

'Clatter along the streets with a pair of fine horses, snub the middle classes, and drive over the commonalty – that is the way to compass wealth and popularity in England,' said Hertford O'Donnell, bitterly; and as the man desired wealth and popularity, he sat before his fire, with a foot on each hob, and a short pipe in his mouth, considering how he might best obtain the means to clatter along the streets in his carriage, and splash plebeians with mud from his wheels like the best.

In Dublin he could, by means of his name and connection, have done well; but then he was not in Dublin, neither did he want to be. The bitterest memories of his life were inseparable from the very name of the Green Island, and he had no desire to return to it.

Besides, in Dublin, heiresses are not quite so plentiful as in London; and an heiress, Hertford O'Donnell had decided, would do more for him then years of steady work.

A rich wife could clear him of debt, introduce him to fashionable practice, afford him that measure of social respectability which a medical bachelor invariably lacks, deliver him from the loneliness of Gerrard Street, and the domination of Mr and Mrs Coles.

To most men, deliberately bartering away their independence for money seems so prosaic a business that they strive to gloss it over even to themselves, and to assign every reason for their choice, save that which is really the influencing one.

Not so, however, with Hertford O'Donnell. He sat beside the fire scoffing over his proposed bargain – thinking of the lady's age, her money bags, her desirable house in town, her seat in the country, her snobbishness, her folly.

'It could be a fitting ending,' he sneered, 'and why I did not settle the matter tonight passes my comprehension. I am not a fool, to be frightened with old women's tales; and yet I must have turned white. I felt I did, and she asked me whether I were ill. And then to think of my being such an idiot as to ask her if she had heard anything like a cry, as though she would be likely to hear that, she with her poor parvenu blood, which I often imagine must have been mixed with some of her father's strong pickling vinegar. What a deuce could I have been dreaming about? I wonder what it really was.' And Hertford O'Donnell pushed his hair back off his forehead, and took another draught from the too familiar tumbler, which was placed conveniently on the chimney-piece.

'After expressly making up my mind to propose, too!' he mentally continued. 'Could it have been conscience – that myth, which somebody, who knew nothing about the matter, said, "Makes cowards of us all"? I don't believe in conscience; and even if there be such a thing capable of being developed by sentiment and cultivation, why should it trouble me? I have no intention of wronging Miss Janice Price Ingot, not the least. Honestly and fairly I shall marry her; honestly and fairly I shall act by her. An old wife is not exactly an ornamental article of furniture in a man's house; and I do not know that the fact of her being well gilded makes her look any handsomer. But she shall have no cause for complaint; and I will go and dine with her tomorrow, and settle the matter.'

Having arrived at which resolution, Mr O'Donnell arose, kicked down the fire – burning hollow – with the heel of his boot, knocked the ashes out of his pipe, emptied his tumbler, and bethought him it was time to go to bed. He was not in the habit of taking his rest so early as a quarter to twelve o'clock; but he felt unusually weary – tired mentally and bodily – and lonely beyond all power of expression.

'The fair Janet would be better than this,' he said, half aloud; and then, with a start and a shiver, and a blanched face, he turned sharply round, while a low, sobbing, wailing cry echoed mournfully through the room. No form of words could give an idea of the sound. The plaintiveness of the Aeolian harp – that plaintiveness which so soon affects and lowers the highest spirits – would have seemed wildly gay in comparison with the sadness of the cry which seemed floating in the air. As the summer wind comes and goes among the trees, so that mournful wail came and went – came and went. It came in a rush of sound, like a gradual crescendo managed by a skilful musician, and died away in a lingering note, so gently that the listener could scarcely tell the exact moment when it faded into utter silence.

I say faded, for it disappeared as the coastline disappears in the twilight, and there was total stillness in the apartment.

Then, for the first time, Hertford O'Donnell looked at his dog, and beholding the creature crouched into a corner beside the fire-place, called upon him to come out.

His voice sounded strange even to himself, and apparently the dog thought so too, for he made no effort to obey the summons.

'Come here, sir,' his master repeated, and then the animal came crawling reluctantly forward with his hair on end, his eyes almost starting from his head, trembling violently, as the surgeon, who caressed him, felt.

'So you heard it, Brian?' he said to the dog. 'And so your ears are sharper than Miss Ingot's, old fellow. It's a mighty queer thing to think of, being favoured with a visit from a Banshee in Gerrard Street; and as the lady has travelled so far, I only wish I knew whether there is any sort of refreshment she would like to take after her long journey.'

He spoke loudly, and with a certain mocking defiance, seeming to think the phantom he addressed would reply; but when he stopped at the end of his sentence, no sound came through the stillness. There was a dead silence in the room – a silence broken only by the falling of cinders on the hearth and the breathing of his dog.

'If my visitor would tell me,' he proceeded, for whom this lamentation is being made, whether for myself, or for some member of my illustrious family, I should feel immensely obliged. It seems too much honour for a poor surgeon to have such attention paid him. Good Heavens! What is that?' he exclaimed, as a ring, loud and peremptory, woke all the echoes in the house, and brought his housekeeper, in a state of distressing dishabille, 'out of her warm bed,' as she subsequently stated, to the head of the staircase.

Across the hall Hertford O'Donnell strode, relieved at the prospect of speaking to any living being. He took no precaution of putting up the chain, but flung the door wide. A dozen burglars would have proved welcome in comparison with that ghostly intruder he had been interviewing; therefore, as has been said, he threw the door wide, admitting a rush of wet, cold air, which made poor Mrs Coles' few remaining teeth chatter in her head.

'Who is there? What do you want?' asked the surgeon, seeing no person, and hearing no voice. 'Who is there? Why the devil can't you speak?'

When even this polite exhortation failed to elicit an answer, he passed out into the night and looked up the street and down the street, to see nothing but the driving rain and the blinking lights.

'If this goes on much longer I shall soon think I must be either mad or drunk,' he muttered, as he re-entered the house and locked and bolted the door once more.

'Lord's sake! What is the matter, sir?' asked Mrs Coles, from the upper flight, careful only to reveal the borders of her nightcap to Mr O'Donnell's admiring gaze. 'Is anybody killed? Have you to go out, sir?'

'It was only a runaway rig,' he answered, trying to reassure himself with an explanation he did not in his heart believe.

'Runaway – I'd run away them!' murmured Mrs Coles, as she retired to the conjugal couch, where Coles was, to quote her own expression, 'snoring like a pig through it all.'

Almost immediately afterwards she heard her master ascend the stairs and close his bedroom door.

'Madam will surely be too much of a gentlewoman to intrude here,' thought the surgeon, scoffing even at his own fears; but when he lay down he did not put out his light, and made Brian leap up and crouch on the coverlet beside him.

The man was fairly frightened, and would have thought it no discredit to his manhood to acknowledge as much. He was not afraid of death, he was not afraid of trouble, he was not afraid of danger; but he was afraid of the Banshee; and as he lay with his hand on the dog's head, he recalled the many stories he had been told concerning this family retainer in the days of his youth.

He had not thought about her for years and years. Never before had he heard her voice himself. When his brother died she had not thought it necessary to travel up to Dublin and give him notice of the impending catastrophe. 'If she had, I would have gone down to

Calgillan, and perhaps saved his life,' considered the surgeon. 'I wonder who this is for? If for me, that will settle my debts and my marriage. If I could be quite certain it was either of the old people, I would start tomorrow.'

Then vaguely his mind wandered on to think of every Banshee story he had ever heard in his life. About the beautiful lady with the wreath of flowers, who sat on the rocks below Red Castle, in the Country Antrim, crying till one of the sons died for love of her; about the Round Chamber at Dunluce, which was swept clean by the Banshee every night; about the bed in a certain great house in Ireland, which was slept in constantly, although no human being ever passed in or out after dark; about that General Officer who, the night before Waterloo, said to a friend, 'I have heard the Banshee, and shall not come off the field alive tomorrow; break the news gently to poor Carry'; and who, nevertheless, coming safe off the field, had subsequently news about poor Carry broken tenderly and pitifully to him; about the lad, who, aloft in the rigging, hearing through the night a sobbing and wailing coming over the waters, went down to the captain and told him he was afraid they were somehow out of their reckoning, just in time to save the ship, which, when morning broke, they found but for his warning would have been on the rocks. It was blowing great guns, and the sea was all in a fret and turmoil, and they could sometimes see in the trough of the waves, as down a valley, the cruel black reefs they had escaped.

On deck the captain stood speaking to the boy who had saved them, and asking how he knew of their danger; and when the lad told him, the captain laughed, and said her ladyship had been outwitted that time.

But the boy answered, with a grave shake of his head, that the warning was either for him or his, and that if he got safe to port there would be bad tidings waiting for him from home; whereupon the captain bade him go below, and get some brandy and lie down.

He got the brandy, and he lay down, but he never rose again; and when the storm abated – when a great calm succeeded to the previous tempest – there was a very solemn funeral at sea; and on their arrival at Liverpool the captain took a journey to Ireland to tell a widowed mother how her only son died, and to bear his few effects to the poor desolate soul.

And Hertford O'Donnell thought again about his own father riding full-chase across country, and hearing, as he galloped by a clump of plantation, something like a sobbing and wailing. The hounds were in full cry, but he still felt, as he afterwards expressed it, that there was something among those trees he could not pass; and so he jumped off his horse, and hung the reins over the branch of a Scotch fir, and beat the cover well, but not a thing could he find in it.

Then, for the first time in his life, Miles O'Donnell turned his horse's head from the hunt, and, within a mile of Calgillan, met a man running to tell him his brother's gun had burst, and injured him mortally.

And he remembered the story also, of how Mary O'Donnell, his great aunt, being married to a young Englishman, heard the Banshee as she sat one evening waiting for his return; and of how she, thinking the bridge by which he often came home unsafe for horse and man, went out in a great panic, to meet and entreat him to go round by the main road for her sake. Sir Edward was riding along in the moonlight, making straight for the bridge, when he beheld a figure dressed all in white crossing it. Then there was a crash, and the figure disappeared.

The lady was rescued and brought back to the hall; but next morning there were two dead bodies within its walls – those of Lady Eyreton and her stillborn son.

Quicker than I write them, these memories chased one another through Hertford O'Donnell's brain; and there was one more terrible memory than any, which would recur to him, concerning an Irish nobleman who, seated alone in his great town house in London, heard the Banshee, and rushed out to get rid of the phantom, which wailed in his ear, nevertheless, as he strode down Piccadilly. And then the surgeon remembered how that nobleman went with a friend to the opera, feeling sure that there no Banshee, unless shed had a box, could find admittance, until suddenly he heard her singing up among the highest part of the scenery, with a terrible mournfulness, and a pathos which made the prima donna's tenderest notes seem harsh by comparison.

As he came out, some quarrel arose between him and a famous fire-eater, against whom he stumbled; and the result was that the next afternoon there was a new Lord, for he was killed in a duel with Captain Bravo.

Memories like these are not the most enlivening possible; they are apt to make a man fanciful, and nervous, and wakeful; but as time ran on, Hertford O'Donnell fell asleep, with his candle still burning, and Brian's cold nose pressed against his hand.

He dreamt of his mother's family – the Hertfords of Artingbury, Yorkshire, far-off relatives of Lord Hertford – so far off that even Mrs O'Donnell held no clue to the genealogical maze.

He thought he was at Artingbury, fishing; that it was a misty summer morning, and the fish rising beautifully. In his dreams he hooked one after another, and the boy who was with him threw them into the basket.

At last there was one more difficult to land than the others; and the boy, in his eagerness to watch the sport, drew nearer and nearer to the bank, while the fisher, intent on his prey, failed to notice his companions' danger.

Suddenly there was a cry, a splash, and the boy disappeared from sight.

Next instance he rose again, however, and then, for the first time, Hertford O'Donnell saw his face.

It was one he knew well.

In a moment he plunged into the water, and struck out for the lad. He had him by the hair, he was turning to bring him back to land, when the stream suddenly changed into a wide, wild, shoreless sea, where the billows were chasing one another with a mad demoniac mirth.

For a while O'Donnell kept the lad and himself afloat. They were swept under the waves, and came up again, only to see larger waves rushing towards them; but through all, the surgeon never loosened his hold, until a tremendous billow, engulfing them both, tore the boy from his grasp.

With the horror of his dream upon him he awoke to hear a voice quite distinctly: 'Go to the hospital – go at once!'

The surgeon started up in bed, rubbing his eyes, and looked around. The candle was flickering faintly in its socket. Brian, with his ears pricked forward, had raised his head at his master's sudden movement.

Everything was quiet, but still those words were ringing in his ear: 'Go to the hospital – go at once!'

The tremendous peal of the bell overnight, and this sentence, seemed to be simultaneous.

That he was wanted at Guy's – wanted imperatively – came to O'Donnell like an inspiration. Neither sense nor reason had anything to do with the conviction that roused him out of bed, and made him dress as speedily as possible, and grope his way down the staircase, Brian following.

He opened the front door, and passed out into the darkness. The rain was over, and the stars were shining as he pursued his way down Newport Market, and thence, winding in and out in a southeasterly direction, through Lincoln's Inn Fields and Old Square to Chancery Lane, whence he proceeded to St Paul's.

Along the deserted streets he resolutely continued his walk. He did not know what he was going to Guy's for. Some instinct was urging him on, and he neither strove to combat nor control it. Only once did the thought of turning back cross his mind, and that was at the archway leading into Old Square. There he had paused for a moment, asking himself whether he were not gone stark, staring mad; but Guy's seemed preferable to the haunted house in Gerrard Street, and he walked resolutely on, determined to say, if any surprise were expressed at his appearance, that he had been sent for.

Sent for? – yea, truly; but by whom?

On through Cannot Street; on over London Bridge, where the lights flickered in the river, and the sullen splash of the water flowing beneath the arches, washing the stone piers, could be heard, now the human din was hushed and lulled to sleep. On, thinking of many things: of the days of his youth; of his dead brother; of his father's heavily encumbered estate; of the fortune his mother had vowed she would leave to some charity rather than to him, if he refused to marry according to her choice; of his wild life in London; of the terrible cry he had heard overnight – that unearthly wail which he could not drive from his memory even when he entered Guy's, and confronted the porter, who said: 'You have been sent for, sir; did you meet the messenger?'

Like one in a dream, Hertford O'Donnell heard him; like one in a dream, also, he asked what was the matter.

'Bad accident, sir; fire; feel off a balcony – unsafe – old building. Mother and child – a son; child with compound fracture of thigh.'

This, the joint information of porter and house-surgeon, mingled together, and made a boom in Mr O'Donnell's ears like the sound of the sea breaking on a shingly shore.

Only one sentence he understood properly – 'Immediate amputation necessary.' At this point he grew cool; he was the careful, cautious, successful surgeon, in a moment.

'The child you say?' he answered. 'Let me see him.'

The Guy's Hospital of today may be different to the Guy's Hertford O'Donnell knew so well. Railways have, I believe, swept away the old operation room; railways may have changed the position of the former accident ward, to reach which, in the days of which I am writing, the two surgeons had to pass a staircase leading to the upper stories.

On the lower step of this staircase, partially in shadow, Hertford O'Donnell beheld, as he came forward, an old woman seated.

An old woman with streaming grey hair, with attenuated arms, with head bowed forward, with scanty clothing, with bare feet; who never looked up at their approach, but sat unnoticing, shaking her head and wringing her hands in an extremity of despair.

'Who is that?' asked Mr O'Donnell, almost involuntarily.

'Who is what?' demanded his companion.

'That – that woman,' was the reply.

'What woman?'

'There – are you blind? – seated on the bottom step of the staircase. What is she doing?' persisted Mr O'Donnell.

'There is no woman near us,' his companion answered, looking at the rising surgeon very much as though he suspected him of seeing double.

'No woman!' scoffed Hertford. 'Do you expect me to disbelieve the evidence of my own eyes?' and he walked up to the figure, meaning to touch it.

But as he assayed to do so, the woman seemed to rise in the air and float away, with her arms stretched high up over her head, uttering such a wail of pain, and agony, and distress, as caused the Irishman's blood to curdle.

'My God! Did you hear that?' he said to his companion.

'What?' was the reply.

Then, although he knew the sound had fallen on deaf ears, he answered: 'The wail of the Banshee! Some of my people are doomed!'

'I trust not,' answered the house-surgeon, who had an idea, nevertheless, that Hertford O'Donnell's Banshee lived in a whisky bottle, and would at some remote day make an end to the rising and clever operator.

With nerves utterly shaken, Mr O'Donnell walked forward to the accident ward. There with his face shaded from the light, lay his patient – a young boy, with a compound fracture of the thing.

In that ward, in the face of actual danger or pain capable of relief, the surgeon had never known faltering or fear; and now he carefully examined the injury, felt the pulse, enquired as to the treatment pursued, and ordered the sufferer to be carried to the operation room.

While he was looking out his instruments he heard the boy lying on the table murmur faintly: 'Tell her not to cry so – tell her not to cry.'

'What is he talking about?' Hertford O'Donnell enquired.

'The nurse says he has been speaking about some woman crying ever since he came in – his mother, most likely,' answered one of the attendants.

'He is delirious then?' observed the surgeon.

'No, sir,' pleaded the boy, excitedly, 'no; it is that woman – that woman with the grey hair. I saw her looking from the upper window before the balcony gave way. She has never left me since, and she won't be quiet, wringing her hands and crying.'

'Can you see her now?' Hertford O'Donnell enquired, stepping to the side of the table. 'Point out where she is.'

Then the lad stretched forth a feeble finger in the direction of the door, where clearly, as he had seen her seated on the stairs, the surgeon saw a woman standing – a woman with grey hair and scanty clothing, and upstretched arms and bare feet.

'A word with you, sir,' O'Donnell said to the house-surgeon, drawing him back from the table. 'I cannot perform this operation: send for some other person. I am ill; I am incapable.'

'But,' pleaded the other, 'there is no time to get anyone else. We sent for Mr West, before we troubled you, but he was out of town, and all the rest of the surgeons live so far away. Mortification may set in at any moment and – .'

'Do you think you require to teach me my business?' was the reply. 'I know the boy's life hangs on a thread, and that is the very reason I cannot operate. I am not fit for it. I tell you I have seen tonight that which unnerves me utterly. My hand is not steady. Send for someone else without delay. Say I am ill – dead! – what you please. Heavens! There she is again, right over the boy! Do you hear her?' and Hertford O'Donnell fell fainting on the floor.

How long he lay in that deathlike swoon I cannot say; but when he returned to consciousness, the principal physician of Guy's was standing beside him in the cold grey light of the Christmas morning.

'The boy?' murmured O'Donnell, faintly.

'Now, my dear fellow, kept yourself quiet,' was the reply.

'The boy?' he repeated, irritably. 'Who operated?'

'No one,' Dr Lanson answered. 'It would have been useless cruelty. Mortification had set in and – '

Hertford O'Donnell turned his face to the wall, and his friend could not see it.

'Do not distress yourself,' went on the physician, kindly. 'Allington says he could not have survived the operation in any case. He was quite delirious from the first, raving about a woman with grey hair and – '

'I know,' Hertford O'Donnell interrupted; 'and the boy had a mother, they told me, or I dreamt it.'

'Yes, she was bruised and shaken, but not seriously injured.'

'Has she blue eyes and fair hair – fair hair all rippling and wavy? Is she white as a lily, with just a faint flush of colour in her cheek? Is she young and trusting and innocent? No; I am wandering. She must be nearly thirty now. Go, for God's sake, and tell me if you can find a woman you could imagine having once been a girl such as I describe.'

'Irish?' asked the doctor; and O'Donnell made a gesture of assent.

'It is she then,' was the reply, 'a woman with the face of an angle.'

'A woman who should have been my wife,' the surgeon answered; 'whose child was my son.'

'Lord help you!' ejaculated the doctor. Then Hertford O'Donnell raised himself from the sofa where they had laid him, and told his companion the story of his life – how there had been a bitter feud between his people and her people – how they were divided by old animosities and by difference of religion – how they had met by stealth, and exchanged rings and vows, all for naught – how is family had insulted hers, so that her father, wishful for her to marry a kinsman of his own, bore her off to a faraway land, and made her write him a letter of eternal farewell – how his own parents had kept all knowledge of the quarrel from him till she was utterly beyond his reach – how they had vowed to discard him unless he agreed to marry according to their wishes – how he left home, and came to London, and sought his fortune. All this Hertford O'Donnell repeated; and when he had finished, the bells were ringing for morning service – ringing loudly, ringing joyfully, 'Peace on earth, goodwill towards men.'

But there was little peace that morning for Hertford O'Donnell. He had to look on the face of his dead son, wherein he beheld, as though reflected, the face of the boy in this dream.

Afterwards, stealthily he followed his friend, and beheld, with her eyes closed, her cheeks pale and pinched, her hair thinner but still falling like a veil over her, the love of his youth, the only woman he had ever loved devotedly and unselfishly.

There is little space left here to tell of how the two met at last – of how the stone of the years seemed suddenly rolled away from the tomb of their past, and their youth arose and returned to them, even amid their tears.

She had been true to him, through persecution, through contumely, through kindness, which was more trying; through shame, and grief, and poverty, she had been loyal to the lover of her youth; and before the New Year dawned there came a letter from Calgillan, saying that the Banshee's wail had been heard there, and praying Hertford, if he were still alive, to let bygones be bygones, in consideration of the long years of estrangement – the anguish and remorse of his afflicted parents.

More than that. Hertford O'Donnell, if a reckless man, was honourable; and so, on the Christmas Day when he was to have proposed for Miss Ingot, he went to that lady, and told her how he had wooed and won, in the years of his youth, one who after many days was miraculously restored to him; and from the hour in which he took her into his confidence, he never thought her either vulgar or foolish, but rather he paid homage to the woman who, when she had heard the whole tale repeated, said, simply 'Ask her to come to me till you can claim her – and God bless you both!'

The Last of Squire Ennismore

CHARLOTTE RIDDELL

'Did I see it myself? No, sir; I did not see it; and my father before me did not see it; nor his father before him, and he was Phil Regan, just the same as myself. But it is true, for all that; just as true as that you are looking at the very place where the whole thing happened. My great-grandfather (and he did not die till he was ninety-eight) used to tell, many and many's the time, how he met the stranger, night after night, walking lonesome-like about the sands where most of the wreckage came ashore.'

'And the old house, then, stood behind that belt of Scotch firs?'

'Yes; and a fine house it was, too. Hearing so much talk about it when a boy, my father said, made him often feel as if he knew every room in the building, though it had all fallen to ruin before he was born. None of the family ever lived in it after the squire went away. Nobody else could be got to stop in the place. There used to be awful noises, as if something was being pitched from the top of the great staircase down in to the hall; and then there would be a sound as if a hundred people were clinking glasses and talking all together at once. And then it seemed as if barrels were rolling in the cellars; and there would be screeches, and howls, and laughing, fit to make your blood run cold. They say there is gold hid away in the cellars; but not one has ever ventured to find it. The very children won't come here to play; and when the men are ploughing the field behind, nothing will make them stay in it, once the day begins to change. When the night is coming on, and the tide creeps in on the sand, more than one thinks he has seen mighty queer things on the shore.'

'But what is it really they think they see? When I asked my landlord to tell me the story from beginning to end, he said he could not remember it; and, at any rate, the whole rigmarole was nonsense, put together to please strangers.'

'And what is he but a stranger himself? And how should he know the doings of real quality like the Ennismores? For they were gentry, every one of them – good old stock; and as for wickedness, you might have searched Ireland through and not found their match. It is a sure thing, though, that if Riley can't tell you the story, I can; for, as I said, my own people were in it, of a manner of speaking. So, if your honour will rest yourself off your feet, on that bit of a bank, I'll set down my creel and give you the whole pedigree of how Squire Ennismore went away from Ardwinsagh.'

It was a lovely day, in the early part of June; and, as the Englishman cast himself on a low ridge of sand, he looked over Ardwinsagh Bay with a feeling of ineffable content. To his left lay the Purple Headland; to his right, a long range of breakers, that went straight out into the Atlantic till they were lost from sight; in front lay the Bay of Ardwinsagh, with its bluish-green water sparkling in the summer sunlight, and here and there breaking over some sunken rock, against which the waves spent themselves in foam.

'You see how the current's set, Sir? That is what makes it dangerous for them as doesn't know the coast, to bathe here at any time, or walk when the tide is flowing. Look how the sea is creeping in now, like a racehorse at the finish. It leaves that tongue of sand bars to the last, and then, before you could look round, it has you up to the middle. That is why I made bold to speak to you; for it is not alone on the account of Squire Ennismore the bay has a bad name. But it is about him and the old house you want to hear. The last mortal being that tried to live in it, my great-grandfather said, was a creature, by name Molly Leary; and she had neither kith nor kin, and begged for her bite and sup, sheltering herself at night in a turf cabin she had built at the back of a ditch. You may be sure she thought herself a made woman when the agent said, "Yes: she might try if she could stop in the house; there was peat and bog-wood," he told her, "and half a crown a week for the winter, and a golden guinea once Easter came," when the house was to be put in order for the family; and his wife gave Molly some warm clothes and a blanket or two; and she was well set up.

'You may be sure she didn't choose the worst room to sleep in; and for a while all went quiet, till one night she was wakened by feeling the bedstead lifted by the four corners and shaken like a carpet. It was a heavy four-post bedstead, with a solid top: and her life seemed to go out of her with the fear. If it had been a ship in a storm off the Headland, it couldn't have pitched worse and then, all

of a sudden, it was dropped with such a bang as nearly drove the
heart into her mouth.

'But that, she said, was nothing to the screaming and laughing,
and hustling and rushing that filled the house. If a hundred people
had been running hard along the passages and tumbling downstairs,
they could not have made greater noise.

'Molly never was able to tell how she got clear of the place; but a
man coming late home from Ballycloyne Fair found the creature
crouched under the old thorn there, with very little on her – saving
your honour's presence. She had a bad fever, and talked about
strange things, and never was the same woman after.'

'But what was the beginning of all this? When did the house first
get the name of being haunted?'

'After the old Squire went away: that was what I purposed telling
you. He did not come here to live regularly till he had got well on
in years. He was near seventy at the time I am talking about; but he
held himself as upright as ever, and rode as hard as the youngest;
and could have drunk a whole roomful under the table, and walked
up to bed as unconcerned as you please at the dead of the night.

'He was a terrible man. You couldn't lay your tongue to a wickedness he had not been in the forefront of – drinking, duelling,
gambling – all manner of sins had been meat and drink to him since
he was a boy almost. But at last he did something in London so bad,
so beyond the beyonds, that he thought he had best come home and
live among people who did not know so much about his goings on
as the English. It was said that he wanted to try and stay in this
world for ever; and that he had got some secret drops that kept him
well and hearty. There was something wonderful queer about him,
anyhow.

'He could hold foot with the youngest; and he was strong, and had
a fine fresh colour in his face; and his eyes were like a hawk's; and
there was not a break in his voice – and him near upon three-score
and ten!

'At last and at long last it came to be the March before he was
seventy – the worst March ever known in all these parts – such
blowing, sleeting, snowing, had not been experienced in the
memory of man; when one blusterous night some foreign vessel
went to bits on the Purple Headland. They say it was an awful
sound to hear the death-cry that went up high above the noise of
the wind; and it was as bad a sight to see the shore there strewed

with corpses of all sorts and sizes, from the little cabin-boy to the grizzled seaman.

'They never knew who they were or where they came from, but some of the men had crosses, and beads, and suchlike, so the priest said they belonged to him, and they were all buried deeply and decently in the chapel graveyard.

'There was not much wreckage of value drifted on shore. Most of what is lost about the Head stays there; but one thing did come into the bay – a puncheon of brandy.

'The Squire claimed it; it was his right to have all that came on his land, and he owned this seashore from the Head to the breakers – every foot – so, in course, he had the brandy; and there was sore ill will because he gave his men nothing, not even a glass of whiskey.

'Well, to make a long story short, that was the most wonderful liquor anybody ever tasted. The gentry came from far and near to take share, and it was cards and dice, and drinking and storytelling night after night – week in, week out. Even on Sundays, God forgive them! The officers would drive over from Ballycloyne, and sit emptying tumbler after tumbler till Monday morning came, for it made beautiful punch.

'But all at once people quit coming – a word went round that the liquor was not all it ought to be. Nobody could say what ailed it, but it got about that in some way men found it did not suit them.

'For one thing, they were losing money very fast.

'They could not make head against the Squire's luck, and a hint was dropped the puncheon ought to have been towed out to sea, and sunk in fifty fathoms of water.

'It was getting to the end of April, and fine, warm weather for the time of year, when first one and then another, and then another still, began to take notice of a stranger who walked the shore alone at night. He was a dark man, the same colour as the drowned crew lying in the chapel graveyard, and had rings in his ears, and wore a strange kind of hat, and cut wonderful antics as he walked, and had an ambling sort of gait, curious to look at. Many tried to talk to him, but he only shook his head; so, as nobody could make out where he came from or what he wanted, they made sure he was the spirit of some poor wretch who was tossing about the Head, longing for a snug corner in holy ground.

'The priest went and tried to get some sense out of him.

' "Is it Christian burial you're wanting?" asked his reverence; but the creature only shook his head.

' "Is it word sent to the wives and daughters you've left orphans and widows, you'd like?" But no; it wasn't that.

' "Is it for sin committed you're doomed to walk this way? Would masses comfort ye? There's a heathen," said his reverence; "Did you ever hear tell of a Christian that shook his head when masses were mentioned?"

' "Perhaps he doesn't understand English, Father," says one of the officers who was there; "Try him with Latin."

'No sooner said than done. The priest started off with such a string of aves and paters that the stranger fairly took to his heels and ran.

' "He is an evil spirit," explained the priest, when he stopped, tired out, "and I have exorcised him."

'But next night my gentleman was back again, as unconcerned as ever.

' "And he'll just have to stay," said his reverence, "For I've got lumbago in the small of my back, and pains in all my joints – never to speak of a hoarseness with standing there shouting; and I don't believe he understood a sentence I said."

'Well, this went on for a while, and people got that frightened of the man, or appearance of a man, they would not go near the sand; till in the end, Squire Ennismore, who had always scoffed at the talk, took it into his head he would go down one night, and see into the rights of the matter. He, maybe, was feeling lonesome, because, as I told your honour before, people had left off coming to the house, and there was nobody for him to drink with.

'Out he goes, then, bold as brass; and there were a few followed him. The man came forward at sight of the Squire and took off his hat with a foreign flourish. Not to be behind in civility, the Squire lifted his.

' "I have come, sir," he said, speaking very loud, to try to make him understand, "to know if you are looking for anything, and whether I can assist you to find it.'

'The man looked at the Squire as if he had taken the greatest liking to him, and took off his hat again.

' "Is it the vessel that was wrecked you are distressed about?"

'There came no answer, only a mournful shake of the head.

' "Well, *I* haven't your ship, you know; it went all to bits months ago; and, as for the sailors, they are snug and sound enough in consecrated ground."

'The man stood and looked at the Squire with a queer sort of smile on his face.

' "What *do* you want?" asked Mr Ennismore in a bit of a passion. "If anything belonging to you went down with the vessel, it's about the Head you ought to be looking for it, not here – unless, indeed, it's after the brandy you're fretting!"

'Now, the Squire had tried him in English and French, and was now speaking a language you'd have thought nobody could understand; but, faith, it seemed natural as kissing to the stranger.

' "Oh! That's where you are from, is it?" said the Squire. "Why couldn't you have told me so at once? I can't give you the brandy, because it mostly is drunk; but come along, and you shall have as stiff a glass of punch as ever crossed your lips." And without more to-do off they went, as sociable as you please, jabbering together in some outlandish tongue that made moderate folks' jaws ache to hear it.

'That was the first night they conversed together, but it wasn't the last. The stranger must have been the height of good company, for the Squire never tired of him. Every evening, regularly, he came up to the house, always dressed the same, always smiling and polite, and then the Squire called for brandy and hot water, and they drank and played cards till cockcrow, talking and laughing into the small hours.

'This went on for weeks and weeks, nobody knowing where the man came from, or where he went; only two things the old housekeeper did know – that the puncheon was nearly empty, and that the Squire's flesh was wasting off him; and she felt so uneasy she went to the priest, but he could give her no manner of comfort.

'She got so concerned at last that she felt bound to listen at the dining-room door; but they always talked in that foreign gibberish, and whether it was blessing or cursing they were at she couldn't tell.

'Well, the upshot of it came one night in July – on the eve of the Squire's birthday – there wasn't a drop of spirit left in the puncheon – no, not as much as would drown a fly. They had drunk the whole lot clean up – and the old woman stood trembling, expecting every minute to hear the bell ring for more brandy, for where was she to get more if they wanted any?

'All at once the Squire and the stranger came out into the hall. It was a full moon, and light as day.

' "I'll go home with you tonight by way of a change," says the Squire.

' "Will you so?" asked the other.

' "That I will," answered the Squire.

' "It is your own choice, you know."

' "Yes; it is my own choice; let us go."

'So they went. And the housekeeper ran up to the window on the great staircase and watched the way they took. Her niece lived there as housemaid, and she came and watched, too; and, after a while, the butler as well. They all turned their faces this way, and looked after their master walking beside the strange man along these very sands. Well, they saw them walk on, and on, and on, and on, till the water took them to their knees, and then to their waists, and then to their armpits, and then to their throats and their heads; but long before that the women and the butler were running out on the shore as fast as they could, shouting for help.'

'Well?' said the Englishman.

'Living or dead, Squire Ennismore never came back again. Next morning, when the tides ebbed again, one walking over the sand saw the print of a cloven foot – that he tracked to the water's edge. Then everybody knew where the Squire had gone, and with whom.'

'And no more search was made?'

'Where would have been the use searching?'

'Not much, I suppose. It's a strange story, anyhow.'

'But true, your honour – every word of it.'

'Oh! I have no doubt of that,' was the satisfactory reply.

The Judge's House

BRAM STOKER

When the time for his examination drew near Malcolm Malcolmson made up his mind to go somewhere to read by himself. He feared the attractions of the seaside, and also he feared completely rural isolation, for of old he knew its charms, and so he determined to find some unpretentious little town where there would be nothing to distract him. He refrained from asking suggestions from any of his friends, for he argued that each would recommend some place of which he had knowledge, and where he had already acquaintances. As Malcolmson wished to avoid friends he had no wish to encumber himself with the attention of friends' friends, and so he determined to look out for a place for himself. He packed a portmanteau with some clothes and all the books he required, and then took ticket for the first name on the local timetable which he did not know.

When at the end of three hours' journey he alighted at Benchurch, he felt satisfied that he had so far obliterated his tracks as to be sure of having a peaceful opportunity of pursuing his studies. He went straight to the one inn which the sleepy little place contained, and put up for the night. Benchurch was a market town, and once in three weeks was crowded to excess, but for the remainder of the twenty-one days it was as attractive as a desert. Malcolmson looked around the day after his arrival to try to find quarters more isolated than even so quiet an inn as the Good Traveller afforded. There was only one place which took his fancy, and it certainly satisfied his wildest ideas regarding quiet; in fact, quiet was not the proper word to apply to it – desolation was the only term conveying any suitable idea of its isolation. It was an old rambling, heavy-built house of the Jacobean style, with heavy gables and windows, unusually small, and set higher than was customary in such houses, and was surrounded with a high brick wall massively built. Indeed, on examination, it looked more like a fortified house than an ordinary dwelling. But all these things pleased Malcolmson. 'Here,' he thought, 'is the very spot I have been looking for, and if I can only get opportunity of using it I shall be happy.' His joy was increased when he realised beyond doubt that it was not at present inhabited.

From the post-office he got the name of the agent, who was rarely surprised at the application to rent a part of the old house. Mr Carnford, the local lawyer and agent, was a genial old gentleman, and frankly confessed his delight at anyone being willing to live in the house.

'To tell you the truth,' said he, 'I should be only too happy, on behalf of the owners, to let anyone have the house rent free for a term of years if only to accustom the people here to see it inhabited. It has been so long empty that some kind of absurd prejudice has grown up about it, and this can be best put down by its occupation – if only,' he added with a sly glance at Malcolmson, 'by a scholar like yourself, who wants its quiet for a time.'

Malcolmson thought it needless to ask the agent about the 'absurd prejudice'; he knew he would get more information, if he should require it, on that subject from other quarters. He paid his three months' rent, got a receipt, and the name of an old woman who would probably undertake to 'do' for him, and came away with the keys in his pocket. He then went to the landlady of the inn, who was a cheerful and most kindly person, and asked her advice as to such stores and provisions as he would be likely to require. She threw up her hands in amazement when he told her where he was going to settle himself.

'Not in the Judge's House!' she said and grew pale as she spoke. He explained the locality of the house, saying that he did not know its name. When he had finished, she answered: 'Aye, sure enough – sure enough the very place. It is the Judge's House sure enough.' He asked her to tell him about the place, why so called, and what there was against it. She told him that it was so called locally because it had been many years before – how long she could not say, as she was herself from another part of the country, but she thought it must have been a hundred years or more – the abode of a judge who was held in great terror on account of his harsh sentences and his hostility to prisoners at Assizes. As to what there was against the house itself she could not tell. She had often asked, but no one could inform her; but there was a general feeling that there was *something*, and for her own part she would not take all the money in Drinkwater's Bank and stay in the house an hour by herself. Then she apologised to Malcolmson for her disturbing talk.

'It is too bad of me, sir, and you – and a young gentleman, too – if you will pardon me saying it, going to live there all alone. If you were my boy – and you'll excuse me for saying it – you wouldn't sleep there a night, not if I had to go there myself and pull the big alarm bell that's on the roof!' The good creature was so manifestly in earnest, and was so kindly in her intentions, that Malcolmson, although amused, was touched. He told her kindly how much he appreciated her interest in him, and added: 'But, my dear Mrs Witham, indeed you need not be concerned about me! A man who is reading for the Mathematical Tripos has too much to think of to be disturbed by any of these mysterious "somethings", and his work is of too exact and prosaic a kind to allow of his having any corner in his mind for mysteries of any kind. Harmonical Progression, Permutations and Combinations, and Elliptic Functions have sufficient mysteries for me!' Mrs Witham kindly undertook to see after his commissions, and he went himself to look for the old woman who had been recommended to him. When he returned to the Judge's House with her, after an interval of a couple of hours, he found Mrs Witham herself waiting with several men and boys carrying parcels, and an upholsterer's man with a bed in a cart, for she said, though tables and chairs might be all very well, a bed that hadn't been aired for maybe fifty years was not proper for young ones to lie on. She was evidently curious to see the inside of the house; and though manifestly so afraid of the 'somethings' that at the slightest sound she clutched on to Malcolmson, whom she never left for a moment, went over the whole place.

After his examination of the house, Malcolmson decided to take up his abode in the great dining-room, which was big enough to serve for all his requirements; and Mrs Witham, with the aid of the charwoman, Mrs Dempster, proceeded to arrange matters. When the hampers were brought in and unpacked, Malcolmson saw that with much kind forethought she had sent from her own kitchen sufficient provisions to last for a few days. Before going she expressed all sorts of kind wishes; and at the door turned and said: 'And perhaps, sir, as the room is big and drafty it might be well to have one of those big screens put round your bed at night – though, truth to tell, I would die myself if I were to be so shut in with all kinds of – of "things" that put their heads round the sides, or over the top, and look on me!' The image which she had called up was too much for her nerves, and she fled incontinently.

Mrs Dempster sniffed in a superior manner as the landlady disappeared, and remarked that for her own part she wasn't afraid of all the bogies in the kingdom.

'I'll tell you what it is, sir,' she said, 'bogies is all kinds and sorts of things – except bogies! Rats and mice, and beetles; and creaky doors, and loose slates, and broken panes, and stiff drawer handles, that stay out when you pull them and then fall down in the middle of the night. Look at the wainscot of the room! It is old – hundreds of years old! Do you think there's no rats and beetles there! And do you imagine, sir, that you won't see none of them? Rats is bogies, I tell you, and bogies is rats; and don't you get to think anything else!'

'Mrs Dempster,' said Malcolmson gravely, making her a polite bow, 'you know more than a Senior Wrangler! And let me say, that, as a mark of esteem for your indubitable soundness of head and heart, I shall, when I go, give you possession of this house, and let you stay here by yourself for the last two months of my tenancy, for four weeks will serve my purpose.'

'Thank you kindly, sir!' she answered, 'but I couldn't sleep away from home a night. I am in Greenhow's Charity, and if I slept a night away from my rooms I should lose all I have got to live on. The rules is very strict; and there's too many watching for a vacancy for me to run any risks in the matter. Only for that, sir, I'd gladly come here and attend on you altogether during your stay.'

'My good woman,' said Malcolmson hastily, 'I have come here on a purpose to obtain solitude; and believe me that I am grateful to the late Greenhow for having organised his admirable charity – whatever it is – that I am perforce denied the opportunity of suffering from such a form of temptation! St Anthony himself could not be more rigid on the point!'

The old woman laughed harshly. 'Ah, you young gentlemen,' she said, 'you don't fear for naught; and belike you'll get all the solitude you want here.' She set to work with her cleaning; and by nightfall, when Malcolmson returned from his walk – he always had one of his books to study as he walked – he found the room swept and tidied, a fire burning on the old hearth, the lamp lit, and the table spread for supper with Mrs Witham's excellent fare. 'This is comfort, indeed,' he said, as he rubbed his hands.

When he had finished his supper, and lifted the tray to the other end of the great oak dining-table, he got out his books again, put fresh wood on the fire, trimmed his lamp, and set himself down to a spell of real hard work. He went on without a pause till about eleven o'clock, when he knocked off for a bit to fix his fire and lamp and to make himself a cup of tea. He had always been a tea-drinker, and during his college life had sat late at work and had taken tea late. The rest was a great luxury to him, and he enjoyed it with a sense of delicious, voluptuous ease. The renewed fire leaped and sparkled, and threw quaint shadows through the great old room; and as he sipped his hot tea he revelled in the sense of isolation from his kind. Then it was that he began to notice for the first time what a noise the rats were making.

'Surely,' he thought, 'they cannot have been at it all the time I was reading. Had they been, I must have noticed it!' Presently, when the noise increased, he satisfied himself that it was really new. It was evident that at first the rats had been frightened at the presence of a stranger, and the light of fire and lamp; but that as the time went on they had grown bolder and were now disporting themselves as was their wont.

How busy they were! and hark to the strange noises! Up and down behind the old wainscot, over the ceiling and under the floor they raced, and gnawed, and scratched! Malcolmson smiled to himself as he recalled to mind the saying of Mrs Dempster, 'Bogies is rats, and rats is bogies!' The tea began to have its effect of intellectual and nervous stimulus, he saw with joy another long spell of work to be done before the night was past, and in the sense of security which it gave him, he allowed himself the luxury of a good look round the room. He took his lamp in one hand, and went all round, wondering that so quaint and beautiful an old house had been so long neglected. The carving of the oak on the panels of the wainscot was fine, and on and round the doors and windows it was beautiful and of rare merit. There were some old pictures on the walls, but they were coated so thick with dust and dirt that he could not distinguish any detail of them, though he held his lamp as high as he could over his head. Here and there as he went round he saw some crack or hole blocked for a moment by the face of a rat with its bright eyes glittering in the light, but in an instant it was gone, and a squeak and a scamper followed. The thing that most struck him, however, was the rope of the great alarm bell on the roof, which hung down in a corner of the room on the right-hand side of the fireplace. He pulled up close to the hearth a great high-backed carved oak chair, and sat down to his last cup of tea. When this was done he made up the fire, and went back to his work, sitting at the corner of the table, having the fire to his left. For a little while the rats disturbed him somewhat with their perpetual scampering, but he got accustomed to the noise as one does to the ticking of the clock or to the roar of moving water; and he became so immersed in his work that everything in the world, except the problem which he was trying to solve, passed away from him.

He suddenly looked up, his problem was still unsolved, and there was in the air that sense of the hour before the dawn, which is so dread to doubtful life. The noise of the rats had ceased. Indeed it seemed to him that it must have ceased but lately and that it was the sudden cessation which had disturbed him. The fire had fallen low, but still it threw out a deep red glow. As he looked he started in spite of his *sang froid*.

There on the great high-backed carved oak chair by the right side of the fireplace sat an enormous rat, steadily glaring at him with baleful eyes. He made a motion to it as though to hunt it away, but it did not stir. Then he made the motion of throwing something. Still it did not stir, but showed its great white teeth angrily, and its cruel eyes shone in the lamplight with an added vindictiveness.

Malcolmson felt amazed, and seizing the poker from the hearth ran at it to kill it. Before, however, he could strike it, the rat, with a squeak that sounded like the concentration of hate, jumped upon the floor, and, running up the rope of the alarm bell, disappeared in the darkness beyond the range of the green-shaded lamp. Instantly, strange to say, the noisy scampering of the rats in the wainscot began again.

By this time Malcolmson's mind was quite off the problem; and as a shrill cockcrow outside told him of the approach of morning, he went to bed and to sleep.

He slept so sound that he was not even waked by Mrs Dempster coming in to make up his room. It was only when she had tided up the place and got his breakfast ready and tapped on the screen which closed in his bed that he woke. He was a little tired still after his night's hard work, but a strong cup of tea soon freshened him up and, taking his book, he went out for his morning walk, bringing with him a few sandwiches lest he should not care to return till dinner time. He found a quiet walk between high elms some way outside the town, and here he spent the greater part of the day studying his Laplace. On his return he looked in to see Mrs Witham and to thank her for her kindness. When she saw him coming through the diamond-paned bay window of her sanctum, she came out to meet him and asked him in. She looked at him searchingly and shook her head as she said: 'You must not overdo it, sir. You are paler this morning than you should be. Too late hours and too hard work on the brain isn't good for any man! But tell me, sir, how did you pass the night? Well, I hope? But, my heart! sir, I was glad when Mrs Dempster told me this morning that you were all right and sleeping sound when she went in.'

'Oh, I was all right,' he answered smiling; 'the "somethings" didn't worry me, as yet. Only the rats; and they had a circus, I tell you, all over the place. There was one wicked looking old devil that sat up on my own chair by the fire and wouldn't go till I took the poker to him, and then he ran up the rope of the alarm bell and got to somewhere up the wall or the ceiling – I couldn't see where, it was so dark.'

'Mercy on us,' said Mrs Witham, 'an old devil, and sitting on a chair by the fireside! Take care, sir! take care! There's many a true word spoken in jest.'

'How do you mean? 'Pon my word I don't understand.'

'An old devil! The old devil, perhaps. There! sir, you needn't laugh,' for Malcolmson had broken into a hearty peal. 'You young folks think it easy to laugh at things that makes older ones shudder. Never mind, sir! never mind. Please God, you'll laugh all the time. It's what I wish you myself!' and the good lady beamed all over in sympathy with his enjoyment, her fears gone for a moment.

'Oh, forgive me!' said Malcolmson presently. 'Don't think me rude, but the idea was too much for me – that the old devil himself was on the chair last night!' And at the thought he laughed again. Then he went home to dinner.

This evening the scampering of the rats began earlier; indeed it had been going on before his arrival, and only ceased while his presence by its freshness disturbed them. After dinner he sat by the fire for a while and had a smoke; and then, having cleared his table, began to work as before. Tonight the rats disturbed him more than they had done on the previous night. How they scampered up and down and under and over! How they squeaked, and scratched, and gnawed! How they, getting bolder by degrees, came to the mouths of their holes and to the chinks and cracks and crannies in the wainscoting till their eyes shone like tiny lamps as the firelight rose and fell. But to him, now doubtless accustomed to them, their eyes were not wicked; only their playfulness touched him. Sometimes the boldest of them made sallies out on the floor or along the mouldings of the wainscot. Now and again as they disturbed him Malcolmson made a sound to frighten them, smiting the table with his hand or giving a fierce 'Hsh, hsh,' so that they fled straightway to their holes.

And so the early part of the night wore on; and despite the noise Malcolmson got more and more immersed in his work.

All at once he stopped, as on the previous night, being overcome by a sudden sense of silence. There was not the faintest sound of gnaw, or scratch, or squeak. The silence was as of the grave. He remembered the odd occurrence of the previous night, and instinctively he looked at the chair standing close by the fireside. And then a very odd sensation thrilled through him.

There, on the great old high-backed carved oak chair beside the fireplace sat the same enormous rat, steadily glaring at him with baleful eyes.

Instinctively he took the nearest thing to his hand, a book of logarithms, and flung it at it. The book was badly aimed and the rat did not stir, so again the poker performance of the previous night was repeated; and again the rat, being closely pursued, fled up the rope of the alarm bell. Strangely, too, the departure of this rat was instantly followed by the renewal of the noise made by the general rat community. On this occasion, as on the previous one, Malcolmson could not see at what part of the room the rat disappeared, for the green shade of his lamp left the upper part of the room in darkness, and the fire had burned low.

On looking at his watch he found it was close on midnight and, not sorry for the *divertissement*, he made up his fire and made himself his nightly pot of tea. He had got through a good spell of work, and thought himself entitled to a cigarette; and so he sat on the great carved oak chair before the fire and enjoyed it. While smoking he began to think that he would like to know where the rat disappeared to, for he had certain ideas for the morrow not entirely disconnected with a rat trap. Accordingly he lit another lamp and placed it so that it would shine well into the right-hand corner of the wall by the fireplace. Then he got all the books he had with him, and placed them handy to throw at the vermin. Finally he lifted the rope of the alarm bell and placed the end of it on the table, fixing the extreme end under the lamp. As he handled it he could not help noticing how pliable it was, especially for so strong a rope, and one not in use. 'You could hang a man with it,' he thought to himself. When his preparations were made he looked around, and said complacently: 'There now, my friend, I think we shall learn something of you this time!' He began his work again, and though as before somewhat disturbed at first by the noise of the rats, soon lost himself in his proposition and problems.

Again he was called to his immediate surroundings suddenly. This time it might not have been the sudden silence only which took his attention; there was a slight movement of the rope, and the lamp moved. Without stirring, he looked to see if his pile of books was within range, and then cast his eye along the rope. As he looked he saw the great rat drop from the rope on the oak armchair and sit there glaring at him. He raised a book in his right hand, and taking careful aim, flung it at the rat. The latter, with a quick movement, sprang aside and dodged the missile. He then took another book, and a third, and flung them one after another at the rat, but each time unsuccessfully. At last, as he stood with a book poised in his hand to throw, the rat squeaked and seemed afraid. This made Malcolmson more than ever eager to strike, and the book flew and struck the rat a resounding blow. It gave a terrified squeak, and turning on his pursuer a look of terrible malevolence, ran up the chair-back and made a great jump to the rope of the alarm bell and ran up it like lightning. The lamp rocked under the sudden strain, but it was a heavy one and did not topple over. Malcolmson kept his eyes on the rat, and saw it by the light of the second lamp leap to a moulding of the wainscot and disappear through a hole in one of the great pictures which hung on the wall, obscured and invisible through its coating of dirt and dust.

'I shall look up my friend's habitation in the morning,' said the student, as he went over to collect his books. 'The third picture from the fireplace; I shall not forget.' He picked up the books one by one, commenting on them as he lifted them. *Conic Sections* he does not mind, nor *Cycloidal Oscillations*, nor the *Principia*, nor *Quaternions*, nor *Thermodynamics*. Now for a book that fetched him!' Malcolmson took it up and looked at it. As he did so he started, and a sudden pallor overspread his face. He looked round uneasily and shivered slightly, as he murmured to himself: 'The Bible my mother gave me! What an odd coincidence.' He sat down to work again, and the rats in the wainscot renewed their gambols. They did not disturb him, however; somehow their presence gave him a sense of companionship. But he could not attend to his work, and after striving to master the subject on which he was engaged, gave it up in despair, and went to bed as the first streak of dawn stole in through the eastern window.

He slept heavily but uneasily, and dreamed much; and when Mrs Dempster woke him late in the morning he seemed ill at ease, and for a few minutes did not seem to realise exactly where he was. His first request rather surprised the servant.

'Mrs Dempster, when I am out today I wish you would get the steps and dust or wash those pictures – specially that one the third from the fireplace – I want to see what they are.'

Late in the afternoon Malcolmson worked at his books in the shaded walk, and the cheerfulness of the previous day came back to him as the day wore on, and he found that his reading was progressing well. He had worked out to a satisfactory conclusion all the problems which had as yet baffled him, and it was in a state of jubilation that he paid a visit to Mrs Witham at the Good Traveller. He found a stranger in the cozy sitting-room with the landlady, who was introduced to him as Dr Thornhill. She was not quite at ease, and this, combined with the doctor's plunging at once into a series of questions, made Malcolmson come to the conclusion that his presence was not an accident, so without preliminary he said: 'Dr Thornhill, I shall with pleasure answer you any question you may choose to ask me if you will answer me one question first.'

The doctor seemed surprised, but he smiled and answered at once, 'Done! What is it?'

'Did Mrs Witham ask you to come here and see me and advise me?'

Dr Thornhill for a moment was taken aback, and Mrs Witham got fiery red and turned away; but the doctor was a frank and ready man, and he answered at once and openly: 'She did, but she didn't intend you to know it. I suppose it was my clumsy haste that made you suspect. She told me that she did not like the idea of your being in that house all by yourself, and that she thought you took too much strong tea. In fact, she wants me to advise you if possible to give up the tea and the very late hours. I was a keen student in my

time, so I suppose I may take the liberty of a college man, and
without offence, advise you not quite as a stranger.'

Malcolmson with a bright smile held out his hand. 'Shake! as they
say in America,' he said. 'I must thank you for your kindness and
Mrs Witham too, and your kindness deserves a return on my part. I
promise to take no more strong tea – no tea at all till you let me –
and I shall go to bed tonight at one o'clock at latest. Will that do?'

'Capital,' said the doctor. 'Now tell us all that you noticed in the
old house,' and so Malcolmson then and there told in minute detail
all that had happened in the last two nights. He was interrupted
every now and then by some exclamation from Mrs Witham, till
finally when he told of the episode of the Bible the landlady's pent-
up emotions found vent in a shriek; and it was not till a stiff glass of
brandy and water had been administered that she grew composed
again. Dr Thornhill listened with a face of growing gravity, and
when the narrative was complete and Mrs Witham had been restored,
he asked: 'The rat always went up the rope of the alarm bell?'

'I suppose you know,' said the doctor after a pause, 'what the rope
is?'

'It is,' said the doctor slowly, 'the very rope which the hangman
used for all the victims of the judge's judicial rancour!' Here he was
interrupted by another scream from Mrs Witham, and steps had to
be taken for her recovery. Malcolmson having looked at his watch,
and found that it was close to his dinner hour, had gone home
before her complete recovery.

When Mrs Witham was herself again she almost assailed the
doctor with angry questions as to what he meant by putting such
horrible ideas into the poor young man's mind. 'He has quite enough
there already to upset him,' she added. Dr Thornhill replied: 'My
dear madam, I had a distinct purpose in it! I wanted to draw his
attention to the bell rope, and to fix it there. It may be that he is in a
highly overwrought state, and has been studying too much, although
I am bound to say that he seems as sound and healthy a young man,
mentally and bodily, as ever I saw – but then the rats – and that
suggestion of the devil.' The doctor shook his head and went on. 'I
would have offered to go and stay the first night with him but that I
felt sure it would have been a cause of offence. He may get in the
night some strange fright or hallucination and if he does I want him
to pull that rope. All alone as he is, it will give us warning, and we
may reach him in time to be of service. I shall be sitting up pretty

late tonight and shall keep my ears open. Do not be alarmed if Benchurch gets a surprise before morning.'

'Oh, doctor, what do you mean? What do you mean?'

'I mean this; that possibly – nay, more probably – we shall hear the great alarm bell from the Judge's House tonight,' and the doctor made about as effective an exit as could be thought of.

When Malcolmson arrived home he found that it was a little after his usual time, and Mrs Dempster had gone away – the rules of Greenhow's Charity were not to be neglected. He was glad to see that the place was bright and tidy with a cheerful fire and a well-trimmed lamp. The evening was colder than might have been expected in April, and a heavy wind was blowing with such rapidly-increasing strength that there was every promise of a storm during the night. For a few minutes after his entrance the noise of the rats ceased; but so soon as they became accustomed to his presence they began again. He was glad to hear them, for he felt once more the feeling of companionship in their noise, and his mind ran back to the strange fact that they only ceased to manifest themselves when that other – the great rat with the baleful eyes – came upon the scene. The reading-lamp only was lit and its green shade kept the ceiling and the upper part of the room in darkness, so that the cheerful light from the hearth spreading over the floor and shining on the white cloth laid over the end of the table was warm and cheery. Malcolmson sat down to his dinner with a good appetite and a buoyant spirit. After his dinner and a cigarette he sat steadily down to work, determined not to let anything disturb him, for he remembered his promise to the doctor, and made up his mind to make the best of the time at his disposal.

For an hour or so he worked all right, and then his thoughts began to wander from his books. The actual circumstances around him, the calls on his physical attention, and his nervous susceptibility were not to be denied. By this time the wind had become a gale, and the gale a storm. The old house, solid though it was, seemed to shake to its foundations, and the storm roared and raged through its many chimneys and its queer old gables, producing strange, unearthly sounds in the empty rooms and corridors. Even the great alarm bell on the roof must have felt the force of the wind, for the rope rose and fell slightly, as though the bell were moved a little from time to time, and the limber rope fell on the oak floor with a hard and hollow sound.

As Malcolmson listened to it he bethought himself of the doctor's words, 'It is the rope which the hangman used for the victims of the judge's judicial rancour,' and he went over to the corner of the fireplace and took it in his hand to look at it. There seemed a sort of deadly interest in it, and as he stood there he lost himself for a moment in speculation as to who these victims were, and the grim wish of the judge to have such a ghastly relic ever under his eyes. As he stood there the swaying of the bell on the roof still lifted the rope now and again; but presently there came a new sensation – a sort of tremor in the rope, as though something was moving along it.

Looking up instinctively Malcolmson saw the great rat coming slowly down towards him, glaring at him steadily. He dropped the rope and started back with a muttered curse, and the rat turning ran up the rope again and disappeared, and at the same instant Malcolmson became conscious that the noise of the other rats, which had ceased for a while, began again.

All this set him thinking, and it occurred to him that he had not investigated the lair of the rat or looked at the pictures, as he had intended. He lit the other lamp without the shade, and, holding it up, went and stood opposite the third picture from the fireplace on the right-hand side where he had seen the rat disappear on the previous night.

At the first glance he started back so suddenly that he almost dropped the lamp, and a deadly pallor overspread his face. His knees shook, and heavy drops of sweat came on his forehead, and he trembled like an aspen. But he was young and plucky, and pulled himself together, and after the pause of a few seconds stepped forward again, raised the lamp, and examined the picture which had been dusted and washed, and now stood out clearly.

It was of a judge dressed in his robes of scarlet and ermine. His face was strong and merciless, evil, crafty, and vindictive, with a sensual mouth, hooked nose of ruddy colour, and shaped like the beak of a bird of prey. The rest of the face was of a cadaverous colour. The eyes were of peculiar brilliance and with a terribly malignant expression. As he looked at them, Malcolmson grew cold, for he saw there the very counterpart of the eyes of the great rat. The lamp almost fell from his hand, he saw the rat with its baleful eyes peering out through the hole in the corner of the picture, and noted the sudden cessation of the noise of the other rats. However, he pulled himself together, and went on with his examination of the picture.

The judge was seated in a great high-backed carved oak chair, on the right-hand side of a great stone fireplace where, in the corner, a rope hung down from the ceiling, its end lying coiled on the floor. With a feeling of something like horror, Malcolmson recognised the scene of the room as it stood, and gazed around him in an awestruck manner as though he expected to find some strange presence behind him. Then he looked over to the corner of the fireplace – and with a loud cry he let the lamp fall from his hand.

There, in the judge's armchair, with the rope hanging behind, sat the rat with the judge's baleful eyes, now intensified and with a fiendish leer. Save for the howling of the storm without there was silence.

The fallen lamp recalled Malcolmson to himself. Fortunately it was of metal, and so the oil was not spilt. However, the practical need of attending to it settled at once his nervous apprehensions. When he had turned it out, he wiped his brow and thought for a moment.

'This will not do,' he said to himself. 'If I go on like this I shall become a crazy fool. This must stop! I promised the doctor I would not take tea. Faith, he was pretty right! My nerves must have been getting into a queer state. Funny I did not notice it. I never felt better in my life. However, it is all right now, and I shall not be such a fool again.'

Then he mixed himself a good stiff glass of brandy and water and resolutely sat down to his work.

It was nearly an hour later when he looked up from his book, disturbed by the sudden stillness. Without, the wind howled and roared louder then ever, and the rain drove in sheets against the windows, beating like hail on the glass; but within there was no sound whatever save the echo of the wind as it roared in the great chimney, and now and then a hiss as a few raindrops found their way down the chimney in a lull of the storm. The fire had fallen low and had ceased to flame, though it threw out a red glow. Malcolmson listened attentively, and presently heard a thin, squeaking noise, very faint. It came from the corner of the room where the rope hung down, and he thought it was the creaking of the rope on the floor as the swaying of the bell raised and lowered it. Looking up, however, he saw in the dim light the great rat clinging to the rope and gnawing it. The rope was already nearly gnawed through – he could see the lighter colour where the strands were laid bare. As he looked the job was completed, and the severed end of the rope fell clattering on the oaken floor, while for an instant the great rat remained like a knob or tassel at the end of the rope, which now began to sway to and fro. Malcolmson felt for a moment another pang of terror as he thought that now the possibility of calling the outer world to his assistance was cut off, but an intense anger took its place, and seizing the book he was reading he hurled it at the rat. The blow was well aimed, but before the missile could reach him the rat dropped off and struck the floor with a soft thud. Malcolmson instantly rushed over towards him, but it darted away and disappeared in the darkness of the shadows of the room. Malcolmson felt that his work was over for the night, and determined then and there to vary the monotony of the proceedings by a hunt for the rat, and took off the green shade of the lamp so as to insure a wider spreading light. As he did so the gloom of the upper part of the room was relieved, and in the new flood of light, great by comparison with the previous darkness, the pictures on the wall stood out boldly. From where he stood, Malcolmson saw right opposite to him the third picture on the wall from the right of the fireplace. He rubbed his eyes in surprise, and then a great fear began to come upon him.

In the centre of the picture was a great irregular patch of brown canvas, as fresh as when it was stretched on the frame. The background was as before, with chair and chimney-corner and rope, but the figure of the judge had disappeared.

Malcolmson, almost in a chill of horror, turned slowly round, and then he began to shake and tremble like a man in a palsy. His strength seemed to have left him, and he was incapable of action or movement, hardly even of thought. He could only see and hear.

There, on the great high-backed carved oak chair sat the judge in his robes of scarlet and ermine, with his baleful eyes glaring vindictively, and a smile of triumph on the resolute, cruel mouth, as he lifted with his hands a *black cap*. Malcolmson felt as if the blood was running from his heart, as one does in moments of prolonged suspense. There was a ringing in his ears. Without, he could hear the roar and howl of the tempest, and through it, swept on the storm, came the striking of midnight by the great chimes in the marketplace. He stood for a space of time that seemed to him endless still as a statue, and with wide-open, horror-struck eyes, breathless. As the clock struck, so the smile of triumph on the judge's face intensified, and at the last stroke of midnight he placed the black cap on his head.

Slowly and deliberately the judge rose from his chair and picked up the piece of the rope of the alarm bell which lay on the floor, drew it through his hands as if he enjoyed its touch, and then deliberately began to knot one end of it, fashioning it into a noose. This he tightened and tested with his foot, pulling hard at it till he was satisfied and then making a running noose of it, which he held in his hand. Then he began to move along the table on the opposite side to Malcolmson keeping his eyes on him until he had passed him, when with a quick movement he stood in front of the door. Malcolmson then began to feel that he was trapped, and tried to think of what he should do. There was some fascination in the judge's eyes, which he never took off him, and he had, perforce, to look. He saw the judge approach – still keeping between him and the door – and raise the noose and throw it towards him as if to entangle him. With a great effort he made a quick movement to one side, and saw the rope fall beside him, and heard it strike the oaken floor. Again the judge raised the noose and tried to ensnare him, ever keeping his baleful eyes fixed on him, and each time by a mighty effort the student just managed to evade it. So this went on for many times, the judge seeming never discouraged nor discomposed at failure, but playing as a cat does with a mouse. At last in despair, which had reached its climax, Malcolmson cast a quick glance round him. The lamp seemed to have blazed up, and there was a fairly good light in the room. At the many rat-holes and in the chinks and crannies of the wainscot he saw the rats' eyes; and this aspect, that was purely physical, gave him a gleam of comfort. He looked round and saw that the rope of the great alarm bell was laden with rats. Every inch of it was covered with them, and more and more were pouring through the small circular hole in the ceiling whence it emerged, so that with their weight the bell was beginning to sway.

Hark! it had swayed till the clapper had touched the bell. The sound was but a tiny one, but the bell was only beginning to sway, and it would increase.

At the sound the judge, who had been keeping his eyes fixed on Malcolmson, looked up, and a scowl of diabolical anger overspread his face. His eyes fairly glowed like hot coals, and he stamped his foot with a sound that seemed to make the house shake. A dreadful peal of thunder broke overhead as he raised the rope again, while the rats kept running up and down the rope as though working against time. This time, instead of throwing it, he drew close to his victim, and held open the noose as he approached. As he came closer there seemed something paralysing in his very presence, and Malcolmson stood rigid as a corpse. He felt the judge's icy fingers touch his throat as he adjusted the rope. The noose tightened – tightened. Then the judge, taking the rigid form of the student in his arms, carried him over and placed him standing in the oak chair, and stepping up beside him, put his hand up and caught the end of the swaying rope of the alarm bell. As he raised his hand the rats fled squeaking, and disappeared through the hole in the ceiling. Taking the end of the noose which was round Malcolmson's neck he tied it to the hanging-bell rope, and then descending pulled away the chair.

*   *   *

When the alarm bell of the Judge's House began to sound, a crowd soon assembled. Lights and torches of various kinds appeared, and soon a silent crowd was hurrying to the spot. They knocked loudly at the door, but there was no reply. Then they burst in the door, and poured into the great dining room, the doctor at the head.

There at the end of the rope of the great alarm bell hung the body of the student, and on the face of the judge in the picture was a malignant smile.

Daniel Crowley and the Ghosts

TRADITIONAL

There lived a man in Cork whose name was Daniel Crowley. He was a coffin-maker by trade, and had a deal of coffins laid by, so that his apprentice might sell them when himself was not at home.

A messenger came to Daniel Crowley's shop one day and told him that there was a man dead at the end of the town, and to send up a coffin for him, or to make one.

Daniel Crowley took down a coffin, put it on a donkey cart, drove to the wake house, went in and told the people of the house that the coffin was there for them. The corpse was laid out on a table in a room next to the kitchen. Five or six women were keeping watch around it; many people were in the kitchen. Daniel Crowley was asked to sit down and commence to shorten the night: that is, to tell stories, amuse himself and others. A tumbler of punch was brought, and he promised to do the best he could.

He began to tell stories and shorten the night. A second glass of punch was brought to him, and he went on telling tales. There was a man at the wake who sang a song: after him another was found, and then another. Then the people asked Daniel Crowley to sing, and he did. The song that he sang was of another nation. He sang about the good people, the fairies. The song pleased the company, they desired him to sing again, and he did not refuse.

Daniel Crowley pleased the company so much with his two songs that a woman who had three daughters wanted to make a match for one of them and get Daniel Crowley as a husband for her. Crowley was a bachelor, well on in years, and had never thought of marrying.

The mother spoke of the match to a woman sitting next to her. The woman shook her head, but the mother said: 'If he takes one of my daughters I'll be glad, for he has money laid by. Do you go and speak to him, but say nothing of me at first.'

The woman went to Daniel Crowley then, and told him that she had a fine, beautiful girl in view, and that now was his time to get a good wife; he'd never have such a chance again.

Crowley rose up in great anger. 'There isn't a woman wearing clothes that I'd marry,' said he. 'There isn't a woman born that could bring me to make two halves of my loaf for her.'

The mother was insulted now and forget herself. She began to abuse Crowley.

'Bad luck to you, you hairy little scoundrel,' said she, 'you might be a grandfather to my child. You are not fit to clean the shoes on her feet. You have only dead people for company day and night; 'tis by them you make your living.'

'Oh, then,' said Daniel Crowley, 'I'd prefer the dead to the living any day if all the living were like you. Besides, I have nothing against the dead. I am getting employment by them and not by the living, for 'tis the dead that want coffins.'

'Bad luck to you, 'tis with the dead you ought to be and not with the living; 'twould be fitter for you to go out of this altogether and go to your dead people.'

'I'd go if I knew how to go to them,' said Crowley.

'Why not invite them to supper?' retorted the woman.

He rose up then, went out, and called: 'Men, women, children, soldiers, sailors, all people that I have ever made coffins for, I invite you tonight to my house, and I'll spend what is needed in giving a feast.'

The people who were watching the dead man on the table saw him smile when he heard the invitation. They ran out of the room in a fright and out of the kitchen, and Daniel Crowley hurried away to his shop as fast as ever his donkey could carry him. On the way he came to a public-house and, going in, bought a pint bottle of whiskey, put it in his pocket, and drove on.

The workshop was locked and the shutters down when he left that evening, but when he came near he saw that all the windows were shining with light, and he was in dread that the building was burning or that robbers were in it. When right there Crowley slipped into a corner of the building opposite, to know could he see what was happening, and soon he saw crowds of men, women, and children walking toward his shop and going in, but none coming out. He was hiding some time when a man tapped him on the shoulder and asked, 'Is it here you are, and we waiting for you? 'Tis a shame to treat company this way. Come now.'

Crowley went with the man to the shop, and as he passed the threshold he saw a great gathering of people. Some were neighbours, people he had known in the past. All were dancing, singing, amusing themselves. He was not long looking on when a man came up to him and said: 'You seem not to know me, Daniel Crowley.'

'I don't know you,' said Crowley. 'How could I?'

'You might then, and you ought to know me, for I am the first man you made a coffin for, and 'twas I gave you the first start in business.'

Soon another came up, a lame man: 'Do you know me, Daniel Crowley?'

'I do not.'

'I am your cousin, and it isn't long since I died.'

'Oh, now I know you well, for you are lame. In God's name,' said Crowley to the cousin, 'how am I to get these people out o' this. What time is it?'

'''Tis early yet, it's hardly eleven o'clock, man.'

Crowley wondered that it was so early.

'Receive them kindly,' said the cousin; 'be good to them, make merriment as you can.'

'I have no money with me to get food or drink for them; 'tis night now, and all places are closed,' answered Crowley.

'Well, do the best you can,' said the cousin.

The fun and dancing went on, and while Daniel Crowley was looking around, examining everything, he saw a woman in the far-off corner. She took no part in the amusement, but seemed very shy in herself.

'Why is that woman so shy – she seems to be afraid?' asked he of the cousin. 'And why doesn't she dance and make merry like others?'

'Oh, 'tis not long since she died, and you gave the coffin, as she had no means of paying for it. She is in dread you'll ask her for the money, or let the company know that she didn't pay,' said the cousin.

The best dancer they had was a piper by the name of John Reardon from the city of Cork. The fiddler was one John Healy. Healy brought no fiddle with him, but he made one, and the way he made it was to take off what flesh he had on his body. He rubbed up and down on his own ribs, each rib having a different note, and he made the loveliest music that Daniel Crowley had ever heard. After that the whole company followed his example. All threw off what flesh they had on them and began to dance jigs and hornpipes in their bare bones. When by chance they struck against one another in dancing, you'd think it was Brandon Mountain that was sinking Mount Eagle, with the noise that was in it.

Daniel Crowley plucked up all his courage to know could he live through the night, but still he thought daylight would never come. There was one man, John Sullivan, that he noticed especially. This man had married twice in his life, and with him came the two women. Crowley saw him taking out the second wife to dance a breakdown, and the two danced so well that the company were delighted, and all the skeletons had their mouths open, laughing. He danced and knocked so much merriment out of them all that his first wife, who was at the end of the house, became jealous and very mad altogether. She ran down to where he was and told him she had a better right to dance with him than the second wife; 'That's not the truth for you,' said the second wife, 'I have a better right than you. When he married me you were a dead woman and he was free, and, besides, I'm a better dancer than what you are, and I will dance with him whether you like it or not.'

'Hold your tongue!' screamed the first wife. 'Sure, you couldn't come to this feast tonight at all but for the loan of another woman's shinbones.'

Sullivan looked at his two wives and asked the second one: 'Isn't it your own shinbones you have?'

'No, they are borrowed. I borrowed a neighbouring woman's shins from her, and 'tis those I have with me tonight.'

'Who is the owner of the shinbones you have under you?' asked the husband.

'They belong to one Catherine Murray. She hadn't a very good name in life.'

'But why didn't you come on your own feet?'

'Oh, I wasn't good myself in life, and I was put under a penalty, and the penalty is that whenever there is a feast or a ball I cannot go to it unless I am able to borrow a pair of shins.'

Sullivan was raging when he found that the shinbones he had been dancing with belonged to a third woman, and she not the best, and he gave a slap to the wife that sent her spinning into a corner.

The woman had relations among the skeletons present, and they were angry when they saw the man strike their friend. 'We'll never let that go with him,' said they. 'We must knock satisfaction out of Sullivan!'

The woman's friends rose up, and, as there were no clubs or weapons, they pulled off their left arms and began to slash and strike with them in terrible fashion. There was an awful battle in one minute.

While this was going on Daniel Crowley was standing below at the end of the room, cold and hungry, not knowing but he'd be killed. As Sullivan was trying to dodge the blows sent against him, he got as far as Daniel Crowley and stepped on his toe without knowing it; Crowley got vexed and gave Sullivan a blow with his fist that drove the head from him and sent it flying to the opposite corner.

When Sullivan saw his head flying off from the blow, he ran, and, catching it, aimed a blow at Daniel Crowley with the head, and aimed so truly that he knocked him under the bench; then, having him at a disadvantage, Sullivan hurried to the bench and began to strangle him. He squeezed his throat and held him so firmly between the bench and the floor that the man lost his senses and couldn't remember a thing more.

When Daniel Crowley came to himself in the morning, his apprentice found him stretched under the bench with an empty bottle under his arm. He was bruised and pounded. His throat was sore where Sullivan had squeezed it; he didn't know how the company broke up, nor when his guests went away.

John Reardon and the Sister Ghosts

TRADITIONAL

Once there was a farmer, a widower, Tom Reardon, who lived near Castlemain. He had an only son, a fine strong boy, who was almost a man, and the boy's name was John. This farmer married a second time, and the stepmother hated the boy and gave him neither rest nor peace. She was turning the father's mind against the son, till at last the farmer resolved to put the son in a place where a ghost was, and this ghost never let any man go without killing him.

One day the father sent the son to the forge with some chains belonging to a plough; he would have two horses ploughing next day.

The boy took the chains to the forge; and it was nearly evening when the father sent him, and the forge was four miles away.

The smith had much work and he hadn't the chains mended till close on to midnight. The smith had two sons, and they didn't wish to let John go, but he said he must go, for he had promised to be home and the father would kill him if he stayed away. They stood before him in the door, but he went in spite of them.

When two miles from the forge a ghost rose up before John, a woman; she attacked him and they fought for two hours, when he put the plough chain round her. She could do nothing then, because what belongs to a plough is blessed. He fastened the chain and dragged the ghost home with him, and told her to go to the bedroom and give the father and stepmother a rough handling, not to spare them.

The ghost beat them till the father cried for mercy, and said if he lived till morning he'd leave the place, and that the wife was the cause of putting John in the way to be killed.

John put food on the table and told the ghost to sit down and eat for herself, but she refused and said he must take her back to the very spot where he found her. John was willing to do that, and he went with her. She told him to come to that place on the following night, that there was a sister of hers, a ghost, a deal more determined and stronger than what herself was.

John told her that maybe the two of them would attack and kill him. She said that they would not, that she wanted his help against the sister, and that he would not be sorry for helping her. He told her he would come, and when he was leaving her she said not to forget the plough chains.

Next morning the father was going to leave the house, but the wife persuaded him to stay. 'That ghost will never walk the way again,' said she. John went the following night, and the ghost was waiting before him on the spot where he fought with her. They walked on together two miles by a different road, and halted. They were talking in that place a while when the sister came and attacked John Reardon, and they were fighting two hours and she was getting the better of the boy, when the first sister put the plough chains around her. He pulled her home with the chains, and the first sister walked along behind them. When John came to the house, he opened the door, and when the father saw the two ghosts he said that if morning overtook him alive he'd leave the son everything, the farm and the house.

The son told the second ghost to go down and give a good turn to the stepmother; 'Let her have a few strong knocks,' said he.

The second ghost barely left life in the stepmother. John had food on the table, but they would not take a bite, and the second sister said he must take her back to the very spot where he met her first. He said he would. She told him that he was the bravest man that ever stood before her, and that she would not threaten him again in the world, and told him to come the next night. He said he would not, for the two might attack and get the better of him. They promised they would not attack, but would help him, for it was to get the upper hand of the youngest and strongest of the sisters that they wanted him, and that he must bring the plough chains, for without them they could do nothing.

He agreed to go if they would give their word not to harm him. They said they would give their word and would help him the best they could.

The next day, when the father was going to leave the place, the wife would not let him. 'Stay where you are,' she said, 'they'll never trouble us again.'

John went the third night, and, when he came, the two sisters were before him, and they walked till they travelled four miles then told him to stop on the green grass at one side and not to be on the road.

They weren't waiting long when the third sister came, and red lightning flashing from her mouth. She went at John, and with the first blow that she gave him put him on his knees. He rose with the help of the two sisters, and for three hours they fought, and the youngest sister was getting the better of the boy when the two others threw the chains around her. The boy dragged her away home with him then, and, when the stepmother saw the three sisters coming, herself and John's father were terrified and they died of fright, the two of them

John put food on the table and told the sisters to come and eat, but they refused, and the youngest told him that he must take her to the spot where he fought with her. All four went to that place, and at parting they promised never to harm him and to put him in the way that he would never need to do a day's work, nor his children after him, if he had any. The eldest sister told him to come on the following night, and to bring a spade with him; she would tell him, she said, her whole history from first to last.

He went, and what she told him was this: Long ago her father was one of the richest men in all Ireland; her mother died when the three sisters were very young, and ten or twelve years after the father died, and left the care of all the wealth and treasures in the castle to herself, telling her to make three equal parts of it, and to let herself and each of the other two sisters have one of those parts. But she was in love with a young man unknown to her father, and one night when the two sisters were fast asleep, and she thought if she killed them she would have the whole fortune for herself and her husband, she took a knife and cut their throats, and when she had them killed she got sorry and did the same to herself. The sentence put on them was that none of the three was to have rest or peace till some man without fear would come and conquer them, and John was the first to attempt this.

She took him then to her father's castle – only the ruins of it were standing, no roof and only some of the walls, and showed where all the riches and treasures were. John, to make sure, took his spade and dug away, dug with what strength was in him, and just before day-break he came to the treasure. That moment the three sisters left good health with him, turned into three doves, and flew away.

He had riches enough for himself and for seven generations after him.

The Canterville Ghost

A Hylo-Idealistic Romance

OSCAR WILDE

CHAPTER I

When Mr Hiram B. Otis, the American Minister, bought Canterville Chase, everyone told him he was doing a very foolish thing, as there was no doubt at all that the place was haunted. Indeed, Lord Canterville himself, who was a man of the most punctilious honour, had felt it his duty to mention the fact to Mr Otis when they came to discuss terms.

'We have not cared to live in the place ourselves,' said Lord Canterville, 'since my grandaunt, the Dowager Duchess of Bolton, was frightened into a fit, from which she never really recovered, by two skeleton hands being placed on her shoulders as she was dressing for dinner, and I feel bound to tell you, Mr Otis, that the ghost has been seen by several living members of my family, as well as by the rector of the parish, the Reverend Augustus Dampier, who is a Fellow of King's College, Cambridge. After the unfortunate accident to the Duchess, none of our younger servants would stay with us, and Lady Canterville often got very little sleep at night, in consequence of the mysterious noises that came from the corridor and the library.'

'My Lord,' answered the minister, 'I will take the furniture and the ghost at a valuation. I come from a modern country, where we have everything that money can buy; and with all our spry young fellows painting the Old World red, and carrying off your best actresses and prima-donnas, I reckon that if there were such a thing as a ghost in Europe, we'd have it at home in a very short time in one of our public museums, or on the road as a show.'

'I fear that the ghost exists,' said Lord Canterville, smiling, 'though it may have resisted the overtures of your enterprising impresarios.

It has been well known for three centuries, since 1584 in fact, and always makes its appearance before the death of any member of our family.'

'Well, so does the family doctor for that matter, Lord Canterville. But there is no such thing, sir, as a ghost, and I guess the laws of nature are not going to be suspended for the British aristocracy.'

'You are certainly very natural in America,' answered Lord Canterville, who did not quite understand Mr Otis's last observation, 'and if you don't mind a ghost in the house, it is all right. Only you must remember I warned you.'

A few weeks after this, the purchase was completed, and at the close of the season the minister and his family went down to Canterville Chase. Mrs Otis, who, as Miss Lucretia R. Tappan, of West 53rd Street, had been a celebrated New York belle, was now a very handsome, middle-aged woman, with fine eyes and a superb profile. Many American ladies on leaving their native land adopt an appearance of chronic ill-health, under the impression that it is a form of European refinement, but Mrs Otis had never fallen into this error. She had a magnificent constitution, and a really wonderful amount of animal spirits. Indeed, in many respects, she was quite English, and was an excellent example of the fact that we have really everything in common with America nowadays, except, of course, language. Her eldest son, christened Washington by his parents in a moment of patriotism, which he never ceased to regret, was a fair-haired, rather good-looking young man, who had qualified himself for American diplomacy by leading the German at the Newport Casino for three successive seasons, and even in London was well known as an excellent dancer. Gardenias and the peerage were his only weaknesses. Otherwise he was extremely sensible. Miss Virginia E. Otis was a little girl of fifteen, lithe and lovely as a fawn, and with a fine freedom in her large blue eyes. She was a wonderful amazon, and had once raced old Lord Bilton on her pony twice round the park, winning by a length and a half, just in front of the Achilles statue, to the huge delight of the young Duke of Cheshire, who proposed for her on the spot, and was sent back to Eton that very night by his guardians, in floods of tears. After Virginia came the twins, who were usually called 'the Stars and Stripes', as they were always getting swished. They were delightful boys, and with the exception of the worthy minister, the only true republicans of the family.

As Canterville Chase is seven miles from Ascot, the nearest railway station, Mr Otis had telegraphed for a waggonette to meet them, and they started on their drive in high spirits. It was a lovely July evening, and the air was delicate with the scent of the pine woods. Now and then they heard a woodpigeon brooding over its own sweet voice, or saw, deep in the rustling fern, the burnished breast of the pheasant. Little squirrels peered at them from the beech trees as they went by, and the rabbits scudded away through the brushwood and over the mossy knolls, with their white tails in the air. As they entered the avenue of Canterville Chase, however, the sky became suddenly overcast with clouds, a curious stillness seemed to hold the atmosphere, a great flight of rooks passed silently over their heads, and, before they reached the house, some big drops of rain had fallen.

Standing on the steps to receive them was an old woman, neatly dressed in black silk, with a white cap and apron. This was Mrs Umney, the housekeeper, whom Mrs Otis, at Lady Canterville's earnest request, had consented to keep on in her former position. She made them each a low curtsey as they alighted and said, in a quaint, old-fashioned manner, 'I bid you welcome to Canterville Chase.' Following her, they passed through the fine Tudor hall into the library, a long, low room, panelled in black oak, at the end of which was a large stained-glass window. Here they found tea laid out for them, and, after taking off their wraps, they sat down and began to look round, while Mrs Umney waited on them.

Suddenly Mrs Otis caught sight of a dull red stain on the floor just by the fireplace and, quite unconscious of what it really signified, said to Mrs Umney, 'I am afraid something has been spilt there.'

'Yes, madam,' replied the old housekeeper in a low voice, 'blood has been spilt on that spot.'

'How horrid,' cried Mrs Otis; 'I don't at all care for bloodstains in a sitting-room. It must be removed at once.'

The old woman smiled, and answered in the same low, mysterious voice, 'It is the blood of Lady Eleanore de Canterville, who was murdered on that very spot by her own husband, Sir Simon de Canterville, in 1575. Sir Simon survived her nine years, and disappeared suddenly under very mysterious circumstances. His body has never been discovered, but his guilty spirit still haunts the Chase. The bloodstain has been much admired by tourists and others, and cannot be removed.'

'That is all nonsense,' cried Washington Otis; 'Pinkerton's

Champion Stain Remover and Paragon Detergent will clean it up in no time,' and before the terrified housekeeper could interfere he had fallen upon his knees, and was rapidly scouring the floor with a small stick of what looked like a black cosmetic. In a few moments no trace of the bloodstain could be seen.

'I knew Pinkerton would do it,' he exclaimed triumphantly, as he looked round at his admiring family; but no sooner had he said these words than a terrible flash of lightning lit up the sombre room, a fearful peal of thunder made them all start to their feet, and Mrs Umney fainted.

'What a monstrous climate!' said the American Minister calmly, as he lit a long cheroot. 'I guess the old country is so over-populated that they have not enough decent weather for everybody. I have always been of opinion that emigration is the only thing for England.'

'My dear Hiram,' cried Mrs Otis, 'what can we do with a woman who faints?'

'Charge it to her like breakages,' answered the minister; 'she won't faint after that;' and in a few moments Mrs Umney certainly came to. There was no doubt, however, that she was extremely upset, and she sternly warned Mr Otis to beware of some trouble coming to the house.

'I have seen things with my own eyes, sir,' she said, 'that would make any Christian's hair stand on end, and many and many a night I have not closed my eyes in sleep for the awful things that are done here.' Mr Otis, however, and his wife warmly assured the honest soul that they were not afraid of ghosts, and, after invoking the blessings of Providence on her new master and mistress, and making arrangements for an increase of salary, the old housekeeper tottered off to her own room.

CHAPTER 2

The storm raged fiercely all that night, but nothing of particular note occurred. The next morning, however, when they came down to breakfast, they found the terrible stain of blood once again on the floor. 'I don't think it can be the fault of the Paragon Detergent,' said Washington, 'for I have tried it with everything. It must be the ghost.' He accordingly rubbed out the stain a second time, but the second morning it appeared again. The third morning also it was there, though the library had been locked up at night by Mr Otis himself, and the key carried upstairs. The whole family were now quite interested; Mr Otis began to suspect that he had been too dogmatic in his denial of the existence of ghosts, Mrs Otis expressed her intention of joining the Psychical Society, and Washington prepared a long letter to Messrs Myers and Podmore on the subject of the Permanence of Sanguineous Stains when connected with Crime. That night all doubts about the objective existence of phantasmata were removed for ever.

The day had been warm and sunny; and, in the cool of the evening, the whole family went out for a drive. They did not return home till nine o'clock, when they had a light supper. The conversation in no way turned upon ghosts, so there were not even those primary conditions of receptive expectation which so often precede the presentation of psychical phenomena. The subjects discussed, as I have since learned from Mr Otis, were merely such as form the ordinary conversation of cultured Americans of the better class, such as the immense superiority of Miss Fanny Davenport over Sarah Bernhardt as an actress; the difficulty of obtaining green corn, buck-wheat cakes and hominy, even in the best English houses; the importance of Boston in the development of the world-soul; the advantages of the baggage-check system in railway travelling; and the sweetness of the New York accent as compared to the London drawl. No mention at all was made of the supernatural, nor was Sir Simon de Canterville alluded to in anyway. At eleven o'clock the family retired, and by half-past all the lights were out. Some time after, Mr Otis was awakened by a curious noise in the corridor, outside his room. It sounded like the clank of metal, and seemed to be coming nearer every moment. He got up at once, struck a match, and looked at the time. It was exactly one o'clock. He was quite calm, and felt his pulse, which was not at all feverish. The strange noise still continued, and with it he heard distinctly the sound of footsteps. He put on his slippers, took a small oblong phial out of his dressing-case, and opened the door. Right in front of him he saw, in the wan moonlight, an old man of terrible aspect. His eyes were as red burning coals; long grey hair fell over his shoulders in matted coils; his garments, which were of antique cut, were soiled and ragged, and from his wrists and ankles hung heavy manacles and rusty gyves.

'My dear sir,' said Mr Otis, 'I really must insist on your oiling those chains, and have brought you for that purpose a small bottle of the Tammany Rising Sun Lubricator. It is said to be completely efficacious upon one application, and there are several testimonials to that effect on the wrapper from some of our most eminent native divines. I shall leave it here for you by the bedroom candles, and will be happy to supply you with more should you require it.' With these words the United States Minister laid the bottle down on a marble table, and, closing his door, retired to rest.

For a moment the Canterville ghost stood quite motionless in natural indignation; then, dashing the bottle violently upon the polished floor, he fled down the corridor, uttering hollow groans, and emitting a ghastly green light. Just, however, as he reached the top of the great oak staircase, a door was flung open, two little white-robed figures appeared, and a large pillow whizzed past his head! There was evidently no time to be lost, so, hastily adopting the Fourth Dimension of Space as a means of escape, he vanished through the wainscoting, and the house became quite quiet.

On reaching a small secret chamber in the left wing, he leaned up against a moonbeam to recover his breath, and began to try and realise his position. Never, in a brilliant and uninterrupted career of three hundred years, had he been so grossly insulted. He thought of the Dowager Duchess, whom he had frightened into a fit as she stood before the glass in her lace and diamonds; of the four house-maids, who had gone off into hysterics when he merely grinned at them through the curtains of one of the spare bedrooms; of the rector of the parish, whose candle he had blown out as he was coming late one night from the library, and who had been under the care of Sir William Gull ever since, a perfect martyr to nervous disorders; and of old Madame de Tremouillac, who, having wakened up one morning early and seen a skeleton seated in an armchair by the fire reading her diary, had been confined to her bed for six weeks with an attack of brain fever, and, on her recovery, had become reconciled to the church, and broken off her connection with that notorious sceptic Monsieur de Voltaire. He remembered the terrible night when the wicked Lord Canterville was found choking in his dressing-room, with the knave of diamonds halfway down his throat, and confessed, just before he died, that he had cheated Charles James Fox out of £50,000 at Crockford's by means of that very card, and swore that the ghost had made him swallow it. All his great achievements came back to him again, from the butler who had shot himself in the pantry because he had seen a green hand tapping at the window pane, to the beautiful Lady Stutfield, who was always obliged to wear a black velvet band round her throat to hide the mark of five fingers burnt upon her white skin, and who drowned herself at last in the carp-pond at the end of the King's Walk. With the enthusiastic egotism of the true artist he went over his most celebrated performances, and smiled bitterly to himself as he recalled to mind his last appearance as 'Red Ruben, or the Strangled Babe', his début as 'Gaunt Gibeon, the Bloodsucker of Bexley Moor', and the furore he had excited one lovely June evening by merely playing ninepins with his own bones upon the lawn-tennis ground. And after all this, some wretched modern Americans were to come and offer him the Rising Sun Lubricator, and throw pillows at his head! It was quite unbearable. Besides, no ghosts in history had ever been treated in this manner. Accordingly, he determined to have vengeance, and remained till daylight in an attitude of deep thought.

CHAPTER 3

The next morning when the Otis family met at breakfast, they discussed the ghost at some length. The United States Minister was naturally a little annoyed to find that his present had not been accepted. 'I have no wish,' he said, 'to do the ghost any personal injury, and I must say that, considering the length of time he has been in the house, I don't think it is at all polite to throw pillows at him' – a very just remark, at which, I am sorry to say, the twins burst into shouts of laughter. 'Upon the other hand,' he continued, 'if he really declines to use the Rising Sun Lubricator, we shall have to take his chains from him. It would be quite impossible to sleep, with such a noise going on outside the bedrooms.'

For the rest of the week, however, they were undisturbed, the only thing that excited any attention being the continual renewal of the bloodstain on the library floor. This certainly was very strange, as the door was always locked at night by Mr Otis, and the windows kept closely barred. The chameleon-like colour, also, of the stain excited a good deal of comment. Some mornings it was a dull (almost Indian) red, then it would be vermilion, then a rich purple, and once when they came down for family prayers, according to the simple rites of the Free American Reformed Episcopalian Church, they found it a bright emerald-green. These kaleidoscopic changes naturally amused the party very much, and bets on the subject were freely made every evening. The only person who did not enter into the joke was little Virginia, who, for some unexplained reason, was always a good deal distressed at the sight of the bloodstain, and very nearly cried the morning it was emerald-green.

The second appearance of the ghost was on Sunday night. Shortly after they had gone to bed they were suddenly alarmed by a fearful crash in the hall. Rushing downstairs, they found that a large suit of old armour had become detached from its stand, and had fallen on the stone floor, while, seated in a high-backed chair, was the Canterville ghost, rubbing his knees with an expression of acute agony on his face. The twins, having brought their peashooters with them, at once discharged two pellets on him, with that accuracy of aim which can only be attained by long and careful practice on a writing-master, while the United States Minister covered him with his revolver, and called upon him, in accordance with Californian etiquette, to hold up his hands! The ghost started up with a wild shriek of rage, and swept through them like a mist, extinguishing Washington Otis's candle as he passed, and so leaving them all in total darkness. On reaching the top of the staircase he recovered himself, and determined to give his celebrated peal of demoniac laughter. This he had on more than one occasion found extremely useful. It was said to have turned Lord Raker's wig grey in a single night, and had certainly made three of Lady Canterville's French governesses give warning before their month was up. He accordingly laughed his most horrible laugh, till the old vaulted roof rang and rang again, but hardly had the fearful echo died away when a door opened, and Mrs Otis came out in a light blue dressing-gown. 'I am afraid you are far from well,' she said, 'and have brought you a bottle of Dr Dobell's tincture. If it is indigestion, you will find it a most excellent remedy.' The ghost glared at her in fury, and began at once to make preparations for turning himself into a large black dog, an accomplishment for which he was justly renowned, and to which the family doctor always attributed the permanent idiocy of Lord Canterville's uncle, the Hon. Thomas Horton. The sound of approaching footsteps, however, made him hesitate in his fell purpose, so he contented himself with becoming faintly phosphorescent, and vanished with a deep churchyard groan, just as the twins had come up to him.

On reaching his room he entirely broke down, and became a prey to the most violent agitation. The vulgarity of the twins, and the gross materialism of Mrs Otis, were naturally extremely annoying, but what really distressed him most was that he had been unable to wear the suit of mail. He had hoped that even modern Americans would be thrilled by the sight of a Spectre In Armour, if for no more sensible reason, at least out of respect for their national poet Longfellow, over whose graceful and attractive poetry he himself had whiled away many a weary hour when the Cantervilles were up in town. Besides, it was his own suit. He had worn it with great success at the Kenilworth tournament, and had been highly complimented on it by no less a person than the Virgin Queen herself. Yet when he had put it on, he had been completely overpowered by the weight of the huge breastplate and steel casque, and had fallen heavily on the stone pavement, barking both his knees severely, and bruising the knuckles of his right hand.

For some days after this he was extremely ill, and hardly stirred out of his room at all, except to keep the bloodstain in proper repair. However, by taking great care of himself, he recovered, and resolved to make a third attempt to frighten the United States Minister and his family. He selected Friday, the 17th of August, for his appearance, and spent most of that day in looking over his wardrobe, ultimately deciding in favour of a large slouched hat with a red feather, a winding-sheet frilled at the wrists and neck, and a rusty dagger. Towards evening a violent storm of rain came on, and the wind was so high that all the windows and doors in the old house shook and rattled. In fact, it was just such weather as he loved. His plan of action was this. He was to make his way quietly to Washington Otis's room, gibber at him from the foot of the bed, and stab himself three times in the throat to the sound of slow music. He bore Washington a special grudge, being quite aware that it was he who was in the habit of removing the famous Canterville bloodstain, by means of Pinkerton's Paragon Detergent. Having reduced the reckless and foolhardy youth to a condition of abject terror, he was then to proceed to the room occupied by the United States Minister and his wife, and there to place a clammy hand on Mrs Otis's forehead, while he hissed into her trembling husband's ear the awful secrets of the charnel-house. With regard to little Virginia, he had not quite made up his mind. She had never insulted him in any way, and was pretty and gentle. A few hollow groans from the wardrobe, he thought, would be more than sufficient, or, if that failed to wake her, he might grabble at the counterpane with palsy-twitching fingers. As for the twins, he was quite determined to teach them a lesson. The first thing to be done was, of course, to sit upon their chests, so as to produce the stifling sensation of nightmare. Then, as their beds were quite close to each other, to stand between them in the form of a green, icy-cold corpse, till they became paralysed with fear, and, finally, to throw off the winding-sheet, and crawl round the room, with white bleached bones and one rolling eyeball, in the character of 'Dumb Daniel, or the Suicide's Skeleton', a role in which he had on more than one occasion produced a great effect, and which he considered quite equal to his famous part of 'Martin the Maniac, or the Masked Mystery'.

At half-past ten he heard the family going to bed. For some time he was disturbed by wild shrieks of laughter from the twins, who, with the light-hearted gaiety of schoolboys, were evidently amusing themselves before they retired to rest, but at a quarter past eleven all was still, and, as midnight sounded, he sallied forth. The owl beat against the window panes, the raven croaked from the old yew tree, and the wind wandered moaning round the house like a lost soul; but the Otis family slept unconscious of their doom, and high above the rain and storm he could hear the steady snoring of the Minister for the United States. He stepped stealthily out of the wainscoting, with an evil smile on his cruel, wrinkled mouth, and the moon hid her face in a cloud as he stole past the great oriel window, where his own arms and those of his murdered wife were blazoned in azure and gold. On and on he glided, like an evil shadow, the very darkness seeming to loathe him as he passed. Once he thought he heard something call, and stopped; but it was only the baying of a dog from the Red Farm, and he went on, muttering strange sixteenth-century curses, and ever and anon brandishing the rusty dagger in the midnight air. Finally he reached the corner of the passage that led to luckless Washington's room. For a moment he paused there, the wind blowing his long grey locks about his head, and twisting into grotesque and fantastic folds the nameless horror of the dead man's shroud. Then the clock struck the quarter, and he felt the time was come. He chuckled to himself, and turned the corner; but no sooner had he done so, than, with a piteous wail of terror, he fell back, and hid his blanched face in his long, bony hands. Right in front of him was standing a horrible spectre, motionless as a carven image, and monstrous as a madman's dream! Its head was bald and burnished; its face round, and fat, and white; and hideous laughter seemed to have writhed its features into an eternal grin. From the eyes streamed rays of scarlet light, the mouth was a wide well of fire, and a hideous garment, like to his own, swathed with its silent snows the Titan form. On its breast was a placard with strange writing in antique characters, some scroll of shame it seemed, some record of wild sins, some awful calendar of crime, and, with its right hand, it bore aloft a falchion of gleaming steel.

Never having seen a ghost before, he naturally was terribly frightened, and, after a second hasty glance at the awful phantom, he fled back to his room, tripping up in his long winding-sheet as he sped down the corridor, and finally dropping the rusty dagger into the minister's jackboots, where it was found in the morning by the butler. Once in the privacy of his own apartment, he flung himself down on a small pallet-bed, and hid his face under the clothes. After a time, however, the brave old Canterville spirit asserted itself, and he determined to go and speak to the other ghost as soon as it was daylight. Accordingly, just as the dawn was touching the hills with silver, he returned towards the spot where he had first laid eyes on the grisly phantom, feeling that, after all, two ghosts were better than one, and that, by the aid of his new friend, he might safely grapple with the twins. On reaching the spot, however, a terrible sight met his gaze. Something had evidently happened to the spectre, for the light had entirely faded from its hollow eyes, the gleaming falchion had fallen from its hand, and it was leaning up against the wall in a strained and uncomfortable attitude. He rushed forward and seized it in his arms, when, to his horror, the head slipped off and rolled on the floor, the body assumed a recumbent posture, and he found himself clasping a white dimity bed-curtain, with a sweeping-brush, a kitchen cleaver, and a hollow turnip lying at his feet! Unable to understand this curious transformation, he clutched the placard with feverish haste, and there, in the grey morning light, he read these fearful words:

The Otis Ghoste
Ye Onlie True and Originale Spook
Beware of Ye Imitations
All others are Counterfeite

The whole thing flashed across him. He had been tricked, foiled and outwitted! The old Canterville look came into his eyes; he ground his toothless gums together; and, raising his withered hands high above his head, swore, according to the picturesque phraseology of the antique school, that when Chanticleer had sounded twice his merry horn, deeds of blood would be wrought, and Murder walk abroad with silent feet.

Hardly had he finished this awful oath when, from the red-tiled roof of a distant homestead, a cock crew. He laughed a long, low, bitter laugh, and waited. Hour after hour he waited, but the cock, for some strange reason, did not crow again. Finally, at half-past seven, the arrival of the housemaids made him give up his fearful vigil, and he stalked back to his room, thinking of his vain hope and baffled purpose. There he consulted several books of ancient chivalry, of which he was exceedingly fond, and found that, on every occasion on which his oath had been used, Chanticleer had always crowed a second time. 'Perdition seize the naughty fowl,' he muttered. 'I have seen the day when, with my stout spear, I would have run him through the gorge, and made him crow for me as 'twere in death!' He then retired to a comfortable lead coffin, and stayed there till evening.

CHAPTER 4

The next day the ghost was very weak and tired. The terrible excitement of the last four weeks was beginning to have its effect. His nerves were completely shattered, and he started at the slightest noise. For five days he kept his room, and at last made up his mind to give up the point of the bloodstain on the library floor. If the Otis family did not want it, they clearly did not deserve it. They were evidently people on a low, material plane of existence, and quite incapable of appreciating the symbolic value of sensuous phenomena. The question of phantasmic apparitions, and the development of astral bodies, was of course quite a different matter, and really not under his control. It was his solemn duty to appear in the corridor once a week, and to gibber from the large oriel window on the first and third Wednesday in every month, and he did not see how he could honourably escape from his obligations. It is quite true that his life had been very evil, but, upon the other hand, he was most conscientious in all things connected with the supernatural. For the next three Saturdays, accordingly, he traversed the corridor as usual between midnight and three o'clock, taking every possible precaution against being either heard or seen. He removed his boots, trod as lightly as possible on the old worm-eaten boards, wore a large black velvet cloak, and was careful to use the Rising Sun Lubricator for oiling his chains. I am bound to acknowledge that it was with a good deal of difficulty that he brought himself to adopt this last mode of protection. However, one night, while the family were at dinner, he slipped into Mr Otis's bedroom and carried off the bottle. He felt a little humiliated at first, but afterwards was sensible enough to see that there was a great deal to be said for the invention, and, to a certain degree, it served his purpose. Still, in spite of everything, he was not left unmolested. Strings were continually being stretched across the corridor, over which he tripped in the dark, and on one occasion, while dressed for the part of 'Black Isaac, or the Huntsman of Hogley Woods', he met with a severe fall, through treading on a butter-slide, which the twins had constructed from the entrance of the Tapestry Chamber to the top of the oak staircase. This last insult so enraged him, that he resolved to make one final effort to assert his dignity and social position, and determined to visit the insolent young Etonians the next night in his celebrated character of 'Reckless Rupert, or the Headless Earl'.

He had not appeared in this disguise for more than seventy years; in fact, not since he had so frightened pretty Lady Barbara Modish by means of it, that she suddenly broke off her engagement with the present Lord Canterville's grandfather, and ran away to Gretna Green with handsome Jack Castleton, declaring that nothing in the world would induce her to marry into a family that allowed such a horrible phantom to walk up and down the terrace at twilight. Poor Jack was afterwards shot in a duel by Lord Canterville on Wandsworth Common, and Lady Barbara died of a broken heart at Tunbridge Wells before the year was out, so, in every way, it had been a great success. It was, however, an extremely difficult 'make-up', if I may use such a theatrical expression in connection with one of the greatest mysteries of the supernatural, or, to employ a more scientific term, the higher-natural world, and it took him fully three hours to make his preparations. At last everything was ready, and he was very pleased with his appearance. The big leather riding-boots that went with the dress were just a little too large for him, and he could only find one of the two horse-pistols, but, on the whole, he was quite satisfied, and at a quarter past one he glided out of the wainscoting and crept down the corridor. On reaching the room occupied by the twins, which I should mention was called the Blue Bedchamber, on account of the colour of its hangings, he found the door just ajar. Wishing to make an effective entrance, he flung it wide open, when a heavy jug of water fell right down on him, wetting him to the skin, and just missing his left shoulder by a couple of inches. At the same moment he heard stifled shrieks of laughter proceeding from the four-post bed. The shock to his nervous system was so great that he fled back to his room as hard as he could go, and the next day he was laid up with a severe cold. The only thing that at all consoled him in the whole affair was the fact that he had not brought his head with him, for, had he done so, the consequences might have been very serious.

He now gave up all hope of ever frightening this rude American family, and contented himself, as a rule, with creeping about the passages in list slippers, with a thick red muffler round his throat for fear of draughts, and a small arquebuse, in case he should be attacked by the twins. The final blow he received occurred on the 19th of September. He had gone downstairs to the great entrance-hall, feeling sure that there, at any rate, he would be quite unmolested, and was amusing himself by making satirical remarks on the large Saroni photographs of the United States Minister and his wife, which had now taken the place of the Canterville family pictures. He was simply but neatly clad in a long shroud, spotted with church-yard mould, had tied up his jaw with a strip of yellow linen, and carried a small lantern and a sexton's spade. In fact, he was dressed for the character of 'Jonas the Graveless, or the Corpse-Snatcher of Chertsey Barn', one of his most remarkable impersonations, and one which the Cantervilles had every reason to remember, as it was the real origin of their quarrel with their neighbour, Lord Rufford. It was about a quarter past two o'clock in the morning, and, as far as he could ascertain, no one was stirring. As he was strolling towards the library, however, to see if there were any traces left of the bloodstain, suddenly there leaped out on him from a dark corner two figures, who waved their arms wildly above their heads, and shrieked out 'boo!' in his ear.

Seized with a panic, which, under the circumstances, was only natural, he rushed for the staircase, but found Washington Otis waiting for him there with the big garden-syringe; and being thus hemmed in by his enemies on every side, and driven almost to bay, he vanished into the great iron stove which, fortunately for him, was not lit, and had to make his way home through the flues and chimneys, arriving at his own room in a terrible state of dirt, disorder and despair.

After this he was not seen again on any nocturnal expedition. The twins lay in wait for him on several occasions, and strewed the passages with nutshells every night to the great annoyance of their parents and the servants, but it was of no avail. It was quite evident that his feelings were so wounded that he would not appear. Mr Otis consequently resumed his great work on the history of the Democratic Party, on which he had been engaged for some years; Mrs Otis organised a wonderful clam bake, which amazed the whole county; the boys took to lacrosse, euchre, poker, and other American national games; and Virginia rode about the lanes on her pony, accompanied by the young Duke of Cheshire, who had come to spend the last week of his holidays at Canterville Chase. It was generally assumed that the ghost had gone away, and, in fact, Mr Otis wrote a letter to that effect to Lord Canterville, who, in reply, expressed his great pleasure at the news, and sent his best congratulations to the minister's worthy wife.

The Otises, however, were deceived, for the ghost was still in the house, and though now almost an invalid, was by no means ready to let matters rest, particularly as he heard that among the guests was the young Duke of Cheshire, whose granduncle, Lord Francis Stilton, had once bet a hundred guineas with Colonel Carbury that he would play dice with the Canterville ghost, and was found the next morning lying on the floor of the cardroom in such a helpless paralytic state, that though he lived on to a great age, he was never able to say anything again but 'Double Sixes'. The story was well known at the time, though, of course, out of respect for the feelings of the two noble families, every attempt was made to hush it up; and a full account of all the circumstances connected with it will be found in the third volume of Lord Tattle's *Recollections of the Prince Regent and his Friends*. The ghost, then, was naturally very anxious to show that he had not lost his influence over the Stiltons, with whom, indeed, he was distantly connected, his own first cousin having been married *en secondes noces* to the Sieur de Bulkeley, from whom, as everyone knows, the Dukes of Cheshire are lineally descended.

Accordingly, he made arrangements for appearing to Virginia's little lover in his celebrated impersonation of 'The Vampire Monk, or the Bloodless Benedictine', a performance so horrible that when old Lady Startup saw it, which she did on one fatal New Year's Eve, in the year 1764, she went off into the most piercing shrieks, which culminated in violent apoplexy, and died in three days, after dis-inheriting the Cantervilles, who were her nearest relations, and leaving all her money to her London apothecary. At the last moment, however, his terror of the twins prevented his leaving his room, and the little Duke slept in peace under the great feathered canopy in the Royal Bedchamber, and dreamed of Virginia.

CHAPTER 5

A few days after this, Virginia and her curly-haired cavalier went out riding on Brockley meadows, where she tore her habit so badly in getting through a hedge, that, on her return home, she made up her mind to go up by the back staircase so as not to be seen. As she was running past the Tapestry Chamber, the door of which happened to be open, she fancied she saw someone inside, and thinking it was her mother's maid, who sometimes used to bring her work there, looked in to ask her to mend her habit. To her immense surprise, however, it was the Canterville Ghost himself! He was sitting by the window, watching the ruined gold of the yellowing trees fly through the air, and the red leaves dancing madly down the long avenue. His head was leaning on his hand, and his whole attitude was one of extreme depression. Indeed, so forlorn, and so much out of repair did he look, that little Virginia, whose first idea had been to run away and lock herself in her room, was filled with pity, and determined to try and comfort him. So light was her footfall, and so deep his melancholy, that he was not aware of her presence till she spoke to him.

'I am so sorry for you,' she said, 'but my brothers are going back to Eton tomorrow, and then, if you behave yourself, no one will annoy you.'

'It is absurd asking me to behave myself,' he answered, looking round in astonishment at the pretty little girl who had ventured to address him, 'quite absurd. I must rattle my chains, and groan through keyholes, and walk about at night, if that is what you mean. It is my only reason for existing.'

'It is no reason at all for existing, and you know you have been very wicked. Mrs Umney told us, the first day we arrived here, that you had killed your wife.'

'Well, I quite admit it,' said the Ghost petulantly, 'but it was a purely family matter, and concerned no one else.'

'It is very wrong to kill anyone,' said Virginia, who at times had a sweet Puritan gravity, caught from some old New England ancestor.

'Oh, I hate the cheap severity of abstract ethics! My wife was very plain, never had my ruffs properly starched, and knew nothing about cookery. Why, there was a buck I had shot in Hogley Woods, a magnificent pricket, and do you know how she had it sent up to table? However, it is no matter now, for it is all over, and I don't think it was very nice of her brothers to starve me to death, though I did kill her.'

'Starve you to death? Oh, Mr Ghost, I mean Sir Simon, are you hungry? I have a sandwich in my case. Would you like it?'

'No, thank you, I never eat anything now; but it is very kind of you, all the same, and you are much nicer than the rest of your horrid, rude, vulgar, dishonest family.'

'Stop!' cried Virginia, stamping her foot, 'it is you who are rude, and horrid, and vulgar, and as for dishonesty, you know you stole the paints out of my box to try and furbish up that ridiculous bloodstain in the library. First you took all my reds, including the vermilion, and I couldn't do any more sunsets, then you took the emerald-green and the chrome-yellow, and finally I had nothing left but indigo and Chinese white, and could only do moonlight scenes, which are always depressing to look at, and not at all easy to paint. I never told on you, though I was very much annoyed, and it was most ridiculous, the whole thing; for who ever heard of emerald-green blood?'

'Well, really,' said the Ghost, rather meekly, 'what was I to do? It is a very difficult thing to get real blood nowadays, and as your brother began it all with his Paragon Detergent, I certainly saw no reason why I should not have your paints. As for colour, that is always a matter of taste: the Cantervilles have blue blood, for instance, the very bluest in England; but I know you Americans don't care for things of this kind.'

'You know nothing about it, and the best thing you can do is to emigrate and improve your mind. My father will be only too happy to give you a free passage, and though there is a heavy duty on spirits

of every kind, there will be no difficulty about the Custom House, as
the officers are all Democrats. Once in New York, you are sure to be
a great success. I know lots of people there who would give a hundred
thousand dollars to have a grandfather, and much more than that to
have a family Ghost.'

'I don't think I should like America.'

'I suppose because we have no ruins and no curiosities,' said
Virginia satirically.

'No ruins! No curiosities!' answered the Ghost; 'you have your
navy and your manners.'

'Good-evening; I will go and ask papa to get the twins an extra
week's holiday.'

'Please don't go, Miss Virginia,' he cried; 'I am so lonely and so
unhappy, and I really don't know what to do. I want to go to sleep
and I cannot.'

'That's quite absurd! You have merely to go to bed and blow out
the candle. It is very difficult sometimes to keep awake, especially at
church, but there is no difficulty at all about sleeping. Why, even
babies know how to do that, and they are not very clever.'

'I have not slept for three hundred years,' he said sadly, and
Virginia's beautiful blue eyes opened in wonder; 'for three hundred
years I have not slept, and I am so tired.'

Virginia grew quite grave, and her little lips trembled like rose-
leaves. She came towards him, and kneeling down at his side, looked
up into his old withered face.

'Poor, poor Ghost,' she murmured; 'have you no place where you
can sleep?'

'Far away beyond the pine woods,' he answered, in a low dreamy
voice, 'there is a little garden. There the grass grows long and deep,
there are the great white stars of the hemlock flower, there the
nightingale sings all night long. All night long he sings, and the
cold, crystal moon looks down, and the yew tree spreads out its giant
arms over the sleepers.'

Virginia's eyes grew dim with tears, and she hid her face in her
hands.

'You mean the Garden of Death,' she whispered.

'Yes, Death. Death must be so beautiful. To lie in the soft brown
earth, with the grasses waving above one's head, and listen to silence.
To have no yesterday, and no tomorrow. To forget time, to forgive
life, to be at peace. You can help me. You can open for me the

portals of Death's house, for Love is always with you, and Love is stronger than Death is.'

Virginia trembled, a cold shudder ran through her, and for a few moments there was silence. She felt as if she was in a terrible dream.

Then the Ghost spoke again, and his voice sounded like the sighing of the wind.

'Have you ever read the old prophecy on the library window?'

'Oh, often,' cried the little girl, looking up; 'I know it quite well. It is painted in curious black letters, and it is difficult to read. There are only six lines:

'When a golden girl can win
Prayer from out the lips of sin,
When the barren almond bears,
And a little child gives away its tears,
Then shall all the house be still
And peace come to Canterville.

But I don't know what they mean.'

'They mean,' he said sadly, 'that you must weep for me for my sins, because I have no tears, and pray with me for my soul, because I have no faith, and then, if you have always been sweet, and good, and gentle, the Angel of Death will have mercy on me. You will see fearful shapes in darkness, and wicked voices will whisper in your ear, but they will not harm you, for against the purity of a little child the powers of hell cannot prevail.'

Virginia made no answer, and the Ghost wrung his hands in wild despair as he looked down at her bowed golden head. Suddenly she stood up, very pale, and with a strange light in her eyes. 'I am not afraid,' she said firmly, 'and I will ask the Angel to have mercy on you.'

He rose from his seat with a faint cry of joy, and taking her hand bent over it with old-fashioned grace and kissed it. His fingers were as cold as ice, and his lips burned like fire, but Virginia did not falter, as he led her across the dusky room. On the faded green tapestry were broidered little huntsmen. They blew their tasselled horns and with their tiny hands waved to her to go back. 'Go back! little Virginia,' they cried, 'go back!' but the Ghost clutched her hand more tightly, and she shut her eyes against them. Horrible animals with lizard tails, and goggle eyes, blinked at her from the carven

chimney-piece, and murmured 'Beware! little Virginia, beware! we
may never see you again,' but the Ghost glided on more swiftly, and
Virginia did not listen. When they reached the end of the room he
stopped, and muttered some words she could not understand. She
opened her eyes, and saw the wall slowly fading away like a mist, and
a great black cavern in front of her. A bitter cold wind swept round
them, and she felt something pulling at her dress. 'Quick, quick,'
cried the Ghost, 'or it will be too late,' and, in a moment, the
wainscoting had closed behind them, and the Tapestry Chamber was
empty.

CHAPTER 6

About ten minutes later, the bell rang for tea, and, as Virginia did
not come down, Mrs Otis sent up one of the footmen to tell her.
After a little time he returned and said that he could not find Miss
Virginia anywhere. As she was in the habit of going out to the
garden every evening to get flowers for the dinner-table, Mrs Otis
was not at all alarmed at first, but when six o'clock struck, and
Virginia did not appear, she became really agitated, and sent the
boys out to look for her, while she herself and Mr Otis searched
every room in the house. At half-past six the boys came back and
said that they could find no trace of their sister anywhere. They
were all now in the greatest state of excitement, and did not know
what to do, when Mr Otis suddenly remembered that, some few
days before, he had given a band of gypsies permission to camp in
the park. He accordingly at once set off for Blackfell Hollow, where
he knew they were, accompanied by his eldest son and two of the
farm-servants. The little Duke of Cheshire, who was perfectly frantic
with anxiety, begged hard to be allowed to go too, but Mr Otis
would not allow him, as he was afraid there might be a scuffle. On
arriving at the spot, however, he found that the gypsies had gone,
and it was evident that their departure had been rather sudden, as
the fire was still burning, and some plates were lying on the grass.
Having sent off Washington and the two men to scour the district,
he ran home, and despatched telegrams to all the police inspectors
in the county, telling them to look out for a little girl who had been
kidnapped by tramps or gypsies. He then ordered his horse to be
brought round, and, after insisting on his wife and the three boys

sitting down to dinner, rode off down the Ascot Road with a groom. He had hardly, however, gone a couple of miles when he heard somebody galloping after him, and, looking round, saw the little Duke coming up on his pony, with his face very flushed and no hat. 'I'm awfully sorry, Mr Otis,' gasped out the boy, 'but I can't eat any dinner as long as Virginia is lost. Please, don't be angry with me; if you had let us be engaged last year, there would never have been all this trouble. You won't send me back, will you? I can't go! I won't go!'

The minister could not help smiling at the handsome young scape-grace, and was a good deal touched at his devotion to Virginia, so leaning down from his horse, he patted him kindly on the shoulders, and said, 'Well, Cecil, if you won't go back I suppose you must come with me, but I must get you a hat at Ascot.'

'Oh, bother my hat! I want Virginia!' cried the little Duke, laughing, and they galloped on to the railway station. There Mr Otis enquired of the station-master if anyone answering the description of Virginia had been seen on the platform, but could get no news of her. The station-master, however, wired up and down the line, and assured him that a strict watch would be kept for her, and, after having bought a hat for the little Duke from a linen-draper, who was just putting up his shutters, Mr Otis rode off to Bexley, a village about four miles away, which he was told was a well-known haunt of the gypsies, as there was a large common next to it. Here they roused up the rural policeman, but could get no information from him, and, after riding all over the common, they turned their horses' heads homewards and reached the Chase about eleven o'clock, dead-tired and almost heartbroken. They found Washington and the twins waiting for them at the gatehouse with lanterns, as the avenue was very dark. Not the slightest trace of Virginia had been discovered. The gypsies had been caught on Brockley meadows, but she was not with them, and they had explained their sudden departure by saying that they had mistaken the date of Chorton Fair, and had gone off in a hurry for fear they might be late. Indeed, they had been quite distressed at hearing of Virginia's disappearance, as they were very grateful to Mr Otis for having allowed them to camp in his park, and four of their number had stayed behind to help in the search. The carp-pond had been dragged, and the whole Chase thoroughly gone over, but without any result. It was evident that, for that night at any rate, Virginia was lost to them; and it was in a state of the deepest depression that Mr Otis and the boys walked up to the house, the groom following behind with the two horses and the pony. In the hall they found a group of frightened servants, and lying on a sofa in the library was poor Mrs Otis, almost out of her mind with terror and anxiety, and having her forehead bathed with eau-de-Cologne by the old housekeeper. Mr Otis at once insisted on her having something to eat, and ordered up supper for the whole party. It was a melancholy meal, as hardly anyone spoke, and even the twins were awestruck and subdued, as they were very fond of their sister. When they had finished, Mr Otis, in spite of the entreaties of the little Duke, ordered them all to bed, saying that nothing more could be done that night, and that he would telegraph in the morning to Scotland Yard for some detectives to be sent down immediately. Just as they were passing out of the dining-room, midnight began to boom from the clock tower, and when the last stroke sounded they heard a crash and a sudden shrill cry; a dreadful peal of thunder shook the house, a strain of unearthly music floated through the air, a panel at the top of the staircase flew back with a loud noise, and out on the landing, looking very pale and white, with a little casket in her hand, stepped Virginia. In a moment they had all rushed up to her. Mrs Otis clasped her passionately in her arms, the Duke smothered her with violent kisses, and the twins executed a wild war-dance round the group.

'Good heavens! child, where have you been?' said Mr Otis, rather angrily, thinking that she had been playing some foolish trick on them. 'Cecil and I have been riding all over the country looking for you, and your mother has been frightened to death. You must never play these practical jokes any more.'

'Except on the Ghost! Except on the Ghost!' shrieked the twins, as they capered about.

'My own darling, thank God you are found; you must never leave my side again,' murmured Mrs Otis, as she kissed the trembling child, and smoothed the tangled gold of her hair.

'Papa,' said Virginia quietly, 'I have been with the Ghost. He is dead, and you must come and see him. He had been very wicked, but he was really sorry for all that he had done, and he gave me this box of beautiful jewels before he died.'

The whole family gazed at her in mute amazement, but she was quite grave and serious; and, turning round, she led them through the opening in the wainscoting down a narrow secret corridor,

Washington following with a lighted candle, which he had caught up from the table. Finally, they came to a great oak door, studded with rusty nails. When Virginia touched it, it swung back on its heavy hinges, and they found themselves in a little low room, with a vaulted ceiling, and one tiny grated window. Imbedded in the wall was a huge iron ring, and chained to it was a gaunt skeleton, that was stretched out at full length on the stone floor, and seemed to be trying to grasp with its long fleshless fingers an old-fashioned trencher and ewer, that were placed just out of its reach. The jug had evidently been once filled with water, as it was covered inside with green mould. There was nothing on the trencher but a pile of dust. Virginia knelt down beside the skeleton, and, folding her little hands together, began to pray silently, while the rest of the party looked on in wonder at the terrible tragedy whose secret was now disclosed to them.

'Hallo!' suddenly exclaimed one of the twins, who had been looking out of the window to try and discover in what wing of the house the room was situated. 'Hallo! the old withered almond tree has blossomed. I can see the flowers quite plainly in the moonlight.'

'God has forgiven him,' said Virginia gravely, as she rose to her feet, and a beautiful light seemed to illumine her face.

'What an angel you are!' cried the young Duke, and he put his arm round her neck and kissed her.

CHAPTER 7

Four days after these curious incidents a funeral started from Canterville Chase at about eleven o'clock at night. The hearse was drawn by eight black horses, each of which carried on its head a great tuft of nodding ostrich-plumes, and the leaden coffin was covered by a rich purple pall, on which was embroidered in gold the Canterville coat-of-arms. By the side of the hearse and the coaches walked the servants with lighted torches, and the whole procession was wonderfully impressive. Lord Canterville was the chief mourner, having come up specially from Wales to attend the funeral, and sat in the first carriage along with little Virginia. Then came the United States Minister and his wife, then Washington and the three boys, and in the last carriage was Mrs Umney. It was generally felt that, as she had been frightened by the ghost for more than fifty years of her life, she had the right to see the last of him. A deep grave had been dug in the corner of the churchyard, just under the old yew tree, and the service was read in the most impressive manner by the Reverend Augustus Dampier. When the ceremony was over, the servants, according to an old custom observed in the Canterville family, extinguished their torches, and, as the coffin was being lowered into the grave, Virginia stepped forward and laid on it a large cross made of white and pink almond-blossoms. As she did so, the moon came out from behind a cloud, and flooded with its silent silver the little churchyard, and from a distant copse a nightingale began to sing. She thought of the ghost's description of the Garden of Death, her eyes became dim with tears, and she hardly spoke a word during the drive home.

The next morning, before Lord Canterville went up to town, Mr Otis had an interview with him on the subject of the jewels the ghost had given to Virginia. They were perfectly magnificent, especially a certain ruby necklace with old Venetian setting, which was really a superb specimen of sixteenth-century work, and their value was so great that Mr Otis felt considerable scruples about allowing his daughter to accept them.

'My lord,' he said, 'I know that in this country mortmain is held to apply to trinkets as well as to land, and it is quite clear to me that these jewels are, or should be, heirlooms in your family. I must beg you, accordingly, to take them to London with you, and to regard them simply as a portion of your property which has been restored to you under certain strange conditions. As for my daughter, she is merely a child, and has as yet, I am glad to say, but little interest in such appurtenances of idle luxury. I am also informed by Mrs Otis, who, I may say, is no mean authority upon art – having had the privilege of spending several winters in Boston when she was a girl – that these gems are of great monetary worth, and if offered for sale would fetch a tall price. Under these circumstances, Lord Canterville, I feel sure that you will recognise how impossible it would be for me to allow them to remain in the possession of any member of my family; and, indeed, all such vain gauds and toys, however suitable or necessary to the dignity of the British aristocracy, would be completely out of place among those who have been brought up on the severe, and I believe immortal, principles of republican simplicity. Perhaps I should mention that Virginia is very anxious that you should allow her to retain the box as a memento of your unfortunate but misguided ancestor. As it is extremely old, and consequently a good deal out of repair, you may perhaps think fit to comply with her request. For my own part, I confess I am a good deal surprised to find a child of mine expressing sympathy with mediaevalism in any form, and can only account for it by the fact that Virginia was born in one of your London suburbs shortly after Mrs Otis had returned from a trip to Athens.'

Lord Canterville listened very gravely to the worthy minister's speech, pulling his grey moustache now and then to hide an involuntary smile, and when Mr Otis had ended, he shook him cordially by the hand, and said, 'My dear sir, your charming little daughter rendered my unlucky ancestor, Sir Simon, a very important service, and I and my family are much indebted to her for her marvellous courage and pluck. The jewels are clearly hers, and, egad, I believe that if I were heartless enough to take them from her, the wicked old fellow would be out of his grave in a fortnight, leading me the devil of a life. As for their being heirlooms, nothing is an heirloom that is not so mentioned in a will or legal document, and the existence of these jewels has been quite unknown. I assure you I have no more claim on them than your butler, and when Miss Virginia grows up I dare say she will be pleased to have pretty things to wear. Besides, you forget, Mr Otis, that you took the furniture and the ghost at a valuation, and anything that belonged to the ghost passed at once into your possession, as, whatever activity Sir Simon may have shown in the corridor at night, in point of law he was really dead, and you acquired his property by purchase.'

Mr Otis was a good deal distressed at Lord Canterville's refusal, and begged him to reconsider his decision, but the good-natured peer was quite firm, and finally induced the minister to allow his daughter to retain the present the ghost had given her, and when, in the spring of 1890, the young Duchess of Cheshire was presented at the Queen's first drawing-room on the occasion of her marriage, her jewels were the universal theme of admiration. For Virginia received the coronet, which is the reward of all good little American girls, and was married to her boy-lover as soon as he came of age. They were both so charming, and they loved each other so much, that every-one was delighted at the match, except the old Marchioness of Dumbleton, who had tried to catch the Duke for one of her seven unmarried daughters, and had given no less than three expensive dinner-parties for that purpose, and, strange to say, Mr Otis himself. Mr Otis was extremely fond of the young Duke personally, but, theoretically, he objected to titles, and, to use his own words, 'was not without apprehension lest, amid the enervating influences of a pleasure-loving aristocracy, the true principles of republican simplicity should be forgotten'. His objections, however, were completely overruled, and I believe that when he walked up the aisle of St George's, Hanover Square, with his daughter leaning on his arm, there was not a prouder man in the whole length and breadth of England.

The Duke and Duchess, after the honeymoon was over, went down to Canterville Chase, and on the day after their arrival they walked over in the afternoon to the lonely churchyard by the pine woods. There had been a great deal of difficulty at first about the inscription on Sir Simon's tombstone, but finally it had been decided to engrave on it simply the initials of the old gentleman's name, and the verse from the library window. The Duchess had brought with her some lovely roses, which she strewed upon the grave, and after they had stood by it for some time they strolled into the ruined chancel of the old abbey. There the Duchess sat down on a fallen pillar, while her husband lay at her feet smoking a cigarette and looking up at her beautiful eyes. Suddenly he threw his cigarette away, took hold of her hand, and said to her, 'Virginia, a wife should have no secrets from her husband.'

'Dear Cecil! I have no secrets from you.'

'Yes, you have,' he answered, smiling, 'you have never told me what happened to you when you were locked up with the ghost.'

'I have never told anyone, Cecil,' said Virginia gravely.

'I know that, but you might tell me.'

'Please don't ask me, Cecil, I cannot tell you. Poor Sir Simon! I owe him a great deal. Yes, don't laugh, Cecil, I really do. He made me see what Life is, and what Death signifies, and why Love is stronger than both.'

The Duke rose and kissed his wife lovingly.

'You can have your secret as long as I have your heart,' he murmured.

'You have always had that, Cecil.'

'And you will tell our children someday, won't you?'

Virginia blushed.